Kid Beowulf™

kid Beowulf

the BLOOD~BOUND Oath

STORY & ART BY
ALEXIS E. FAJARDO

COLOR BY
JOSE MARI FLORES

PROLOGUE COLOR BY
BRIAN KOLM

Andrews McMeel
PUBLISHING®

FOR MY GRANDFATHER

contents

prologue...........................vii

part one: the past...................1

part two: the present...............59

part three: the future.............127

more to explore....................192

world map..........................194

map of daneland....................196

key terms..........................197

character glossary.................198

family tree........................203

beowulf: origins of the epic poem......204

monster slayers....................206

how to draw beowulf................208

anatomy of a page..................210

fun facts..........................214

bibliography.......................216

sneak peak.........................217
kid beowulf: the song of roland

PROLOGUE

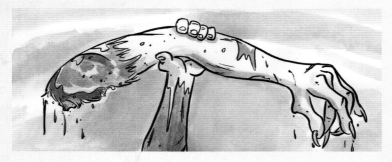

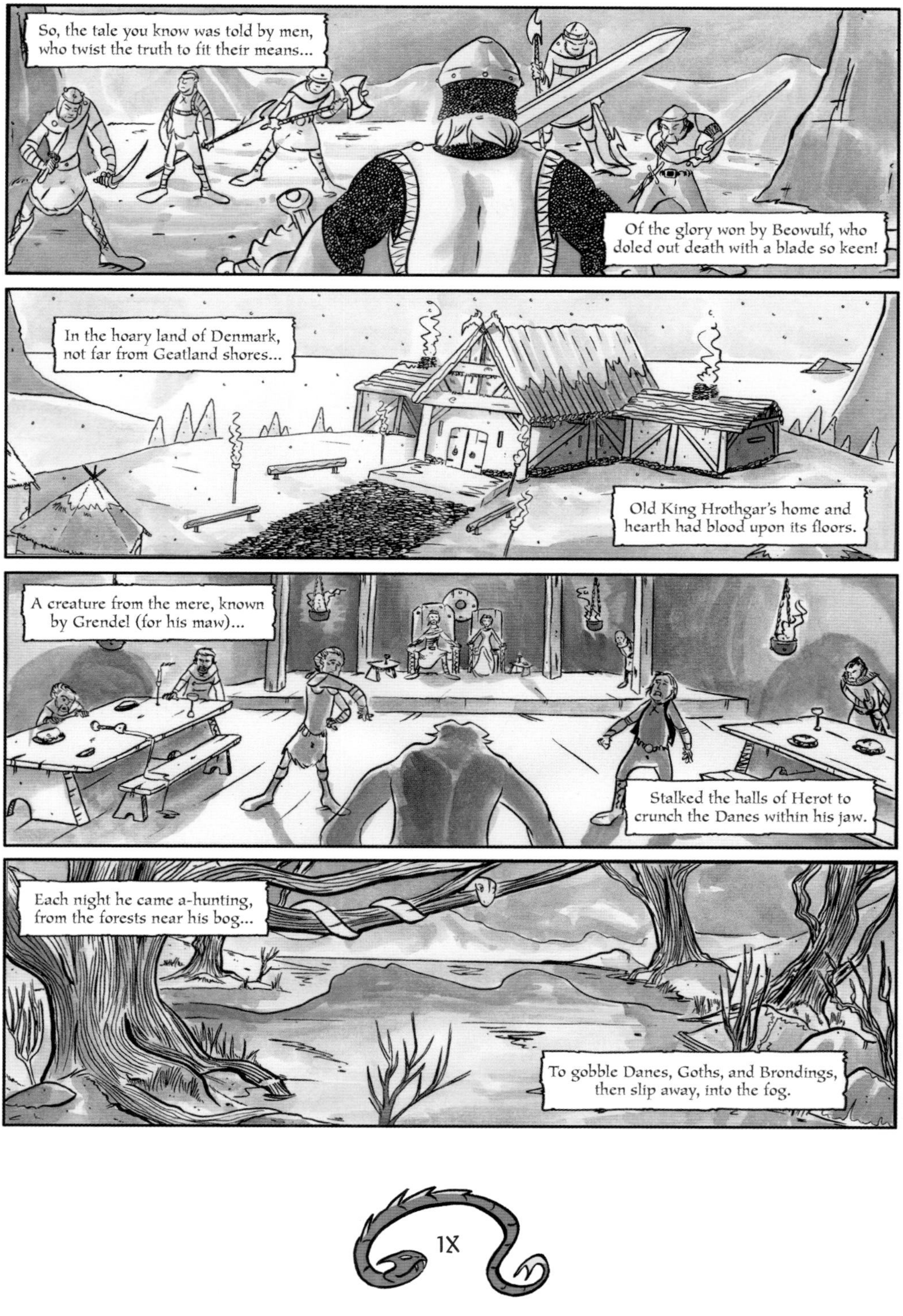
So, the tale you know was told by men, who twist the truth to fit their means...
Of the glory won by Beowulf, who doled out death with a blade so keen!
In the hoary land of Denmark, not far from Geatland shores...
Old King Hrothgar's home and hearth had blood upon its floors.
A creature from the mere, known by Grendel (for his maw)...
Stalked the halls of Herot to crunch the Danes within his jaw.
Each night he came a-hunting, from the forests near his bog...
To gobble Danes, Goths, and Brondings, then slip away, into the fog.

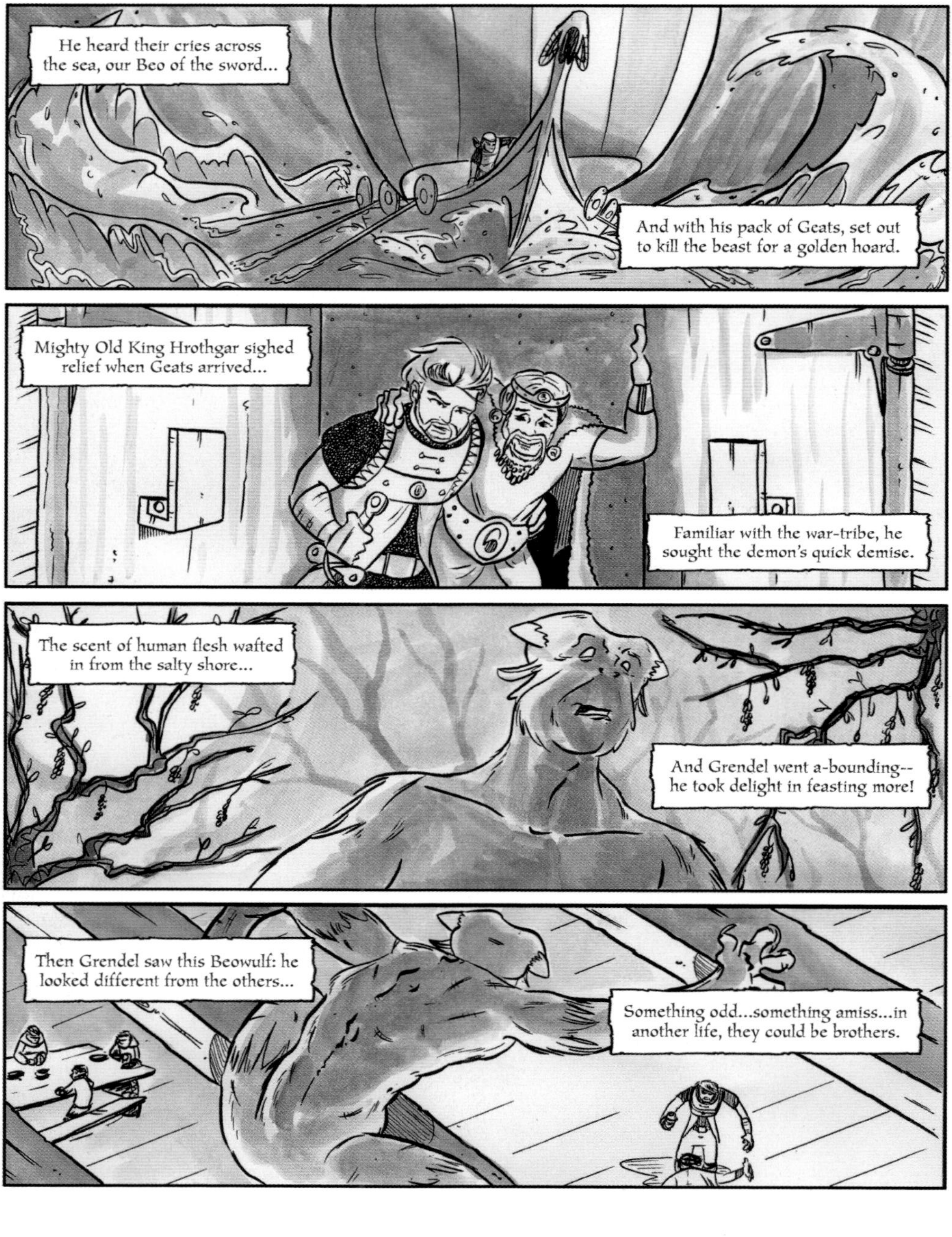
He heard their cries across the sea, our Beo of the sword...
And with his pack of Geats, set out to kill the beast for a golden hoard.
Mighty Old King Hrothgar sighed relief when Geats arrived...
Familiar with the war-tribe, he sought the demon's quick demise.
The scent of human flesh wafted in from the salty shore...
And Grendel went a-bounding-- he took delight in feasting more!
Then Grendel saw this Beowulf: he looked different from the others...
Something odd...something amiss...in another life, they could be brothers.

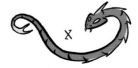

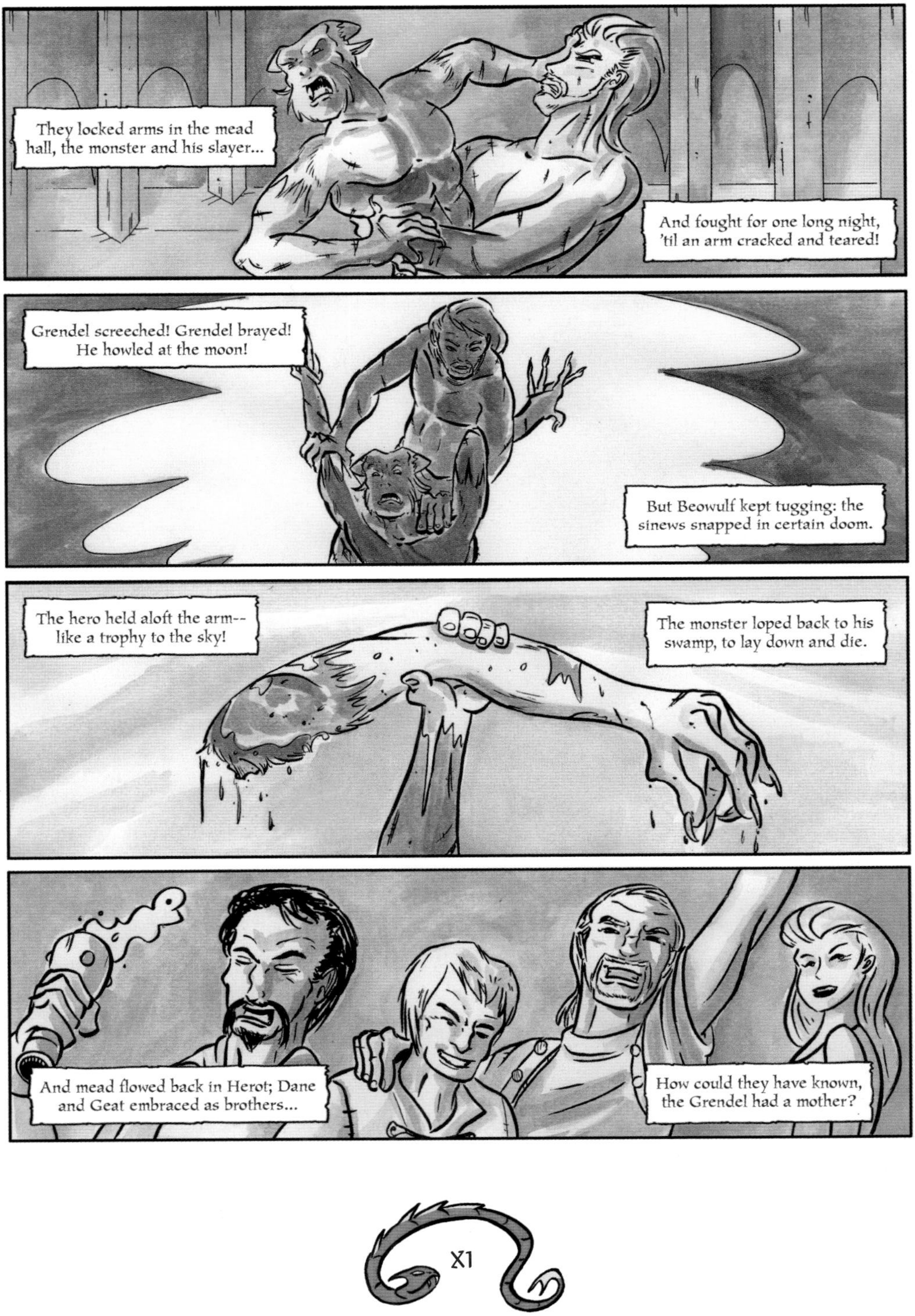
They locked arms in the mead hall, the monster and his slayer...
And fought for one long night, 'til an arm cracked and teared!
Grendel screeched! Grendel brayed! He howled at the moon!
But Beowulf kept tugging: the sinews snapped in certain doom.
The hero held aloft the arm-- like a trophy to the sky!
The monster loped back to his swamp, to lay down and die.
And mead flowed back in Herot; Dane and Geat embraced as brothers...
How could they have known, the Grendel had a mother?

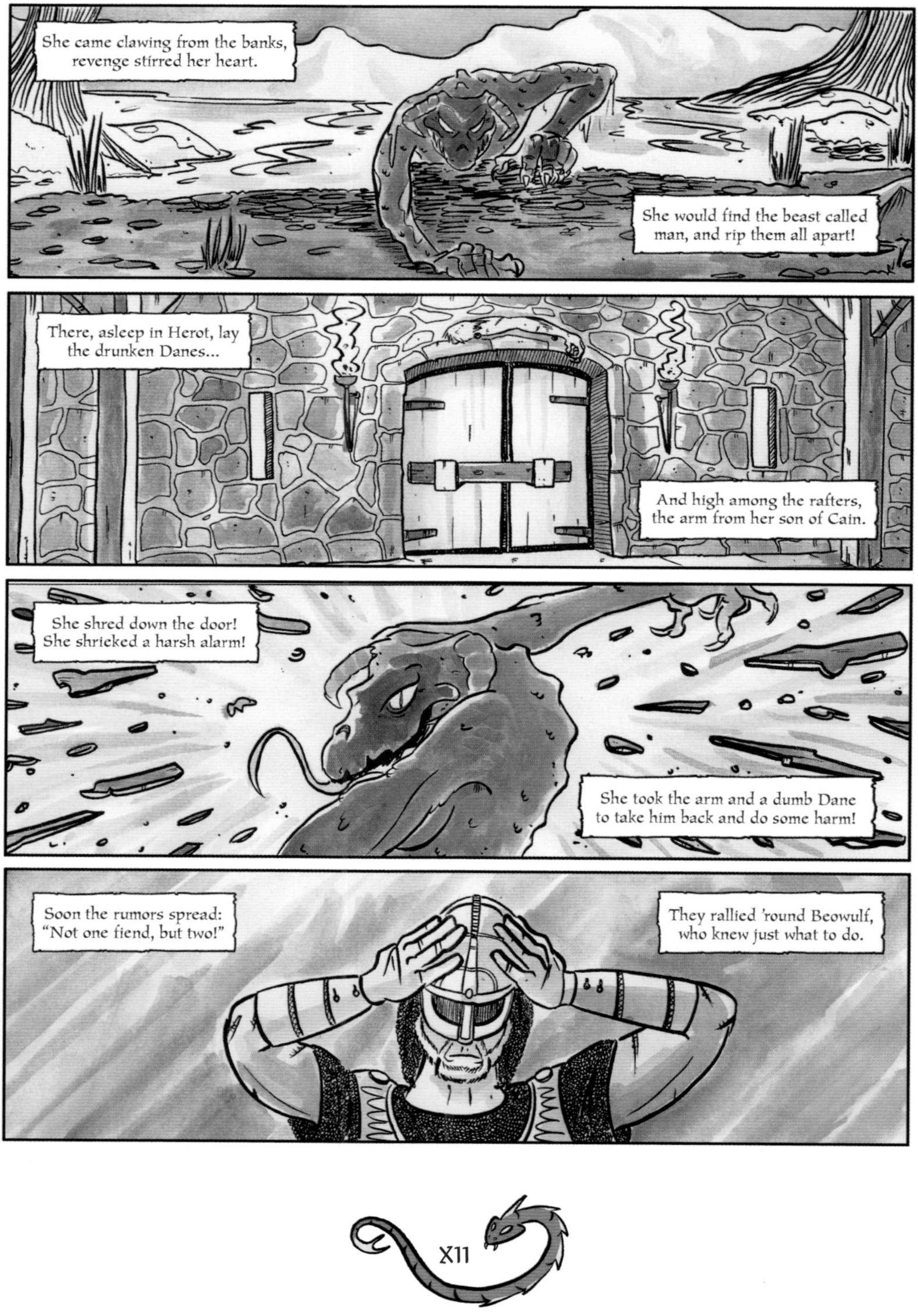
She came clawing from the banks, revenge stirred her heart.
She would find the beast called man, and rip them all apart!
There, asleep in Herot, lay the drunken Danes...
And high among the rafters, the arm from her son of Cain.
She shred down the door! She shrieked a harsh alarm!
She took the arm and a dumb Dane to take him back and do some harm!
Soon the rumors spread: "Not one fiend, but two!"
They rallied 'round Beowulf, who knew just what to do.

the Blood-Bound Oath

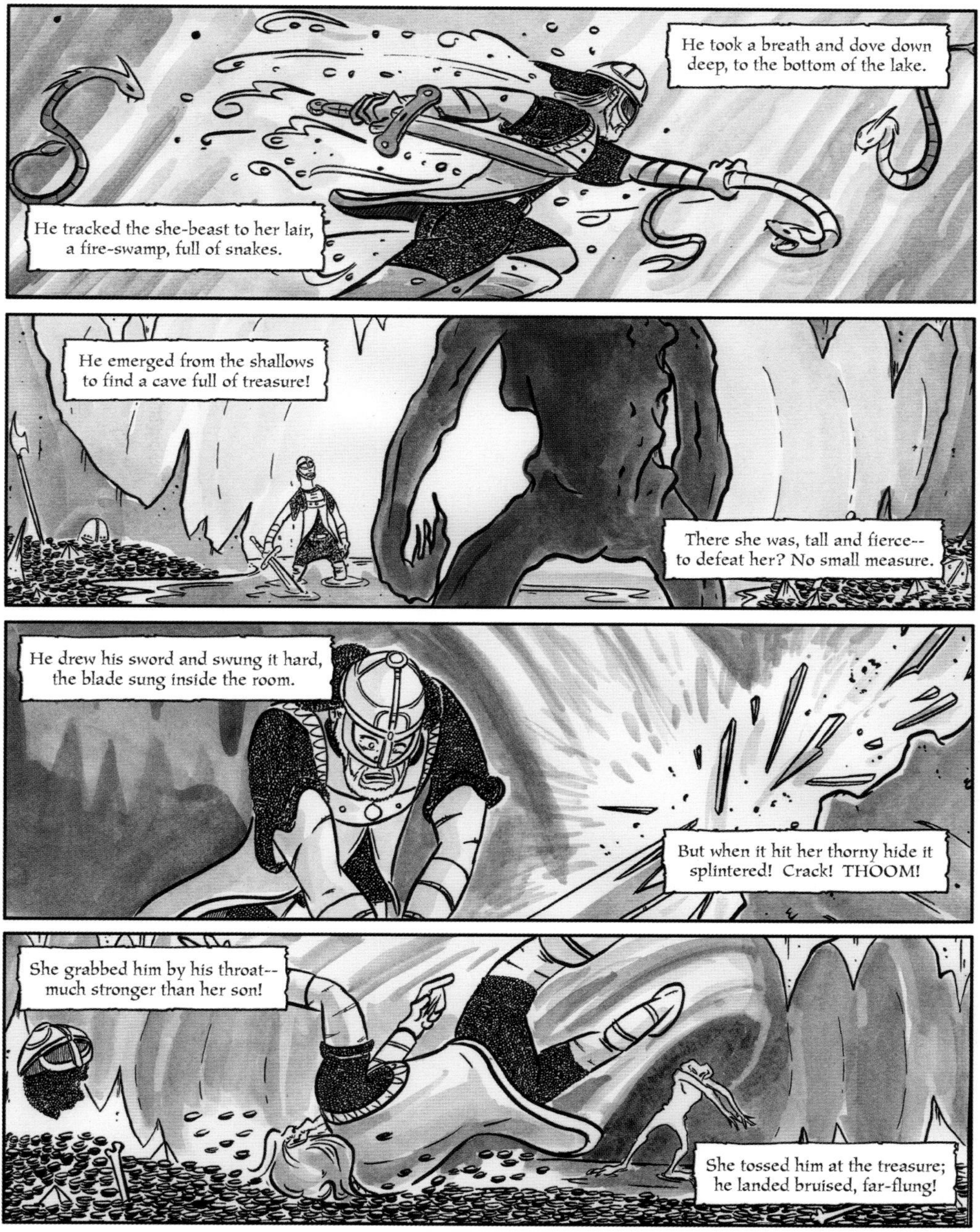
He tracked the she-beast to her lair, a fire-swamp, full of snakes.
He took a breath and dove down deep, to the bottom of the lake.
He emerged from the shallows to find a cave full of treasure!
There she was, tall and fierce-- to defeat her? No small measure.
He drew his sword and swung it hard, the blade sung inside the room.
But when it hit her thorny hide it splintered! Crack! THOOM!
She grabbed him by his throat-- much stronger than her son!
She tossed him at the treasure; he landed bruised, far-flung!

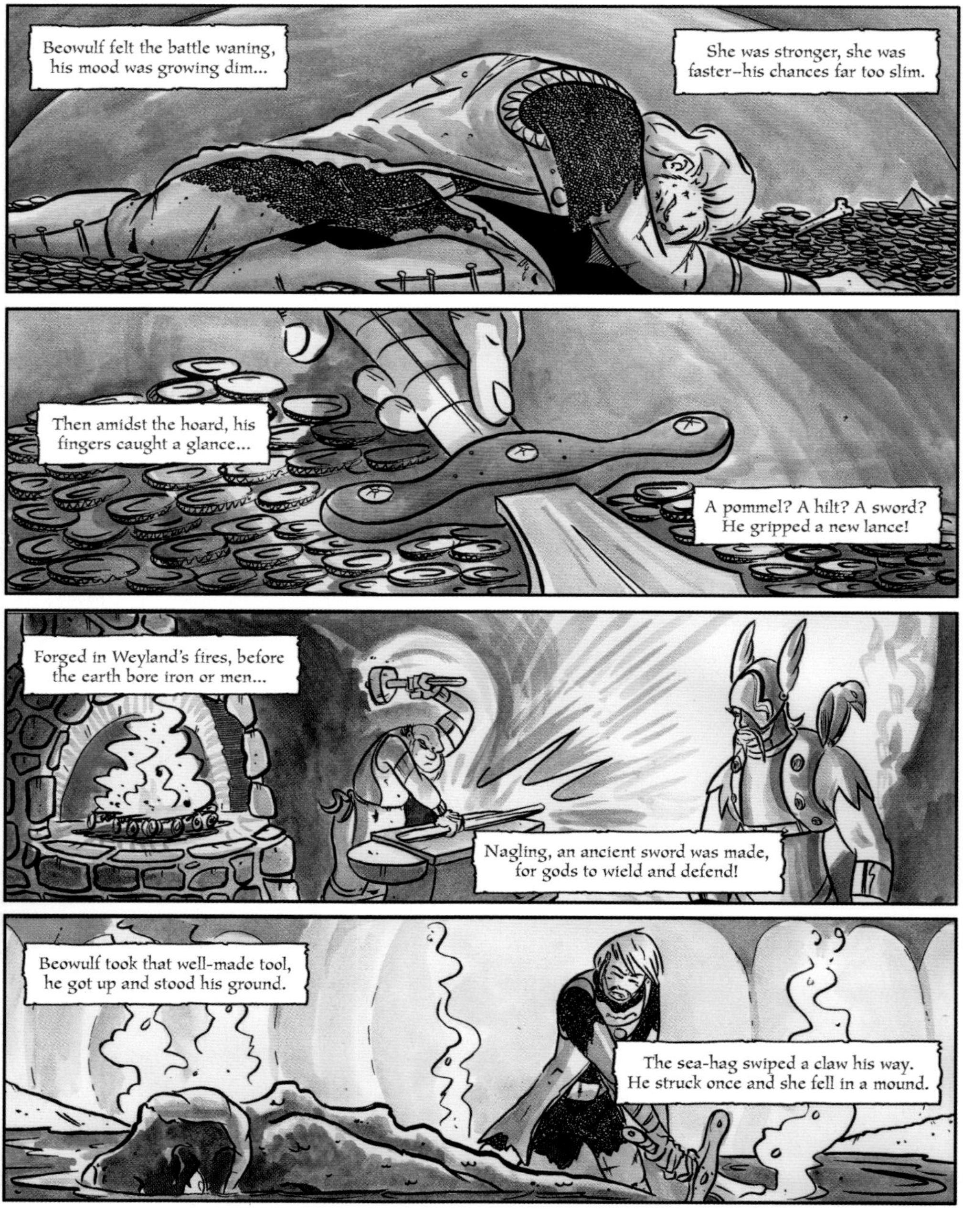
Beowulf felt the battle waning, his mood was growing dim...
She was stronger, she was faster–his chances far too slim.
Then amidst the hoard, his fingers caught a glance...
A pommel? A hilt? A sword? He gripped a new lance!
Forged in Weyland's fires, before the earth bore iron or men...
Nagling, an ancient sword was made, for gods to wield and defend!
Beowulf took that well-made tool, he got up and stood his ground.
The sea-hag swiped a claw his way. He struck once and she fell in a mound.

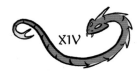

the blood-bound oath

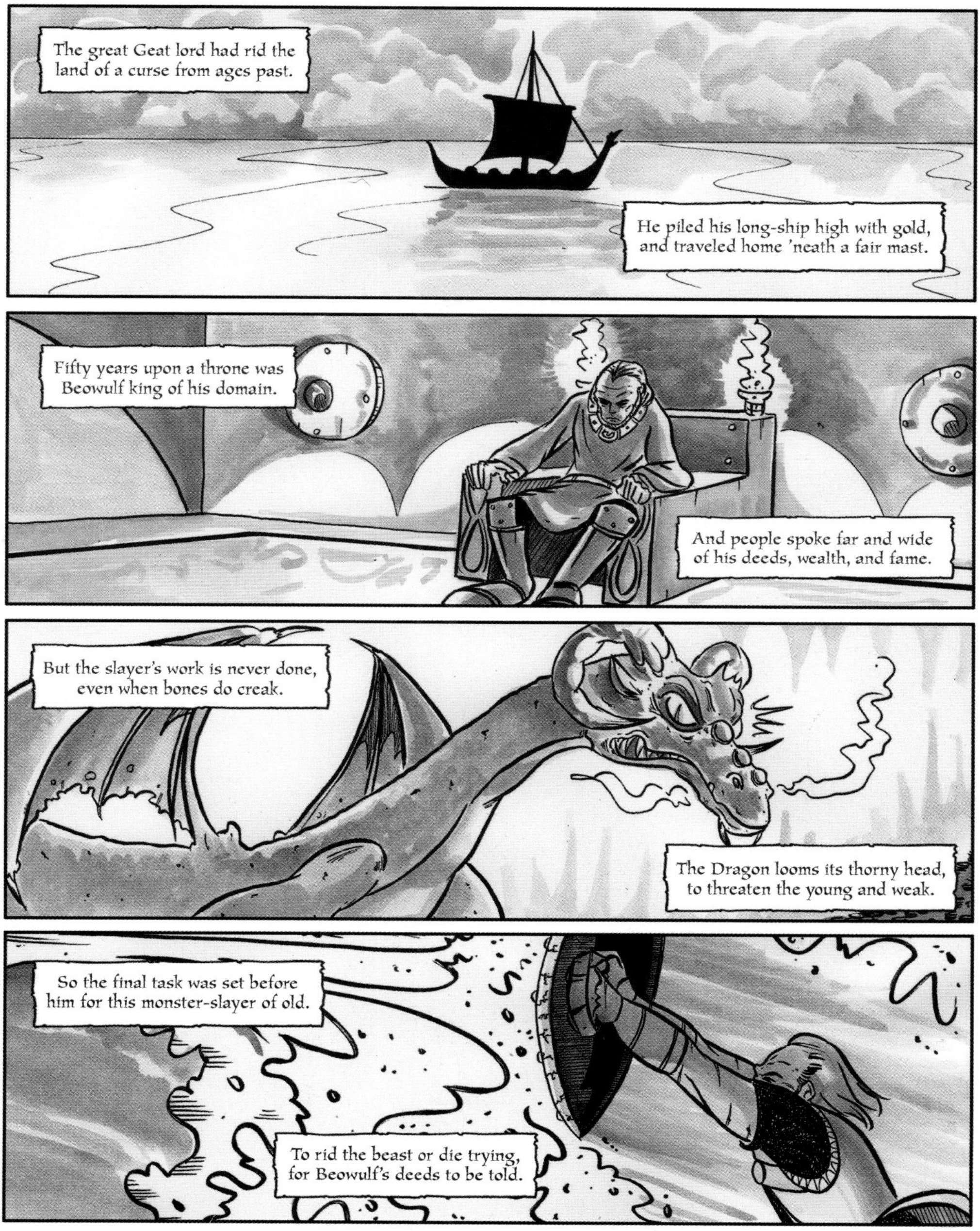
The great Geat lord had rid the land of a curse from ages past.
He piled his long-ship high with gold, and traveled home 'neath a fair mast.
Fifty years upon a throne was Beowulf king of his domain.
And people spoke far and wide of his deeds, wealth, and fame.
But the slayer's work is never done, even when bones do creak.
The Dragon looms its thorny head, to threaten the young and weak.
So the final task was set before him for this monster-slayer of old.
To rid the beast or die trying, for Beowulf's deeds to be told.

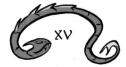

At least, that's as men have told it--
as I said, they twist the truth.
Too blind to know the proper tale
of a king's run-rampant youth...

part one

the past

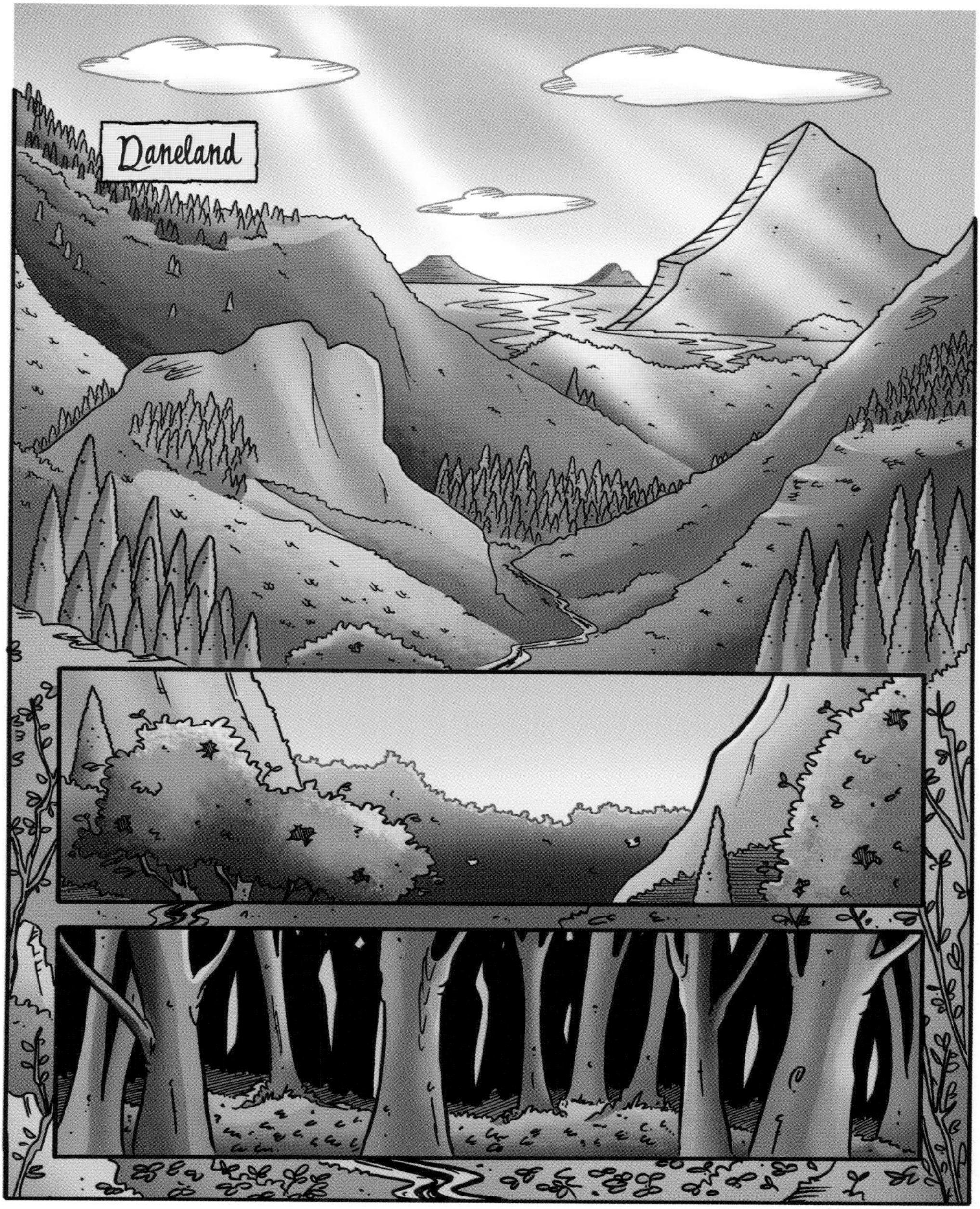
Daneland

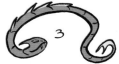

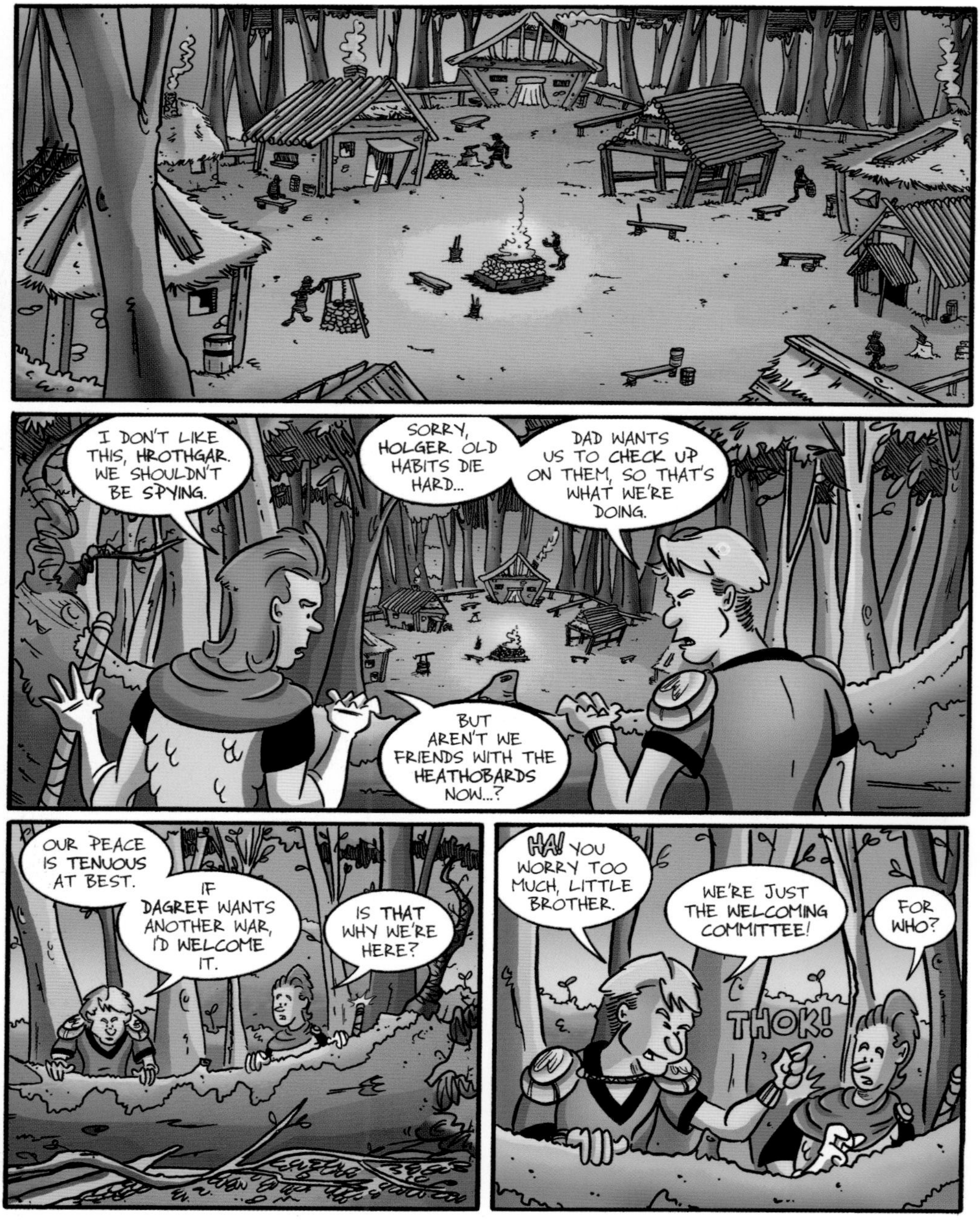

I DON'T LIKE THIS, HROTHGAR. WE SHOULDN'T BE SPYING.
SORRY, HOLGER. OLD HABITS DIE HARD...
DAD WANTS US TO CHECK UP ON THEM, SO THAT'S WHAT WE'RE DOING.
BUT AREN'T WE FRIENDS WITH THE HEATHOBARDS NOW...?
OUR PEACE IS TENUOUS AT BEST.
IF DAGREF WANTS ANOTHER WAR, I'D WELCOME IT.
IS THAT WHY WE'RE HERE?
HA! YOU WORRY TOO MUCH, LITTLE BROTHER.
WE'RE JUST THE WELCOMING COMMITTEE!
FOR WHO?
THOK!

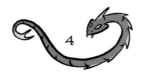

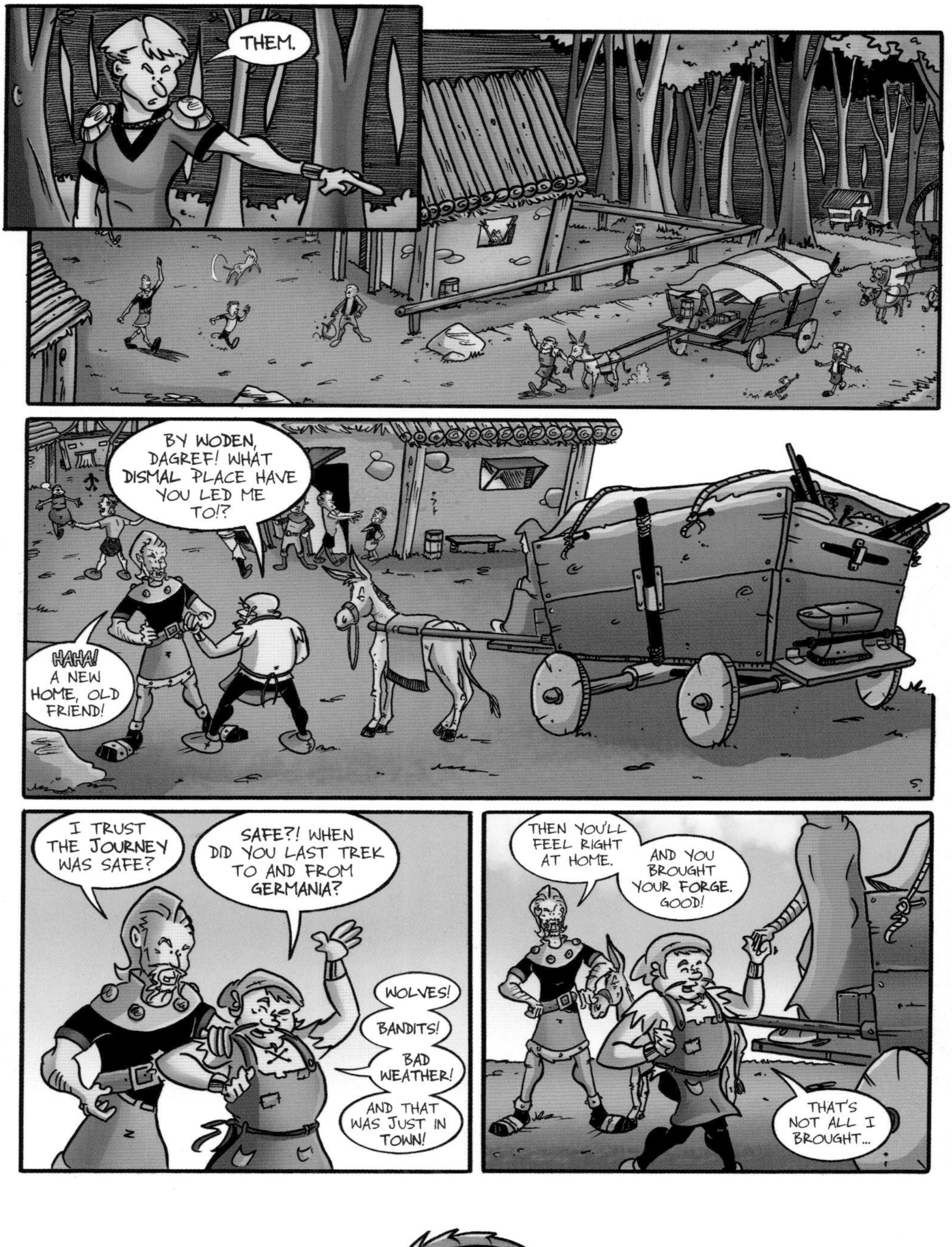
THEM.
BY WODEN, DAGREF! WHAT DISMAL PLACE HAVE YOU LED ME TO!?
HAHA! A NEW HOME, OLD FRIEND!
I TRUST THE JOURNEY WAS SAFE?
SAFE?! WHEN DID YOU LAST TREK TO AND FROM GERMANIA?
WOLVES!
BANDITS!
BAD WEATHER!
AND THAT WAS JUST IN TOWN!
THEN YOU'LL FEEL RIGHT AT HOME.
AND YOU BROUGHT YOUR FORGE. GOOD!
THAT'S NOT ALL I BROUGHT...

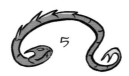

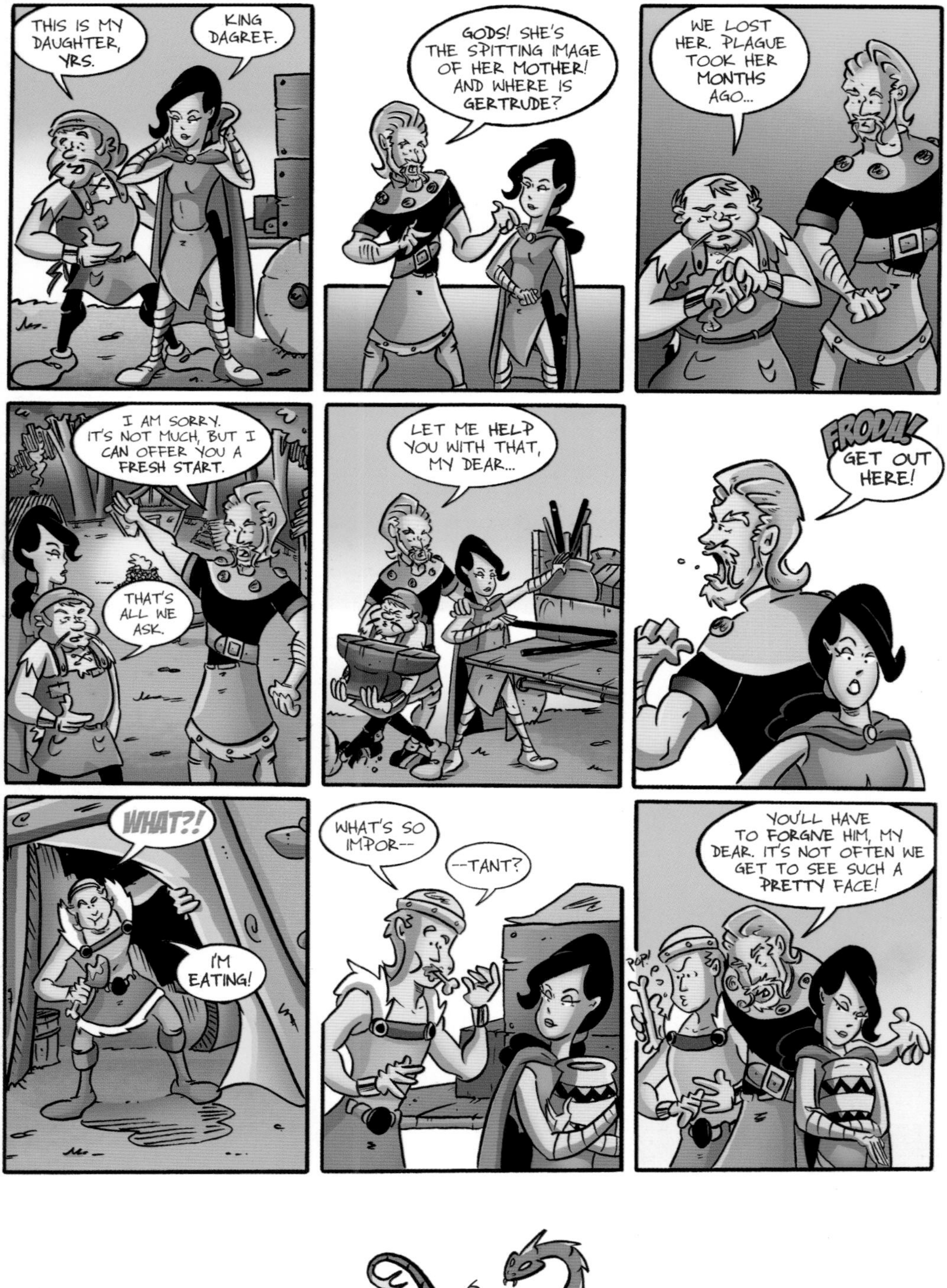
THIS IS MY DAUGHTER, YRS.
KING DAGREF.
GODS! SHE'S THE SPITTING IMAGE OF HER MOTHER! AND WHERE IS GERTRUDE?
WE LOST HER. PLAGUE TOOK HER MONTHS AGO...
I AM SORRY. IT'S NOT MUCH, BUT I CAN OFFER YOU A FRESH START.
THAT'S ALL WE ASK.
LET ME HELP YOU WITH THAT, MY DEAR...
FRODA! GET OUT HERE!
WHAT?!
I'M EATING!
WHAT'S SO IMPOR--
--TANT?
YOU'LL HAVE TO FORGIVE HIM, MY DEAR. IT'S NOT OFTEN WE GET TO SEE SUCH A PRETTY FACE!
POP!

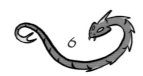

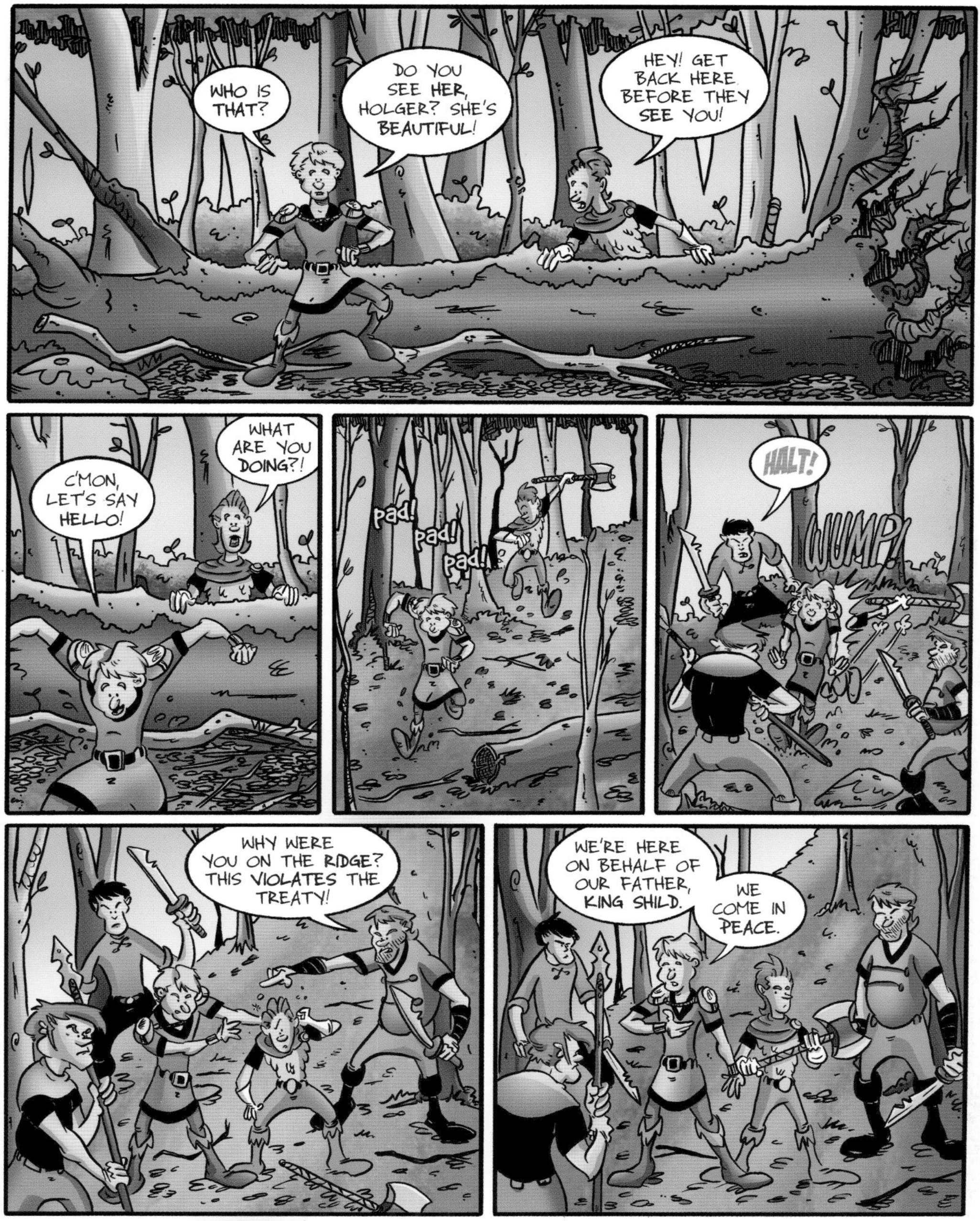
WHO IS THAT?
DO YOU SEE HER, HOLGER? SHE'S BEAUTIFUL!
HEY! GET BACK HERE BEFORE THEY SEE YOU!
C'MON, LET'S SAY HELLO!
WHAT ARE YOU DOING?!
pad! pad! pad!
HALT!
WUMP!
WHY WERE YOU ON THE RIDGE? THIS VIOLATES THE TREATY!
WE'RE HERE ON BEHALF OF OUR FATHER, KING SHILD.
WE COME IN PEACE.

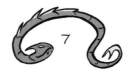

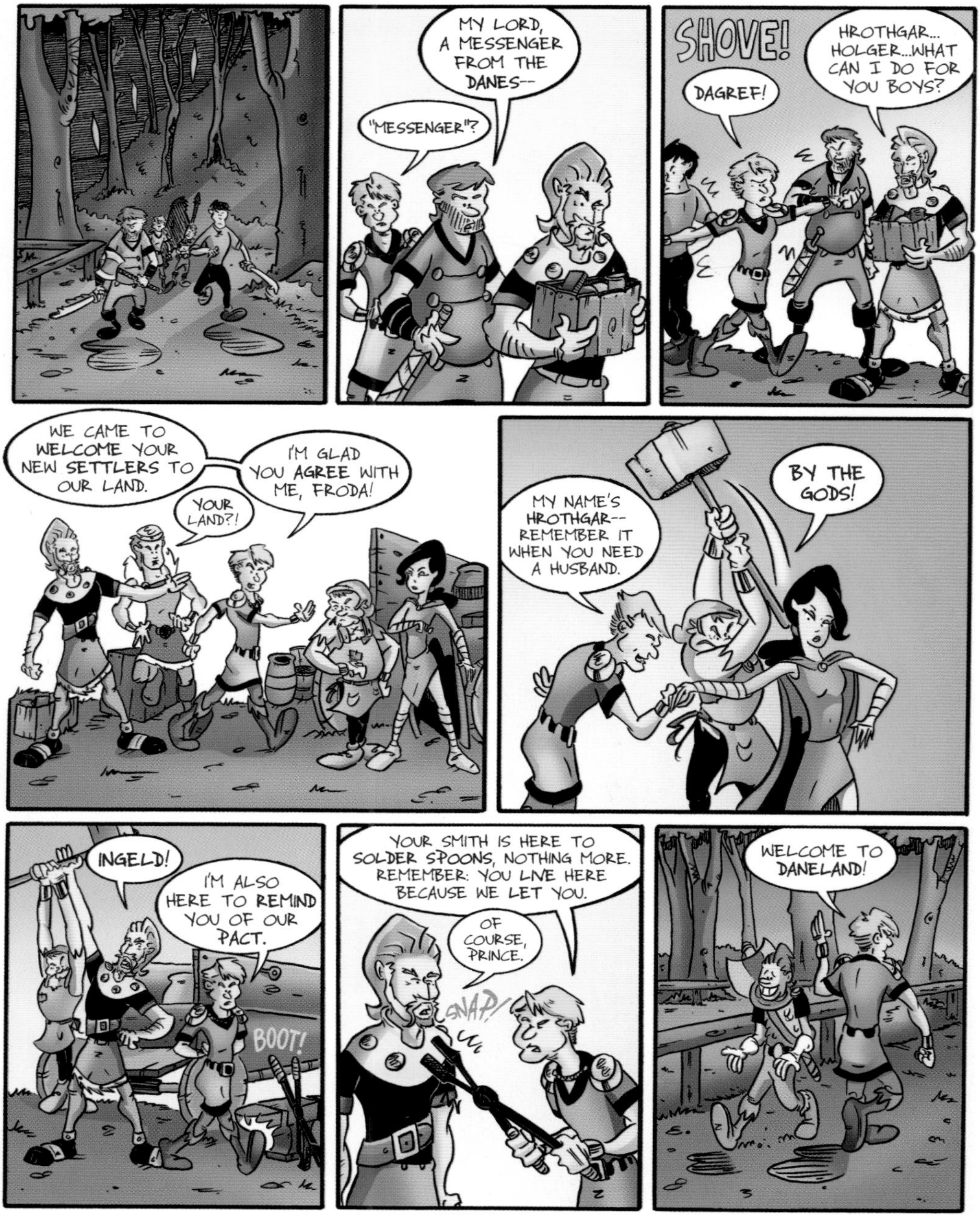
MY LORD, A MESSENGER FROM THE DANES--
"MESSENGER"?
SHOVE!
DAGREF!
HROTHGAR... HOLGER...WHAT CAN I DO FOR YOU BOYS?
WE CAME TO WELCOME YOUR NEW SETTLERS TO OUR LAND.
YOUR LAND?!
I'M GLAD YOU AGREE WITH ME, FRODA!
MY NAME'S HROTHGAR-- REMEMBER IT WHEN YOU NEED A HUSBAND.
BY THE GODS!
INGELD!
I'M ALSO HERE TO REMIND YOU OF OUR PACT.
BOOT!
YOUR SMITH IS HERE TO SOLDER SPOONS, NOTHING MORE. REMEMBER: YOU LIVE HERE BECAUSE WE LET YOU.
OF COURSE, PRINCE.
SNAP!
WELCOME TO DANELAND!

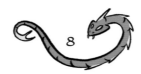

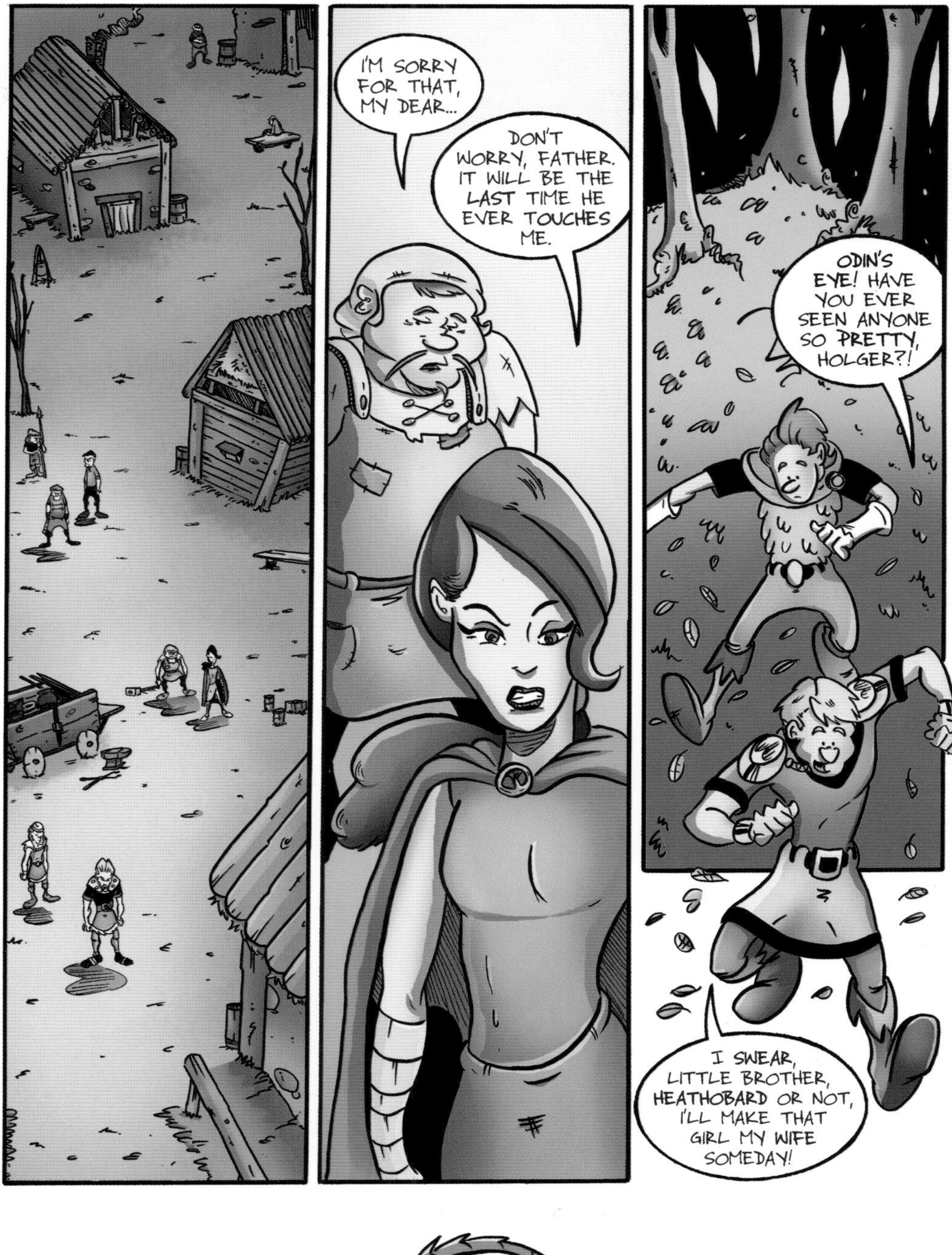
I'M SORRY FOR THAT, MY DEAR...
DON'T WORRY, FATHER. IT WILL BE THE LAST TIME HE EVER TOUCHES ME.
ODIN'S EYE! HAVE YOU EVER SEEN ANYONE SO PRETTY, HOLGER?!
I SWEAR, LITTLE BROTHER, HEATHOBARD OR NOT, I'LL MAKE THAT GIRL MY WIFE SOMEDAY!

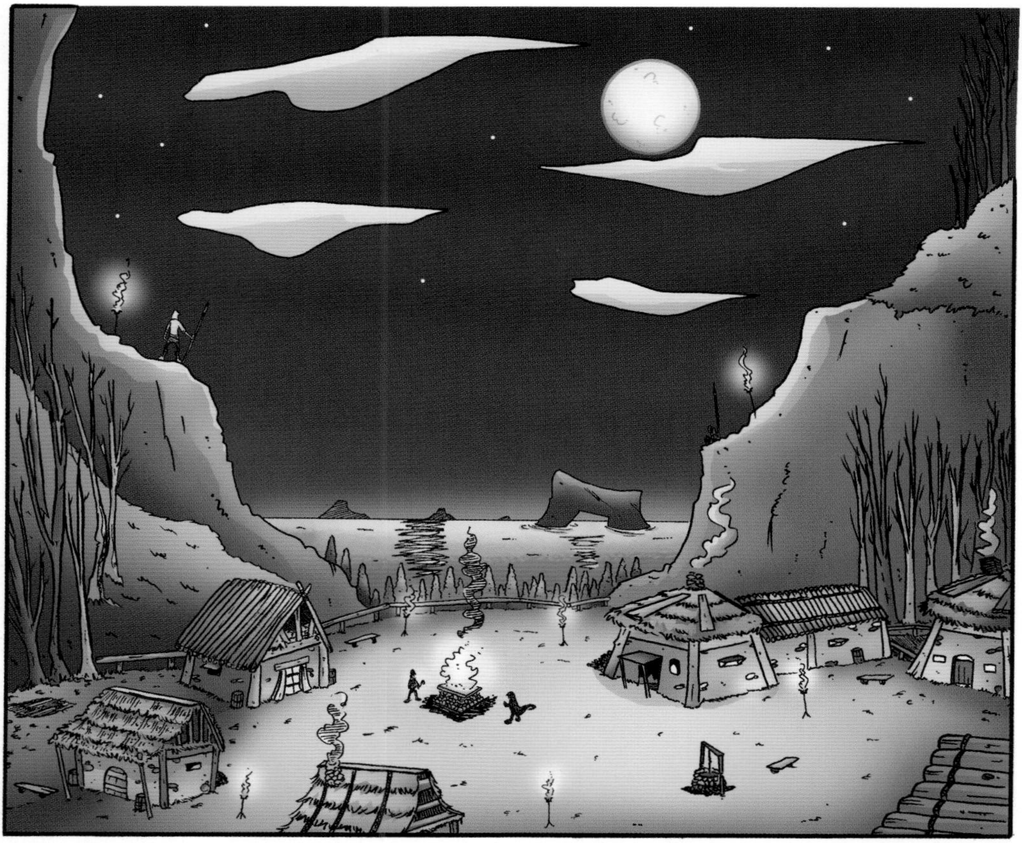

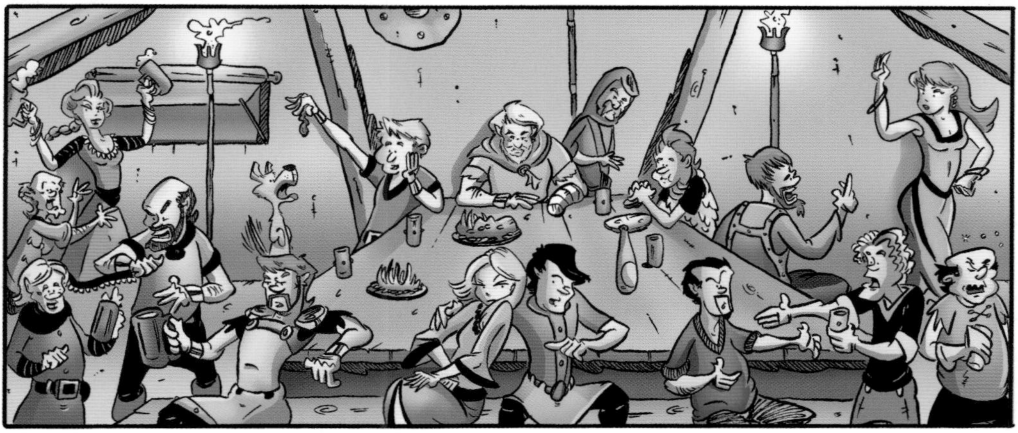

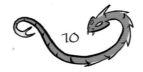

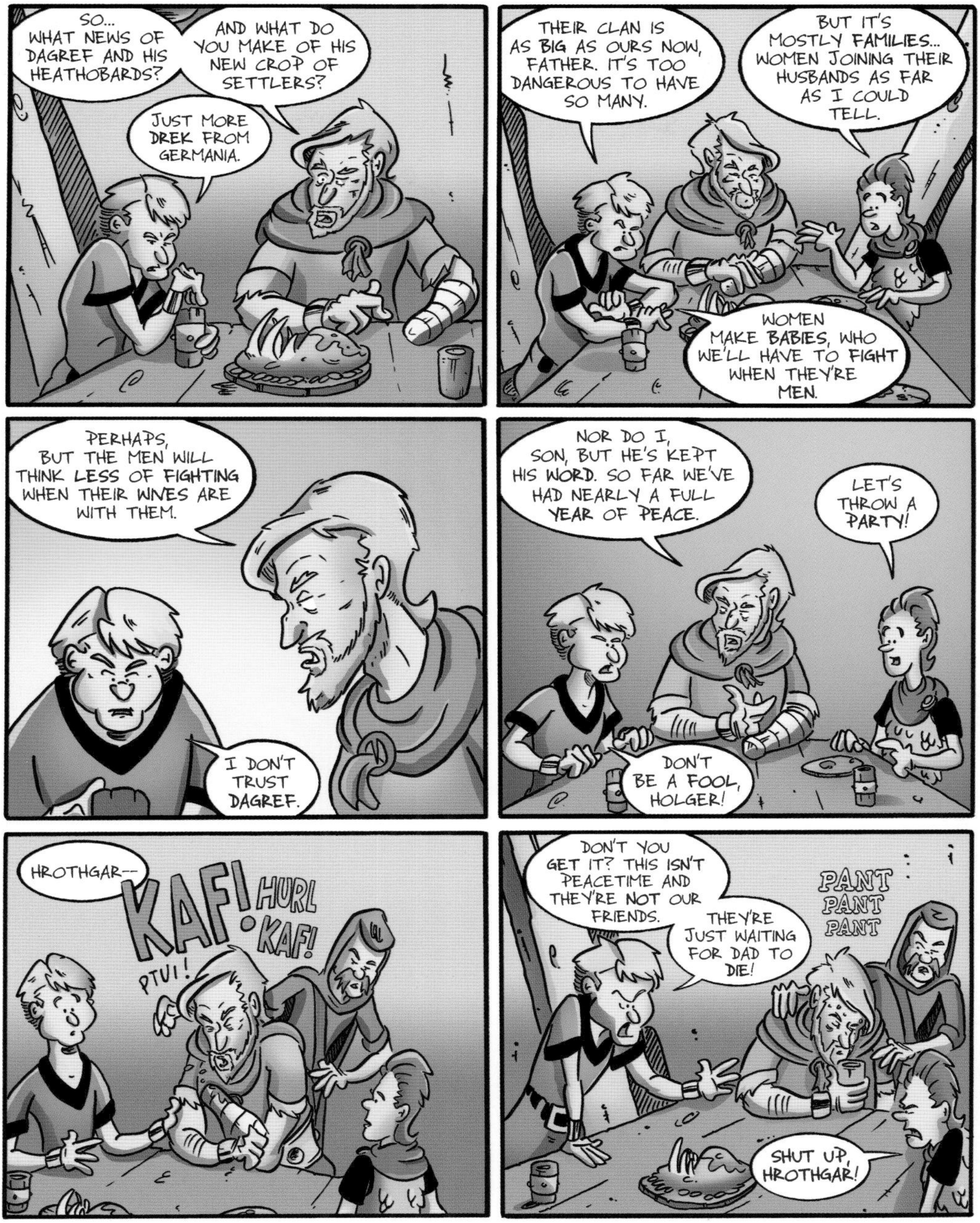
SO... WHAT NEWS OF DAGREF AND HIS HEATHOBARDS?
AND WHAT DO YOU MAKE OF HIS NEW CROP OF SETTLERS?
JUST MORE DREK FROM GERMANIA.
THEIR CLAN IS AS BIG AS OURS NOW, FATHER. IT'S TOO DANGEROUS TO HAVE SO MANY.
BUT IT'S MOSTLY FAMILIES... WOMEN JOINING THEIR HUSBANDS AS FAR AS I COULD TELL.
WOMEN MAKE BABIES, WHO WE'LL HAVE TO FIGHT WHEN THEY'RE MEN.
PERHAPS, BUT THE MEN WILL THINK LESS OF FIGHTING WHEN THEIR WIVES ARE WITH THEM.
I DON'T TRUST DAGREF.
NOR DO I, SON, BUT HE'S KEPT HIS WORD. SO FAR WE'VE HAD NEARLY A FULL YEAR OF PEACE.
LET'S THROW A PARTY!
DON'T BE A FOOL, HOLGER!
HROTHGAR--
KAF!
HURL
KAF!
PTUI!
DON'T YOU GET IT? THIS ISN'T PEACETIME AND THEY'RE NOT OUR FRIENDS.
THEY'RE JUST WAITING FOR DAD TO DIE!
PANT
PANT
PANT
SHUT UP, HROTHGAR!

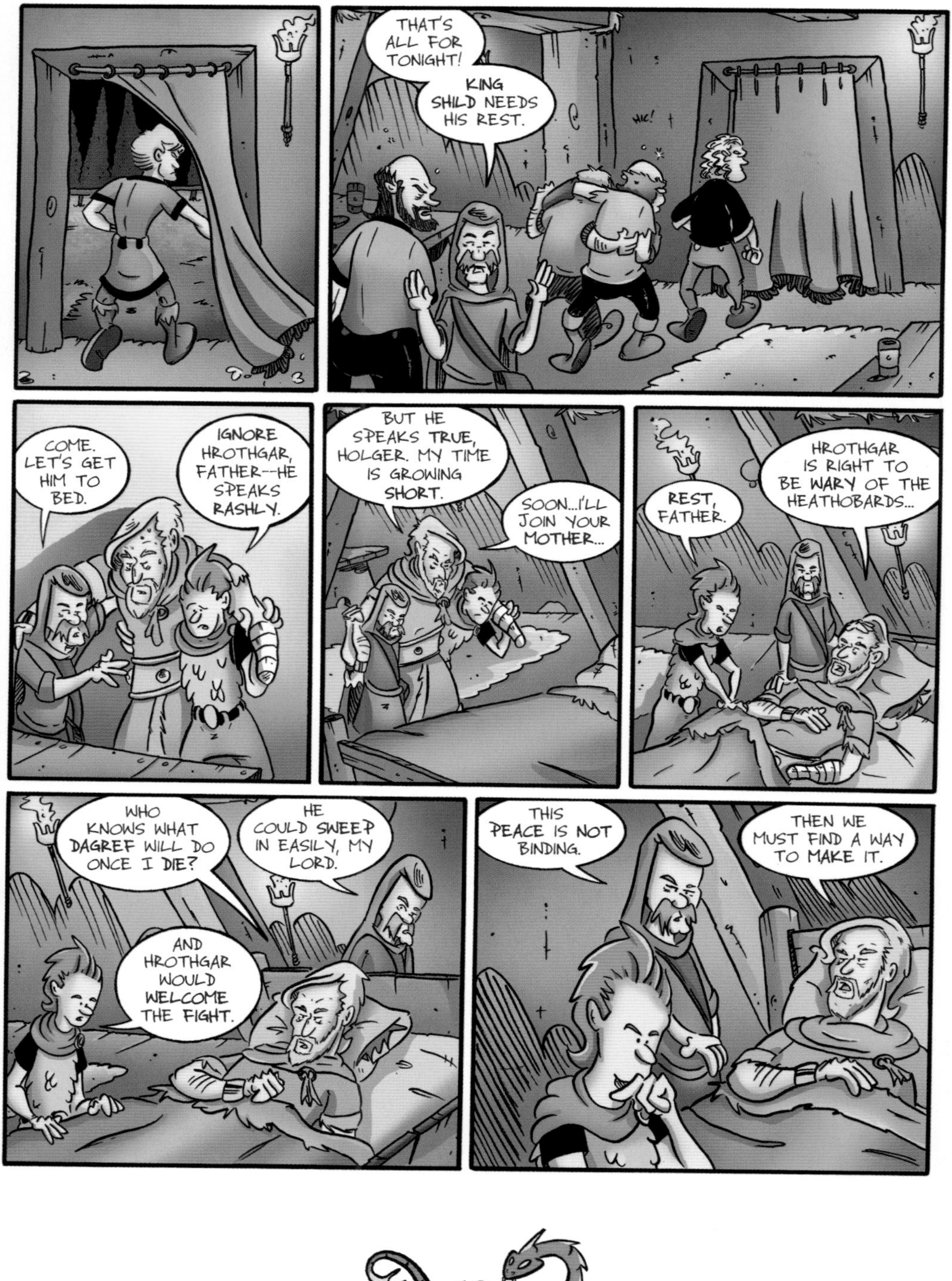
THAT'S ALL FOR TONIGHT!
KING SHILD NEEDS HIS REST.
HIC!
COME. LET'S GET HIM TO BED.
IGNORE HROTHGAR, FATHER--HE SPEAKS RASHLY.
BUT HE SPEAKS TRUE, HOLGER. MY TIME IS GROWING SHORT.
SOON...I'LL JOIN YOUR MOTHER...
REST, FATHER.
HROTHGAR IS RIGHT TO BE WARY OF THE HEATHOBARDS...
WHO KNOWS WHAT DAGREF WILL DO ONCE I DIE?
HE COULD SWEEP IN EASILY, MY LORD.
AND HROTHGAR WOULD WELCOME THE FIGHT.
THIS PEACE IS NOT BINDING.
THEN WE MUST FIND A WAY TO MAKE IT.

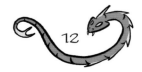

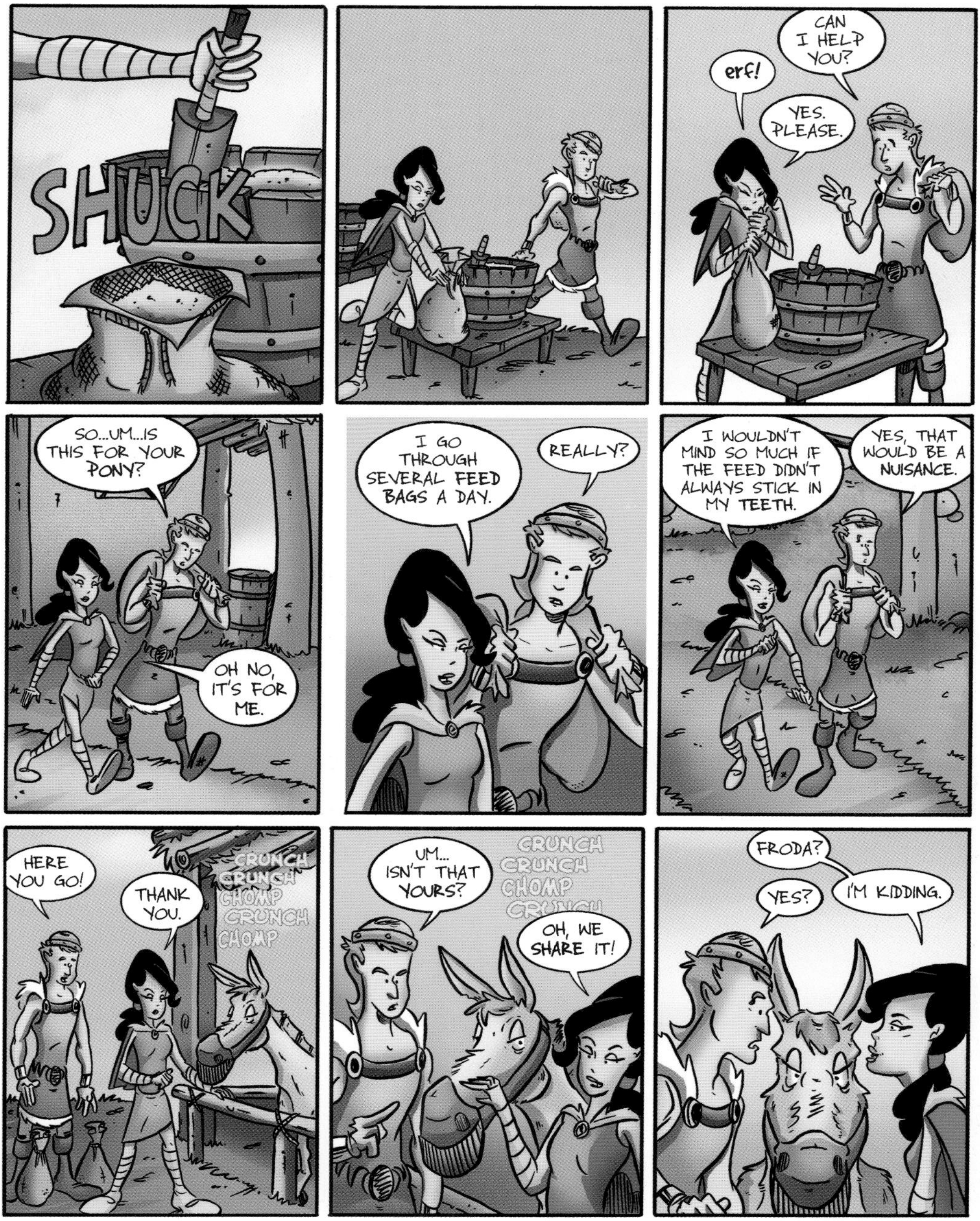
SHUCK
CAN I HELP YOU?
erf!
YES. PLEASE.
SO...UM...IS THIS FOR YOUR PONY?
OH NO, IT'S FOR ME.
I GO THROUGH SEVERAL FEED BAGS A DAY.
REALLY?
I WOULDN'T MIND SO MUCH IF THE FEED DIDN'T ALWAYS STICK IN MY TEETH.
YES, THAT WOULD BE A NUISANCE.
HERE YOU GO!
THANK YOU.
CRUNCH CRUNCH CHOMP CRUNCH CHOMP
UM... ISN'T THAT YOURS?
CRUNCH CRUNCH CHOMP
OH, WE SHARE IT!
FRODA?
YES?
I'M KIDDING.

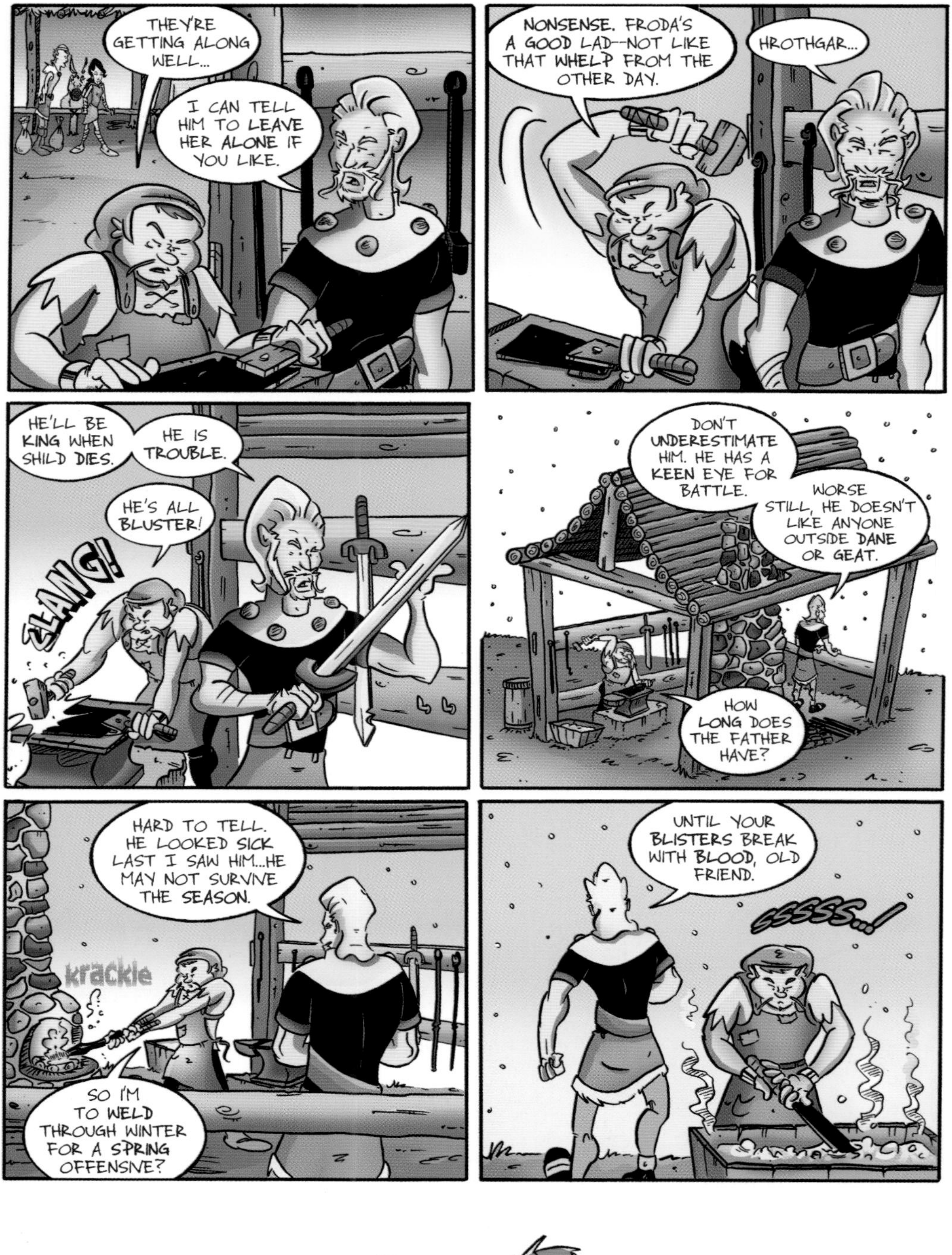
THEY'RE GETTING ALONG WELL...
I CAN TELL HIM TO LEAVE HER ALONE IF YOU LIKE.
NONSENSE. FRODA'S A GOOD LAD--NOT LIKE THAT WHELP FROM THE OTHER DAY.
HROTHGAR...
HE'LL BE KING WHEN SHILD DIES.
HE IS TROUBLE.
HE'S ALL BLUSTER!
CLANG!
DON'T UNDERESTIMATE HIM. HE HAS A KEEN EYE FOR BATTLE.
WORSE STILL, HE DOESN'T LIKE ANYONE OUTSIDE DANE OR GEAT.
HOW LONG DOES THE FATHER HAVE?
HARD TO TELL. HE LOOKED SICK LAST I SAW HIM...HE MAY NOT SURVIVE THE SEASON.
krackle
SO I'M TO WELD THROUGH WINTER FOR A SPRING OFFENSIVE?
UNTIL YOUR BLISTERS BREAK WITH BLOOD, OLD FRIEND.
SSSSS...!

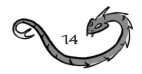

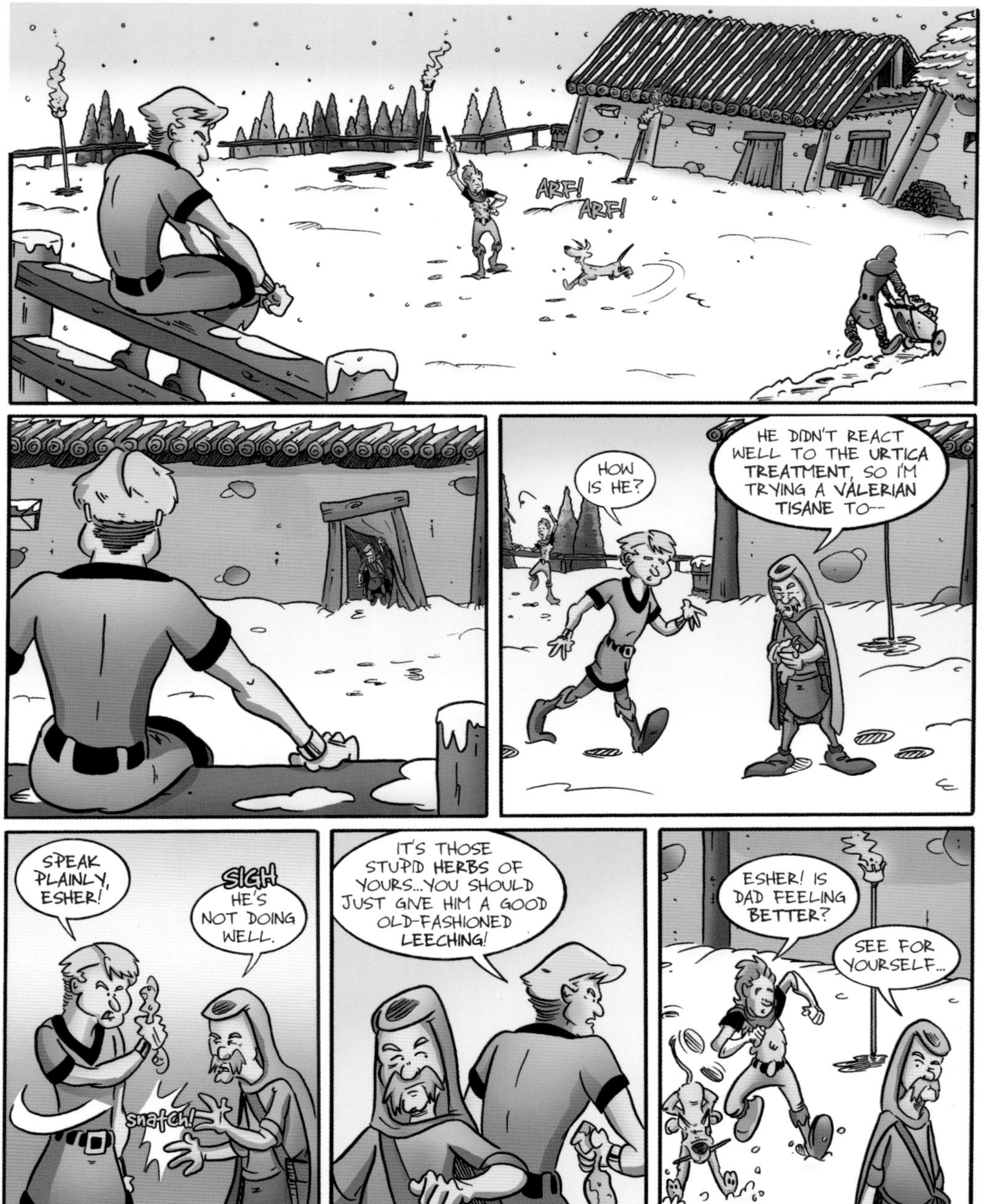
ARF!
ARF!
HOW IS HE?
HE DIDN'T REACT WELL TO THE URTICA TREATMENT, SO I'M TRYING A VALERIAN TISANE TO--
SPEAK PLAINLY, ESHER!
SIGH
HE'S NOT DOING WELL.
snatch!
IT'S THOSE STUPID HERBS OF YOURS...YOU SHOULD JUST GIVE HIM A GOOD OLD-FASHIONED LEECHING!
ESHER! IS DAD FEELING BETTER?
SEE FOR YOURSELF...

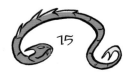

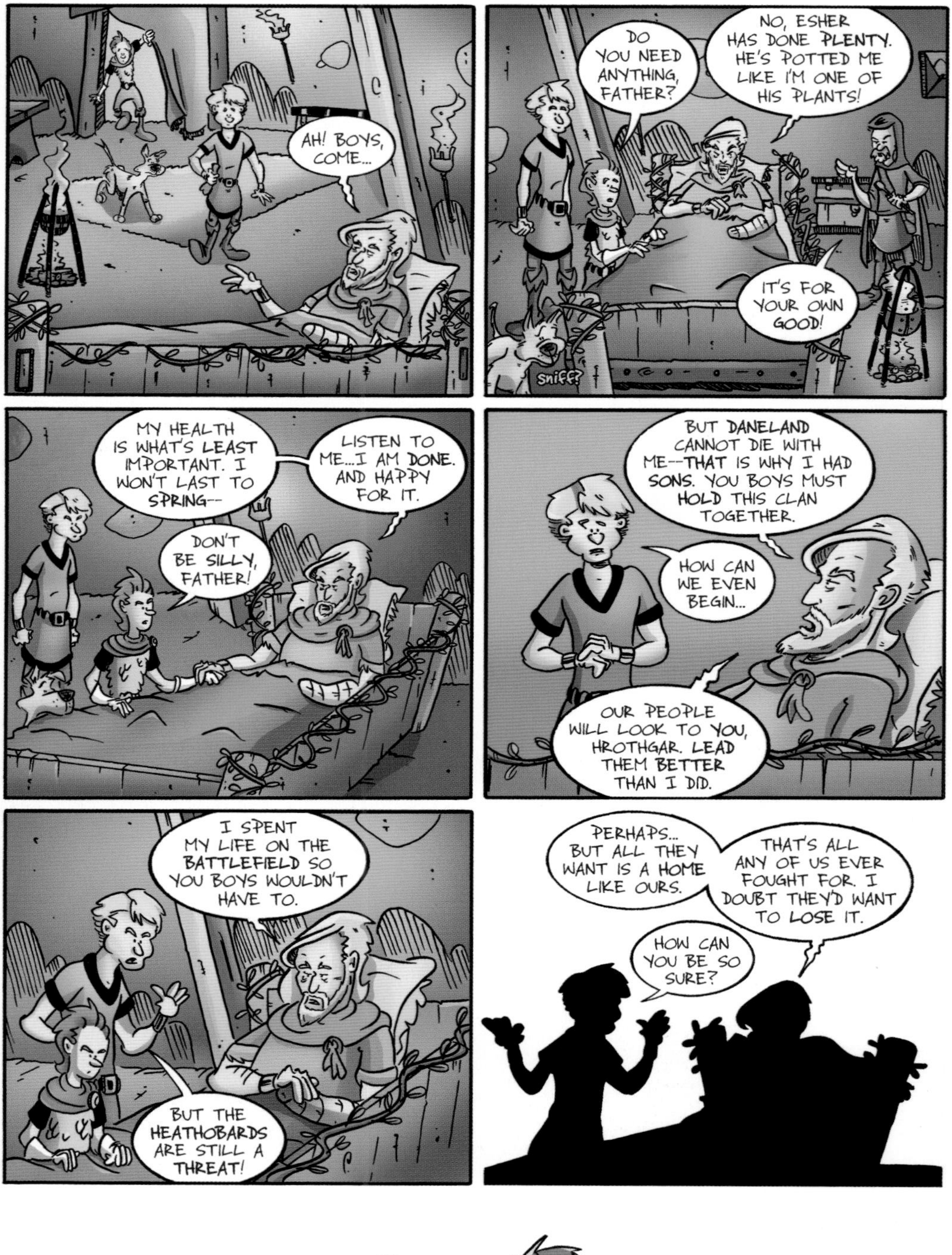
AH! BOYS, COME...
DO YOU NEED ANYTHING, FATHER?
NO, ESHER HAS DONE PLENTY. HE'S POTTED ME LIKE I'M ONE OF HIS PLANTS!
IT'S FOR YOUR OWN GOOD!
SNIFF?
MY HEALTH IS WHAT'S LEAST IMPORTANT. I WON'T LAST TO SPRING--
LISTEN TO ME...I AM DONE. AND HAPPY FOR IT.
DON'T BE SILLY, FATHER!
BUT DANELAND CANNOT DIE WITH ME--THAT IS WHY I HAD SONS. YOU BOYS MUST HOLD THIS CLAN TOGETHER.
HOW CAN WE EVEN BEGIN...
OUR PEOPLE WILL LOOK TO YOU, HROTHGAR. LEAD THEM BETTER THAN I DID.
I SPENT MY LIFE ON THE BATTLEFIELD SO YOU BOYS WOULDN'T HAVE TO.
BUT THE HEATHOBARDS ARE STILL A THREAT!
PERHAPS... BUT ALL THEY WANT IS A HOME LIKE OURS.
THAT'S ALL ANY OF US EVER FOUGHT FOR. I DOUBT THEY'D WANT TO LOSE IT.
HOW CAN YOU BE SO SURE?

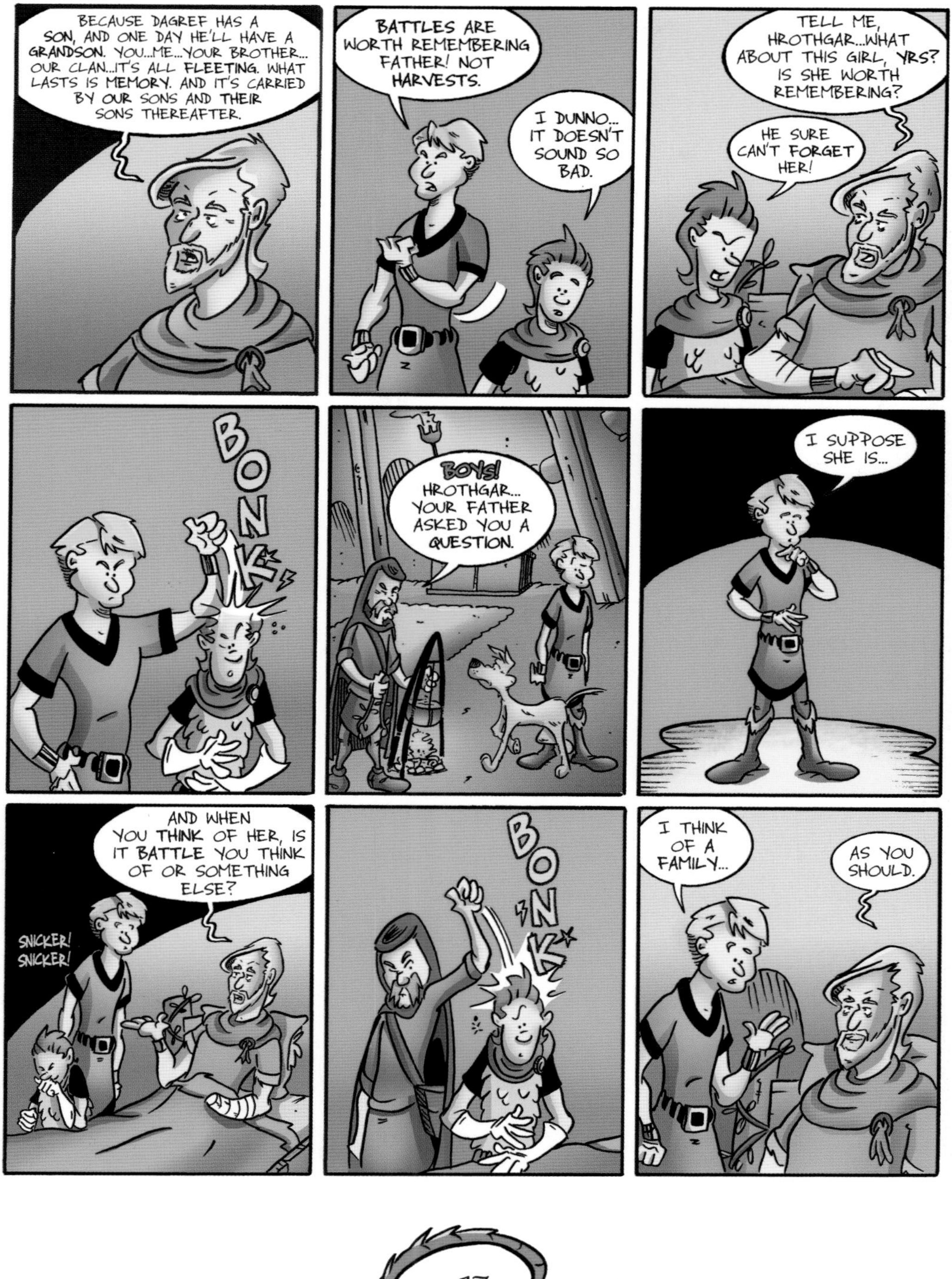
BECAUSE DAGREF HAS A SON, AND ONE DAY HE'LL HAVE A GRANDSON. YOU...ME...YOUR BROTHER... OUR CLAN...IT'S ALL FLEETING. WHAT LASTS IS MEMORY. AND IT'S CARRIED BY OUR SONS AND THEIR SONS THEREAFTER.
BATTLES ARE WORTH REMEMBERING FATHER! NOT HARVESTS.
I DUNNO... IT DOESN'T SOUND SO BAD.
TELL ME, HROTHGAR...WHAT ABOUT THIS GIRL, YRS? IS SHE WORTH REMEMBERING?
HE SURE CAN'T FORGET HER!
BONK
BOYS! HROTHGAR... YOUR FATHER ASKED YOU A QUESTION.
I SUPPOSE SHE IS...
AND WHEN YOU THINK OF HER, IS IT BATTLE YOU THINK OF OR SOMETHING ELSE?
SNICKER! SNICKER!
BONK
I THINK OF A FAMILY...
AS YOU SHOULD.

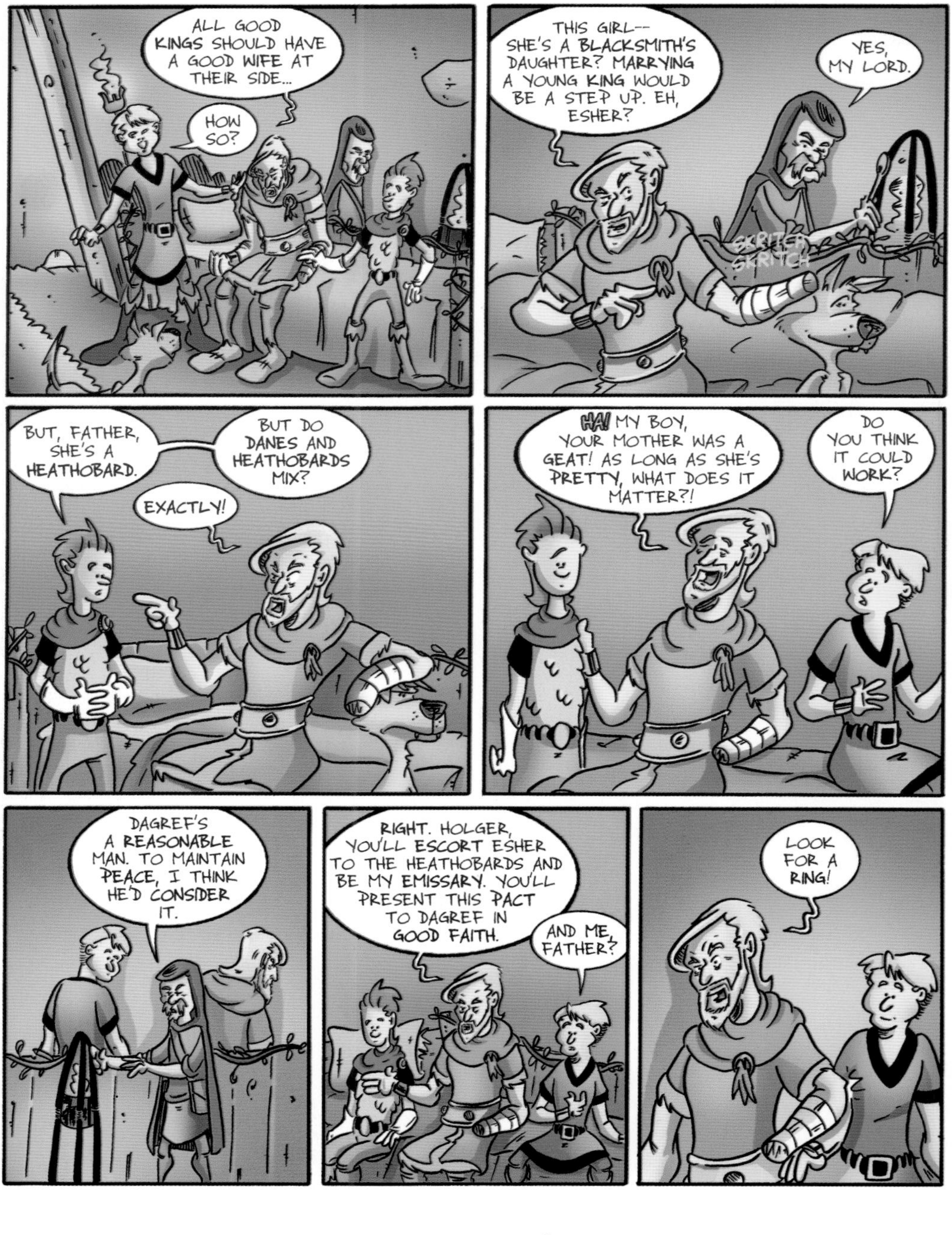
ALL GOOD KINGS SHOULD HAVE A GOOD WIFE AT THEIR SIDE...
HOW SO?
THIS GIRL-- SHE'S A BLACKSMITH'S DAUGHTER? MARRYING A YOUNG KING WOULD BE A STEP UP. EH, ESHER?
YES, MY LORD.
SKRITCH SKRITCH
BUT, FATHER, SHE'S A HEATHOBARD.
BUT DO DANES AND HEATHOBARDS MIX?
EXACTLY!
HA! MY BOY, YOUR MOTHER WAS A GEAT! AS LONG AS SHE'S PRETTY, WHAT DOES IT MATTER?!
DO YOU THINK IT COULD WORK?
DAGREF'S A REASONABLE MAN. TO MAINTAIN PEACE, I THINK HE'D CONSIDER IT.
RIGHT. HOLGER, YOU'LL ESCORT ESHER TO THE HEATHOBARDS AND BE MY EMISSARY. YOU'LL PRESENT THIS PACT TO DAGREF IN GOOD FAITH.
AND ME, FATHER?
LOOK FOR A RING!

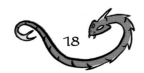

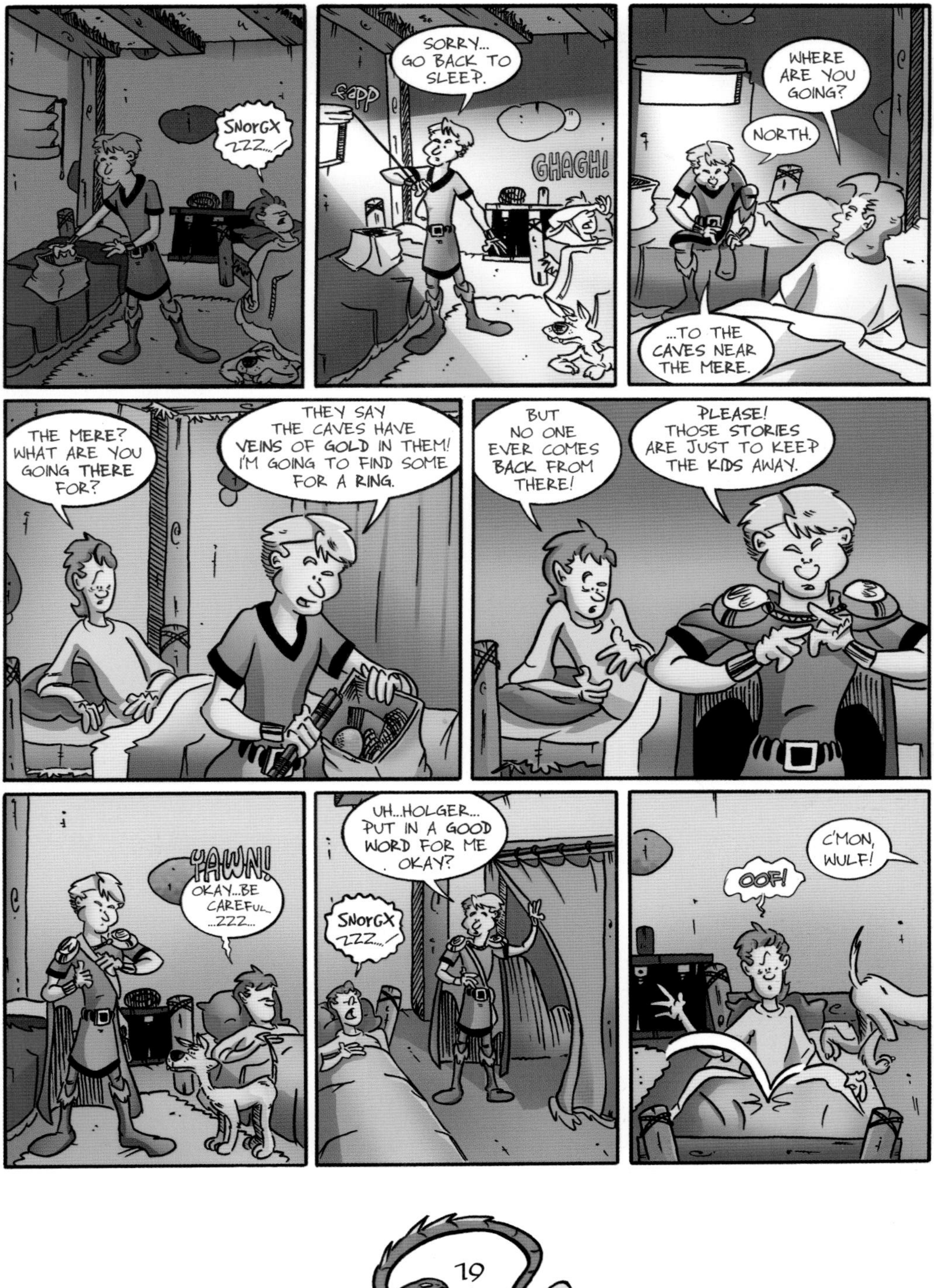
SNorGX ZZZ...!
SORRY... GO BACK TO SLEEP.
GHAGH!
WHERE ARE YOU GOING?
NORTH.
...TO THE CAVES NEAR THE MERE.
THE MERE? WHAT ARE YOU GOING THERE FOR?
THEY SAY THE CAVES HAVE VEINS OF GOLD IN THEM! I'M GOING TO FIND SOME FOR A RING.
BUT NO ONE EVER COMES BACK FROM THERE!
PLEASE! THOSE STORIES ARE JUST TO KEEP THE KIDS AWAY.
YAWN!
OKAY...BE CAREFUL... ...ZZZ...
UH...HOLGER... PUT IN A GOOD WORD FOR ME OKAY?
SNorGX ZZZ...!
OOF!
C'MON, WULF!

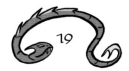

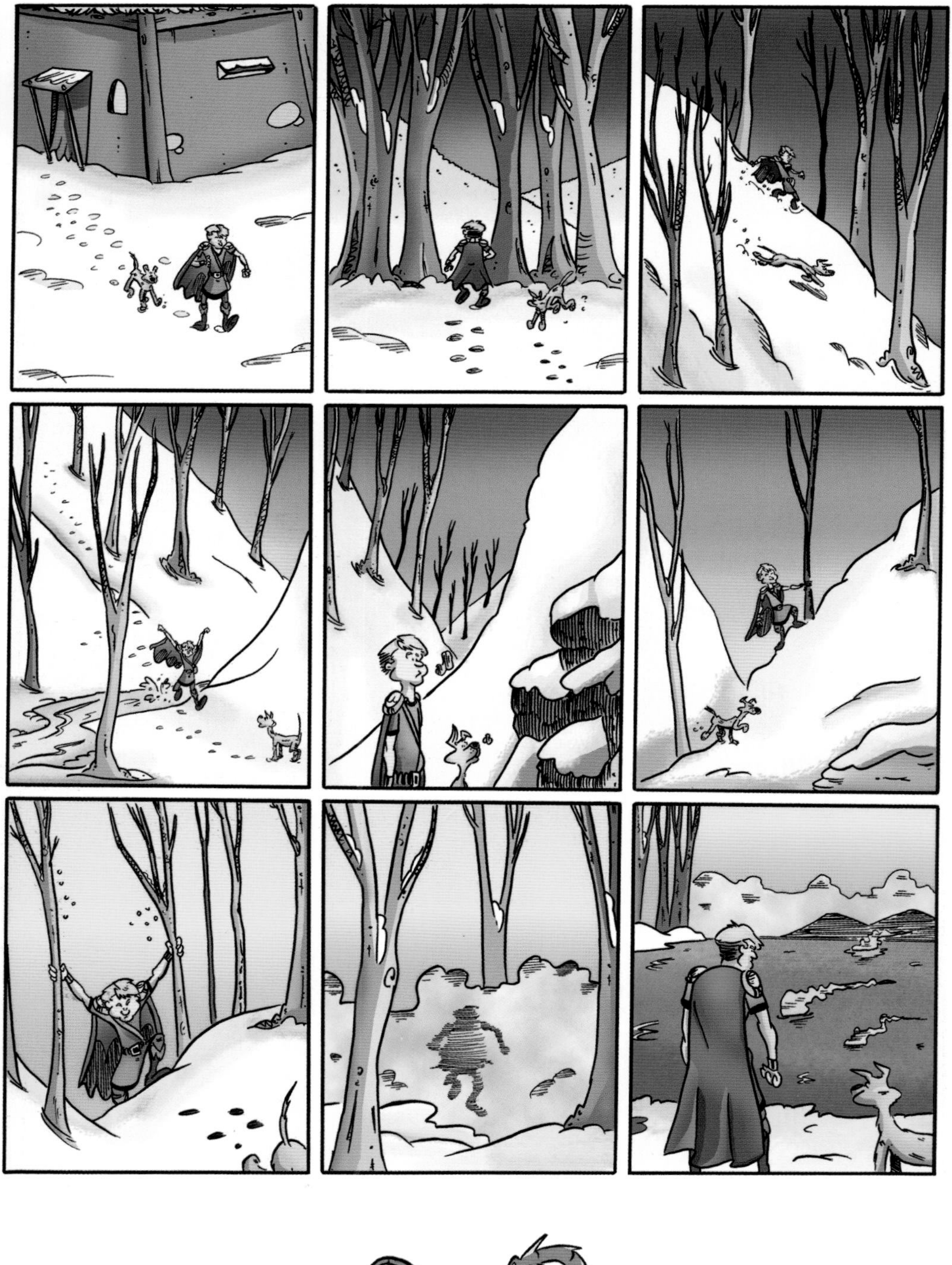

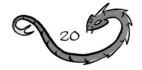

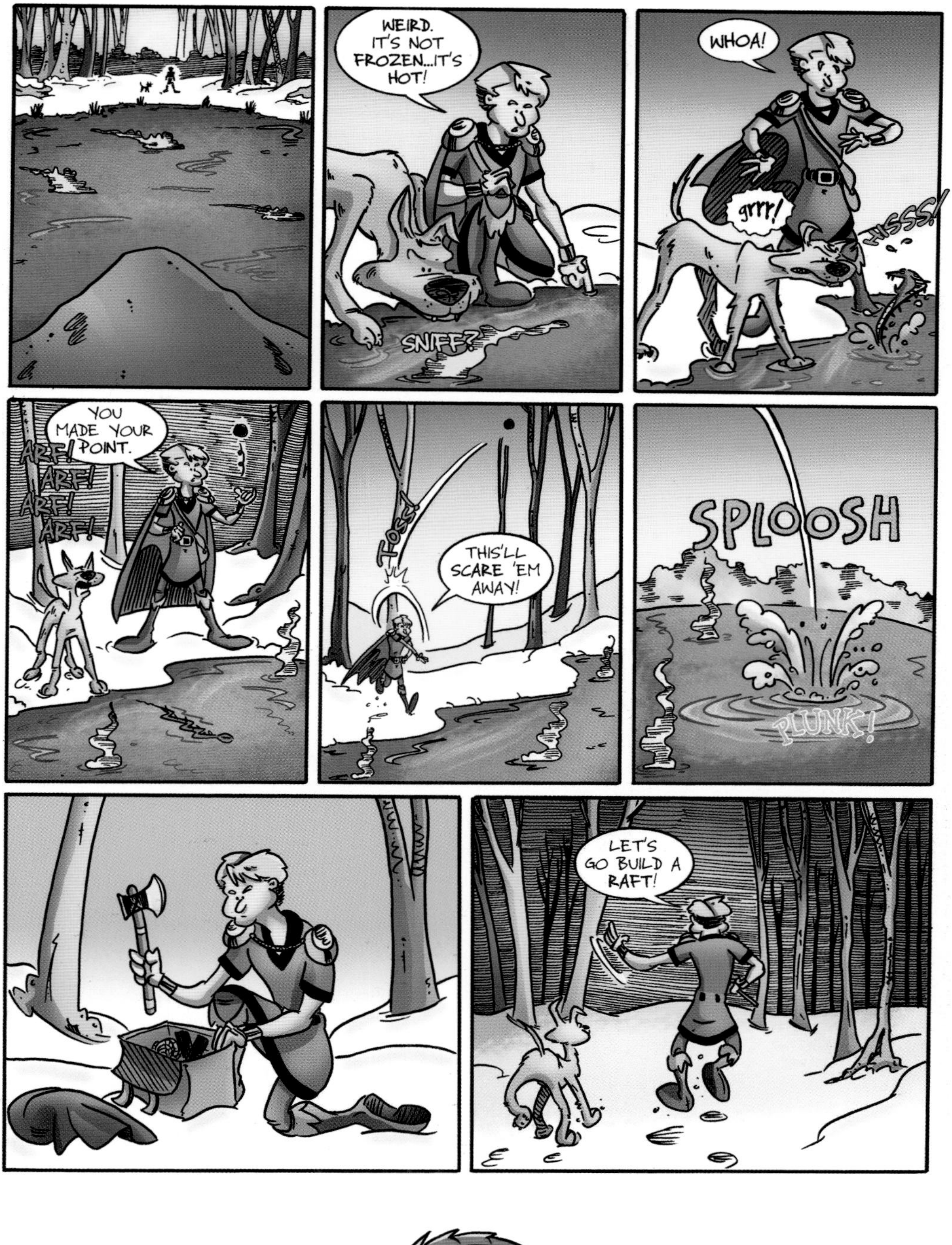
WEIRD. IT'S NOT FROZEN...IT'S HOT!
SNIFF?
WHOA!
grrr!
HISSSS!
YOU MADE YOUR POINT.
ARF! ARF! ARF! ARF!
TOSS
THIS'LL SCARE 'EM AWAY!
SPLOOSH
PLUNK!
LET'S GO BUILD A RAFT!

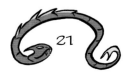

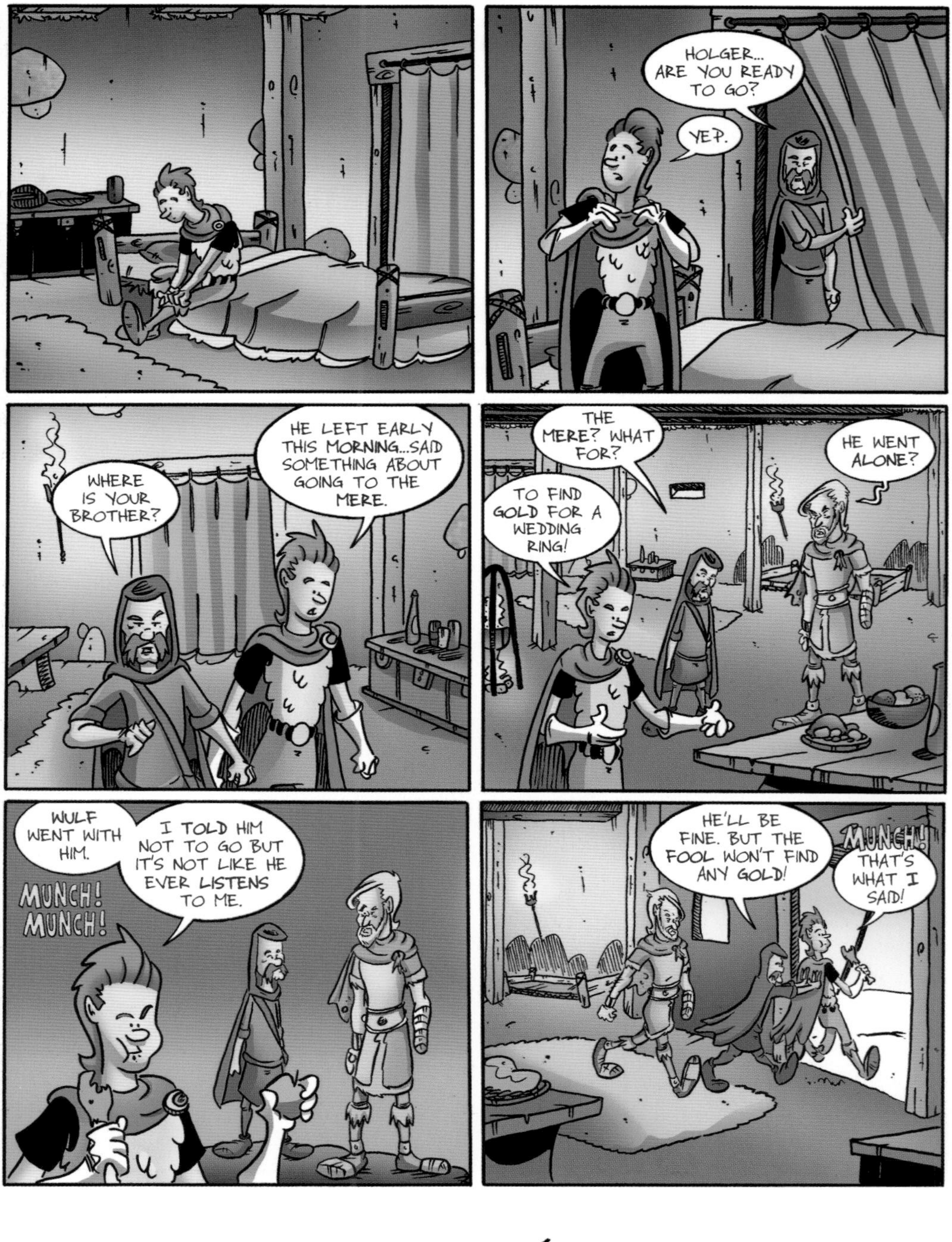
HOLGER... ARE YOU READY TO GO?
YEP.
WHERE IS YOUR BROTHER?
HE LEFT EARLY THIS MORNING...SAID SOMETHING ABOUT GOING TO THE MERE.
THE MERE? WHAT FOR?
TO FIND GOLD FOR A WEDDING RING!
HE WENT ALONE?
WULF WENT WITH HIM.
I TOLD HIM NOT TO GO BUT IT'S NOT LIKE HE EVER LISTENS TO ME.
MUNCH! MUNCH!
HE'LL BE FINE. BUT THE FOOL WON'T FIND ANY GOLD!
MUNCH!
THAT'S WHAT I SAID!

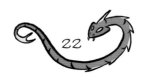

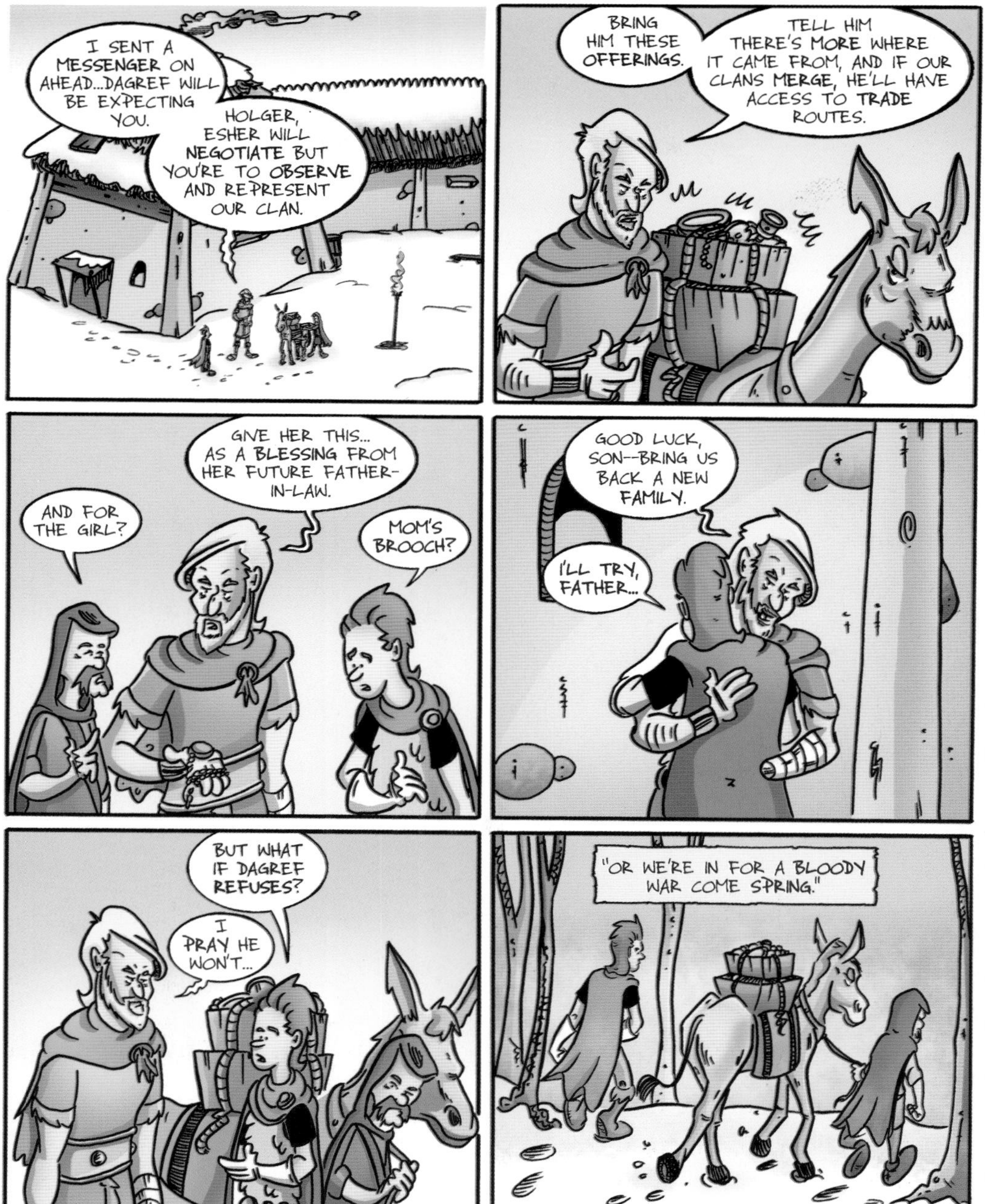
I SENT A MESSENGER ON AHEAD...DAGREF WILL BE EXPECTING YOU.
HOLGER, ESHER WILL NEGOTIATE BUT YOU'RE TO OBSERVE AND REPRESENT OUR CLAN.
BRING HIM THESE OFFERINGS.
TELL HIM THERE'S MORE WHERE IT CAME FROM, AND IF OUR CLANS MERGE, HE'LL HAVE ACCESS TO TRADE ROUTES.
AND FOR THE GIRL?
GIVE HER THIS... AS A BLESSING FROM HER FUTURE FATHER-IN-LAW.
MOM'S BROOCH?
GOOD LUCK, SON--BRING US BACK A NEW FAMILY.
I'LL TRY, FATHER...
BUT WHAT IF DAGREF REFUSES?
I PRAY HE WON'T...
"OR WE'RE IN FOR A BLOODY WAR COME SPRING."

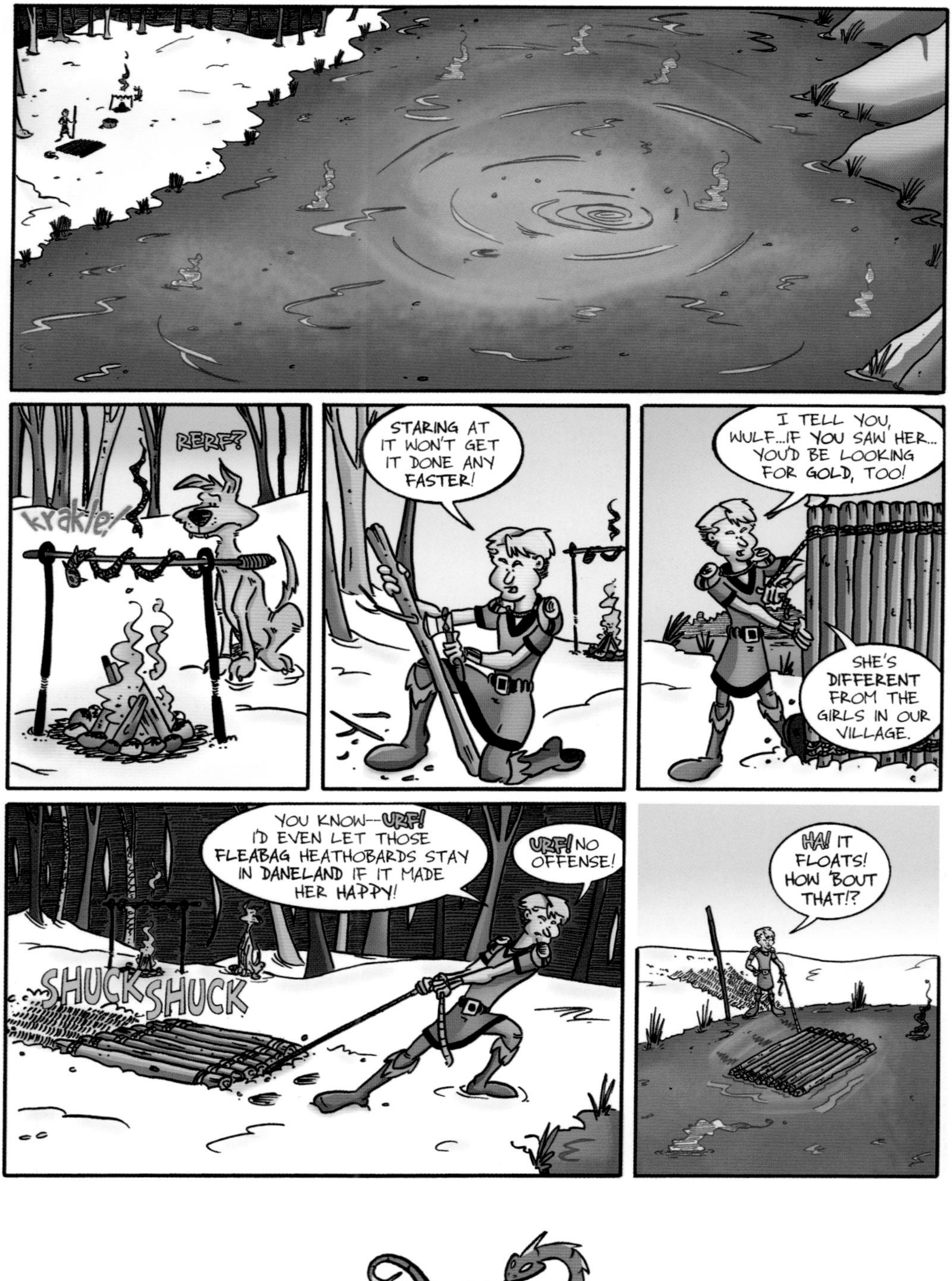
RERF?
KRAKLE!
STARING AT IT WON'T GET IT DONE ANY FASTER!
I TELL YOU, WULF...IF YOU SAW HER... YOU'D BE LOOKING FOR GOLD, TOO!
SHE'S DIFFERENT FROM THE GIRLS IN OUR VILLAGE.
YOU KNOW--URF! I'D EVEN LET THOSE FLEABAG HEATHOBARDS STAY IN DANELAND IF IT MADE HER HAPPY!
URF! NO OFFENSE!
SHUCK SHUCK
HA! IT FLOATS! HOW 'BOUT THAT!?

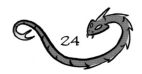

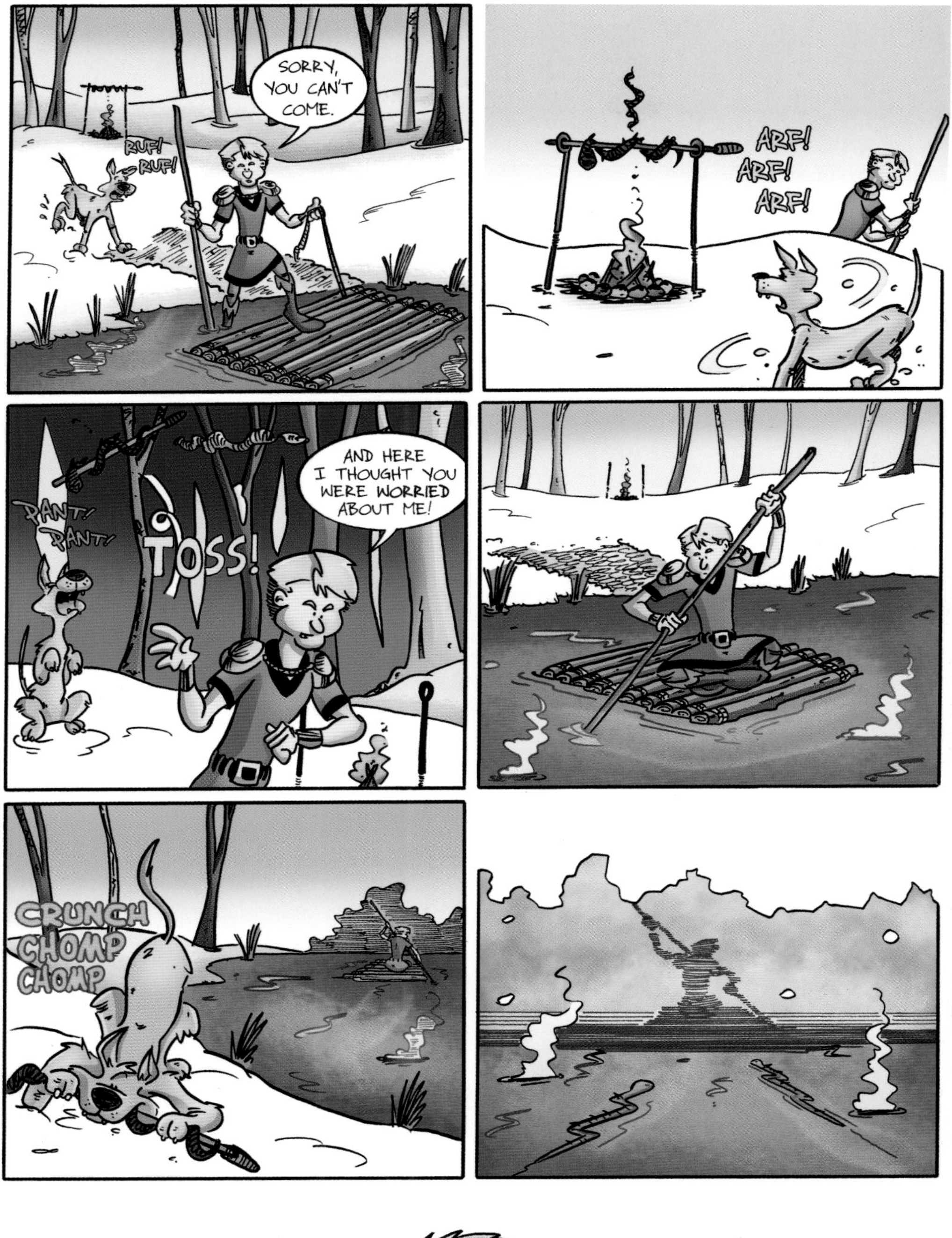
SORRY, YOU CAN'T COME.
RUF! RUF!
ARF! ARF! ARF!
PANT! PANT!
TOSS!
AND HERE I THOUGHT YOU WERE WORRIED ABOUT ME!
CRUNCH CHOMP CHOMP

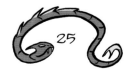

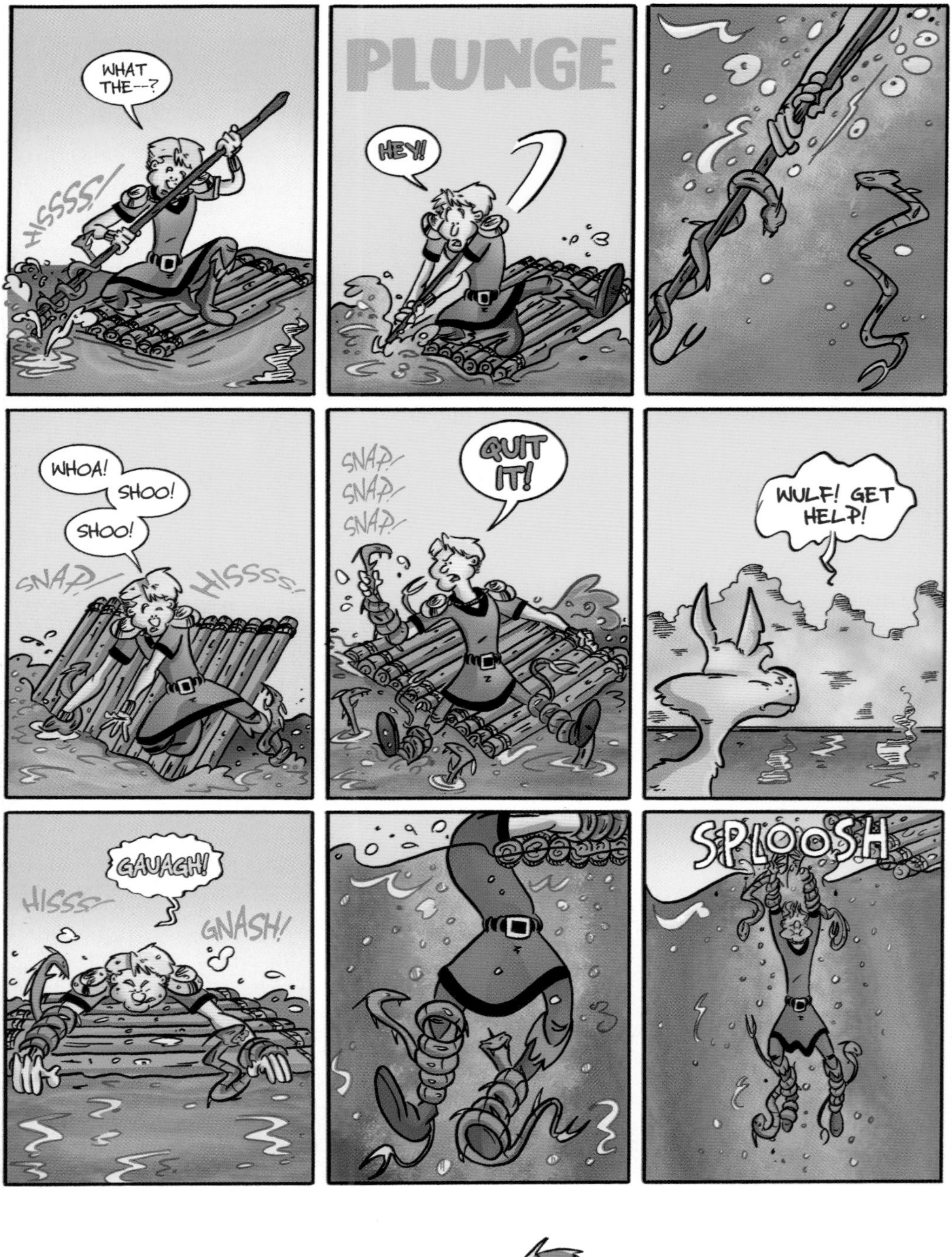
WHAT THE--?
HISSSS!
PLUNGE
HEY!
WHOA!
SHOO!
SHOO!
SNAP!
HISSSS!
SNAP!
SNAP!
SNAP!
QUIT IT!
WULF! GET HELP!
GAUAGH!
HISSS
GNASH!
SPLOOSH

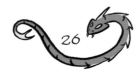

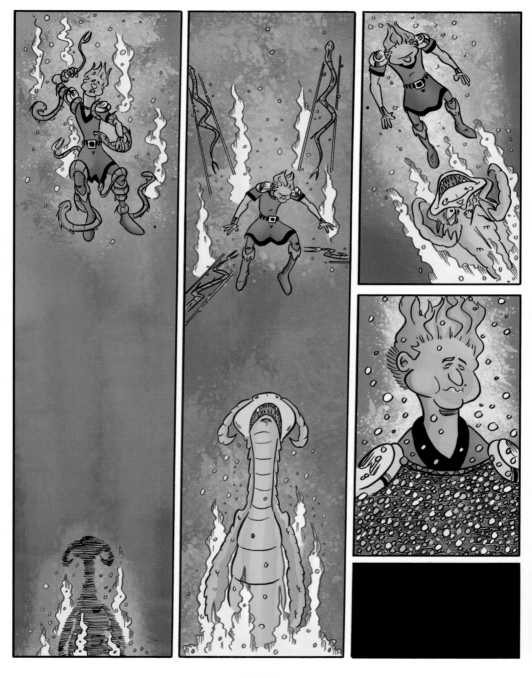

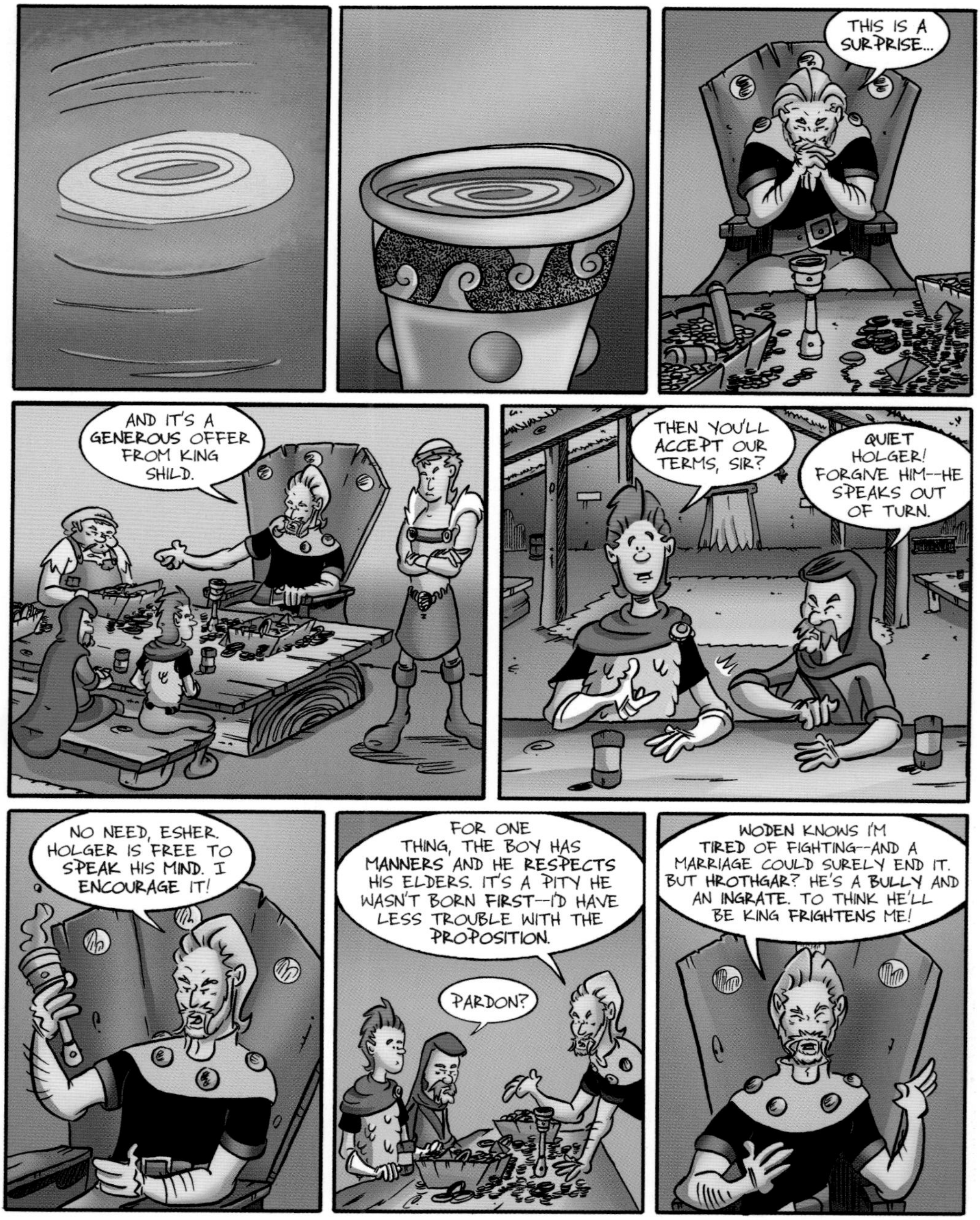
THIS IS A SURPRISE...
AND IT'S A GENEROUS OFFER FROM KING SHILD.
THEN YOU'LL ACCEPT OUR TERMS, SIR?
QUIET HOLGER! FORGIVE HIM--HE SPEAKS OUT OF TURN.
NO NEED, ESHER. HOLGER IS FREE TO SPEAK HIS MIND. I ENCOURAGE IT!
FOR ONE THING, THE BOY HAS MANNERS AND HE RESPECTS HIS ELDERS. IT'S A PITY HE WASN'T BORN FIRST--I'D HAVE LESS TROUBLE WITH THE PROPOSITION.
PARDON?
WODEN KNOWS I'M TIRED OF FIGHTING--AND A MARRIAGE COULD SURELY END IT. BUT HROTHGAR? HE'S A BULLY AND AN INGRATE. TO THINK HE'LL BE KING FRIGHTENS ME!

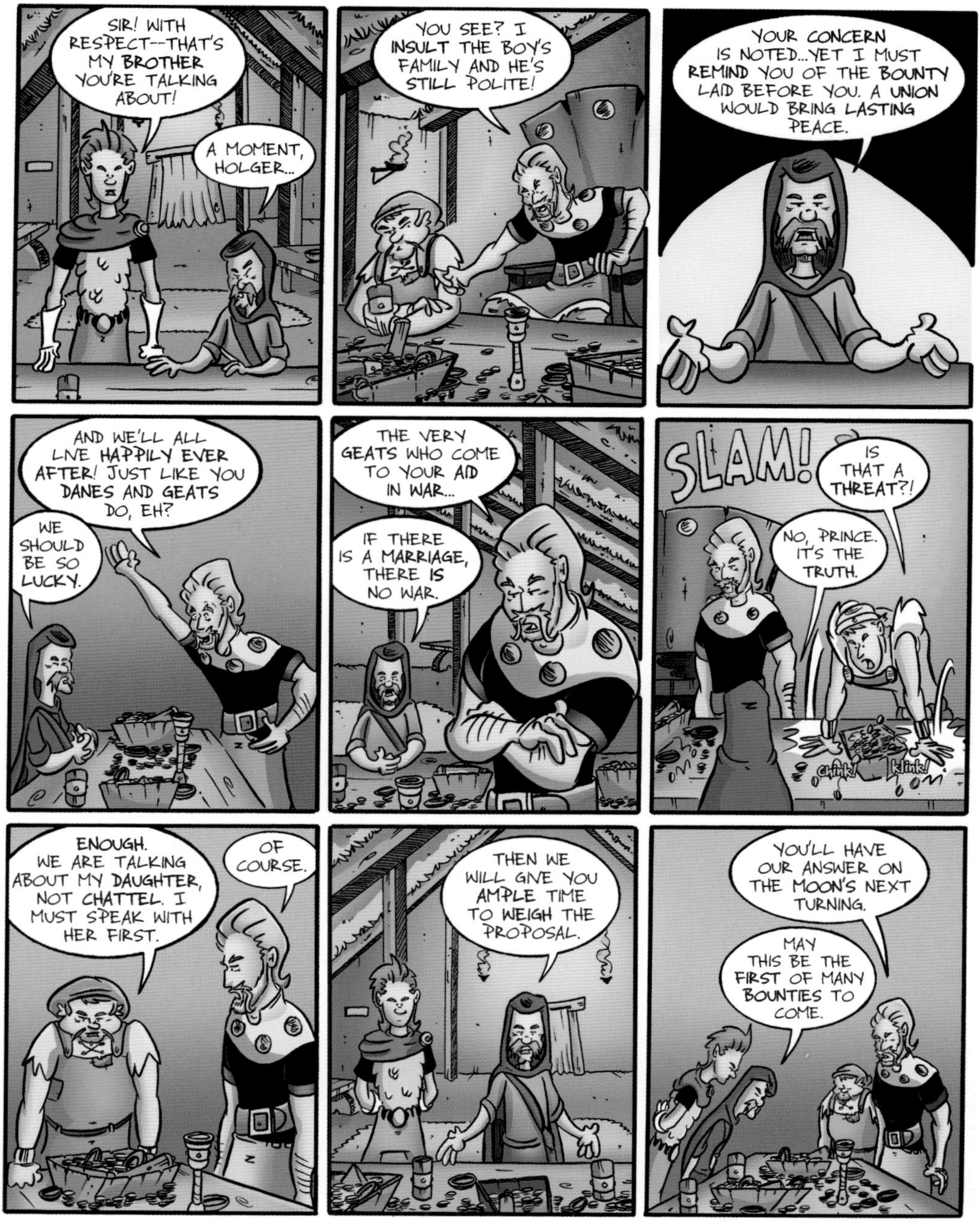
SIR! WITH RESPECT--THAT'S MY BROTHER YOU'RE TALKING ABOUT!
A MOMENT, HOLGER...
YOU SEE? I INSULT THE BOY'S FAMILY AND HE'S STILL POLITE!
YOUR CONCERN IS NOTED...YET I MUST REMIND YOU OF THE BOUNTY LAID BEFORE YOU. A UNION WOULD BRING LASTING PEACE.
AND WE'LL ALL LIVE HAPPILY EVER AFTER! JUST LIKE YOU DANES AND GEATS DO, EH?
WE SHOULD BE SO LUCKY.
THE VERY GEATS WHO COME TO YOUR AID IN WAR...
IF THERE IS A MARRIAGE, THERE IS NO WAR.
SLAM!
IS THAT A THREAT?!
NO, PRINCE. IT'S THE TRUTH.
chink!
klink!
ENOUGH. WE ARE TALKING ABOUT MY DAUGHTER, NOT CHATTEL. I MUST SPEAK WITH HER FIRST.
OF COURSE.
THEN WE WILL GIVE YOU AMPLE TIME TO WEIGH THE PROPOSAL.
YOU'LL HAVE OUR ANSWER ON THE MOON'S NEXT TURNING.
MAY THIS BE THE FIRST OF MANY BOUNTIES TO COME.

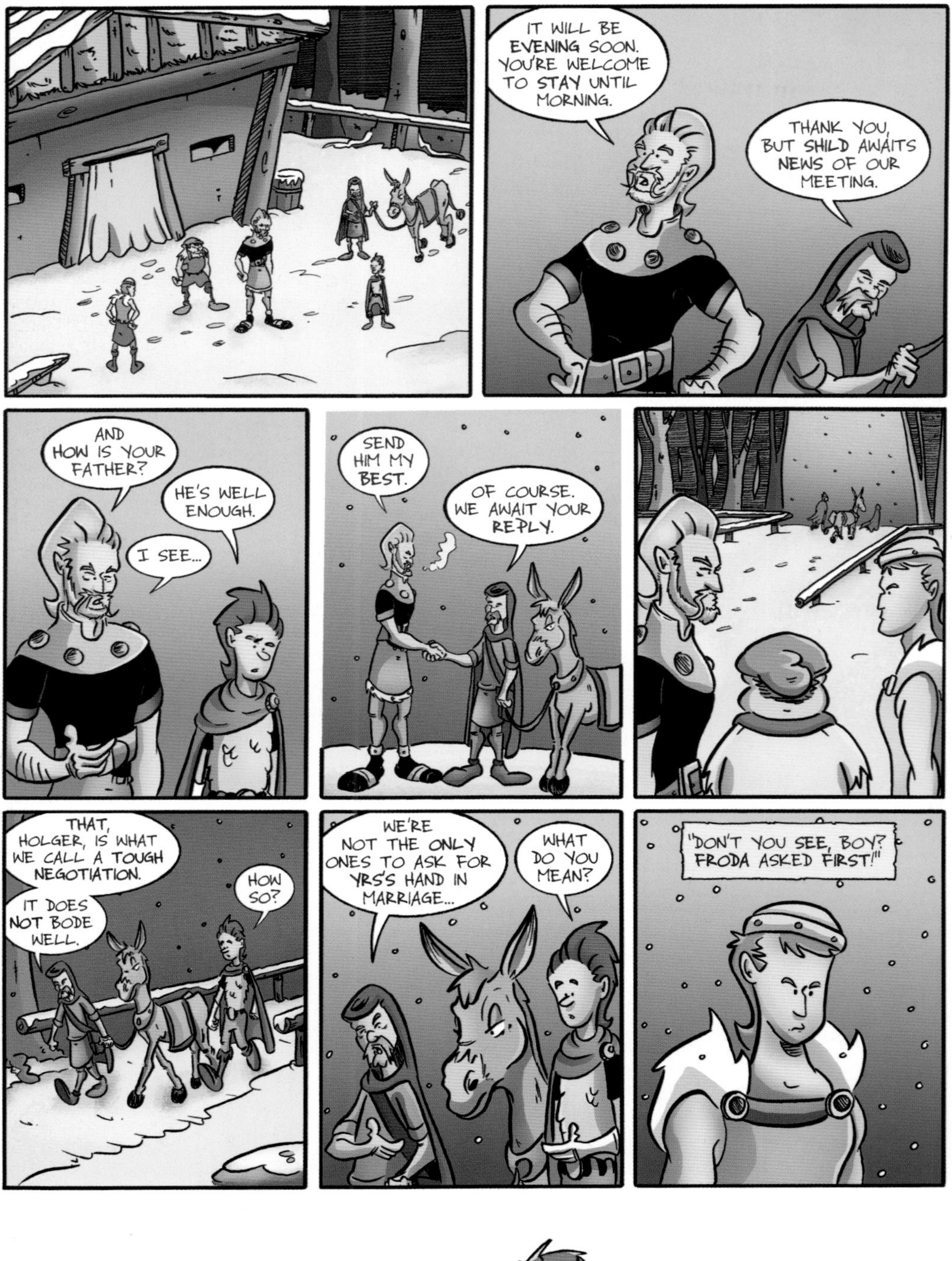
IT WILL BE EVENING SOON. YOU'RE WELCOME TO STAY UNTIL MORNING.
THANK YOU, BUT SHILD AWAITS NEWS OF OUR MEETING.
AND HOW IS YOUR FATHER?
HE'S WELL ENOUGH.
I SEE...
SEND HIM MY BEST.
OF COURSE. WE AWAIT YOUR REPLY.
THAT, HOLGER, IS WHAT WE CALL A TOUGH NEGOTIATION.
IT DOES NOT BODE WELL.
HOW SO?
WE'RE NOT THE ONLY ONES TO ASK FOR YRS'S HAND IN MARRIAGE...
WHAT DO YOU MEAN?
"DON'T YOU SEE, BOY? FRODA ASKED FIRST!"

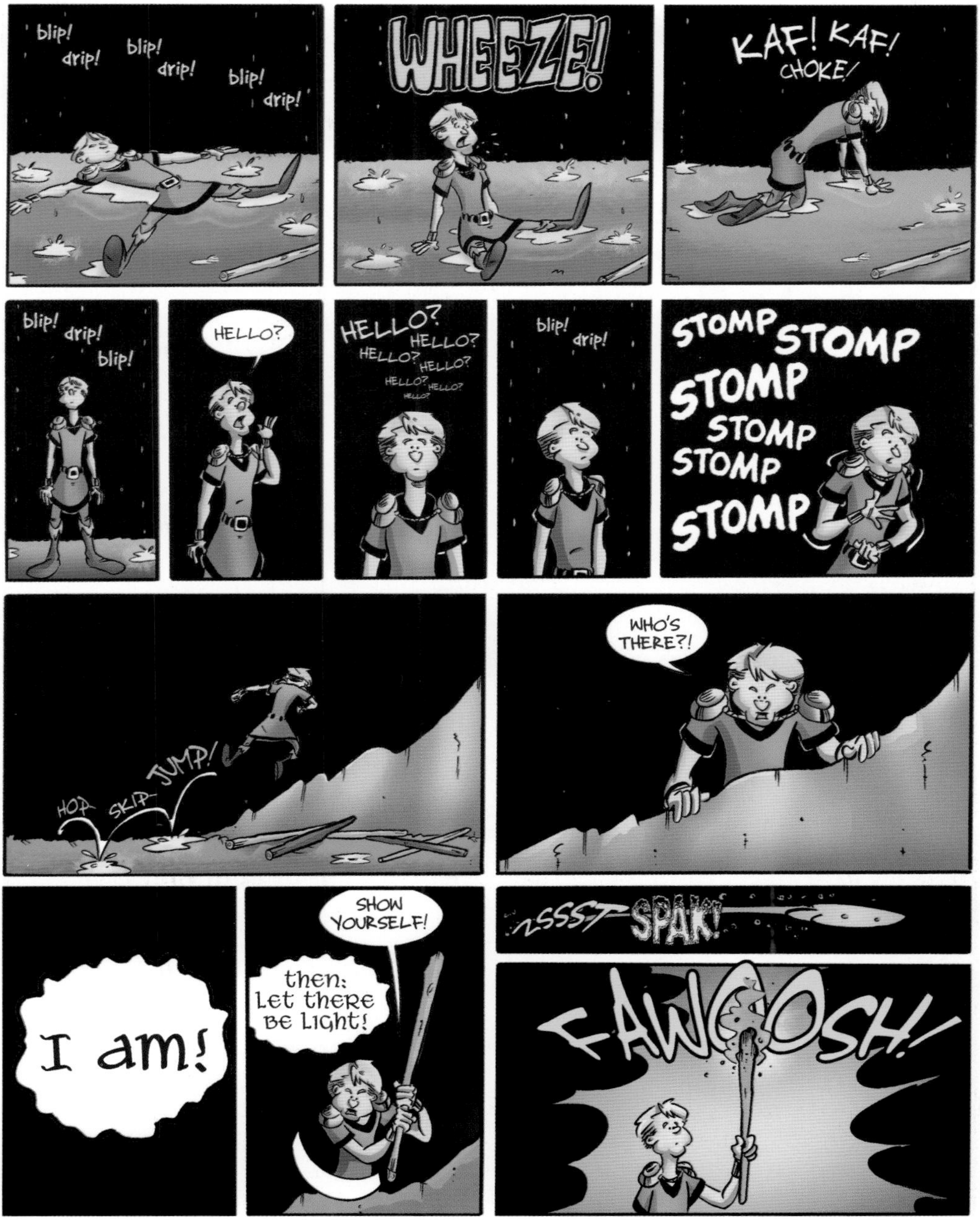
blip!
drip!
blip!
drip!
blip!
drip!
WHEEZE!
KAF! KAF!
CHOKE!
blip! drip!
blip!
HELLO?
HELLO?
HELLO?
HELLO?
HELLO?
HELLO?
HELLO?
HELLO?
blip! drip!
STOMP STOMP
STOMP
STOMP
STOMP
STOMP
HOP SKIP JUMP!
WHO'S THERE?!
I am!
SHOW YOURSELF!
then: Let there be Light!
ZSSST SPAK!
FAWOOSH!

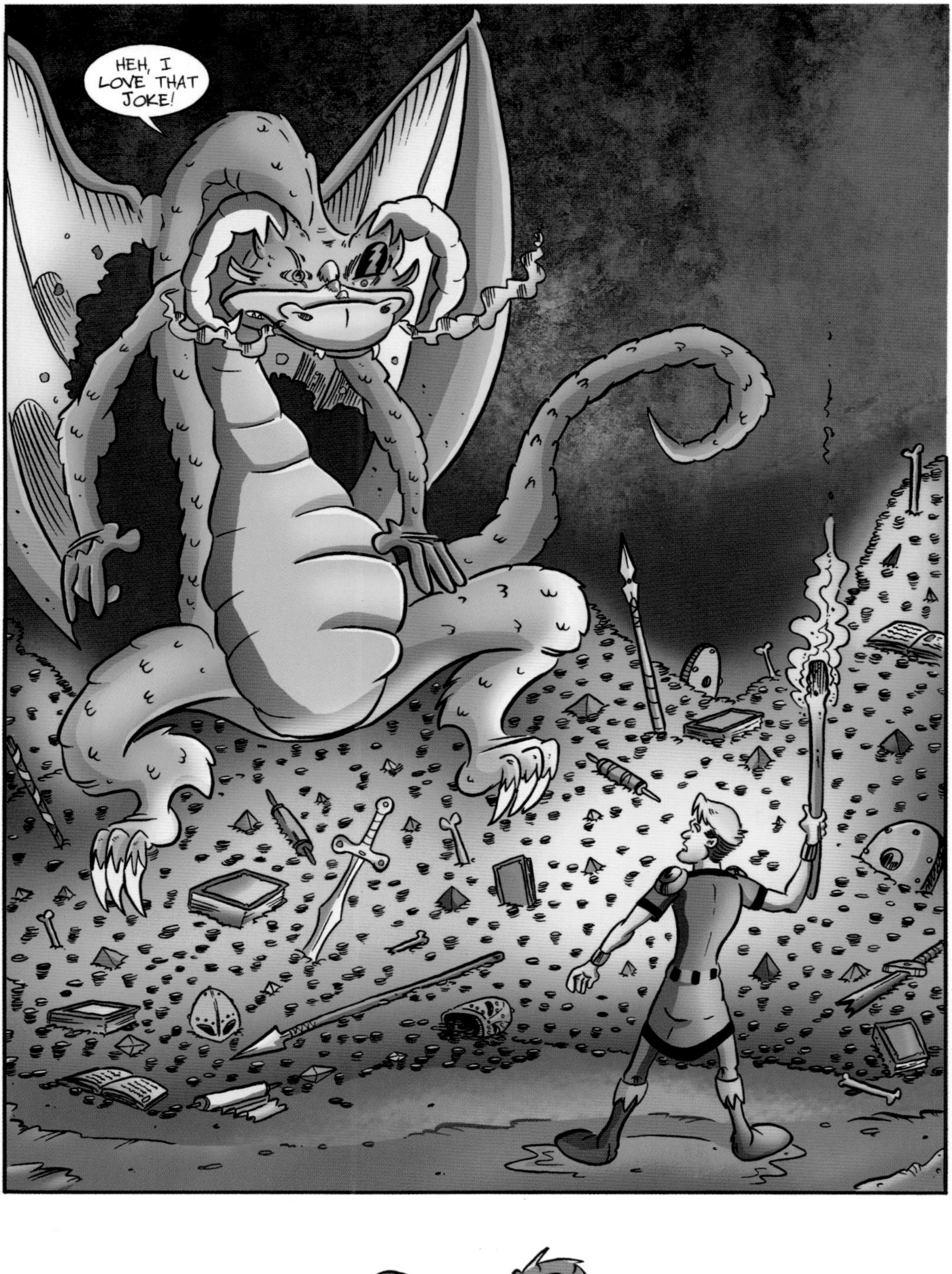
HEH, I LOVE THAT JOKE!

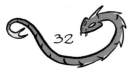

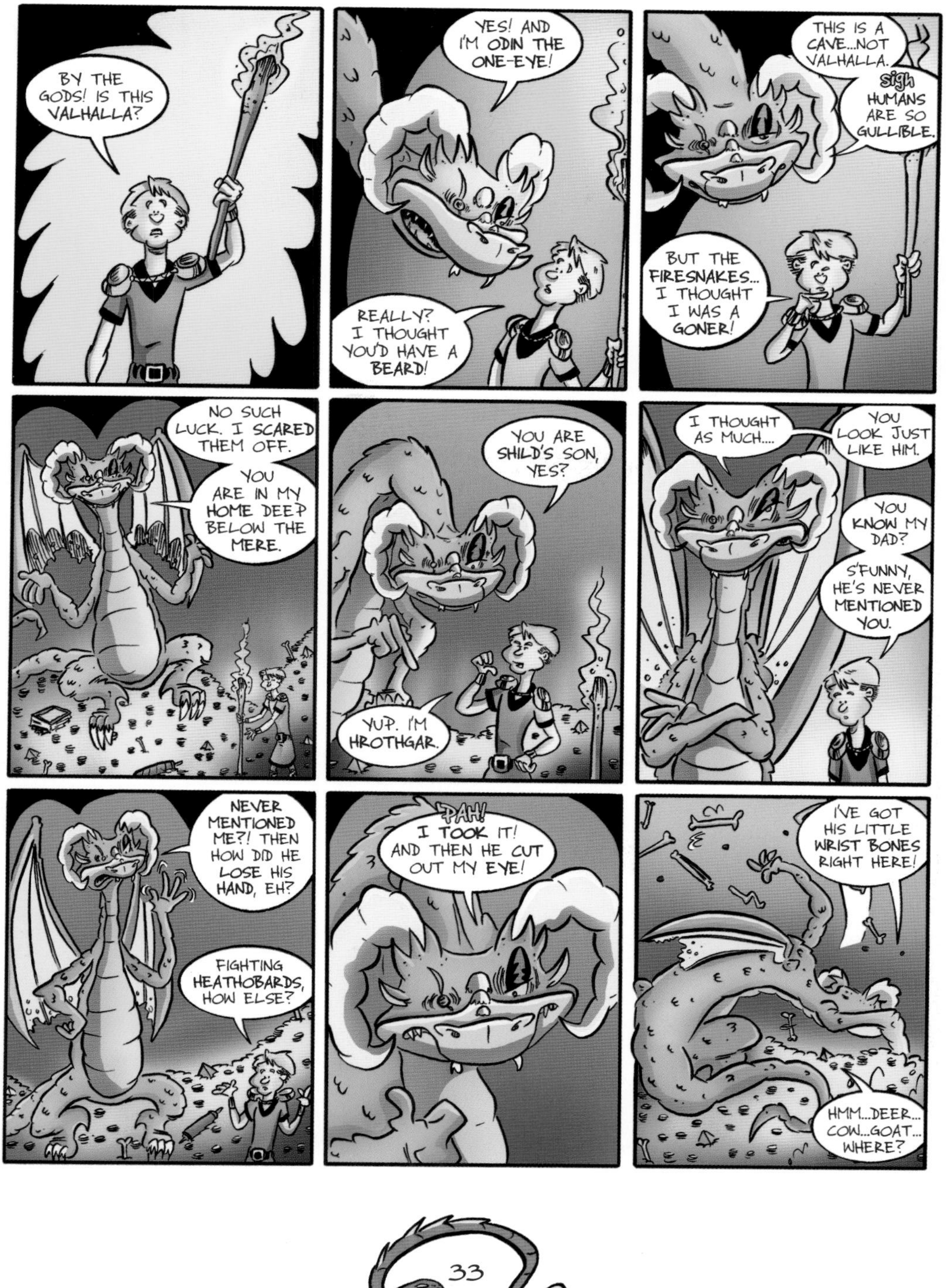
BY THE GODS! IS THIS VALHALLA?
YES! AND I'M ODIN THE ONE-EYE!
REALLY? I THOUGHT YOU'D HAVE A BEARD!
THIS IS A CAVE...NOT VALHALLA.
sigh HUMANS ARE SO GULLIBLE.
BUT THE FIRESNAKES... I THOUGHT I WAS A GONER!
NO SUCH LUCK. I SCARED THEM OFF.
YOU ARE IN MY HOME DEEP BELOW THE MERE.
YOU ARE SHILD'S SON, YES?
YUP. I'M HROTHGAR.
I THOUGHT AS MUCH....
YOU LOOK JUST LIKE HIM.
YOU KNOW MY DAD?
S'FUNNY, HE'S NEVER MENTIONED YOU.
NEVER MENTIONED ME?! THEN HOW DID HE LOSE HIS HAND, EH?
FIGHTING HEATHOBARDS, HOW ELSE?
PAH!
I TOOK IT! AND THEN HE CUT OUT MY EYE!
I'VE GOT HIS LITTLE WRIST BONES RIGHT HERE!
HMM...DEER... COW...GOAT... WHERE?

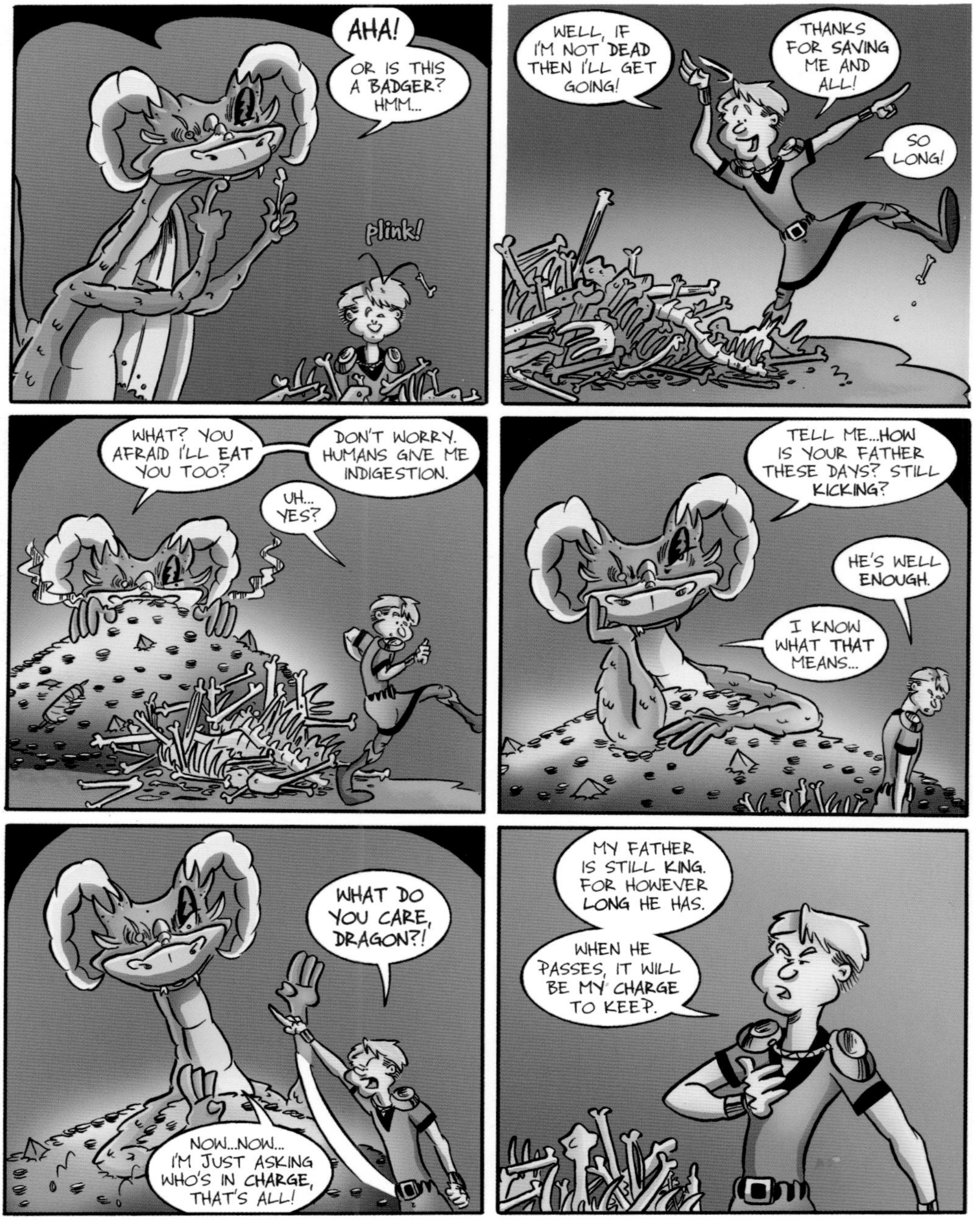
AHA!
OR IS THIS A BADGER? HMM...
plink!
WELL, IF I'M NOT DEAD THEN I'LL GET GOING!
THANKS FOR SAVING ME AND ALL!
SO LONG!
WHAT? YOU AFRAID I'LL EAT YOU TOO?
DON'T WORRY. HUMANS GIVE ME INDIGESTION.
UH... YES?
TELL ME...HOW IS YOUR FATHER THESE DAYS? STILL KICKING?
HE'S WELL ENOUGH.
I KNOW WHAT THAT MEANS...
WHAT DO YOU CARE, DRAGON?!
NOW...NOW... I'M JUST ASKING WHO'S IN CHARGE, THAT'S ALL!
MY FATHER IS STILL KING. FOR HOWEVER LONG HE HAS.
WHEN HE PASSES, IT WILL BE MY CHARGE TO KEEP.

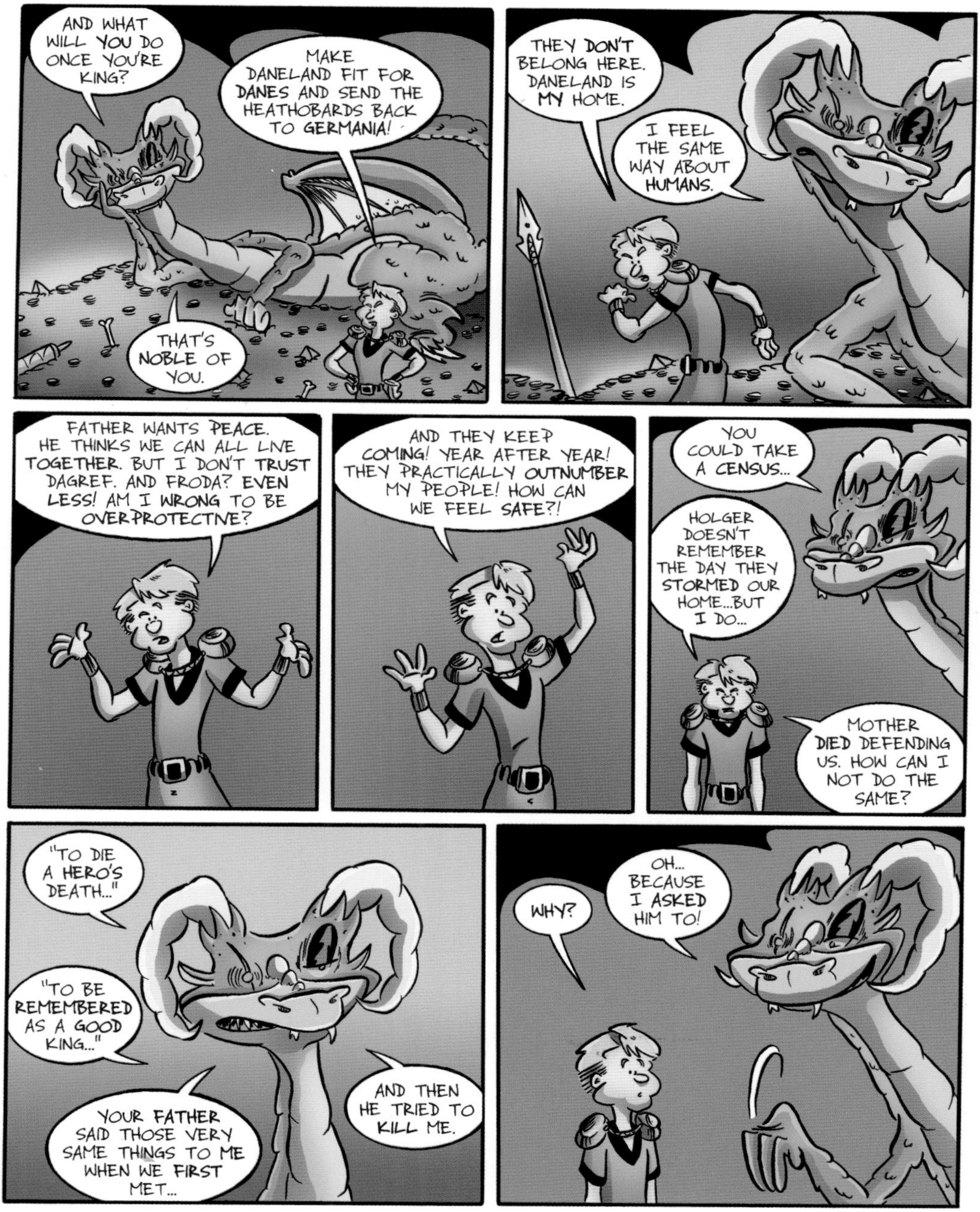
AND WHAT WILL YOU DO ONCE YOU'RE KING?
MAKE DANELAND FIT FOR DANES AND SEND THE HEATHOBARDS BACK TO GERMANIA!
THAT'S NOBLE OF YOU.
THEY DON'T BELONG HERE. DANELAND IS MY HOME.
I FEEL THE SAME WAY ABOUT HUMANS.
FATHER WANTS PEACE. HE THINKS WE CAN ALL LIVE TOGETHER. BUT I DON'T TRUST DAGREF. AND FRODA? EVEN LESS! AM I WRONG TO BE OVERPROTECTIVE?
AND THEY KEEP COMING! YEAR AFTER YEAR! THEY PRACTICALLY OUTNUMBER MY PEOPLE! HOW CAN WE FEEL SAFE?!
YOU COULD TAKE A CENSUS...
HOLGER DOESN'T REMEMBER THE DAY THEY STORMED OUR HOME...BUT I DO...
MOTHER DIED DEFENDING US. HOW CAN I NOT DO THE SAME?
"TO DIE A HERO'S DEATH..."
"TO BE REMEMBERED AS A GOOD KING..."
YOUR FATHER SAID THOSE VERY SAME THINGS TO ME WHEN WE FIRST MET...
AND THEN HE TRIED TO KILL ME.
WHY?
OH... BECAUSE I ASKED HIM TO!

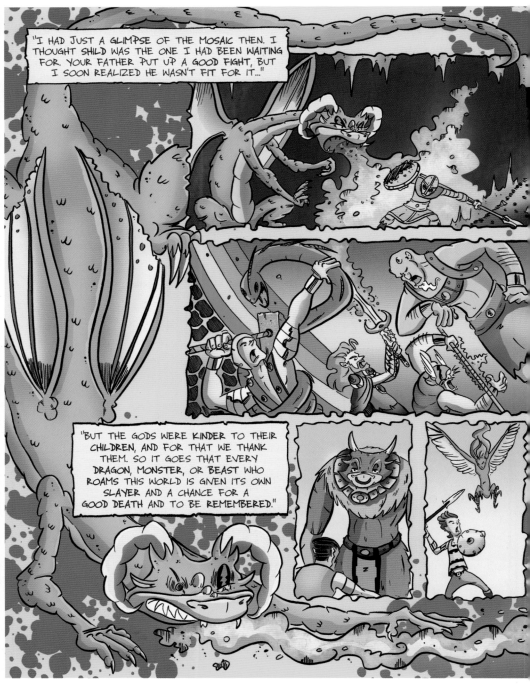

"I HAD JUST A GLIMPSE OF THE MOSAIC THEN. I THOUGHT SHILD WAS THE ONE I HAD BEEN WAITING FOR. YOUR FATHER PUT UP A GOOD FIGHT, BUT I SOON REALIZED HE WASN'T FIT FOR IT..."

"BUT THE GODS WERE KINDER TO THEIR CHILDREN, AND FOR THAT WE THANK THEM. SO IT GOES THAT EVERY DRAGON, MONSTER, OR BEAST WHO ROAMS THIS WORLD IS GIVEN ITS OWN SLAYER AND A CHANCE FOR A GOOD DEATH AND TO BE REMEMBERED."

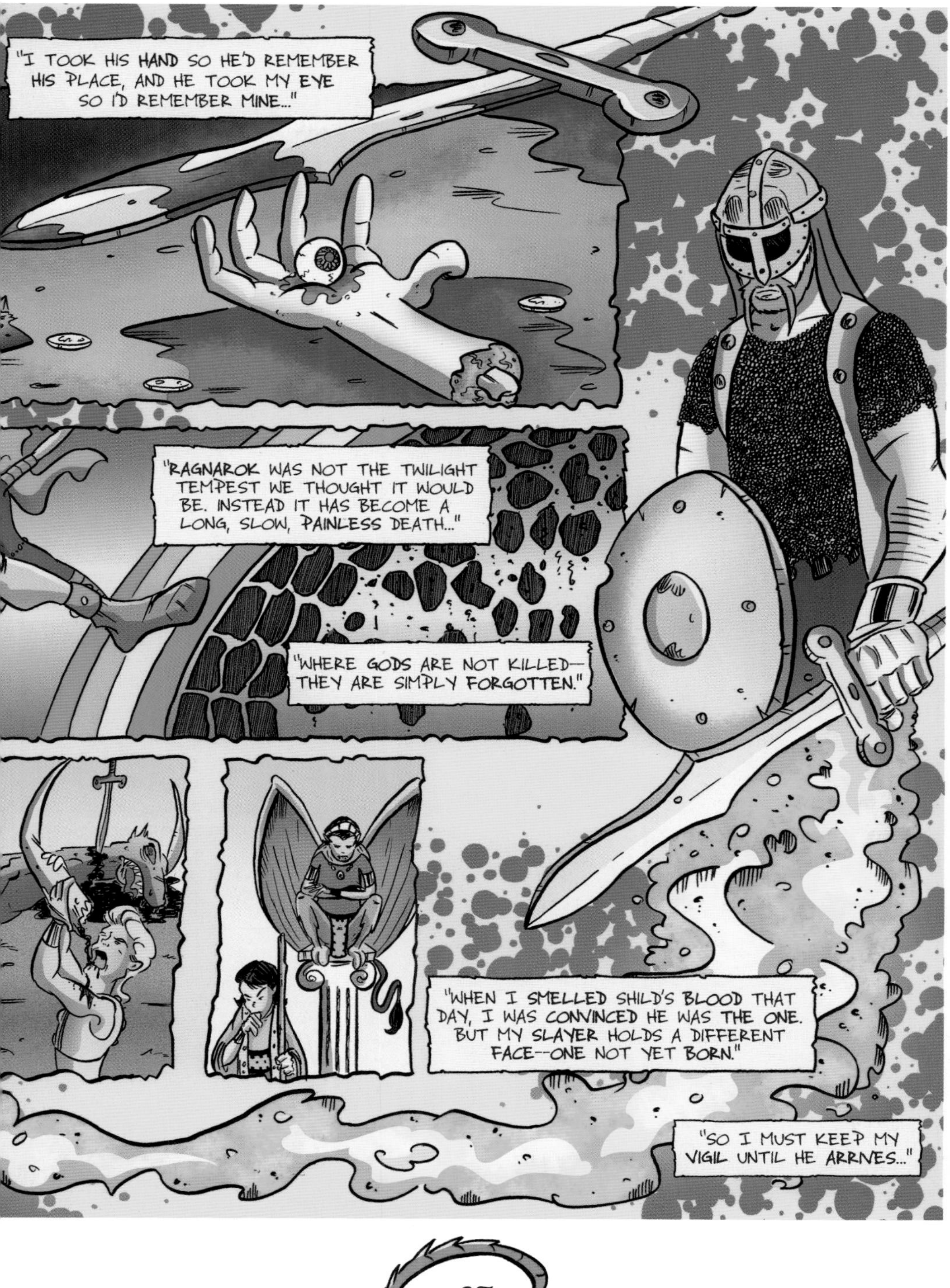
"I TOOK HIS HAND SO HE'D REMEMBER HIS PLACE, AND HE TOOK MY EYE SO I'D REMEMBER MINE..."
"RAGNAROK WAS NOT THE TWILIGHT TEMPEST WE THOUGHT IT WOULD BE. INSTEAD IT HAS BECOME A LONG, SLOW, PAINLESS DEATH..."
"WHERE GODS ARE NOT KILLED--THEY ARE SIMPLY FORGOTTEN."
"WHEN I SMELLED SHILD'S BLOOD THAT DAY, I WAS CONVINCED HE WAS THE ONE. BUT MY SLAYER HOLDS A DIFFERENT FACE--ONE NOT YET BORN."
"SO I MUST KEEP MY VIGIL UNTIL HE ARRIVES..."

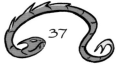

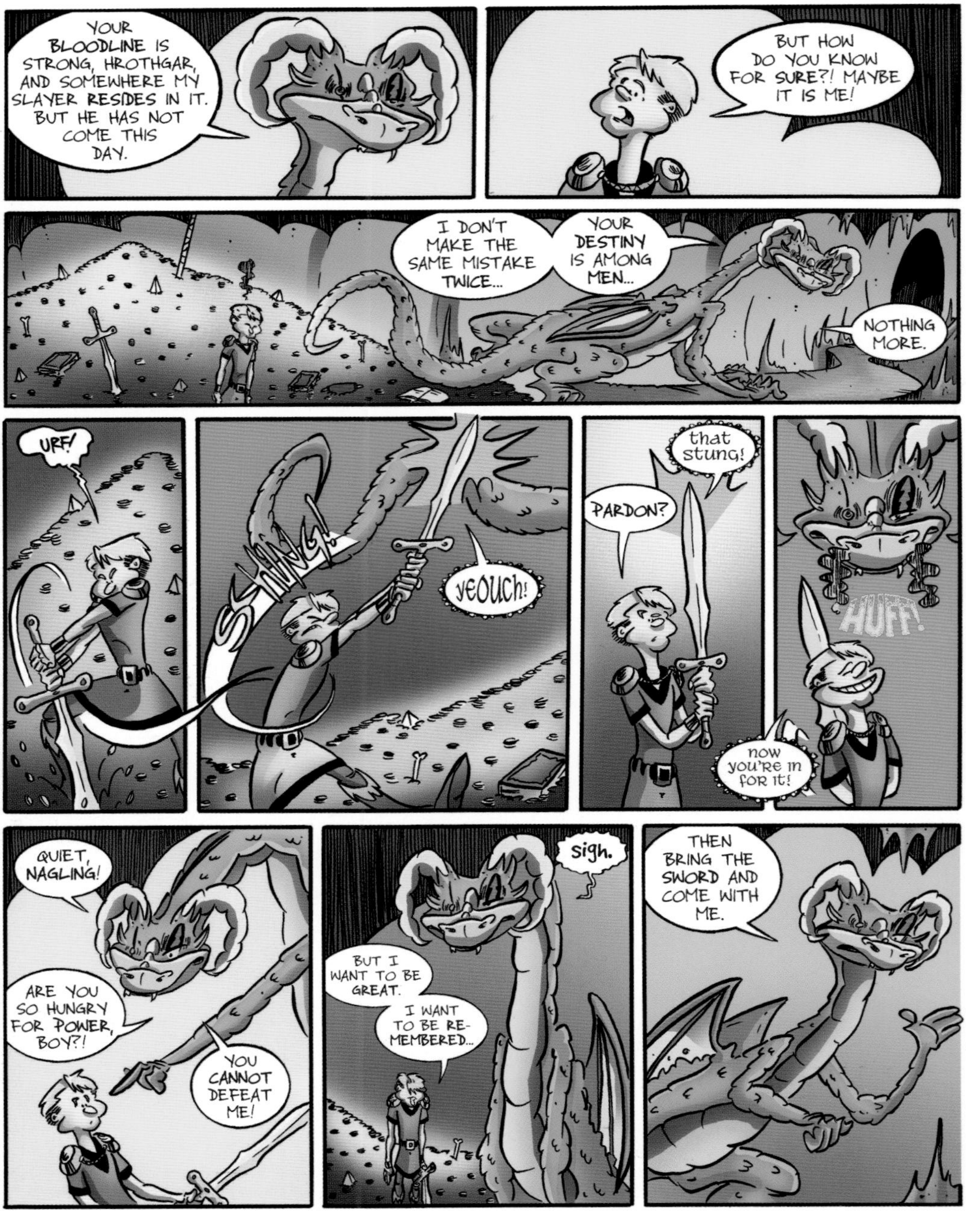
YOUR BLOODLINE IS STRONG, HROTHGAR, AND SOMEWHERE MY SLAYER RESIDES IN IT. BUT HE HAS NOT COME THIS DAY.
BUT HOW DO YOU KNOW FOR SURE?! MAYBE IT IS ME!
I DON'T MAKE THE SAME MISTAKE TWICE...
YOUR DESTINY IS AMONG MEN...
NOTHING MORE.
URF!
SHING!
yEOUCH!
that stung!
PARDON?
HUFF!
now you're in for it!
QUIET, NAGLING!
ARE YOU SO HUNGRY FOR POWER, BOY?!
YOU CANNOT DEFEAT ME!
Sigh.
BUT I WANT TO BE GREAT.
I WANT TO BE RE-MEMBERED...
THEN BRING THE SWORD AND COME WITH ME.

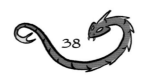

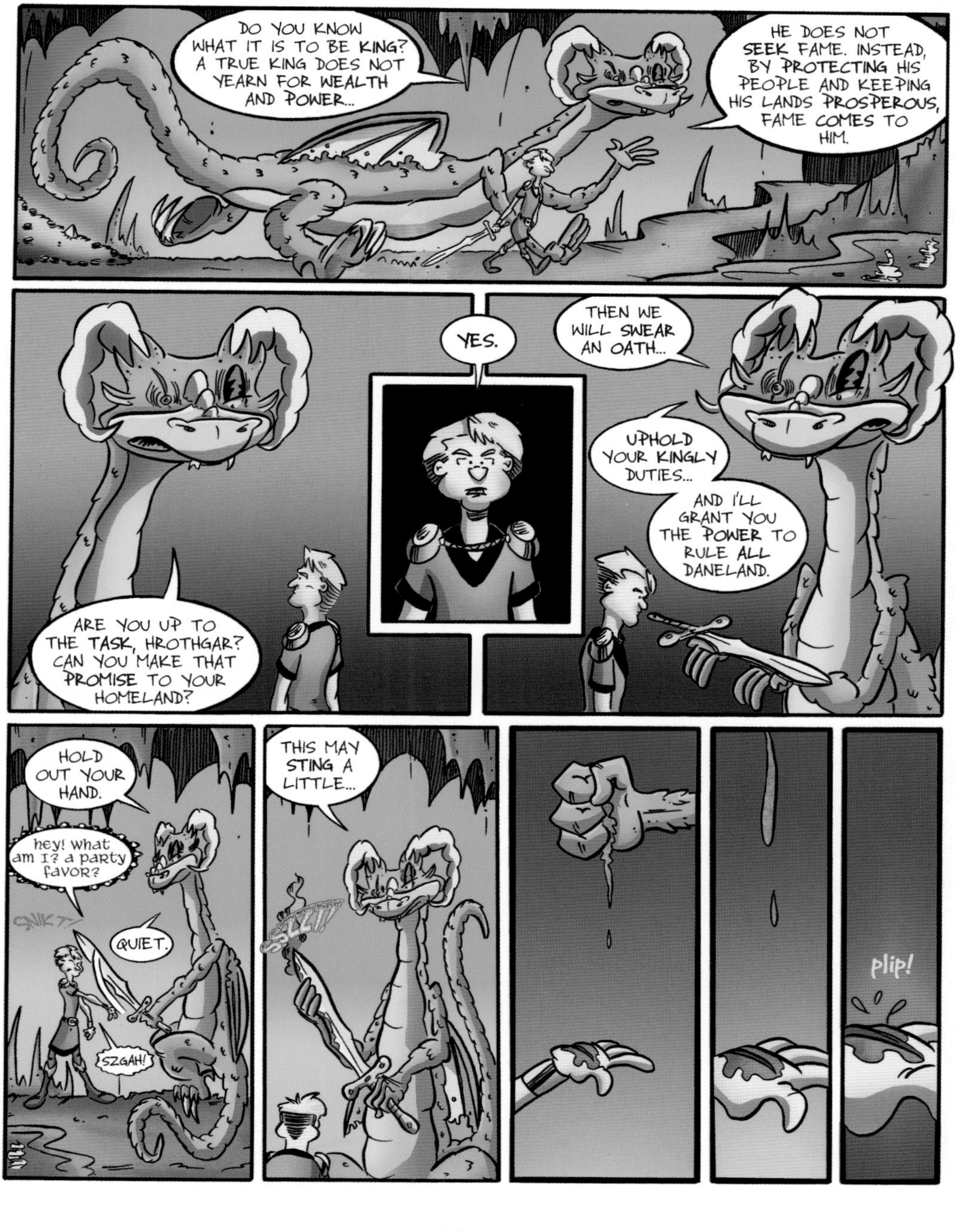
DO YOU KNOW WHAT IT IS TO BE KING? A TRUE KING DOES NOT YEARN FOR WEALTH AND POWER...
HE DOES NOT SEEK FAME. INSTEAD, BY PROTECTING HIS PEOPLE AND KEEPING HIS LANDS PROSPEROUS, FAME COMES TO HIM.
ARE YOU UP TO THE TASK, HROTHGAR? CAN YOU MAKE THAT PROMISE TO YOUR HOMELAND?
YES.
THEN WE WILL SWEAR AN OATH...
UPHOLD YOUR KINGLY DUTIES...
AND I'LL GRANT YOU THE POWER TO RULE ALL DANELAND.
HOLD OUT YOUR HAND.
hey! what am I? a party favor?
QUIET.
SZGAH!
THIS MAY STING A LITTLE...
plip!

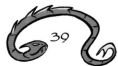

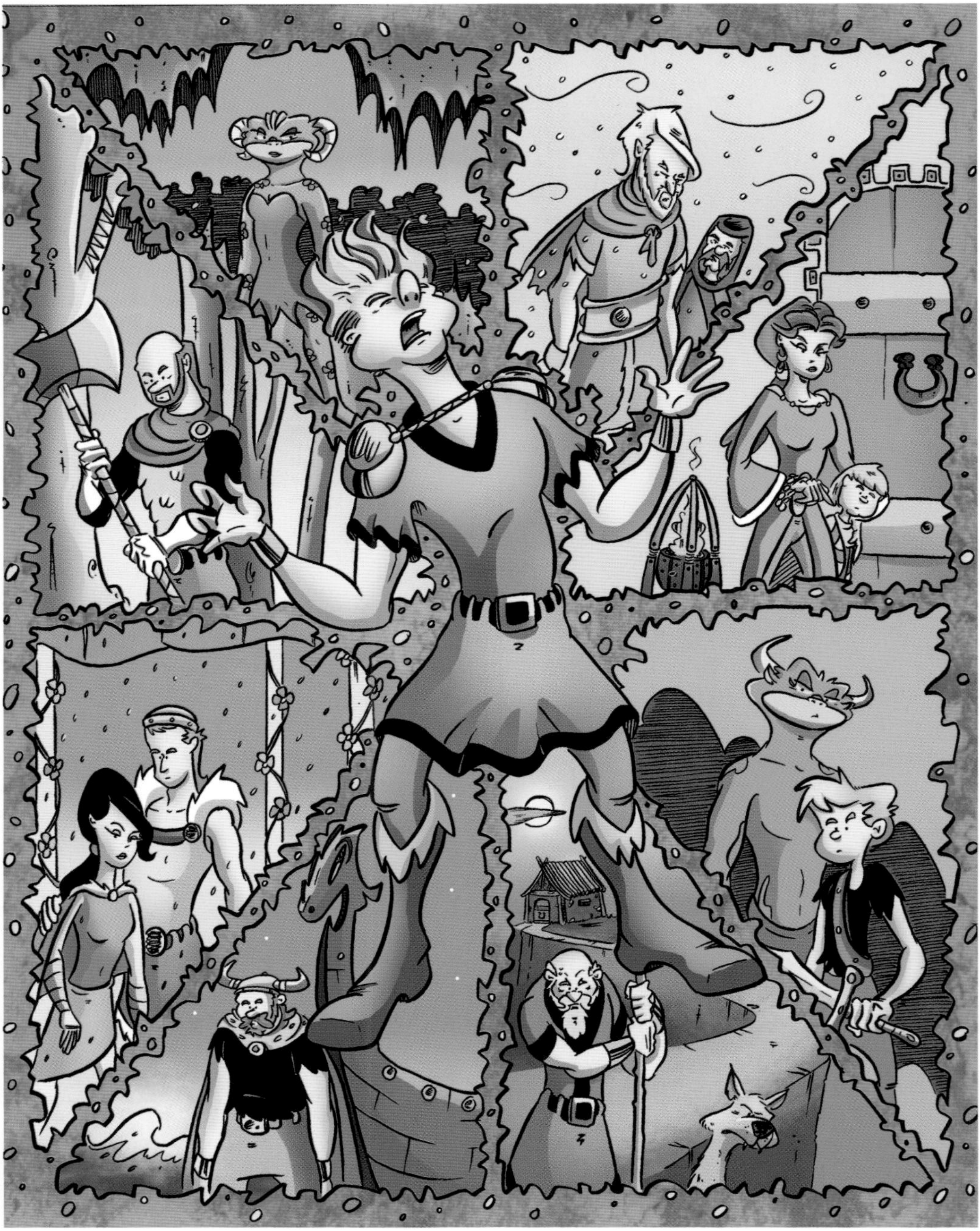

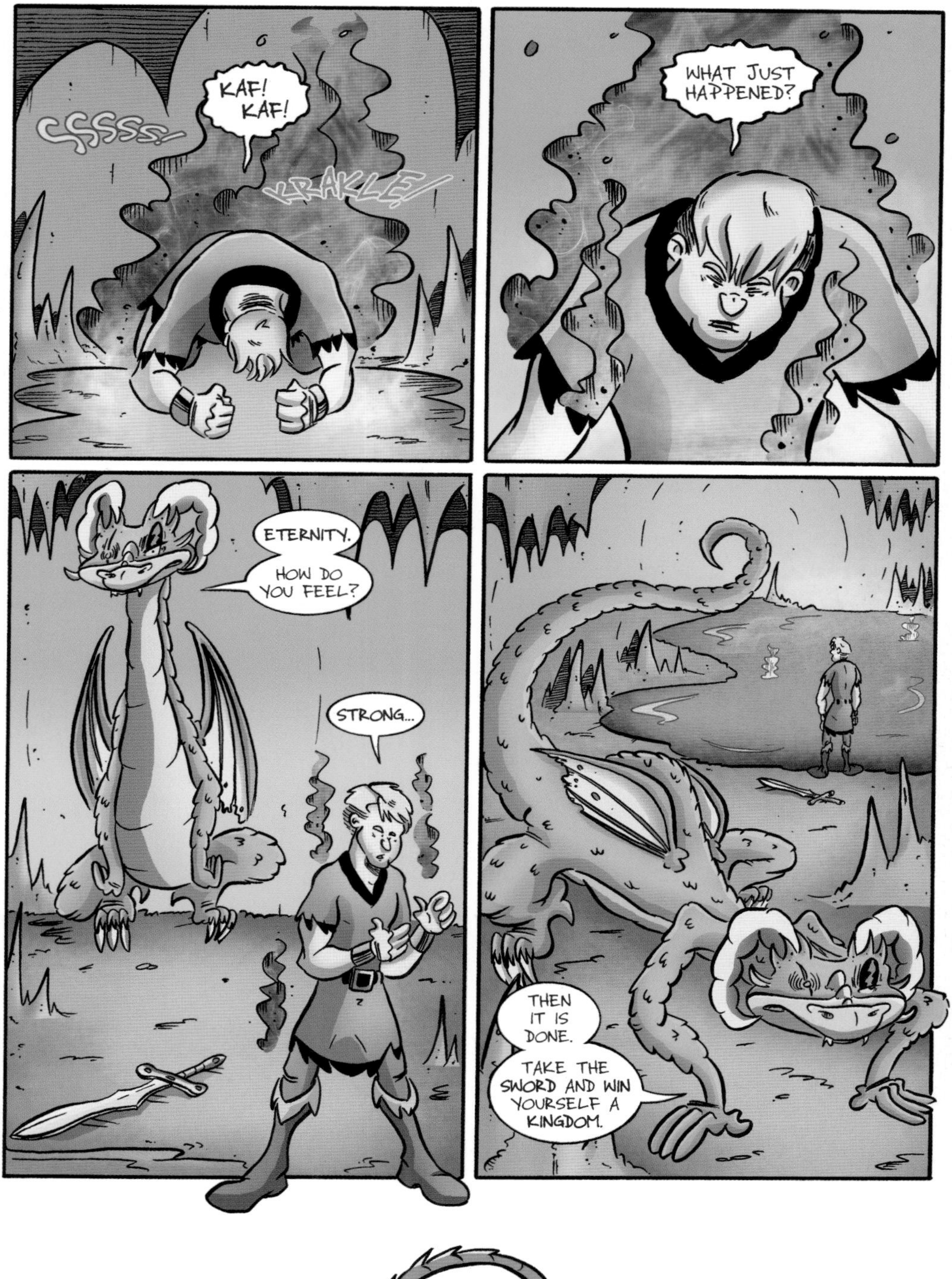
CSSSS!
KAF! KAF!
KRAKLE!
WHAT JUST HAPPENED?
ETERNITY.
HOW DO YOU FEEL?
STRONG...
THEN IT IS DONE.
TAKE THE SWORD AND WIN YOURSELF A KINGDOM.

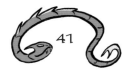

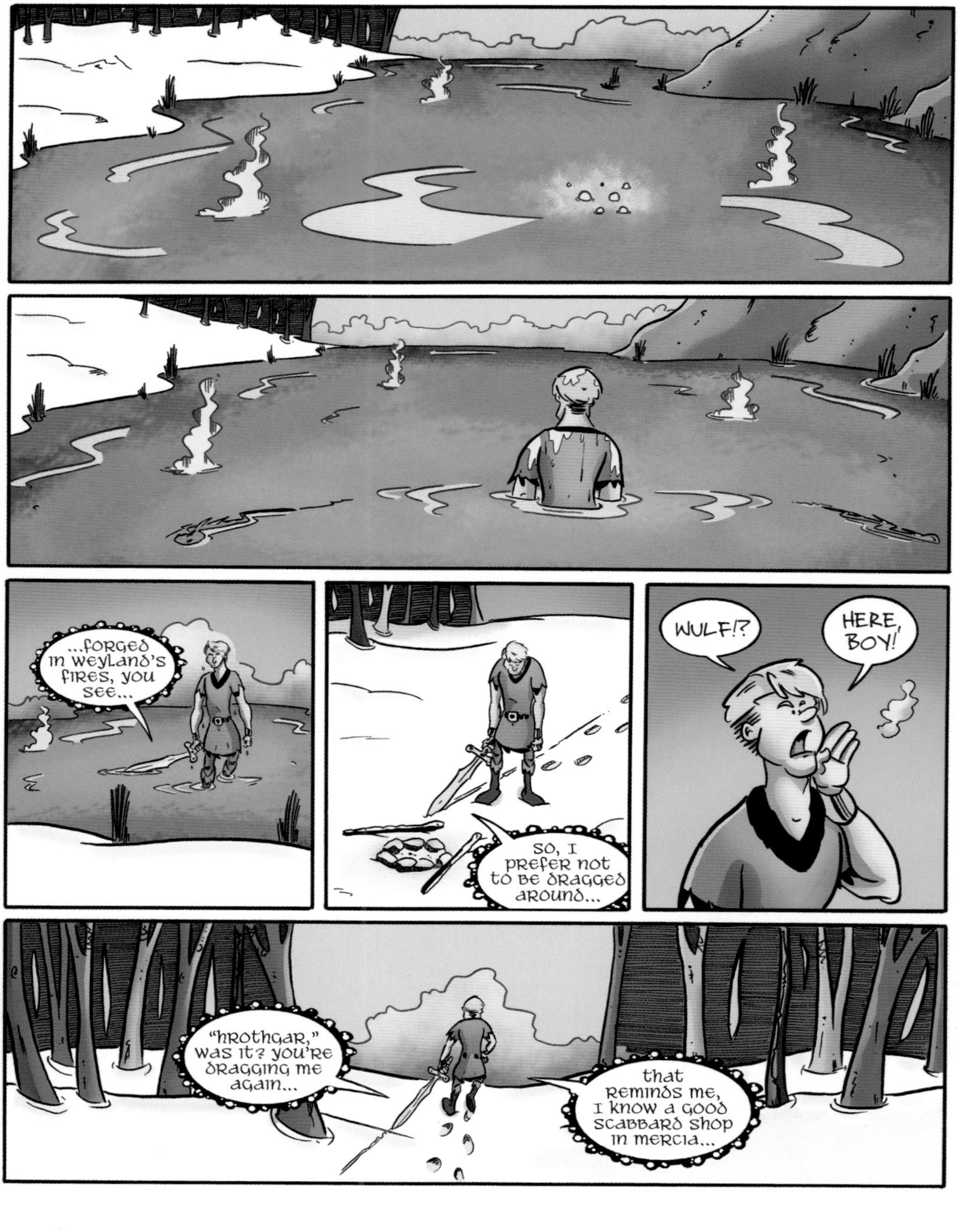
...forged in weyland's fires, you see...
so, I prefer not to be dragged around...
WULF!?
HERE, BOY!
"hrothgar," was it? you're dragging me again...
that reminds me, I know a good scabbard shop in mercia...

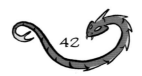

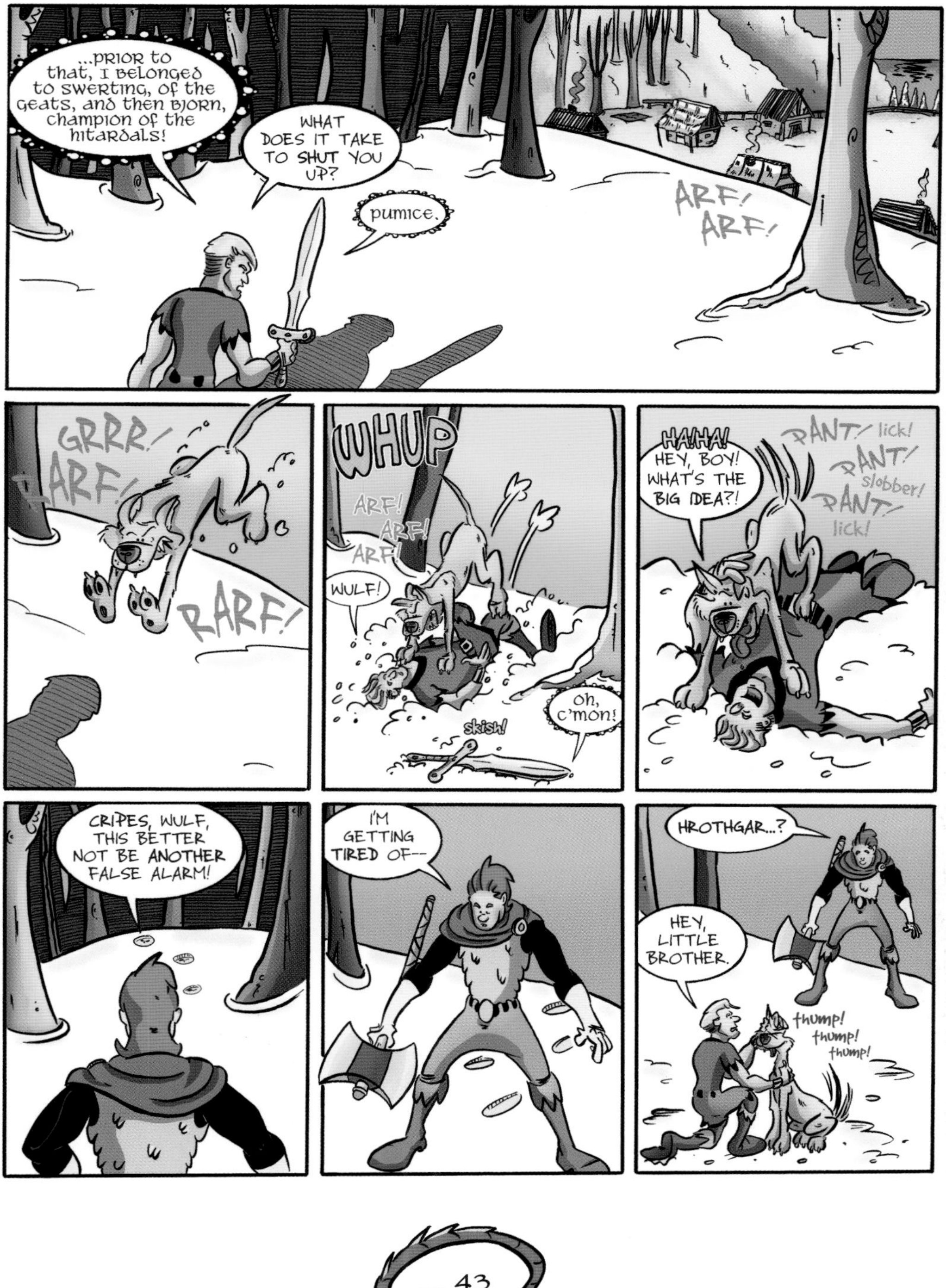
...PRIOR TO that, I BELONGED TO SWERTING, OF THE GEATS, AND THEN BJORN, CHAMPION OF THE HITARDALS!
WHAT DOES IT TAKE TO SHUT YOU UP?
pumice.
ARF! ARF!
GRRR!
RARF!
RARF!
WHUP
ARF! ARF! ARF!
WULF!
oh, c'mon!
skish!
HAHA!
HEY, BOY! WHAT'S THE BIG IDEA?!
PANT! lick!
PANT! slobber!
PANT! lick!
CRIPES, WULF, THIS BETTER NOT BE ANOTHER FALSE ALARM!
I'M GETTING TIRED OF--
HROTHGAR...?
HEY, LITTLE BROTHER.
thump! thump! thump!

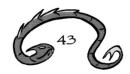

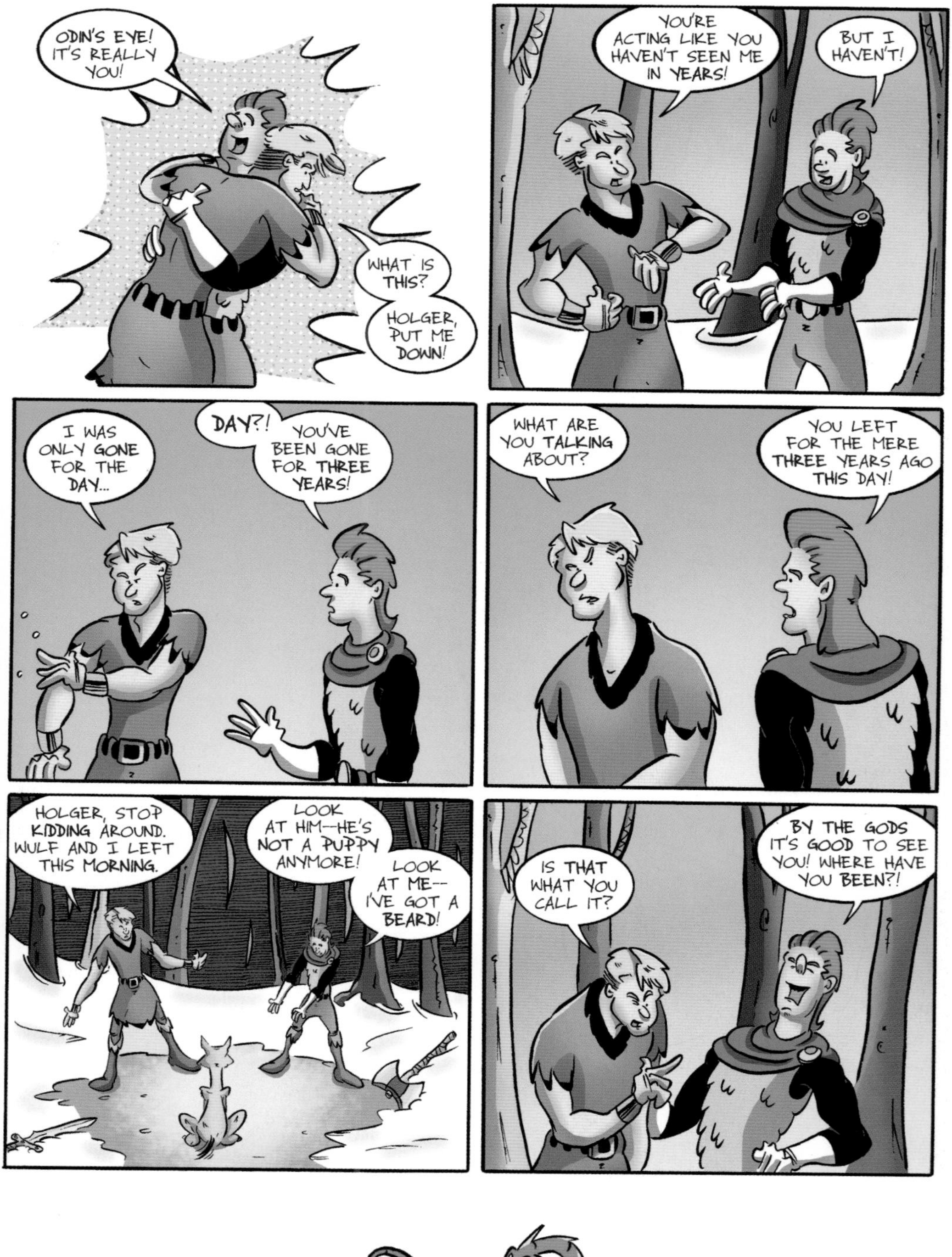
ODIN'S EYE! IT'S REALLY YOU!
WHAT IS THIS?
HOLGER, PUT ME DOWN!
YOU'RE ACTING LIKE YOU HAVEN'T SEEN ME IN YEARS!
BUT I HAVEN'T!
I WAS ONLY GONE FOR THE DAY...
DAY?!
YOU'VE BEEN GONE FOR THREE YEARS!
WHAT ARE YOU TALKING ABOUT?
YOU LEFT FOR THE MERE THREE YEARS AGO THIS DAY!
HOLGER, STOP KIDDING AROUND. WULF AND I LEFT THIS MORNING.
LOOK AT HIM--HE'S NOT A PUPPY ANYMORE!
LOOK AT ME--I'VE GOT A BEARD!
BY THE GODS IT'S GOOD TO SEE YOU! WHERE HAVE YOU BEEN?!
IS THAT WHAT YOU CALL IT?

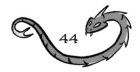

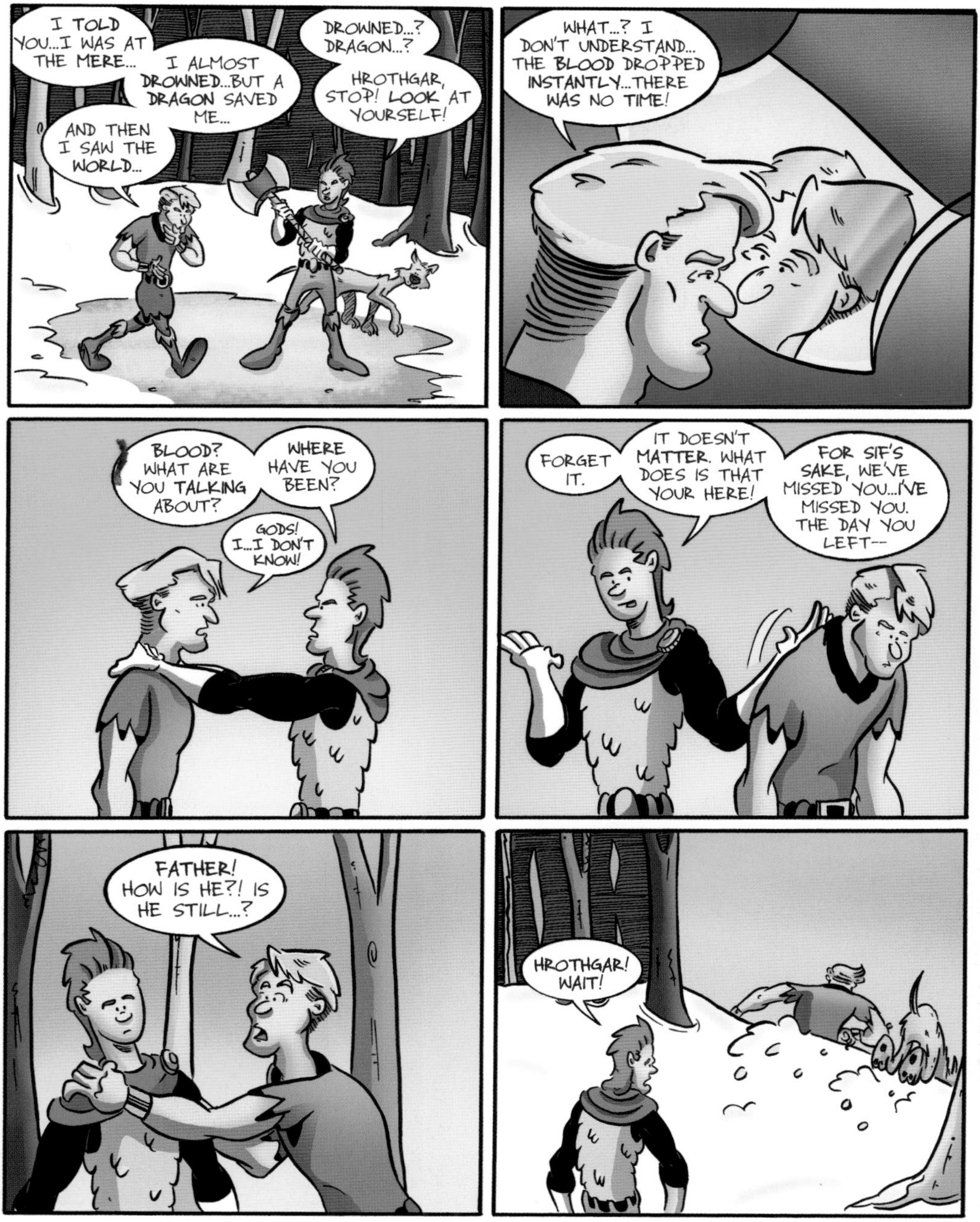
I TOLD YOU...I WAS AT THE MERE...
I ALMOST DROWNED...BUT A DRAGON SAVED ME...
AND THEN I SAW THE WORLD...
DROWNED...? DRAGON...?
HROTHGAR, STOP! LOOK AT YOURSELF!
WHAT...? I DON'T UNDERSTAND... THE BLOOD DROPPED INSTANTLY...THERE WAS NO TIME!
BLOOD? WHAT ARE YOU TALKING ABOUT?
WHERE HAVE YOU BEEN?
GODS! I...I DON'T KNOW!
FORGET IT.
IT DOESN'T MATTER. WHAT DOES IS THAT YOUR HERE!
FOR SIF'S SAKE, WE'VE MISSED YOU...I'VE MISSED YOU. THE DAY YOU LEFT--
FATHER! HOW IS HE?! IS HE STILL...?
HROTHGAR! WAIT!

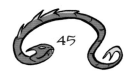

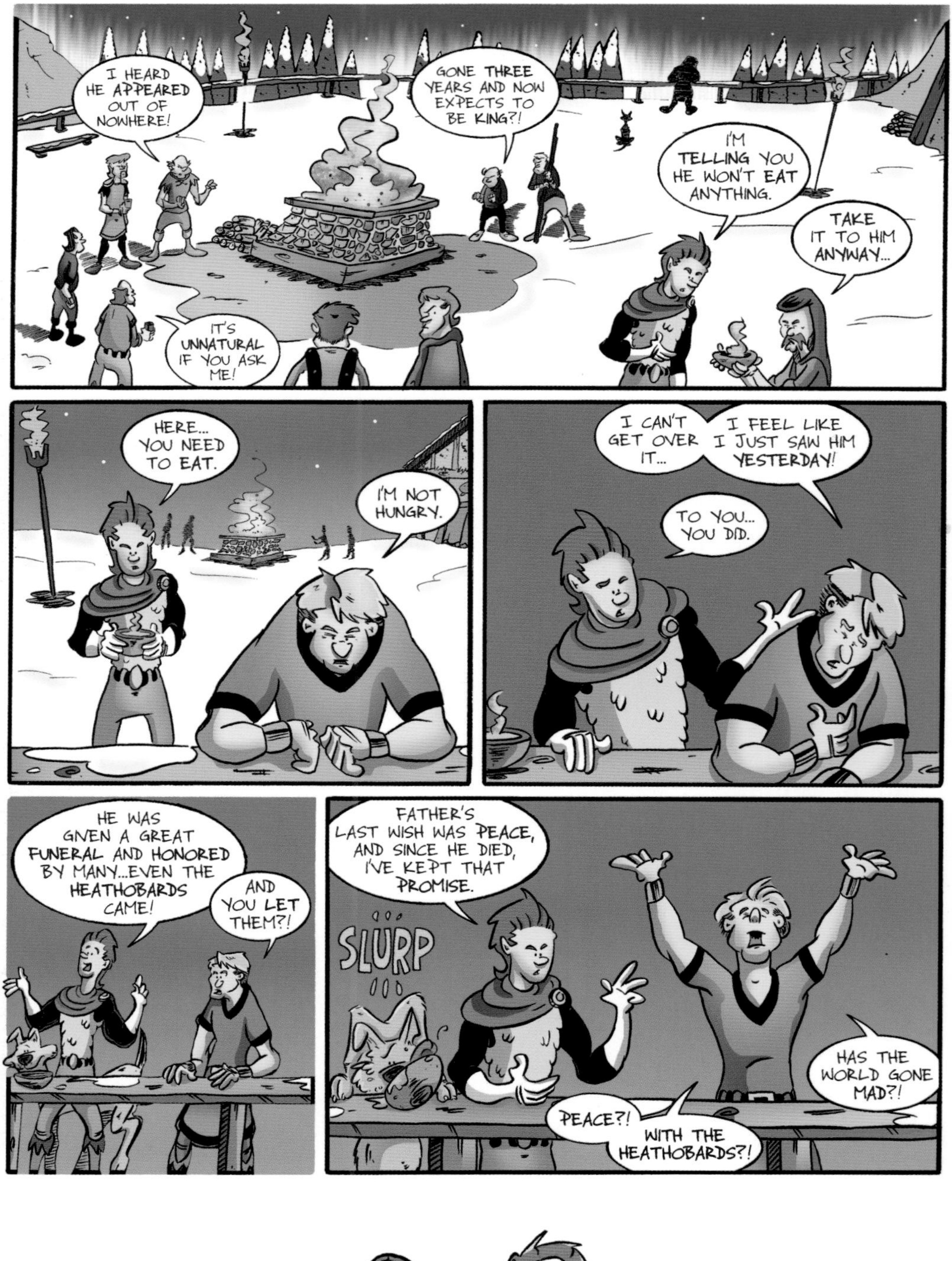
I HEARD HE APPEARED OUT OF NOWHERE!
GONE THREE YEARS AND NOW EXPECTS TO BE KING?!
I'M TELLING YOU HE WON'T EAT ANYTHING.
TAKE IT TO HIM ANYWAY...
IT'S UNNATURAL IF YOU ASK ME!
HERE... YOU NEED TO EAT.
I'M NOT HUNGRY.
I CAN'T GET OVER IT...
I FEEL LIKE I JUST SAW HIM YESTERDAY!
TO YOU... YOU DID.
HE WAS GIVEN A GREAT FUNERAL AND HONORED BY MANY...EVEN THE HEATHOBARDS CAME!
AND YOU LET THEM?!
FATHER'S LAST WISH WAS PEACE, AND SINCE HE DIED, I'VE KEPT THAT PROMISE.
SLURP
HAS THE WORLD GONE MAD?!
PEACE?!
WITH THE HEATHOBARDS?!

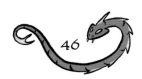

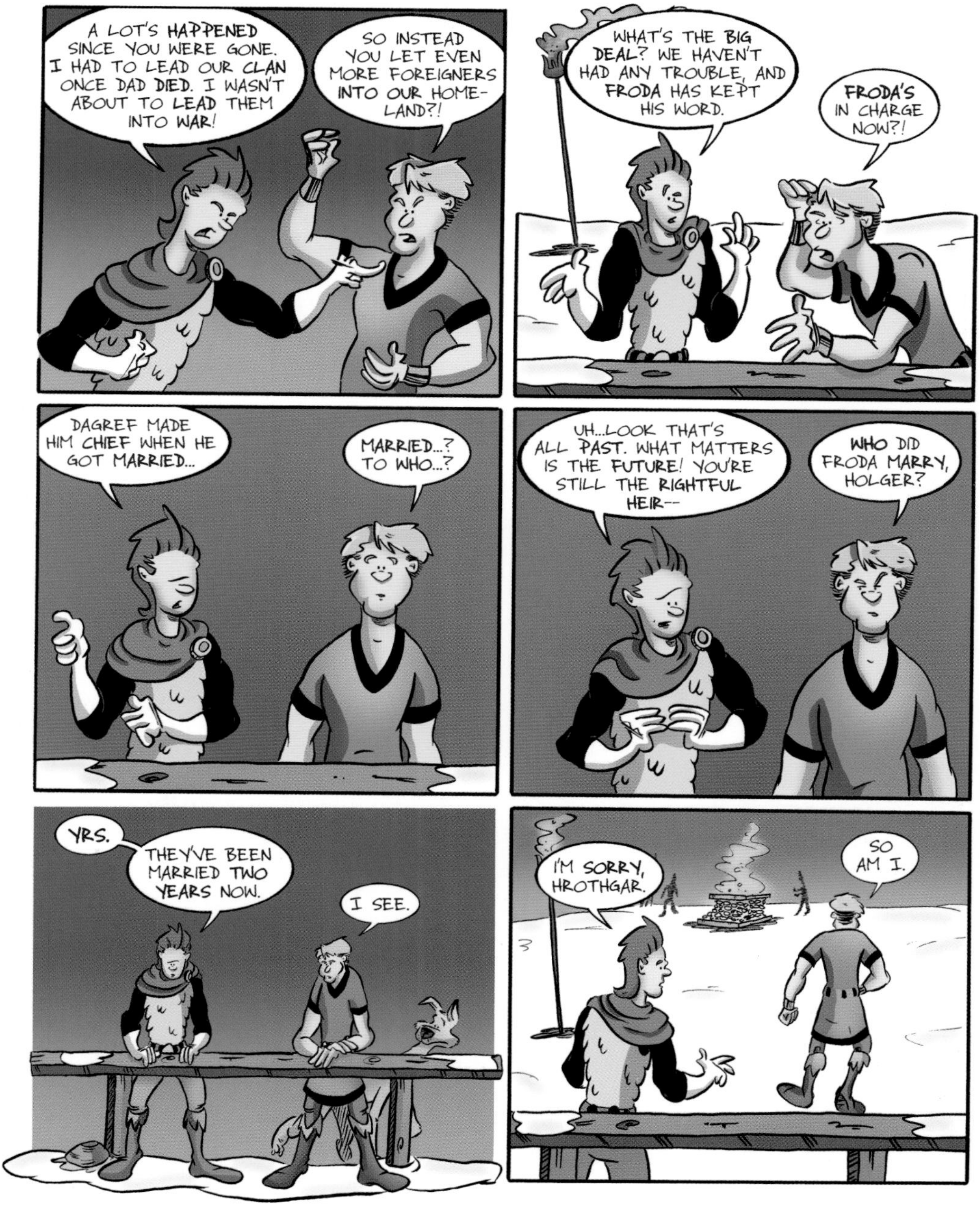
A LOT'S HAPPENED SINCE YOU WERE GONE. I HAD TO LEAD OUR CLAN ONCE DAD DIED. I WASN'T ABOUT TO LEAD THEM INTO WAR!
SO INSTEAD YOU LET EVEN MORE FOREIGNERS INTO OUR HOME-LAND?!
WHAT'S THE BIG DEAL? WE HAVEN'T HAD ANY TROUBLE, AND FRODA HAS KEPT HIS WORD.
FRODA'S IN CHARGE NOW?!
DAGREF MADE HIM CHIEF WHEN HE GOT MARRIED...
MARRIED...? TO WHO...?
UH...LOOK THAT'S ALL PAST. WHAT MATTERS IS THE FUTURE! YOU'RE STILL THE RIGHTFUL HEIR--
WHO DID FRODA MARRY, HOLGER?
YRS.
THEY'VE BEEN MARRIED TWO YEARS NOW.
I SEE.
I'M SORRY, HROTHGAR.
SO AM I.

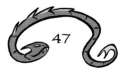

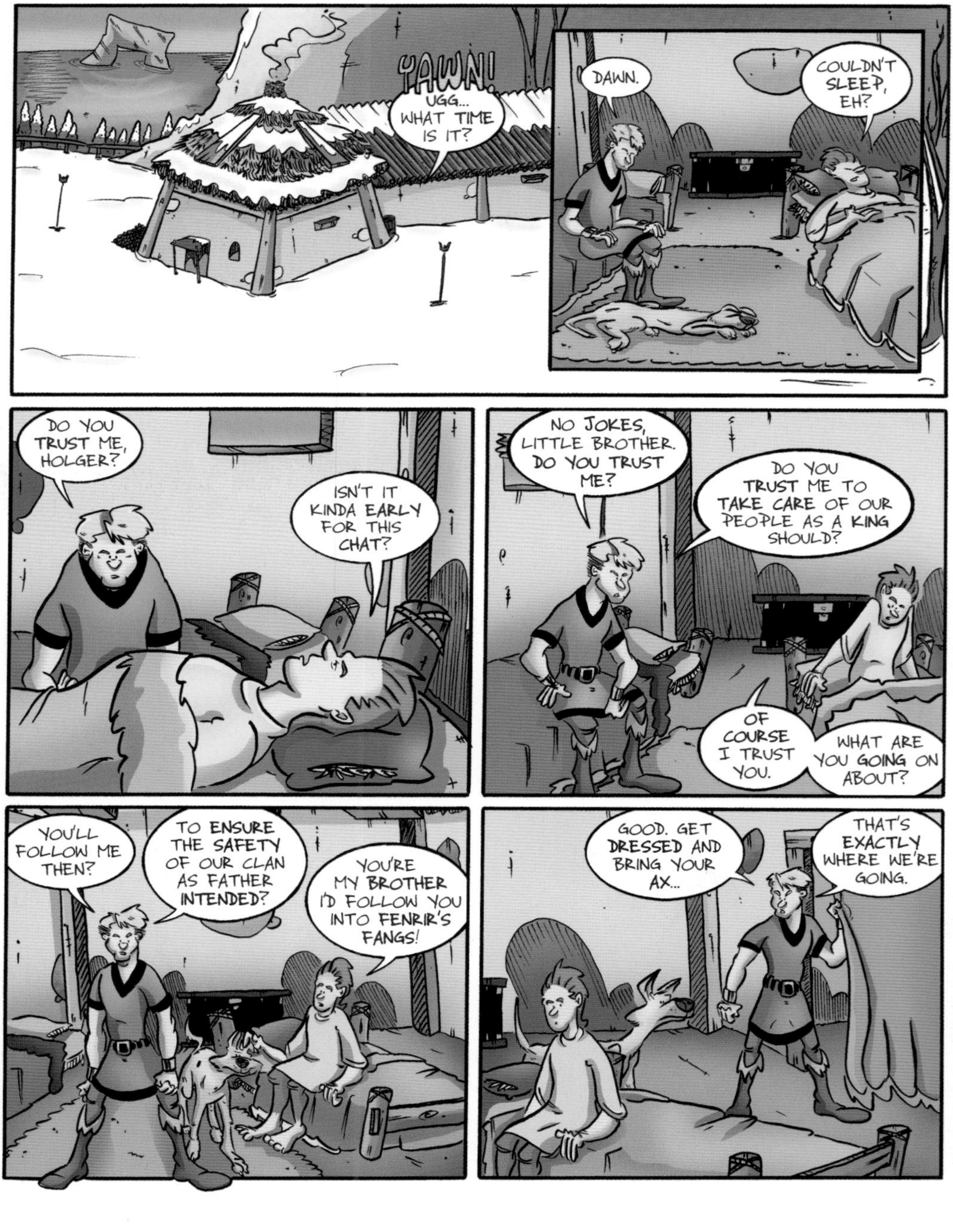
YAWN!
UGG... WHAT TIME IS IT?
DAWN.
COULDN'T SLEEP, EH?
DO YOU TRUST ME, HOLGER?
ISN'T IT KINDA EARLY FOR THIS CHAT?
NO JOKES, LITTLE BROTHER. DO YOU TRUST ME?
DO YOU TRUST ME TO TAKE CARE OF OUR PEOPLE AS A KING SHOULD?
OF COURSE I TRUST YOU.
WHAT ARE YOU GOING ON ABOUT?
YOU'LL FOLLOW ME THEN?
TO ENSURE THE SAFETY OF OUR CLAN AS FATHER INTENDED?
YOU'RE MY BROTHER I'D FOLLOW YOU INTO FENRIR'S FANGS!
GOOD. GET DRESSED AND BRING YOUR AX...
THAT'S EXACTLY WHERE WE'RE GOING.

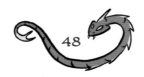

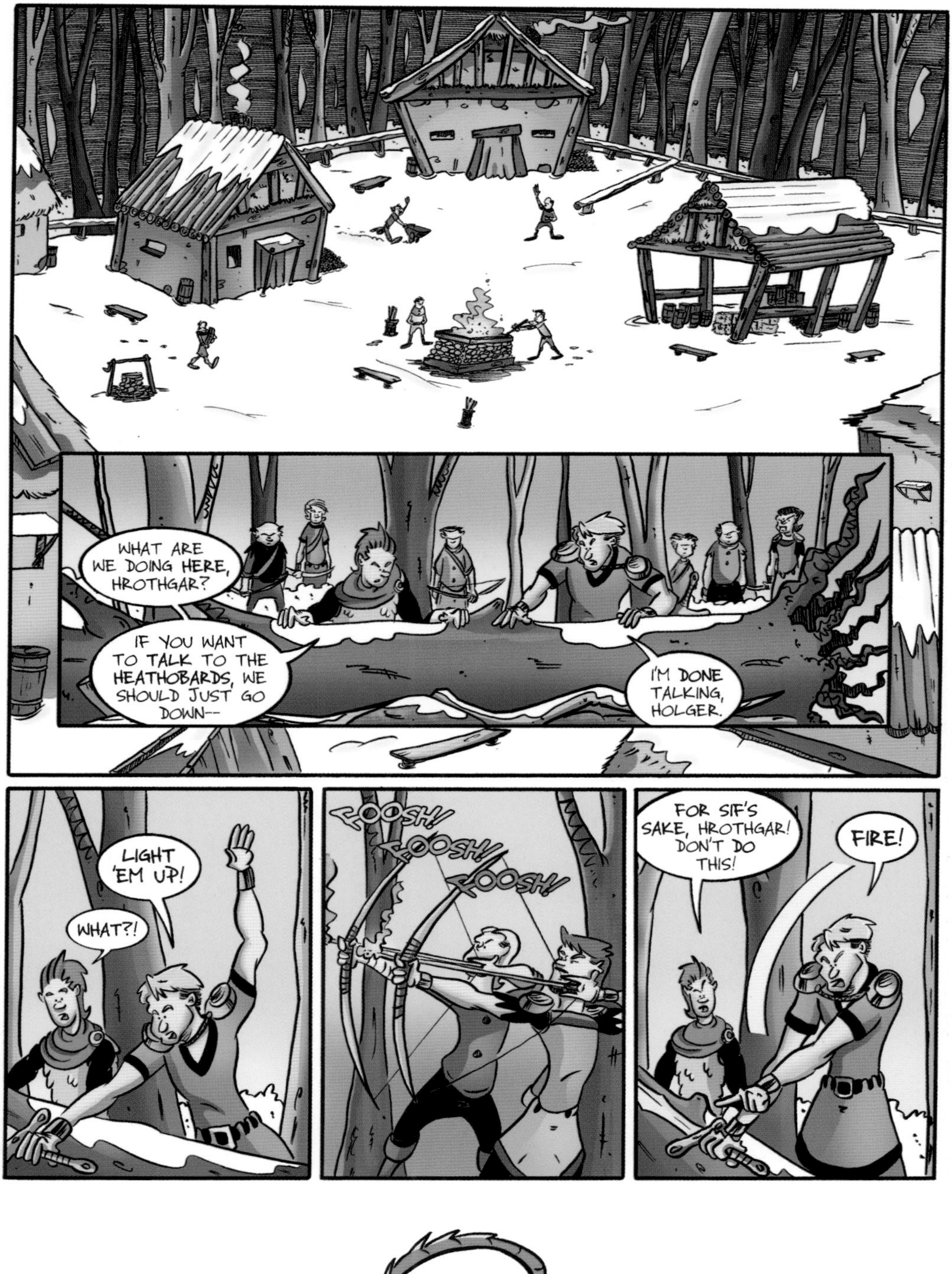
WHAT ARE WE DOING HERE, HROTHGAR?
IF YOU WANT TO TALK TO THE HEATHOBARDS, WE SHOULD JUST GO DOWN--
I'M DONE TALKING, HOLGER.
LIGHT 'EM UP!
WHAT?!
FOOSH!
FOOSH!
FOOSH!
FOR SIF'S SAKE, HROTHGAR! DON'T DO THIS!
FIRE!

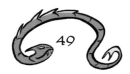

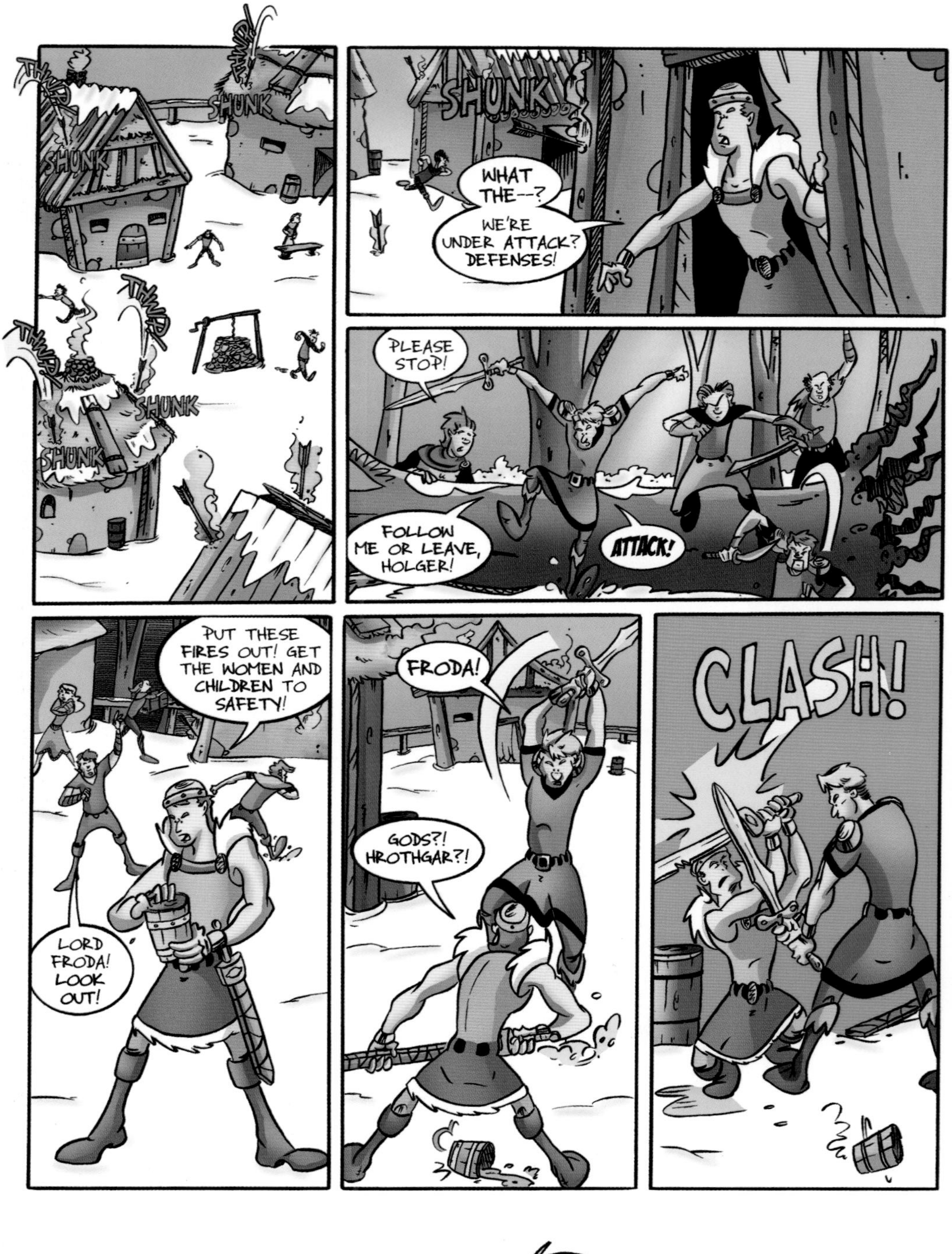
THWP
SHUNK
THWP
SHUNK
THWP
THWP
SHUNK
SHUNK
SHUNK
WHAT THE--?
WE'RE UNDER ATTACK? DEFENSES!
PLEASE STOP!
FOLLOW ME OR LEAVE, HOLGER!
ATTACK!
PUT THESE FIRES OUT! GET THE WOMEN AND CHILDREN TO SAFETY!
LORD FRODA! LOOK OUT!
FRODA!
GODS?! HROTHGAR?!
CLASH!

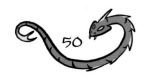

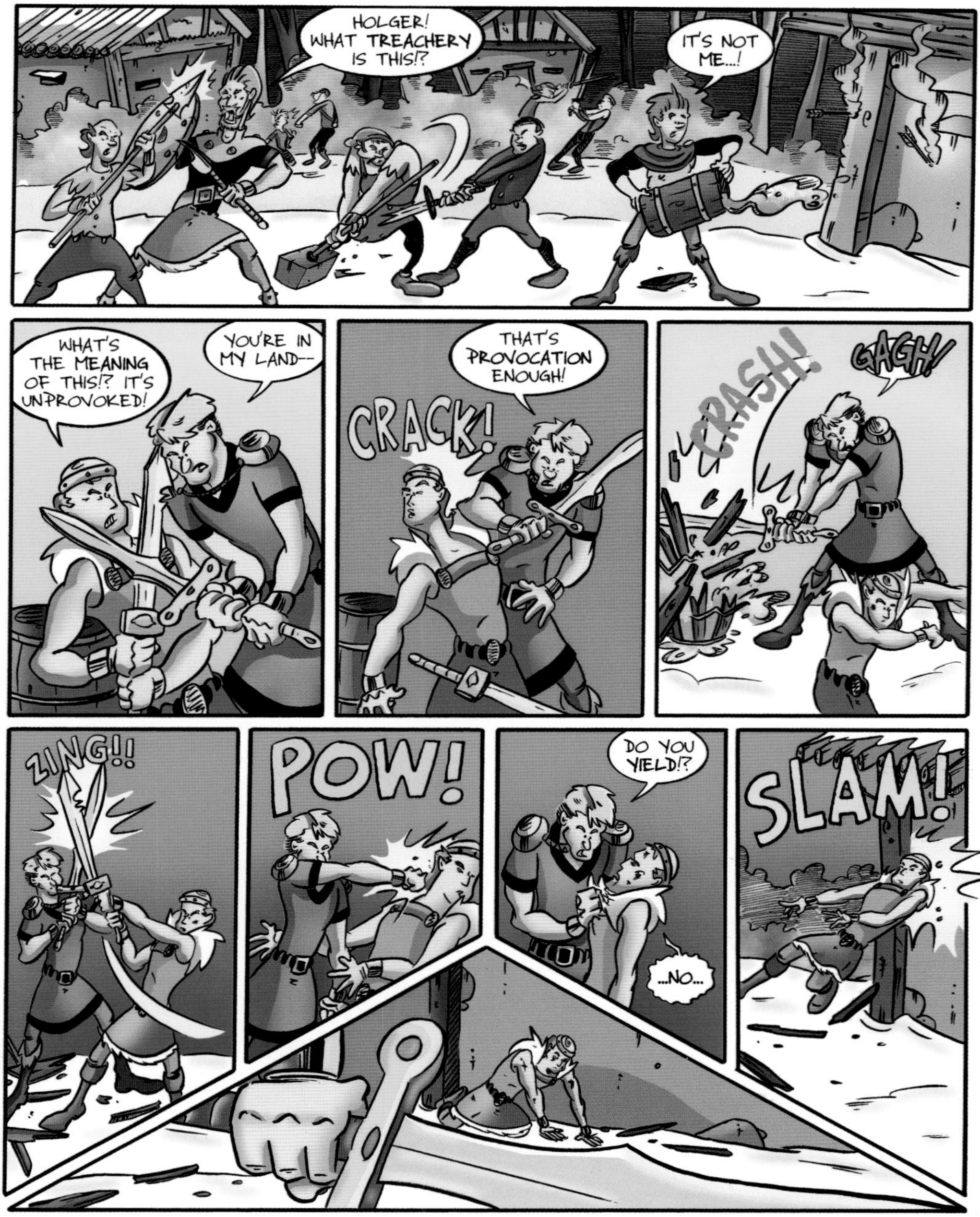
HOLGER! WHAT TREACHERY IS THIS!?
IT'S NOT ME...!
WHAT'S THE MEANING OF THIS!? IT'S UNPROVOKED!
YOU'RE IN MY LAND--
CRACK!
THAT'S PROVOCATION ENOUGH!
CRASH!
GAGH!
ZING!!
POW!
DO YOU YIELD!?
...NO...
SLAM!

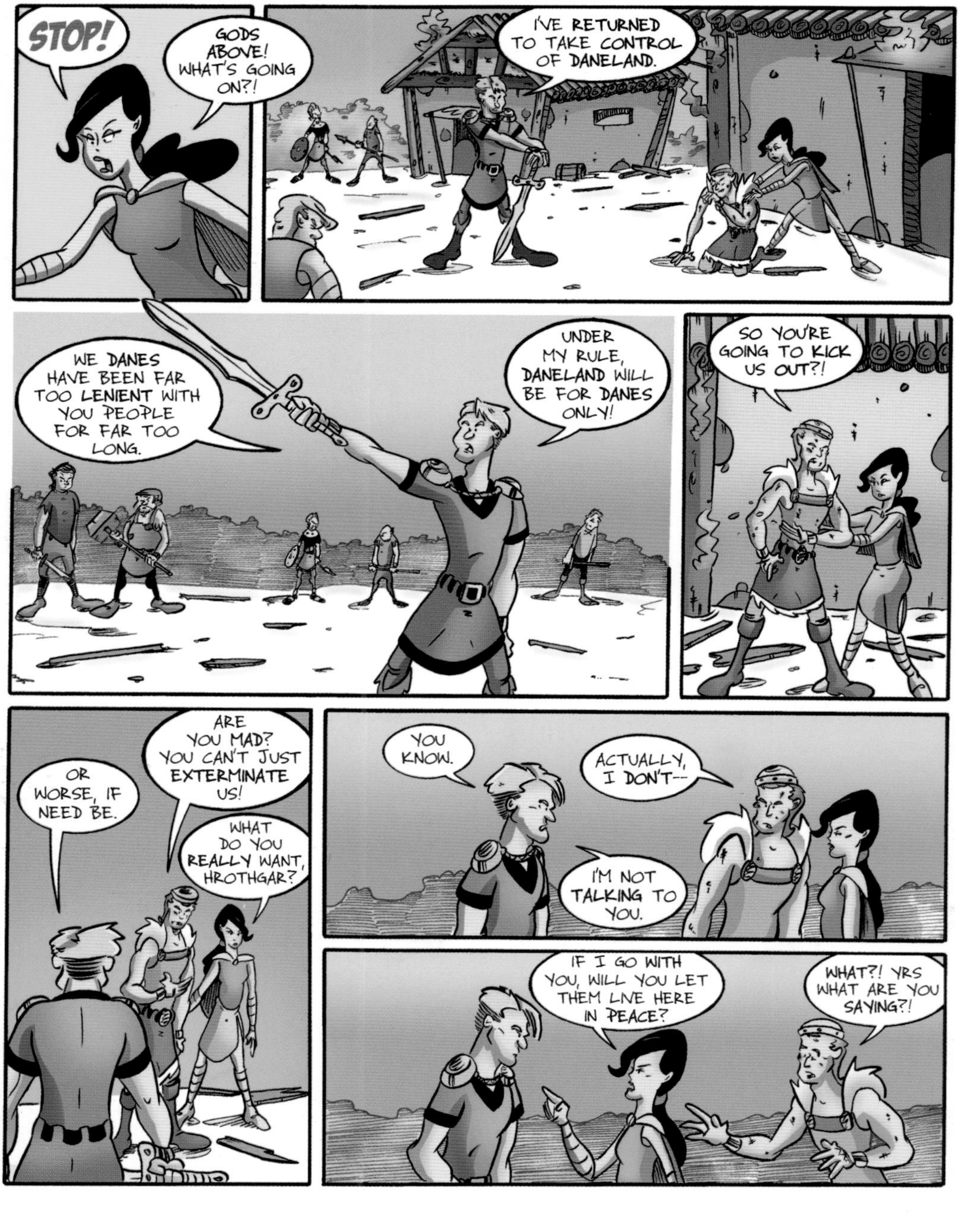
STOP!
GODS ABOVE! WHAT'S GOING ON?!
I'VE RETURNED TO TAKE CONTROL OF DANELAND.
UNDER MY RULE, DANELAND WILL BE FOR DANES ONLY!
WE DANES HAVE BEEN FAR TOO LENIENT WITH YOU PEOPLE FOR FAR TOO LONG.
SO YOU'RE GOING TO KICK US OUT?!
ARE YOU MAD? YOU CAN'T JUST EXTERMINATE US!
OR WORSE, IF NEED BE.
WHAT DO YOU REALLY WANT, HROTHGAR?
YOU KNOW.
ACTUALLY, I DON'T--
I'M NOT TALKING TO YOU.
IF I GO WITH YOU, WILL YOU LET THEM LIVE HERE IN PEACE?
WHAT?! YRS WHAT ARE YOU SAYING?!

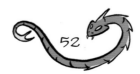

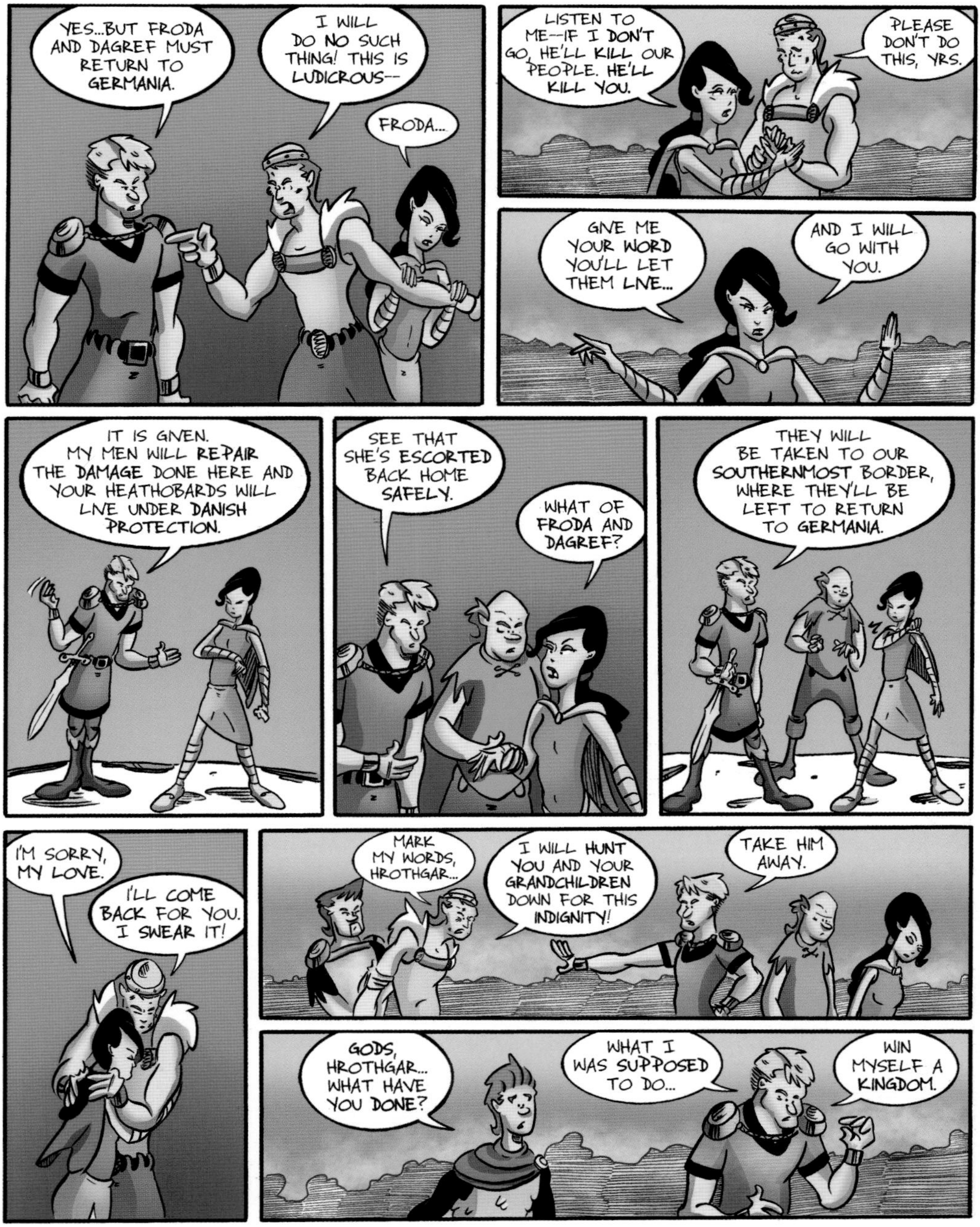
YES...BUT FRODA AND DAGREF MUST RETURN TO GERMANIA.
I WILL DO NO SUCH THING! THIS IS LUDICROUS--
FRODA...
LISTEN TO ME--IF I DON'T GO, HE'LL KILL OUR PEOPLE. HE'LL KILL YOU.
PLEASE DON'T DO THIS, YRS.
GIVE ME YOUR WORD YOU'LL LET THEM LIVE...
AND I WILL GO WITH YOU.
IT IS GIVEN. MY MEN WILL REPAIR THE DAMAGE DONE HERE AND YOUR HEATHOBARDS WILL LIVE UNDER DANISH PROTECTION.
SEE THAT SHE'S ESCORTED BACK HOME SAFELY.
WHAT OF FRODA AND DAGREF?
THEY WILL BE TAKEN TO OUR SOUTHERNMOST BORDER, WHERE THEY'LL BE LEFT TO RETURN TO GERMANIA.
I'M SORRY, MY LOVE.
I'LL COME BACK FOR YOU. I SWEAR IT!
MARK MY WORDS, HROTHGAR...
I WILL HUNT YOU AND YOUR GRANDCHILDREN DOWN FOR THIS INDIGNITY!
TAKE HIM AWAY.
GODS, HROTHGAR... WHAT HAVE YOU DONE?
WHAT I WAS SUPPOSED TO DO...
WIN MYSELF A KINGDOM.

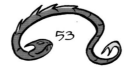

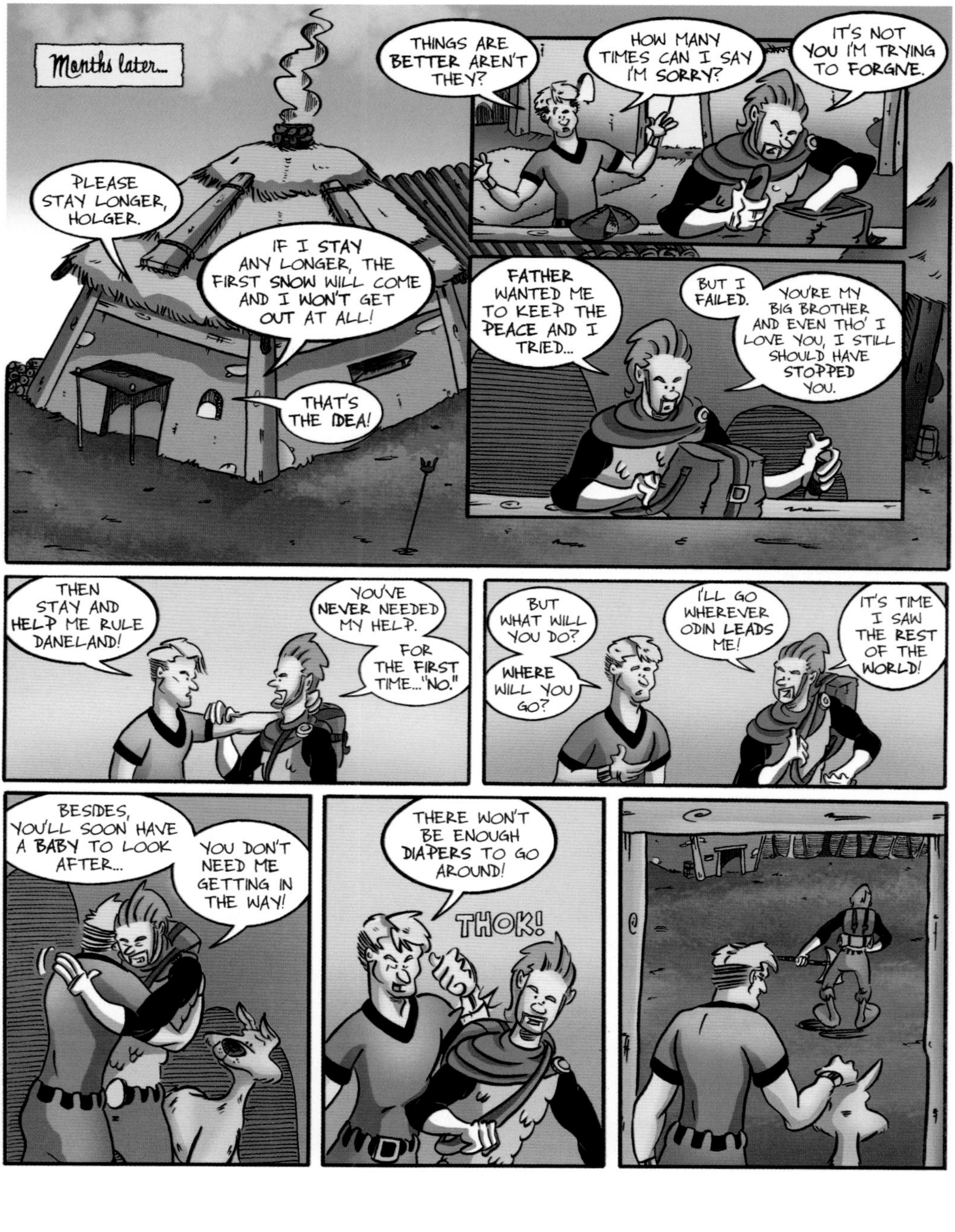
Months later...
PLEASE STAY LONGER, HOLGER.
IF I STAY ANY LONGER, THE FIRST SNOW WILL COME AND I WON'T GET OUT AT ALL!
THAT'S THE IDEA!
THINGS ARE BETTER AREN'T THEY?
HOW MANY TIMES CAN I SAY I'M SORRY?
IT'S NOT YOU I'M TRYING TO FORGIVE.
FATHER WANTED ME TO KEEP THE PEACE AND I TRIED...
BUT I FAILED.
YOU'RE MY BIG BROTHER AND EVEN THO' I LOVE YOU, I STILL SHOULD HAVE STOPPED YOU.
THEN STAY AND HELP ME RULE DANELAND!
YOU'VE NEVER NEEDED MY HELP.
FOR THE FIRST TIME..."NO."
BUT WHAT WILL YOU DO?
WHERE WILL YOU GO?
I'LL GO WHEREVER ODIN LEADS ME!
IT'S TIME I SAW THE REST OF THE WORLD!
BESIDES, YOU'LL SOON HAVE A BABY TO LOOK AFTER...
YOU DON'T NEED ME GETTING IN THE WAY!
THERE WON'T BE ENOUGH DIAPERS TO GO AROUND!
THOK!

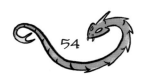

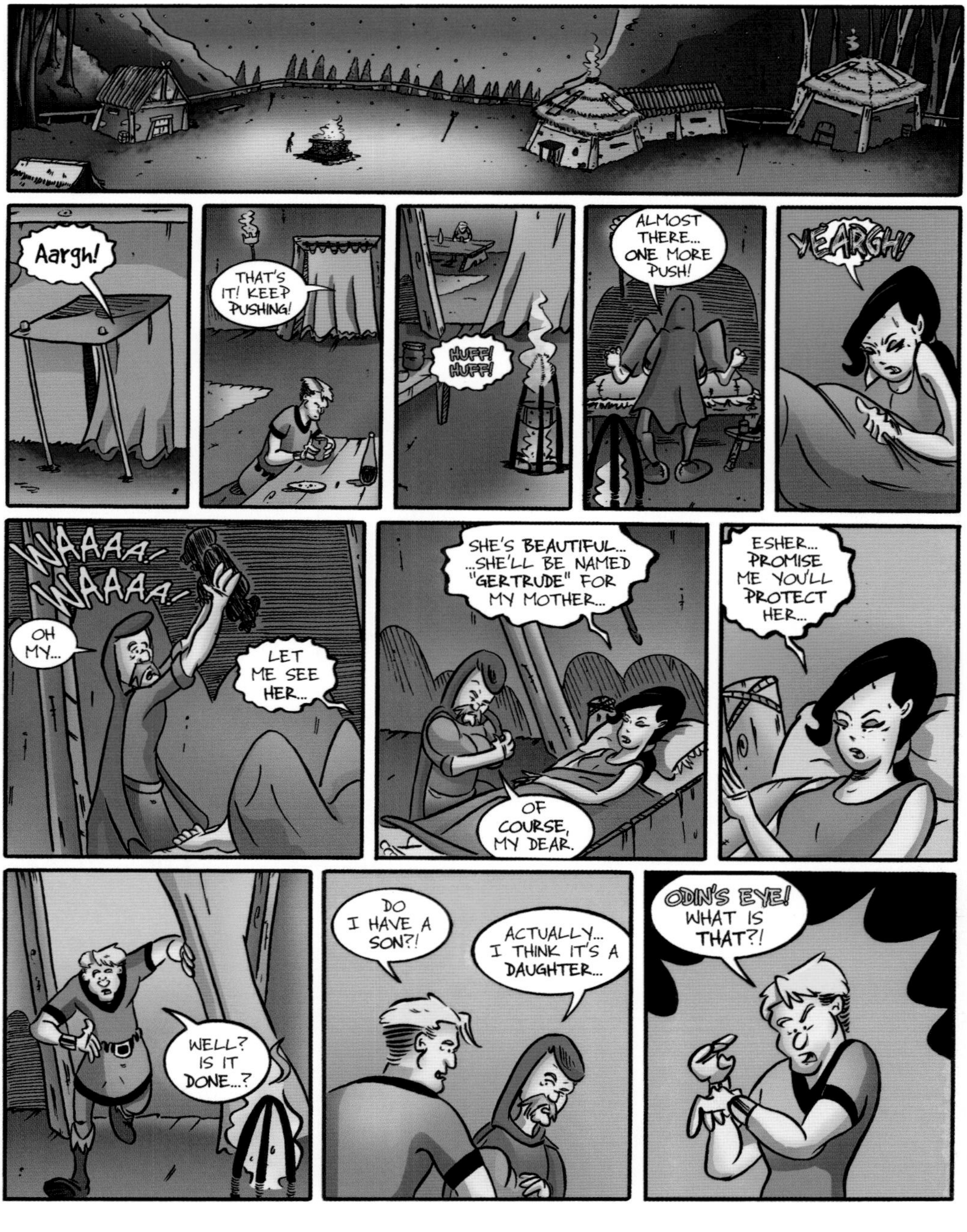
Aargh!
THAT'S IT! KEEP PUSHING!
HUFF! HUFF!
ALMOST THERE... ONE MORE PUSH!
YEARGH!
WAAAA! WAAAA!
OH MY...
LET ME SEE HER...
SHE'S BEAUTIFUL... ...SHE'LL BE NAMED "GERTRUDE" FOR MY MOTHER...
OF COURSE, MY DEAR.
ESHER... PROMISE ME YOU'LL PROTECT HER...
WELL? IS IT DONE...?
DO I HAVE A SON?!
ACTUALLY... I THINK IT'S A DAUGHTER...
ODIN'S EYE! WHAT IS THAT?!

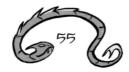

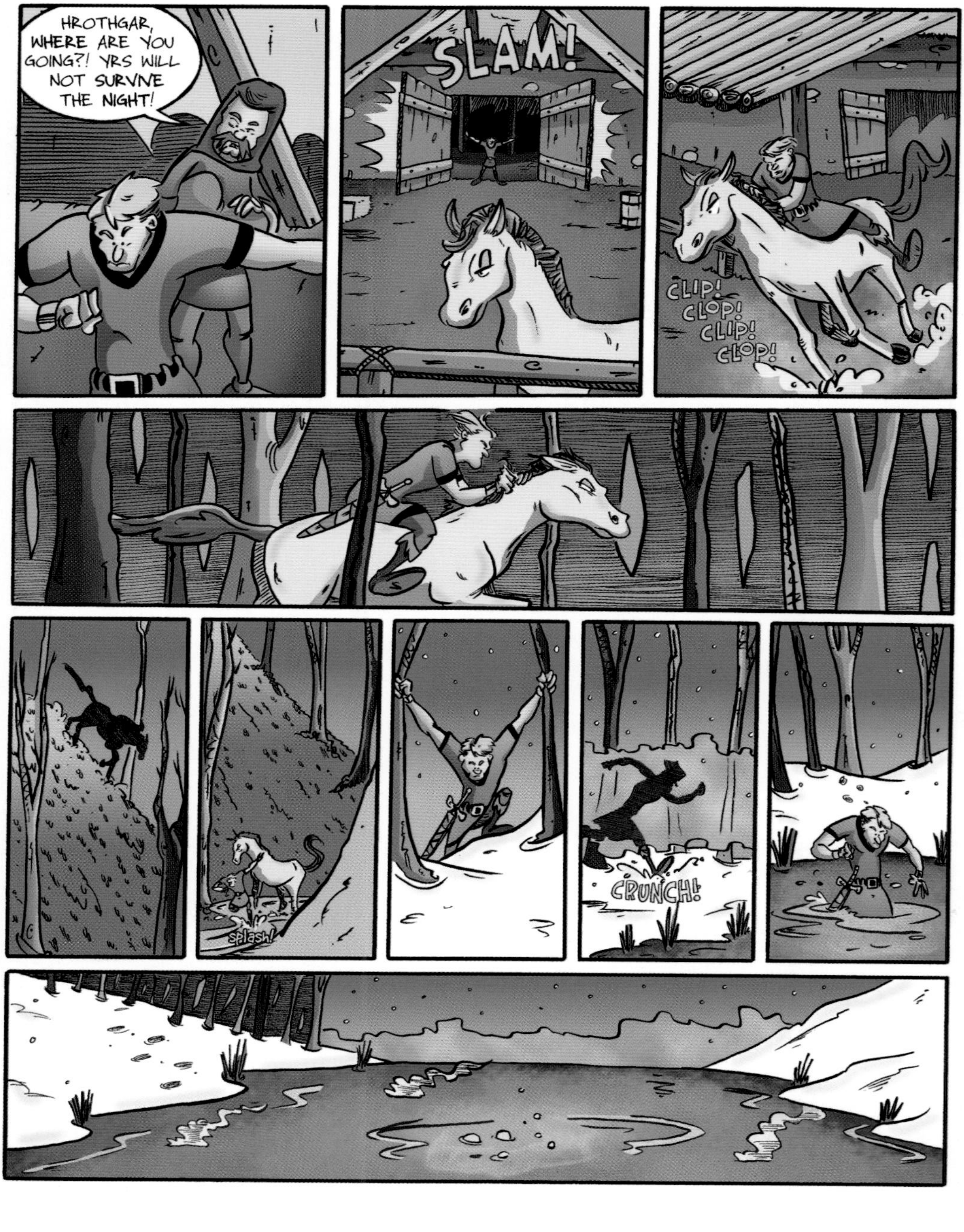
HROTHGAR, WHERE ARE YOU GOING?! YRS WILL NOT SURVIVE THE NIGHT!
SLAM!
CLIP! CLOP! CLIP! CLOP!
SPLASH!
CRUNCH!

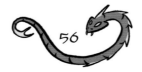

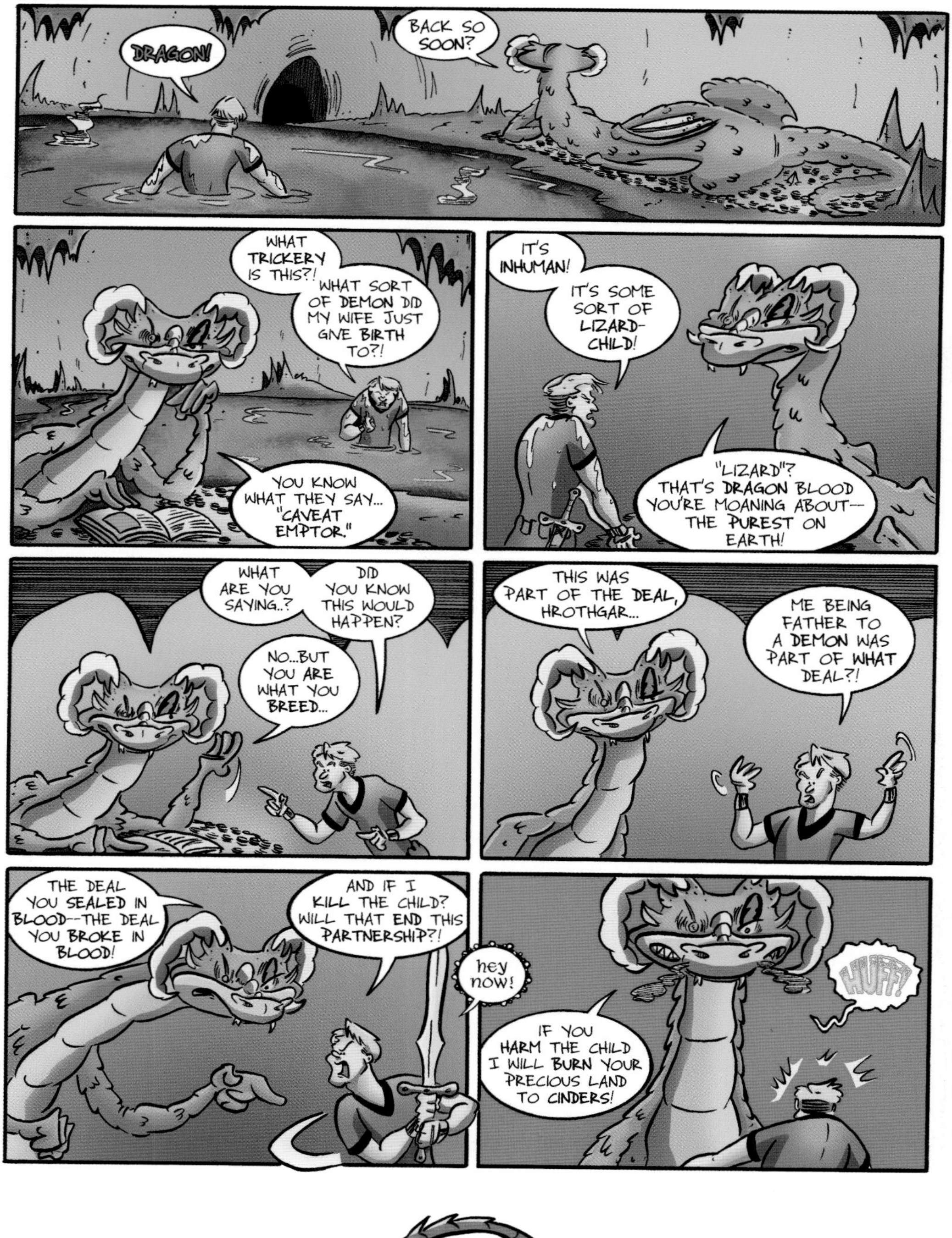
DRAGON!
BACK SO SOON?
WHAT TRICKERY IS THIS?!
WHAT SORT OF DEMON DID MY WIFE JUST GIVE BIRTH TO?!
YOU KNOW WHAT THEY SAY... "CAVEAT EMPTOR."
IT'S INHUMAN!
IT'S SOME SORT OF LIZARD-CHILD!
"LIZARD"? THAT'S DRAGON BLOOD YOU'RE MOANING ABOUT-- THE PUREST ON EARTH!
WHAT ARE YOU SAYING..?
DID YOU KNOW THIS WOULD HAPPEN?
NO...BUT YOU ARE WHAT YOU BREED...
THIS WAS PART OF THE DEAL, HROTHGAR...
ME BEING FATHER TO A DEMON WAS PART OF WHAT DEAL?!
THE DEAL YOU SEALED IN BLOOD--THE DEAL YOU BROKE IN BLOOD!
AND IF I KILL THE CHILD? WILL THAT END THIS PARTNERSHIP?!
hey now!
IF YOU HARM THE CHILD I WILL BURN YOUR PRECIOUS LAND TO CINDERS!
HUFF!

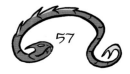

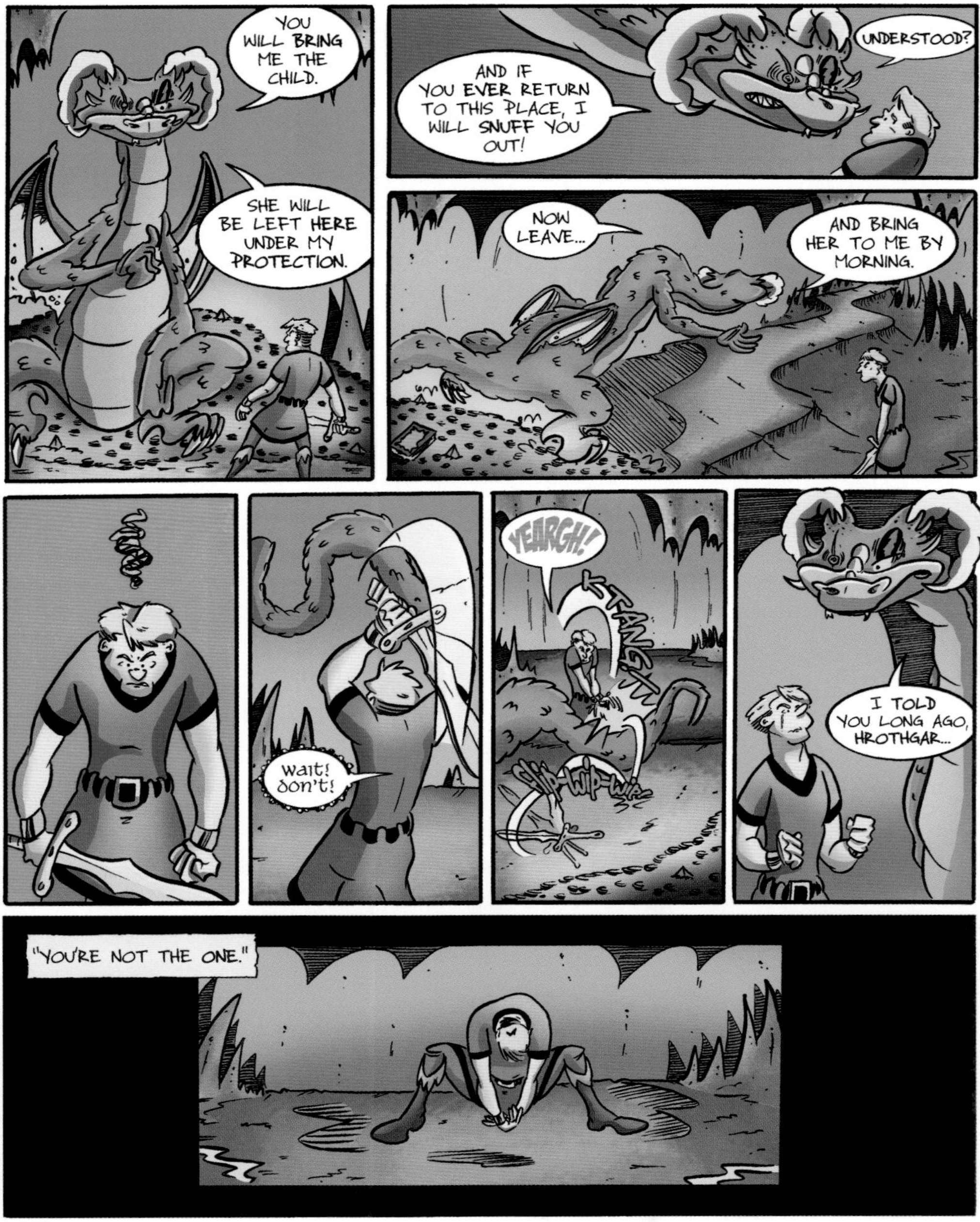
YOU WILL BRING ME THE CHILD.
SHE WILL BE LEFT HERE UNDER MY PROTECTION.
AND IF YOU EVER RETURN TO THIS PLACE, I WILL SNUFF YOU OUT!
UNDERSTOOD?
NOW LEAVE...
AND BRING HER TO ME BY MORNING.
wait! don't!
YEARGH!
KTANG!!
I TOLD YOU LONG AGO, HROTHGAR...
"YOU'RE NOT THE ONE."

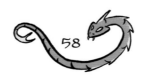

part two

the present

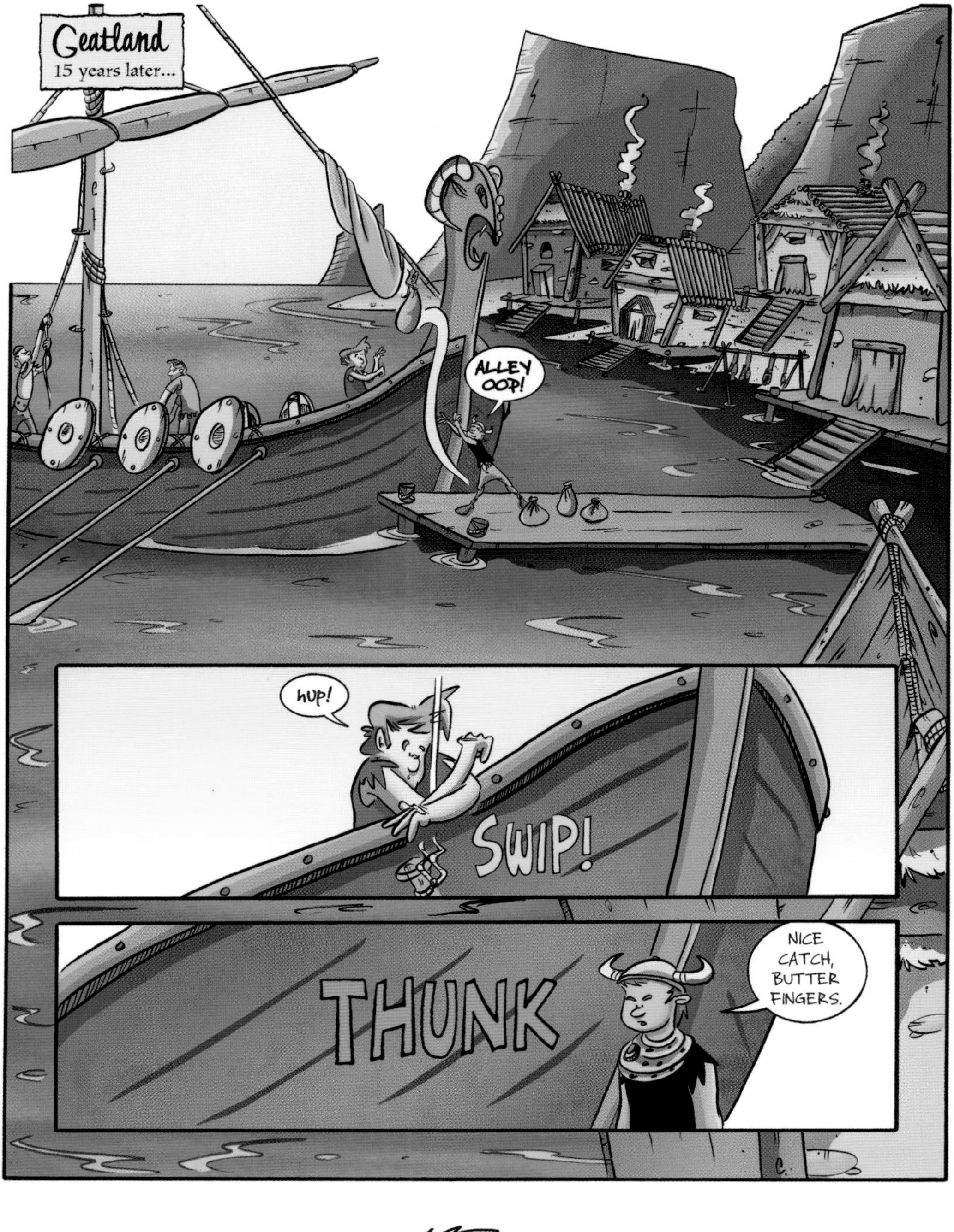
Geatland
15 years later...
ALLEY OOP!
hup!
SWIP!
THUNK
NICE CATCH, BUTTER FINGERS.

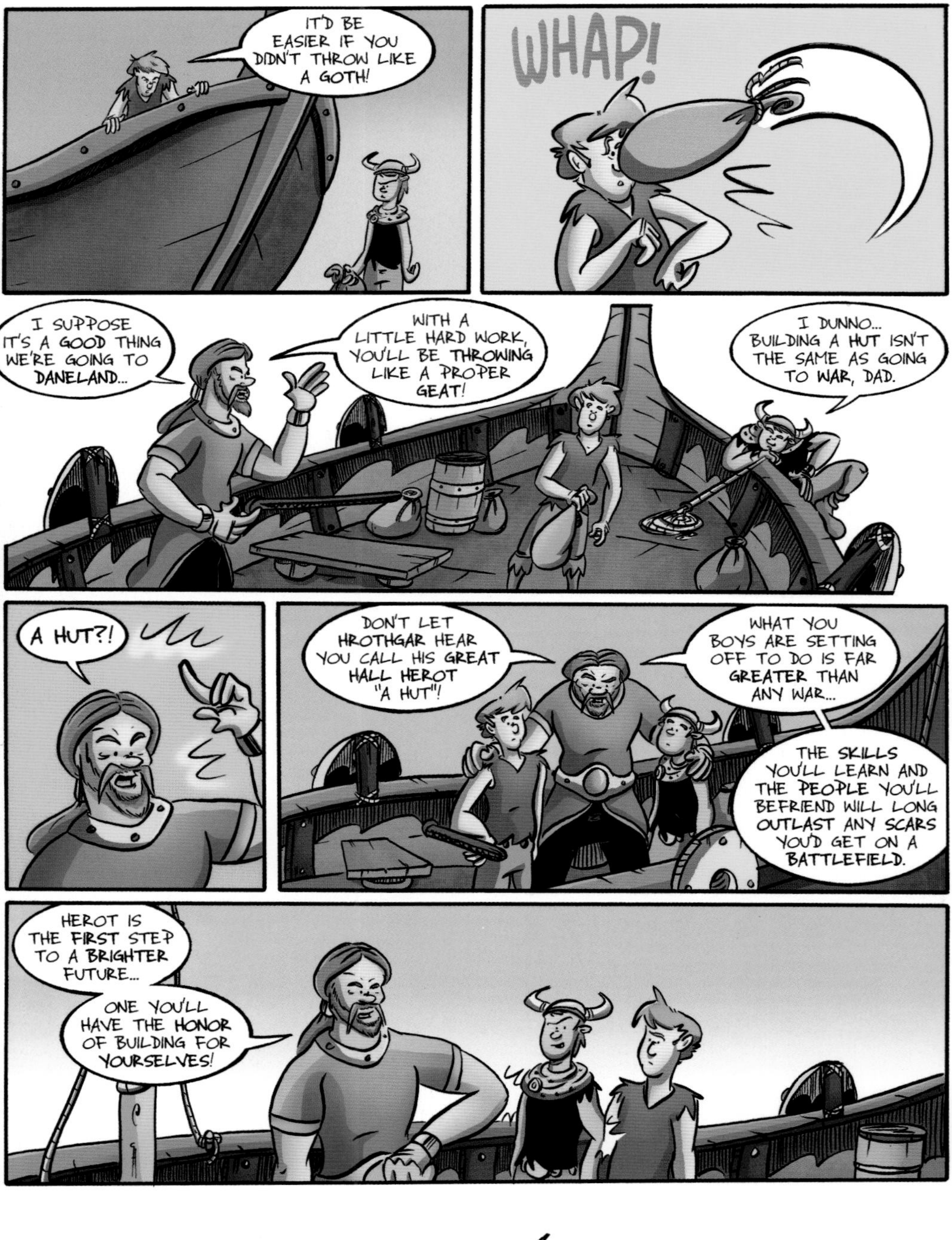
IT'D BE EASIER IF YOU DIDN'T THROW LIKE A GOTH!
WHAP!
I SUPPOSE IT'S A GOOD THING WE'RE GOING TO DANELAND...
WITH A LITTLE HARD WORK, YOU'LL BE THROWING LIKE A PROPER GEAT!
I DUNNO... BUILDING A HUT ISN'T THE SAME AS GOING TO WAR, DAD.
A HUT?!
DON'T LET HROTHGAR HEAR YOU CALL HIS GREAT HALL HEROT "A HUT"!
WHAT YOU BOYS ARE SETTING OFF TO DO IS FAR GREATER THAN ANY WAR...
THE SKILLS YOU'LL LEARN AND THE PEOPLE YOU'LL BEFRIEND WILL LONG OUTLAST ANY SCARS YOU'D GET ON A BATTLEFIELD.
HEROT IS THE FIRST STEP TO A BRIGHTER FUTURE...
ONE YOU'LL HAVE THE HONOR OF BUILDING FOR YOURSELVES!

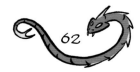

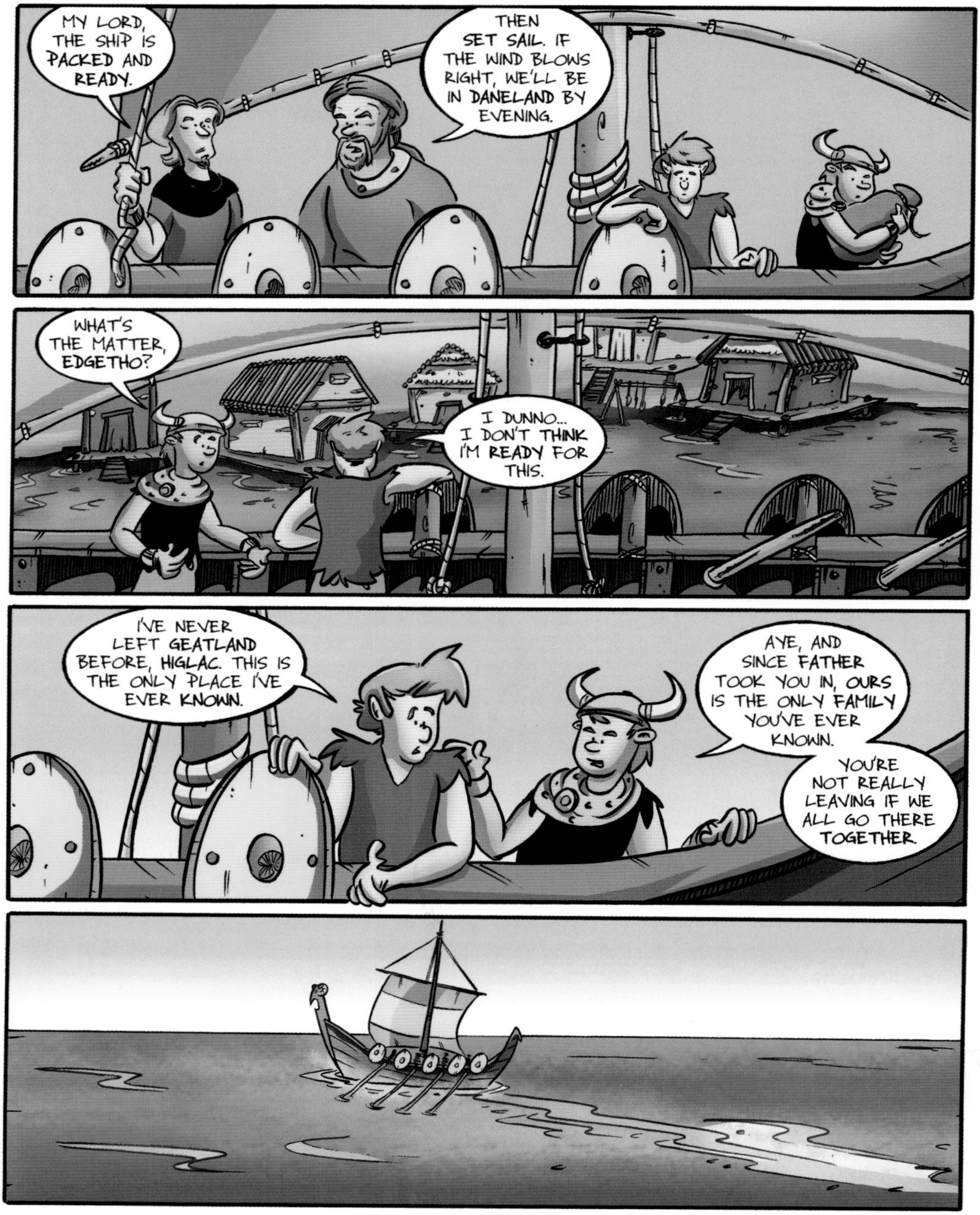
MY LORD, THE SHIP IS PACKED AND READY.
THEN SET SAIL. IF THE WIND BLOWS RIGHT, WE'LL BE IN DANELAND BY EVENING.
WHAT'S THE MATTER, EDGETHO?
I DUNNO... I DON'T THINK I'M READY FOR THIS.
I'VE NEVER LEFT GEATLAND BEFORE, HIGLAC. THIS IS THE ONLY PLACE I'VE EVER KNOWN.
AYE, AND SINCE FATHER TOOK YOU IN, OURS IS THE ONLY FAMILY YOU'VE EVER KNOWN.
YOU'RE NOT REALLY LEAVING IF WE ALL GO THERE TOGETHER.

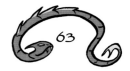

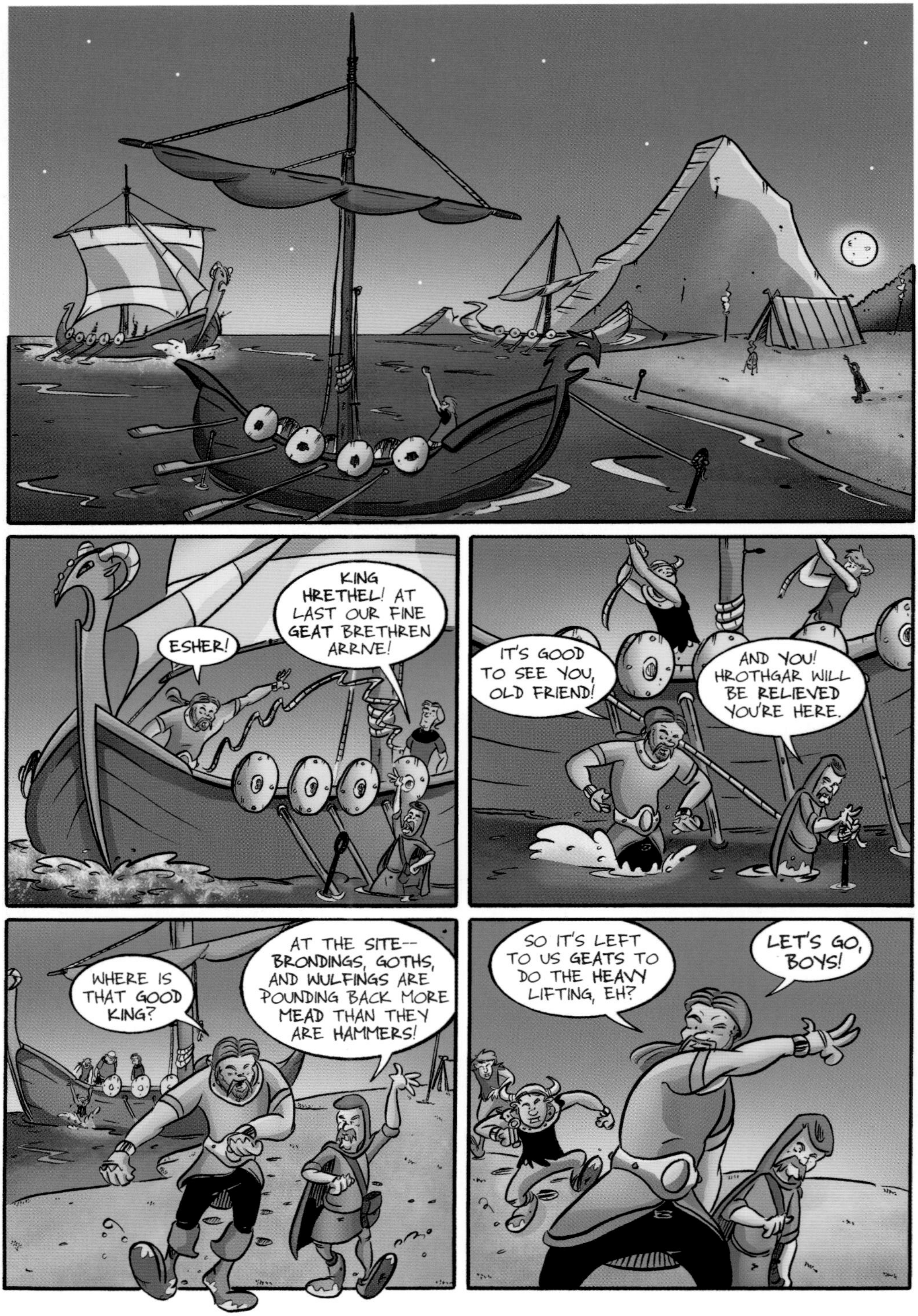
ESHER!
KING HRETHEL! AT LAST OUR FINE GEAT BRETHREN ARRIVE!
IT'S GOOD TO SEE YOU, OLD FRIEND!
AND YOU! HROTHGAR WILL BE RELIEVED YOU'RE HERE.
WHERE IS THAT GOOD KING?
AT THE SITE-- BRONDINGS, GOTHS, AND WULFINGS ARE POUNDING BACK MORE MEAD THAN THEY ARE HAMMERS!
SO IT'S LEFT TO US GEATS TO DO THE HEAVY LIFTING, EH?
LET'S GO, BOYS!

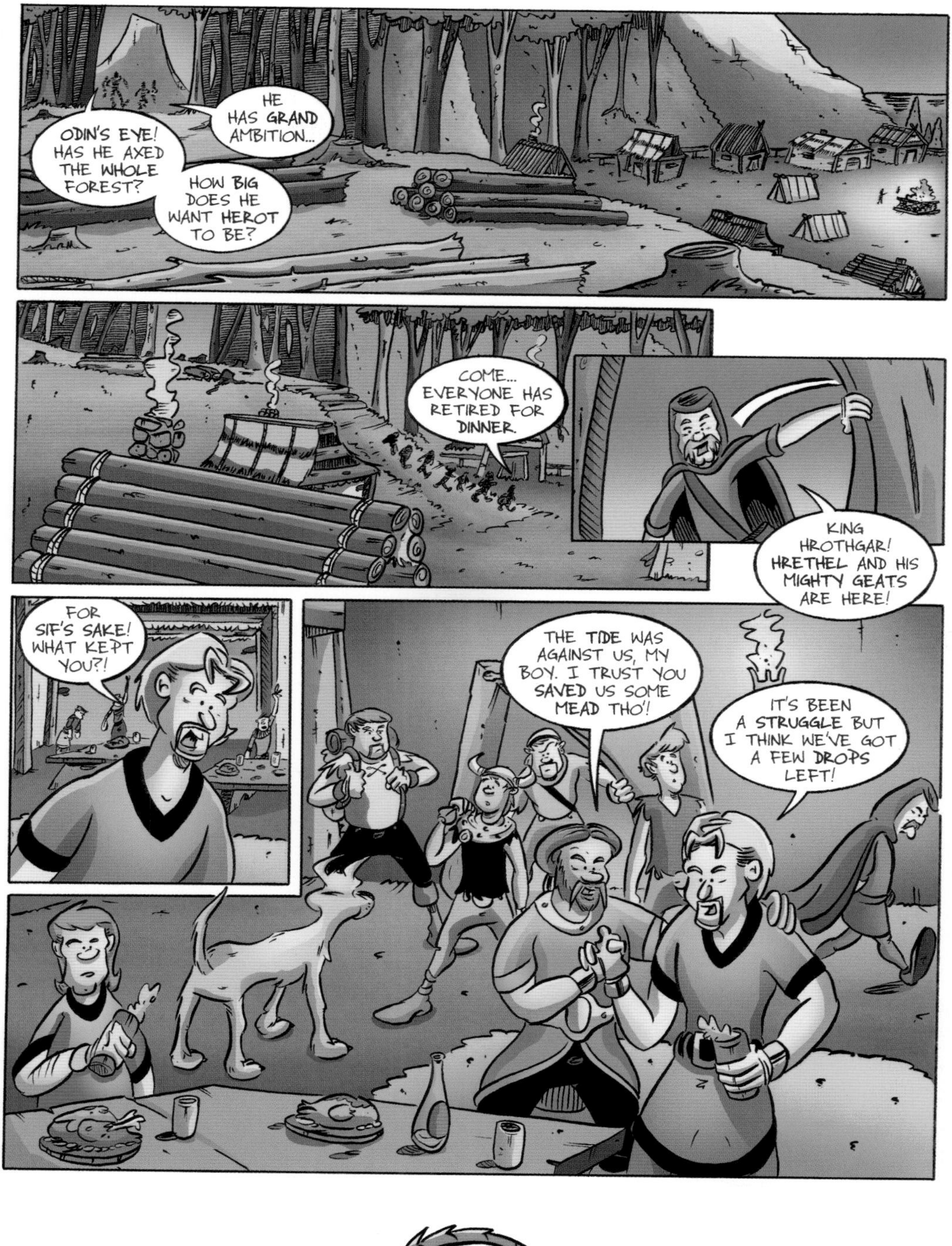
ODIN'S EYE! HAS HE AXED THE WHOLE FOREST?
HE HAS GRAND AMBITION...
HOW BIG DOES HE WANT HEROT TO BE?
COME... EVERYONE HAS RETIRED FOR DINNER.
KING HROTHGAR! HRETHEL AND HIS MIGHTY GEATS ARE HERE!
FOR SIF'S SAKE! WHAT KEPT YOU?!
THE TIDE WAS AGAINST US, MY BOY. I TRUST YOU SAVED US SOME MEAD THO'!
IT'S BEEN A STRUGGLE BUT I THINK WE'VE GOT A FEW DROPS LEFT!

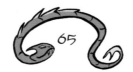

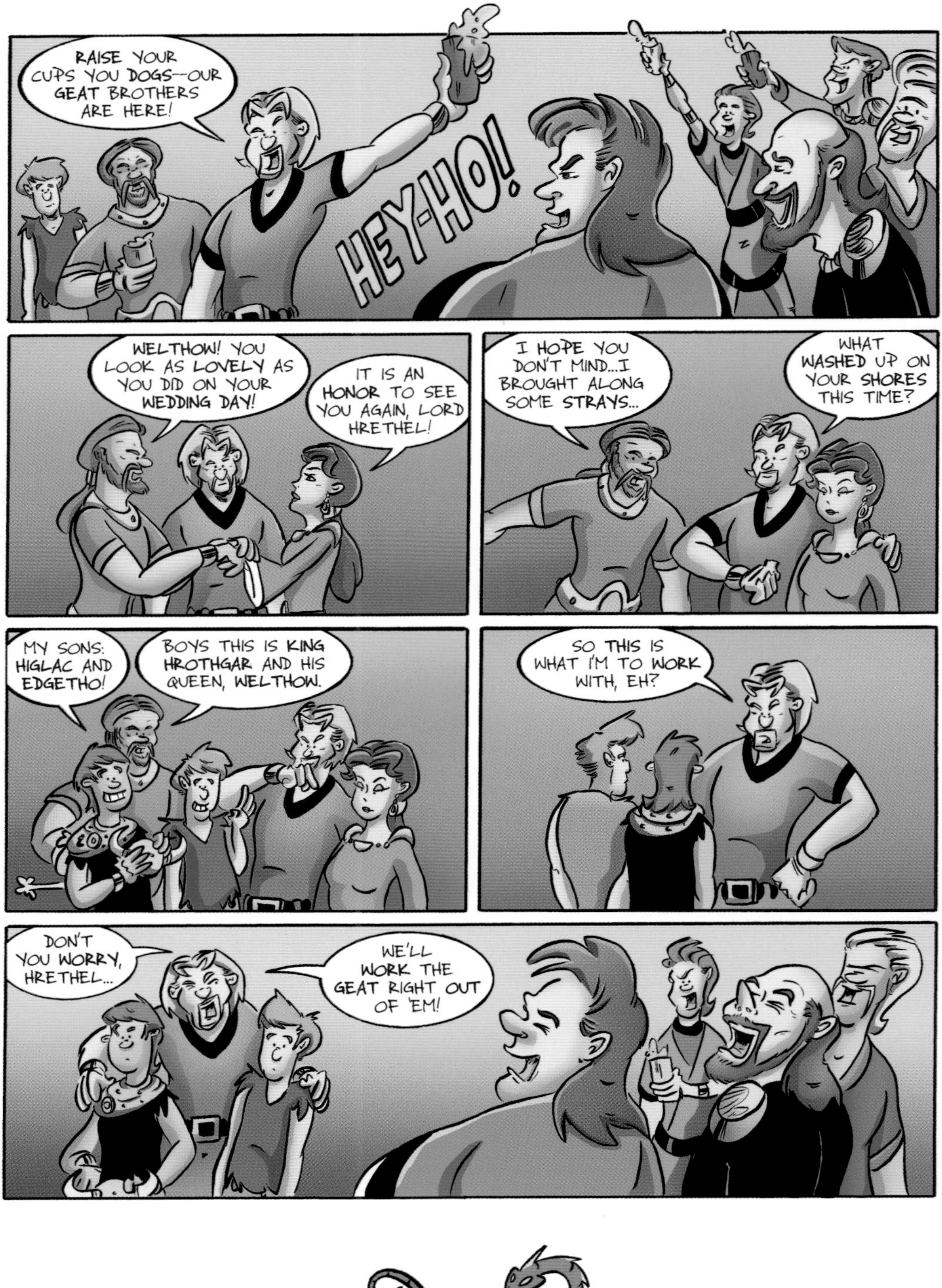
RAISE YOUR CUPS YOU DOGS--OUR GEAT BROTHERS ARE HERE!
HEY-HO!
WELTHOW! YOU LOOK AS LOVELY AS YOU DID ON YOUR WEDDING DAY!
IT IS AN HONOR TO SEE YOU AGAIN, LORD HRETHEL!
I HOPE YOU DON'T MIND...I BROUGHT ALONG SOME STRAYS...
WHAT WASHED UP ON YOUR SHORES THIS TIME?
MY SONS: HIGLAC AND EDGETHO!
BOYS THIS IS KING HROTHGAR AND HIS QUEEN, WELTHOW.
SO THIS IS WHAT I'M TO WORK WITH, EH?
DON'T YOU WORRY, HRETHEL...
WE'LL WORK THE GEAT RIGHT OUT OF 'EM!

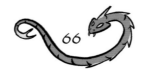

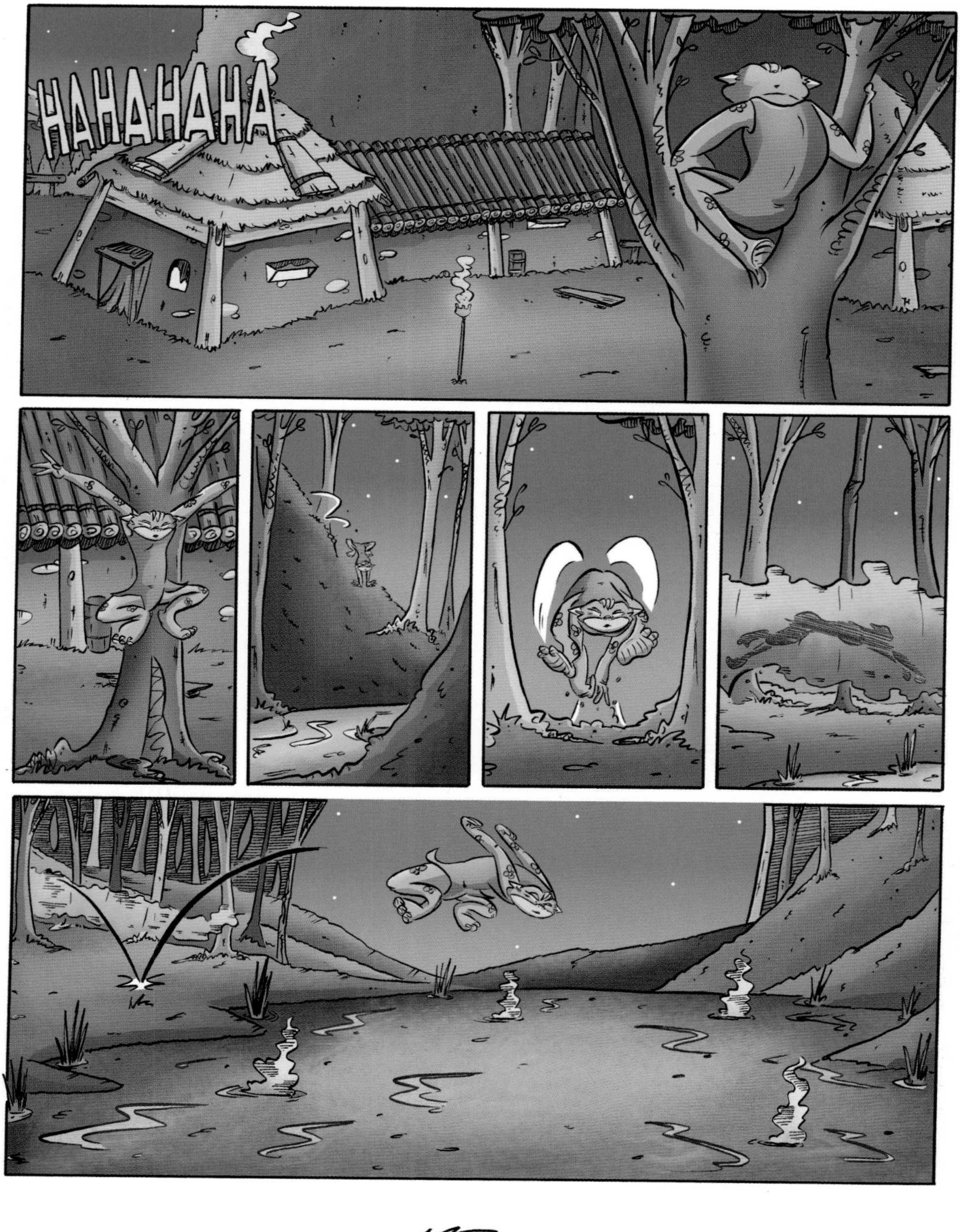
HAHAHAHA

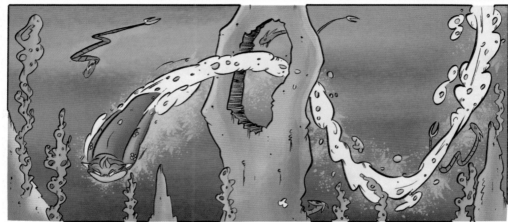

YOU'RE LATE.

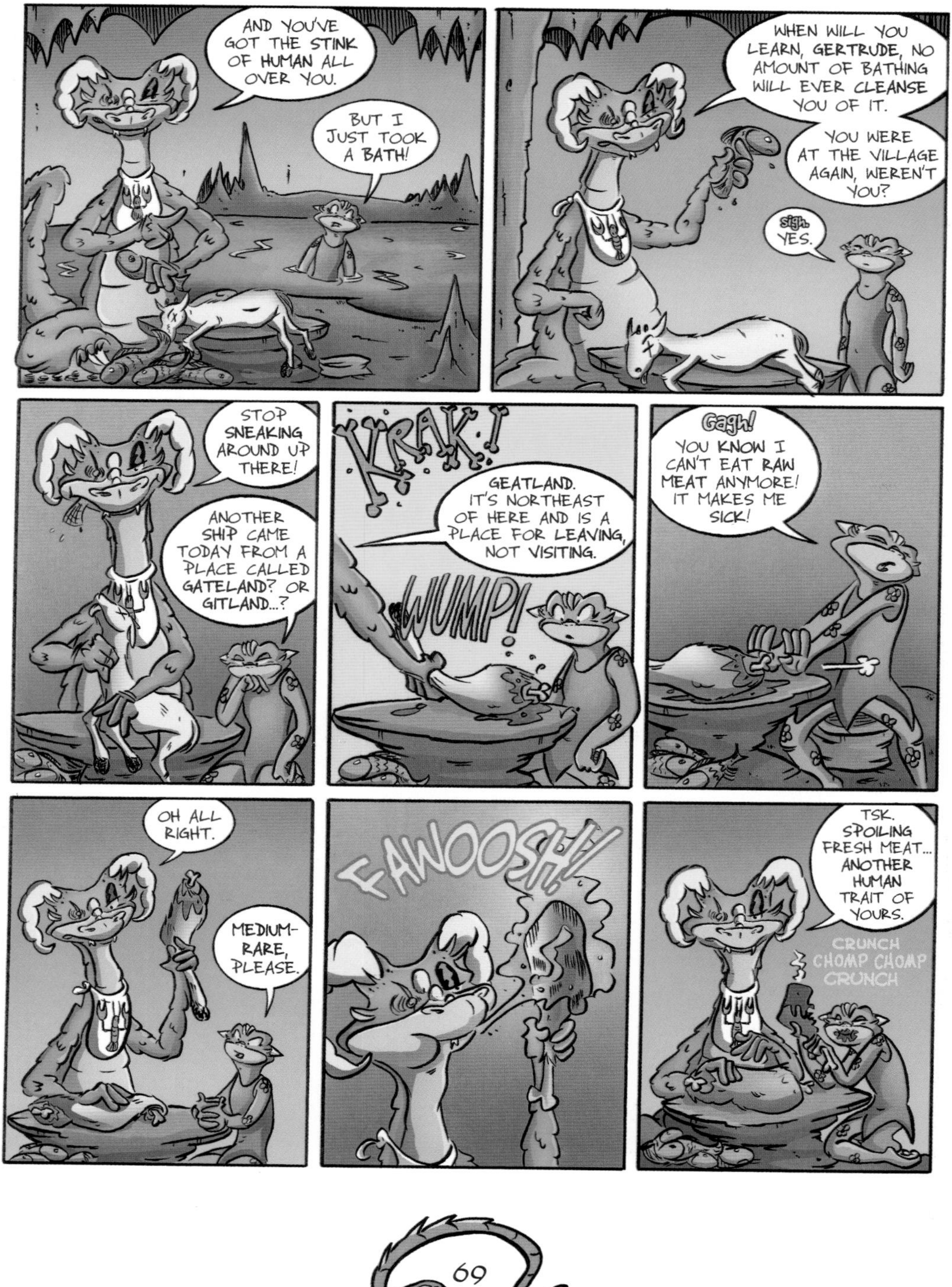
AND YOU'VE GOT THE STINK OF HUMAN ALL OVER YOU.
BUT I JUST TOOK A BATH!
WHEN WILL YOU LEARN, GERTRUDE, NO AMOUNT OF BATHING WILL EVER CLEANSE YOU OF IT.
YOU WERE AT THE VILLAGE AGAIN, WEREN'T YOU?
sigh. YES.
STOP SNEAKING AROUND UP THERE!
ANOTHER SHIP CAME TODAY FROM A PLACE CALLED GATELAND? OR GITLAND...?
KRAK!
GEATLAND. IT'S NORTHEAST OF HERE AND IS A PLACE FOR LEAVING, NOT VISITING.
WUMP!
Gagh!
YOU KNOW I CAN'T EAT RAW MEAT ANYMORE! IT MAKES ME SICK!
OH ALL RIGHT.
MEDIUM-RARE, PLEASE.
FAWOOSH!
TSK. SPOILING FRESH MEAT... ANOTHER HUMAN TRAIT OF YOURS.
CRUNCH CHOMP CHOMP CRUNCH

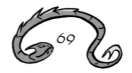

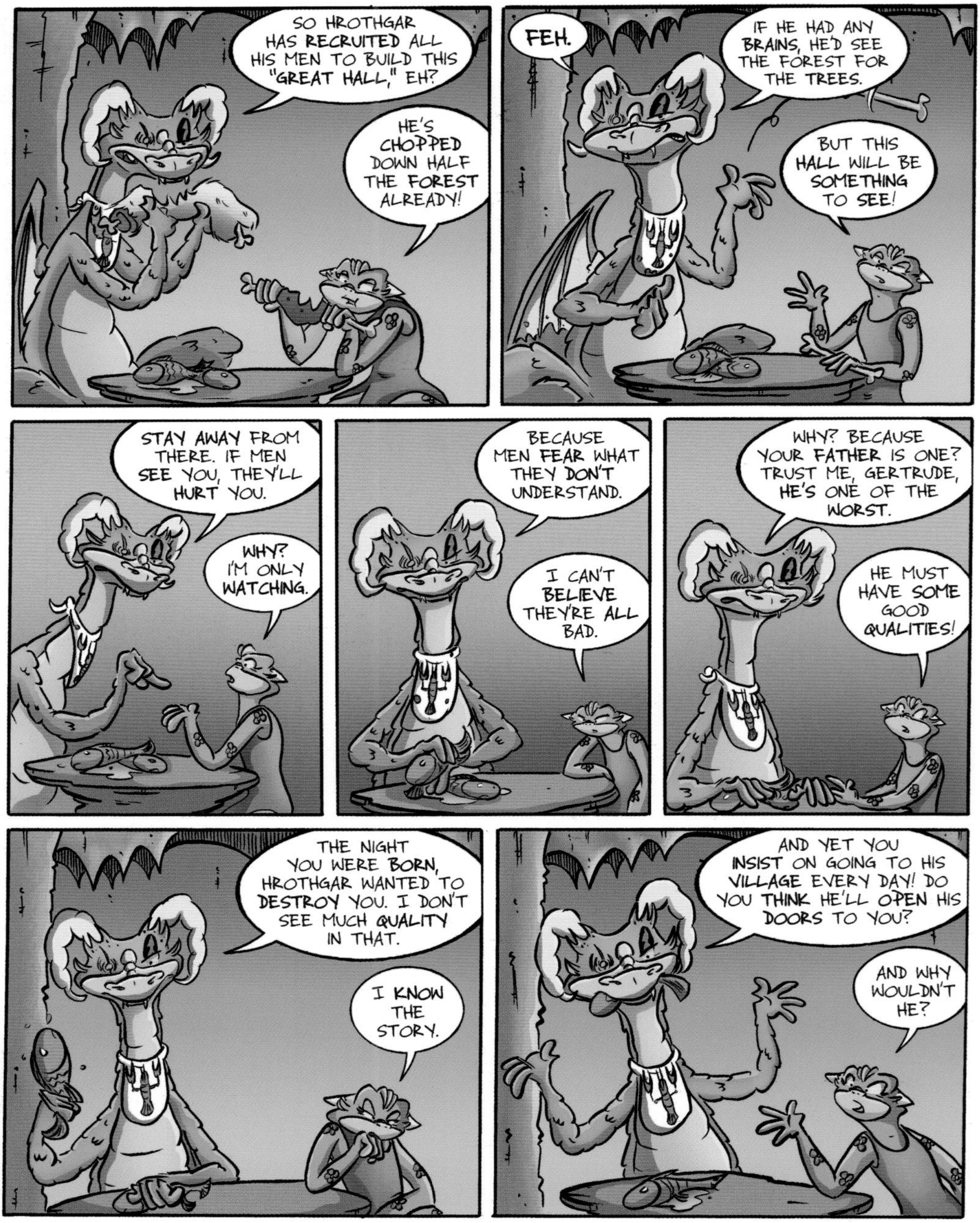
SO HROTHGAR HAS RECRUITED ALL HIS MEN TO BUILD THIS "GREAT HALL," EH?
HE'S CHOPPED DOWN HALF THE FOREST ALREADY!
FEH.
IF HE HAD ANY BRAINS, HE'D SEE THE FOREST FOR THE TREES.
BUT THIS HALL WILL BE SOMETHING TO SEE!
STAY AWAY FROM THERE. IF MEN SEE YOU, THEY'LL HURT YOU.
WHY? I'M ONLY WATCHING.
BECAUSE MEN FEAR WHAT THEY DON'T UNDERSTAND.
I CAN'T BELIEVE THEY'RE ALL BAD.
WHY? BECAUSE YOUR FATHER IS ONE? TRUST ME, GERTRUDE, HE'S ONE OF THE WORST.
HE MUST HAVE SOME GOOD QUALITIES!
THE NIGHT YOU WERE BORN, HROTHGAR WANTED TO DESTROY YOU. I DON'T SEE MUCH QUALITY IN THAT.
I KNOW THE STORY.
AND YET YOU INSIST ON GOING TO HIS VILLAGE EVERY DAY! DO YOU THINK HE'LL OPEN HIS DOORS TO YOU?
AND WHY WOULDN'T HE?

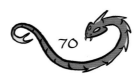

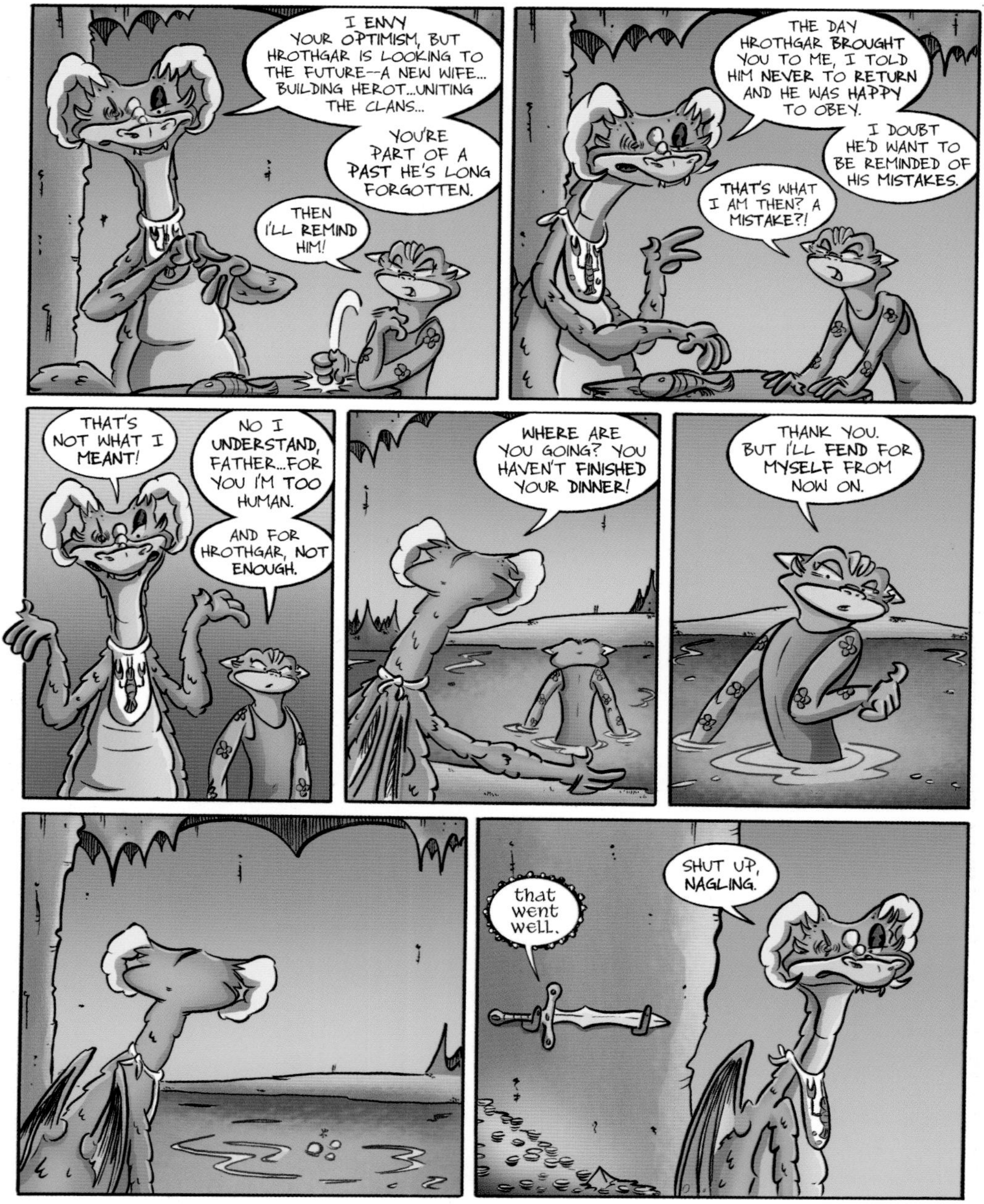
I ENVY YOUR OPTIMISM, BUT HROTHGAR IS LOOKING TO THE FUTURE--A NEW WIFE... BUILDING HEROT...UNITING THE CLANS...
YOU'RE PART OF A PAST HE'S LONG FORGOTTEN.
THEN I'LL REMIND HIM!
THE DAY HROTHGAR BROUGHT YOU TO ME, I TOLD HIM NEVER TO RETURN AND HE WAS HAPPY TO OBEY.
I DOUBT HE'D WANT TO BE REMINDED OF HIS MISTAKES.
THAT'S WHAT I AM THEN? A MISTAKE?!
THAT'S NOT WHAT I MEANT!
NO I UNDERSTAND, FATHER...FOR YOU I'M TOO HUMAN.
AND FOR HROTHGAR, NOT ENOUGH.
WHERE ARE YOU GOING? YOU HAVEN'T FINISHED YOUR DINNER!
THANK YOU. BUT I'LL FEND FOR MYSELF FROM NOW ON.
that went well.
SHUT UP, NAGLING.

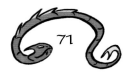

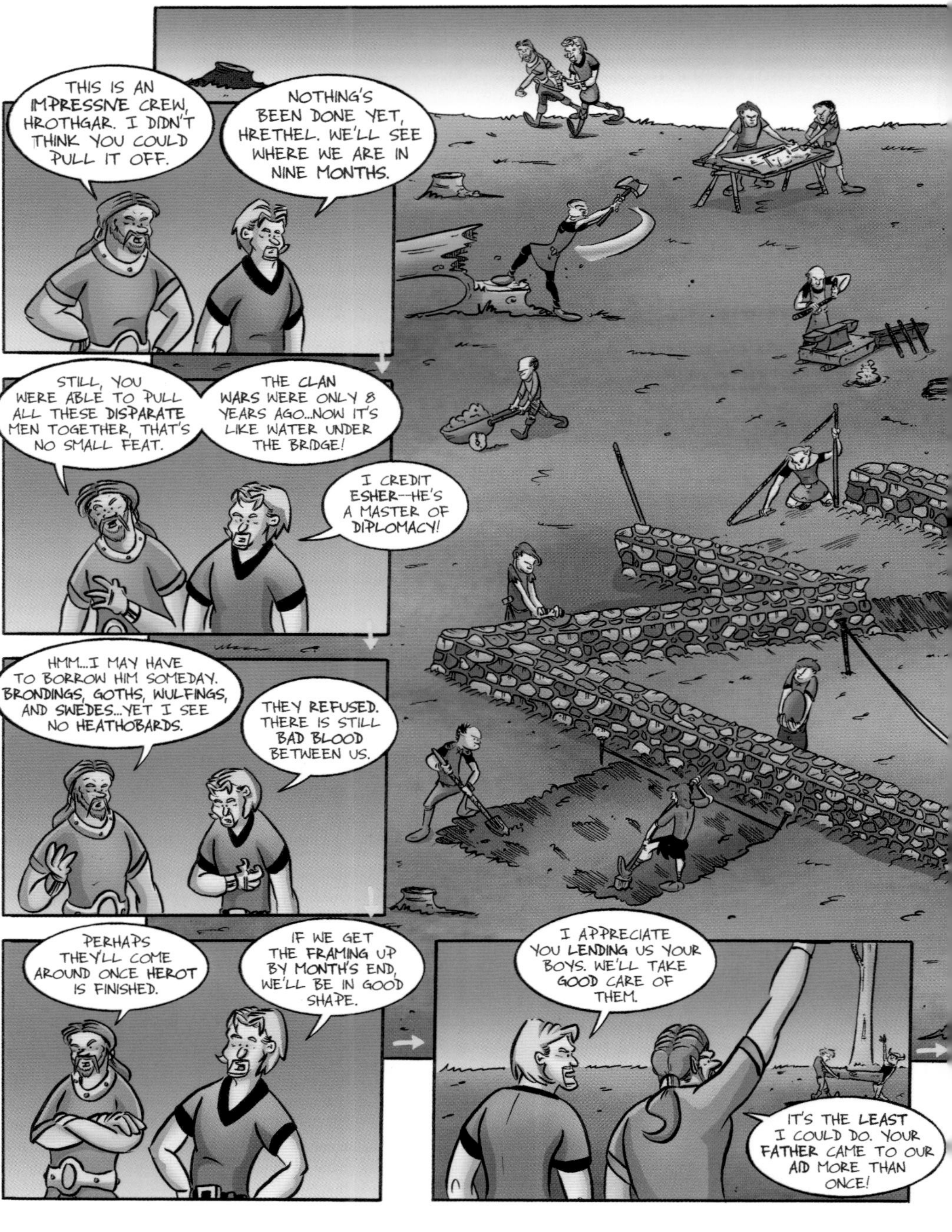
THIS IS AN IMPRESSIVE CREW, HROTHGAR. I DIDN'T THINK YOU COULD PULL IT OFF.
NOTHING'S BEEN DONE YET, HRETHEL. WE'LL SEE WHERE WE ARE IN NINE MONTHS.
STILL, YOU WERE ABLE TO PULL ALL THESE DISPARATE MEN TOGETHER, THAT'S NO SMALL FEAT.
THE CLAN WARS WERE ONLY 8 YEARS AGO...NOW IT'S LIKE WATER UNDER THE BRIDGE!
I CREDIT ESHER--HE'S A MASTER OF DIPLOMACY!
HMM...I MAY HAVE TO BORROW HIM SOMEDAY. BRONDINGS, GOTHS, WULFINGS, AND SWEDES...YET I SEE NO HEATHOBARDS.
THEY REFUSED. THERE IS STILL BAD BLOOD BETWEEN US.
PERHAPS THEY'LL COME AROUND ONCE HEROT IS FINISHED.
IF WE GET THE FRAMING UP BY MONTH'S END, WE'LL BE IN GOOD SHAPE.
I APPRECIATE YOU LENDING US YOUR BOYS. WE'LL TAKE GOOD CARE OF THEM.
IT'S THE LEAST I COULD DO. YOUR FATHER CAME TO OUR AID MORE THAN ONCE!

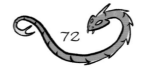

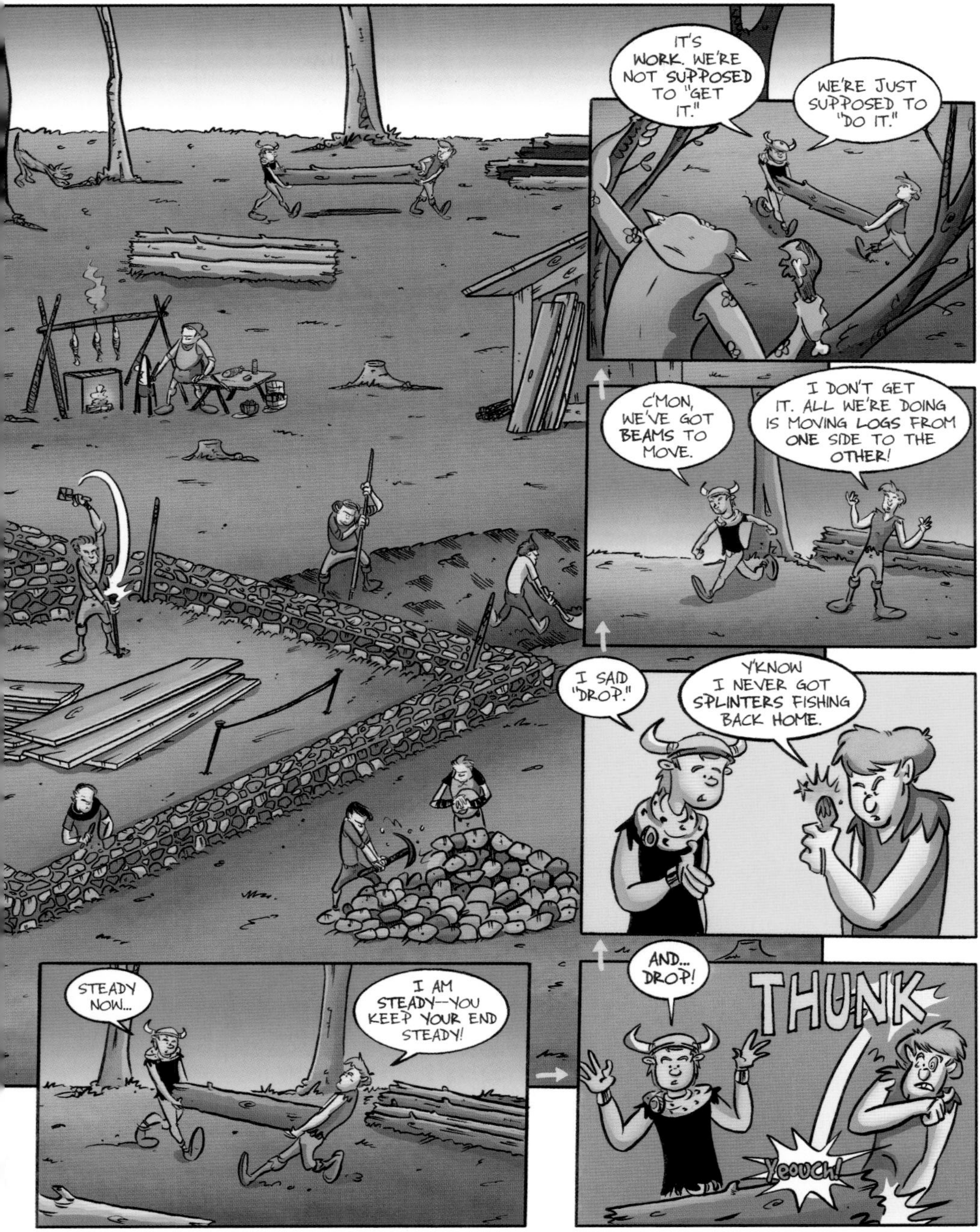
STEADY NOW...
I AM STEADY--YOU KEEP YOUR END STEADY!
AND... DROP!
THUNK
YEOUCH!
I SAID "DROP."
Y'KNOW I NEVER GOT SPLINTERS FISHING BACK HOME.
C'MON, WE'VE GOT BEAMS TO MOVE.
I DON'T GET IT. ALL WE'RE DOING IS MOVING LOGS FROM ONE SIDE TO THE OTHER!
IT'S WORK. WE'RE NOT SUPPOSED TO "GET IT."
WE'RE JUST SUPPOSED TO "DO IT."

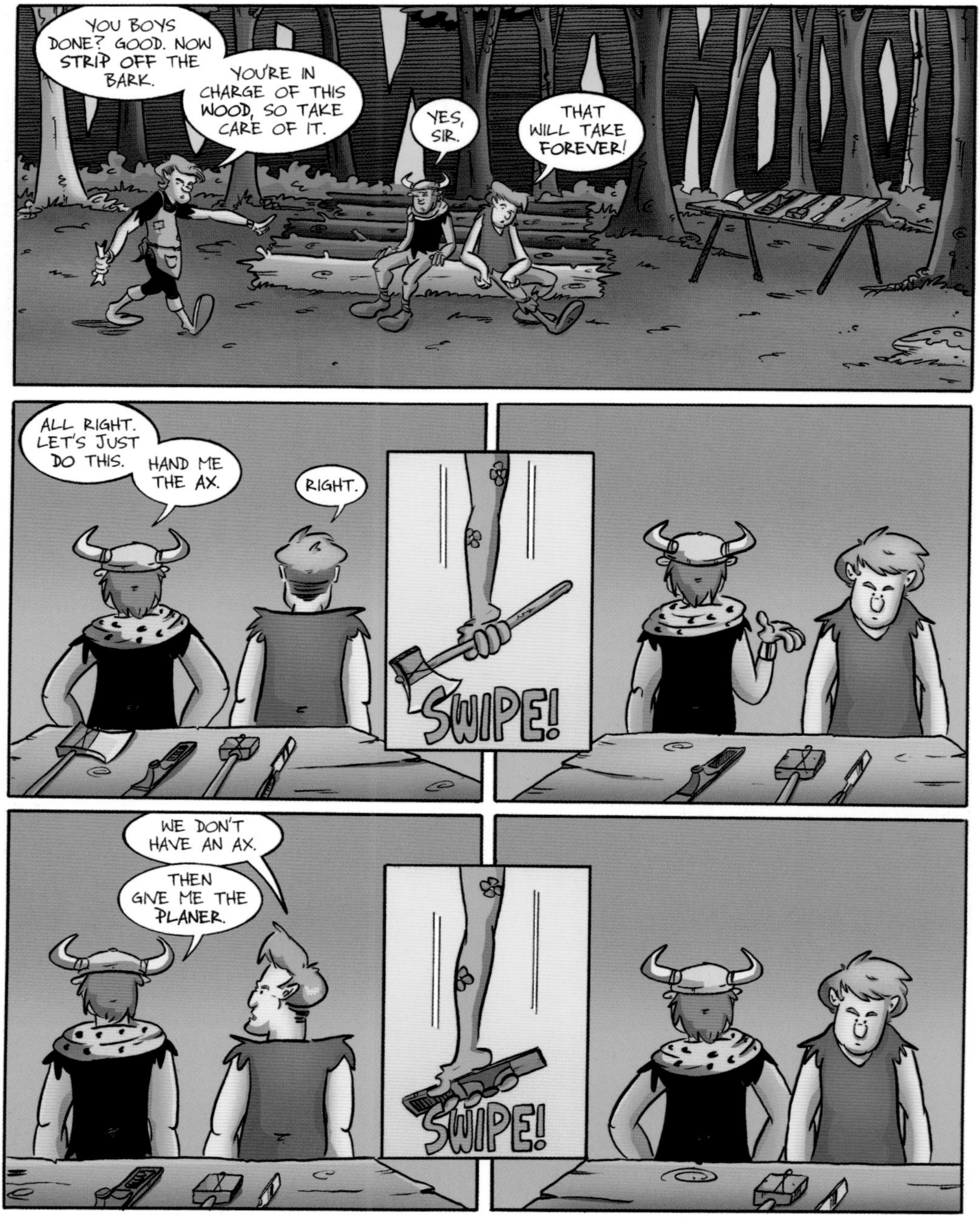
YOU BOYS DONE? GOOD. NOW STRIP OFF THE BARK.
YOU'RE IN CHARGE OF THIS WOOD, SO TAKE CARE OF IT.
YES, SIR.
THAT WILL TAKE FOREVER!
ALL RIGHT. LET'S JUST DO THIS.
HAND ME THE AX.
RIGHT.
SWIPE!
WE DON'T HAVE AN AX.
THEN GIVE ME THE PLANER.
SWIPE!

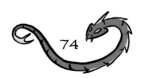

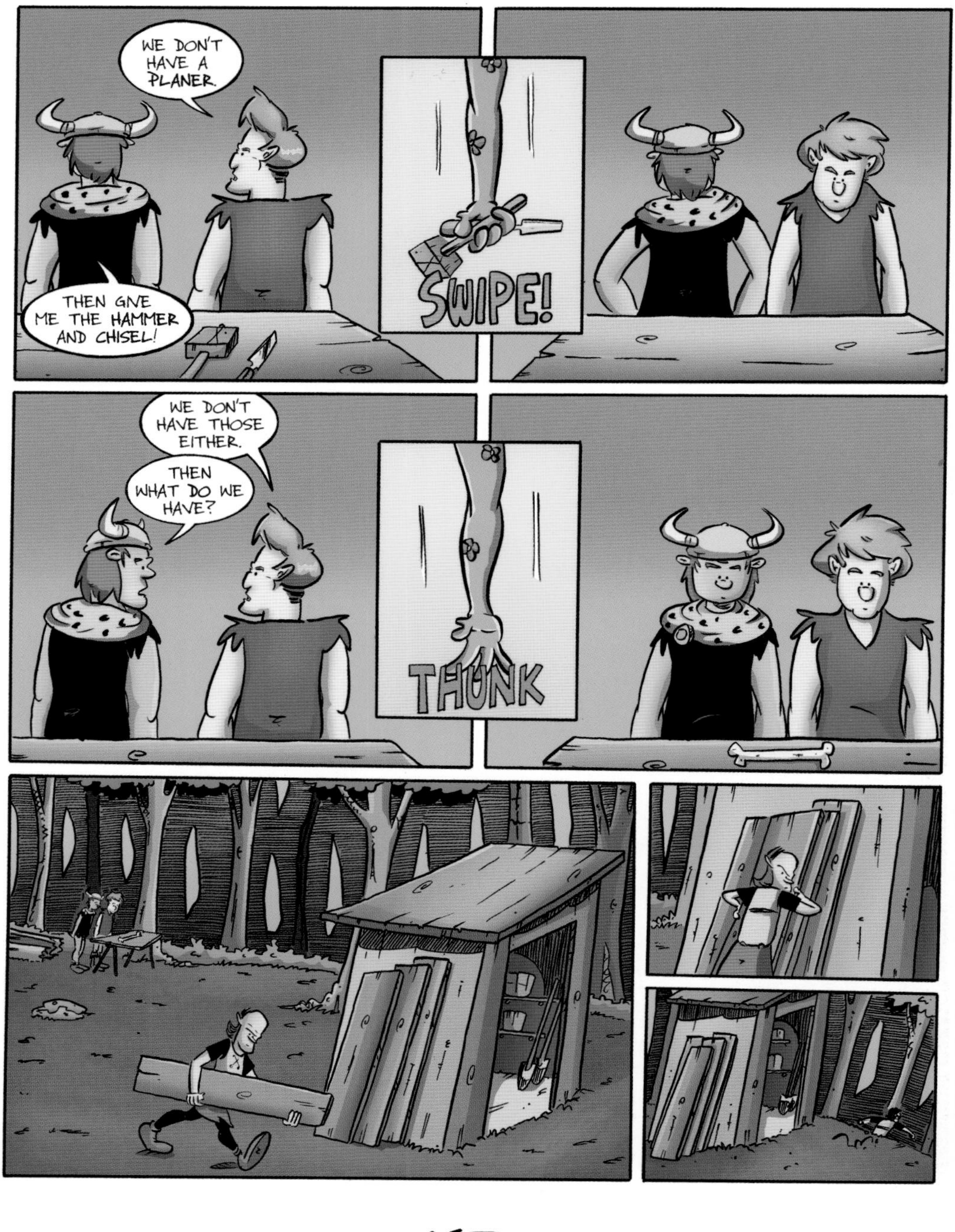
WE DON'T HAVE A PLANER.
THEN GIVE ME THE HAMMER AND CHISEL!
SWIPE!
WE DON'T HAVE THOSE EITHER.
THEN WHAT DO WE HAVE?
THUNK

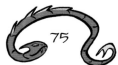

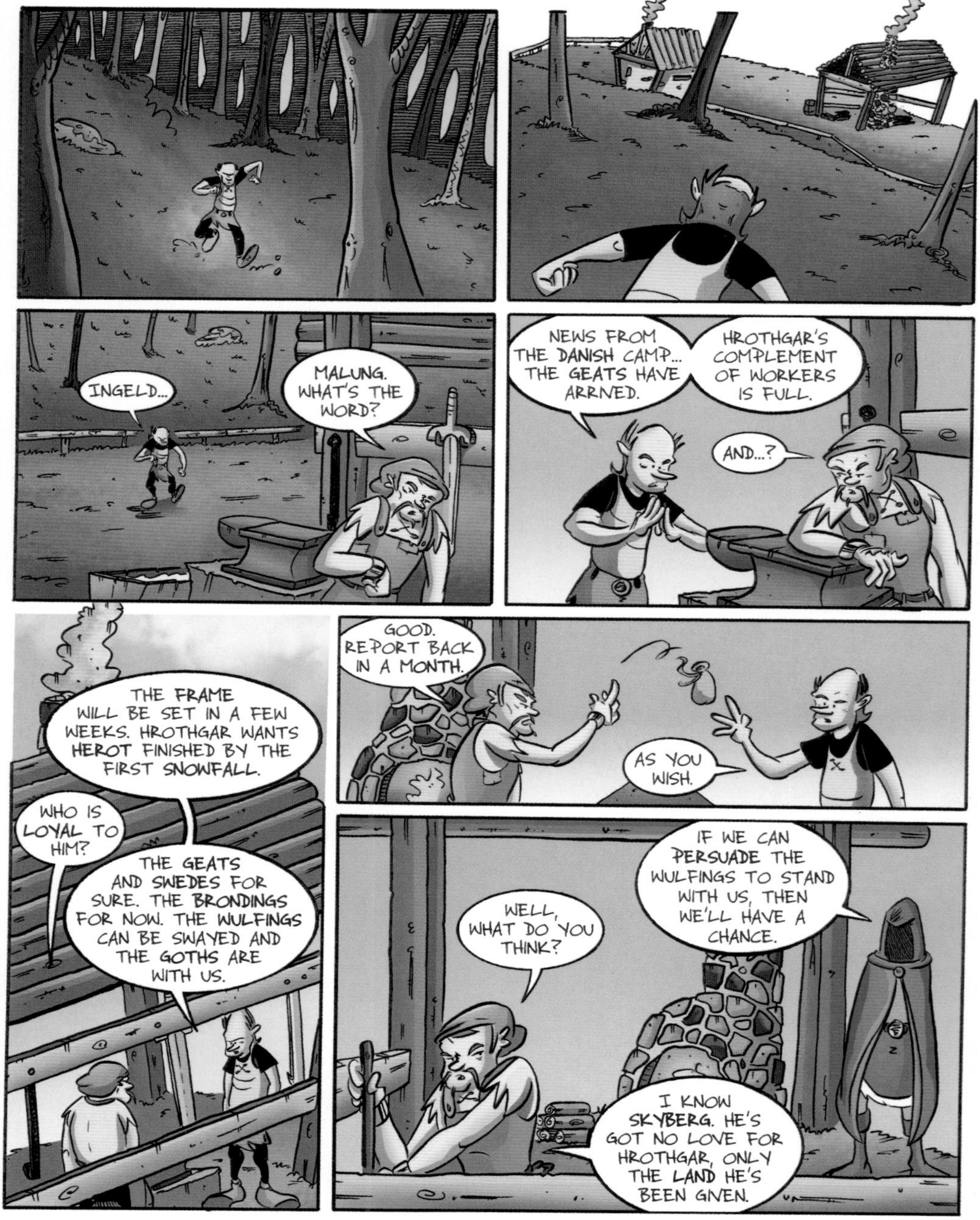
INGELD...
MALUNG. WHAT'S THE WORD?
NEWS FROM THE DANISH CAMP... THE GEATS HAVE ARRIVED.
HROTHGAR'S COMPLEMENT OF WORKERS IS FULL.
AND...?
THE FRAME WILL BE SET IN A FEW WEEKS. HROTHGAR WANTS HEROT FINISHED BY THE FIRST SNOWFALL.
WHO IS LOYAL TO HIM?
THE GEATS AND SWEDES FOR SURE. THE BRONDINGS FOR NOW. THE WULFINGS CAN BE SWAYED AND THE GOTHS ARE WITH US.
GOOD. REPORT BACK IN A MONTH.
AS YOU WISH.
WELL, WHAT DO YOU THINK?
IF WE CAN PERSUADE THE WULFINGS TO STAND WITH US, THEN WE'LL HAVE A CHANCE.
I KNOW SKYBERG. HE'S GOT NO LOVE FOR HROTHGAR, ONLY THE LAND HE'S BEEN GIVEN.

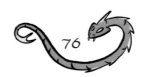

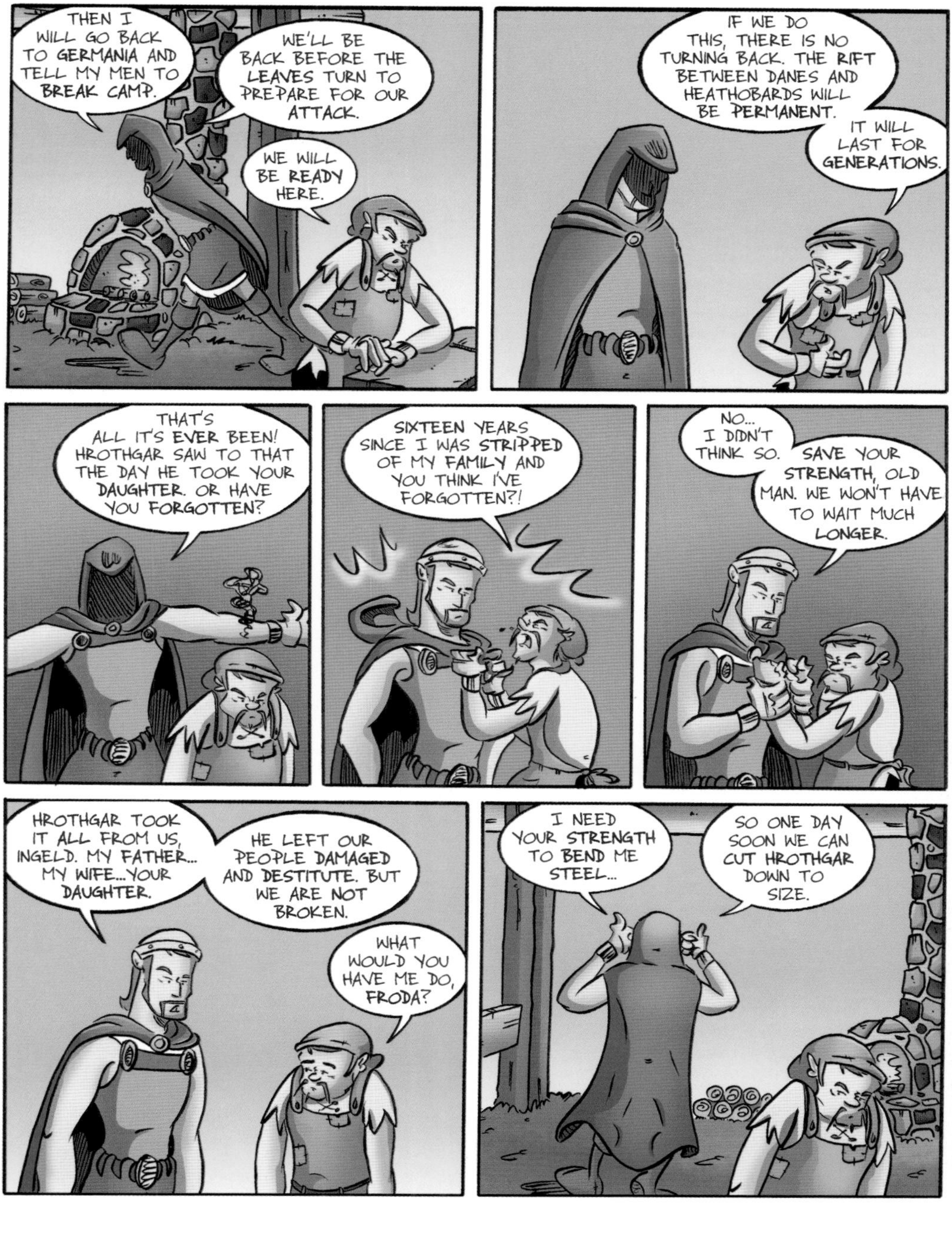
THEN I WILL GO BACK TO GERMANIA AND TELL MY MEN TO BREAK CAMP.
WE'LL BE BACK BEFORE THE LEAVES TURN TO PREPARE FOR OUR ATTACK.
WE WILL BE READY HERE.
IF WE DO THIS, THERE IS NO TURNING BACK. THE RIFT BETWEEN DANES AND HEATHOBARDS WILL BE PERMANENT.
IT WILL LAST FOR GENERATIONS.
THAT'S ALL IT'S EVER BEEN! HROTHGAR SAW TO THAT THE DAY HE TOOK YOUR DAUGHTER. OR HAVE YOU FORGOTTEN?
SIXTEEN YEARS SINCE I WAS STRIPPED OF MY FAMILY AND YOU THINK I'VE FORGOTTEN?!
NO... I DIDN'T THINK SO.
SAVE YOUR STRENGTH, OLD MAN. WE WON'T HAVE TO WAIT MUCH LONGER.
HROTHGAR TOOK IT ALL FROM US, INGELD. MY FATHER... MY WIFE...YOUR DAUGHTER.
HE LEFT OUR PEOPLE DAMAGED AND DESTITUTE. BUT WE ARE NOT BROKEN.
WHAT WOULD YOU HAVE ME DO, FRODA?
I NEED YOUR STRENGTH TO BEND ME STEEL...
SO ONE DAY SOON WE CAN CUT HROTHGAR DOWN TO SIZE.

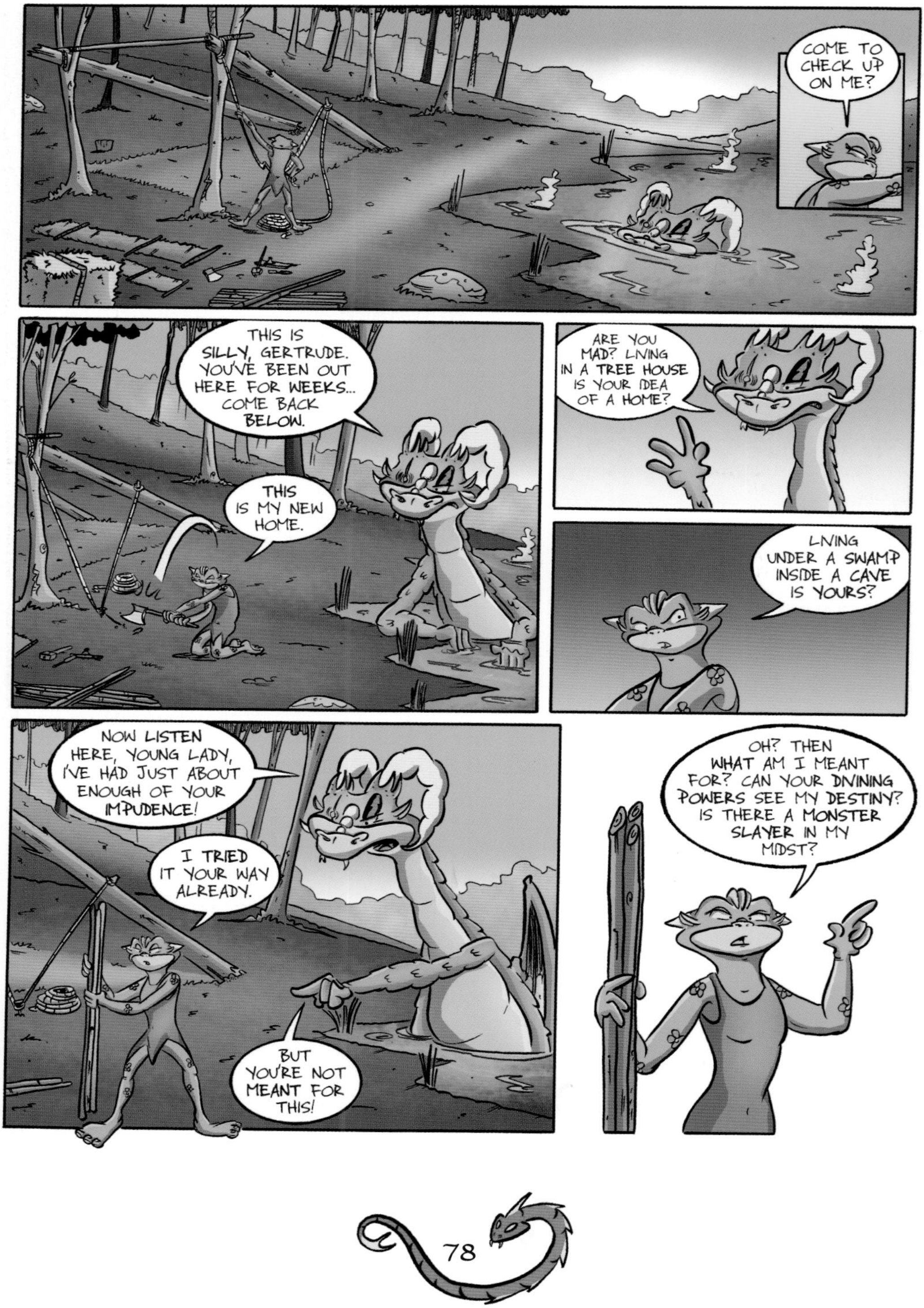
COME TO CHECK UP ON ME?
THIS IS SILLY, GERTRUDE. YOU'VE BEEN OUT HERE FOR WEEKS... COME BACK BELOW.
THIS IS MY NEW HOME.
ARE YOU MAD? LIVING IN A TREE HOUSE IS YOUR IDEA OF A HOME?
LIVING UNDER A SWAMP INSIDE A CAVE IS YOURS?
NOW LISTEN HERE, YOUNG LADY, I'VE HAD JUST ABOUT ENOUGH OF YOUR IMPUDENCE!
I TRIED IT YOUR WAY ALREADY.
BUT YOU'RE NOT MEANT FOR THIS!
OH? THEN WHAT AM I MEANT FOR? CAN YOUR DIVINING POWERS SEE MY DESTINY? IS THERE A MONSTER SLAYER IN MY MIDST?

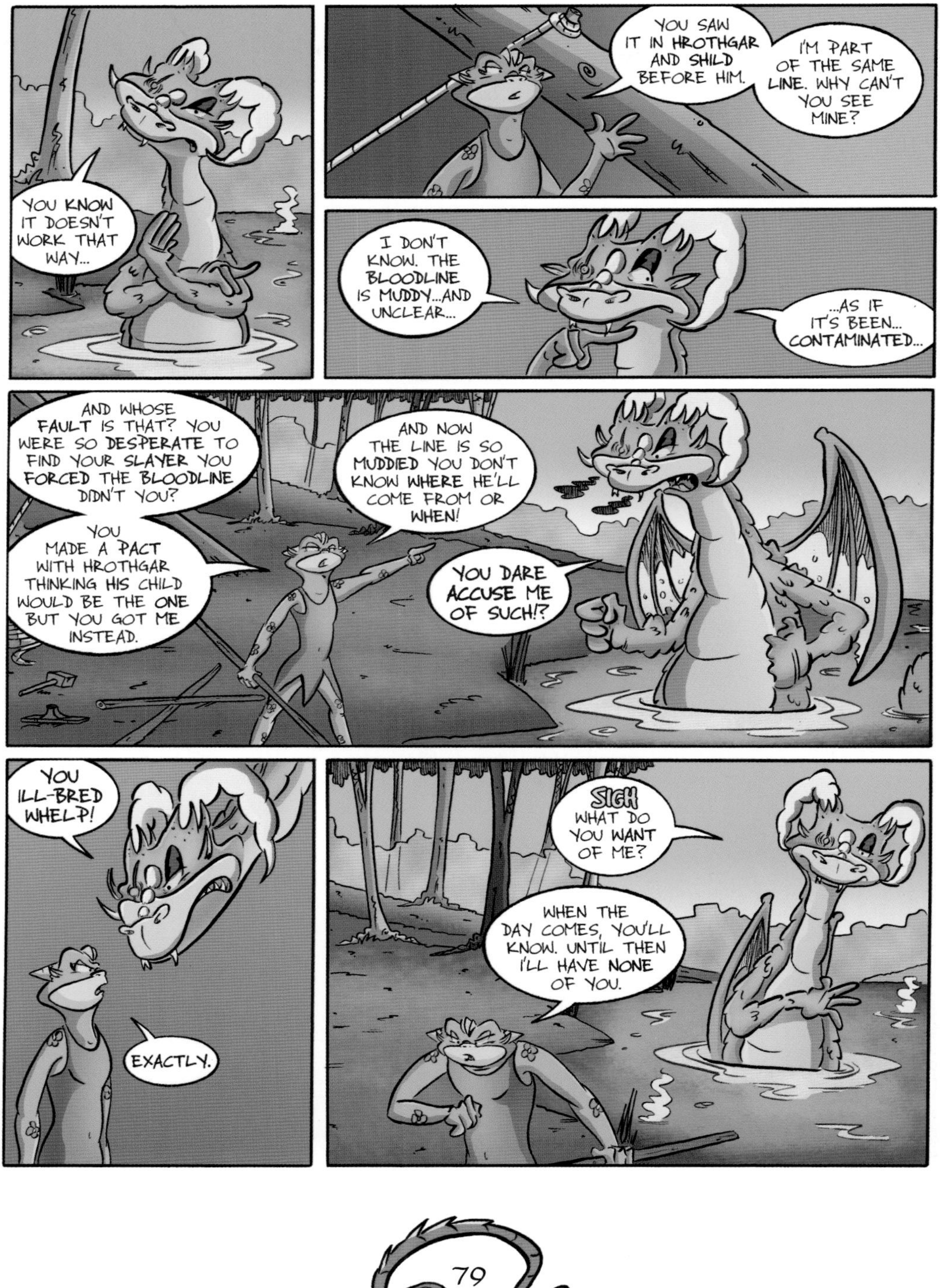
YOU KNOW IT DOESN'T WORK THAT WAY...
YOU SAW IT IN HROTHGAR AND SHILD BEFORE HIM.
I'M PART OF THE SAME LINE. WHY CAN'T YOU SEE MINE?
I DON'T KNOW. THE BLOODLINE IS MUDDY...AND UNCLEAR...
...AS IF IT'S BEEN... CONTAMINATED...
AND WHOSE FAULT IS THAT? YOU WERE SO DESPERATE TO FIND YOUR SLAYER YOU FORCED THE BLOODLINE DIDN'T YOU?
YOU MADE A PACT WITH HROTHGAR THINKING HIS CHILD WOULD BE THE ONE BUT YOU GOT ME INSTEAD.
AND NOW THE LINE IS SO MUDDIED YOU DON'T KNOW WHERE HE'LL COME FROM OR WHEN!
YOU DARE ACCUSE ME OF SUCH!?
YOU ILL-BRED WHELP!
EXACTLY.
SIGH
WHAT DO YOU WANT OF ME?
WHEN THE DAY COMES, YOU'LL KNOW. UNTIL THEN I'LL HAVE NONE OF YOU.

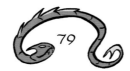

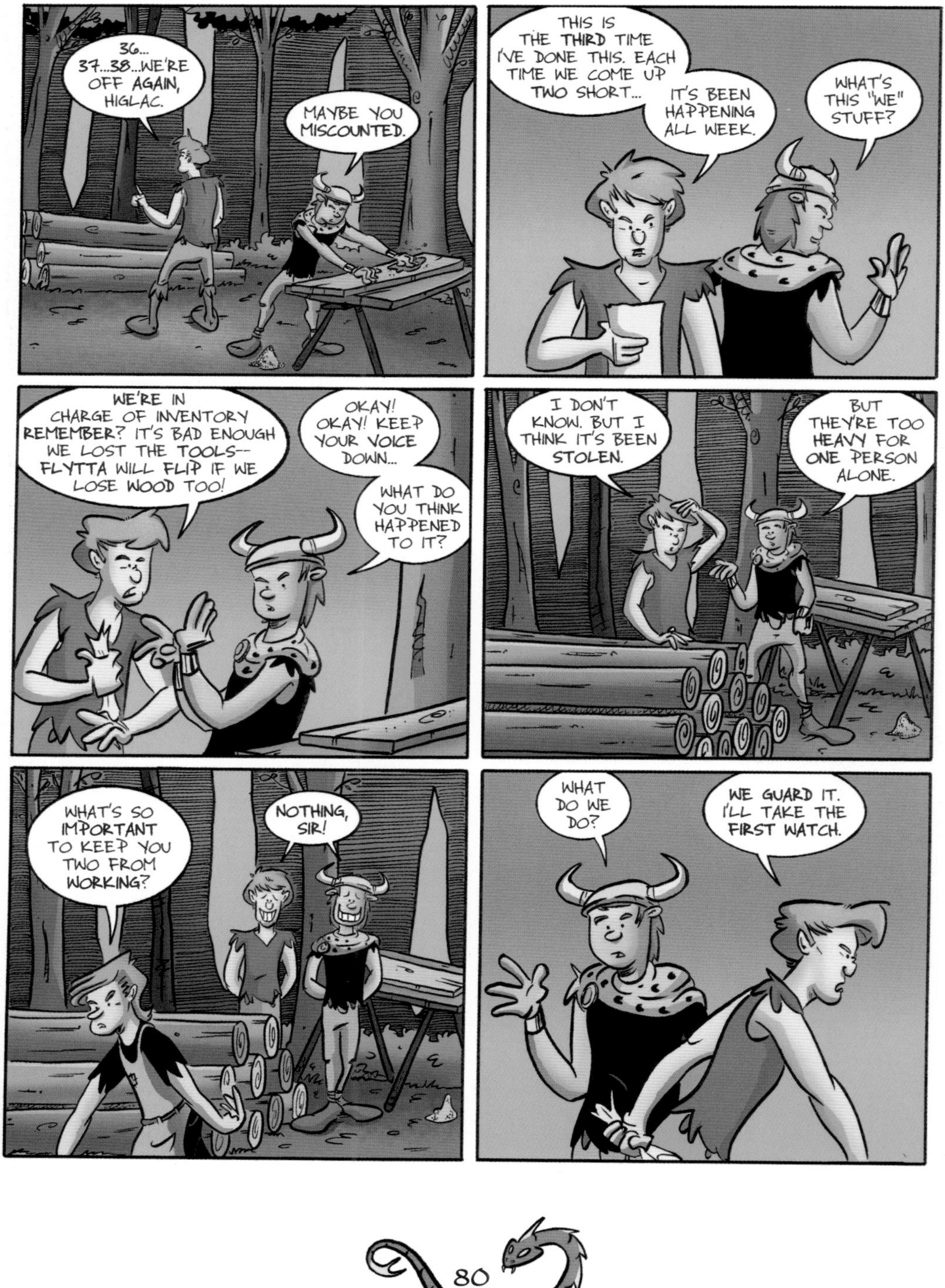
36...
37...38...WE'RE OFF AGAIN, HIGLAC.
MAYBE YOU MISCOUNTED.
THIS IS THE THIRD TIME I'VE DONE THIS. EACH TIME WE COME UP TWO SHORT...
IT'S BEEN HAPPENING ALL WEEK.
WHAT'S THIS "WE" STUFF?
WE'RE IN CHARGE OF INVENTORY REMEMBER? IT'S BAD ENOUGH WE LOST THE TOOLS-- FLYTTA WILL FLIP IF WE LOSE WOOD TOO!
OKAY! OKAY! KEEP YOUR VOICE DOWN...
WHAT DO YOU THINK HAPPENED TO IT?
I DON'T KNOW. BUT I THINK IT'S BEEN STOLEN.
BUT THEY'RE TOO HEAVY FOR ONE PERSON ALONE.
WHAT'S SO IMPORTANT TO KEEP YOU TWO FROM WORKING?
NOTHING, SIR!
WHAT DO WE DO?
WE GUARD IT. I'LL TAKE THE FIRST WATCH.

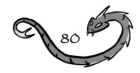

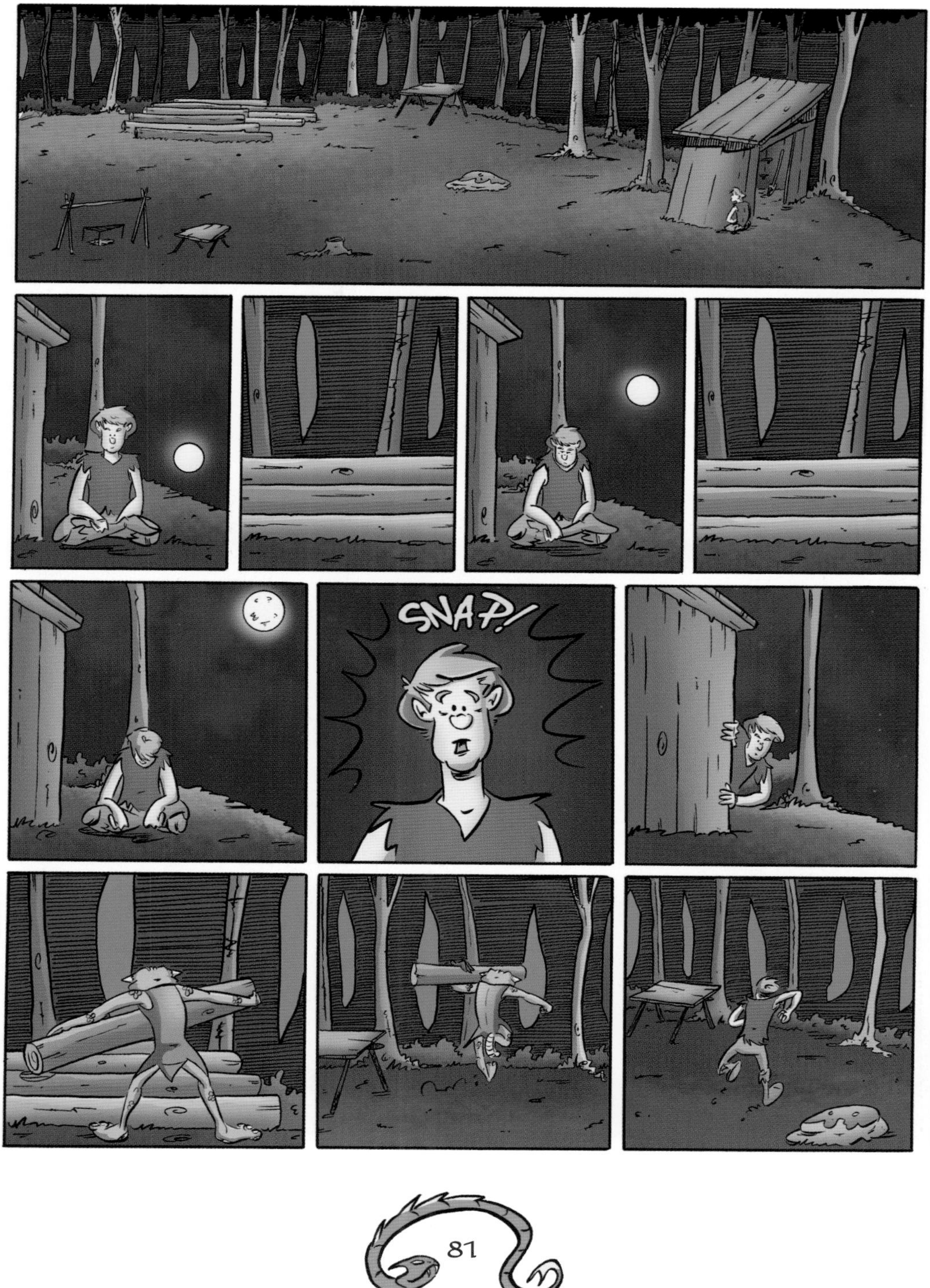
SNAP!

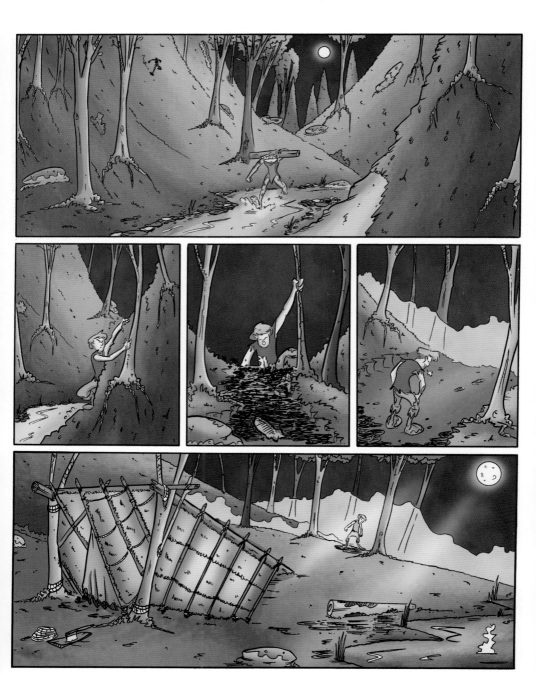

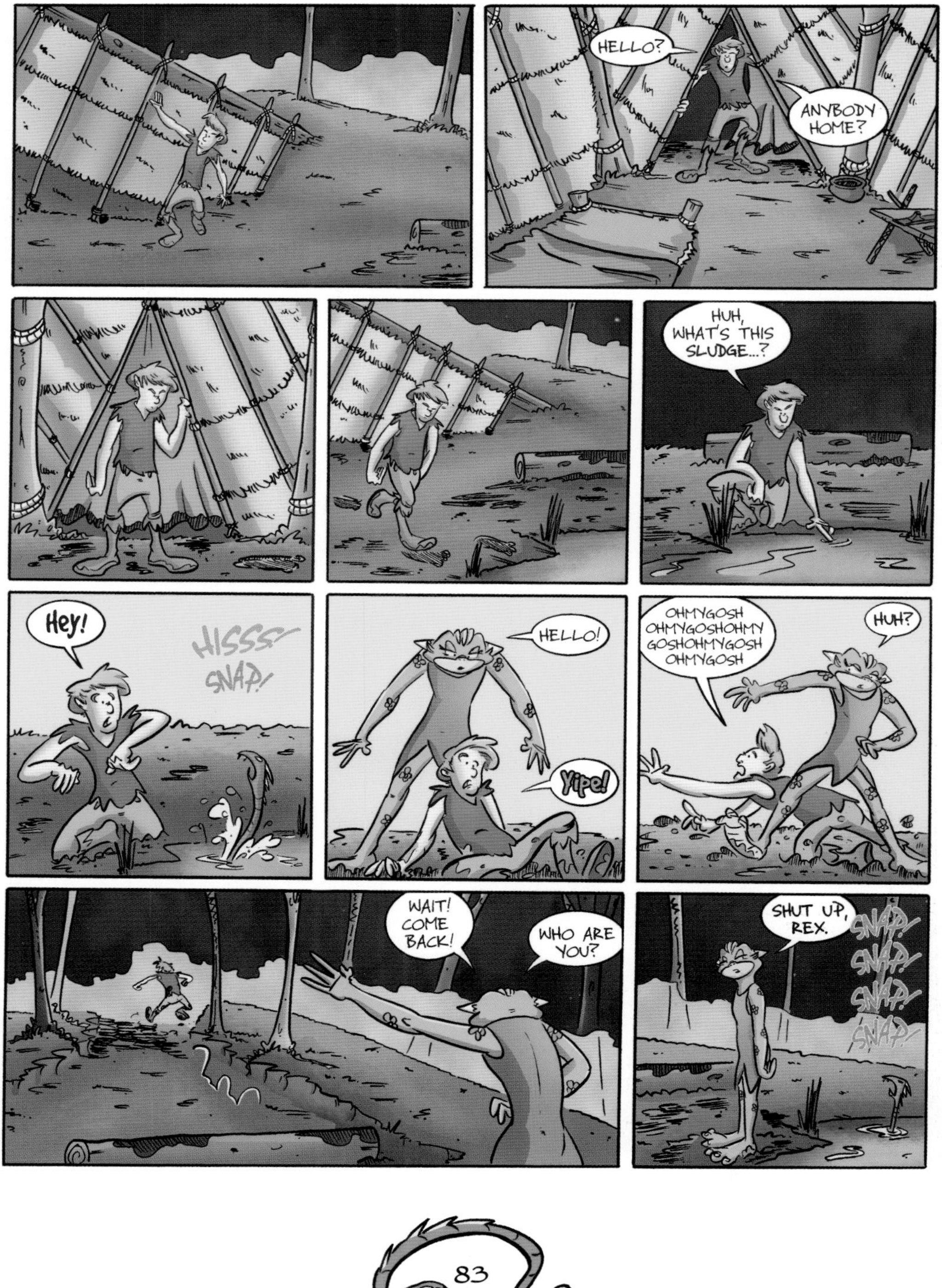
HELLO?
ANYBODY HOME?
HUH, WHAT'S THIS SLUDGE...?
Hey!
HISSS
SNAP!
HELLO!
Yipe!
OHMYGOSH OHMYGOSHOHMY GOSHOHMYGOSH OHMYGOSH
HUH?
WAIT! COME BACK!
WHO ARE YOU?
SHUT UP, REX.
SNAP!
SNAP!
SNAP!
SNAP!

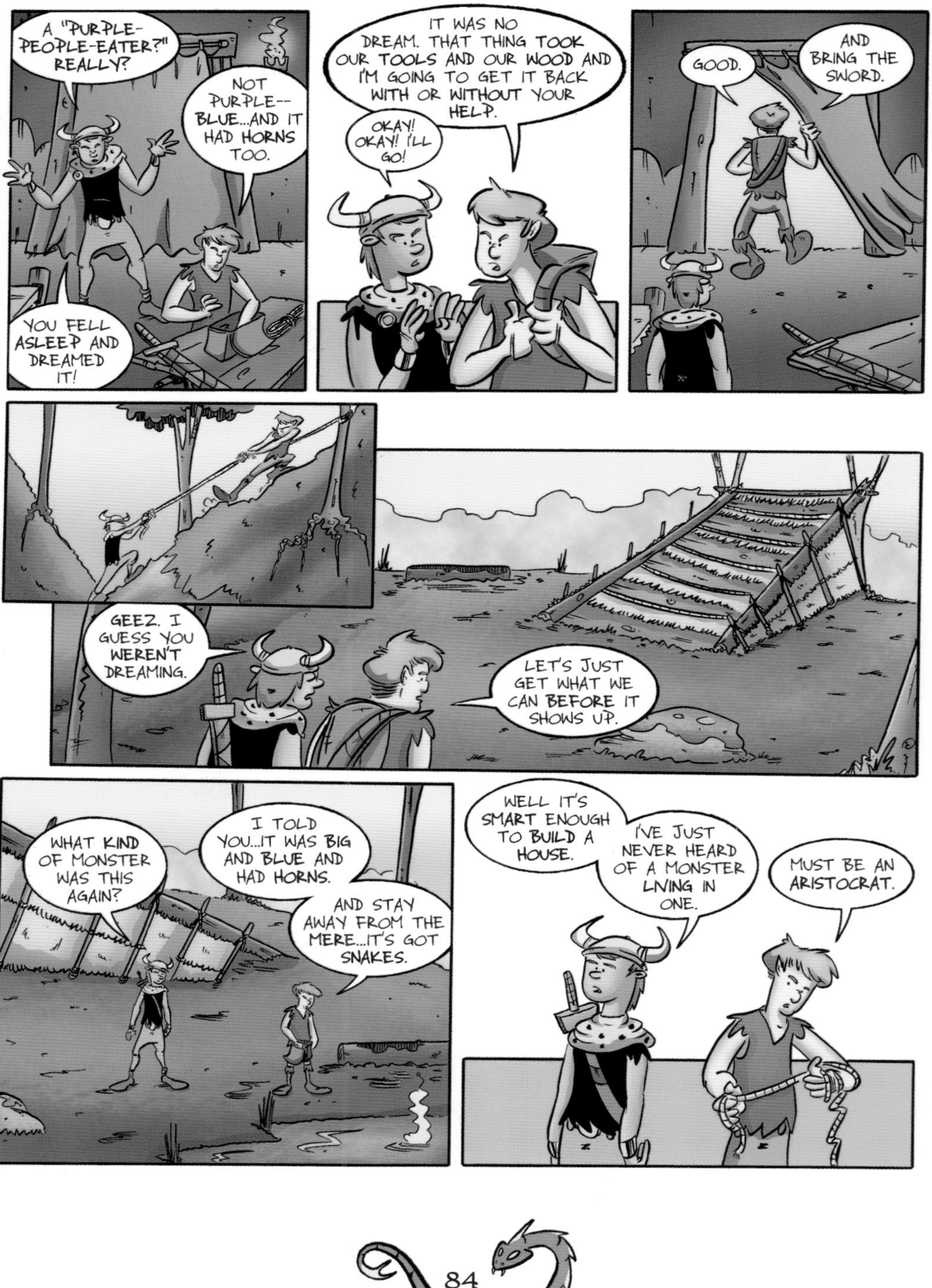

A "PURPLE-PEOPLE-EATER?" REALLY?
NOT PURPLE--BLUE...AND IT HAD HORNS TOO.
YOU FELL ASLEEP AND DREAMED IT!
IT WAS NO DREAM. THAT THING TOOK OUR TOOLS AND OUR WOOD AND I'M GOING TO GET IT BACK WITH OR WITHOUT YOUR HELP.
OKAY! OKAY! I'LL GO!
GOOD.
AND BRING THE SWORD.
GEEZ. I GUESS YOU WEREN'T DREAMING.
LET'S JUST GET WHAT WE CAN BEFORE IT SHOWS UP.
WHAT KIND OF MONSTER WAS THIS AGAIN?
I TOLD YOU...IT WAS BIG AND BLUE AND HAD HORNS.
AND STAY AWAY FROM THE MERE...IT'S GOT SNAKES.
WELL IT'S SMART ENOUGH TO BUILD A HOUSE.
I'VE JUST NEVER HEARD OF A MONSTER LIVING IN ONE.
MUST BE AN ARISTOCRAT.

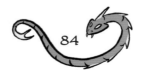

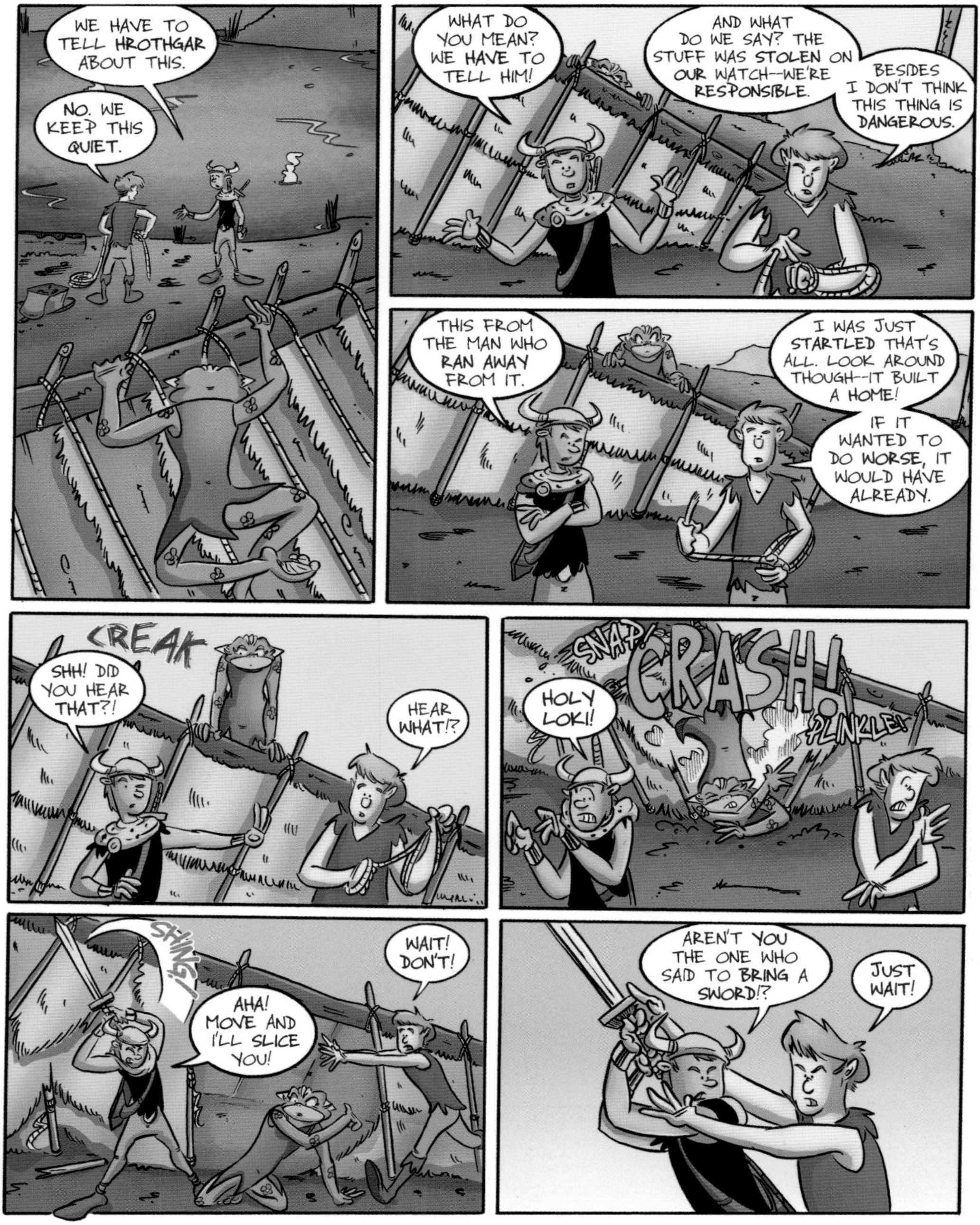
WE HAVE TO TELL HROTHGAR ABOUT THIS.
NO. WE KEEP THIS QUIET.
WHAT DO YOU MEAN? WE HAVE TO TELL HIM!
AND WHAT DO WE SAY? THE STUFF WAS STOLEN ON OUR WATCH--WE'RE RESPONSIBLE.
BESIDES I DON'T THINK THIS THING IS DANGEROUS.
THIS FROM THE MAN WHO RAN AWAY FROM IT.
I WAS JUST STARTLED THAT'S ALL. LOOK AROUND THOUGH--IT BUILT A HOME!
IF IT WANTED TO DO WORSE, IT WOULD HAVE ALREADY.
CREAK
SHH! DID YOU HEAR THAT?!
HEAR WHAT!?
SNAP!
CRASH!
HOLY LOKI!
PLINKLE!
SHING!
WAIT! DON'T!
AHA! MOVE AND I'LL SLICE YOU!
AREN'T YOU THE ONE WHO SAID TO BRING A SWORD!?
JUST WAIT!

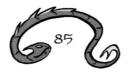

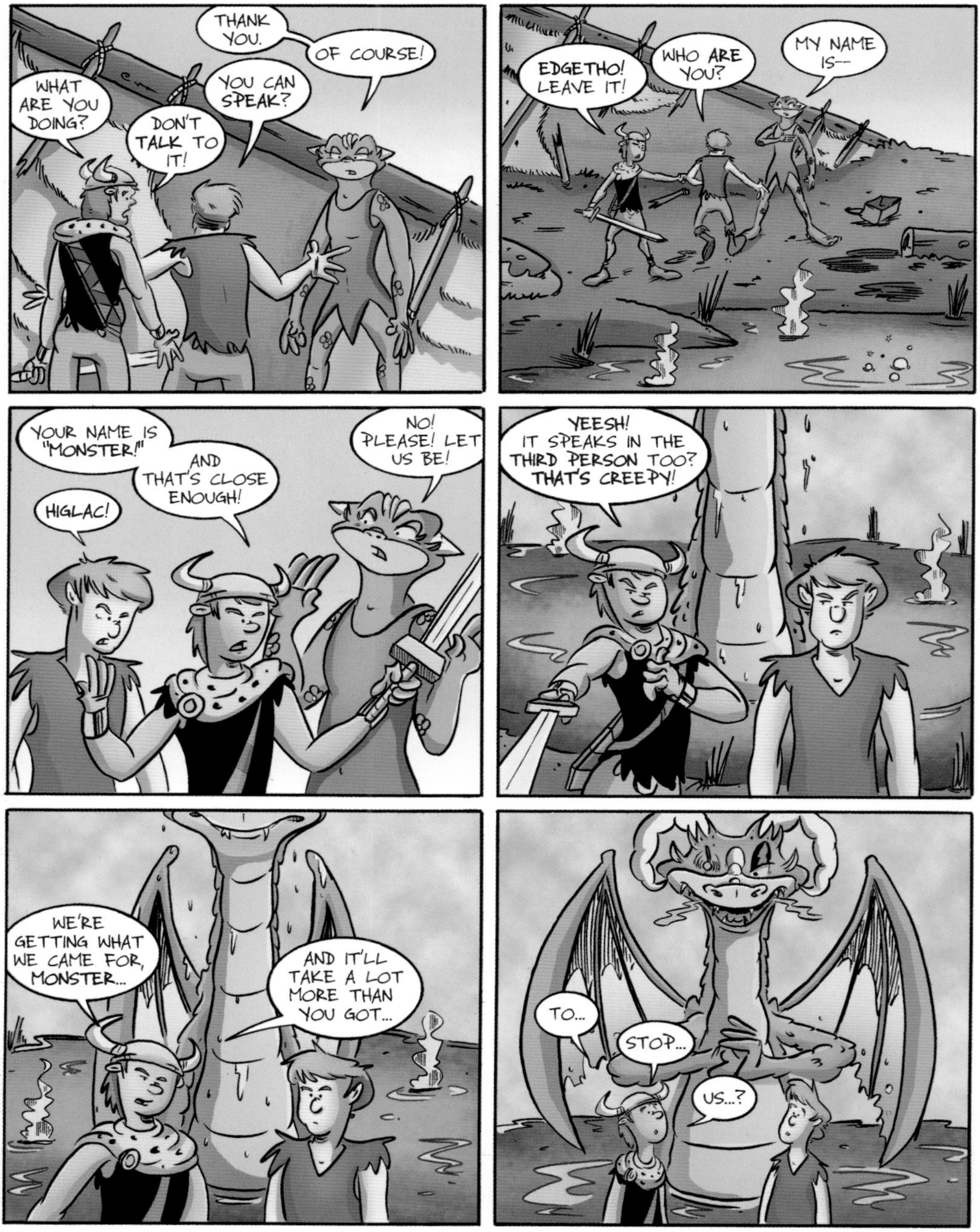
WHAT ARE YOU DOING?
DON'T TALK TO IT!
YOU CAN SPEAK?
THANK YOU.
OF COURSE!
EDGETHO! LEAVE IT!
WHO ARE YOU?
MY NAME IS--
YOUR NAME IS "MONSTER!"
AND THAT'S CLOSE ENOUGH!
HIGLAC!
NO! PLEASE! LET US BE!
YEESH! IT SPEAKS IN THE THIRD PERSON TOO? THAT'S CREEPY!
WE'RE GETTING WHAT WE CAME FOR, MONSTER...
AND IT'LL TAKE A LOT MORE THAN YOU GOT...
TO...
STOP...
US...?

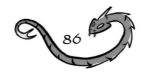

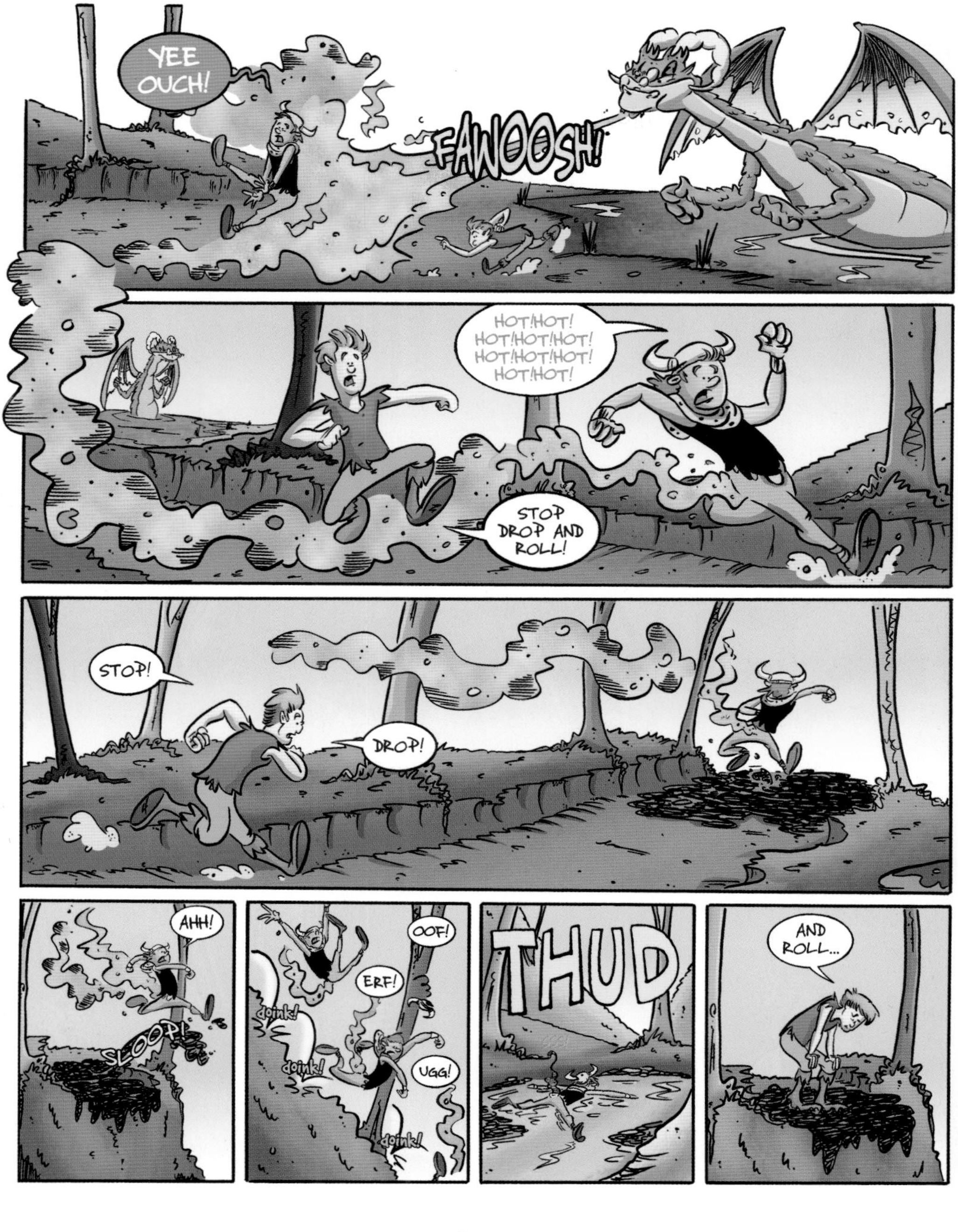
YEE OUCH!
FAWOOSH!
HOT!HOT!
HOT!HOT!HOT!
HOT!HOT!HOT!
HOT!HOT!
STOP DROP AND ROLL!
STOP!
DROP!
AHH!
SLOOP!
OOF!
ERF!
doink!
doink!
UGG!
doink!
THUD
AND ROLL...

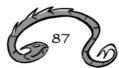

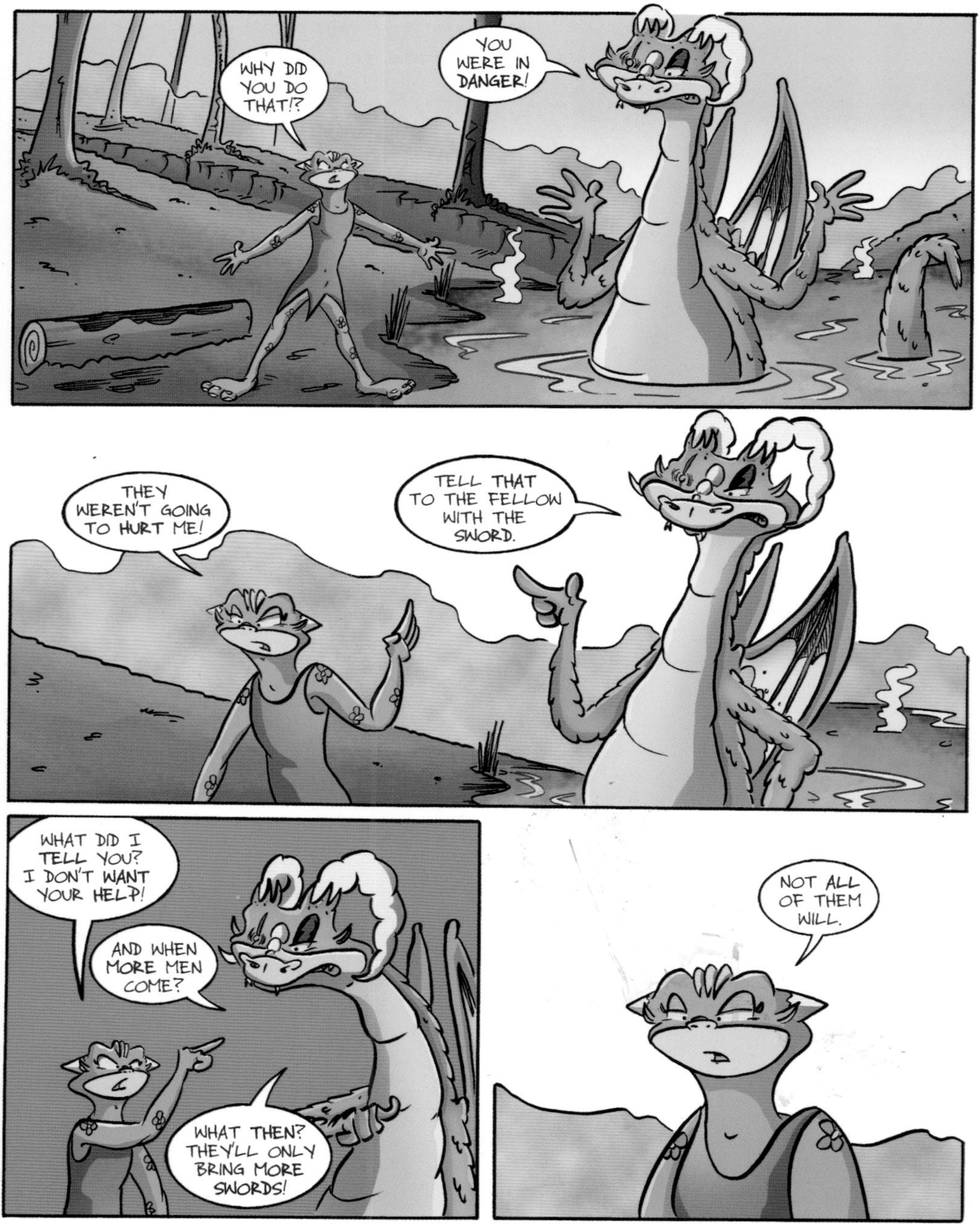
WHY DID YOU DO THAT!?
YOU WERE IN DANGER!
THEY WEREN'T GOING TO HURT ME!
TELL THAT TO THE FELLOW WITH THE SWORD.
WHAT DID I TELL YOU? I DON'T WANT YOUR HELP!
AND WHEN MORE MEN COME?
WHAT THEN? THEY'LL ONLY BRING MORE SWORDS!
NOT ALL OF THEM WILL.

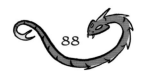

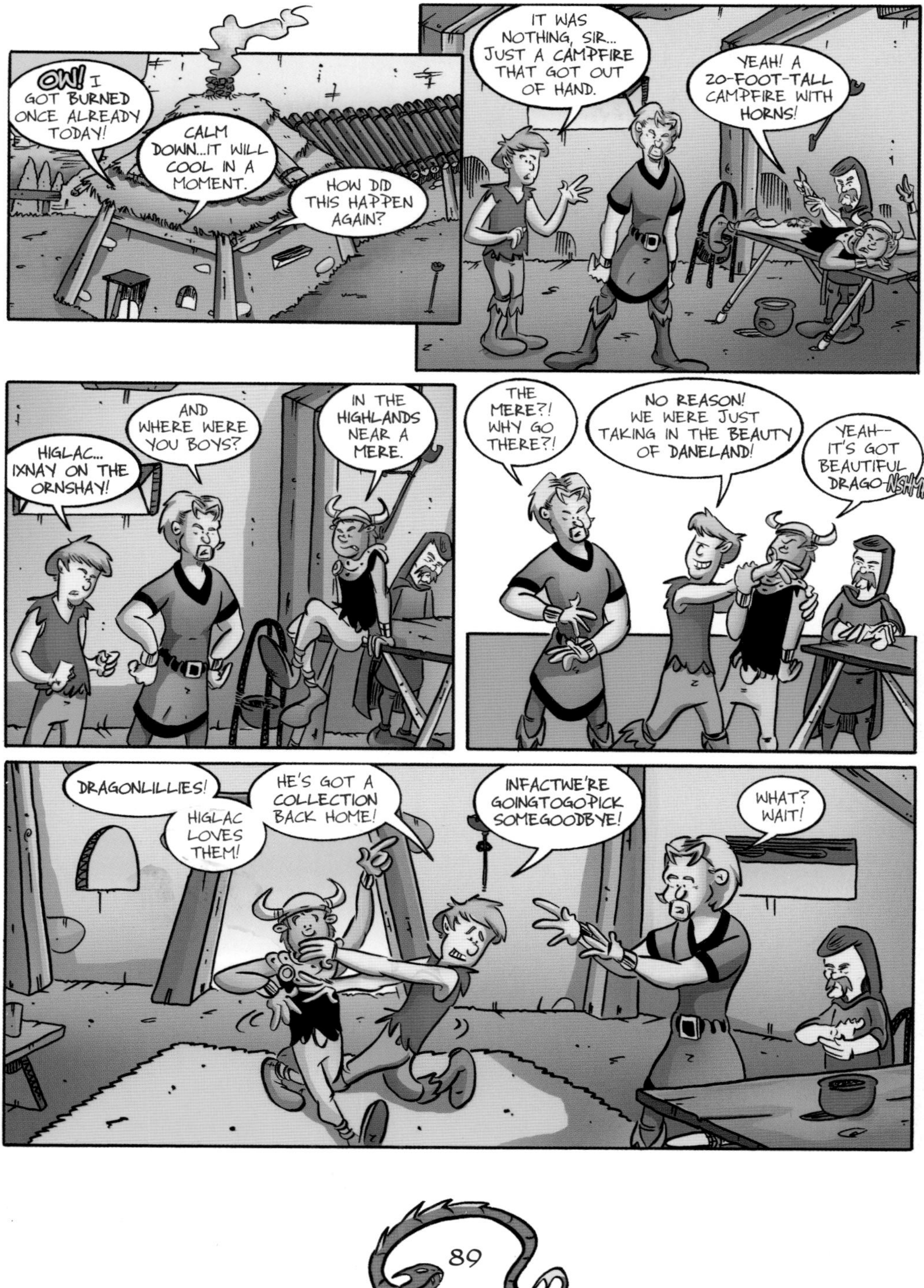
OW! I GOT BURNED ONCE ALREADY TODAY!
CALM DOWN...IT WILL COOL IN A MOMENT.
HOW DID THIS HAPPEN AGAIN?
IT WAS NOTHING, SIR... JUST A CAMPFIRE THAT GOT OUT OF HAND.
YEAH! A 20-FOOT-TALL CAMPFIRE WITH HORNS!
HIGLAC... IXNAY ON THE ORNSHAY!
AND WHERE WERE YOU BOYS?
IN THE HIGHLANDS NEAR A MERE.
THE MERE?! WHY GO THERE?!
NO REASON! WE WERE JUST TAKING IN THE BEAUTY OF DANELAND!
YEAH-- IT'S GOT BEAUTIFUL DRAGO-NSHMF..!
DRAGONLILLIES!
HIGLAC LOVES THEM!
HE'S GOT A COLLECTION BACK HOME!
INFACTWE'RE GOINGTOGOPICK SOMEGOODBYE!
WHAT? WAIT!

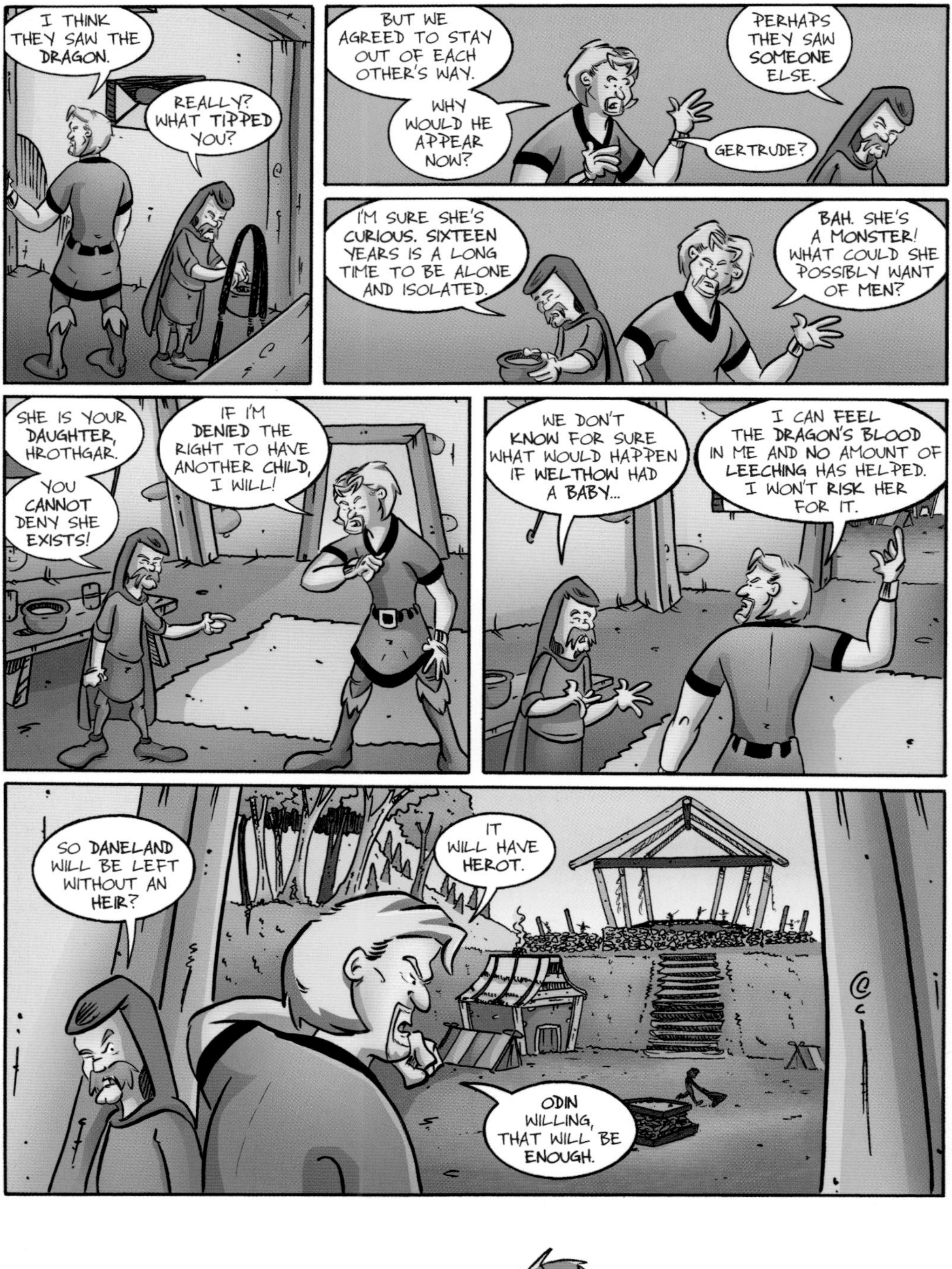
I THINK THEY SAW THE DRAGON.
REALLY? WHAT TIPPED YOU?
BUT WE AGREED TO STAY OUT OF EACH OTHER'S WAY.
WHY WOULD HE APPEAR NOW?
PERHAPS THEY SAW SOMEONE ELSE.
GERTRUDE?
I'M SURE SHE'S CURIOUS. SIXTEEN YEARS IS A LONG TIME TO BE ALONE AND ISOLATED.
BAH. SHE'S A MONSTER! WHAT COULD SHE POSSIBLY WANT OF MEN?
SHE IS YOUR DAUGHTER, HROTHGAR.
YOU CANNOT DENY SHE EXISTS!
IF I'M DENIED THE RIGHT TO HAVE ANOTHER CHILD, I WILL!
WE DON'T KNOW FOR SURE WHAT WOULD HAPPEN IF WELTHOW HAD A BABY...
I CAN FEEL THE DRAGON'S BLOOD IN ME AND NO AMOUNT OF LEECHING HAS HELPED. I WON'T RISK HER FOR IT.
SO DANELAND WILL BE LEFT WITHOUT AN HEIR?
IT WILL HAVE HEROT.
ODIN WILLING, THAT WILL BE ENOUGH.

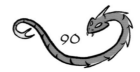

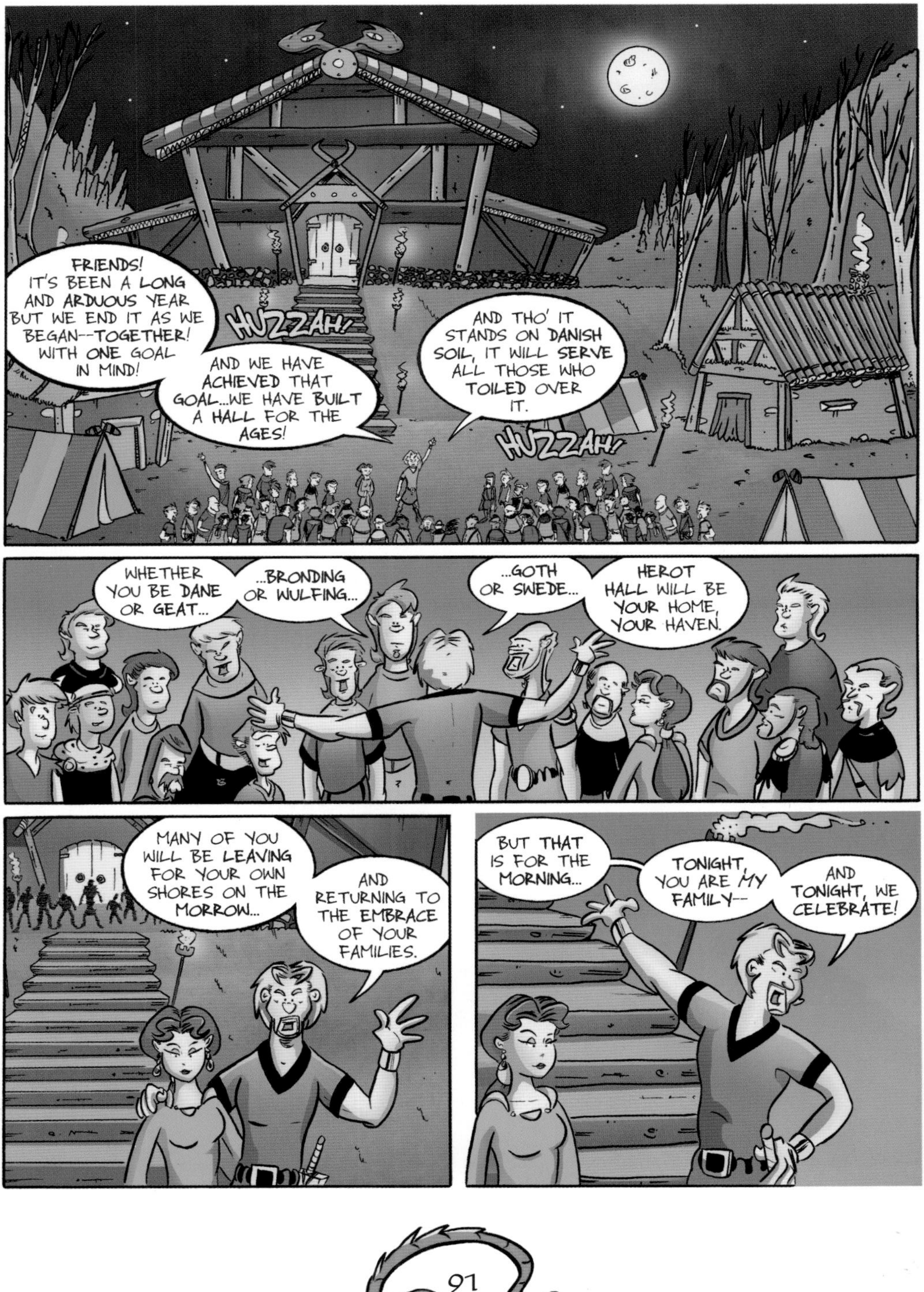
FRIENDS! IT'S BEEN A LONG AND ARDUOUS YEAR BUT WE END IT AS WE BEGAN--TOGETHER! WITH ONE GOAL IN MIND!
HUZZAH!
AND WE HAVE ACHIEVED THAT GOAL...WE HAVE BUILT A HALL FOR THE AGES!
AND THO' IT STANDS ON DANISH SOIL, IT WILL SERVE ALL THOSE WHO TOILED OVER IT.
HUZZAH!
WHETHER YOU BE DANE OR GEAT...
...BRONDING OR WULFING...
...GOTH OR SWEDE...
HEROT HALL WILL BE YOUR HOME, YOUR HAVEN.
MANY OF YOU WILL BE LEAVING FOR YOUR OWN SHORES ON THE MORROW...
AND RETURNING TO THE EMBRACE OF YOUR FAMILIES.
BUT THAT IS FOR THE MORNING...
TONIGHT, YOU ARE MY FAMILY--
AND TONIGHT, WE CELEBRATE!

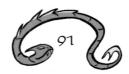

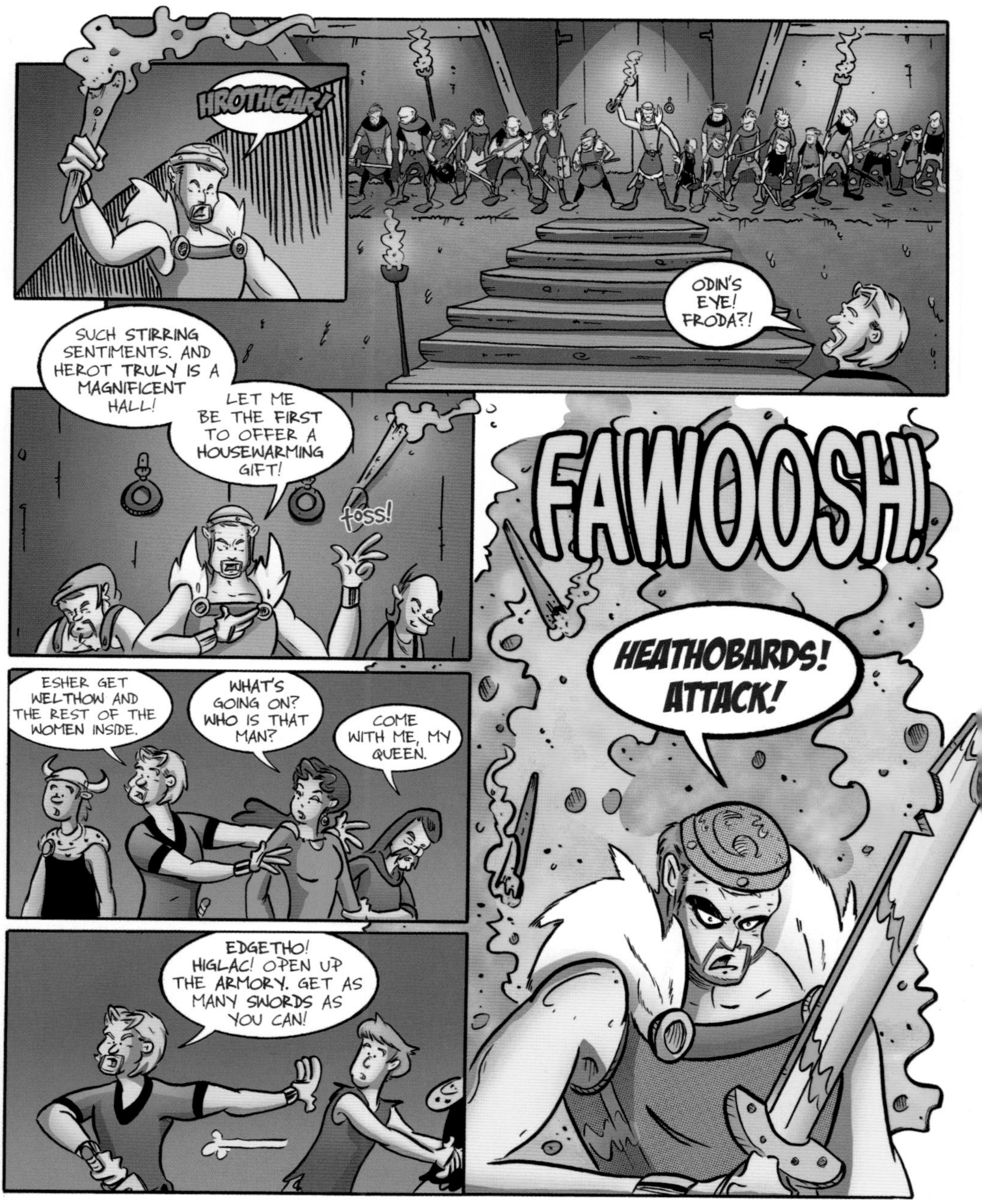
HROTHGAR!
ODIN'S EYE! FRODA?!
SUCH STIRRING SENTIMENTS. AND HEROT TRULY IS A MAGNIFICENT HALL!
LET ME BE THE FIRST TO OFFER A HOUSEWARMING GIFT!
toss!
FAWOOSH!
HEATHOBARDS! ATTACK!
ESHER GET WELTHOW AND THE REST OF THE WOMEN INSIDE.
WHAT'S GOING ON? WHO IS THAT MAN?
COME WITH ME, MY QUEEN.
EDGETHO! HIGLAC! OPEN UP THE ARMORY. GET AS MANY SWORDS AS YOU CAN!

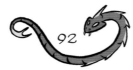

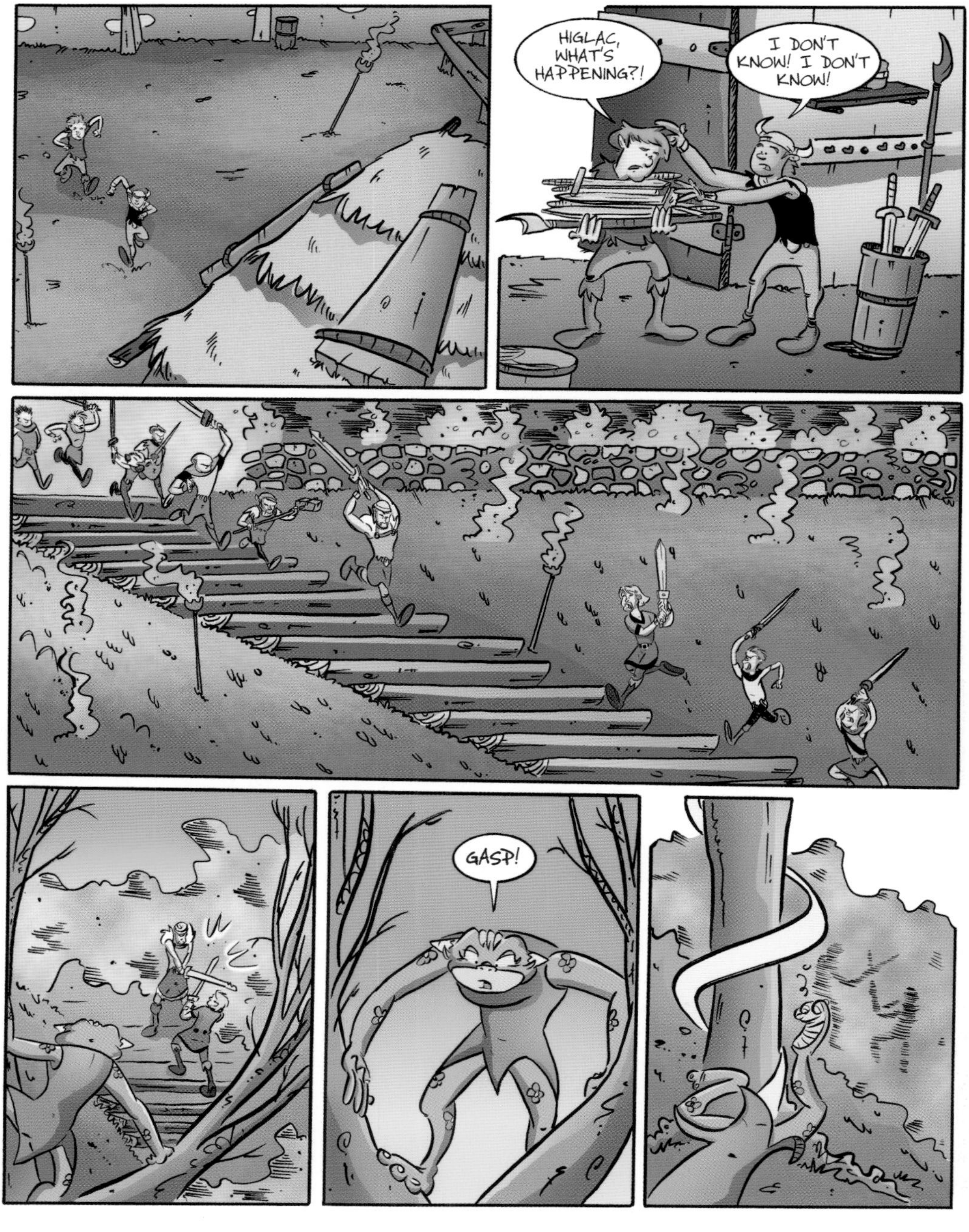
HIGLAC, WHAT'S HAPPENING?!
I DON'T KNOW! I DON'T KNOW!
GASP!

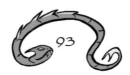

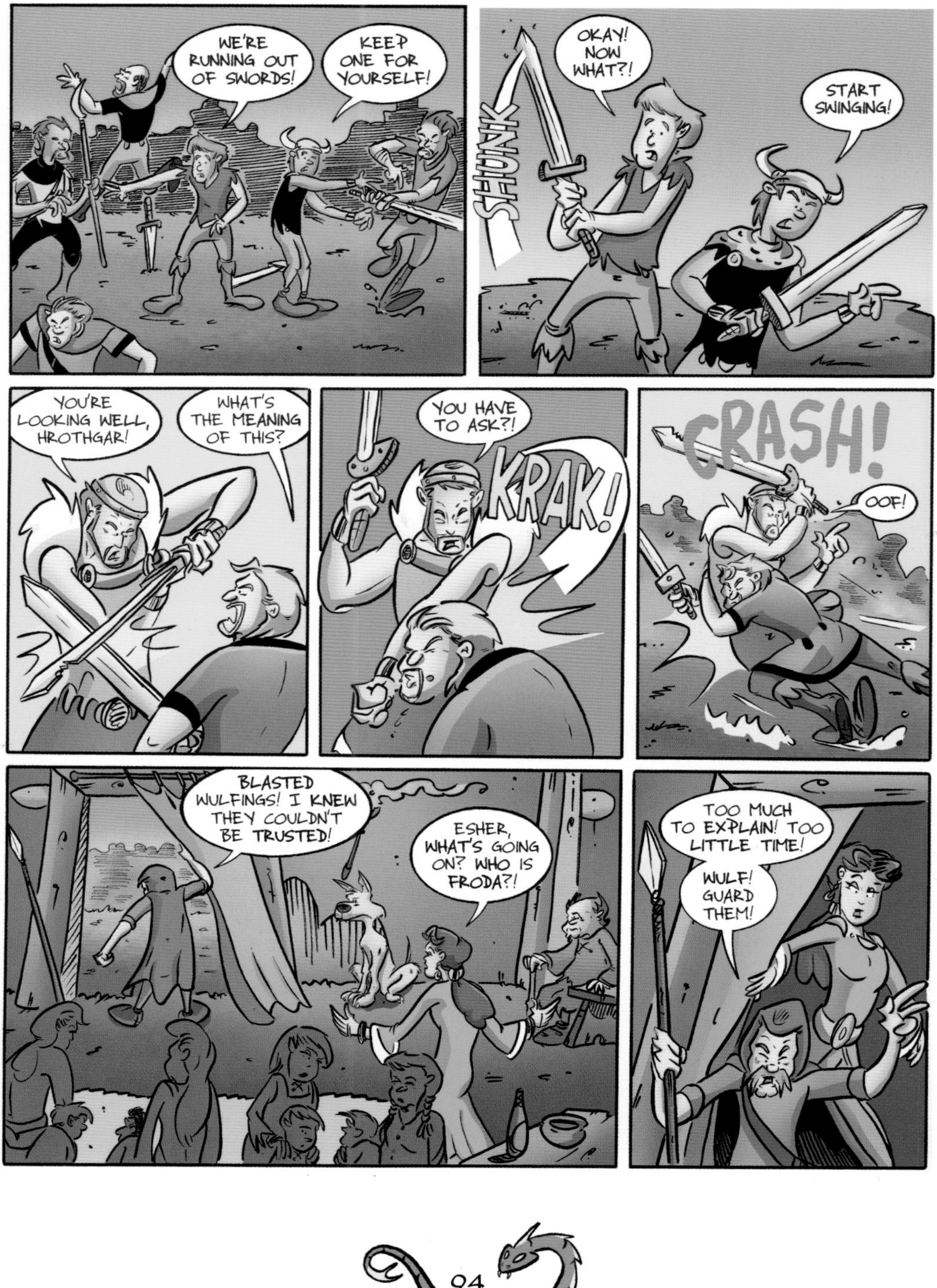
WE'RE RUNNING OUT OF SWORDS!
KEEP ONE FOR YOURSELF!
SHUNK
OKAY! NOW WHAT?!
START SWINGING!
YOU'RE LOOKING WELL, HROTHGAR!
WHAT'S THE MEANING OF THIS?
YOU HAVE TO ASK?!
KRAK!
CRASH!
OOF!
BLASTED WULFINGS! I KNEW THEY COULDN'T BE TRUSTED!
ESHER, WHAT'S GOING ON? WHO IS FRODA?!
TOO MUCH TO EXPLAIN! TOO LITTLE TIME!
WULF! GUARD THEM!

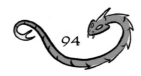

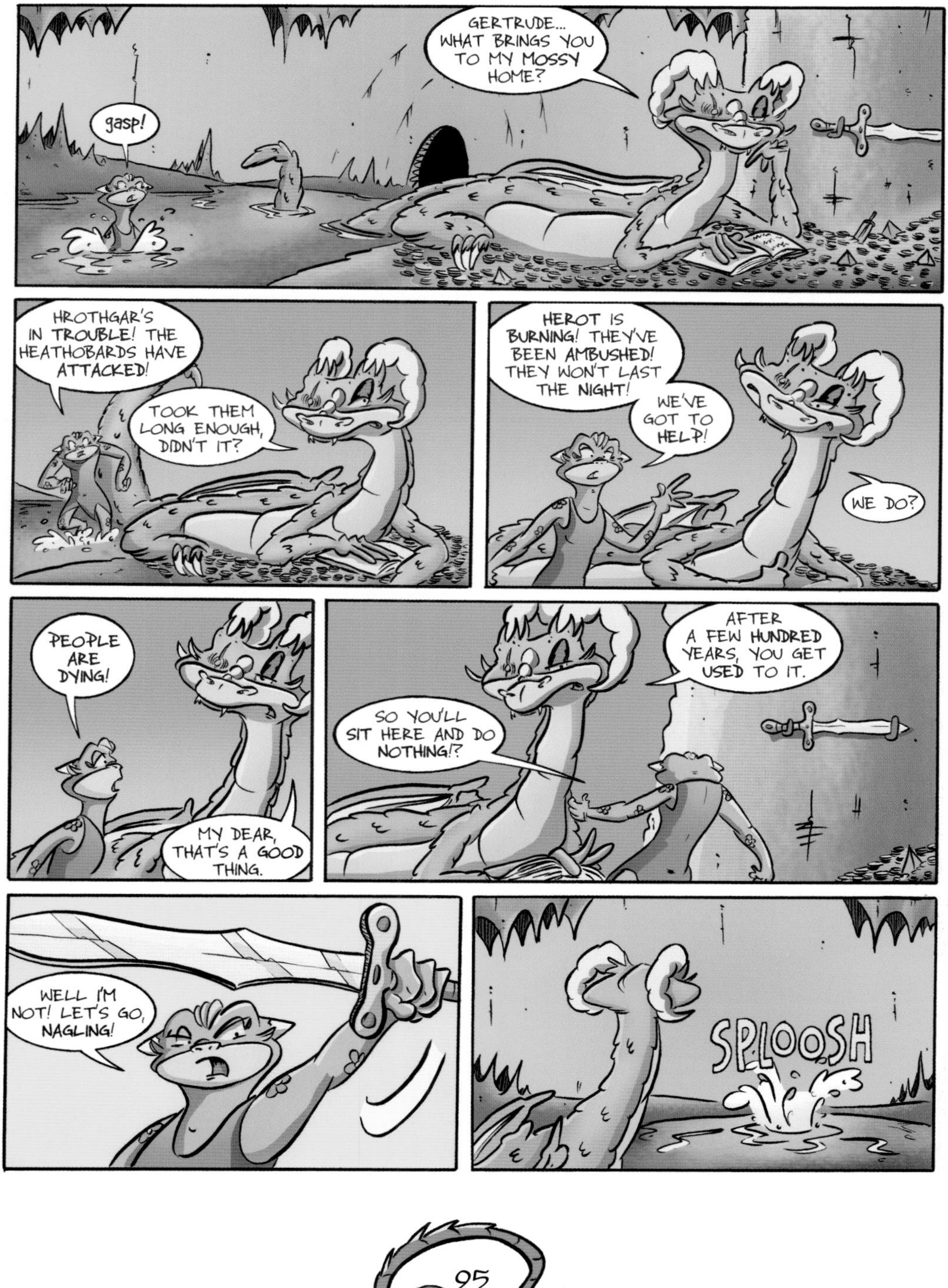
gasp!
GERTRUDE... WHAT BRINGS YOU TO MY MOSSY HOME?
HROTHGAR'S IN TROUBLE! THE HEATHOBARDS HAVE ATTACKED!
TOOK THEM LONG ENOUGH, DIDN'T IT?
HEROT IS BURNING! THEY'VE BEEN AMBUSHED! THEY WON'T LAST THE NIGHT!
WE'VE GOT TO HELP!
WE DO?
PEOPLE ARE DYING!
MY DEAR, THAT'S A GOOD THING.
AFTER A FEW HUNDRED YEARS, YOU GET USED TO IT.
SO YOU'LL SIT HERE AND DO NOTHING!?
WELL I'M NOT! LET'S GO, NAGLING!
SPLOOSH

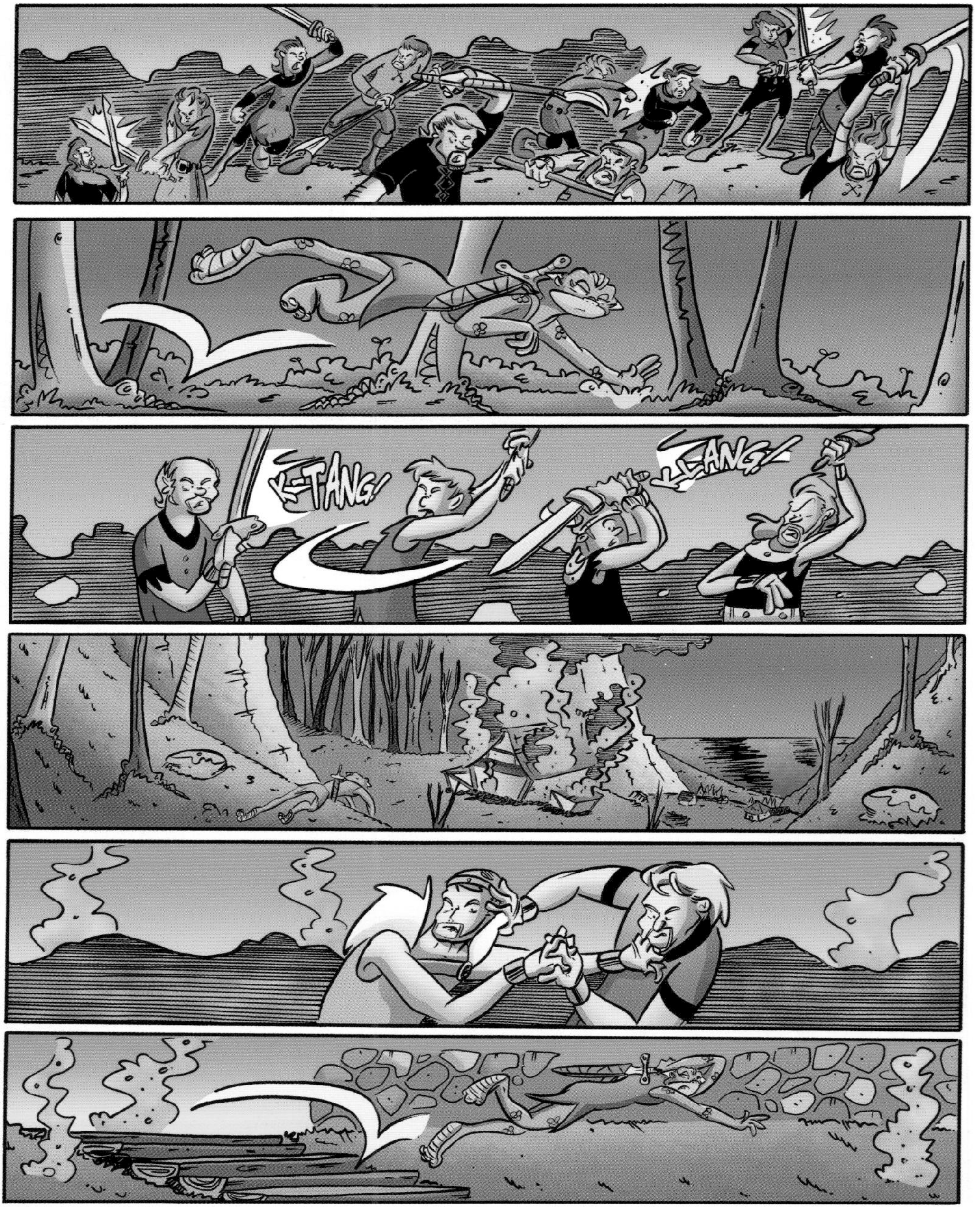
K-TANG!
K-LANG!

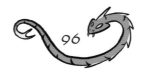

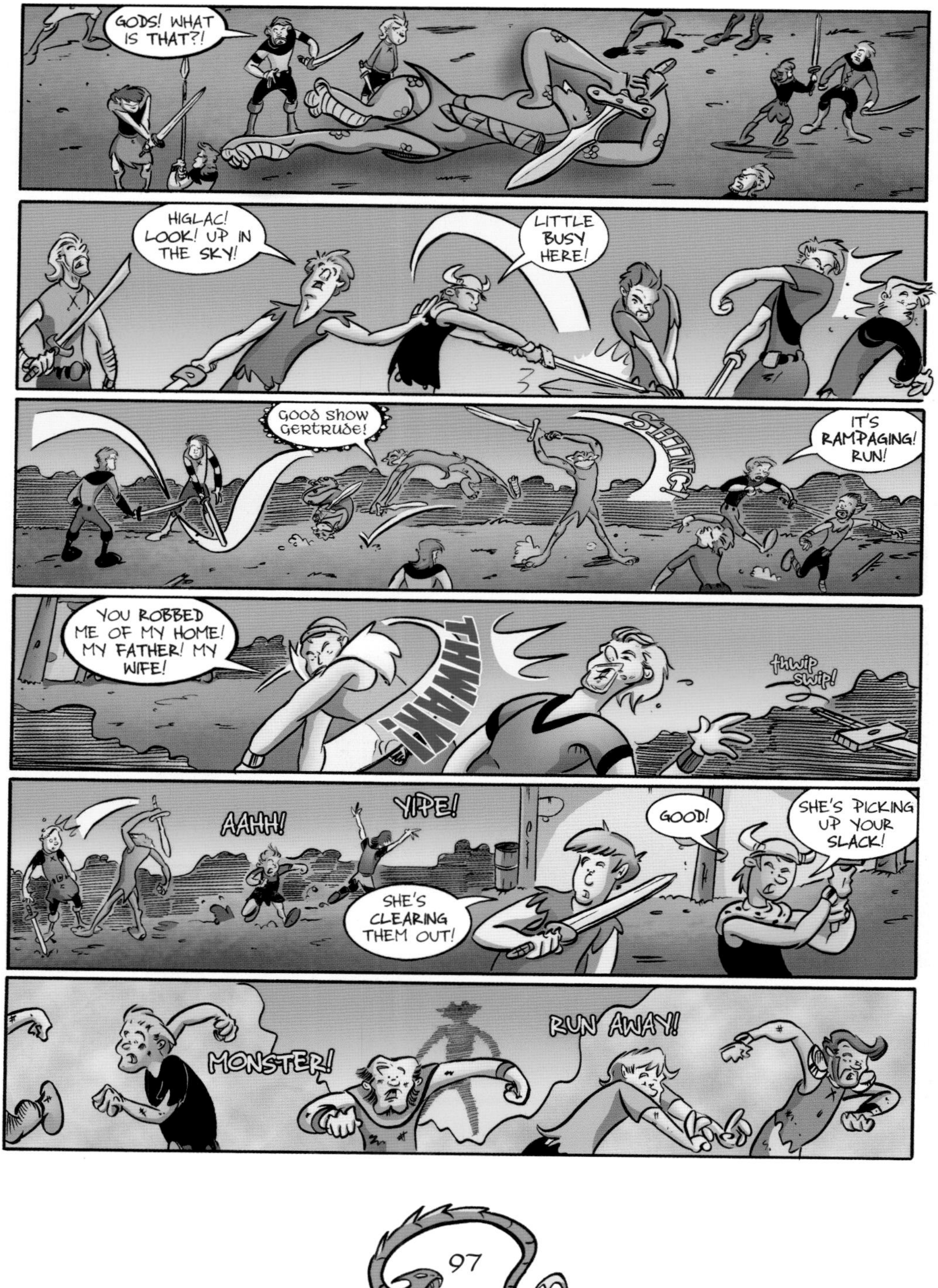
GODS! WHAT IS THAT?!
HIGLAC! LOOK! UP IN THE SKY!
LITTLE BUSY HERE!
GOOD SHOW GERTRUDE!
SHING
IT'S RAMPAGING! RUN!
YOU ROBBED ME OF MY HOME! MY FATHER! MY WIFE!
THWAK!
thwip swip!
AAHH!
YIPE!
SHE'S CLEARING THEM OUT!
GOOD!
SHE'S PICKING UP YOUR SLACK!
MONSTER!
RUN AWAY!

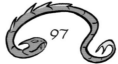

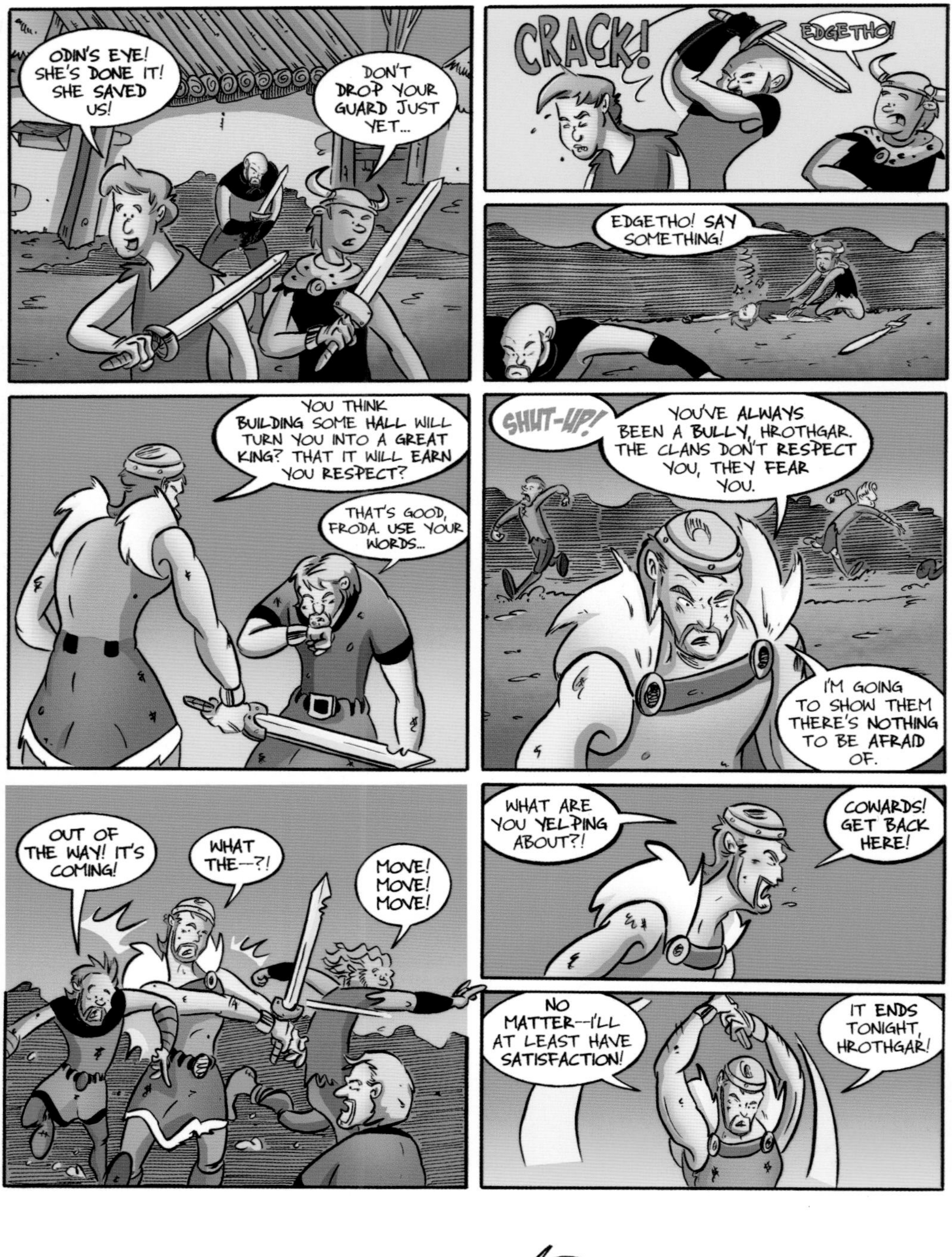
ODIN'S EYE! SHE'S DONE IT! SHE SAVED US!
DON'T DROP YOUR GUARD JUST YET...
CRACK!
EDGETHO!
EDGETHO! SAY SOMETHING!
YOU THINK BUILDING SOME HALL WILL TURN YOU INTO A GREAT KING? THAT IT WILL EARN YOU RESPECT?
THAT'S GOOD, FRODA. USE YOUR WORDS...
SHUT-UP!
YOU'VE ALWAYS BEEN A BULLY, HROTHGAR. THE CLANS DON'T RESPECT YOU, THEY FEAR YOU.
I'M GOING TO SHOW THEM THERE'S NOTHING TO BE AFRAID OF.
OUT OF THE WAY! IT'S COMING!
WHAT THE--?!
MOVE! MOVE! MOVE!
WHAT ARE YOU YELPING ABOUT?!
COWARDS! GET BACK HERE!
NO MATTER--I'LL AT LEAST HAVE SATISFACTION!
IT ENDS TONIGHT, HROTHGAR!

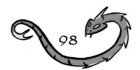

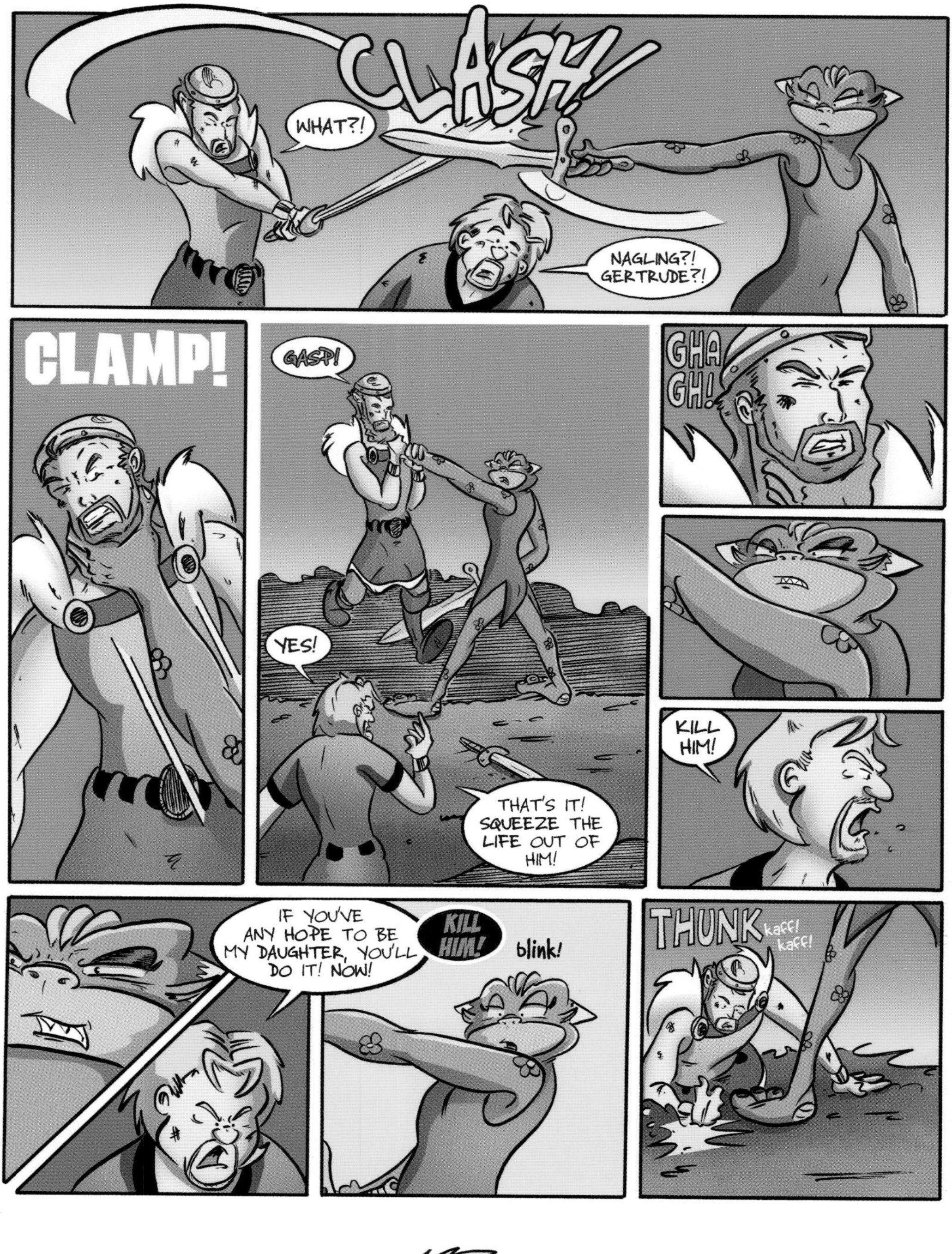
CLASH!
WHAT?!
NAGLING?! GERTRUDE?!
CLAMP!
GASP!
YES!
THAT'S IT! SQUEEZE THE LIFE OUT OF HIM!
GHAGH!
KILL HIM!
IF YOU'VE ANY HOPE TO BE MY DAUGHTER, YOU'LL DO IT! NOW!
KILL HIM!
blink!
THUNK
kaff! kaff!

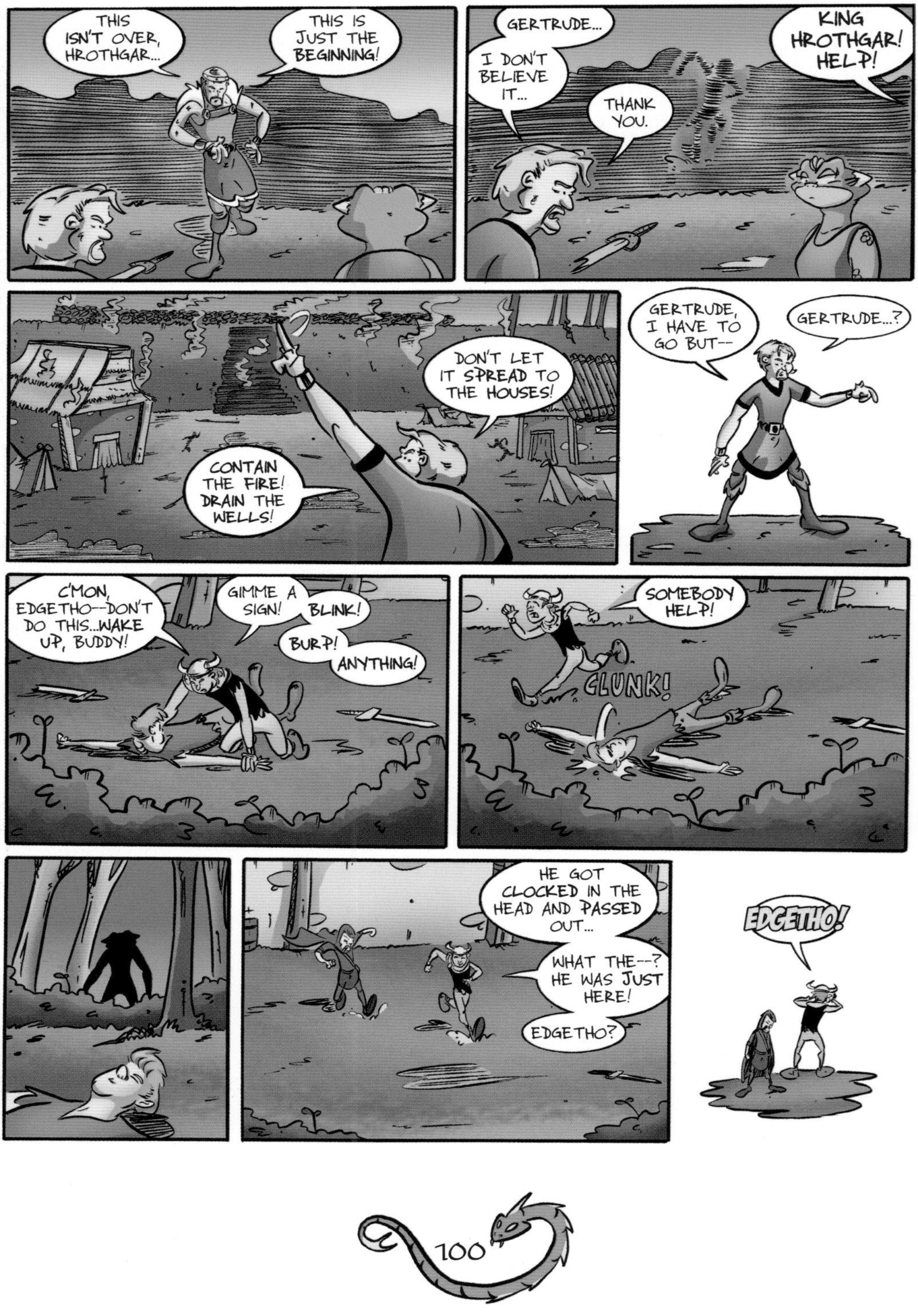
THIS ISN'T OVER, HROTHGAR...
THIS IS JUST THE BEGINNING!
GERTRUDE...
I DON'T BELIEVE IT...
THANK YOU.
KING HROTHGAR! HELP!
DON'T LET IT SPREAD TO THE HOUSES!
CONTAIN THE FIRE! DRAIN THE WELLS!
GERTRUDE, I HAVE TO GO BUT--
GERTRUDE...?
C'MON, EDGETHO--DON'T DO THIS...WAKE UP, BUDDY!
GIMME A SIGN!
BLINK!
BURP!
ANYTHING!
SOMEBODY HELP!
CLUNK!
HE GOT CLOCKED IN THE HEAD AND PASSED OUT...
WHAT THE--? HE WAS JUST HERE!
EDGETHO?
EDGETHO!

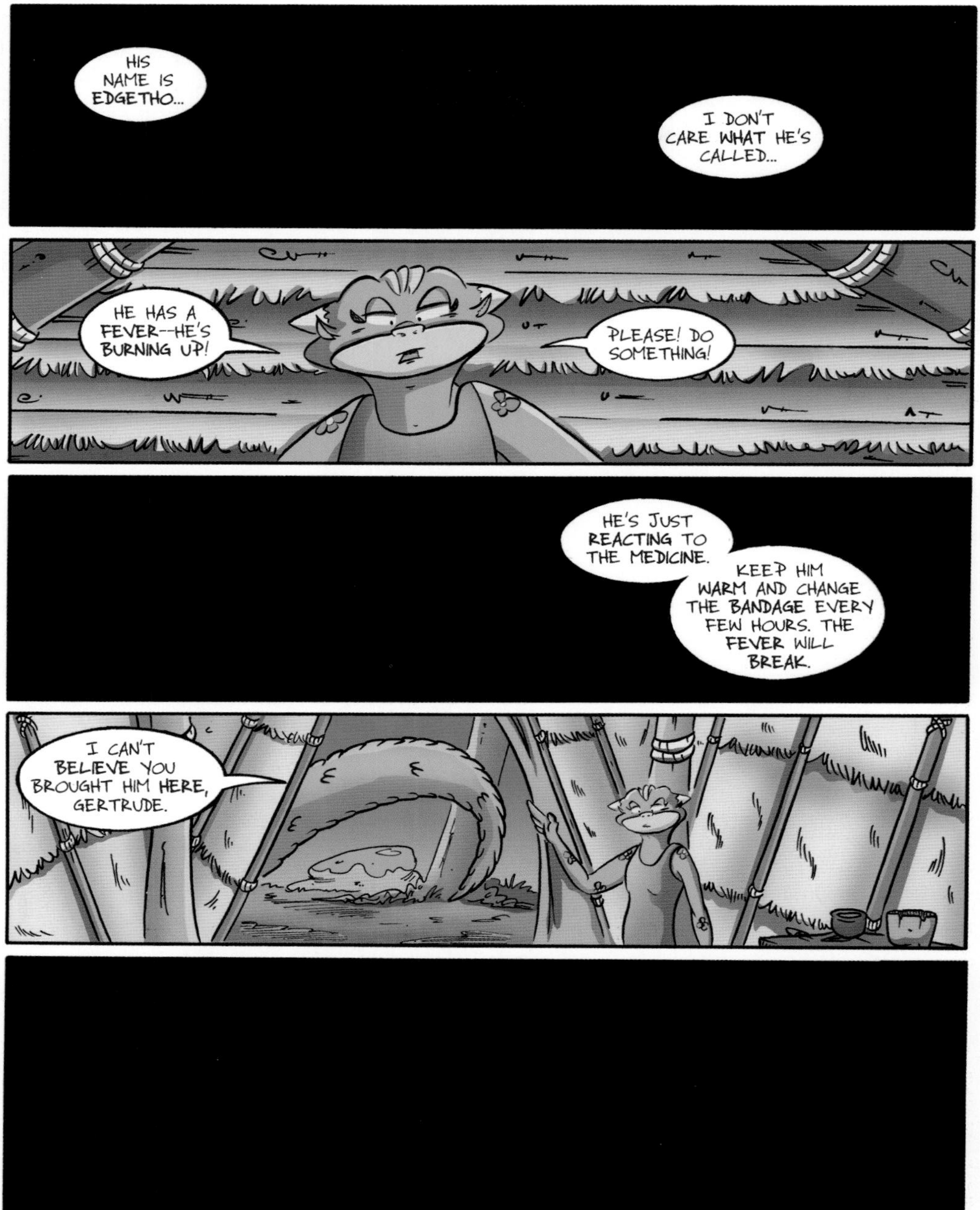
HIS NAME IS EDGETHO...
I DON'T CARE WHAT HE'S CALLED...
HE HAS A FEVER--HE'S BURNING UP!
PLEASE! DO SOMETHING!
HE'S JUST REACTING TO THE MEDICINE.
KEEP HIM WARM AND CHANGE THE BANDAGE EVERY FEW HOURS. THE FEVER WILL BREAK.
I CAN'T BELIEVE YOU BROUGHT HIM HERE, GERTRUDE.

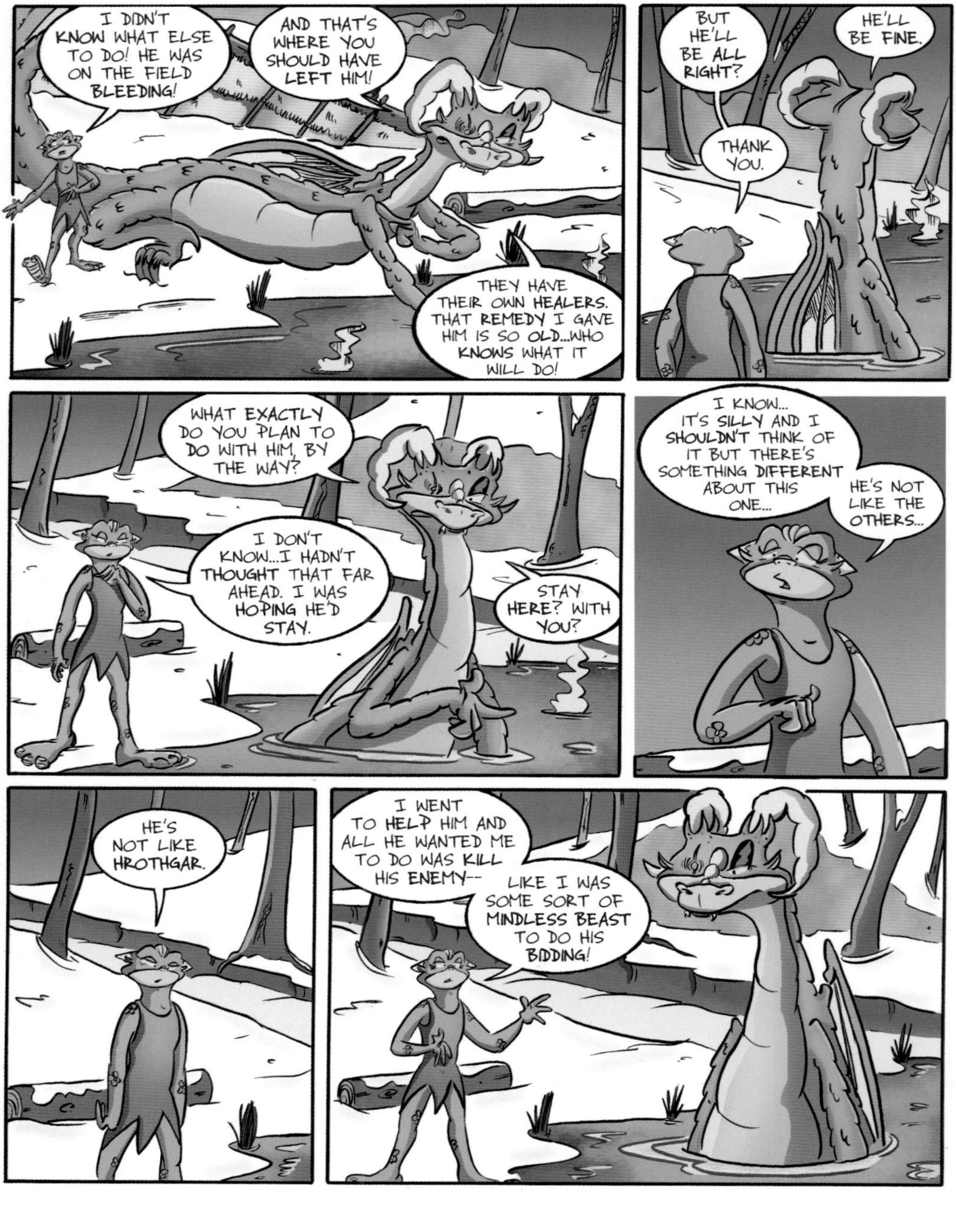
I DIDN'T KNOW WHAT ELSE TO DO! HE WAS ON THE FIELD BLEEDING!
AND THAT'S WHERE YOU SHOULD HAVE LEFT HIM!
THEY HAVE THEIR OWN HEALERS. THAT REMEDY I GAVE HIM IS SO OLD...WHO KNOWS WHAT IT WILL DO!
BUT HE'LL BE ALL RIGHT?
HE'LL BE FINE.
THANK YOU.
WHAT EXACTLY DO YOU PLAN TO DO WITH HIM, BY THE WAY?
I DON'T KNOW...I HADN'T THOUGHT THAT FAR AHEAD. I WAS HOPING HE'D STAY.
STAY HERE? WITH YOU?
I KNOW... IT'S SILLY AND I SHOULDN'T THINK OF IT BUT THERE'S SOMETHING DIFFERENT ABOUT THIS ONE...
HE'S NOT LIKE THE OTHERS...
HE'S NOT LIKE HROTHGAR.
I WENT TO HELP HIM AND ALL HE WANTED ME TO DO WAS KILL HIS ENEMY--
LIKE I WAS SOME SORT OF MINDLESS BEAST TO DO HIS BIDDING!

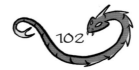

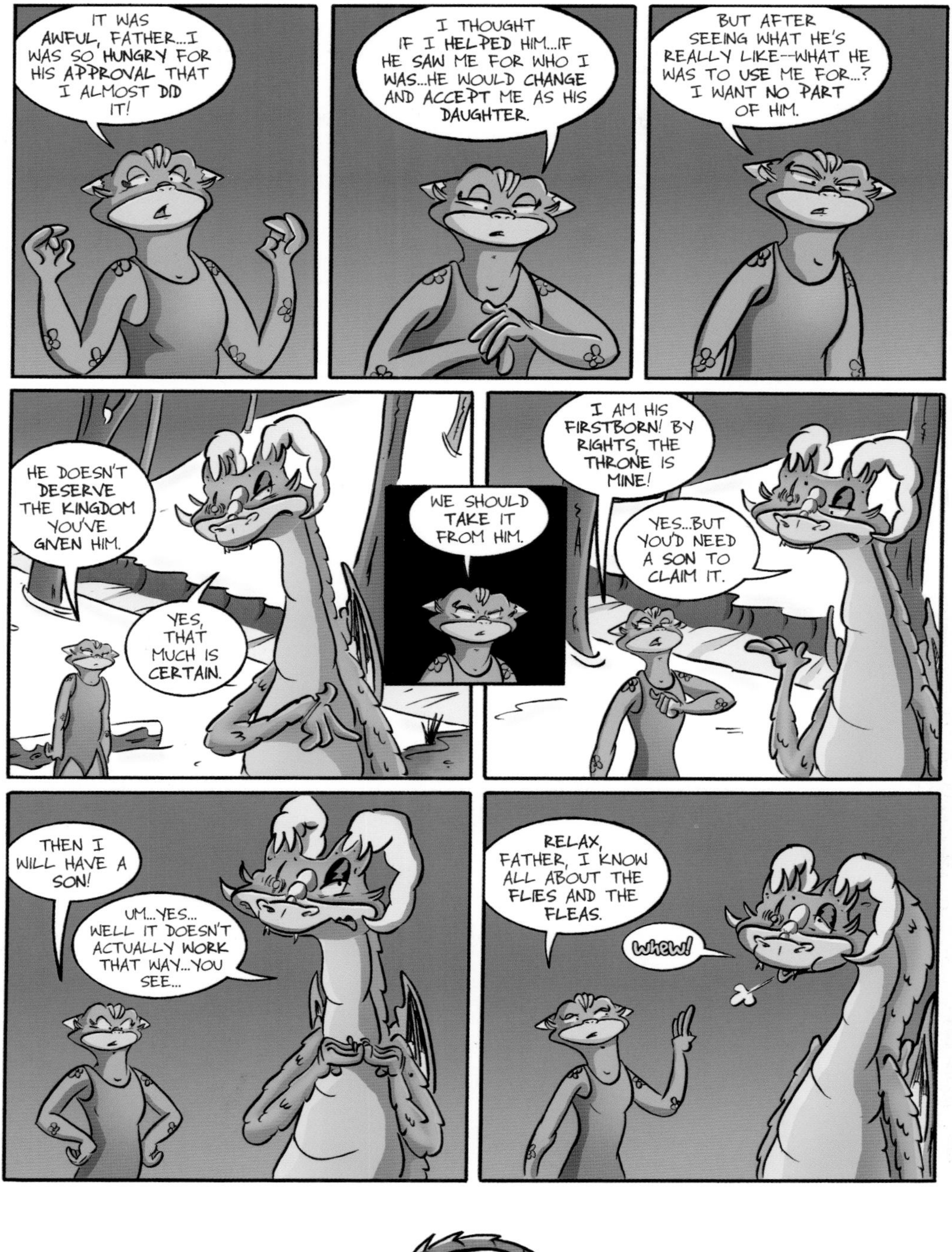
IT WAS AWFUL, FATHER...I WAS SO HUNGRY FOR HIS APPROVAL THAT I ALMOST DID IT!
I THOUGHT IF I HELPED HIM...IF HE SAW ME FOR WHO I WAS...HE WOULD CHANGE AND ACCEPT ME AS HIS DAUGHTER.
BUT AFTER SEEING WHAT HE'S REALLY LIKE--WHAT HE WAS TO USE ME FOR...? I WANT NO PART OF HIM.
HE DOESN'T DESERVE THE KINGDOM YOU'VE GIVEN HIM.
YES, THAT MUCH IS CERTAIN.
WE SHOULD TAKE IT FROM HIM.
I AM HIS FIRSTBORN! BY RIGHTS, THE THRONE IS MINE!
YES...BUT YOU'D NEED A SON TO CLAIM IT.
THEN I WILL HAVE A SON!
UM...YES... WELL IT DOESN'T ACTUALLY WORK THAT WAY...YOU SEE...
RELAX, FATHER, I KNOW ALL ABOUT THE FLIES AND THE FLEAS.
WHEW!

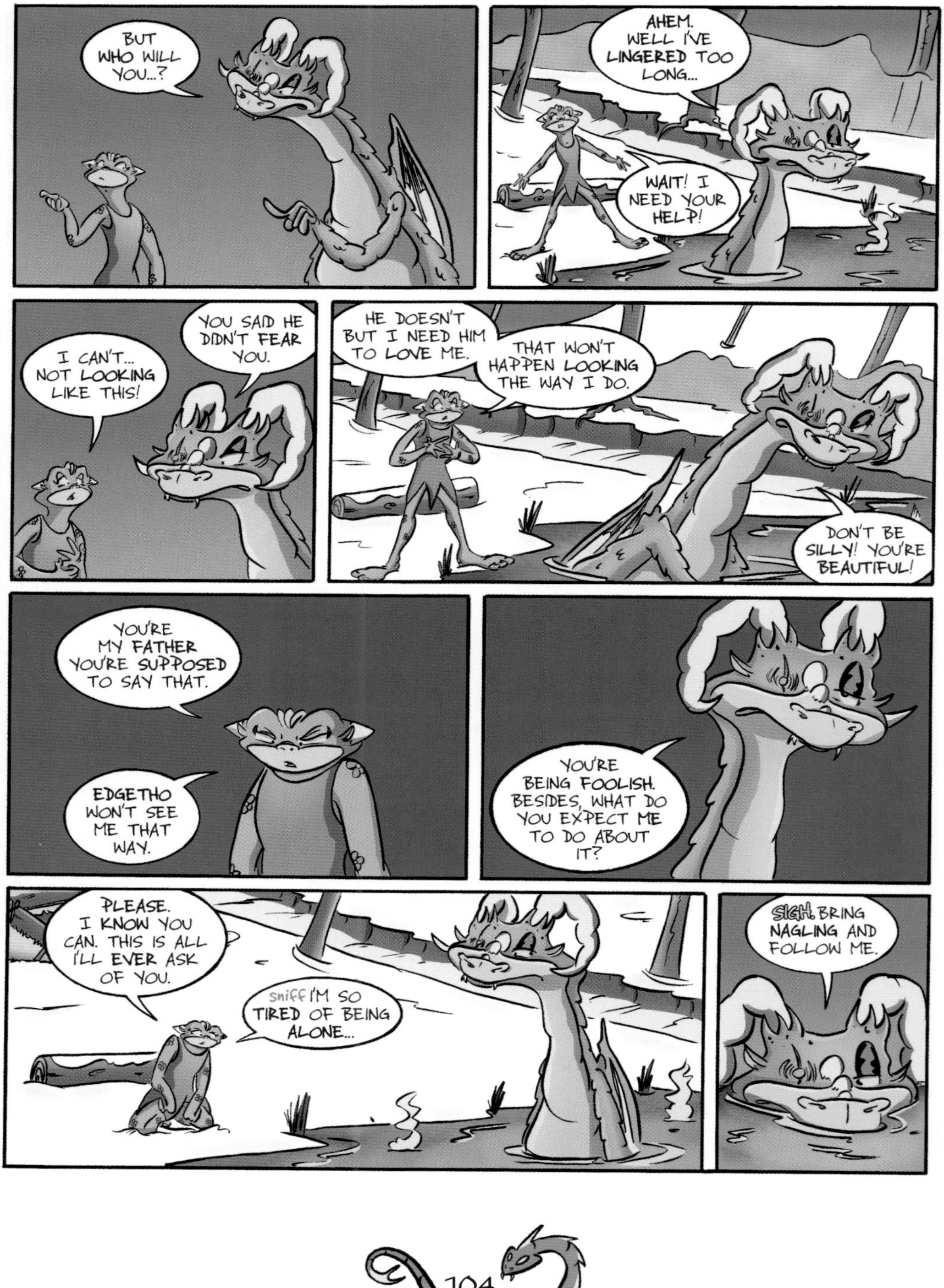
BUT WHO WILL YOU...?
AHEM. WELL I'VE LINGERED TOO LONG...
WAIT! I NEED YOUR HELP!
I CAN'T... NOT LOOKING LIKE THIS!
YOU SAID HE DIDN'T FEAR YOU.
HE DOESN'T BUT I NEED HIM TO LOVE ME.
THAT WON'T HAPPEN LOOKING THE WAY I DO.
DON'T BE SILLY! YOU'RE BEAUTIFUL!
YOU'RE MY FATHER YOU'RE SUPPOSED TO SAY THAT.
EDGETHO WON'T SEE ME THAT WAY.
YOU'RE BEING FOOLISH. BESIDES, WHAT DO YOU EXPECT ME TO DO ABOUT IT?
PLEASE. I KNOW YOU CAN. THIS IS ALL I'LL EVER ASK OF YOU.
sniff I'M SO TIRED OF BEING ALONE...
SIGH. BRING NAGLING AND FOLLOW ME.

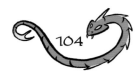

THE TRANSFORMATION WILL NOT BE PERMANENT.

SO WHAT WILL YOU DO WHEN HE DISCOVERS YOUR TRUE NATURE?

I KNOW.

BY THEN, HE WILL LOVE ME.

GERTRUDE, THE CHILD THAT COMES OF THIS UNION WILL BE BOTH MAN AND MONSTER--

NO DIFFERENT FROM YOUR-SELF.

YOU ARE BRINGING IT INTO A WORLD OF PAIN.

I WILL LOVE THE CHILD. I WILL PROTECT IT.

THEN YOU'LL BE A BETTER PARENT THAN ME.

CLEAN ME THIS TIME, WOULD YOU?

QUIET.

SNIKT!

SKKT!

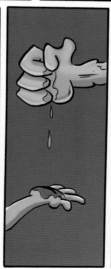

plip!

105

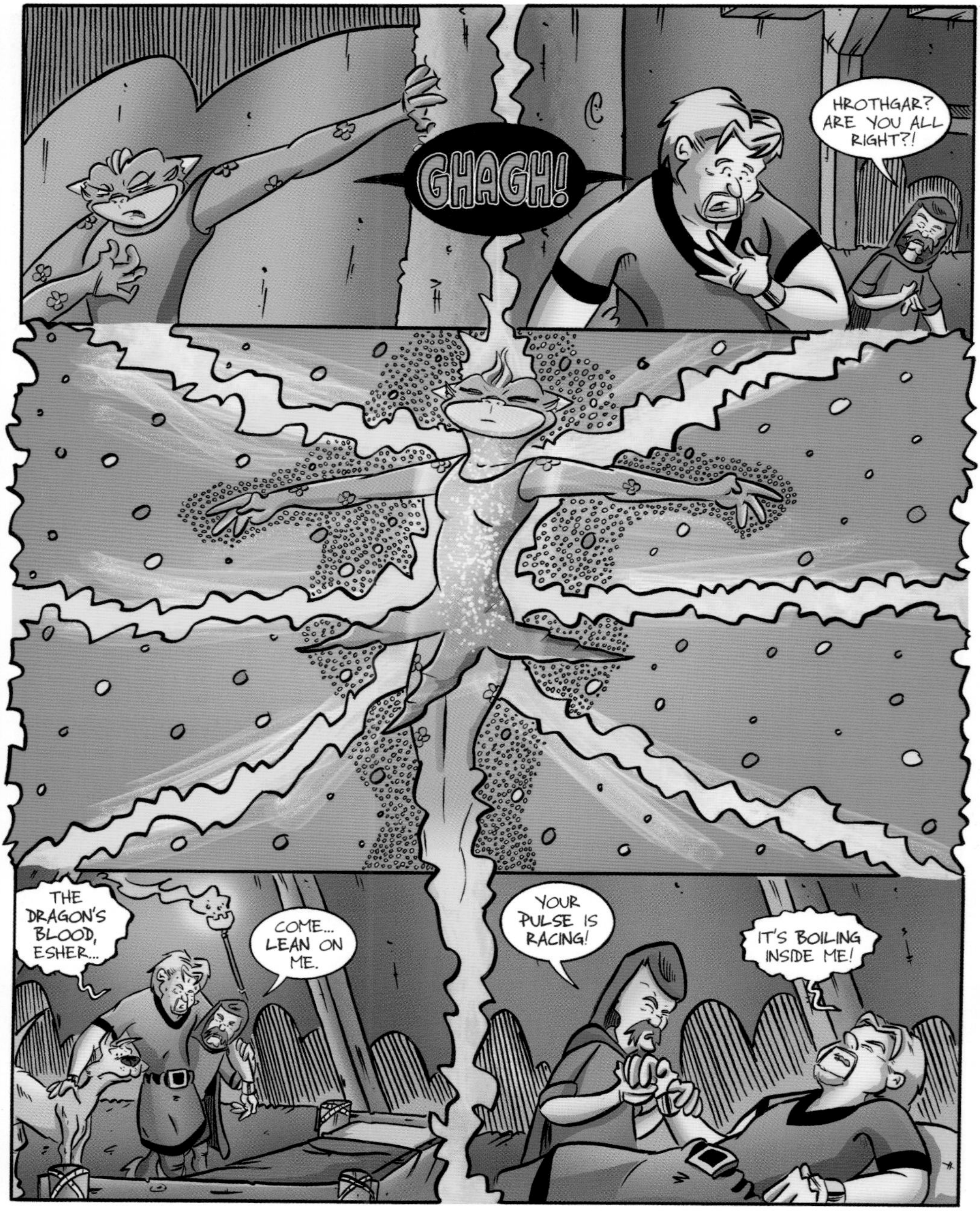
GHAGH!
HROTHGAR? ARE YOU ALL RIGHT?!
THE DRAGON'S BLOOD, ESHER...
COME... LEAN ON ME.
YOUR PULSE IS RACING!
IT'S BOILING INSIDE ME!

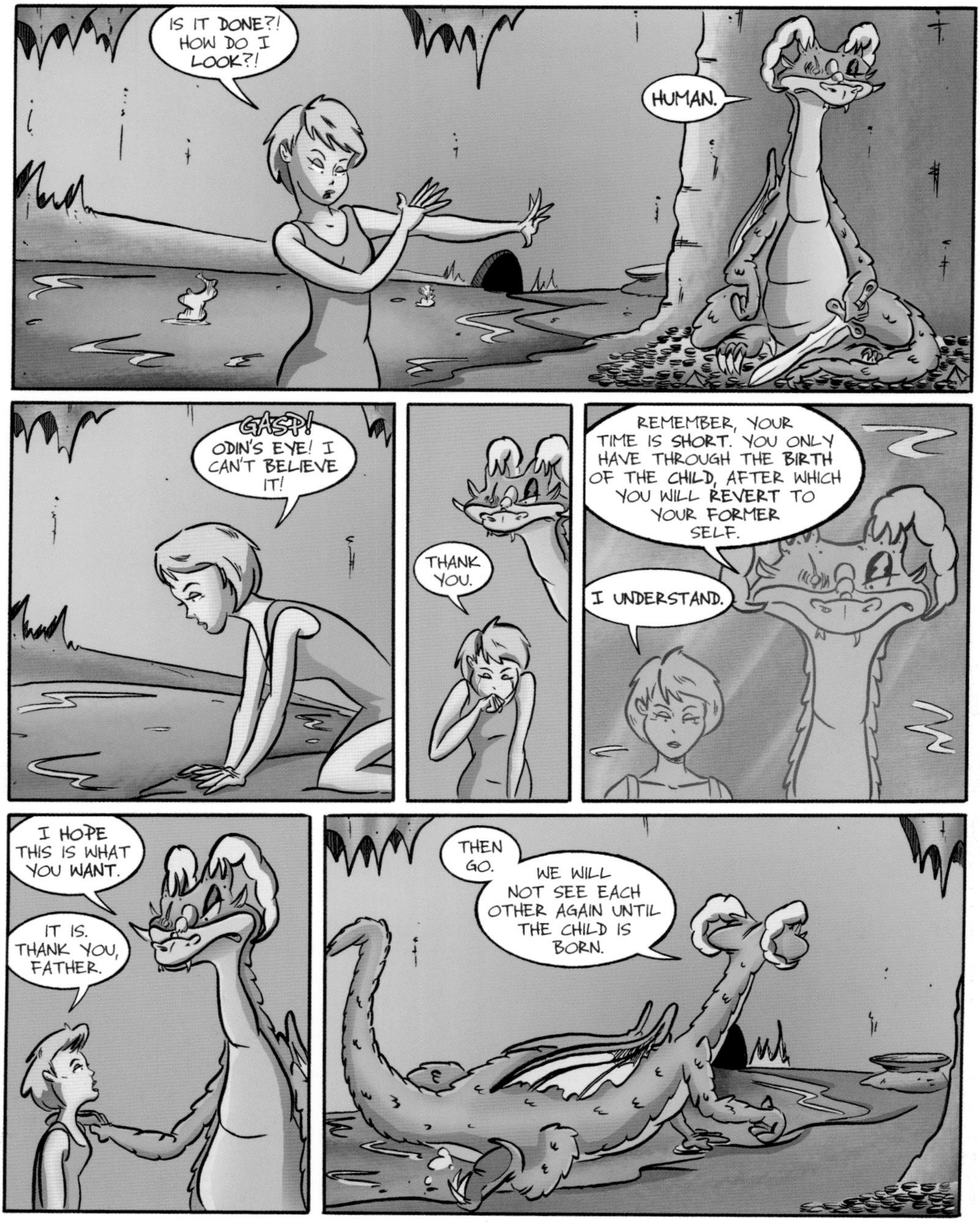
IS IT DONE?! HOW DO I LOOK?!
HUMAN.
GASP!
ODIN'S EYE! I CAN'T BELIEVE IT!
THANK YOU.
REMEMBER, YOUR TIME IS SHORT. YOU ONLY HAVE THROUGH THE BIRTH OF THE CHILD, AFTER WHICH YOU WILL REVERT TO YOUR FORMER SELF.
I UNDERSTAND.
I HOPE THIS IS WHAT YOU WANT.
IT IS. THANK YOU, FATHER.
THEN GO.
WE WILL NOT SEE EACH OTHER AGAIN UNTIL THE CHILD IS BORN.

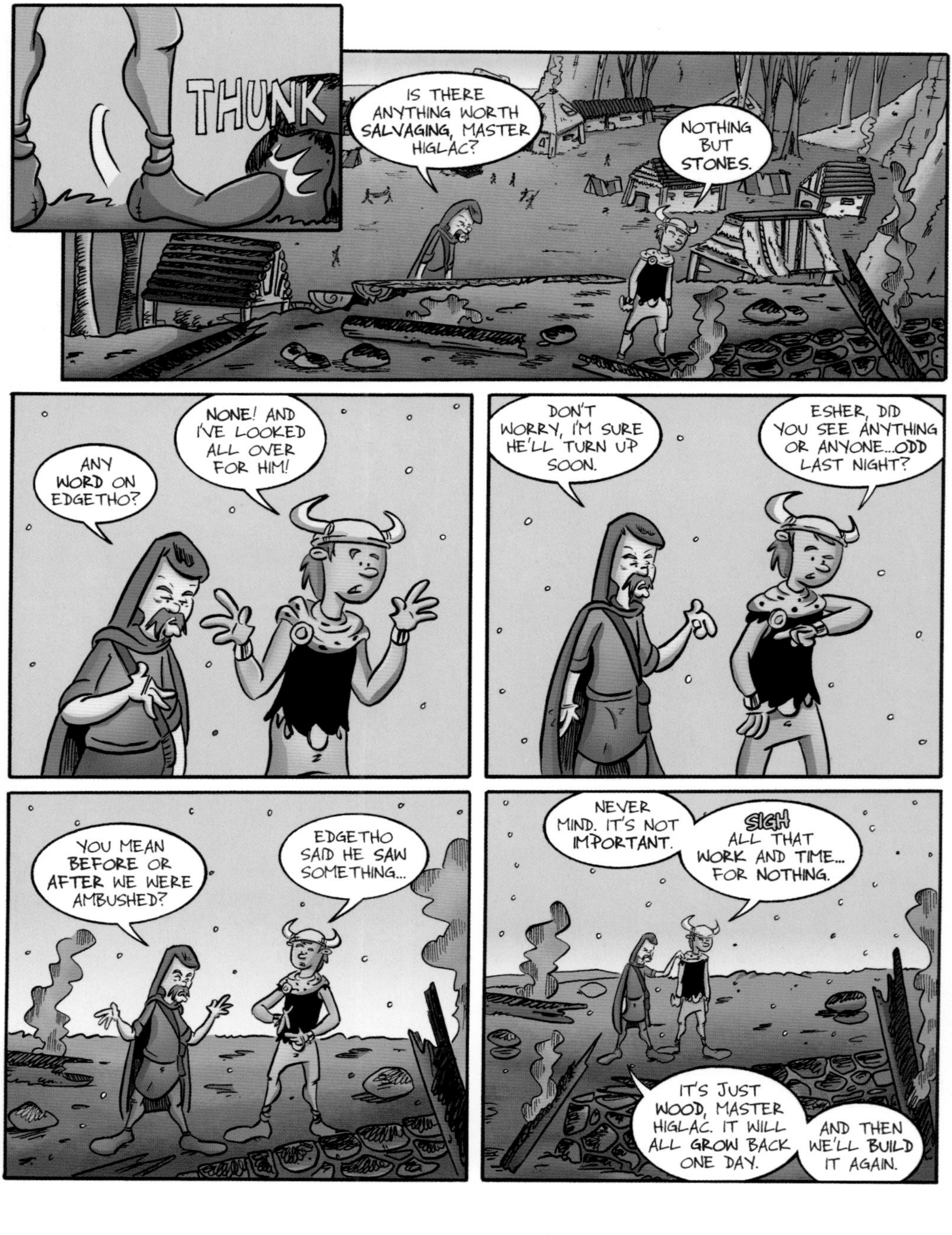
THUNK
IS THERE ANYTHING WORTH SALVAGING, MASTER HIGLAC?
NOTHING BUT STONES.
ANY WORD ON EDGETHO?
NONE! AND I'VE LOOKED ALL OVER FOR HIM!
DON'T WORRY, I'M SURE HE'LL TURN UP SOON.
ESHER, DID YOU SEE ANYTHING OR ANYONE...ODD LAST NIGHT?
YOU MEAN BEFORE OR AFTER WE WERE AMBUSHED?
EDGETHO SAID HE SAW SOMETHING...
NEVER MIND. IT'S NOT IMPORTANT.
SIGH
ALL THAT WORK AND TIME... FOR NOTHING.
IT'S JUST WOOD, MASTER HIGLAC. IT WILL ALL GROW BACK ONE DAY.
AND THEN WE'LL BUILD IT AGAIN.

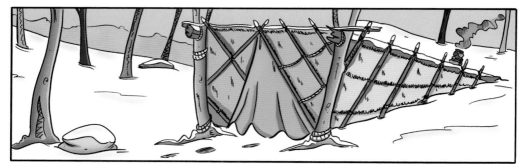

EDGETHO!

EDGETHO!

EDGETHO!

HEY!

OOF!

TRIP!

ARE YOU OKAY? LET ME HELP YOU.

THANK YOU.

SURE...YOU HAVE SOFT HANDS...

CRUNCH!

AAHH! HEH...AND A STRONG GRIP!

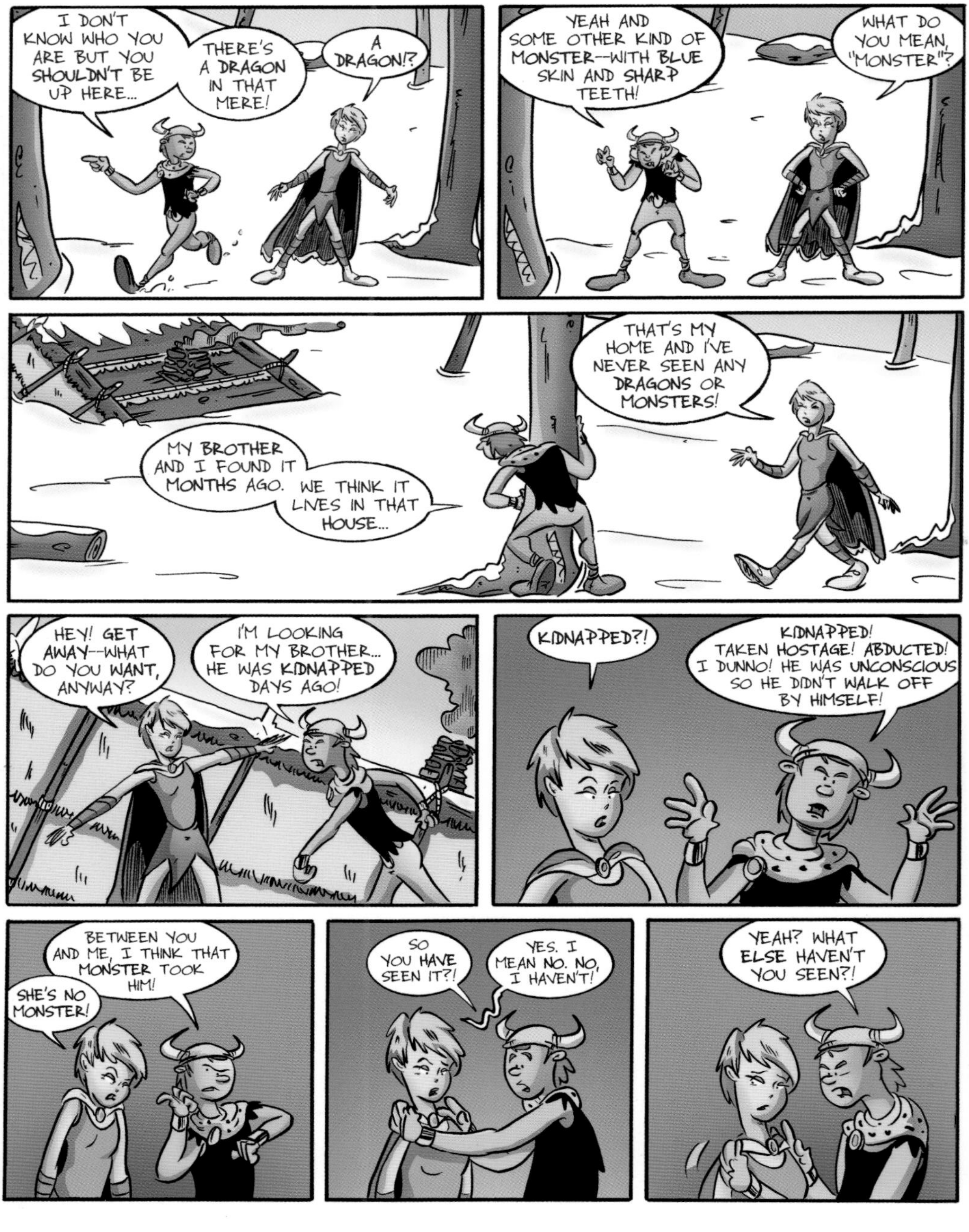
I DON'T KNOW WHO YOU ARE BUT YOU SHOULDN'T BE UP HERE...
THERE'S A DRAGON IN THAT MERE!
A DRAGON!?
YEAH AND SOME OTHER KIND OF MONSTER--WITH BLUE SKIN AND SHARP TEETH!
WHAT DO YOU MEAN, "MONSTER"?
THAT'S MY HOME AND I'VE NEVER SEEN ANY DRAGONS OR MONSTERS!
MY BROTHER AND I FOUND IT MONTHS AGO.
WE THINK IT LIVES IN THAT HOUSE...
HEY! GET AWAY--WHAT DO YOU WANT, ANYWAY?
I'M LOOKING FOR MY BROTHER... HE WAS KIDNAPPED DAYS AGO!
KIDNAPPED?!
KIDNAPPED! TAKEN HOSTAGE! ABDUCTED! I DUNNO! HE WAS UNCONSCIOUS SO HE DIDN'T WALK OFF BY HIMSELF!
BETWEEN YOU AND ME, I THINK THAT MONSTER TOOK HIM!
SHE'S NO MONSTER!
SO YOU HAVE SEEN IT?!
YES. I MEAN NO. NO, I HAVEN'T!
YEAH? WHAT ELSE HAVEN'T YOU SEEN?!

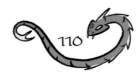

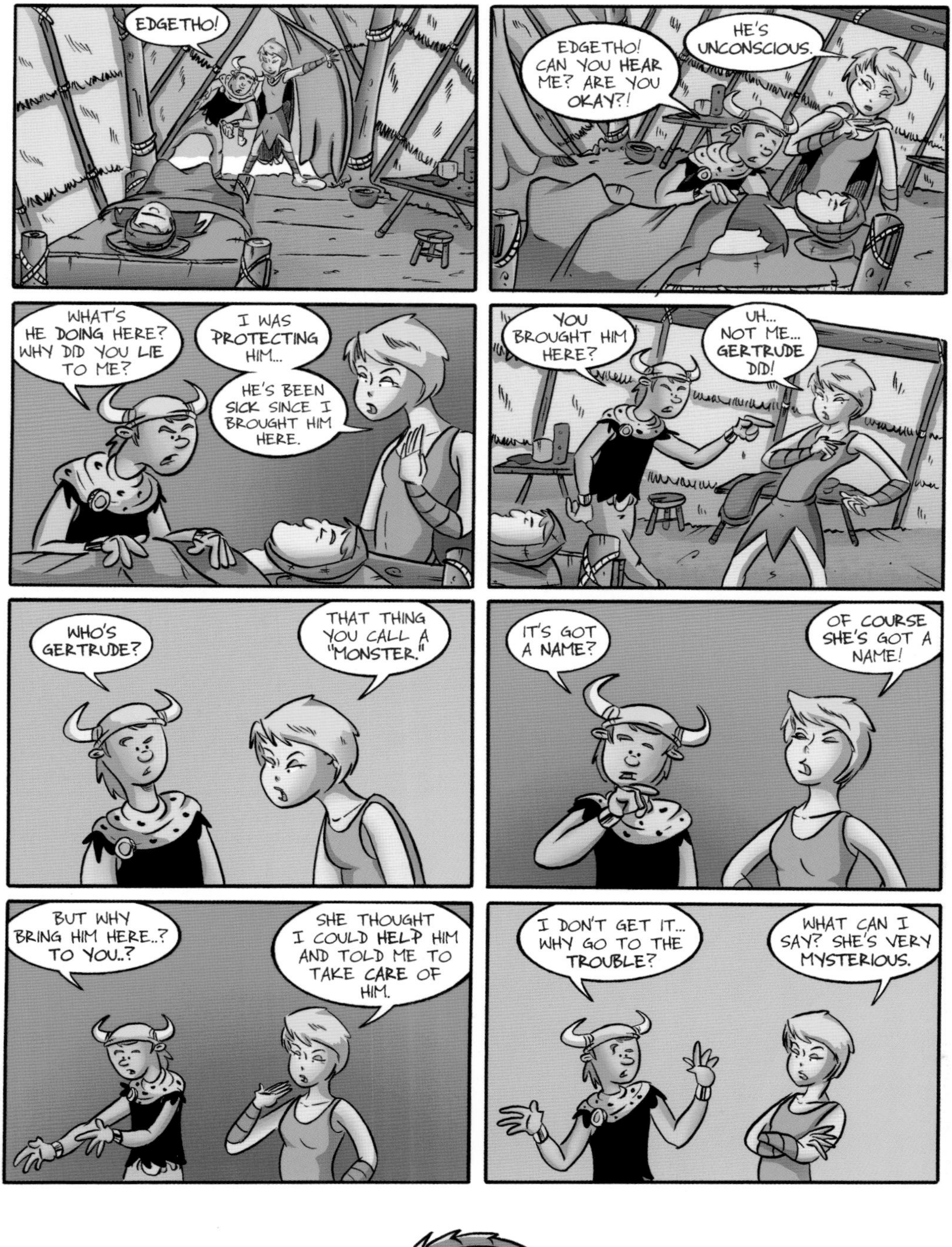
EDGETHO!
EDGETHO! CAN YOU HEAR ME? ARE YOU OKAY?!
HE'S UNCONSCIOUS.
WHAT'S HE DOING HERE? WHY DID YOU LIE TO ME?
I WAS PROTECTING HIM...
HE'S BEEN SICK SINCE I BROUGHT HIM HERE.
YOU BROUGHT HIM HERE?
UH... NOT ME... GERTRUDE DID!
WHO'S GERTRUDE?
THAT THING YOU CALL A "MONSTER."
IT'S GOT A NAME?
OF COURSE SHE'S GOT A NAME!
BUT WHY BRING HIM HERE..? TO YOU..?
SHE THOUGHT I COULD HELP HIM AND TOLD ME TO TAKE CARE OF HIM.
I DON'T GET IT... WHY GO TO THE TROUBLE?
WHAT CAN I SAY? SHE'S VERY MYSTERIOUS.

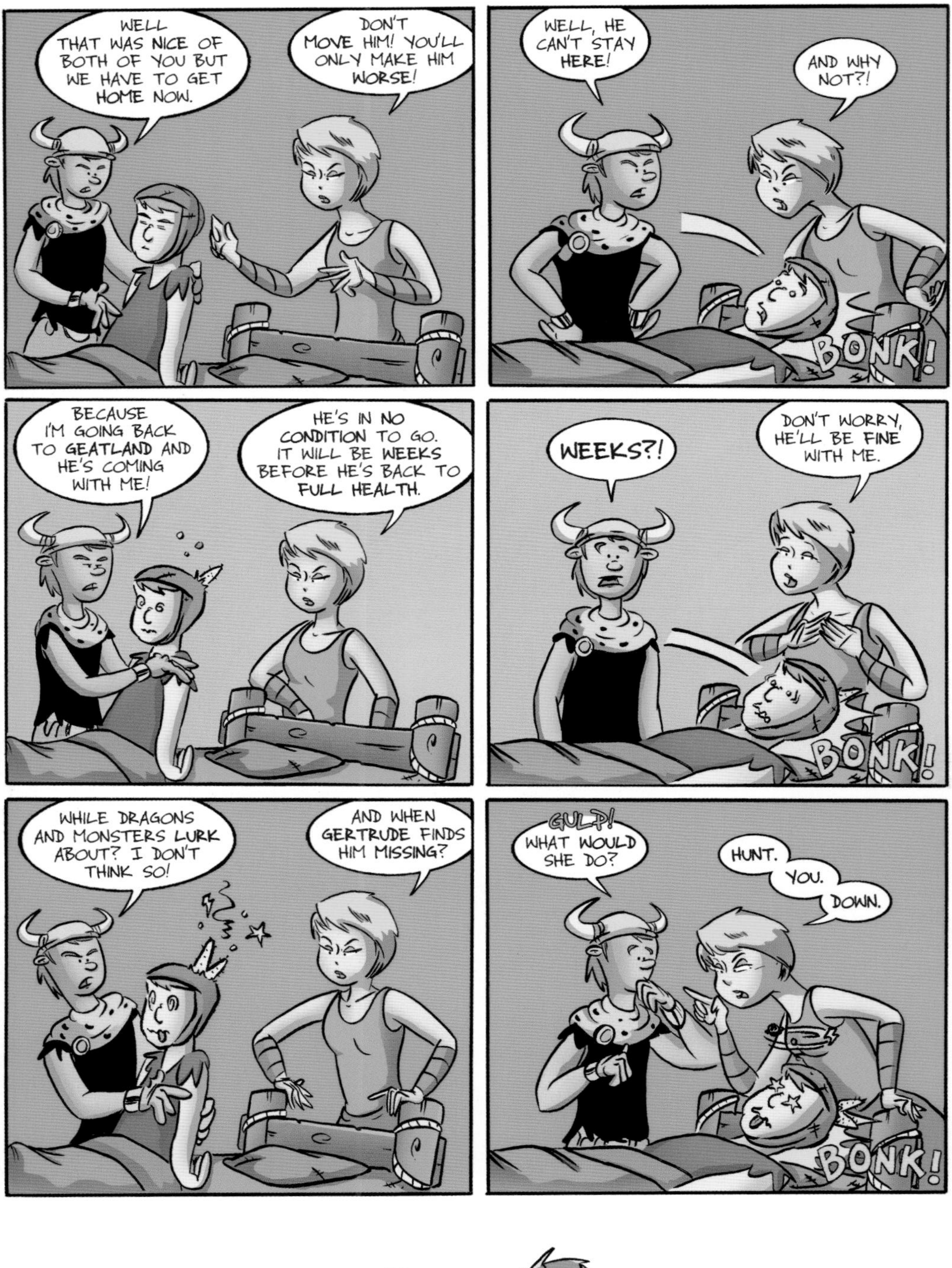
WELL THAT WAS NICE OF BOTH OF YOU BUT WE HAVE TO GET HOME NOW.
DON'T MOVE HIM! YOU'LL ONLY MAKE HIM WORSE!
WELL, HE CAN'T STAY HERE!
AND WHY NOT?!
BONK!
BECAUSE I'M GOING BACK TO GEATLAND AND HE'S COMING WITH ME!
HE'S IN NO CONDITION TO GO. IT WILL BE WEEKS BEFORE HE'S BACK TO FULL HEALTH.
WEEKS?!
DON'T WORRY, HE'LL BE FINE WITH ME.
BONK!
WHILE DRAGONS AND MONSTERS LURK ABOUT? I DON'T THINK SO!
AND WHEN GERTRUDE FINDS HIM MISSING?
GULP!
WHAT WOULD SHE DO?
HUNT.
YOU.
DOWN.
BONK!

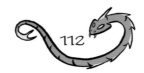

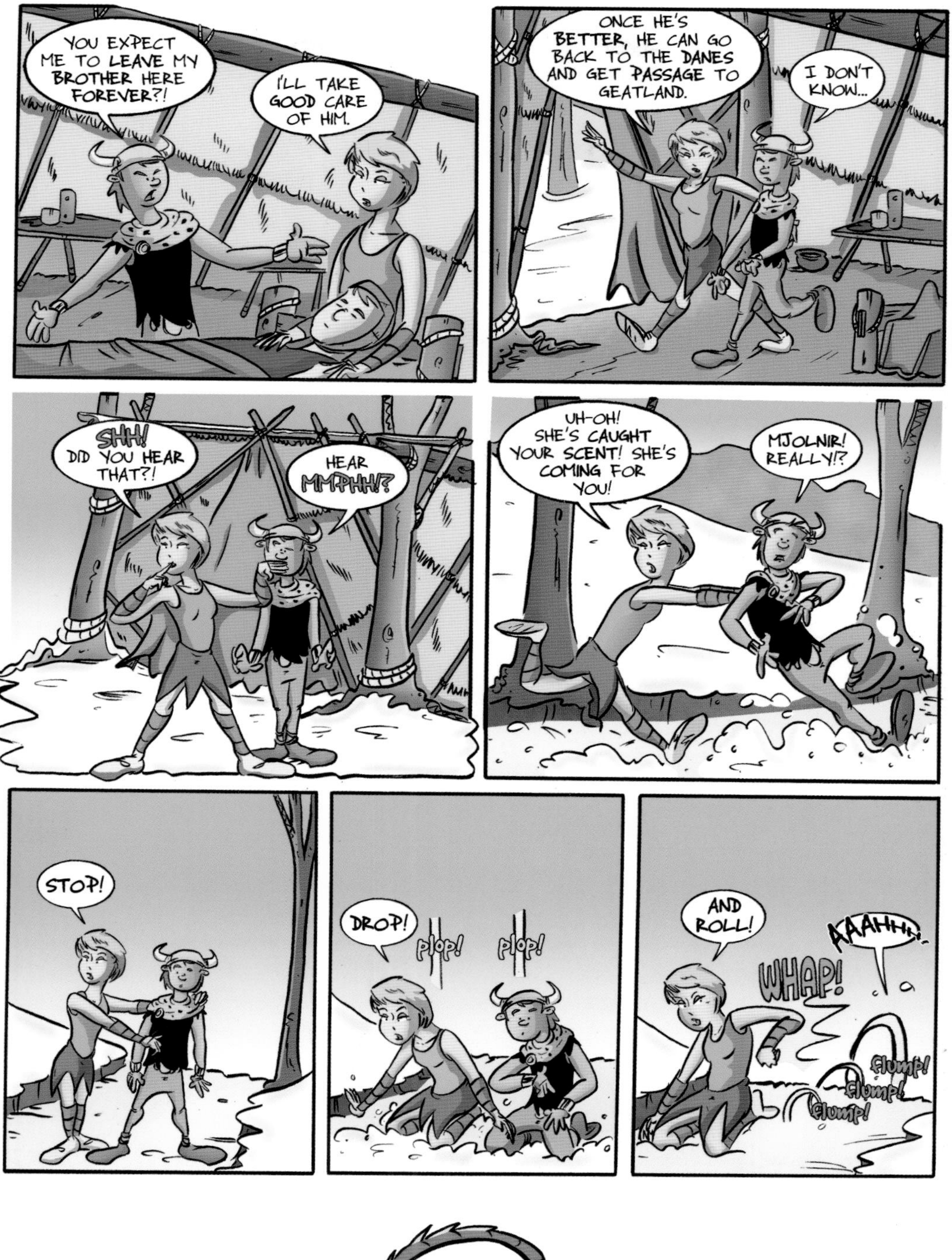
YOU EXPECT ME TO LEAVE MY BROTHER HERE FOREVER?!
I'LL TAKE GOOD CARE OF HIM.
ONCE HE'S BETTER, HE CAN GO BACK TO THE DANES AND GET PASSAGE TO GEATLAND.
I DON'T KNOW...
SHH! DID YOU HEAR THAT?!
HEAR MMPHH!?
UH-OH! SHE'S CAUGHT YOUR SCENT! SHE'S COMING FOR YOU!
MJOLNIR! REALLY!?
STOP!
DROP!
plop!
plop!
AND ROLL!
WHAP!
AAAHH...
flump!
flump!
flump!

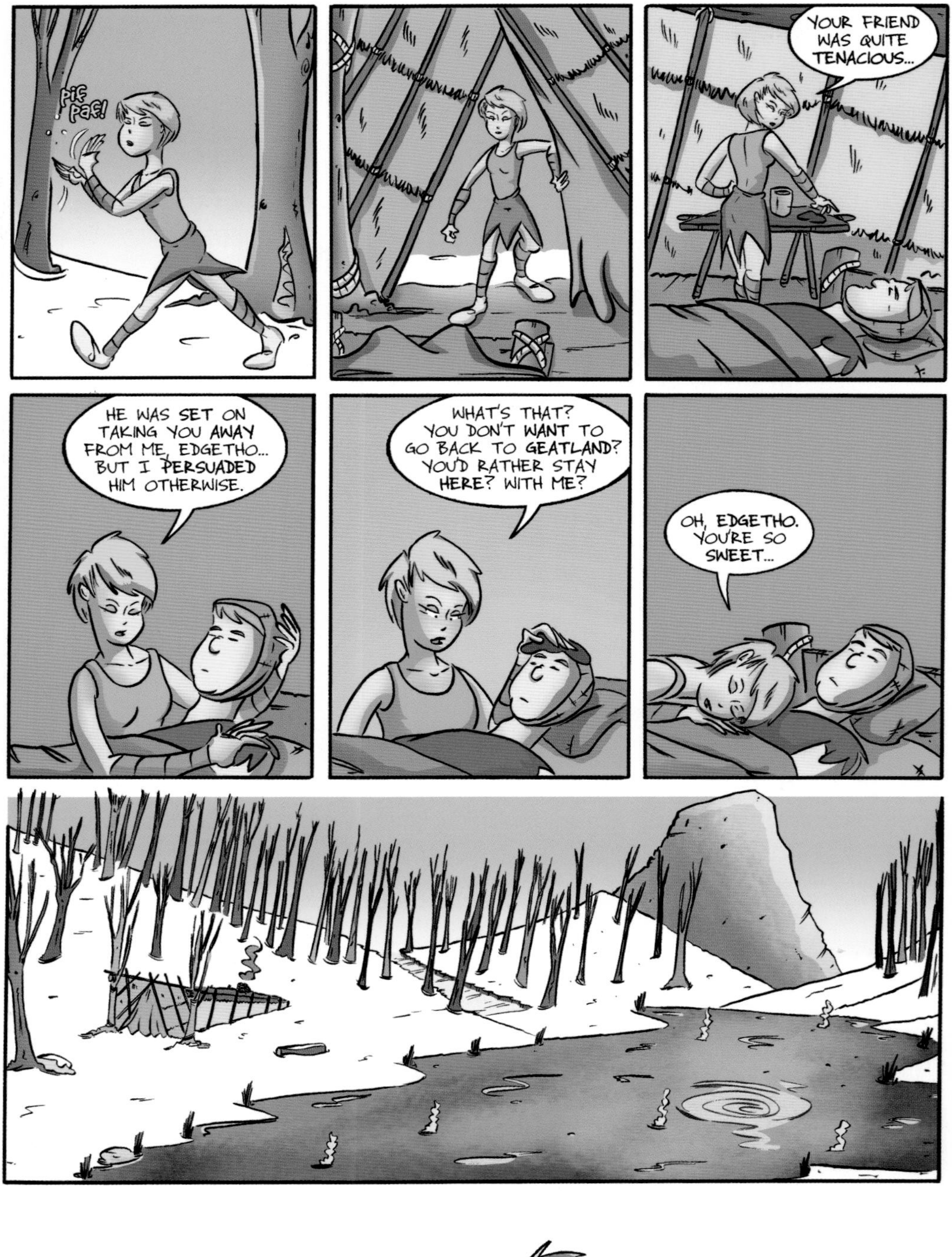
PIF PAF!
YOUR FRIEND WAS QUITE TENACIOUS...
HE WAS SET ON TAKING YOU AWAY FROM ME, EDGETHO... BUT I PERSUADED HIM OTHERWISE.
WHAT'S THAT? YOU DON'T WANT TO GO BACK TO GEATLAND? YOU'D RATHER STAY HERE? WITH ME?
OH, EDGETHO. YOU'RE SO SWEET...

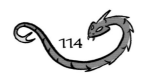

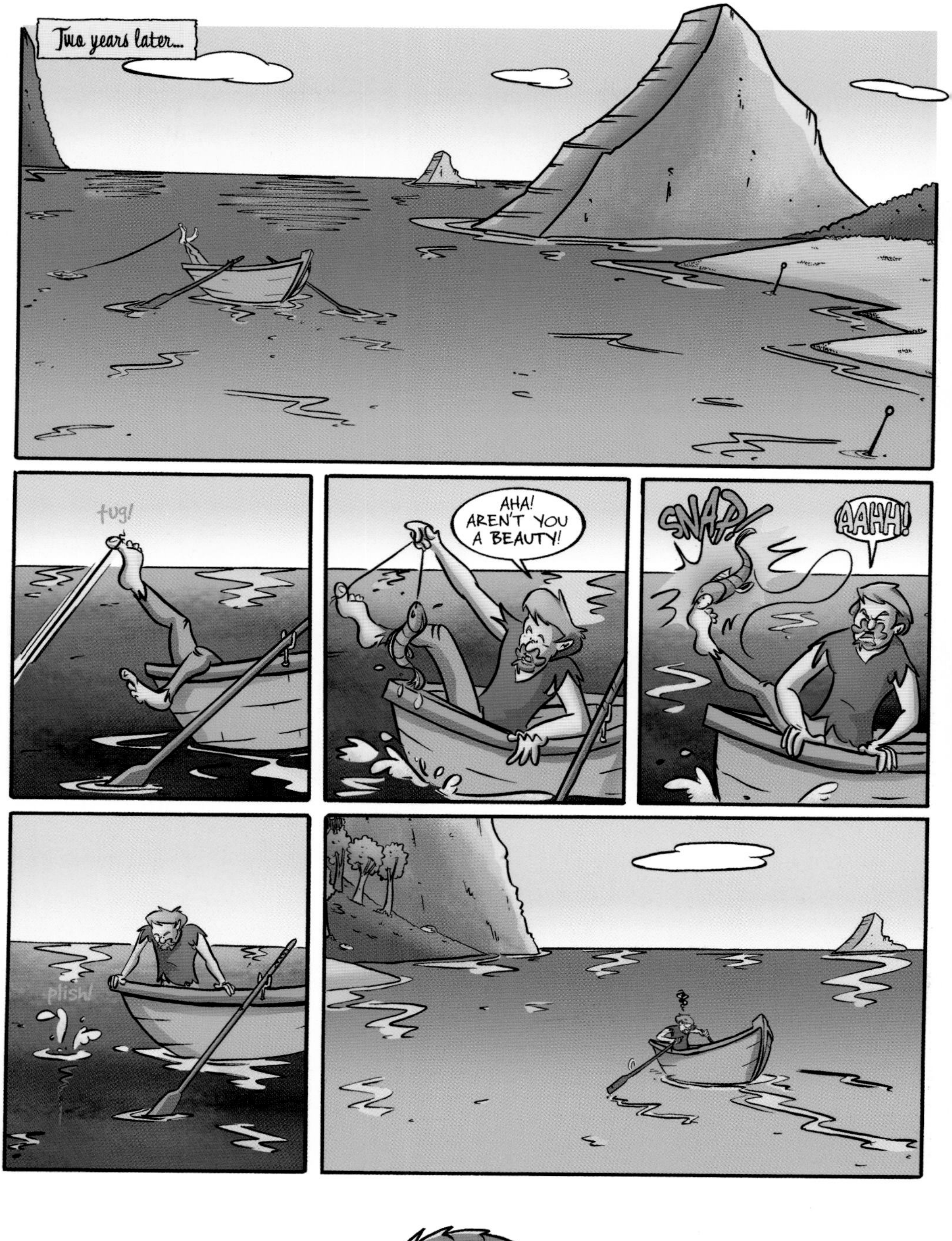
Two years later...
tug!
AHA! AREN'T YOU A BEAUTY!
SNAP!
AAHH!
plish!

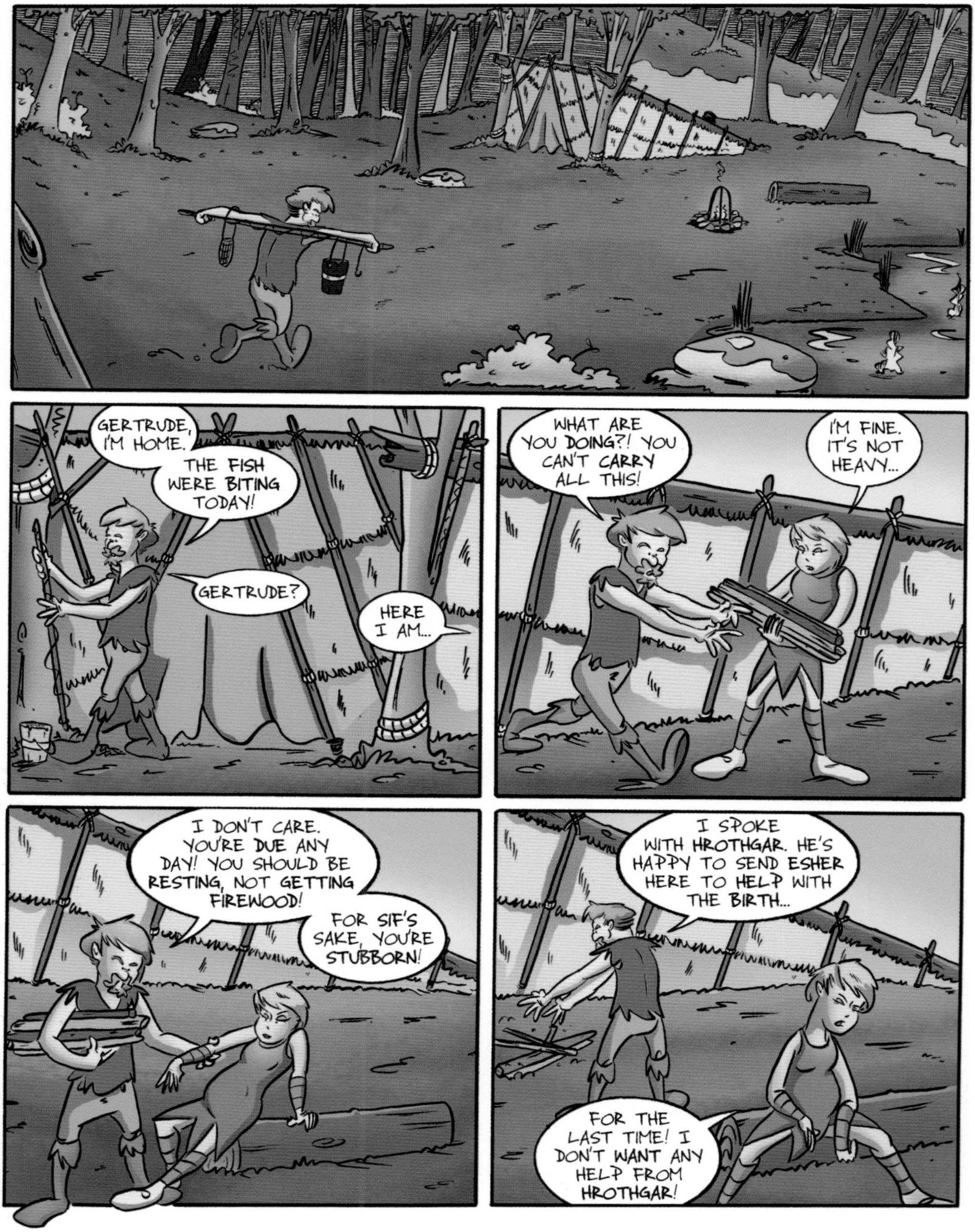
GERTRUDE, I'M HOME.
THE FISH WERE BITING TODAY!
GERTRUDE?
HERE I AM...
WHAT ARE YOU DOING?! YOU CAN'T CARRY ALL THIS!
I'M FINE. IT'S NOT HEAVY...
I DON'T CARE. YOU'RE DUE ANY DAY! YOU SHOULD BE RESTING, NOT GETTING FIREWOOD!
FOR SIF'S SAKE, YOU'RE STUBBORN!
I SPOKE WITH HROTHGAR. HE'S HAPPY TO SEND ESHER HERE TO HELP WITH THE BIRTH...
FOR THE LAST TIME! I DON'T WANT ANY HELP FROM HROTHGAR!

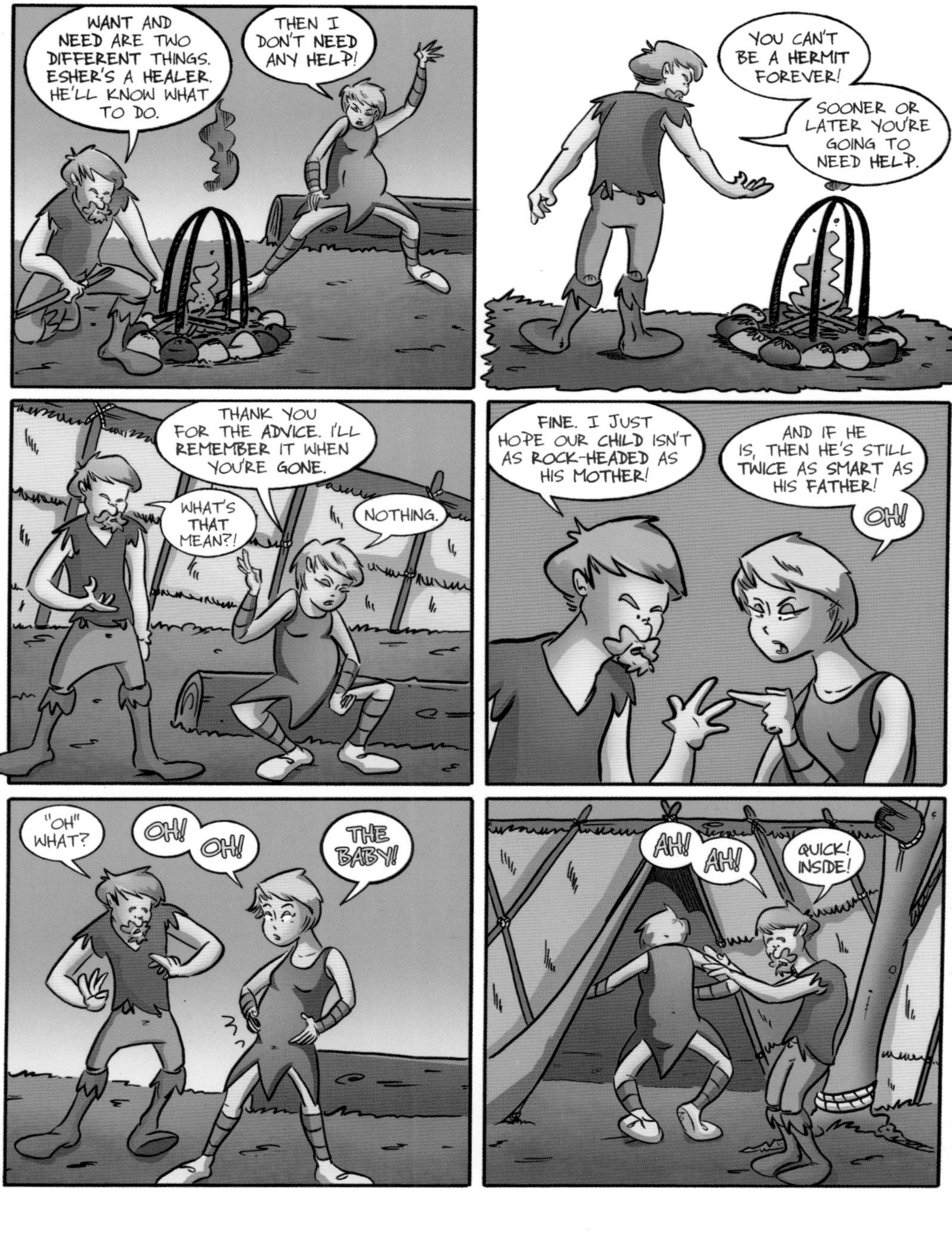
WANT AND NEED ARE TWO DIFFERENT THINGS. ESHER'S A HEALER. HE'LL KNOW WHAT TO DO.
THEN I DON'T NEED ANY HELP!
YOU CAN'T BE A HERMIT FOREVER!
SOONER OR LATER YOU'RE GOING TO NEED HELP.
THANK YOU FOR THE ADVICE. I'LL REMEMBER IT WHEN YOU'RE GONE.
WHAT'S THAT MEAN?!
NOTHING.
FINE. I JUST HOPE OUR CHILD ISN'T AS ROCK-HEADED AS HIS MOTHER!
AND IF HE IS, THEN HE'S STILL TWICE AS SMART AS HIS FATHER!
OH!
"OH" WHAT?
OH!
OH!
THE BABY!
AH!
AH!
QUICK! INSIDE!

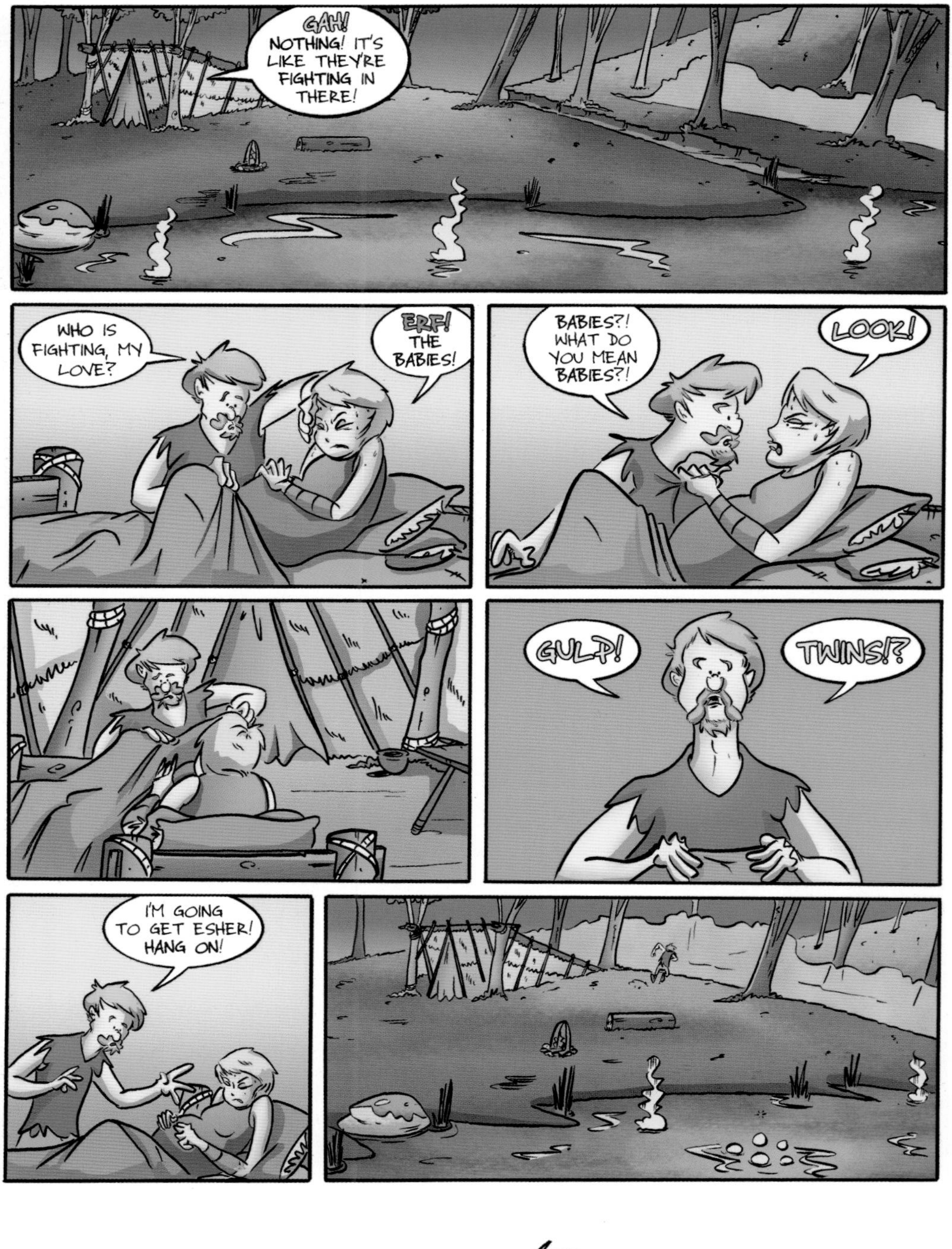
GAH!
NOTHING! IT'S LIKE THEY'RE FIGHTING IN THERE!
WHO IS FIGHTING, MY LOVE?
ERF! THE BABIES!
BABIES?! WHAT DO YOU MEAN BABIES?!
LOOK!
GULP!
TWINS!?
I'M GOING TO GET ESHER! HANG ON!

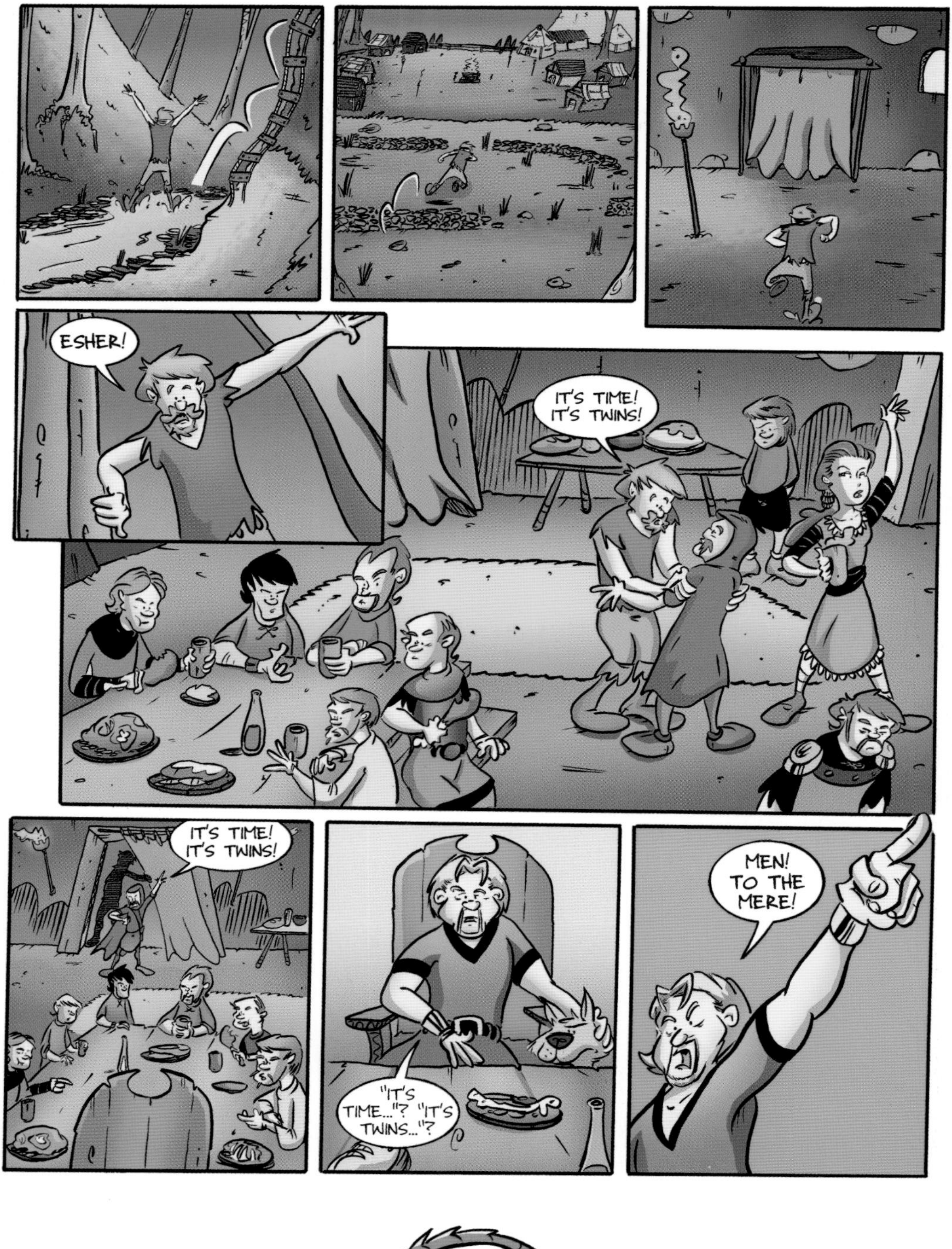
ESHER!
IT'S TIME! IT'S TWINS!
IT'S TIME! IT'S TWINS!
"IT'S TIME..."? "IT'S TWINS..."?
MEN! TO THE MERE!

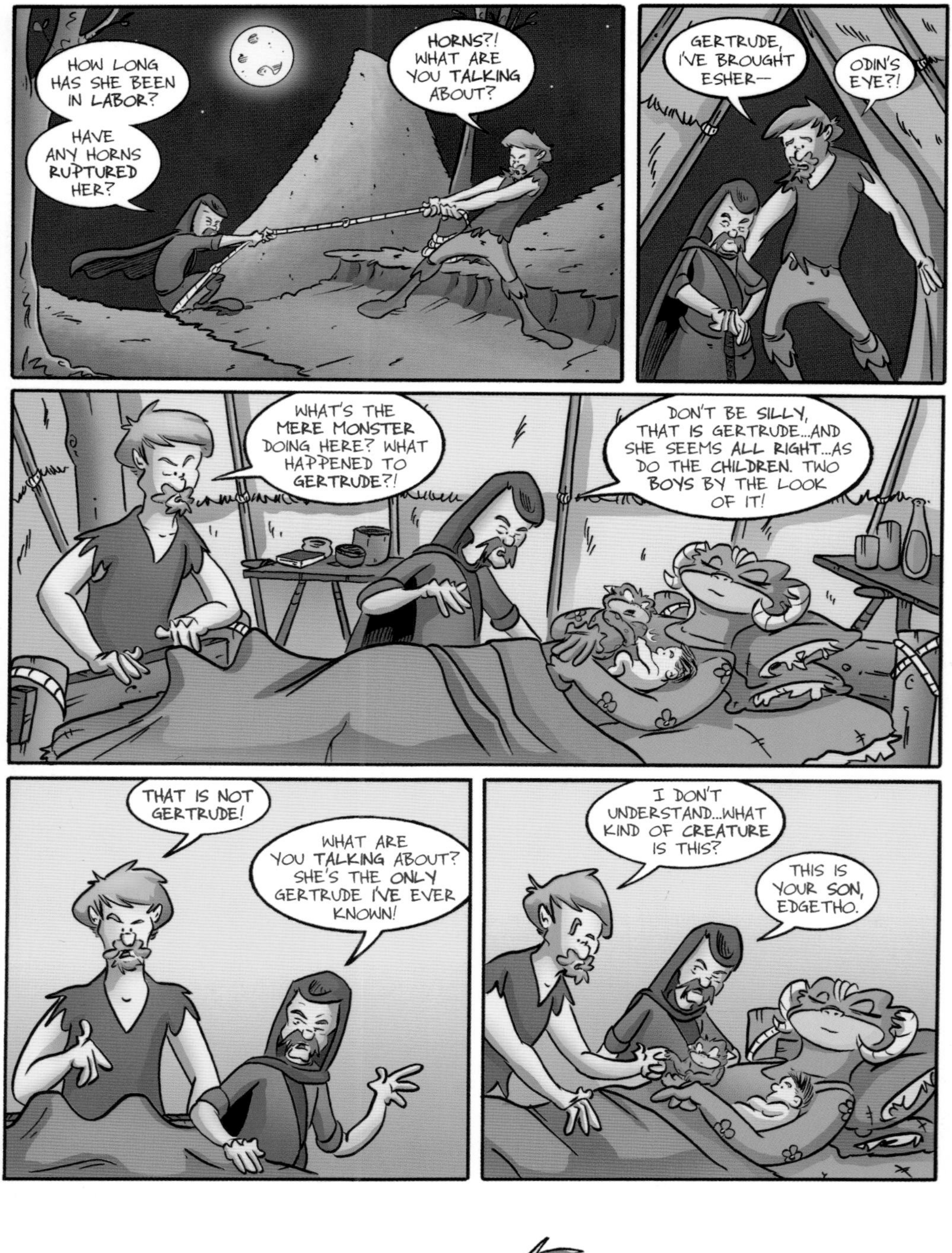
HOW LONG HAS SHE BEEN IN LABOR?
HAVE ANY HORNS RUPTURED HER?
HORNS?! WHAT ARE YOU TALKING ABOUT?
GERTRUDE, I'VE BROUGHT ESHER--
ODIN'S EYE?!
WHAT'S THE MERE MONSTER DOING HERE? WHAT HAPPENED TO GERTRUDE?!
DON'T BE SILLY, THAT IS GERTRUDE...AND SHE SEEMS ALL RIGHT...AS DO THE CHILDREN. TWO BOYS BY THE LOOK OF IT!
THAT IS NOT GERTRUDE!
WHAT ARE YOU TALKING ABOUT? SHE'S THE ONLY GERTRUDE I'VE EVER KNOWN!
I DON'T UNDERSTAND...WHAT KIND OF CREATURE IS THIS?
THIS IS YOUR SON, EDGETHO.

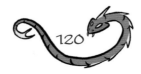

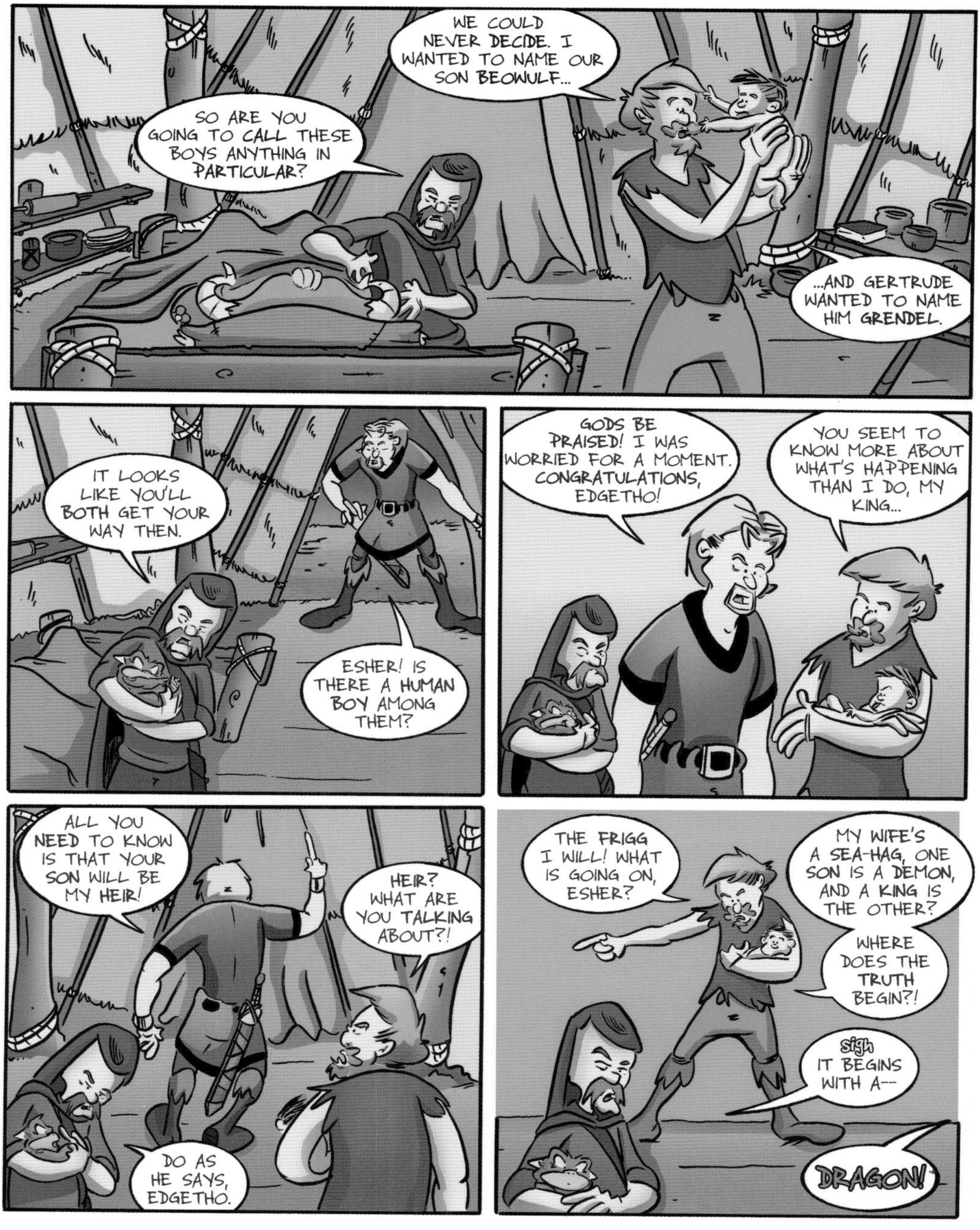
SO ARE YOU GOING TO CALL THESE BOYS ANYTHING IN PARTICULAR?
WE COULD NEVER DECIDE. I WANTED TO NAME OUR SON BEOWULF...
...AND GERTRUDE WANTED TO NAME HIM GRENDEL.
IT LOOKS LIKE YOU'LL BOTH GET YOUR WAY THEN.
ESHER! IS THERE A HUMAN BOY AMONG THEM?
GODS BE PRAISED! I WAS WORRIED FOR A MOMENT. CONGRATULATIONS, EDGETHO!
YOU SEEM TO KNOW MORE ABOUT WHAT'S HAPPENING THAN I DO, MY KING...
ALL YOU NEED TO KNOW IS THAT YOUR SON WILL BE MY HEIR!
HEIR? WHAT ARE YOU TALKING ABOUT?!
DO AS HE SAYS, EDGETHO.
THE FRIGG I WILL! WHAT IS GOING ON, ESHER?
MY WIFE'S A SEA-HAG, ONE SON IS A DEMON, AND A KING IS THE OTHER?
WHERE DOES THE TRUTH BEGIN?!
sigh
IT BEGINS WITH A--
DRAGON!

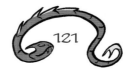

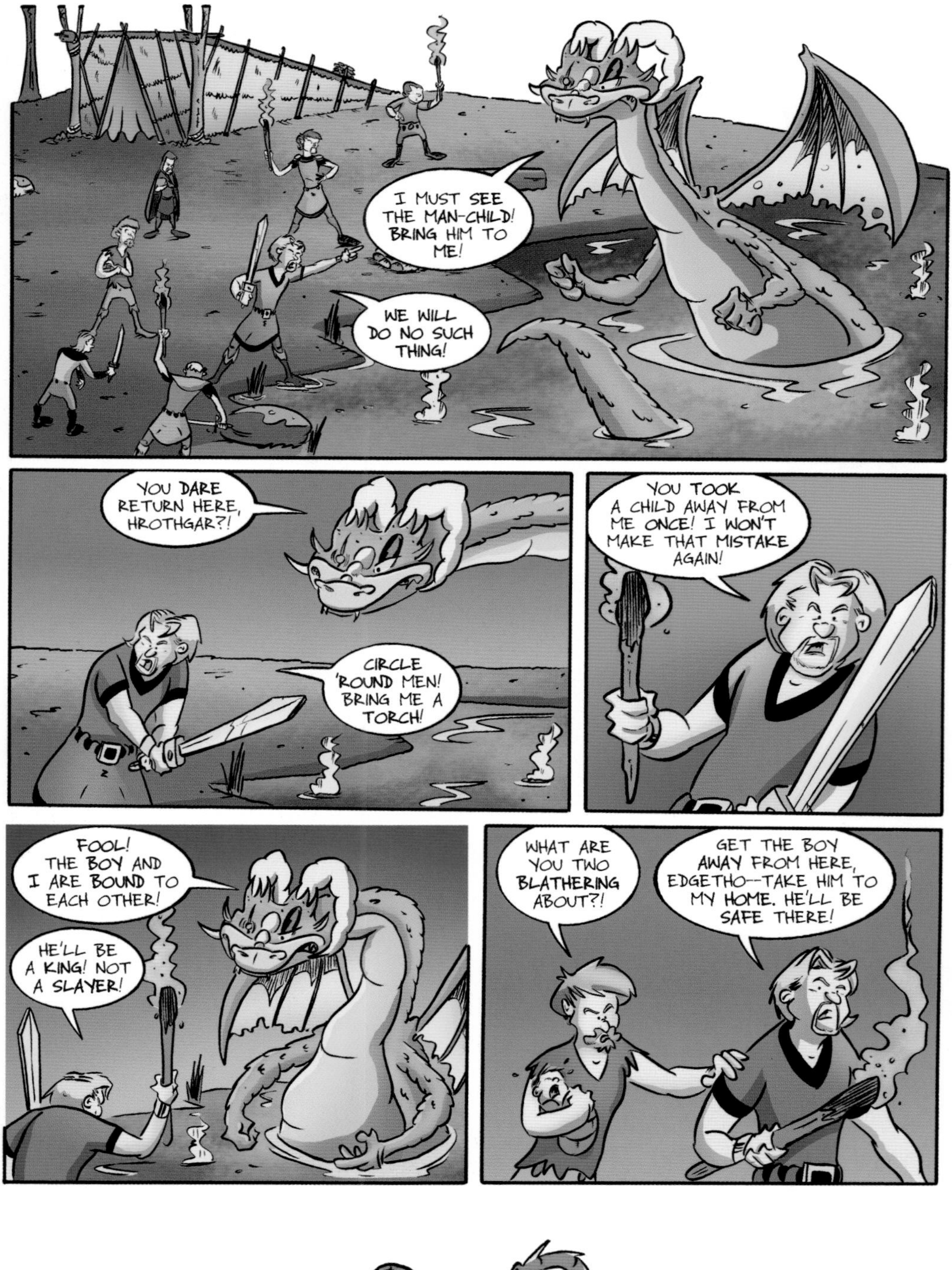
I MUST SEE THE MAN-CHILD! BRING HIM TO ME!
WE WILL DO NO SUCH THING!
YOU DARE RETURN HERE, HROTHGAR?!
CIRCLE 'ROUND MEN! BRING ME A TORCH!
YOU TOOK A CHILD AWAY FROM ME ONCE! I WON'T MAKE THAT MISTAKE AGAIN!
FOOL! THE BOY AND I ARE BOUND TO EACH OTHER!
HE'LL BE A KING! NOT A SLAYER!
WHAT ARE YOU TWO BLATHERING ABOUT?!
GET THE BOY AWAY FROM HERE, EDGETHO--TAKE HIM TO MY HOME. HE'LL BE SAFE THERE!

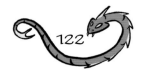

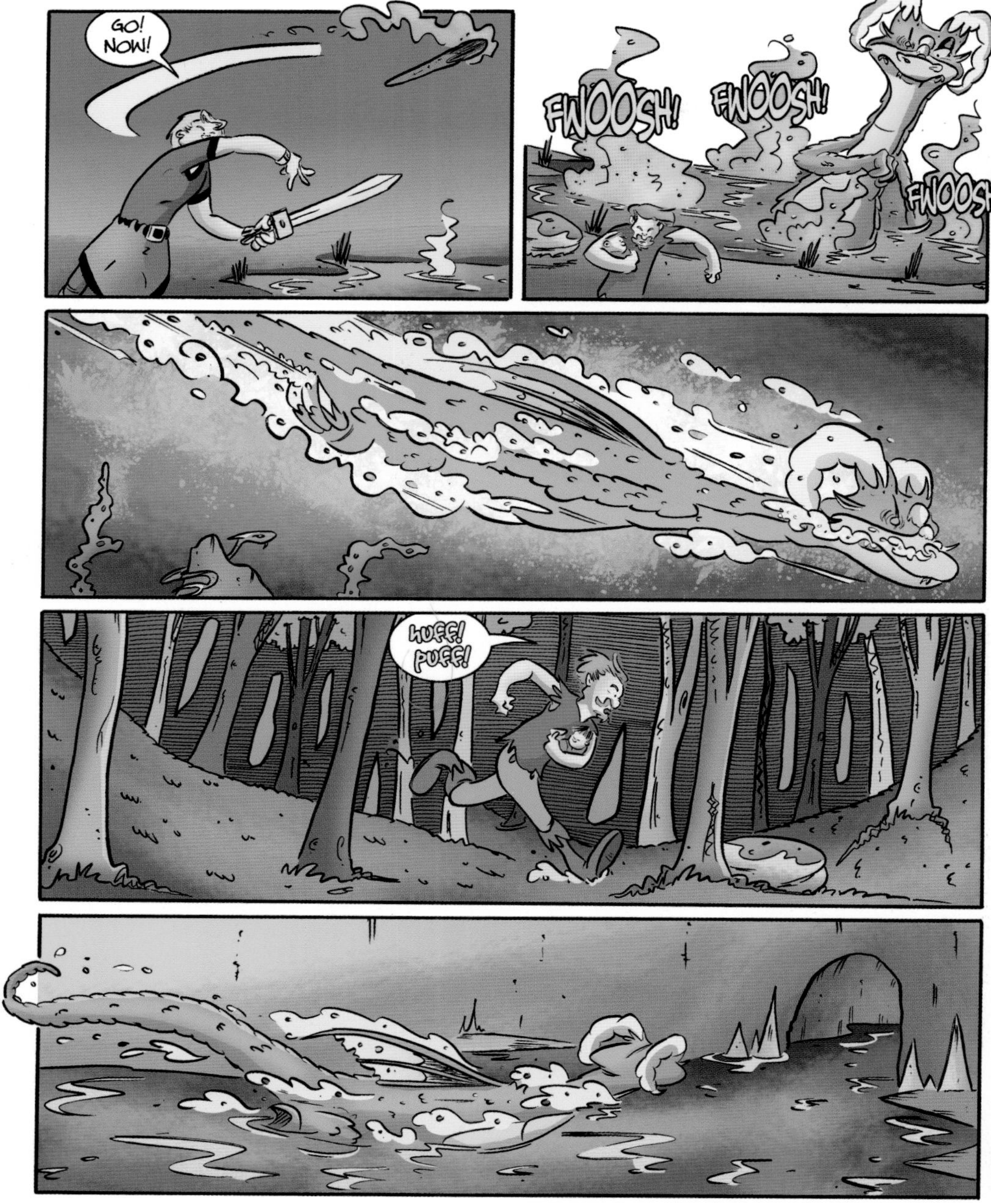
GO! NOW!
FWOOSH!
FWOOSH!
FWOOSH!
HUFF! PUFF!

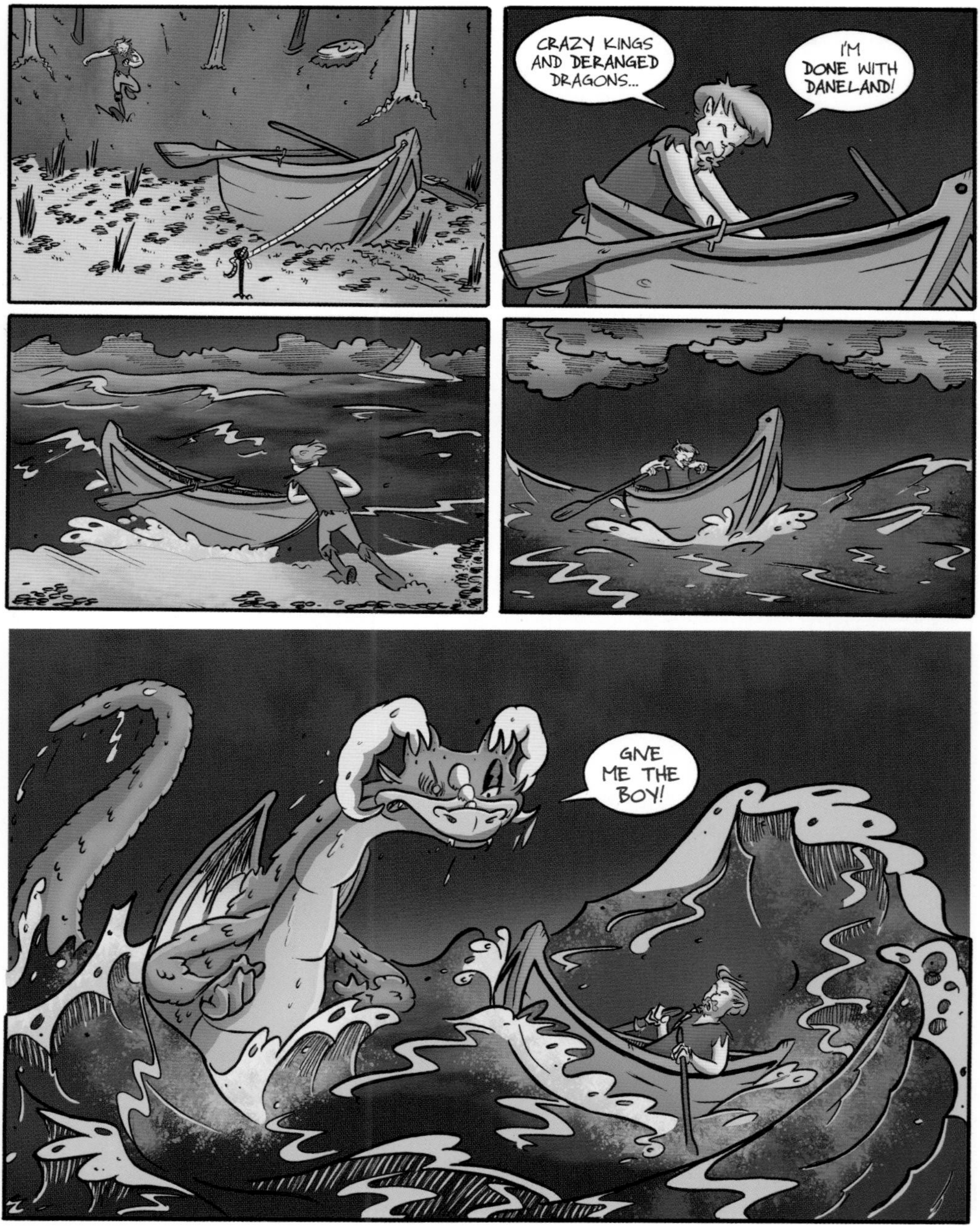
CRAZY KINGS AND DERANGED DRAGONS...
I'M DONE WITH DANELAND!
GIVE ME THE BOY!

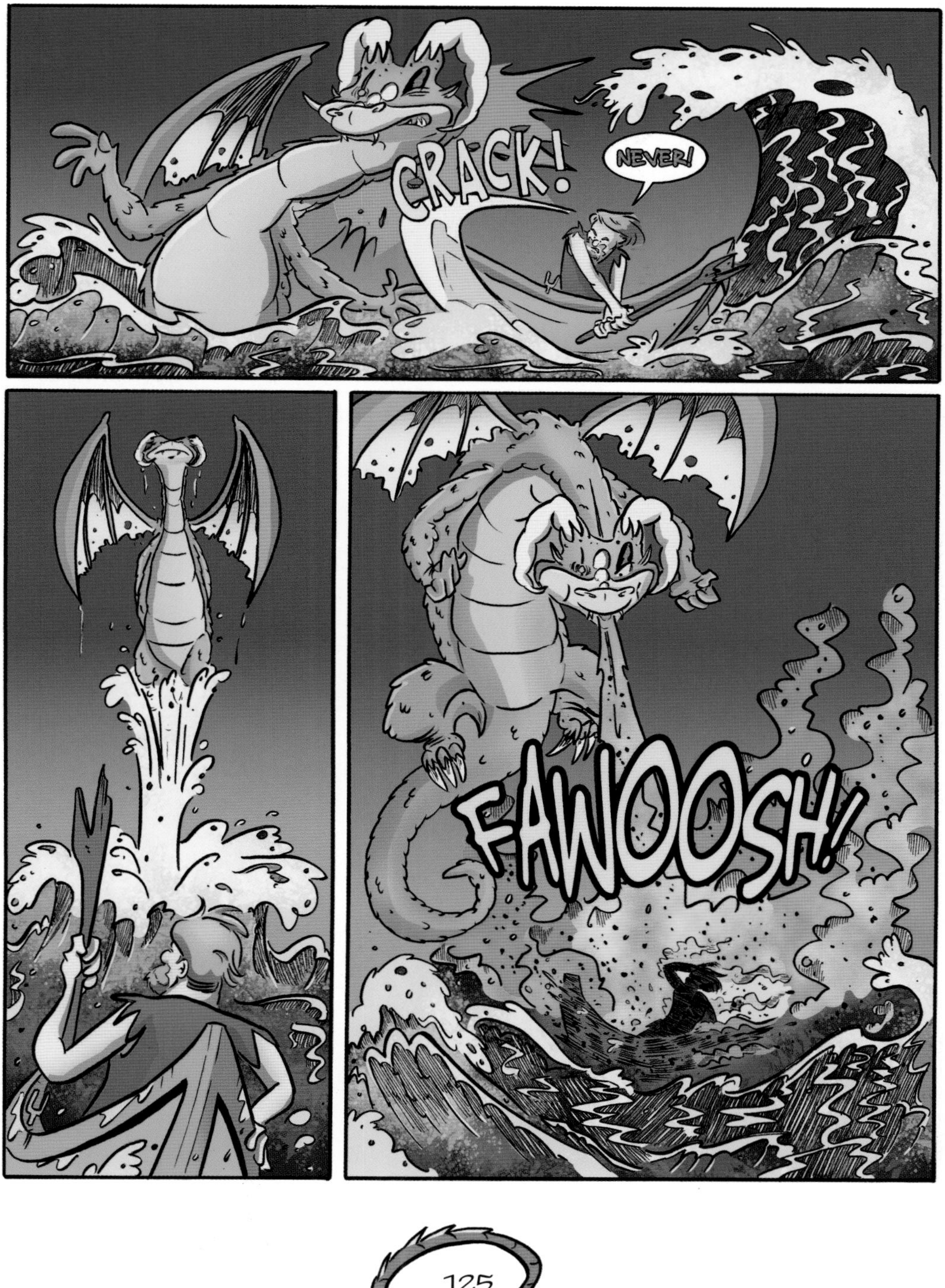
CRACK!
NEVER!
FAWOOSH!

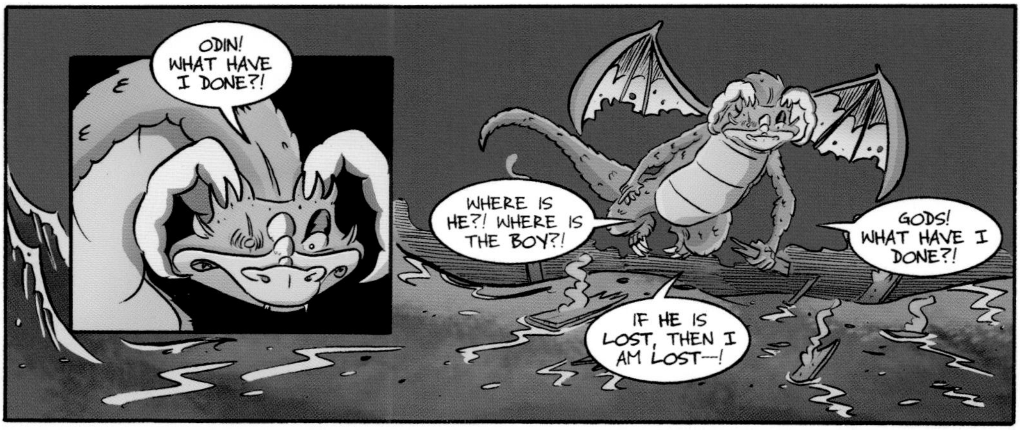
ODIN! WHAT HAVE I DONE?!
WHERE IS HE?! WHERE IS THE BOY?!
GODS! WHAT HAVE I DONE?!
IF HE IS LOST, THEN I AM LOST--!

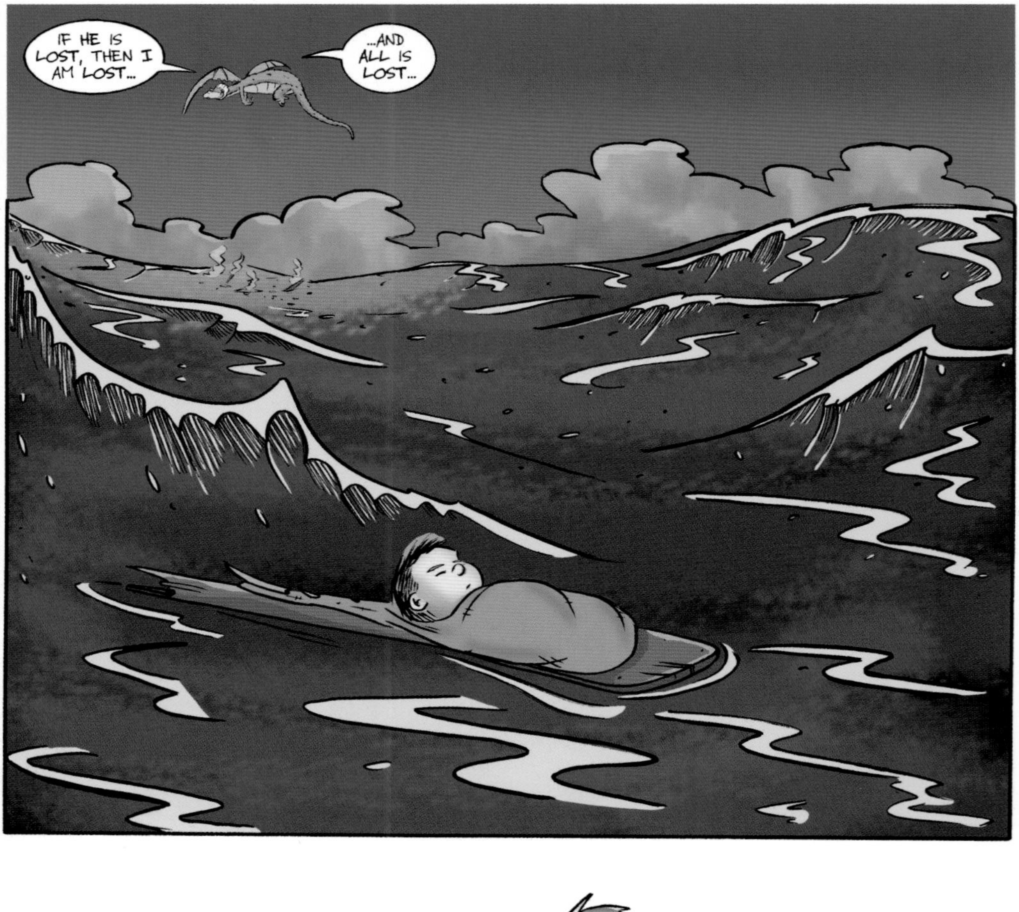
IF HE IS LOST, THEN I AM LOST...
...AND ALL IS LOST...

part three

the future

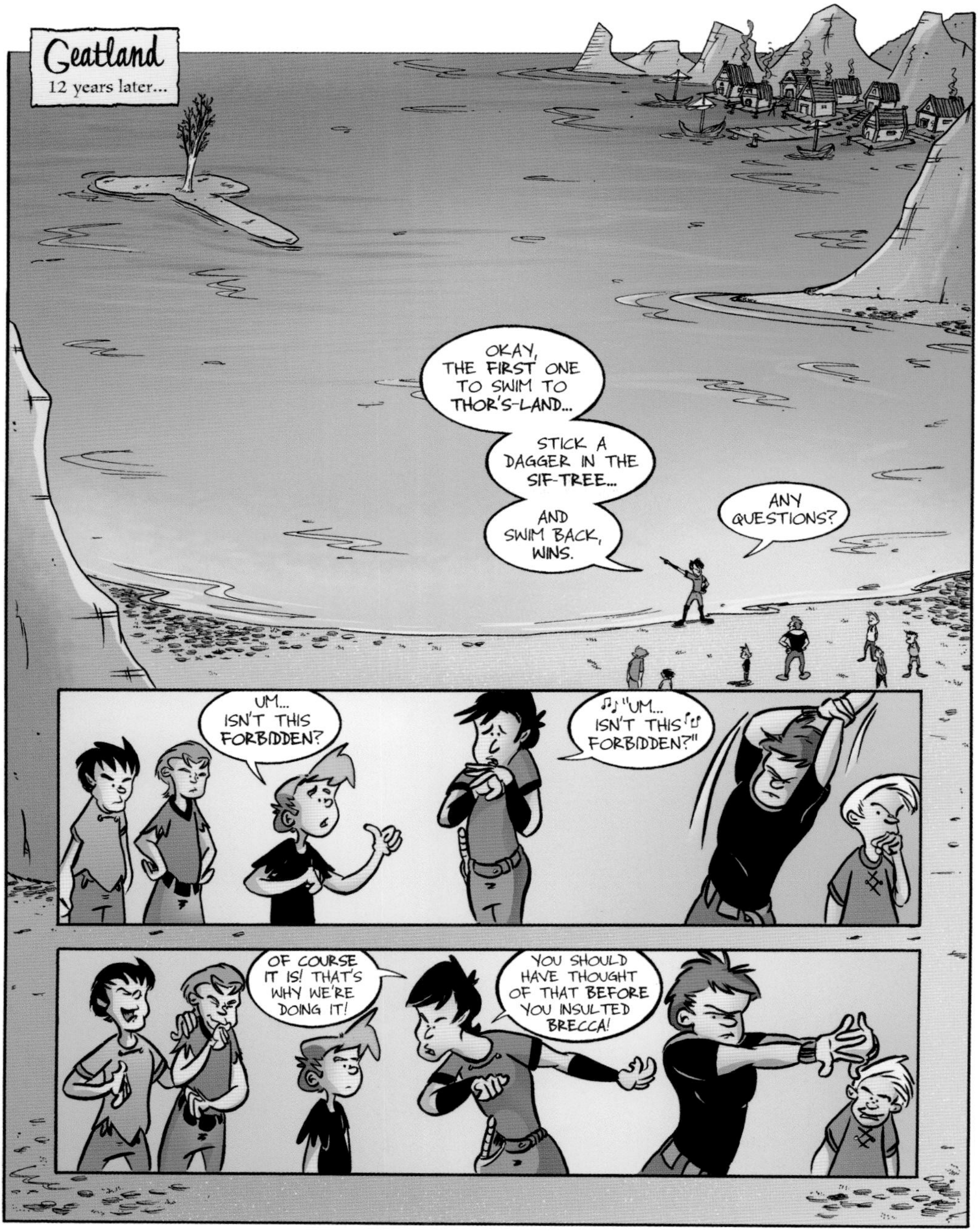
Geatland
12 years later...
OKAY, THE FIRST ONE TO SWIM TO THOR'S-LAND...
STICK A DAGGER IN THE SIF-TREE...
AND SWIM BACK, WINS.
ANY QUESTIONS?
UM... ISN'T THIS FORBIDDEN?
♫♪ "UM... ISN'T THIS ♪♫ FORBIDDEN?"
OF COURSE IT IS! THAT'S WHY WE'RE DOING IT!
YOU SHOULD HAVE THOUGHT OF THAT BEFORE YOU INSULTED BRECCA!

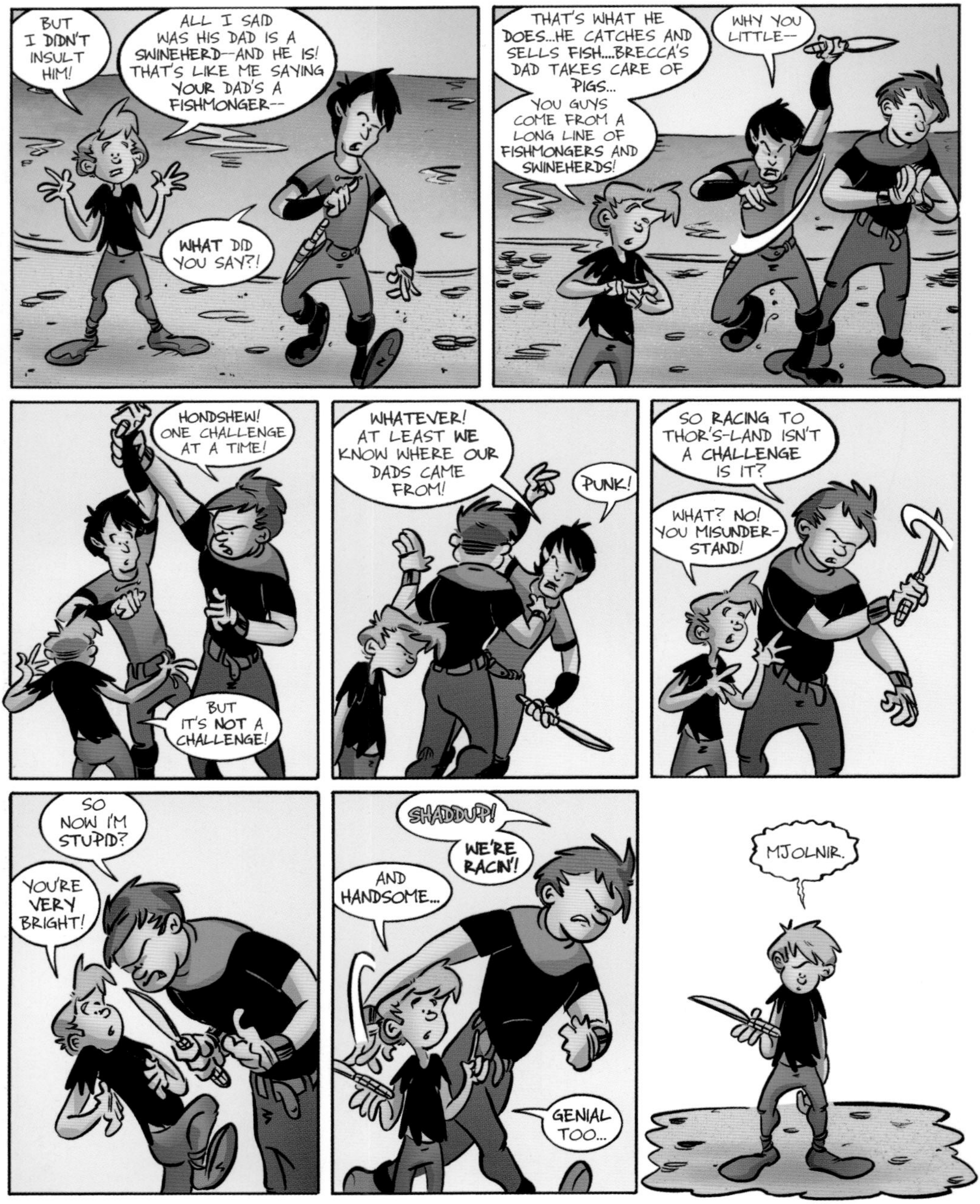
BUT I DIDN'T INSULT HIM!
ALL I SAID WAS HIS DAD IS A SWINEHERD--AND HE IS! THAT'S LIKE ME SAYING YOUR DAD'S A FISHMONGER--
WHAT DID YOU SAY?!
THAT'S WHAT HE DOES...HE CATCHES AND SELLS FISH....BRECCA'S DAD TAKES CARE OF PIGS...
YOU GUYS COME FROM A LONG LINE OF FISHMONGERS AND SWINEHERDS!
WHY YOU LITTLE--
HONDSHEW! ONE CHALLENGE AT A TIME!
BUT IT'S NOT A CHALLENGE!
WHATEVER! AT LEAST WE KNOW WHERE OUR DADS CAME FROM!
PUNK!
SO RACING TO THOR'S-LAND ISN'T A CHALLENGE IS IT?
WHAT? NO! YOU MISUNDER-STAND!
SO NOW I'M STUPID?
YOU'RE VERY BRIGHT!
SHADDUP!
WE'RE RACIN'!
AND HANDSOME...
GENIAL TOO...
MJOLNIR.

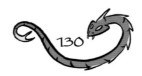

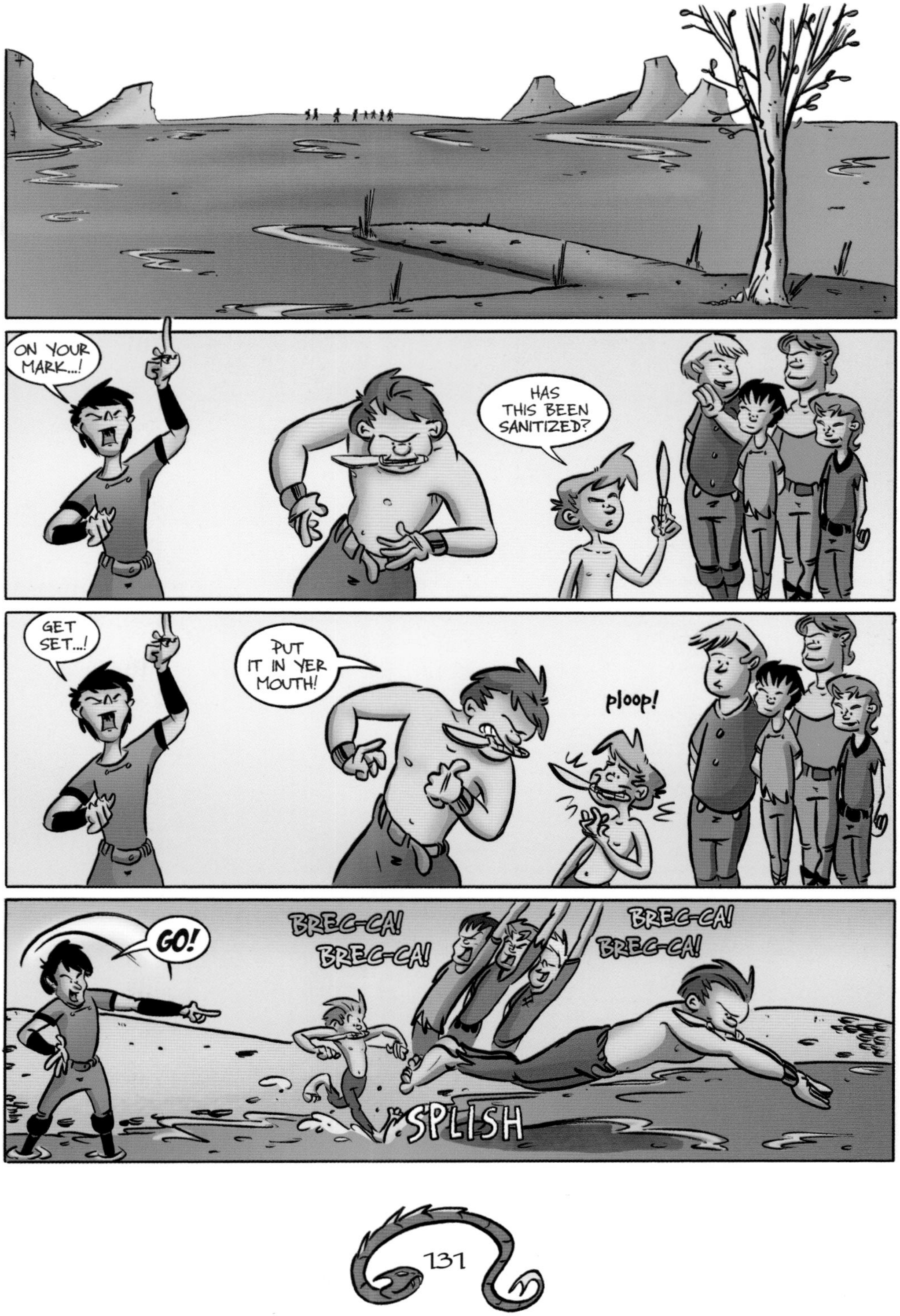
ON YOUR MARK...!
HAS THIS BEEN SANITIZED?
GET SET...!
PUT IT IN YER MOUTH!
ploop!
GO!
BREC-CA!
BREC-CA!
BREC-CA!
BREC-CA!
SPLISH

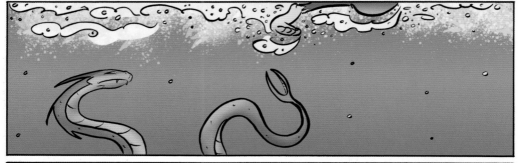

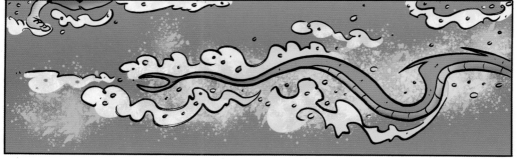

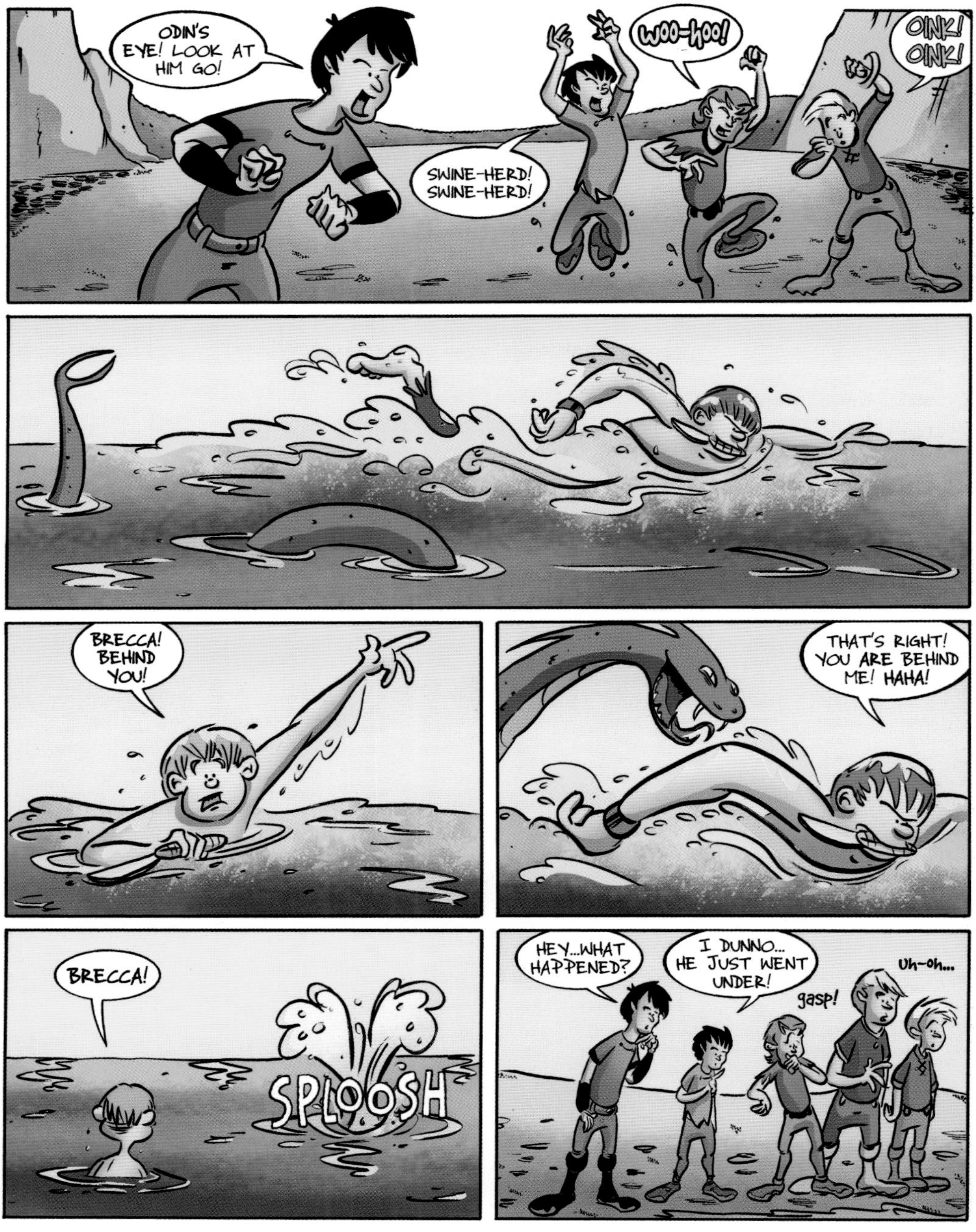
ODIN'S EYE! LOOK AT HIM GO!
SWINE-HERD! SWINE-HERD!
WOO-HOO!
OINK! OINK!
BRECCA! BEHIND YOU!
THAT'S RIGHT! YOU ARE BEHIND ME! HAHA!
BRECCA!
SPLOOSH
HEY...WHAT HAPPENED?
I DUNNO... HE JUST WENT UNDER!
gasp!
Uh-oh...

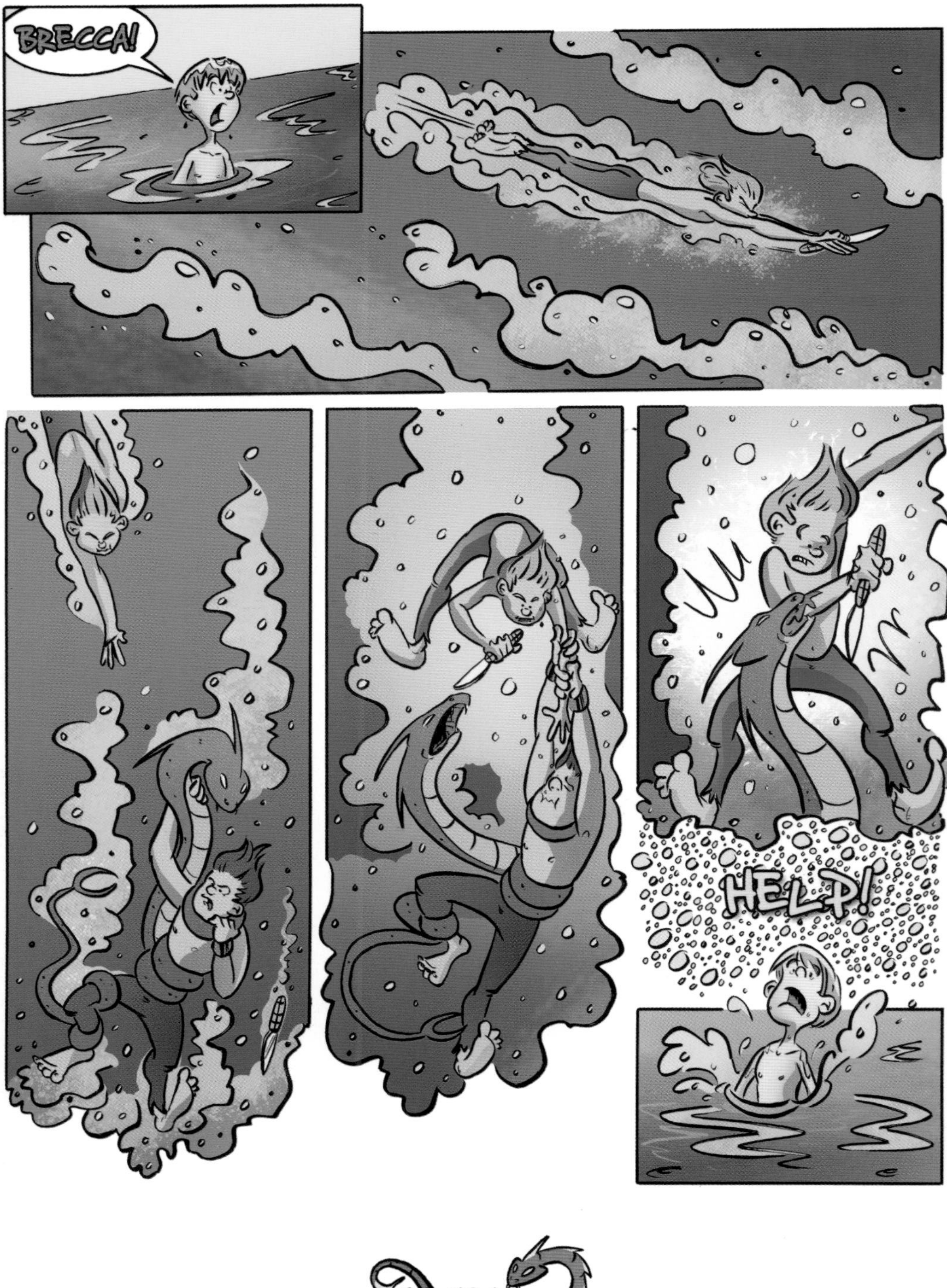
BRECCA!
HELP!

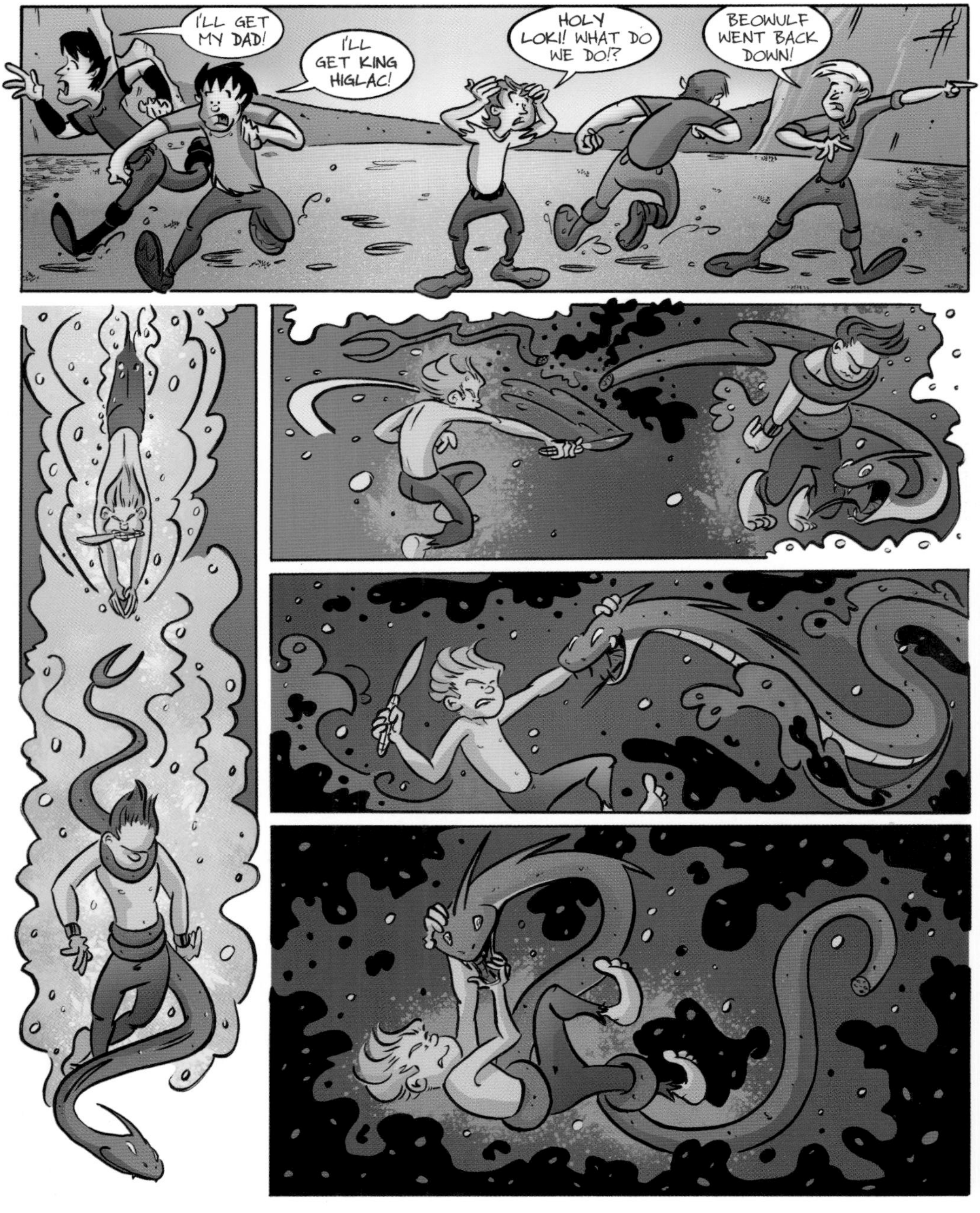
I'LL GET MY DAD!
I'LL GET KING HIGLAC!
HOLY LOKI! WHAT DO WE DO!?
BEOWULF WENT BACK DOWN!

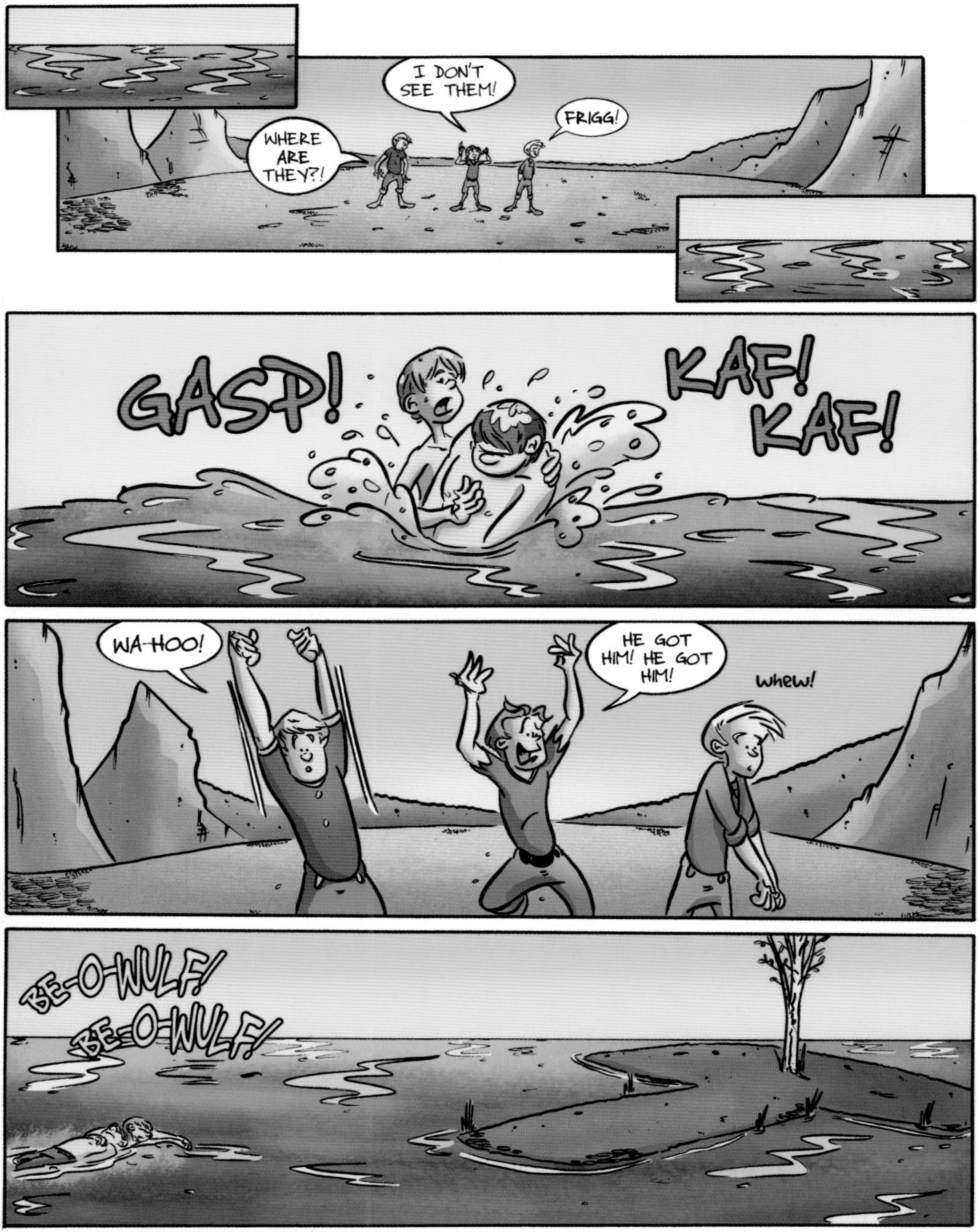
WHERE ARE THEY?!
I DON'T SEE THEM!
FRIGG!
GASP!
KAF! KAF!
WA-HOO!
HE GOT HIM! HE GOT HIM!
whew!
BE-O-WULF!
BE-O-WULF!

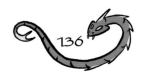

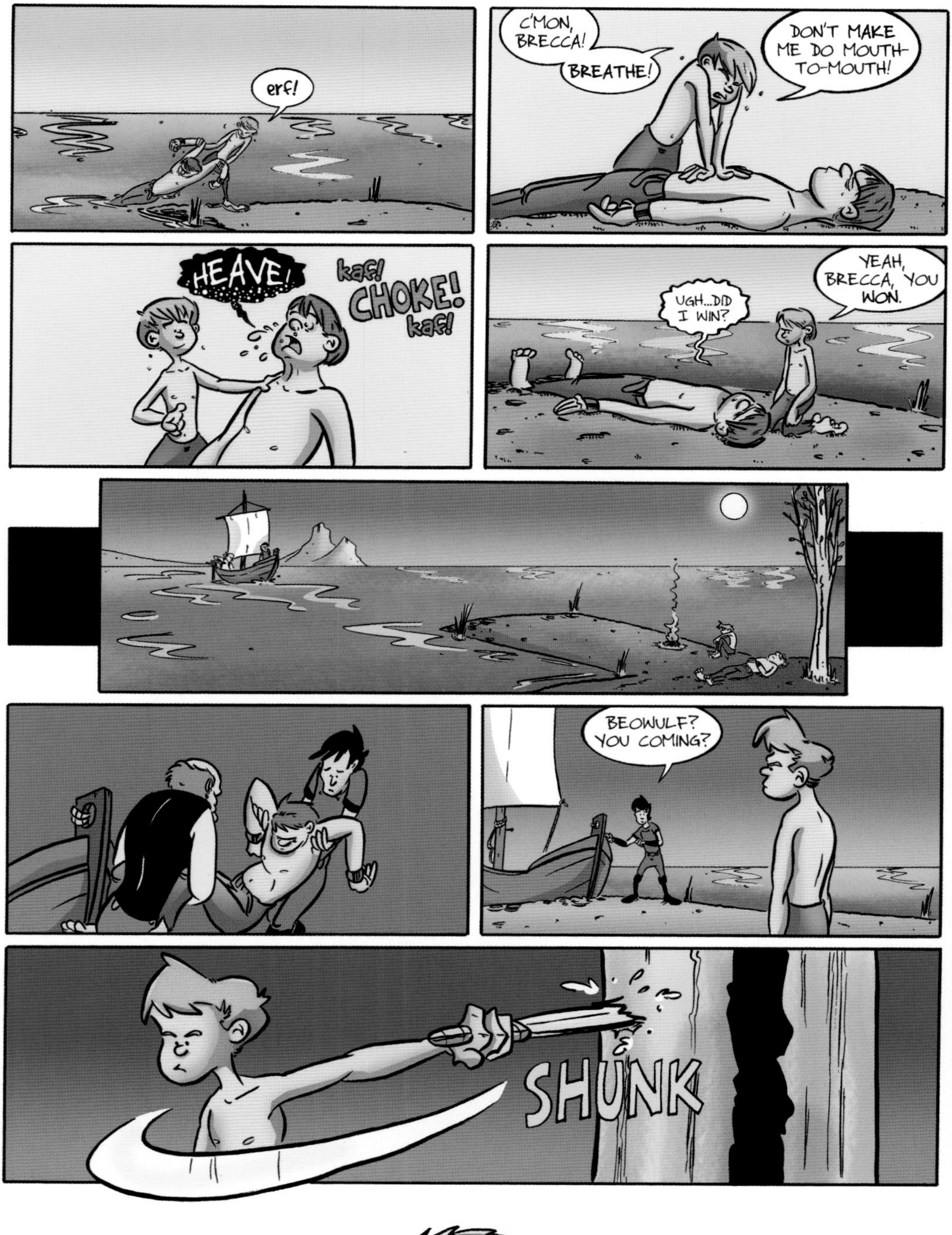
erf!
C'MON, BRECCA!
BREATHE!
DON'T MAKE ME DO MOUTH-TO-MOUTH!
HEAVE!
kaf!
CHOKE!
kaf!
UGH...DID I WIN?
YEAH, BRECCA, YOU WON.
BEOWULF? YOU COMING?
SHUNK

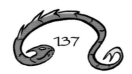

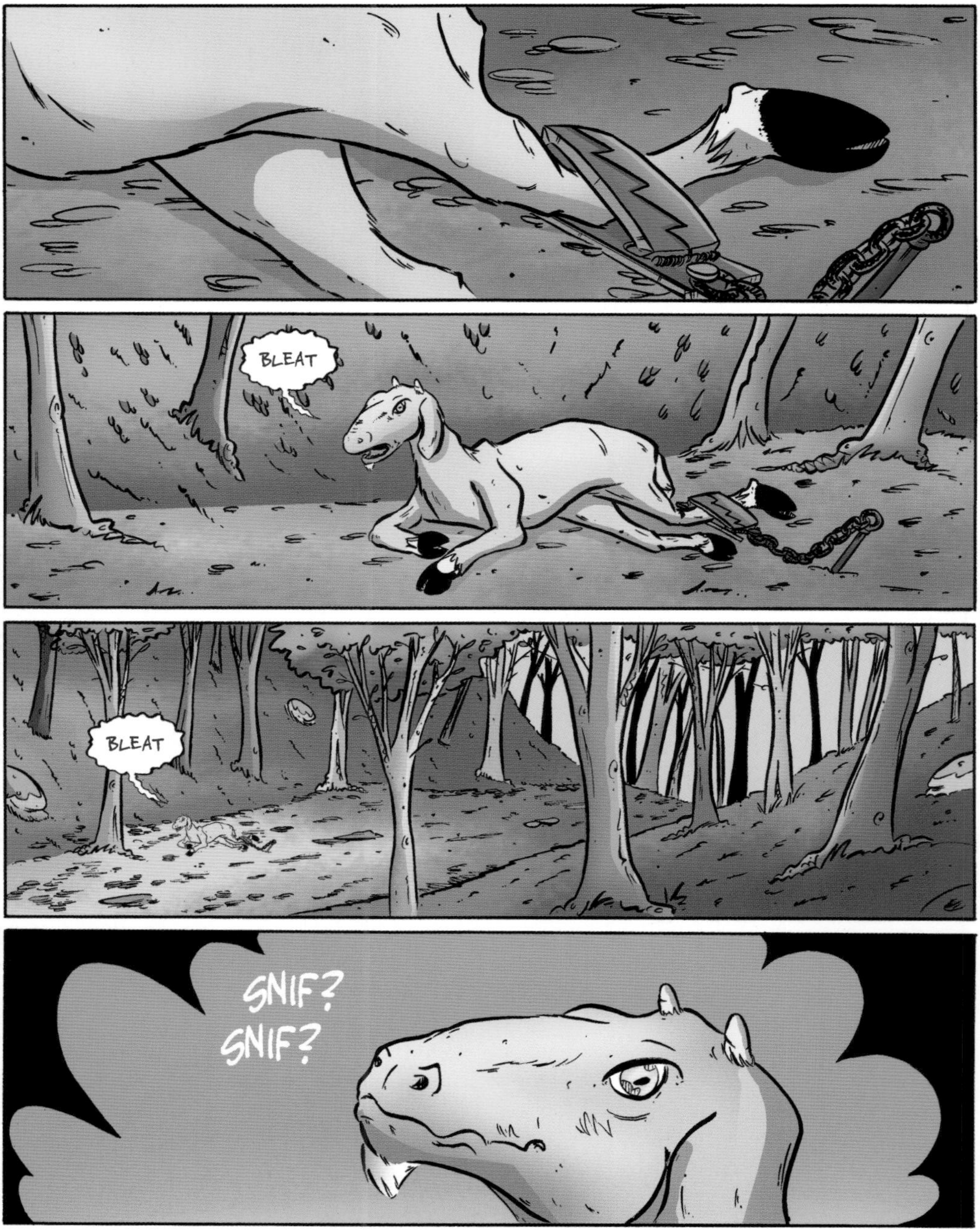
BLEAT
BLEAT
SNIF?
SNIF?

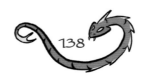

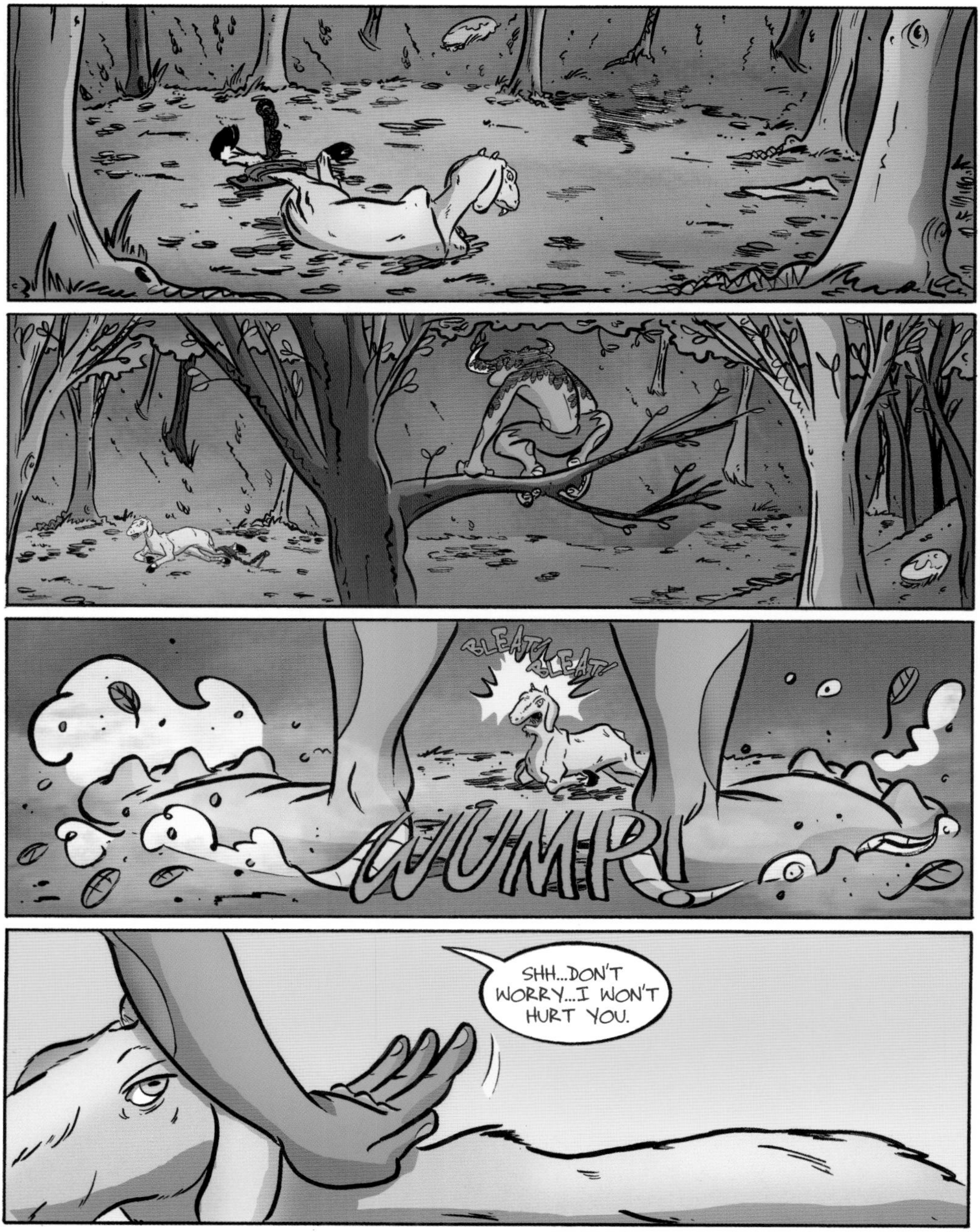
BLEAT! BLEAT!
WUMP!
SHH...DON'T WORRY...I WON'T HURT YOU.

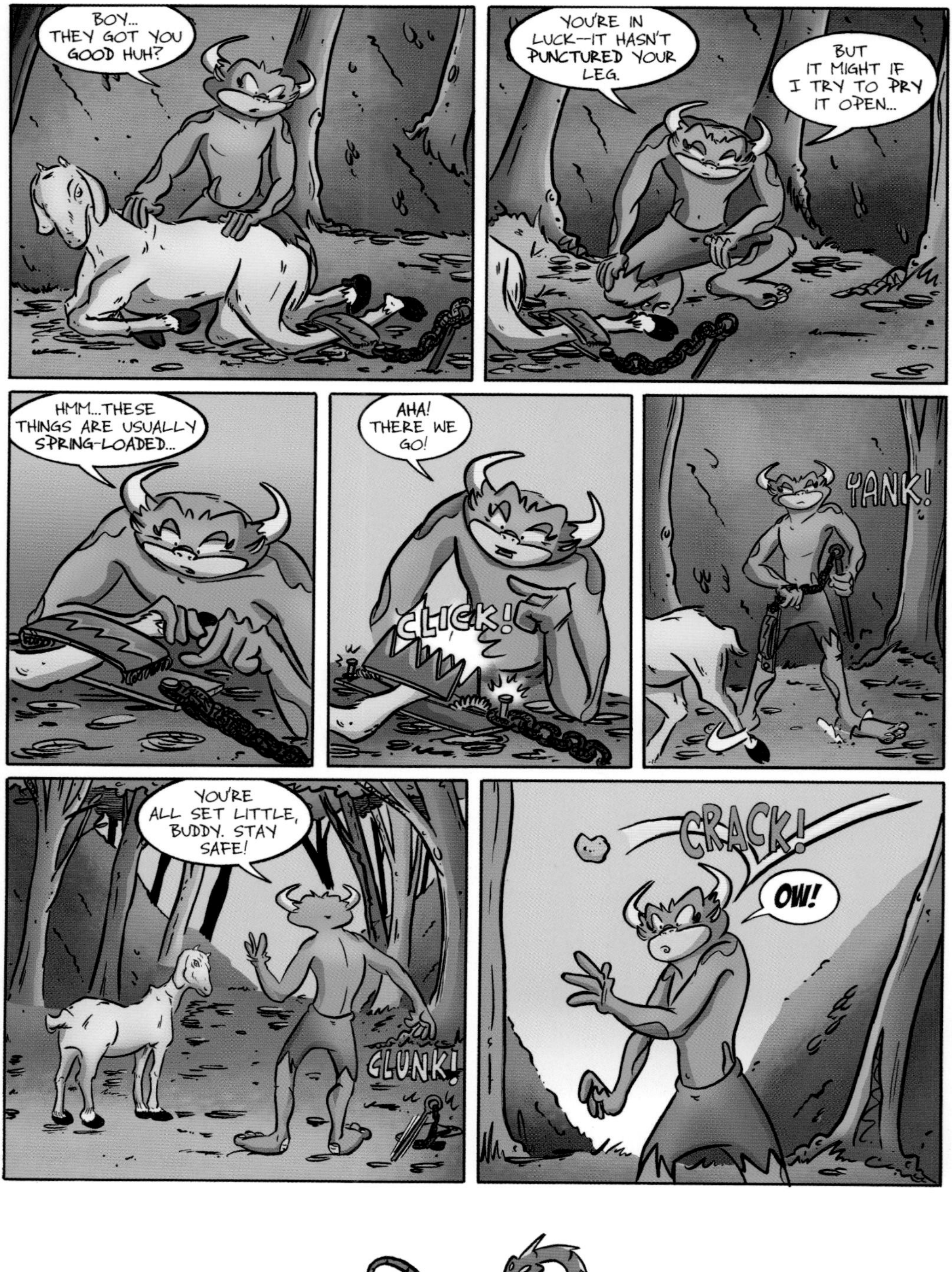
BOY... THEY GOT YOU GOOD HUH?
YOU'RE IN LUCK--IT HASN'T PUNCTURED YOUR LEG.
BUT IT MIGHT IF I TRY TO PRY IT OPEN...
HMM...THESE THINGS ARE USUALLY SPRING-LOADED...
AHA! THERE WE GO!
CLICK!
YANK!
YOU'RE ALL SET LITTLE, BUDDY. STAY SAFE!
CLUNK!
CRACK!
OW!

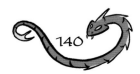

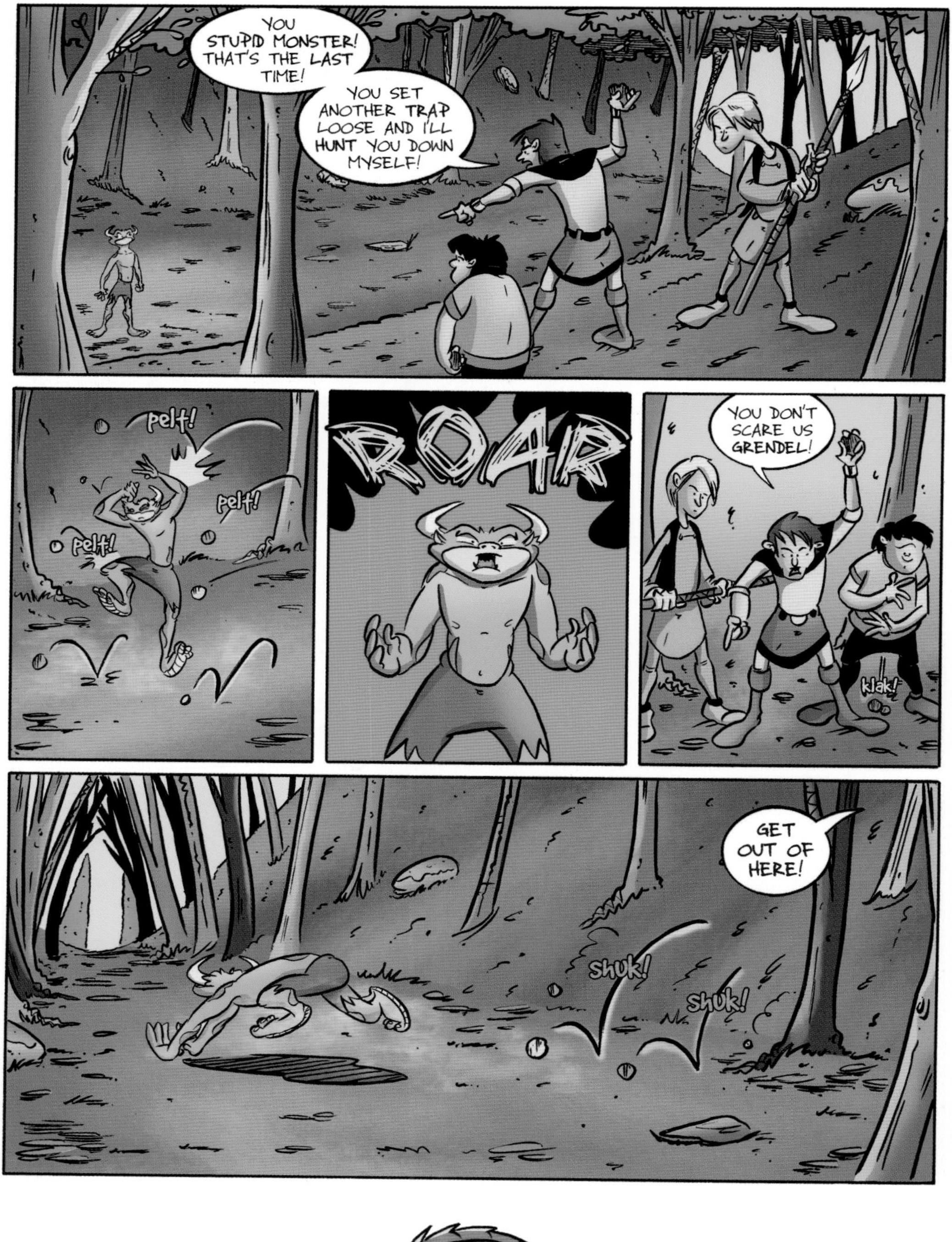

YOU STUPID MONSTER! THAT'S THE LAST TIME!
YOU SET ANOTHER TRAP LOOSE AND I'LL HUNT YOU DOWN MYSELF!
pelt!
pelt!
pelt!
ROAR
YOU DON'T SCARE US GRENDEL!
klak!
GET OUT OF HERE!
SHUK!
SHUK!

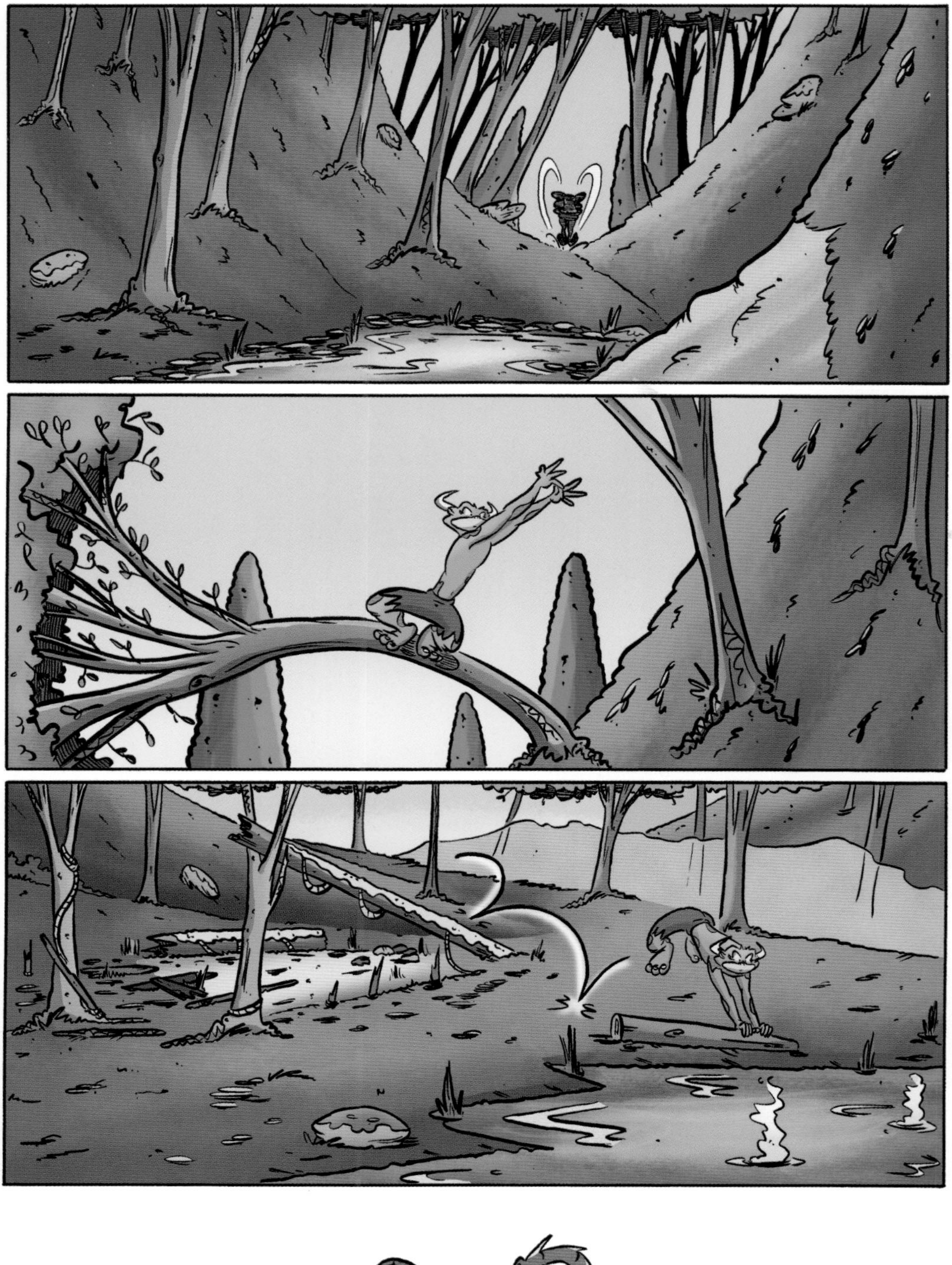

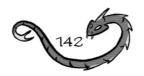

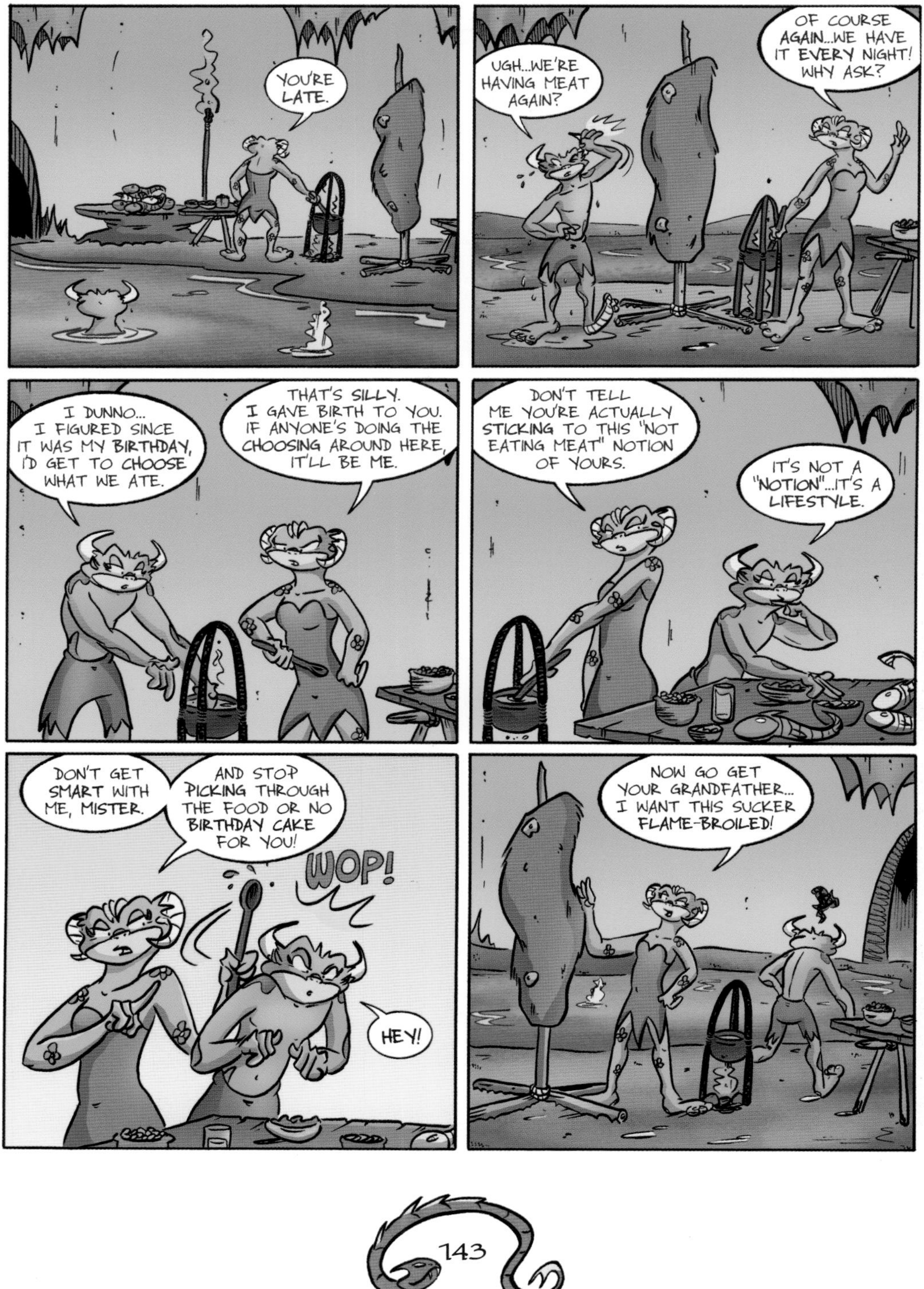
YOU'RE LATE.
UGH...WE'RE HAVING MEAT AGAIN?
OF COURSE AGAIN...WE HAVE IT EVERY NIGHT! WHY ASK?
I DUNNO... I FIGURED SINCE IT WAS MY BIRTHDAY, I'D GET TO CHOOSE WHAT WE ATE.
THAT'S SILLY. I GAVE BIRTH TO YOU. IF ANYONE'S DOING THE CHOOSING AROUND HERE, IT'LL BE ME.
DON'T TELL ME YOU'RE ACTUALLY STICKING TO THIS "NOT EATING MEAT" NOTION OF YOURS.
IT'S NOT A "NOTION"...IT'S A LIFESTYLE.
DON'T GET SMART WITH ME, MISTER.
AND STOP PICKING THROUGH THE FOOD OR NO BIRTHDAY CAKE FOR YOU!
WOP!
HEY!
NOW GO GET YOUR GRANDFATHER... I WANT THIS SUCKER FLAME-BROILED!

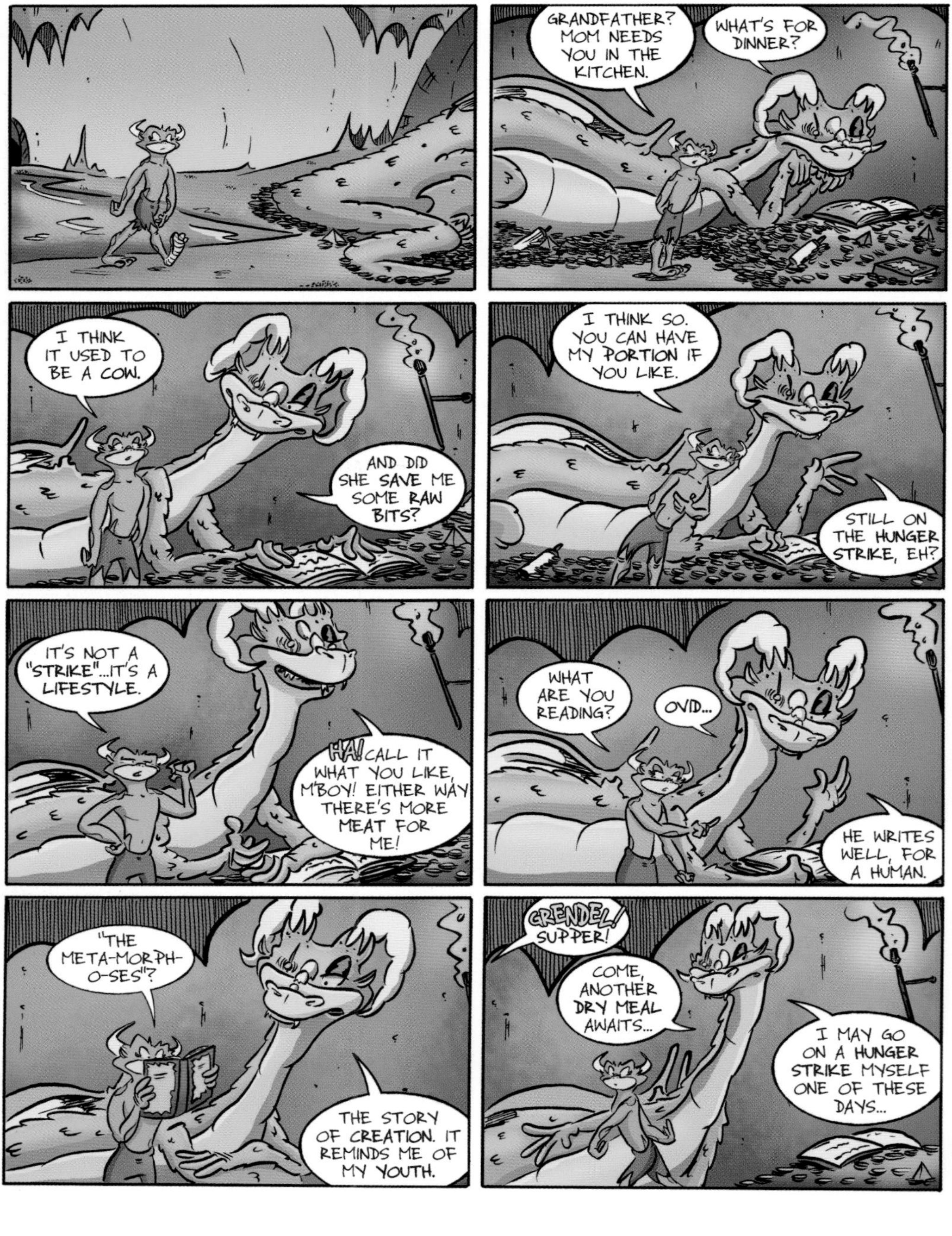
GRANDFATHER? MOM NEEDS YOU IN THE KITCHEN.
WHAT'S FOR DINNER?
I THINK IT USED TO BE A COW.
AND DID SHE SAVE ME SOME RAW BITS?
I THINK SO. YOU CAN HAVE MY PORTION IF YOU LIKE.
STILL ON THE HUNGER STRIKE, EH?
IT'S NOT A "STRIKE"...IT'S A LIFESTYLE.
HA! CALL IT WHAT YOU LIKE, M'BOY! EITHER WAY THERE'S MORE MEAT FOR ME!
WHAT ARE YOU READING?
OVID...
HE WRITES WELL, FOR A HUMAN.
"THE META-MORPH-O-SES"?
THE STORY OF CREATION. IT REMINDS ME OF MY YOUTH.
GRENDEL! SUPPER!
COME, ANOTHER DRY MEAL AWAITS...
I MAY GO ON A HUNGER STRIKE MYSELF ONE OF THESE DAYS...

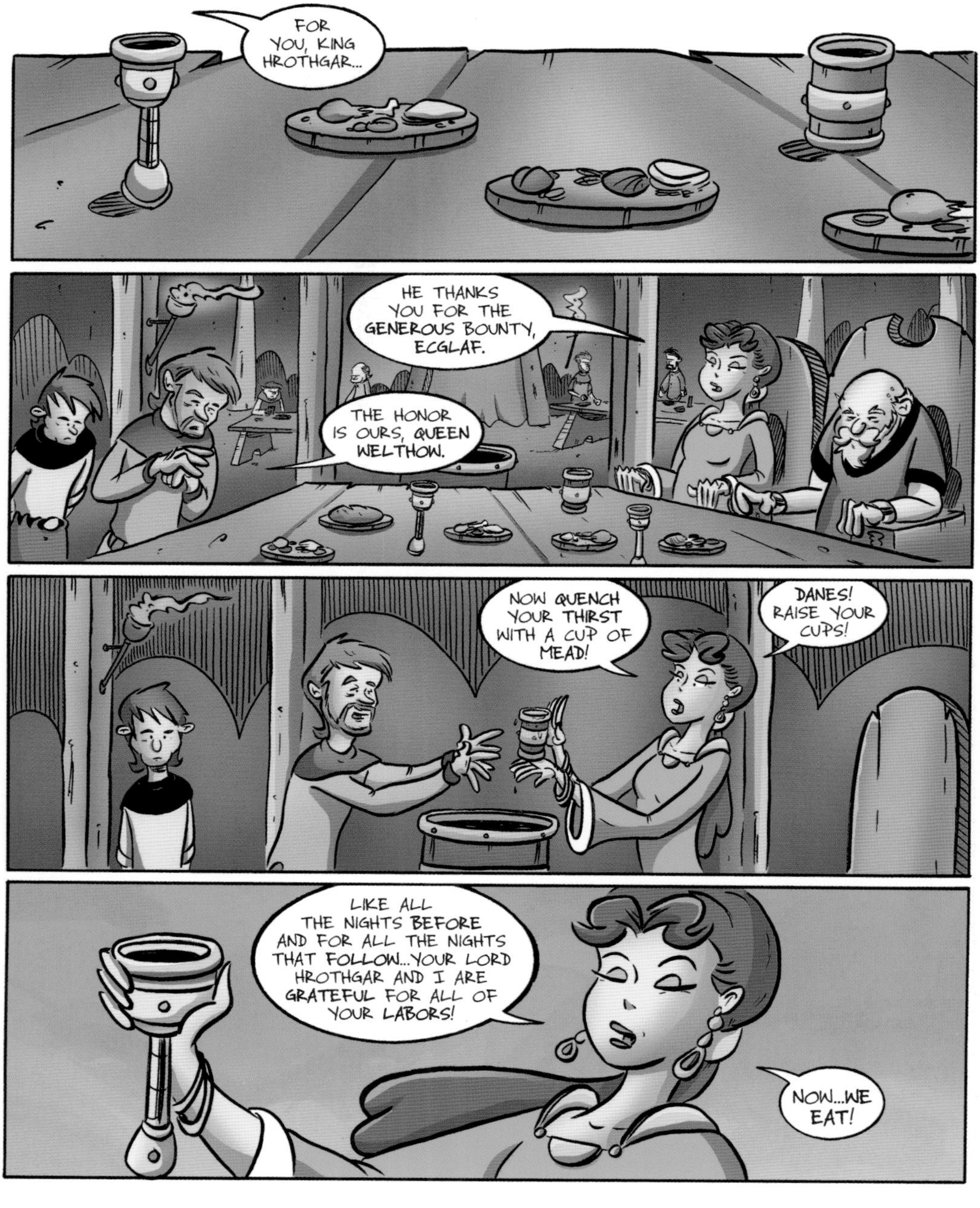
FOR YOU, KING HROTHGAR...
HE THANKS YOU FOR THE GENEROUS BOUNTY, ECGLAF.
THE HONOR IS OURS, QUEEN WELTHOW.
NOW QUENCH YOUR THIRST WITH A CUP OF MEAD!
DANES! RAISE YOUR CUPS!
LIKE ALL THE NIGHTS BEFORE AND FOR ALL THE NIGHTS THAT FOLLOW...YOUR LORD HROTHGAR AND I ARE GRATEFUL FOR ALL OF YOUR LABORS!
NOW...WE EAT!

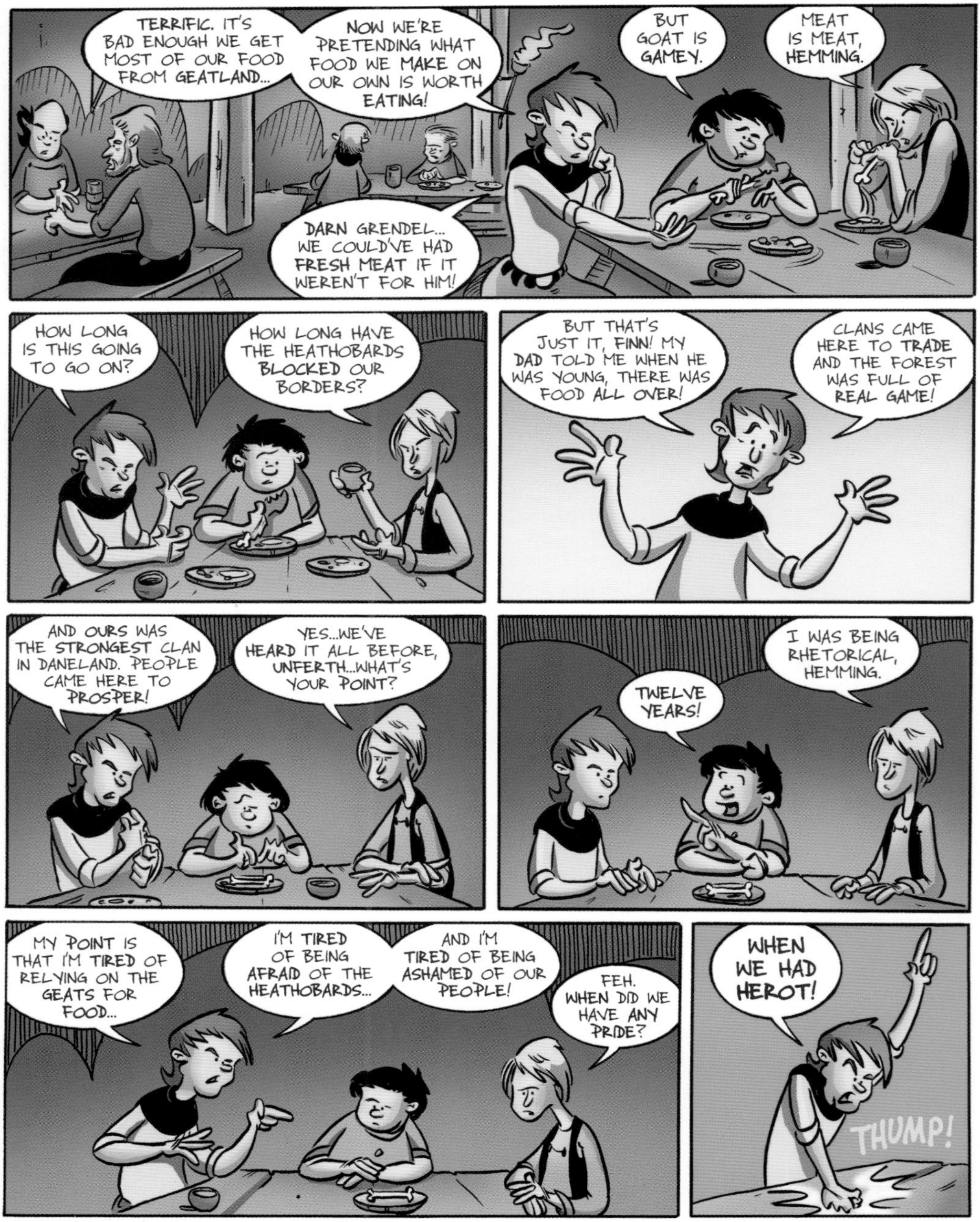
TERRIFIC. IT'S BAD ENOUGH WE GET MOST OF OUR FOOD FROM GEATLAND...
NOW WE'RE PRETENDING WHAT FOOD WE MAKE ON OUR OWN IS WORTH EATING!
DARN GRENDEL... WE COULD'VE HAD FRESH MEAT IF IT WEREN'T FOR HIM!
BUT GOAT IS GAMEY.
MEAT IS MEAT, HEMMING.
HOW LONG IS THIS GOING TO GO ON?
HOW LONG HAVE THE HEATHOBARDS BLOCKED OUR BORDERS?
BUT THAT'S JUST IT, FINN! MY DAD TOLD ME WHEN HE WAS YOUNG, THERE WAS FOOD ALL OVER!
CLANS CAME HERE TO TRADE AND THE FOREST WAS FULL OF REAL GAME!
AND OURS WAS THE STRONGEST CLAN IN DANELAND. PEOPLE CAME HERE TO PROSPER!
YES...WE'VE HEARD IT ALL BEFORE, UNFERTH...WHAT'S YOUR POINT?
TWELVE YEARS!
I WAS BEING RHETORICAL, HEMMING.
MY POINT IS THAT I'M TIRED OF RELYING ON THE GEATS FOR FOOD...
I'M TIRED OF BEING AFRAID OF THE HEATHOBARDS...
AND I'M TIRED OF BEING ASHAMED OF OUR PEOPLE!
FEH. WHEN DID WE HAVE ANY PRIDE?
WHEN WE HAD HEROT!
THUMP!

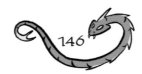

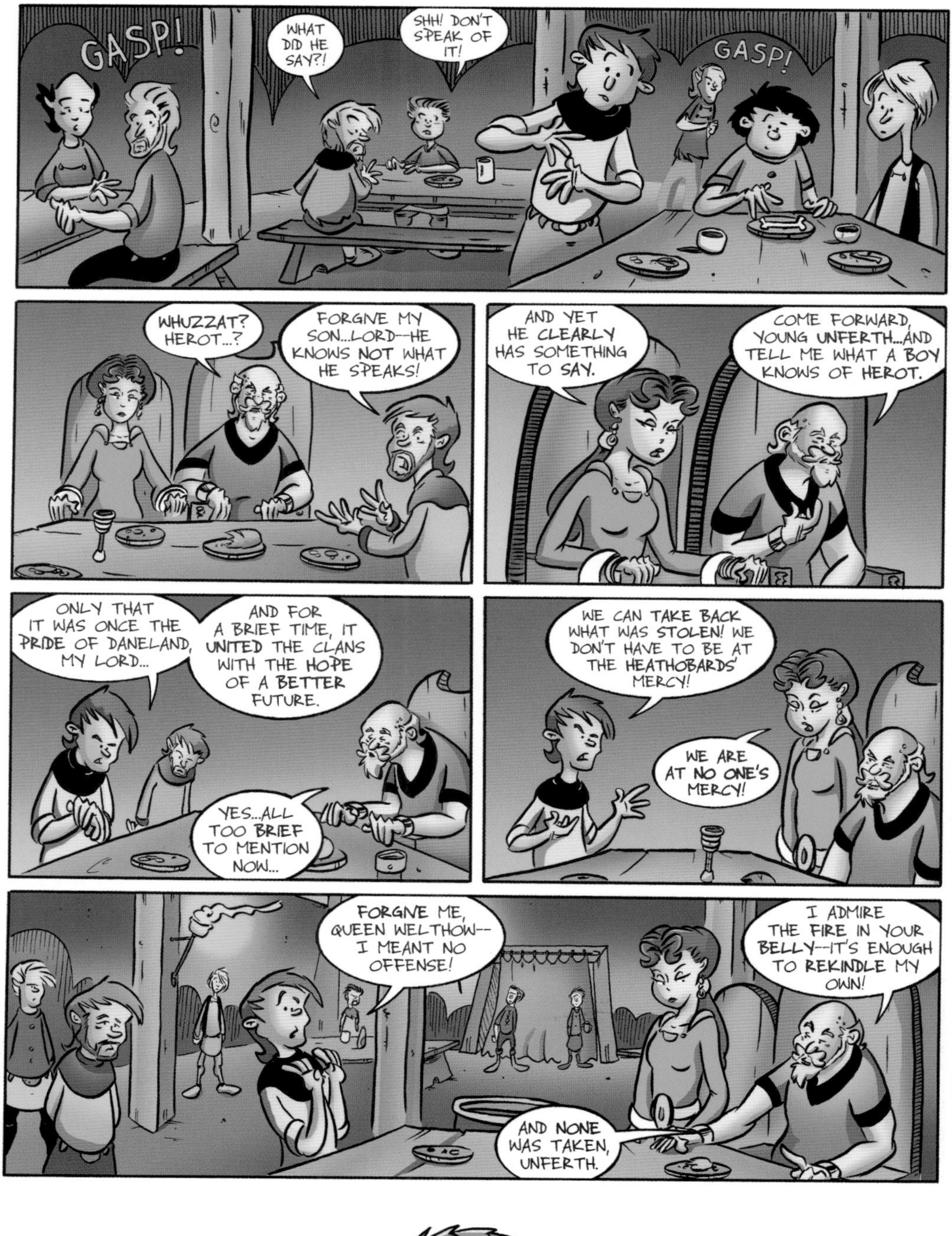
GASP!
WHAT DID HE SAY?!
SHH! DON'T SPEAK OF IT!
GASP!
WHUZZAT? HEROT...?
FORGIVE MY SON...LORD--HE KNOWS NOT WHAT HE SPEAKS!
AND YET HE CLEARLY HAS SOMETHING TO SAY.
COME FORWARD, YOUNG UNFERTH...AND TELL ME WHAT A BOY KNOWS OF HEROT.
ONLY THAT IT WAS ONCE THE PRIDE OF DANELAND, MY LORD...
AND FOR A BRIEF TIME, IT UNITED THE CLANS WITH THE HOPE OF A BETTER FUTURE.
YES...ALL TOO BRIEF TO MENTION NOW...
WE CAN TAKE BACK WHAT WAS STOLEN! WE DON'T HAVE TO BE AT THE HEATHOBARDS' MERCY!
WE ARE AT NO ONE'S MERCY!
FORGIVE ME, QUEEN WELTHOW--I MEANT NO OFFENSE!
I ADMIRE THE FIRE IN YOUR BELLY--IT'S ENOUGH TO REKINDLE MY OWN!
AND NONE WAS TAKEN, UNFERTH.

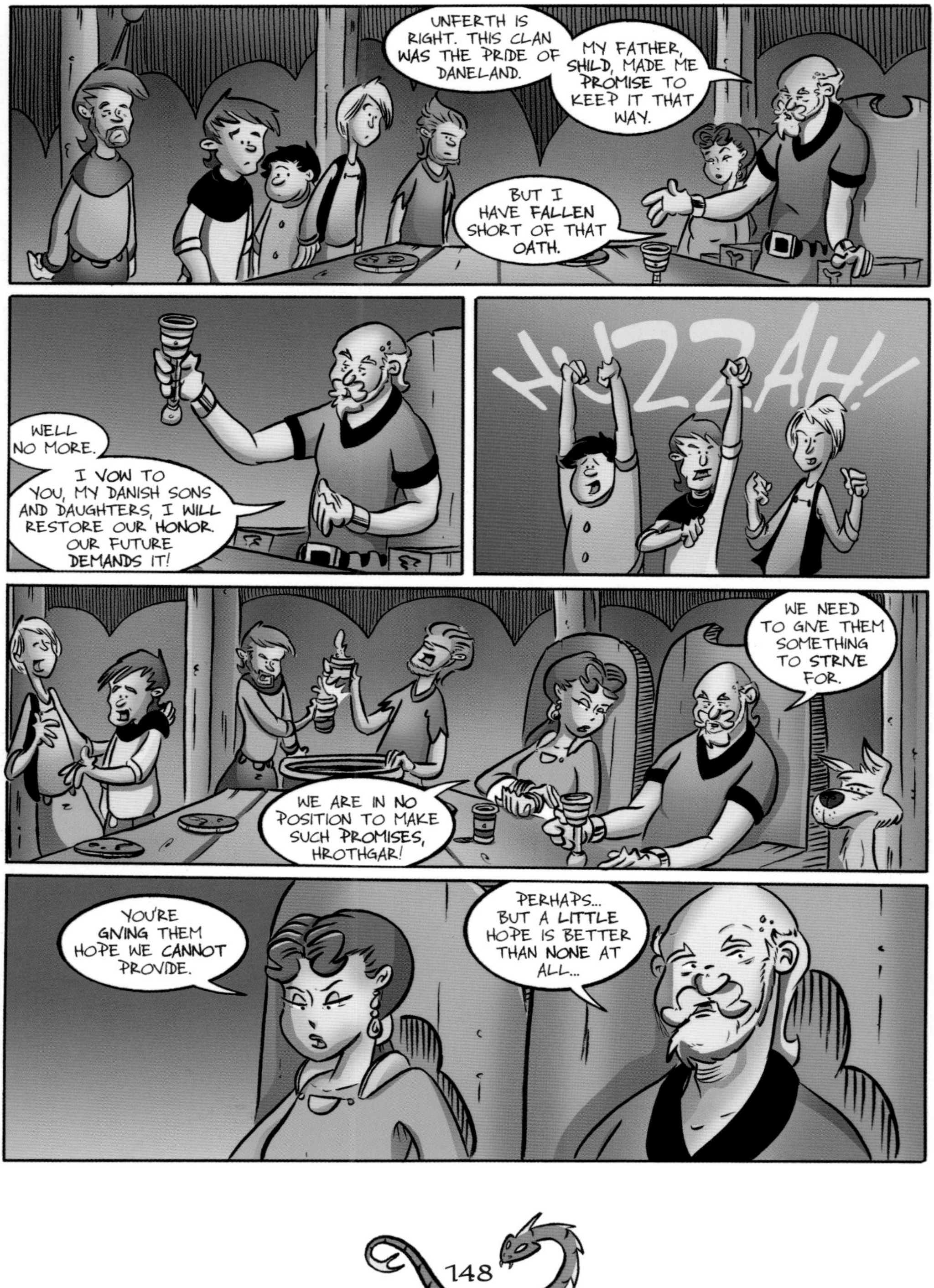
UNFERTH IS RIGHT. THIS CLAN WAS THE PRIDE OF DANELAND.
MY FATHER, SHILD, MADE ME PROMISE TO KEEP IT THAT WAY.
BUT I HAVE FALLEN SHORT OF THAT OATH.
WELL NO MORE.
I VOW TO YOU, MY DANISH SONS AND DAUGHTERS, I WILL RESTORE OUR HONOR. OUR FUTURE DEMANDS IT!
HUZZAH!
WE NEED TO GIVE THEM SOMETHING TO STRIVE FOR.
WE ARE IN NO POSITION TO MAKE SUCH PROMISES, HROTHGAR!
YOU'RE GIVING THEM HOPE WE CANNOT PROVIDE.
PERHAPS... BUT A LITTLE HOPE IS BETTER THAN NONE AT ALL...

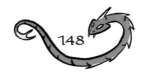

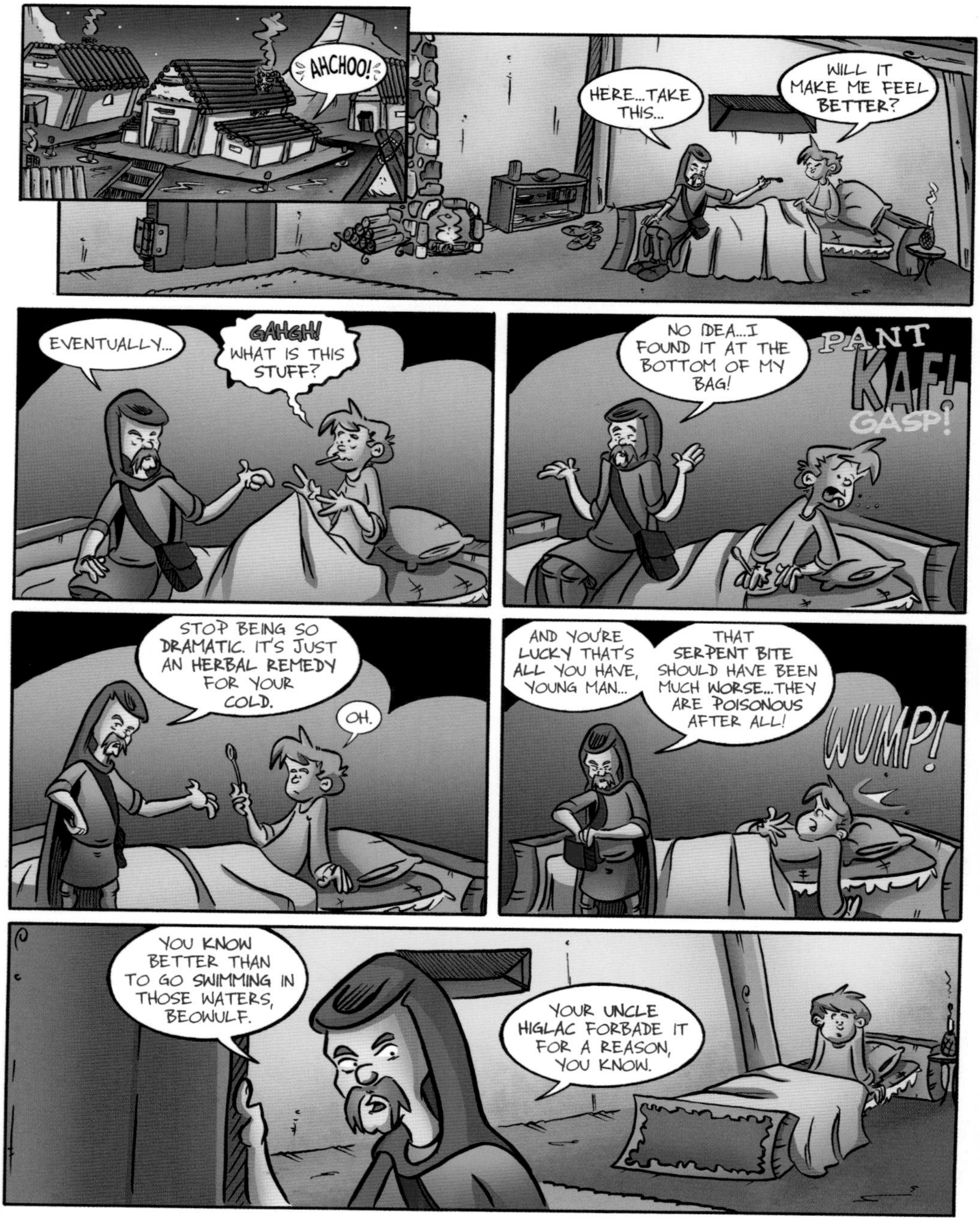
AHCHOO!
HERE...TAKE THIS...
WILL IT MAKE ME FEEL BETTER?
EVENTUALLY...
GAHGH! WHAT IS THIS STUFF?
NO IDEA...I FOUND IT AT THE BOTTOM OF MY BAG!
PANT
KAF!
GASP!
STOP BEING SO DRAMATIC. IT'S JUST AN HERBAL REMEDY FOR YOUR COLD.
OH.
AND YOU'RE LUCKY THAT'S ALL YOU HAVE, YOUNG MAN...
THAT SERPENT BITE SHOULD HAVE BEEN MUCH WORSE...THEY ARE POISONOUS AFTER ALL!
WUMP!
YOU KNOW BETTER THAN TO GO SWIMMING IN THOSE WATERS, BEOWULF.
YOUR UNCLE HIGLAC FORBADE IT FOR A REASON, YOU KNOW.

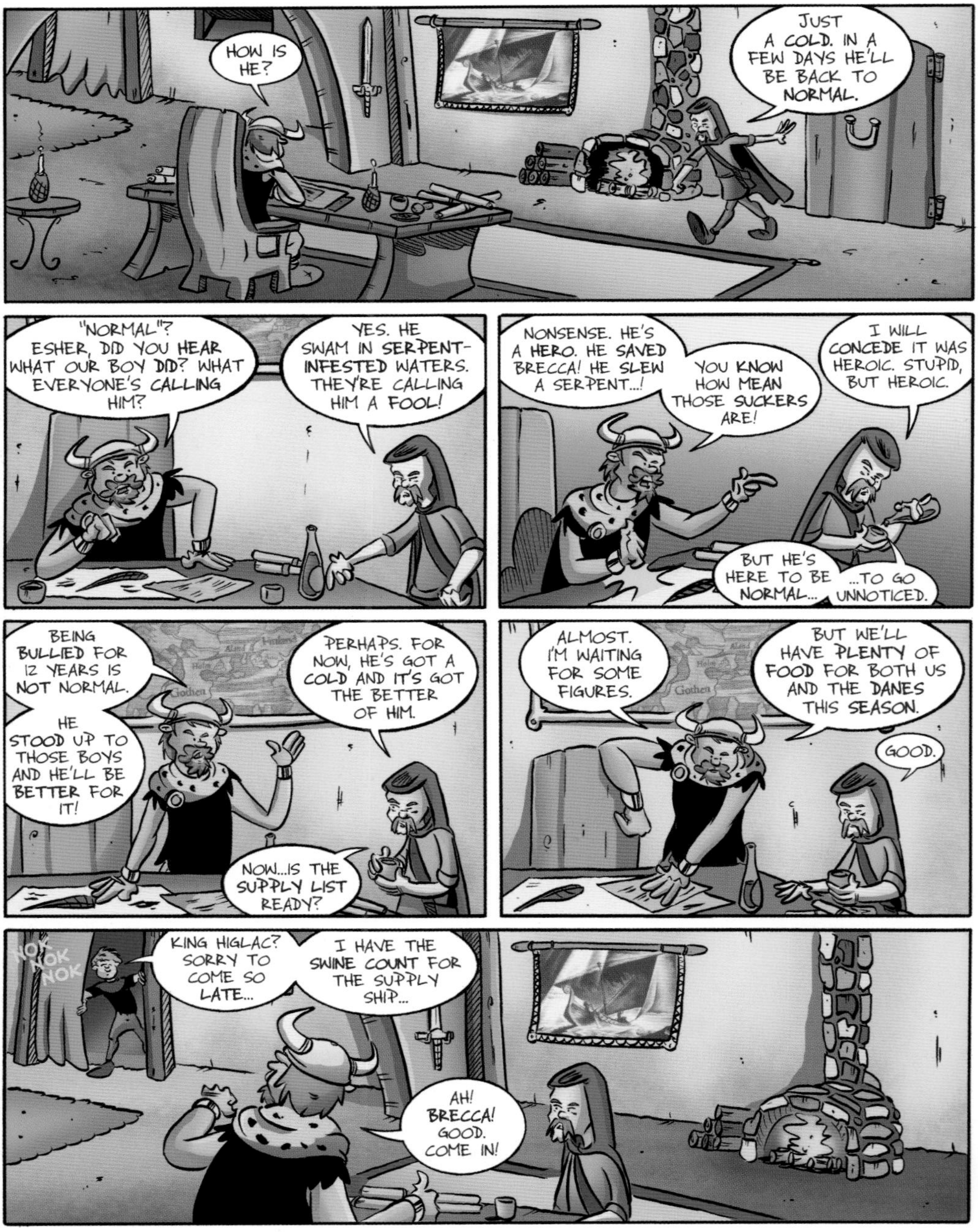
HOW IS HE?
JUST A COLD. IN A FEW DAYS HE'LL BE BACK TO NORMAL.
"NORMAL"? ESHER, DID YOU HEAR WHAT OUR BOY DID? WHAT EVERYONE'S CALLING HIM?
YES. HE SWAM IN SERPENT-INFESTED WATERS. THEY'RE CALLING HIM A FOOL!
NONSENSE. HE'S A HERO. HE SAVED BRECCA! HE SLEW A SERPENT...!
YOU KNOW HOW MEAN THOSE SUCKERS ARE!
I WILL CONCEDE IT WAS HEROIC. STUPID, BUT HEROIC.
BUT HE'S HERE TO BE NORMAL...
...TO GO UNNOTICED.
BEING BULLIED FOR 12 YEARS IS NOT NORMAL.
HE STOOD UP TO THOSE BOYS AND HE'LL BE BETTER FOR IT!
PERHAPS. FOR NOW, HE'S GOT A COLD AND IT'S GOT THE BETTER OF HIM.
NOW...IS THE SUPPLY LIST READY?
ALMOST. I'M WAITING FOR SOME FIGURES.
BUT WE'LL HAVE PLENTY OF FOOD FOR BOTH US AND THE DANES THIS SEASON.
GOOD.
NOK NOK NOK
KING HIGLAC? SORRY TO COME SO LATE...
I HAVE THE SWINE COUNT FOR THE SUPPLY SHIP...
AH! BRECCA! GOOD. COME IN!

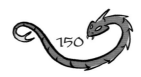

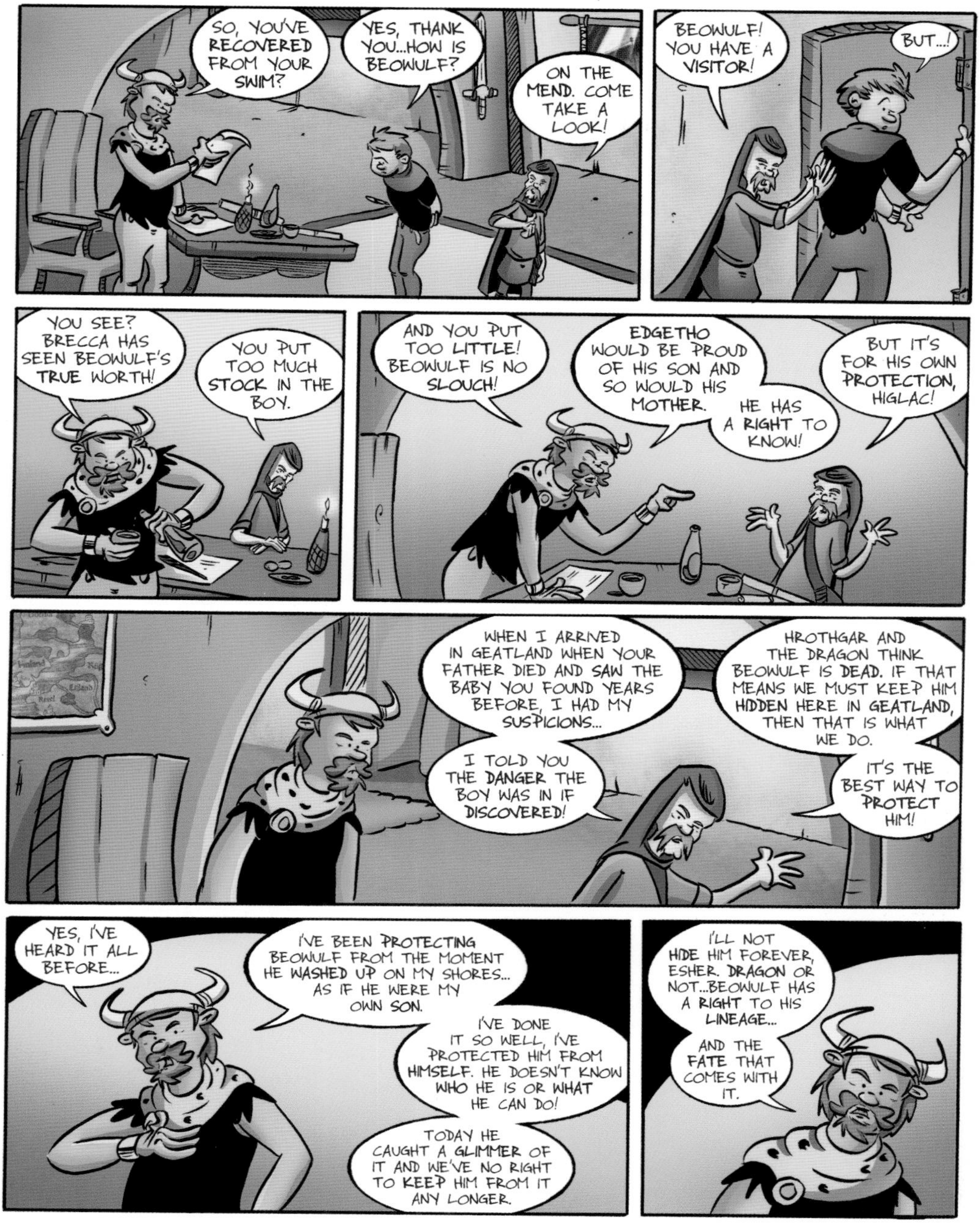
SO, YOU'VE RECOVERED FROM YOUR SWIM?
YES, THANK YOU...HOW IS BEOWULF?
ON THE MEND. COME TAKE A LOOK!
BEOWULF! YOU HAVE A VISITOR!
BUT...!
YOU SEE? BRECCA HAS SEEN BEOWULF'S TRUE WORTH!
YOU PUT TOO MUCH STOCK IN THE BOY.
AND YOU PUT TOO LITTLE! BEOWULF IS NO SLOUCH!
EDGETHO WOULD BE PROUD OF HIS SON AND SO WOULD HIS MOTHER.
HE HAS A RIGHT TO KNOW!
BUT IT'S FOR HIS OWN PROTECTION, HIGLAC!
WHEN I ARRIVED IN GEATLAND WHEN YOUR FATHER DIED AND SAW THE BABY YOU FOUND YEARS BEFORE, I HAD MY SUSPICIONS...
I TOLD YOU THE DANGER THE BOY WAS IN IF DISCOVERED!
HROTHGAR AND THE DRAGON THINK BEOWULF IS DEAD. IF THAT MEANS WE MUST KEEP HIM HIDDEN HERE IN GEATLAND, THEN THAT IS WHAT WE DO.
IT'S THE BEST WAY TO PROTECT HIM!
YES, I'VE HEARD IT ALL BEFORE...
I'VE BEEN PROTECTING BEOWULF FROM THE MOMENT HE WASHED UP ON MY SHORES... AS IF HE WERE MY OWN SON.
I'VE DONE IT SO WELL, I'VE PROTECTED HIM FROM HIMSELF. HE DOESN'T KNOW WHO HE IS OR WHAT HE CAN DO!
TODAY HE CAUGHT A GLIMMER OF IT AND WE'VE NO RIGHT TO KEEP HIM FROM IT ANY LONGER.
I'LL NOT HIDE HIM FOREVER, ESHER. DRAGON OR NOT...BEOWULF HAS A RIGHT TO HIS LINEAGE...
AND THE FATE THAT COMES WITH IT.

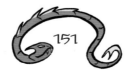

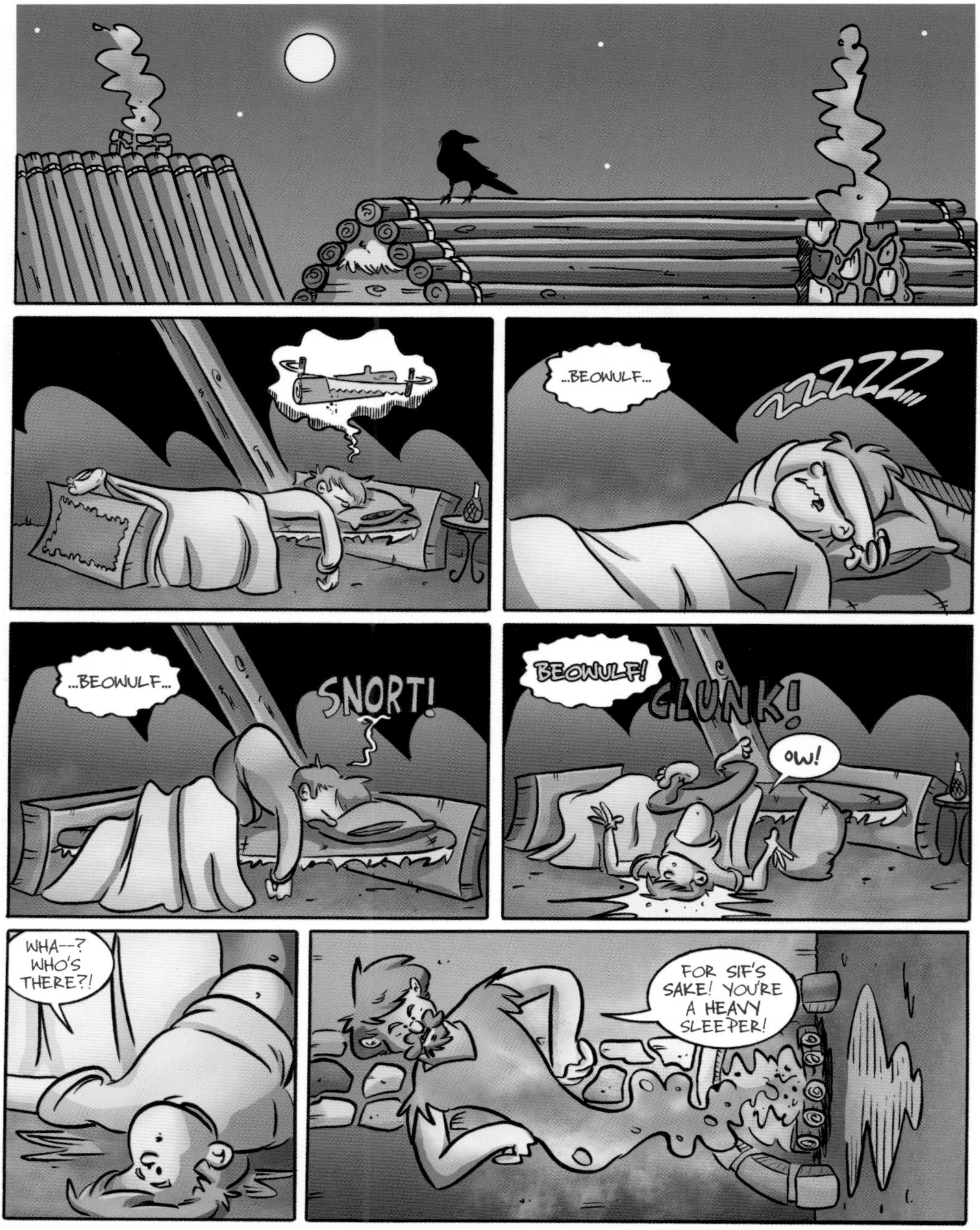
...BEOWULF...
ZZZZZZ
...BEOWULF...
SNORT!
BEOWULF!
CLUNK!
OW!
WHA--? WHO'S THERE?!
FOR SIF'S SAKE! YOU'RE A HEAVY SLEEPER!

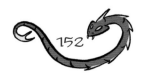

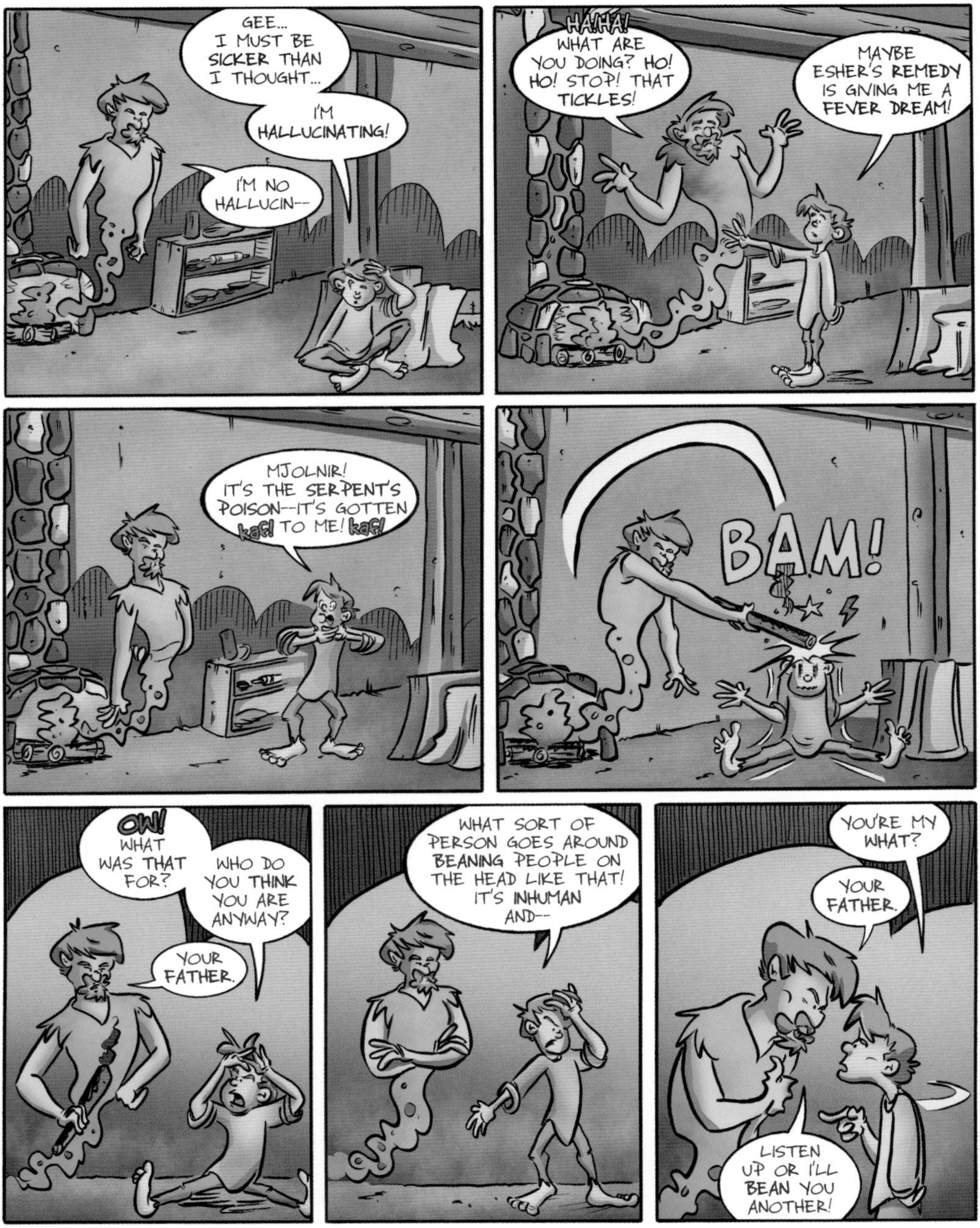
GEE... I MUST BE SICKER THAN I THOUGHT...
I'M HALLUCINATING!
I'M NO HALLUCIN--
HA! HA! WHAT ARE YOU DOING? HO! HO! STOP! THAT TICKLES!
MAYBE ESHER'S REMEDY IS GIVING ME A FEVER DREAM!
MJOLNIR! IT'S THE SERPENT'S POISON--IT'S GOTTEN kaf! TO ME! kaf!
BAM!
OW! WHAT WAS THAT FOR?
WHO DO YOU THINK YOU ARE ANYWAY?
YOUR FATHER.
WHAT SORT OF PERSON GOES AROUND BEANING PEOPLE ON THE HEAD LIKE THAT! IT'S INHUMAN AND--
YOU'RE MY WHAT?
YOUR FATHER.
LISTEN UP OR I'LL BEAN YOU ANOTHER!

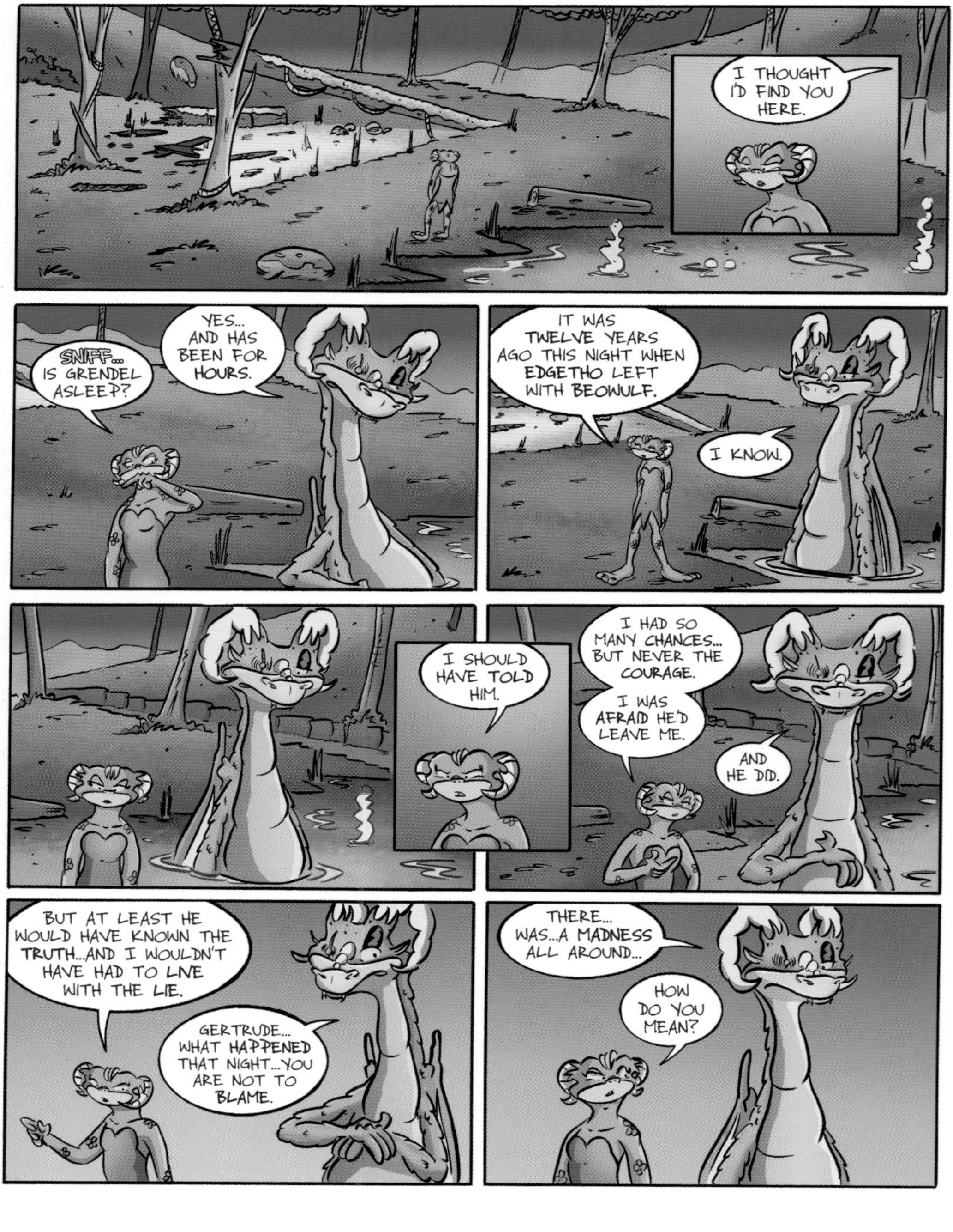
I THOUGHT I'D FIND YOU HERE.
SNIFF... IS GRENDEL ASLEEP?
YES... AND HAS BEEN FOR HOURS.
IT WAS TWELVE YEARS AGO THIS NIGHT WHEN EDGETHO LEFT WITH BEOWULF.
I KNOW.
I SHOULD HAVE TOLD HIM.
I HAD SO MANY CHANCES... BUT NEVER THE COURAGE.
I WAS AFRAID HE'D LEAVE ME.
AND HE DID.
BUT AT LEAST HE WOULD HAVE KNOWN THE TRUTH...AND I WOULDN'T HAVE HAD TO LIVE WITH THE LIE.
GERTRUDE... WHAT HAPPENED THAT NIGHT...YOU ARE NOT TO BLAME.
THERE... WAS...A MADNESS ALL AROUND...
HOW DO YOU MEAN?

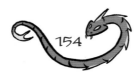

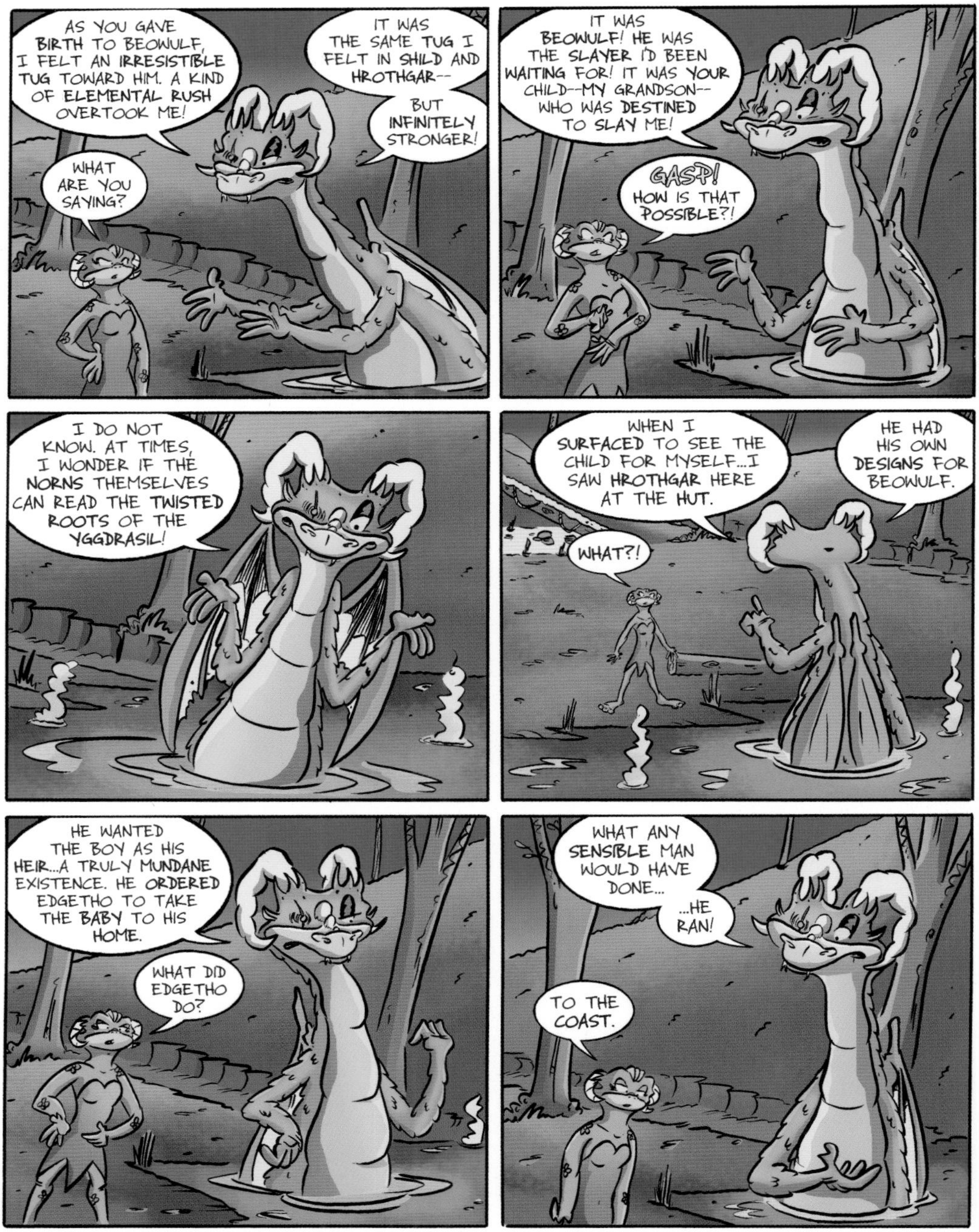
AS YOU GAVE BIRTH TO BEOWULF, I FELT AN IRRESISTIBLE TUG TOWARD HIM. A KIND OF ELEMENTAL RUSH OVERTOOK ME!
IT WAS THE SAME TUG I FELT IN SHILD AND HROTHGAR--
BUT INFINITELY STRONGER!
WHAT ARE YOU SAYING?
IT WAS BEOWULF! HE WAS THE SLAYER I'D BEEN WAITING FOR! IT WAS YOUR CHILD--MY GRANDSON--WHO WAS DESTINED TO SLAY ME!
GASP! HOW IS THAT POSSIBLE?!
I DO NOT KNOW. AT TIMES, I WONDER IF THE NORNS THEMSELVES CAN READ THE TWISTED ROOTS OF THE YGGDRASIL!
WHEN I SURFACED TO SEE THE CHILD FOR MYSELF...I SAW HROTHGAR HERE AT THE HUT.
HE HAD HIS OWN DESIGNS FOR BEOWULF.
WHAT?!
HE WANTED THE BOY AS HIS HEIR...A TRULY MUNDANE EXISTENCE. HE ORDERED EDGETHO TO TAKE THE BABY TO HIS HOME.
WHAT DID EDGETHO DO?
WHAT ANY SENSIBLE MAN WOULD HAVE DONE...
...HE RAN!
TO THE COAST.

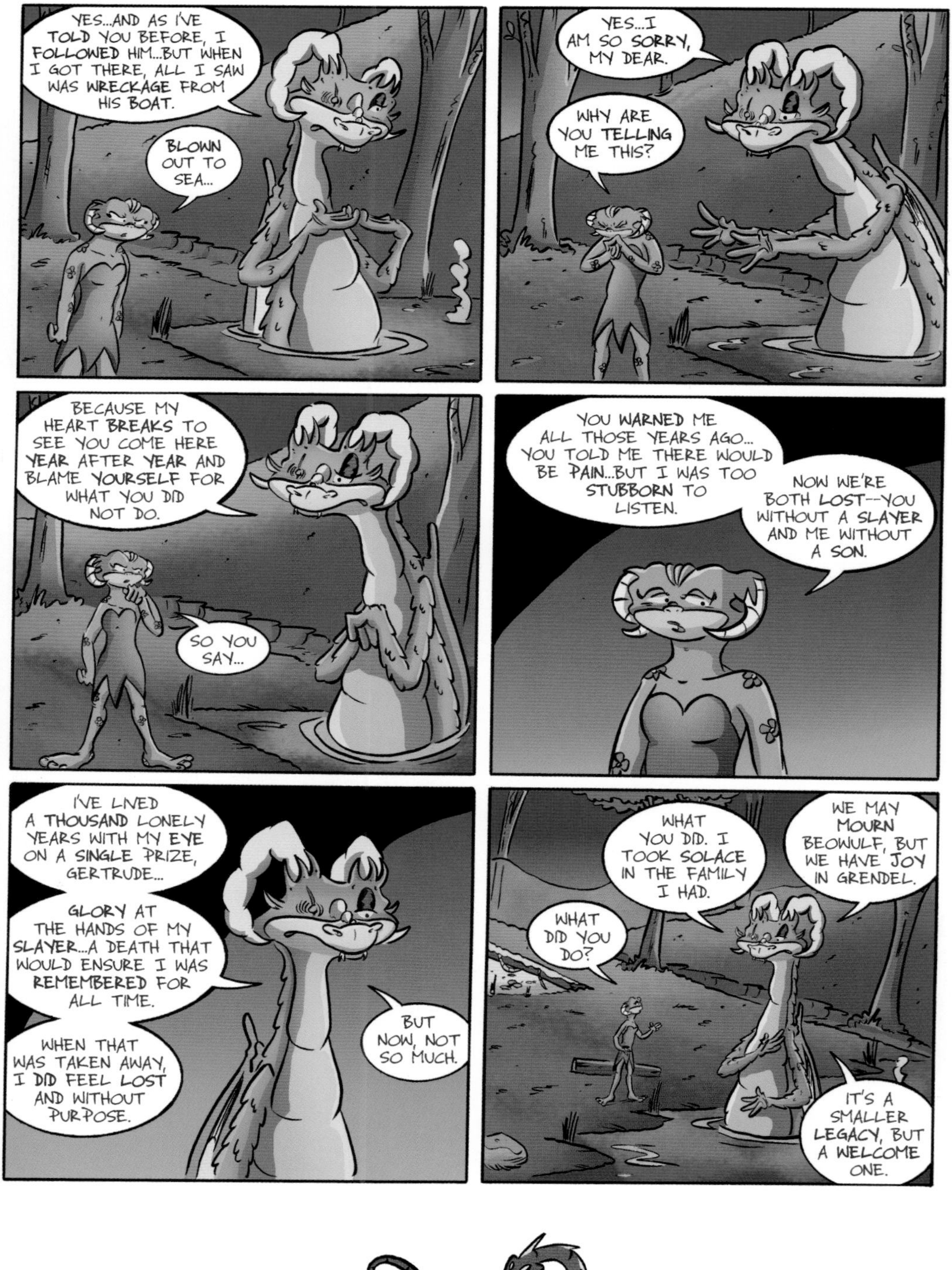
YES...AND AS I'VE TOLD YOU BEFORE, I FOLLOWED HIM...BUT WHEN I GOT THERE, ALL I SAW WAS WRECKAGE FROM HIS BOAT.
BLOWN OUT TO SEA...
YES...I AM SO SORRY, MY DEAR.
WHY ARE YOU TELLING ME THIS?
BECAUSE MY HEART BREAKS TO SEE YOU COME HERE YEAR AFTER YEAR AND BLAME YOURSELF FOR WHAT YOU DID NOT DO.
SO YOU SAY...
YOU WARNED ME ALL THOSE YEARS AGO... YOU TOLD ME THERE WOULD BE PAIN...BUT I WAS TOO STUBBORN TO LISTEN.
NOW WE'RE BOTH LOST--YOU WITHOUT A SLAYER AND ME WITHOUT A SON.
I'VE LIVED A THOUSAND LONELY YEARS WITH MY EYE ON A SINGLE PRIZE, GERTRUDE...
GLORY AT THE HANDS OF MY SLAYER...A DEATH THAT WOULD ENSURE I WAS REMEMBERED FOR ALL TIME.
WHEN THAT WAS TAKEN AWAY, I DID FEEL LOST AND WITHOUT PURPOSE.
BUT NOW, NOT SO MUCH.
WHAT DID YOU DO?
WHAT YOU DID. I TOOK SOLACE IN THE FAMILY I HAD.
WE MAY MOURN BEOWULF, BUT WE HAVE JOY IN GRENDEL.
IT'S A SMALLER LEGACY, BUT A WELCOME ONE.

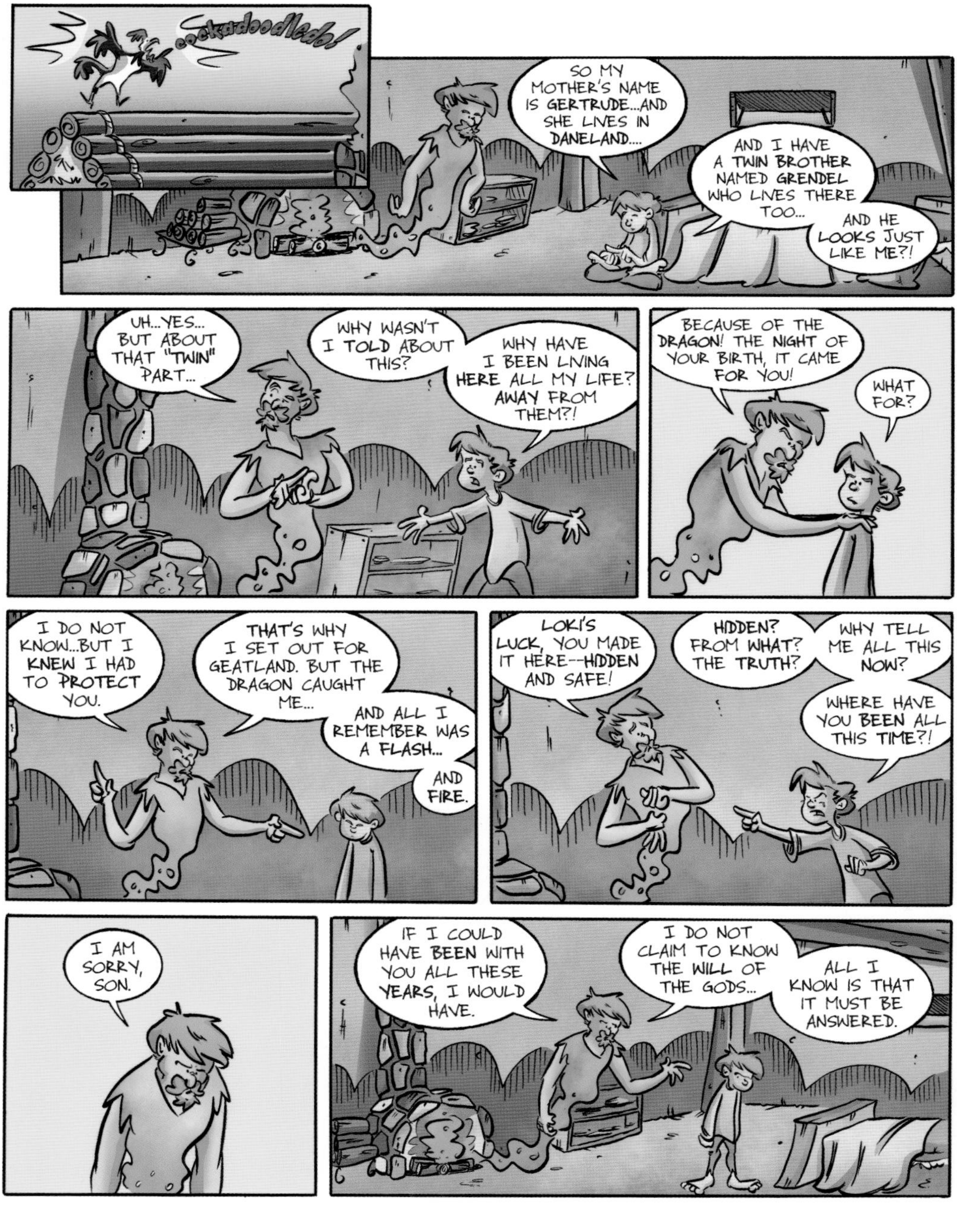
cockadoodledo!
SO MY MOTHER'S NAME IS GERTRUDE...AND SHE LIVES IN DANELAND....
AND I HAVE A TWIN BROTHER NAMED GRENDEL WHO LIVES THERE TOO...
AND HE LOOKS JUST LIKE ME?!
UH...YES... BUT ABOUT THAT "TWIN" PART...
WHY WASN'T I TOLD ABOUT THIS?
WHY HAVE I BEEN LIVING HERE ALL MY LIFE? AWAY FROM THEM?!
BECAUSE OF THE DRAGON! THE NIGHT OF YOUR BIRTH, IT CAME FOR YOU!
WHAT FOR?
I DO NOT KNOW...BUT I KNEW I HAD TO PROTECT YOU.
THAT'S WHY I SET OUT FOR GEATLAND. BUT THE DRAGON CAUGHT ME...
AND ALL I REMEMBER WAS A FLASH...
AND FIRE.
LOKI'S LUCK, YOU MADE IT HERE--HIDDEN AND SAFE!
HIDDEN? FROM WHAT? THE TRUTH?
WHY TELL ME ALL THIS NOW?
WHERE HAVE YOU BEEN ALL THIS TIME?!
I AM SORRY, SON.
IF I COULD HAVE BEEN WITH YOU ALL THESE YEARS, I WOULD HAVE.
I DO NOT CLAIM TO KNOW THE WILL OF THE GODS...
ALL I KNOW IS THAT IT MUST BE ANSWERED.

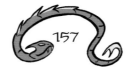

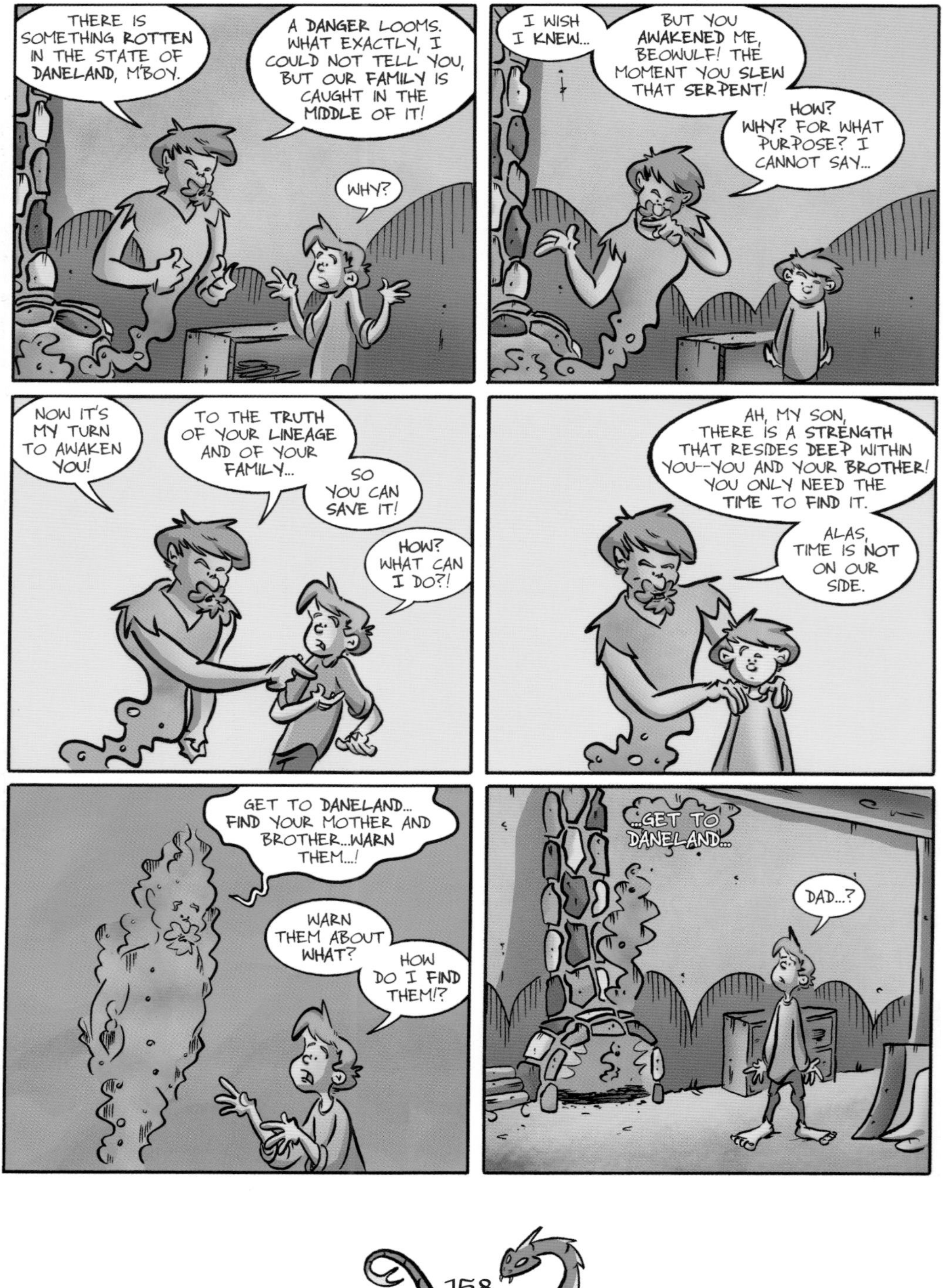
THERE IS SOMETHING ROTTEN IN THE STATE OF DANELAND, M'BOY.
A DANGER LOOMS. WHAT EXACTLY, I COULD NOT TELL YOU, BUT OUR FAMILY IS CAUGHT IN THE MIDDLE OF IT!
WHY?
I WISH I KNEW...
BUT YOU AWAKENED ME, BEOWULF! THE MOMENT YOU SLEW THAT SERPENT!
HOW? WHY? FOR WHAT PURPOSE? I CANNOT SAY...
NOW IT'S MY TURN TO AWAKEN YOU!
TO THE TRUTH OF YOUR LINEAGE AND OF YOUR FAMILY...
SO YOU CAN SAVE IT!
HOW? WHAT CAN I DO?!
AH, MY SON, THERE IS A STRENGTH THAT RESIDES DEEP WITHIN YOU--YOU AND YOUR BROTHER! YOU ONLY NEED THE TIME TO FIND IT.
ALAS, TIME IS NOT ON OUR SIDE.
GET TO DANELAND... FIND YOUR MOTHER AND BROTHER...WARN THEM...!
WARN THEM ABOUT WHAT?
HOW DO I FIND THEM!?
...GET TO DANELAND...
DAD...?

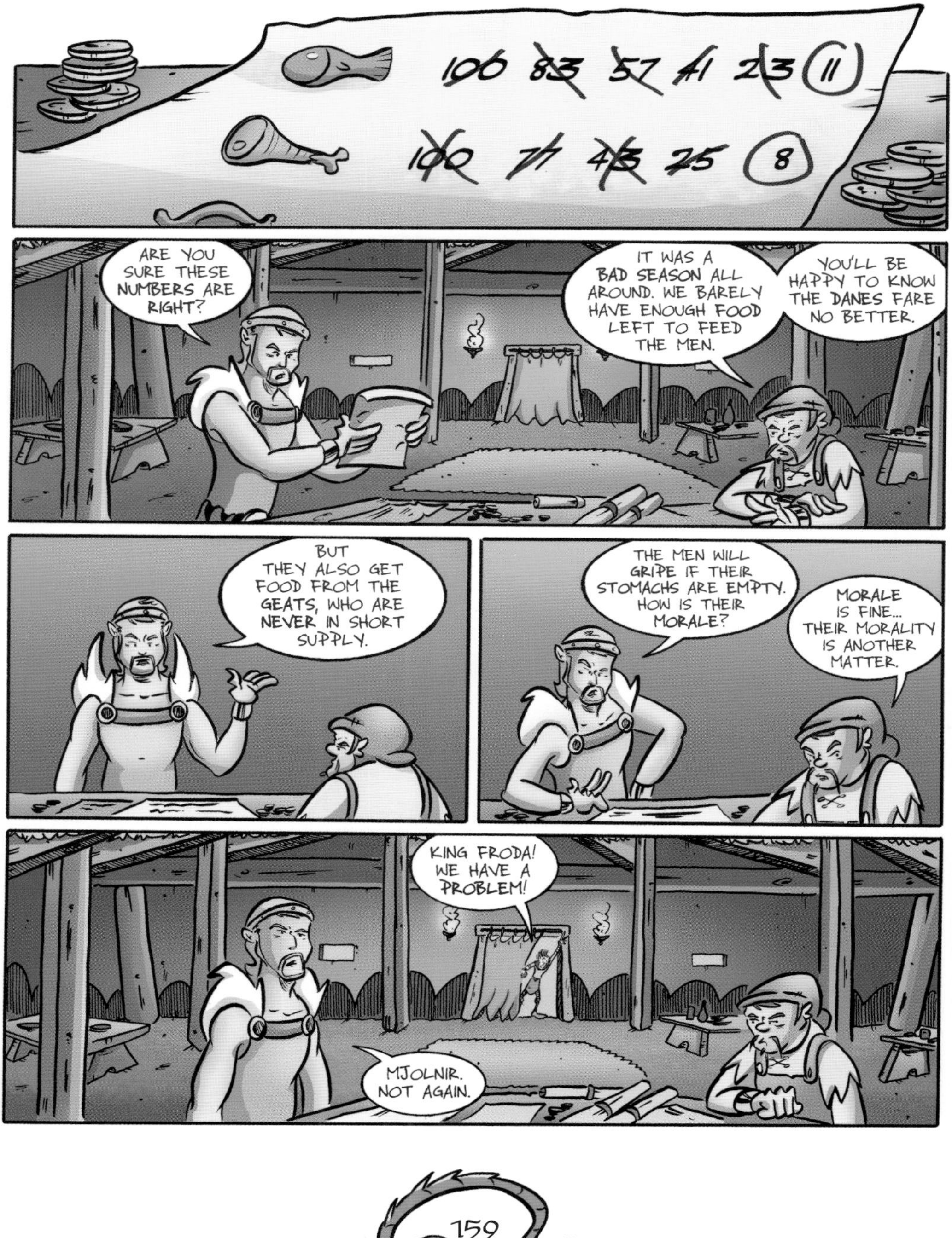
100 83 57 41 23 11
100 71 43 25 8
ARE YOU SURE THESE NUMBERS ARE RIGHT?
IT WAS A BAD SEASON ALL AROUND. WE BARELY HAVE ENOUGH FOOD LEFT TO FEED THE MEN.
YOU'LL BE HAPPY TO KNOW THE DANES FARE NO BETTER.
BUT THEY ALSO GET FOOD FROM THE GEATS, WHO ARE NEVER IN SHORT SUPPLY.
THE MEN WILL GRIPE IF THEIR STOMACHS ARE EMPTY. HOW IS THEIR MORALE?
MORALE IS FINE... THEIR MORALITY IS ANOTHER MATTER.
KING FRODA! WE HAVE A PROBLEM!
MJOLNIR. NOT AGAIN.

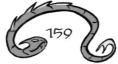

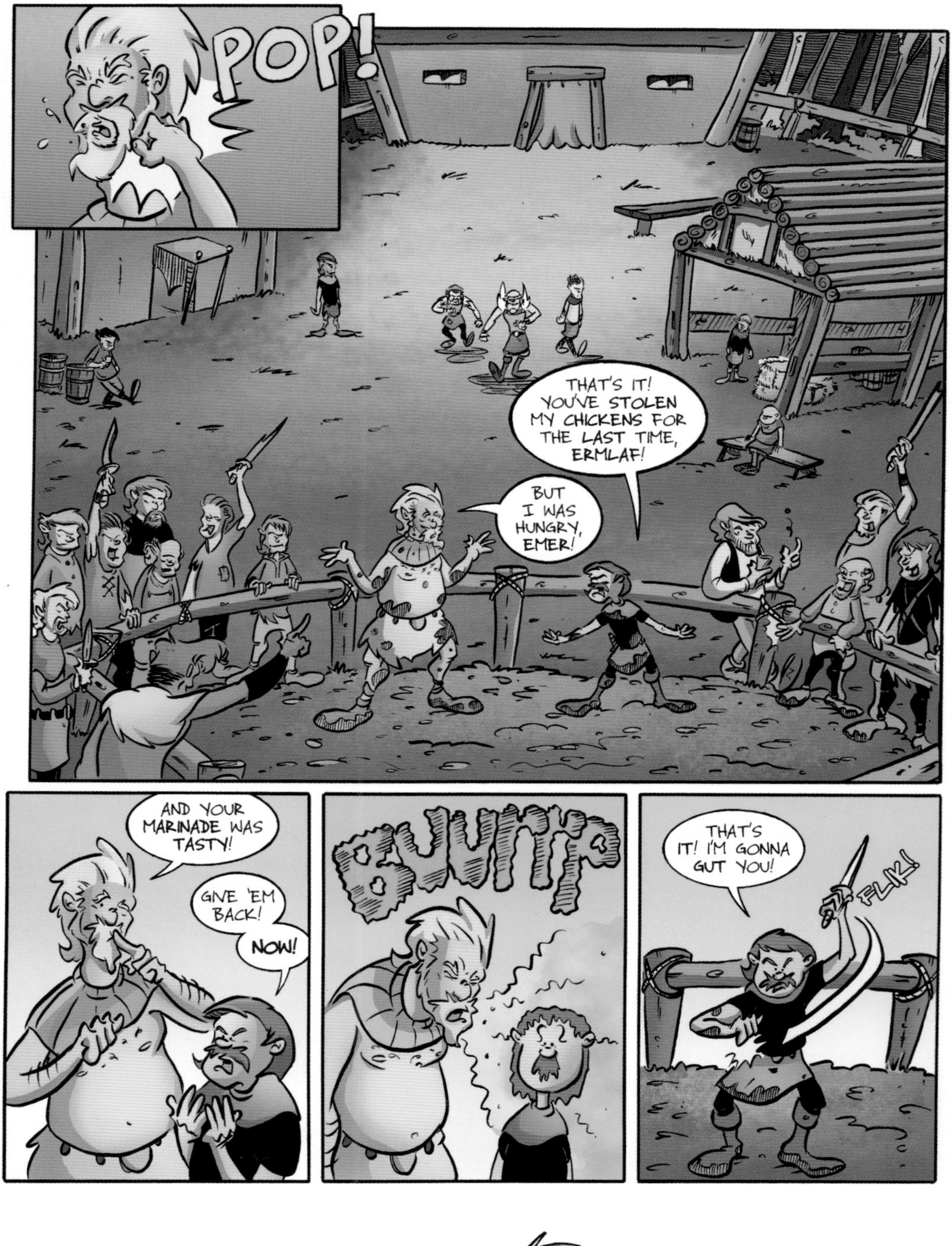
POP!
THAT'S IT! YOU'VE STOLEN MY CHICKENS FOR THE LAST TIME, ERMLAF!
BUT I WAS HUNGRY, EMER!
AND YOUR MARINADE WAS TASTY!
GIVE 'EM BACK!
NOW!
BUURP
THAT'S IT! I'M GONNA GUT YOU!
FLIK!

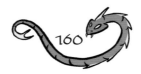

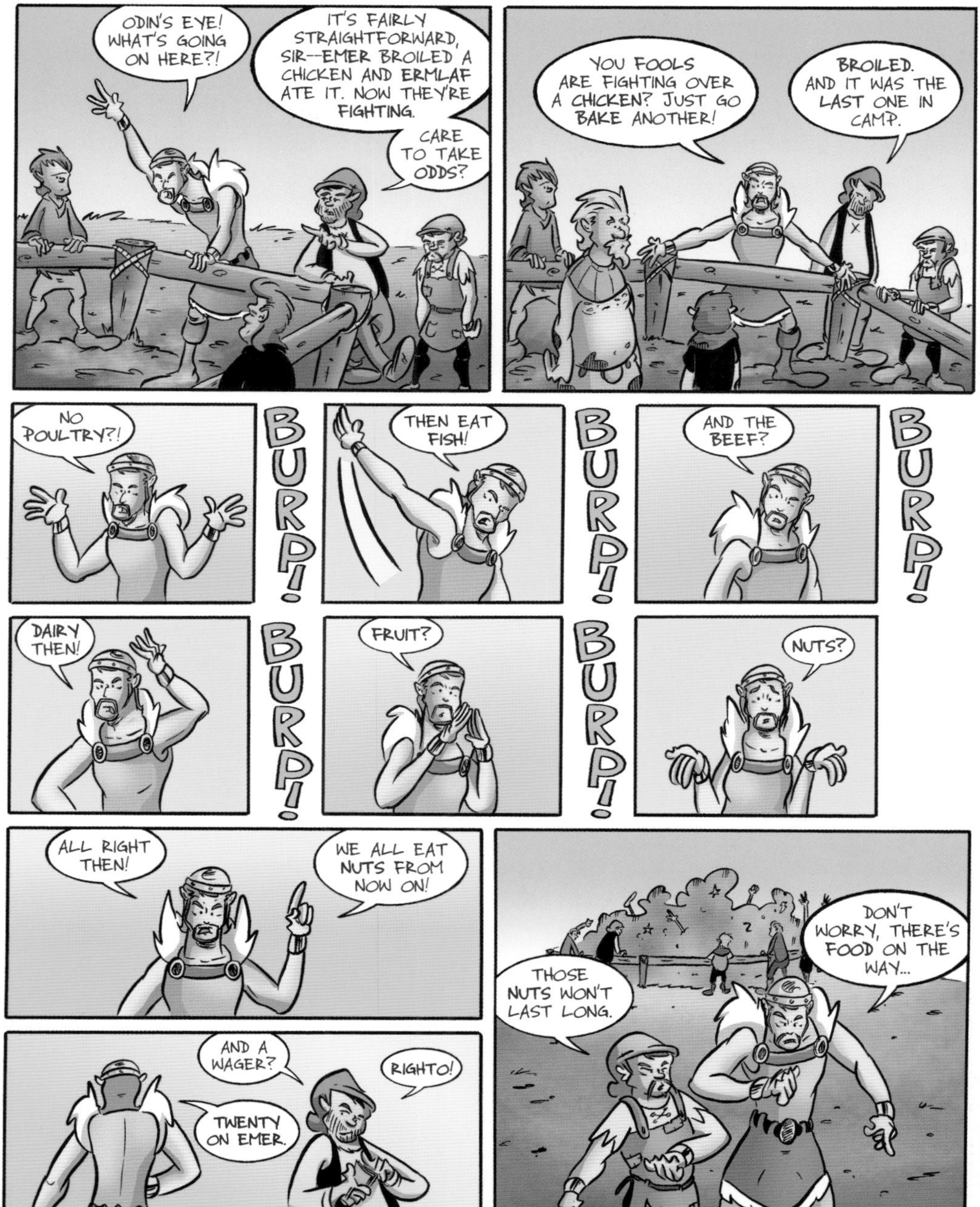
ODIN'S EYE! WHAT'S GOING ON HERE?!
IT'S FAIRLY STRAIGHTFORWARD, SIR--EMER BROILED A CHICKEN AND ERMLAF ATE IT. NOW THEY'RE FIGHTING.
CARE TO TAKE ODDS?
YOU FOOLS ARE FIGHTING OVER A CHICKEN? JUST GO BAKE ANOTHER!
BROILED. AND IT WAS THE LAST ONE IN CAMP.
NO POULTRY?!
BURP!
THEN EAT FISH!
BURP!
AND THE BEEF?
BURP!
DAIRY THEN!
BURP!
FRUIT?
BURP!
NUTS?
ALL RIGHT THEN!
WE ALL EAT NUTS FROM NOW ON!
AND A WAGER?
TWENTY ON EMER.
RIGHTO!
THOSE NUTS WON'T LAST LONG.
DON'T WORRY, THERE'S FOOD ON THE WAY...

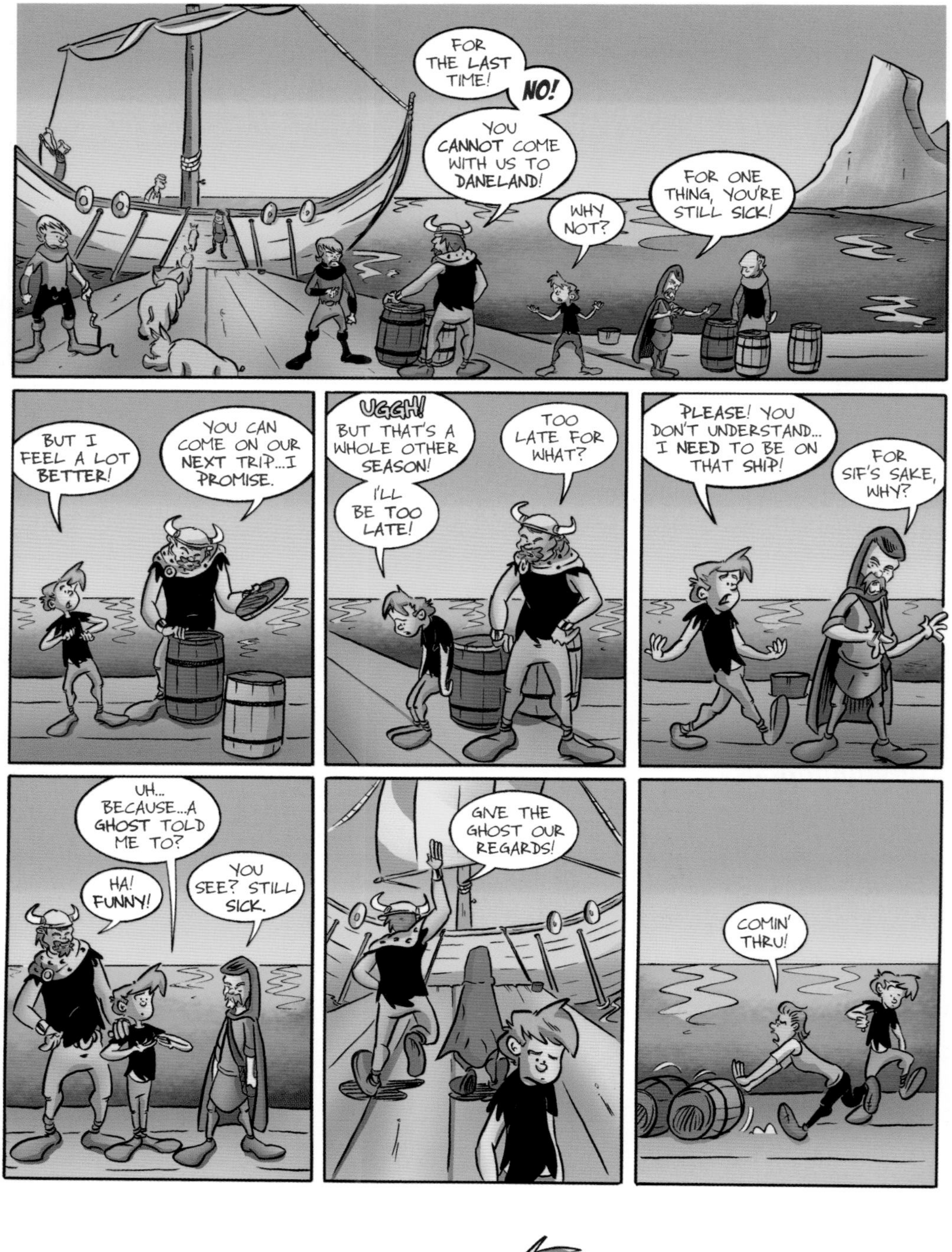
FOR THE LAST TIME!
NO!
YOU CANNOT COME WITH US TO DANELAND!
WHY NOT?
FOR ONE THING, YOU'RE STILL SICK!
BUT I FEEL A LOT BETTER!
YOU CAN COME ON OUR NEXT TRIP...I PROMISE.
UGGH!
BUT THAT'S A WHOLE OTHER SEASON!
I'LL BE TOO LATE!
TOO LATE FOR WHAT?
PLEASE! YOU DON'T UNDERSTAND... I NEED TO BE ON THAT SHIP!
FOR SIF'S SAKE, WHY?
UH... BECAUSE...A GHOST TOLD ME TO?
HA! FUNNY!
YOU SEE? STILL SICK.
GIVE THE GHOST OUR REGARDS!
COMIN' THRU!

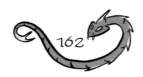

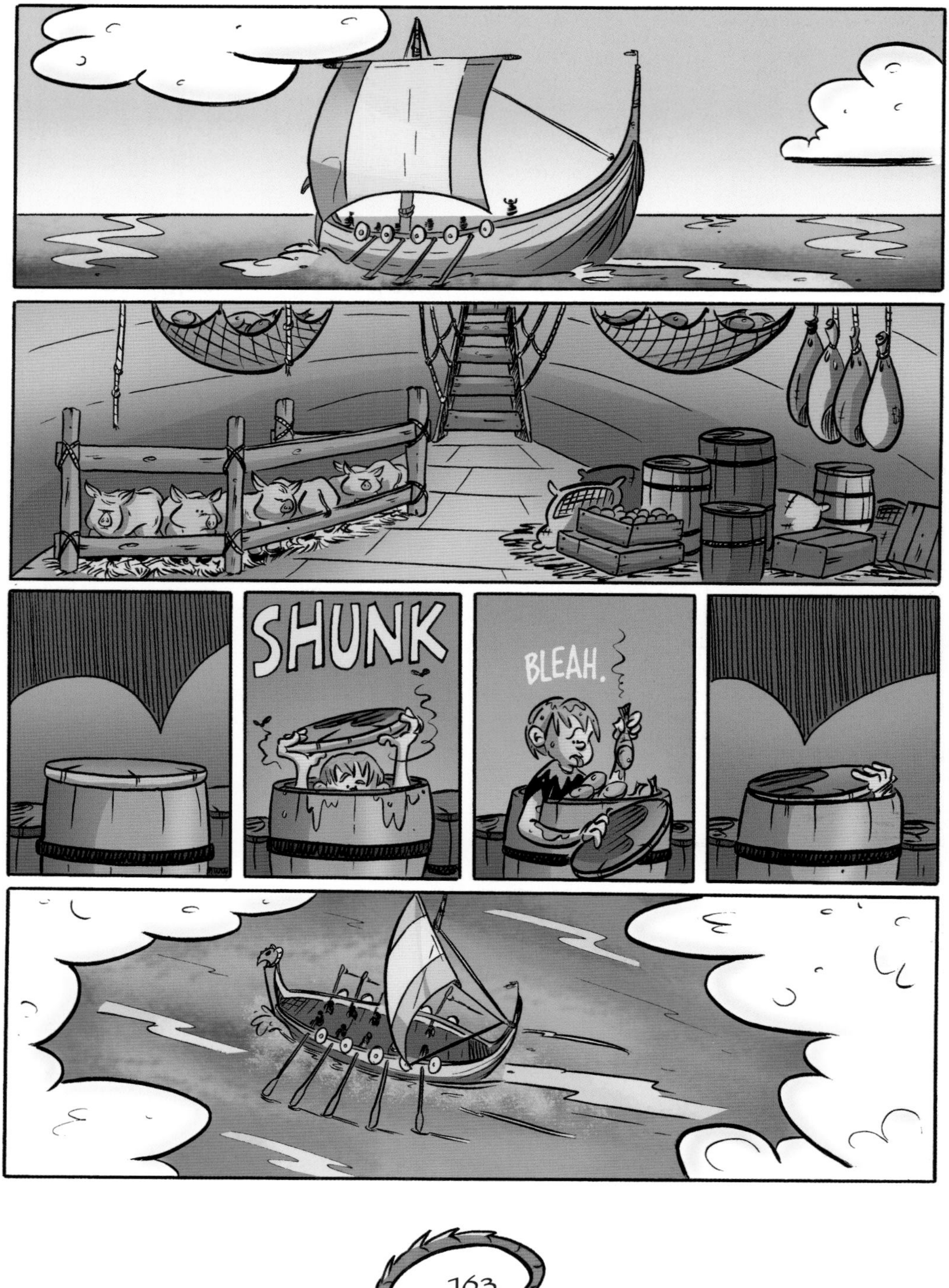
SHUNK
BLEAH.

I THOUGHT WE DISCUSSED THIS, HROTHGAR...

YOU TOLD ME NOT TO GO. THAT ISN'T A DISCUSSION.

FINE, THEN...TELL ME WHY YOU SHOULD.

I MADE A PROMISE.

YES! A RIDICULOUS PROMISE TO OUR PEOPLE--

NO. NOT TO THEM... IT WAS TO HIM...

...TO THE DRAGON.

YEARS AGO... WHEN MY FATHER WAS STILL KING...I MADE A DEAL WITH THE DRAGON.

HE PROMISED ME THE POWER TO RULE ALL DANELAND IF I DID IT AS MY FATHER HAD...JUSTLY AND WITH COMPASSION.

AND SO YOU HAVE!

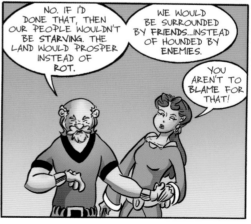

NO. IF I'D DONE THAT, THEN OUR PEOPLE WOULDN'T BE STARVING. THE LAND WOULD PROSPER INSTEAD OF ROT.

WE WOULD BE SURROUNDED BY FRIENDS...INSTEAD OF HOUNDED BY ENEMIES.

YOU AREN'T TO BLAME FOR THAT!

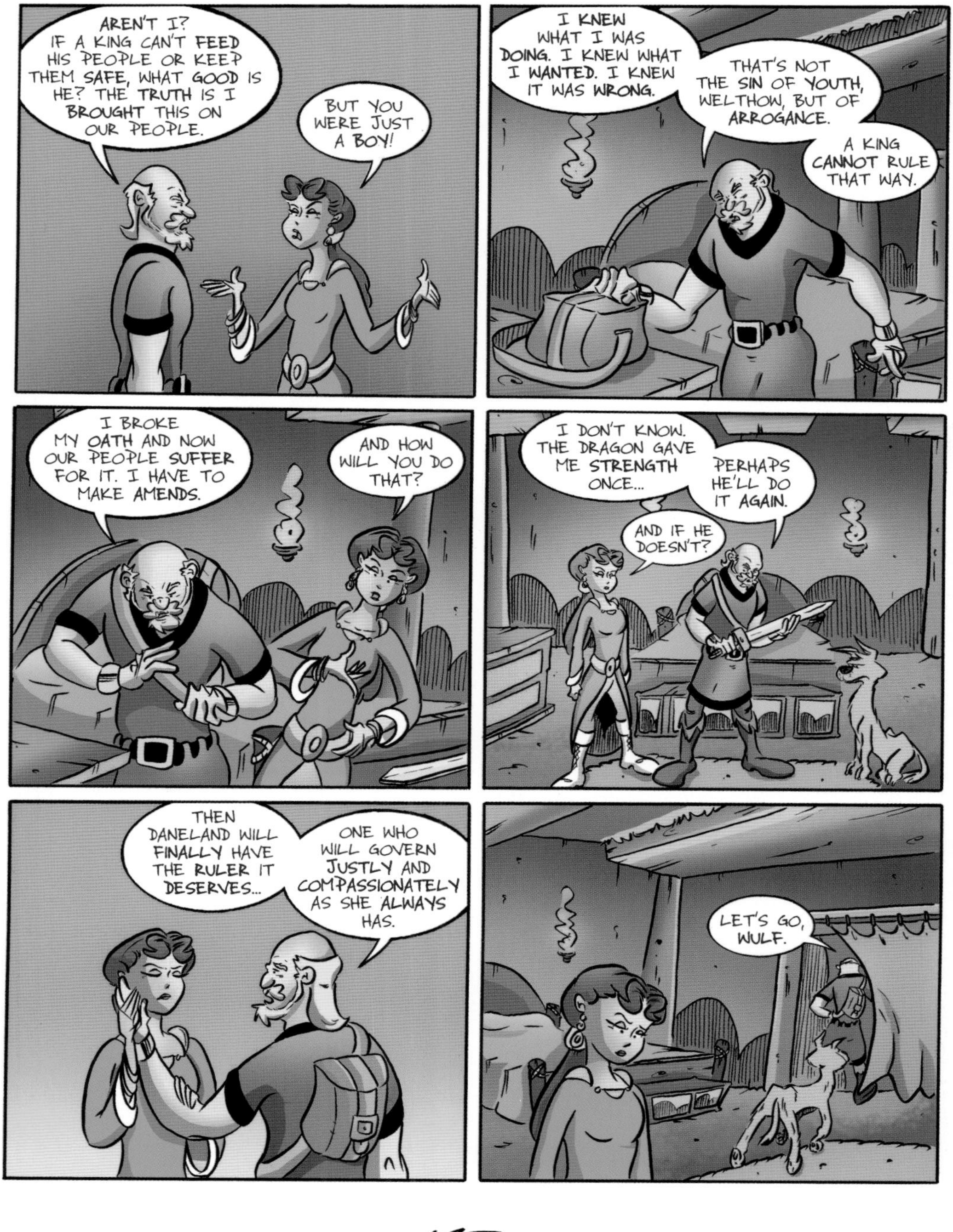
AREN'T I? IF A KING CAN'T FEED HIS PEOPLE OR KEEP THEM SAFE, WHAT GOOD IS HE? THE TRUTH IS I BROUGHT THIS ON OUR PEOPLE.
BUT YOU WERE JUST A BOY!
I KNEW WHAT I WAS DOING. I KNEW WHAT I WANTED. I KNEW IT WAS WRONG.
THAT'S NOT THE SIN OF YOUTH, WELTHOW, BUT OF ARROGANCE.
A KING CANNOT RULE THAT WAY.
I BROKE MY OATH AND NOW OUR PEOPLE SUFFER FOR IT. I HAVE TO MAKE AMENDS.
AND HOW WILL YOU DO THAT?
I DON'T KNOW. THE DRAGON GAVE ME STRENGTH ONCE...
PERHAPS HE'LL DO IT AGAIN.
AND IF HE DOESN'T?
THEN DANELAND WILL FINALLY HAVE THE RULER IT DESERVES...
ONE WHO WILL GOVERN JUSTLY AND COMPASSIONATELY AS SHE ALWAYS HAS.
LET'S GO, WULF.

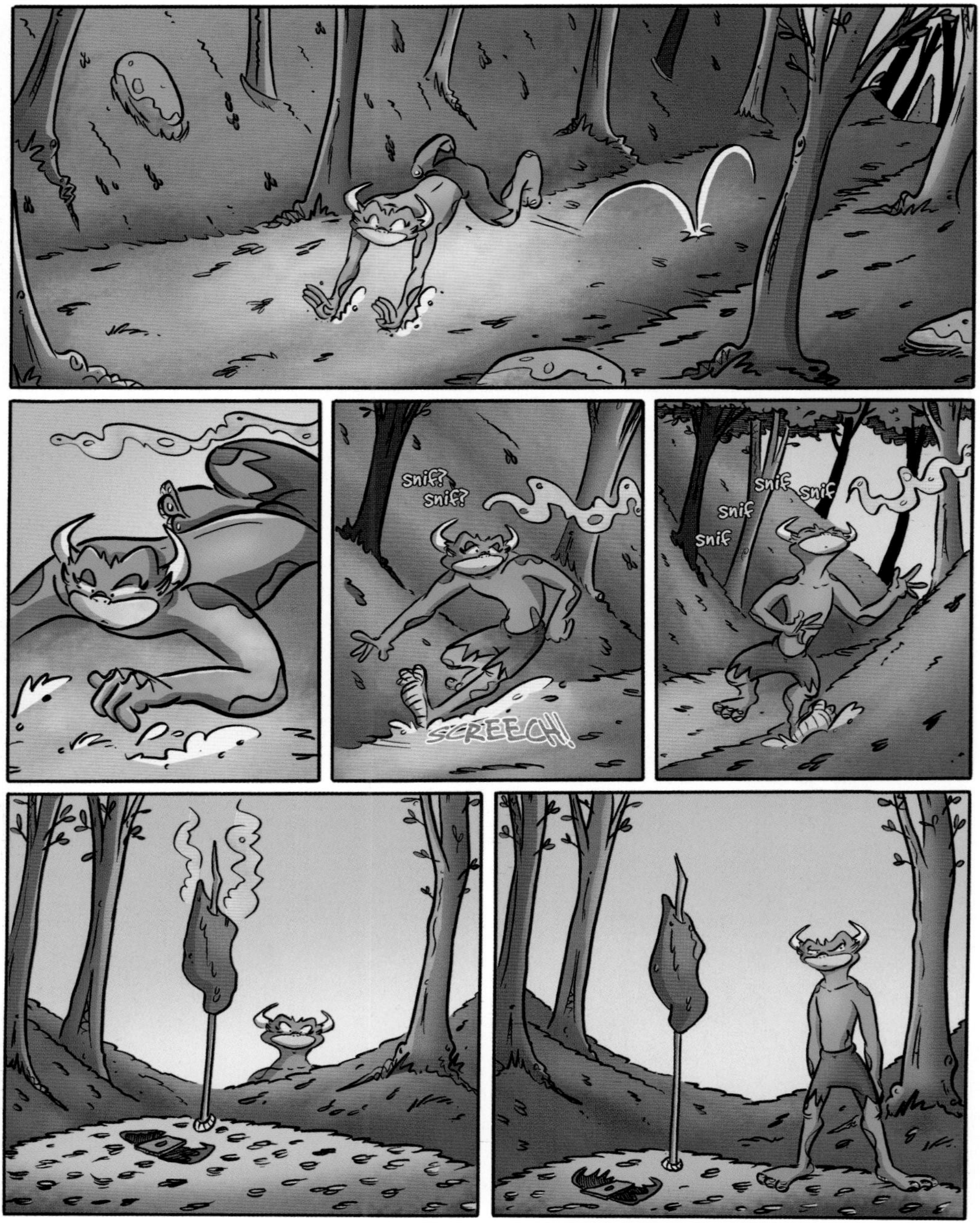
snif?
snif?
SCREECH!
snif
snif
snif
snif

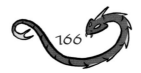

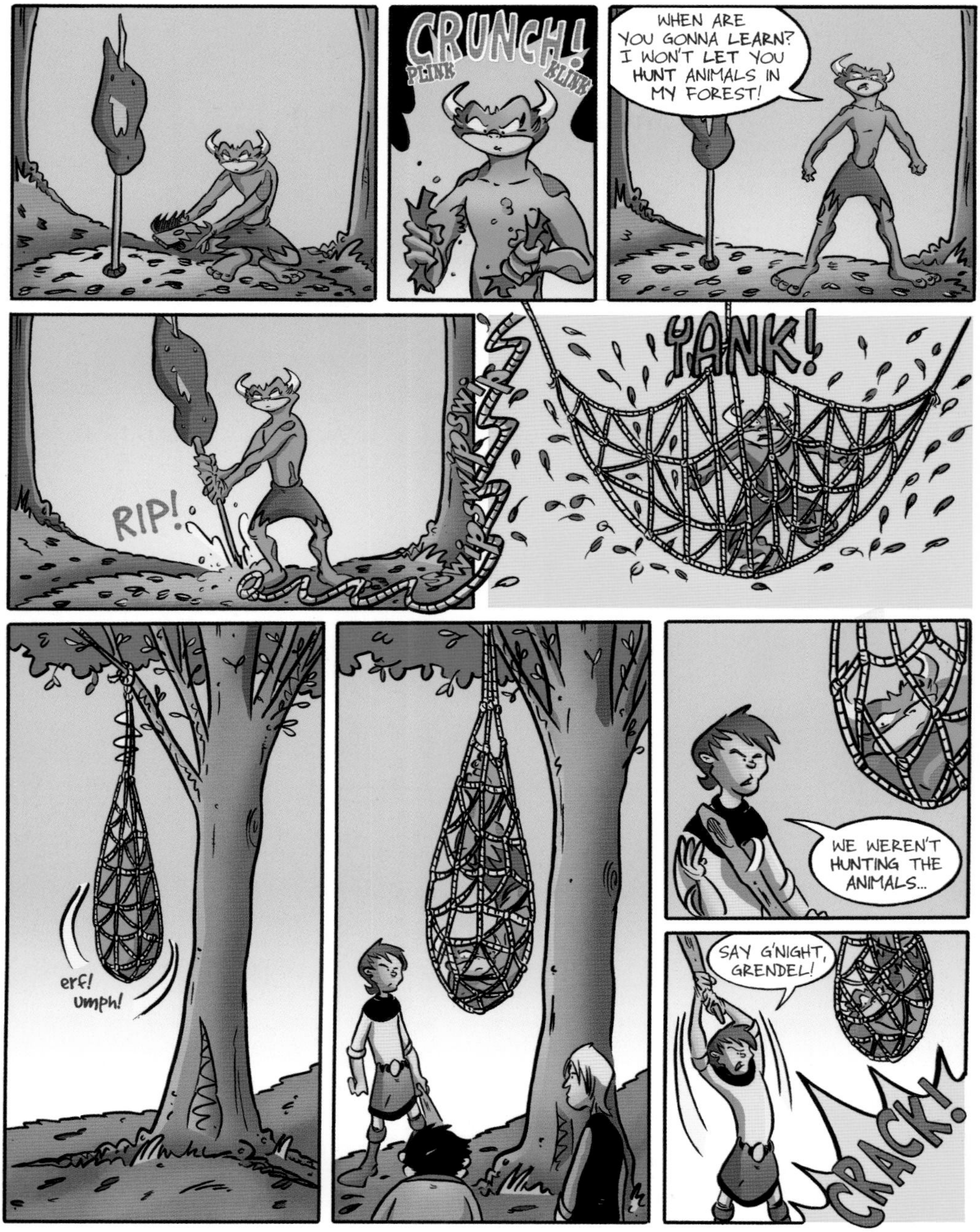
CRUNCH!
PLINK
KLINK
WHEN ARE YOU GONNA LEARN? I WON'T LET YOU HUNT ANIMALS IN MY FOREST!
RIP!
SWIPSWIPSWIPS
YANK!
erf!
umph!
WE WEREN'T HUNTING THE ANIMALS...
SAY G'NIGHT, GRENDEL!
CRACK!

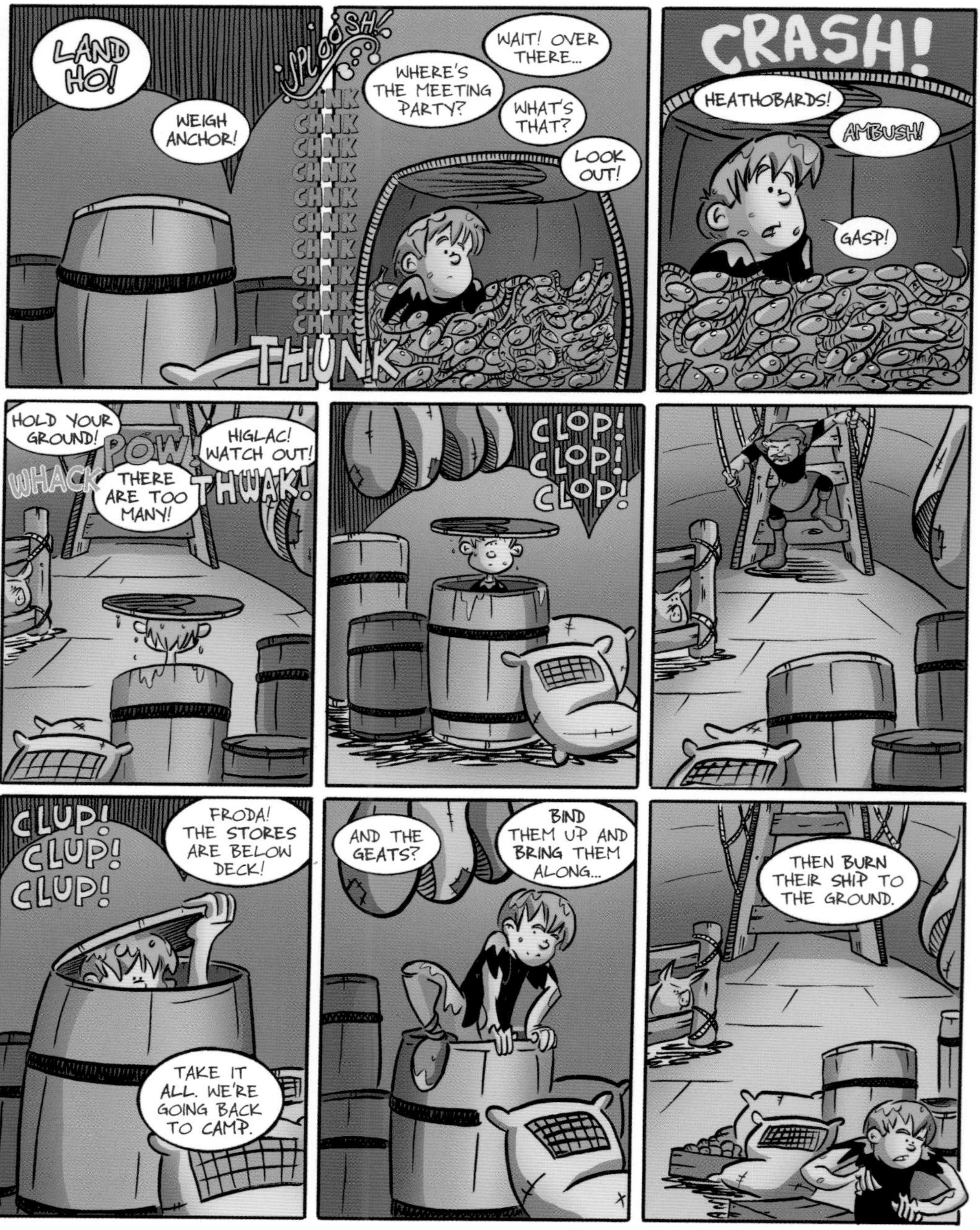
LAND HO!
WEIGH ANCHOR!
SPLOOSH!
CHNK CHNK CHNK CHNK CHNK CHNK CHNK CHNK CHNK CHNK
THUNK
WHERE'S THE MEETING PARTY?
WAIT! OVER THERE...
WHAT'S THAT?
LOOK OUT!
CRASH!
HEATHOBARDS!
AMBUSH!
GASP!
HOLD YOUR GROUND!
POW!
WHACK
THERE ARE TOO MANY!
HIGLAC! WATCH OUT!
THWAK!
CLOP! CLOP! CLOP!
CLUP! CLUP! CLUP!
FRODA! THE STORES ARE BELOW DECK!
TAKE IT ALL. WE'RE GOING BACK TO CAMP.
AND THE GEATS?
BIND THEM UP AND BRING THEM ALONG...
THEN BURN THEIR SHIP TO THE GROUND.

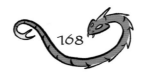

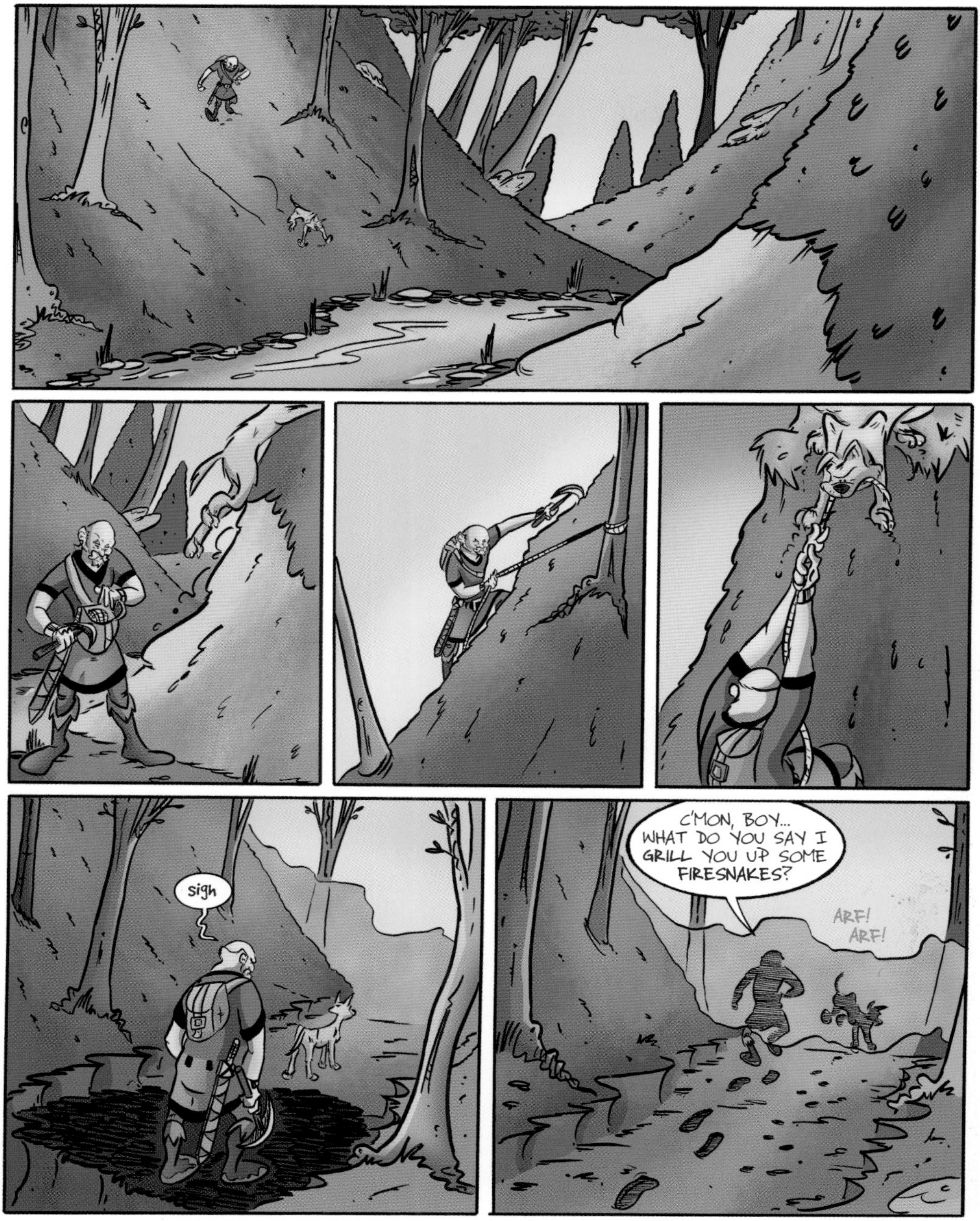
sigh
C'MON, BOY... WHAT DO YOU SAY I GRILL YOU UP SOME FIRESNAKES?
ARF! ARF!

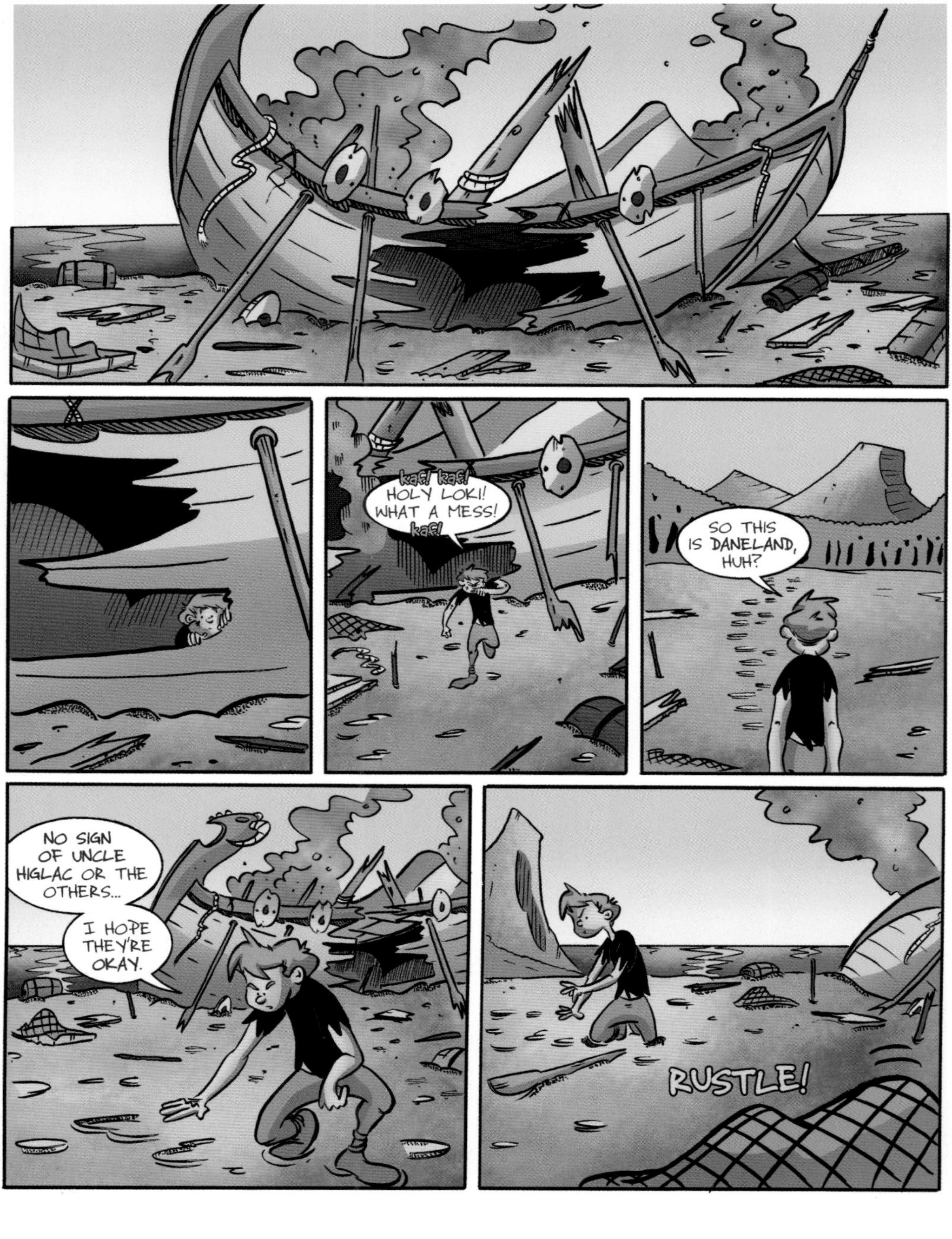
KAF! KAF!
HOLY LOKI! WHAT A MESS!
KAF!
SO THIS IS DANELAND, HUH?
NO SIGN OF UNCLE HIGLAC OR THE OTHERS...
I HOPE THEY'RE OKAY.
RUSTLE!

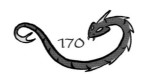

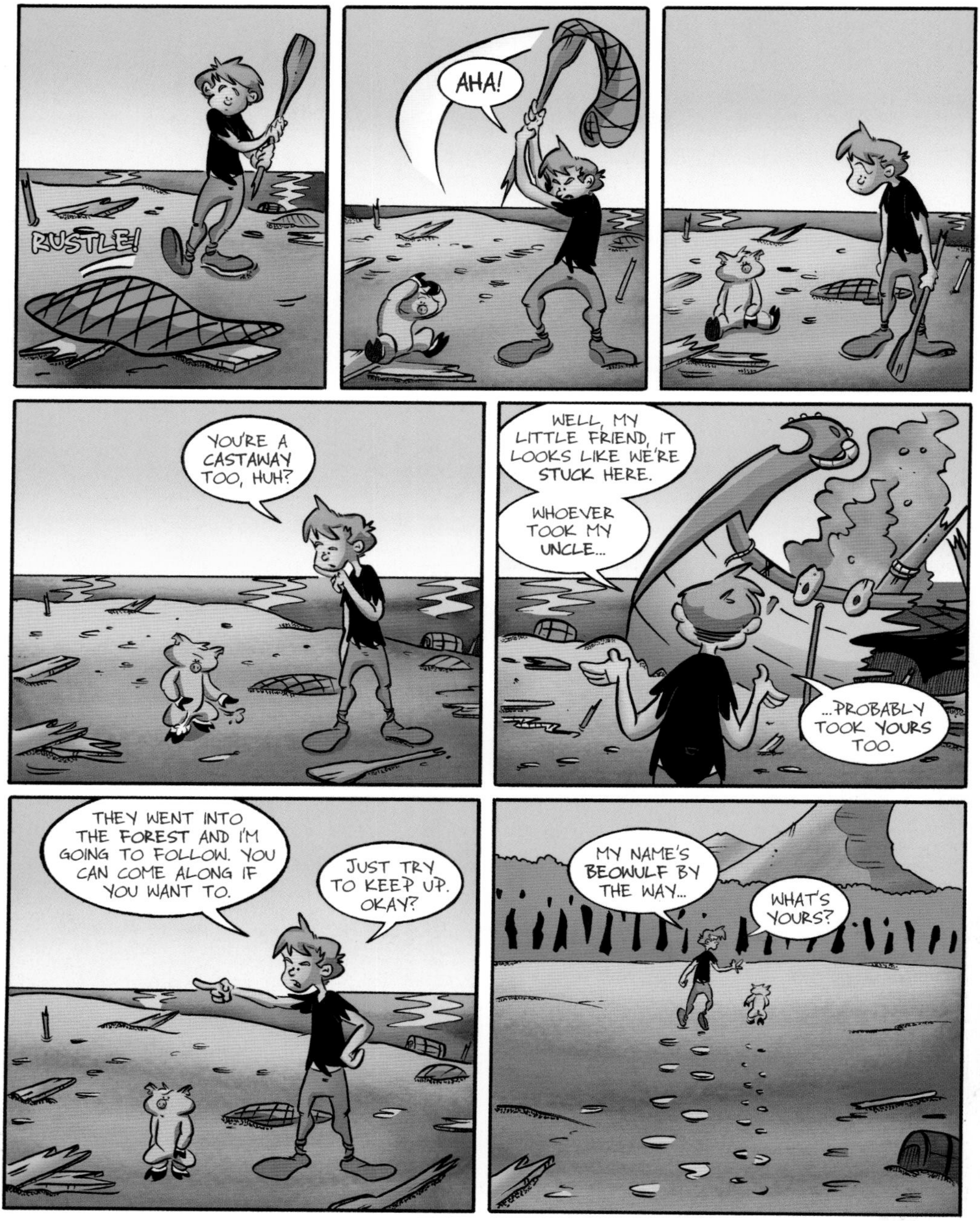
RUSTLE!
AHA!
YOU'RE A CASTAWAY TOO, HUH?
WELL, MY LITTLE FRIEND, IT LOOKS LIKE WE'RE STUCK HERE.
WHOEVER TOOK MY UNCLE...
...PROBABLY TOOK YOURS TOO.
THEY WENT INTO THE FOREST AND I'M GOING TO FOLLOW. YOU CAN COME ALONG IF YOU WANT TO.
JUST TRY TO KEEP UP. OKAY?
MY NAME'S BEOWULF BY THE WAY...
WHAT'S YOURS?

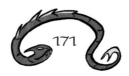

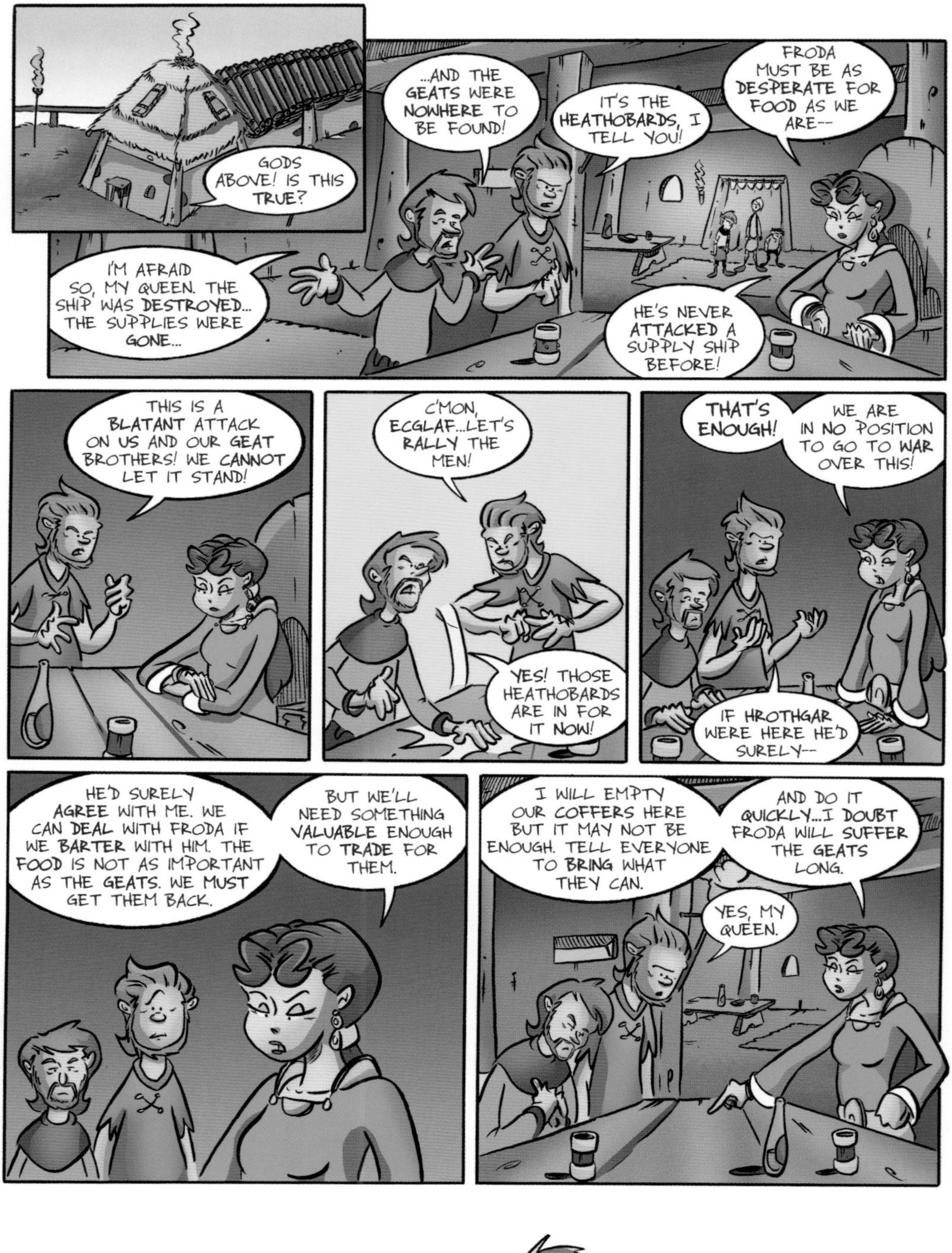
GODS ABOVE! IS THIS TRUE?
I'M AFRAID SO, MY QUEEN. THE SHIP WAS DESTROYED... THE SUPPLIES WERE GONE...
...AND THE GEATS WERE NOWHERE TO BE FOUND!
IT'S THE HEATHOBARDS, I TELL YOU!
FRODA MUST BE AS DESPERATE FOR FOOD AS WE ARE--
HE'S NEVER ATTACKED A SUPPLY SHIP BEFORE!
THIS IS A BLATANT ATTACK ON US AND OUR GEAT BROTHERS! WE CANNOT LET IT STAND!
C'MON, ECGLAF...LET'S RALLY THE MEN!
YES! THOSE HEATHOBARDS ARE IN FOR IT NOW!
THAT'S ENOUGH!
WE ARE IN NO POSITION TO GO TO WAR OVER THIS!
IF HROTHGAR WERE HERE HE'D SURELY--
HE'D SURELY AGREE WITH ME. WE CAN DEAL WITH FRODA IF WE BARTER WITH HIM. THE FOOD IS NOT AS IMPORTANT AS THE GEATS. WE MUST GET THEM BACK.
BUT WE'LL NEED SOMETHING VALUABLE ENOUGH TO TRADE FOR THEM.
I WILL EMPTY OUR COFFERS HERE BUT IT MAY NOT BE ENOUGH. TELL EVERYONE TO BRING WHAT THEY CAN.
AND DO IT QUICKLY...I DOUBT FRODA WILL SUFFER THE GEATS LONG.
YES, MY QUEEN.

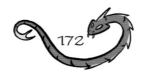

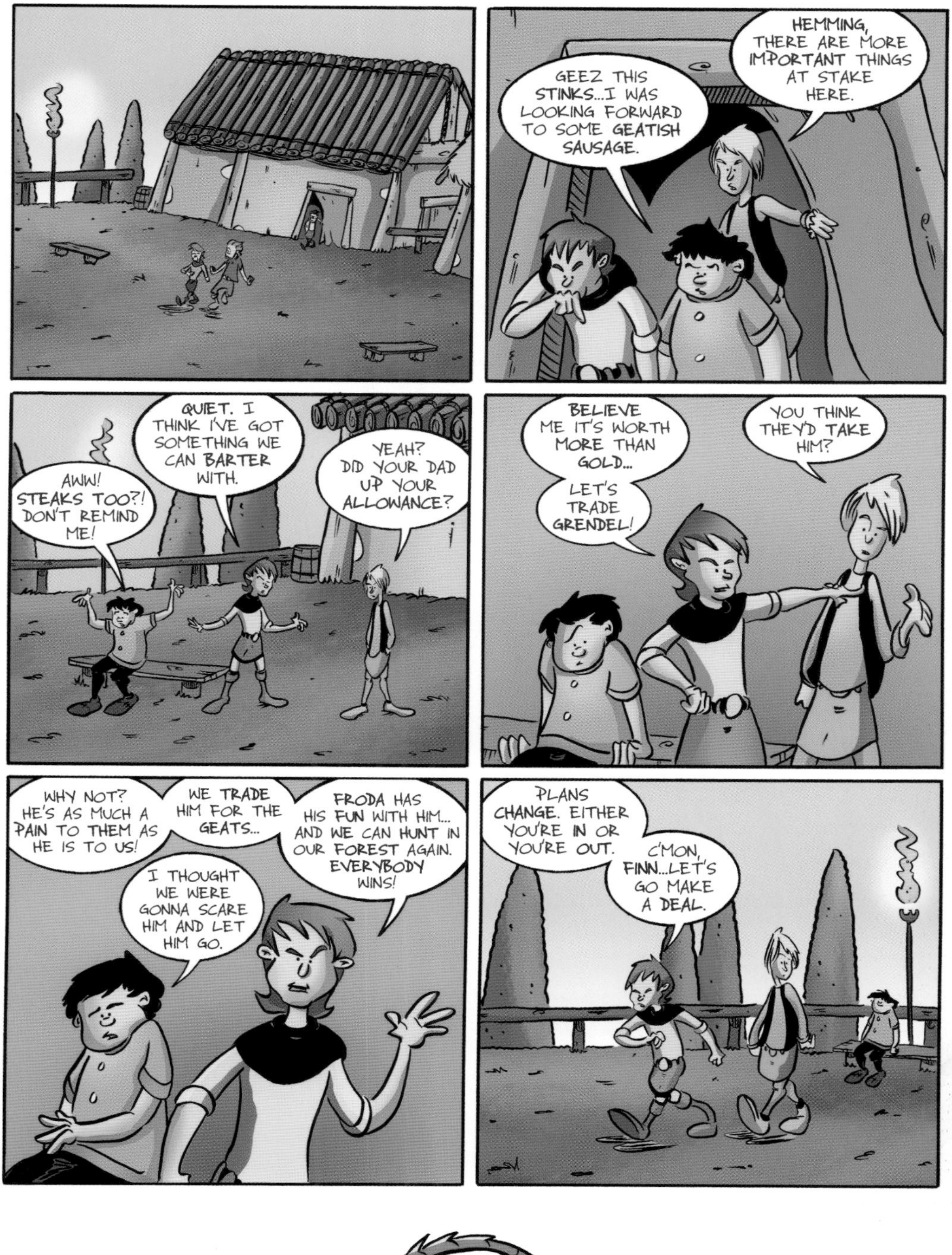
GEEZ THIS STINKS...I WAS LOOKING FORWARD TO SOME GEATISH SAUSAGE.
HEMMING, THERE ARE MORE IMPORTANT THINGS AT STAKE HERE.
AWW! STEAKS TOO?! DON'T REMIND ME!
QUIET. I THINK I'VE GOT SOMETHING WE CAN BARTER WITH.
YEAH? DID YOUR DAD UP YOUR ALLOWANCE?
BELIEVE ME IT'S WORTH MORE THAN GOLD...
LET'S TRADE GRENDEL!
YOU THINK THEY'D TAKE HIM?
WHY NOT? HE'S AS MUCH A PAIN TO THEM AS HE IS TO US!
WE TRADE HIM FOR THE GEATS...
FRODA HAS HIS FUN WITH HIM... AND WE CAN HUNT IN OUR FOREST AGAIN. EVERYBODY WINS!
I THOUGHT WE WERE GONNA SCARE HIM AND LET HIM GO.
PLANS CHANGE. EITHER YOU'RE IN OR YOU'RE OUT.
C'MON, FINN...LET'S GO MAKE A DEAL.

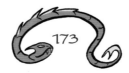

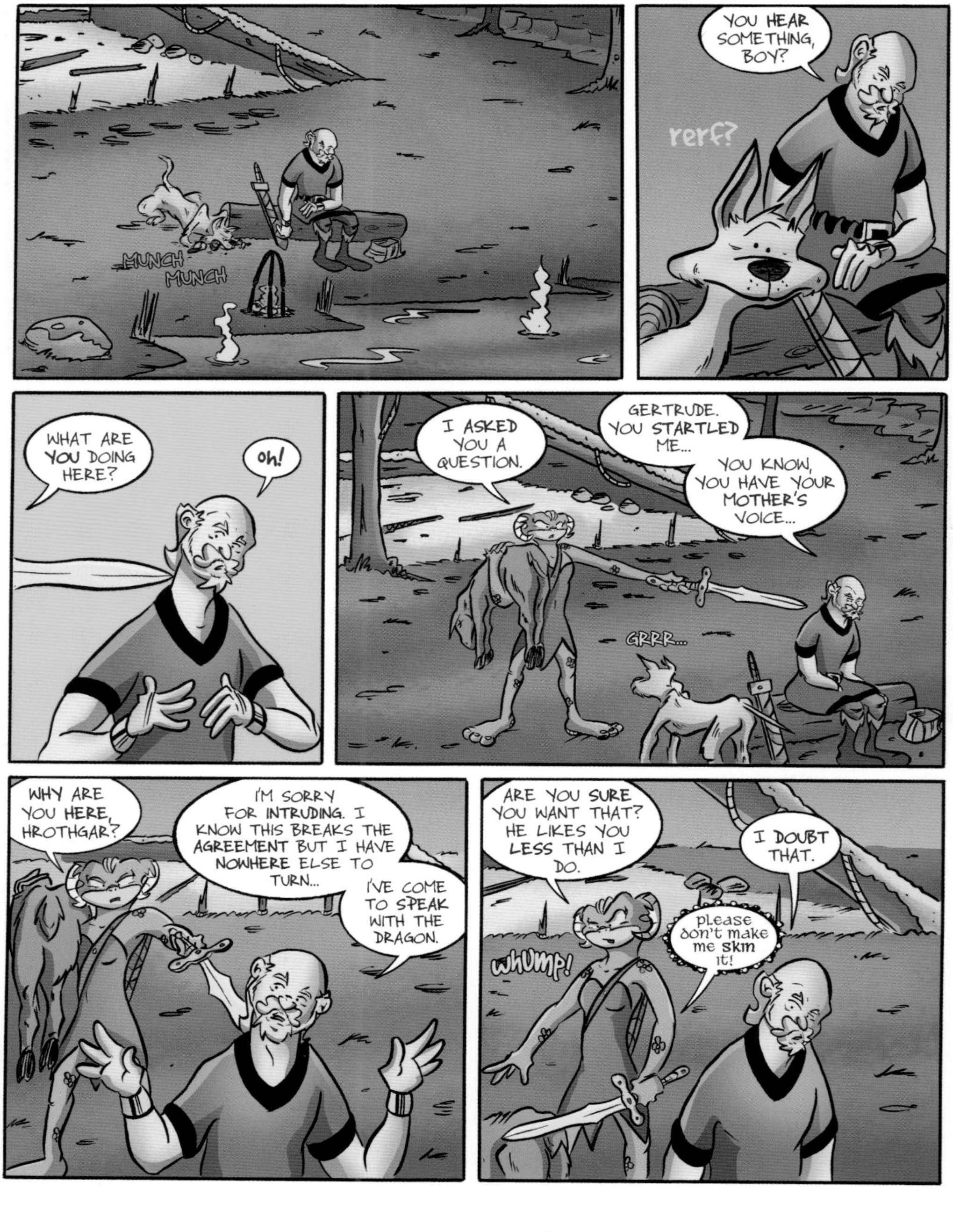
MUNCH
MUNCH
YOU HEAR SOMETHING, BOY?
rerf?
WHAT ARE YOU DOING HERE?
oh!
I ASKED YOU A QUESTION.
GERTRUDE. YOU STARTLED ME...
YOU KNOW, YOU HAVE YOUR MOTHER'S VOICE...
GRRR...
WHY ARE YOU HERE, HROTHGAR?
I'M SORRY FOR INTRUDING. I KNOW THIS BREAKS THE AGREEMENT BUT I HAVE NOWHERE ELSE TO TURN...
I'VE COME TO SPEAK WITH THE DRAGON.
ARE YOU SURE YOU WANT THAT? HE LIKES YOU LESS THAN I DO.
I DOUBT THAT.
WHUMP!
please don't make me skin it!

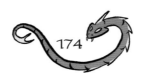

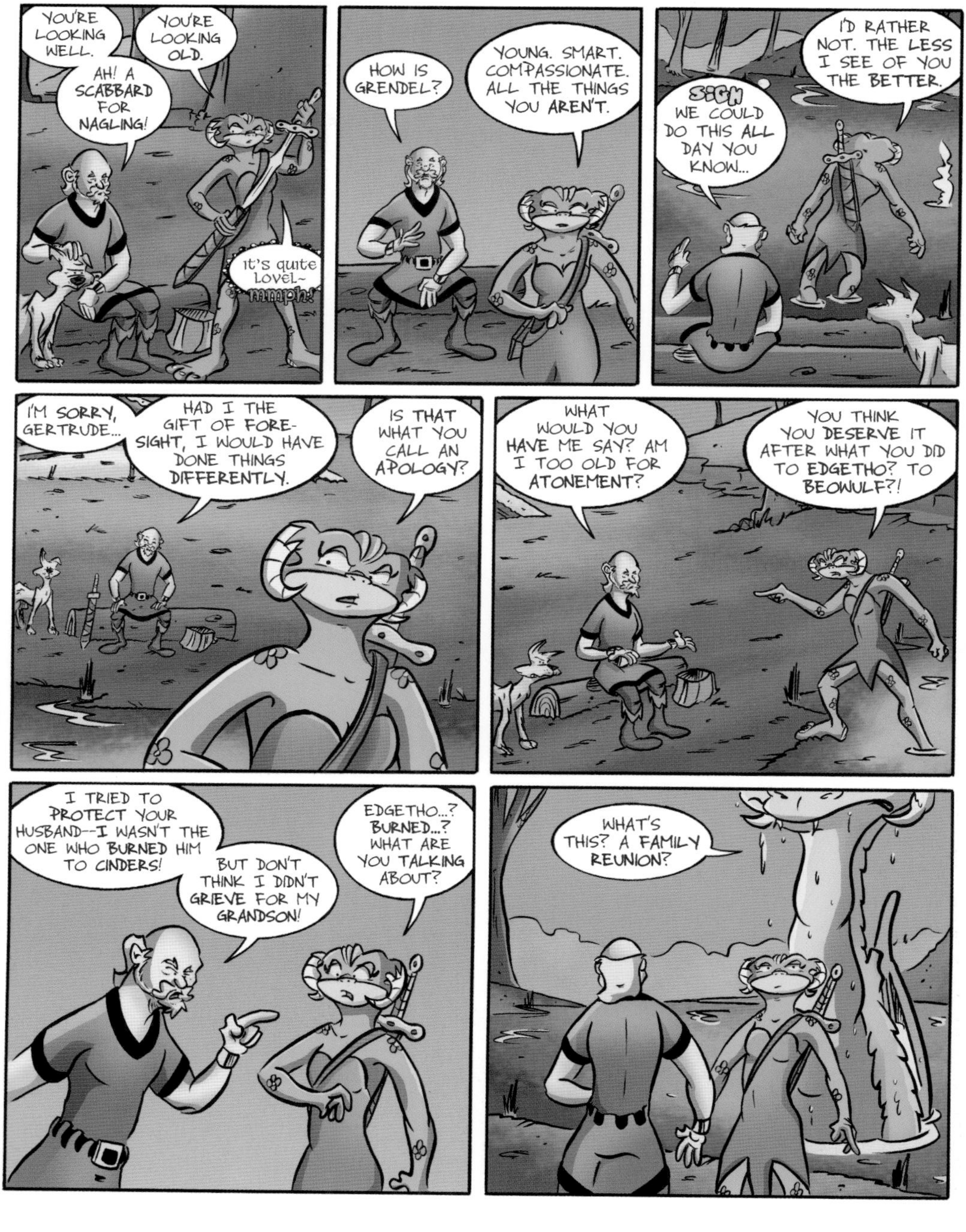
YOU'RE LOOKING WELL.
YOU'RE LOOKING OLD.
AH! A SCABBARD FOR NAGLING!
IT'S QUITE LOVEL~ mmph!
HOW IS GRENDEL?
YOUNG. SMART. COMPASSIONATE. ALL THE THINGS YOU AREN'T.
I'D RATHER NOT. THE LESS I SEE OF YOU THE BETTER.
SIGH
WE COULD DO THIS ALL DAY YOU KNOW...
I'M SORRY, GERTRUDE...
HAD I THE GIFT OF FORE-SIGHT, I WOULD HAVE DONE THINGS DIFFERENTLY.
IS THAT WHAT YOU CALL AN APOLOGY?
WHAT WOULD YOU HAVE ME SAY? AM I TOO OLD FOR ATONEMENT?
YOU THINK YOU DESERVE IT AFTER WHAT YOU DID TO EDGETHO? TO BEOWULF?!
I TRIED TO PROTECT YOUR HUSBAND--I WASN'T THE ONE WHO BURNED HIM TO CINDERS!
BUT DON'T THINK I DIDN'T GRIEVE FOR MY GRANDSON!
EDGETHO...? BURNED...? WHAT ARE YOU TALKING ABOUT?
WHAT'S THIS? A FAMILY REUNION?

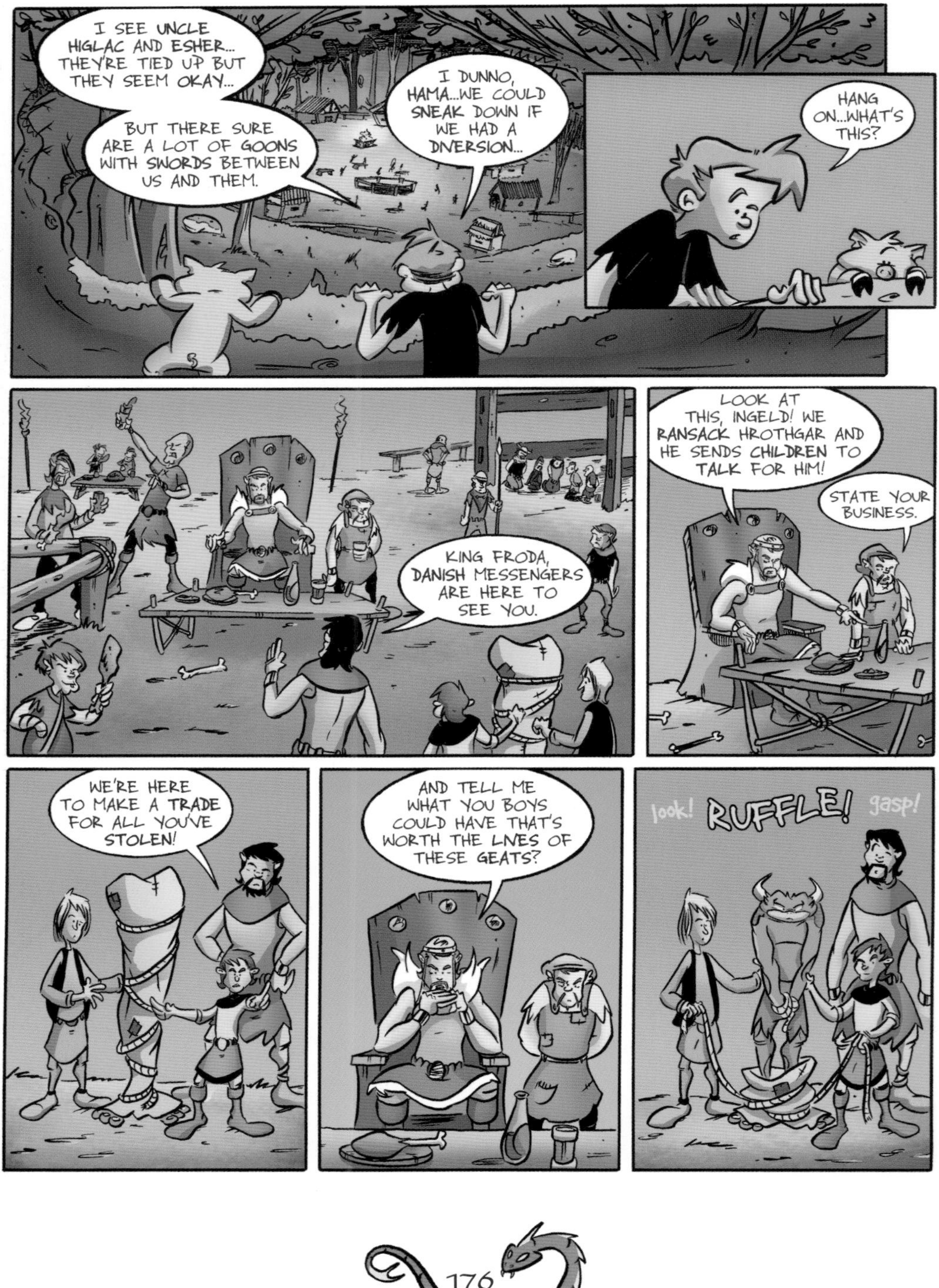
I SEE UNCLE HIGLAC AND ESHER... THEY'RE TIED UP BUT THEY SEEM OKAY...
BUT THERE SURE ARE A LOT OF GOONS WITH SWORDS BETWEEN US AND THEM.
I DUNNO, HAMA...WE COULD SNEAK DOWN IF WE HAD A DIVERSION...
HANG ON...WHAT'S THIS?
KING FRODA, DANISH MESSENGERS ARE HERE TO SEE YOU.
LOOK AT THIS, INGELD! WE RANSACK HROTHGAR AND HE SENDS CHILDREN TO TALK FOR HIM!
STATE YOUR BUSINESS.
WE'RE HERE TO MAKE A TRADE FOR ALL YOU'VE STOLEN!
AND TELL ME WHAT YOU BOYS COULD HAVE THAT'S WORTH THE LIVES OF THESE GEATS?
look!
RUFFLE!
gasp!

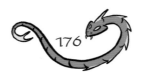

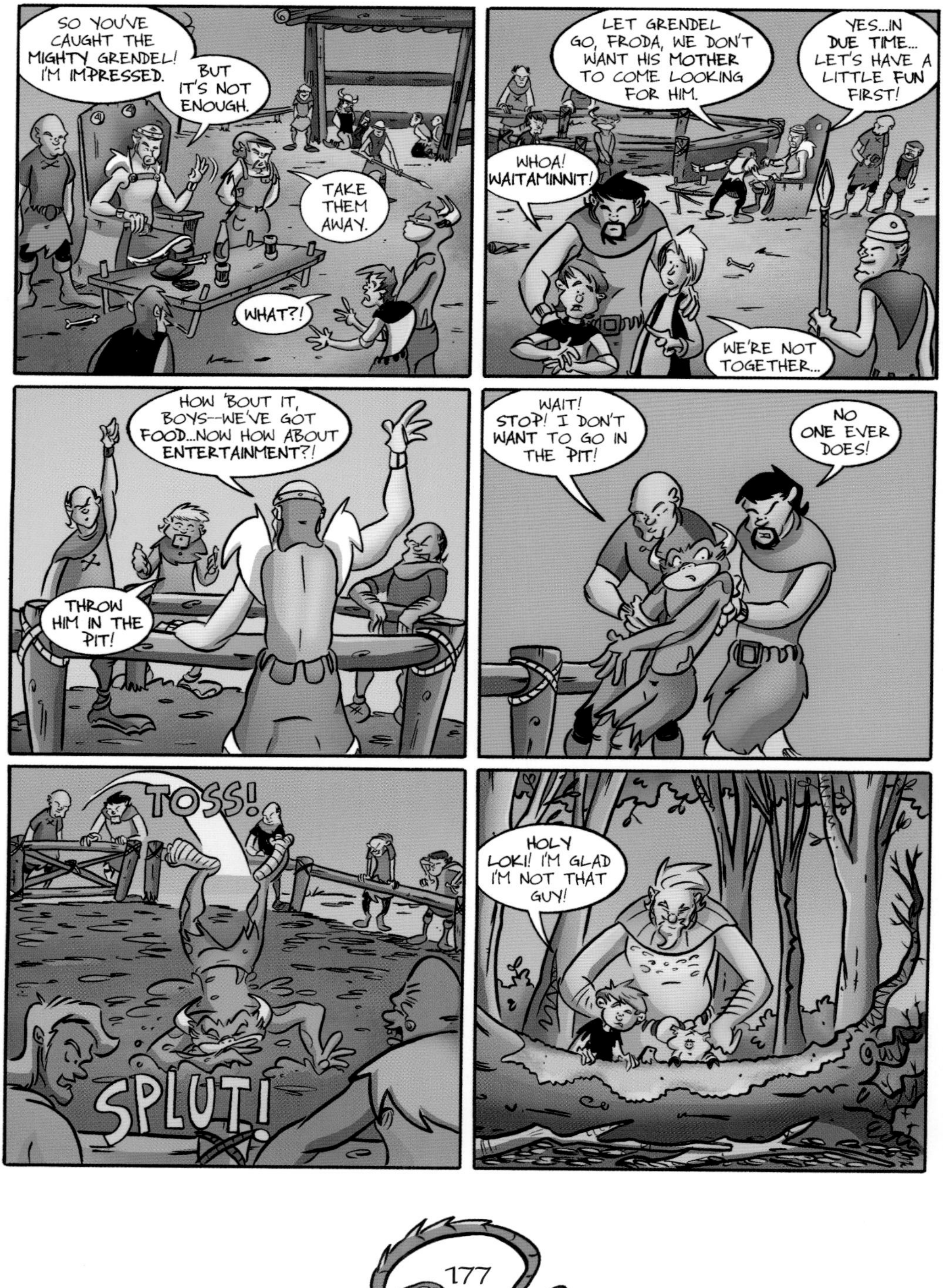
SO YOU'VE CAUGHT THE MIGHTY GRENDEL! I'M IMPRESSED.
BUT IT'S NOT ENOUGH.
TAKE THEM AWAY.
WHAT?!
LET GRENDEL GO, FRODA, WE DON'T WANT HIS MOTHER TO COME LOOKING FOR HIM.
YES...IN DUE TIME... LET'S HAVE A LITTLE FUN FIRST!
WHOA! WAITAMINNIT!
WE'RE NOT TOGETHER...
HOW 'BOUT IT, BOYS--WE'VE GOT FOOD...NOW HOW ABOUT ENTERTAINMENT?!
THROW HIM IN THE PIT!
WAIT! STOP! I DON'T WANT TO GO IN THE PIT!
NO ONE EVER DOES!
TOSS!
SPLUT!
HOLY LOKI! I'M GLAD I'M NOT THAT GUY!

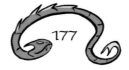

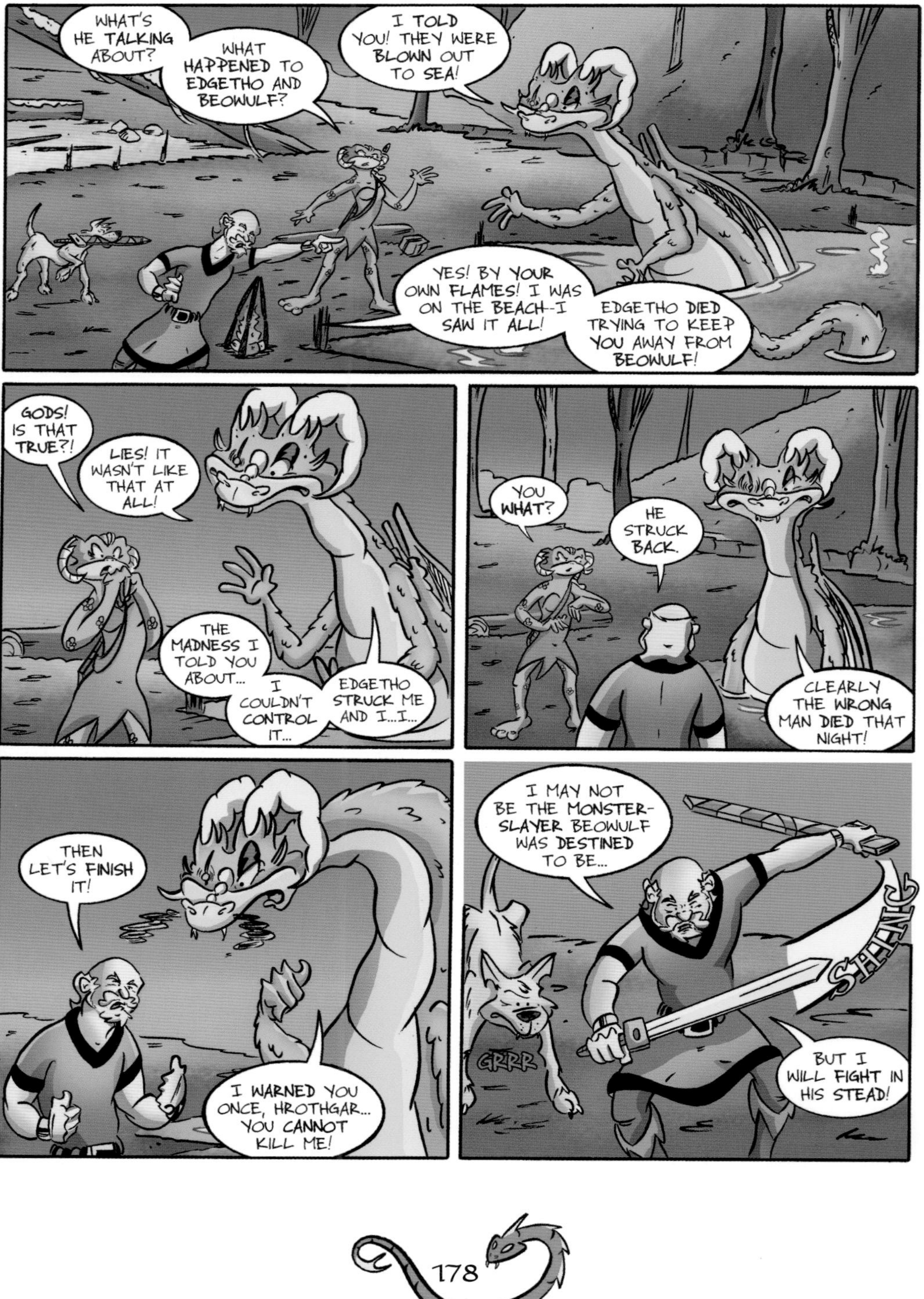
WHAT'S HE TALKING ABOUT?
WHAT HAPPENED TO EDGETHO AND BEOWULF?
I TOLD YOU! THEY WERE BLOWN OUT TO SEA!
YES! BY YOUR OWN FLAMES! I WAS ON THE BEACH--I SAW IT ALL!
EDGETHO DIED TRYING TO KEEP YOU AWAY FROM BEOWULF!
GODS! IS THAT TRUE?!
LIES! IT WASN'T LIKE THAT AT ALL!
THE MADNESS I TOLD YOU ABOUT...
EDGETHO STRUCK ME AND I...I...
I COULDN'T CONTROL IT...
YOU WHAT?
HE STRUCK BACK.
CLEARLY THE WRONG MAN DIED THAT NIGHT!
THEN LET'S FINISH IT!
I WARNED YOU ONCE, HROTHGAR... YOU CANNOT KILL ME!
I MAY NOT BE THE MONSTER-SLAYER BEOWULF WAS DESTINED TO BE...
SHHING
GRRR
BUT I WILL FIGHT IN HIS STEAD!

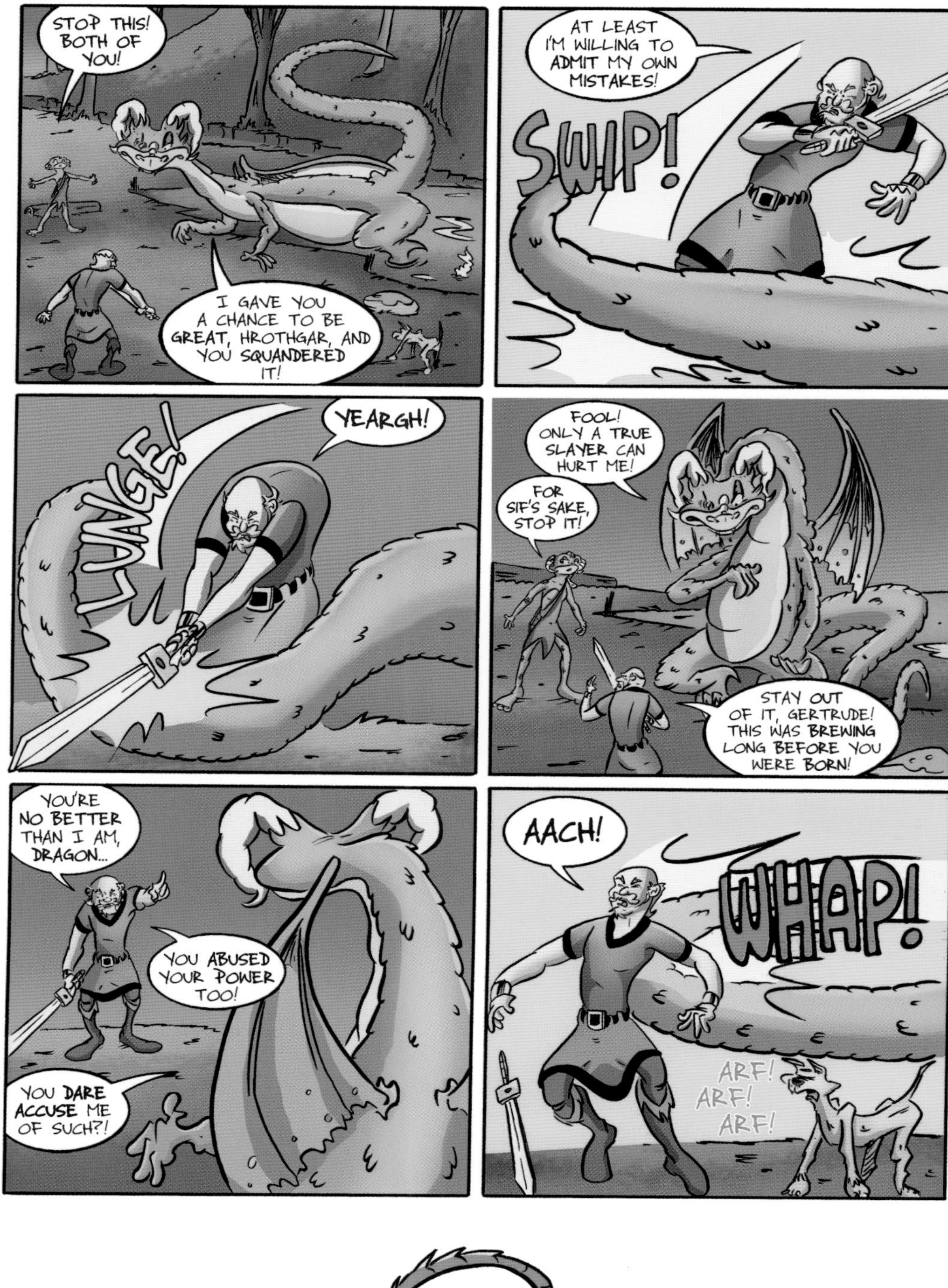
STOP THIS! BOTH OF YOU!
I GAVE YOU A CHANCE TO BE GREAT, HROTHGAR, AND YOU SQUANDERED IT!
AT LEAST I'M WILLING TO ADMIT MY OWN MISTAKES!
SWIP!
LUNGE!
YEARGH!
FOOL! ONLY A TRUE SLAYER CAN HURT ME!
FOR SIF'S SAKE, STOP IT!
STAY OUT OF IT, GERTRUDE! THIS WAS BREWING LONG BEFORE YOU WERE BORN!
YOU'RE NO BETTER THAN I AM, DRAGON...
YOU ABUSED YOUR POWER TOO!
YOU DARE ACCUSE ME OF SUCH?!
AACH!
WHAP!
ARF! ARF! ARF!

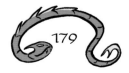

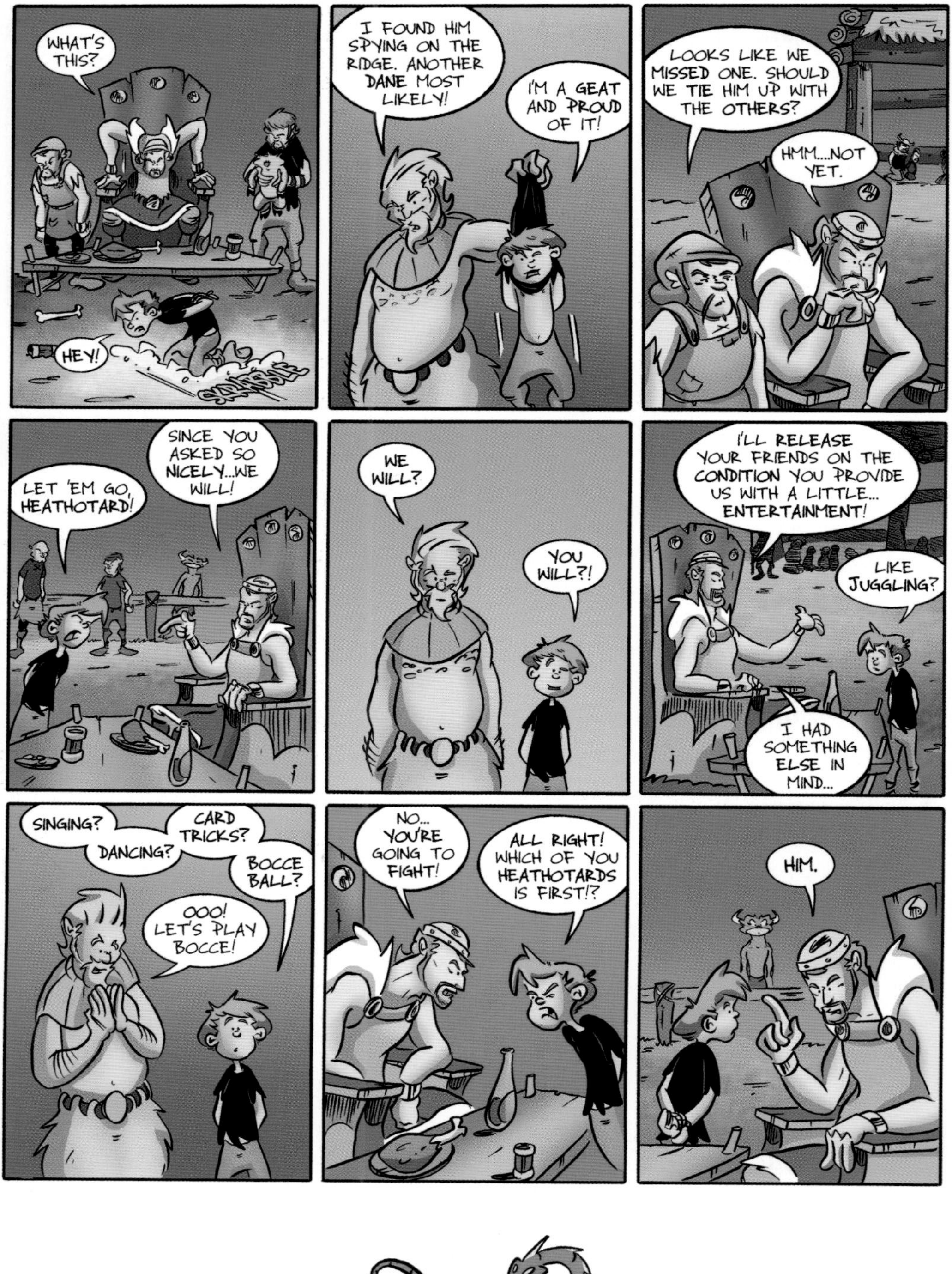
WHAT'S THIS?
HEY!
I FOUND HIM SPYING ON THE RIDGE. ANOTHER DANE MOST LIKELY!
I'M A GEAT AND PROUD OF IT!
LOOKS LIKE WE MISSED ONE. SHOULD WE TIE HIM UP WITH THE OTHERS?
HMM...NOT YET.
LET 'EM GO, HEATHOTARD!
SINCE YOU ASKED SO NICELY...WE WILL!
WE WILL?
YOU WILL?!
I'LL RELEASE YOUR FRIENDS ON THE CONDITION YOU PROVIDE US WITH A LITTLE... ENTERTAINMENT!
LIKE JUGGLING?
I HAD SOMETHING ELSE IN MIND...
SINGING?
DANCING?
CARD TRICKS?
BOCCE BALL?
OOO! LET'S PLAY BOCCE!
NO... YOU'RE GOING TO FIGHT!
ALL RIGHT! WHICH OF YOU HEATHOTARDS IS FIRST!?
HIM.

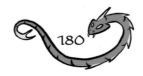

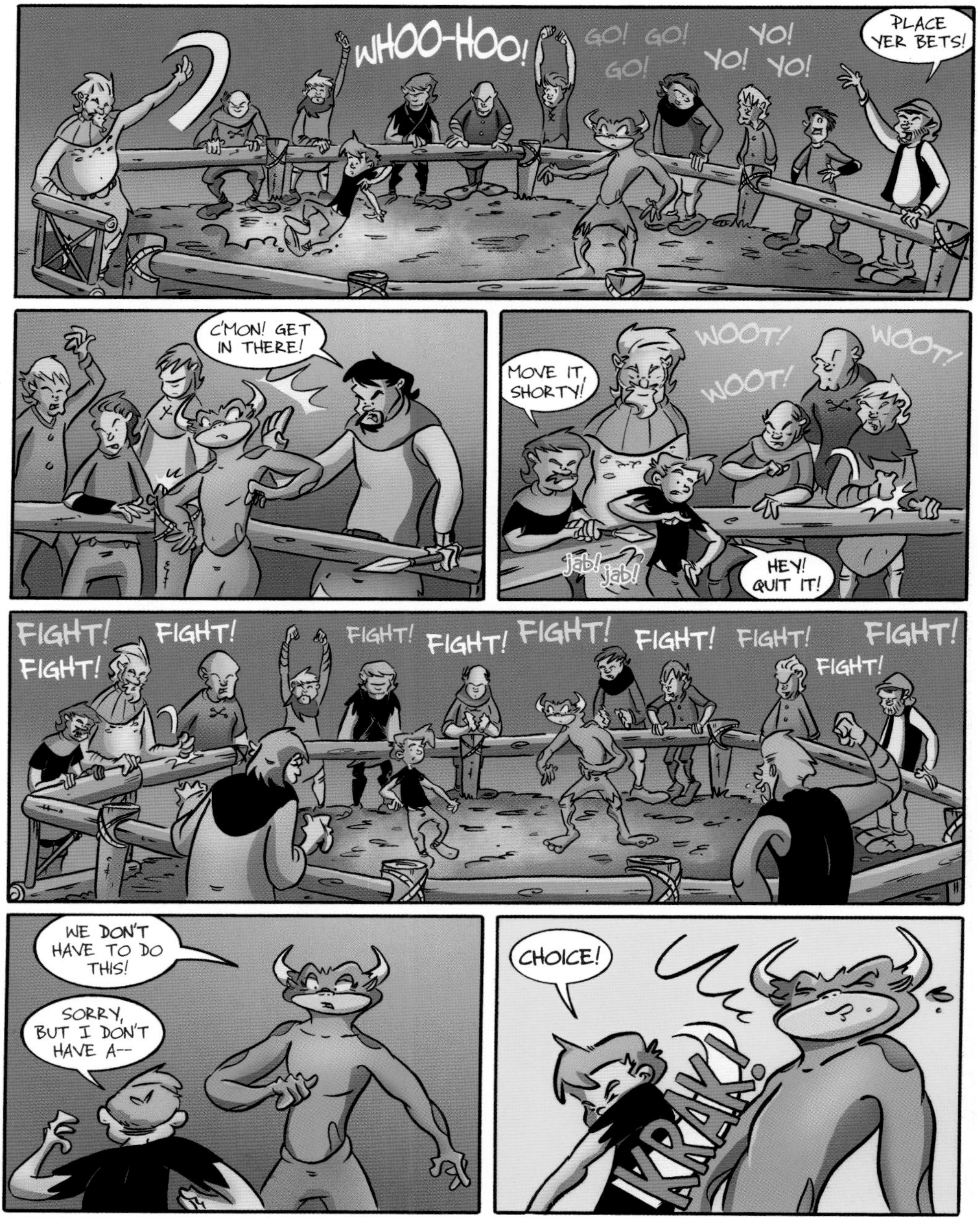
WHOO-HOO!
GO! GO! GO!
YO! YO! YO!
PLACE YER BETS!
C'MON! GET IN THERE!
MOVE IT, SHORTY!
WOOT! WOOT! WOOT!
jab! jab!
HEY! QUIT IT!
FIGHT! FIGHT! FIGHT! FIGHT! FIGHT! FIGHT! FIGHT! FIGHT! FIGHT! FIGHT!
WE DON'T HAVE TO DO THIS!
SORRY, BUT I DON'T HAVE A--
CHOICE!
KRAK!

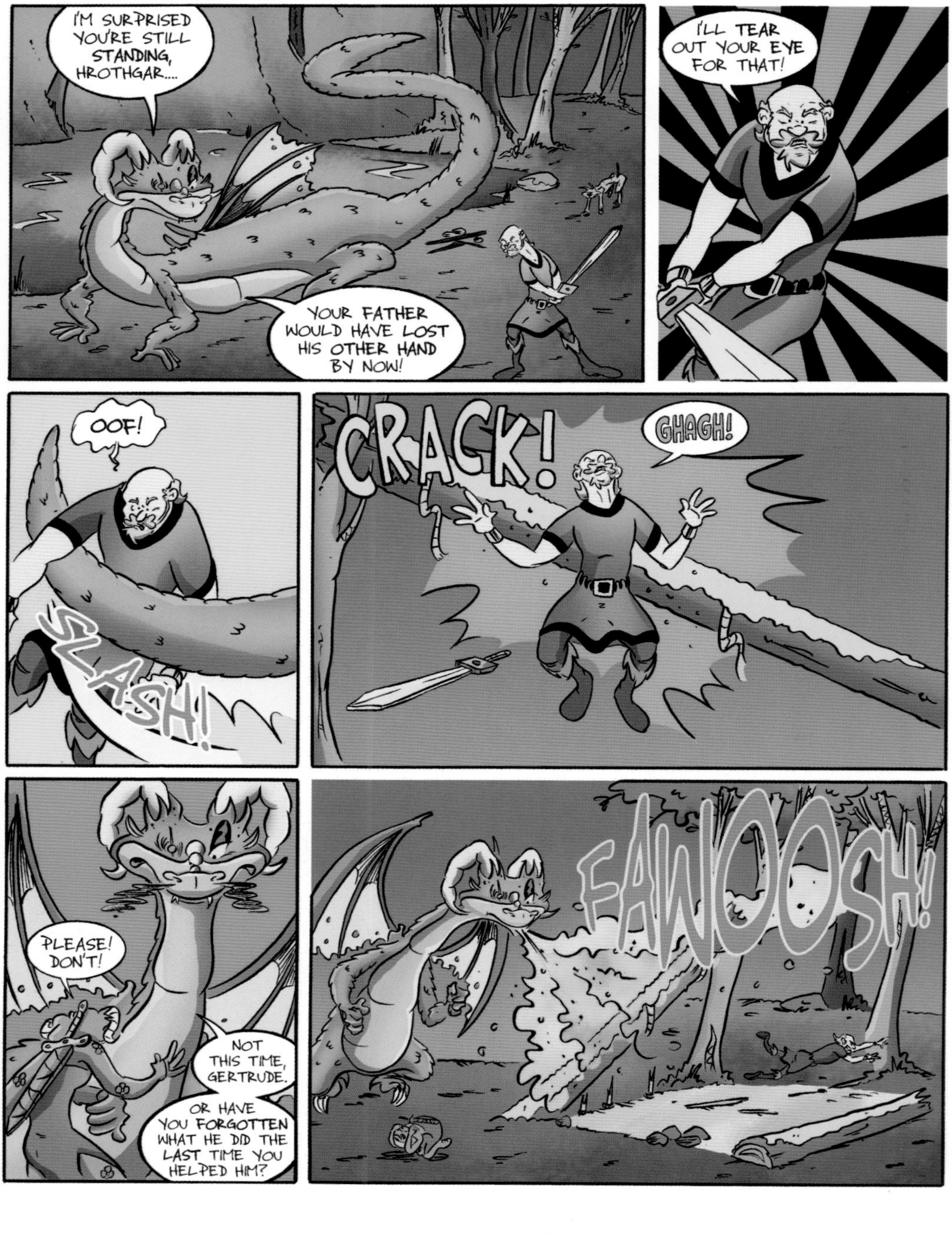
I'M SURPRISED YOU'RE STILL STANDING, HROTHGAR....
YOUR FATHER WOULD HAVE LOST HIS OTHER HAND BY NOW!
I'LL TEAR OUT YOUR EYE FOR THAT!
OOF!
SLASH!
CRACK!
GHAGH!
PLEASE! DON'T!
NOT THIS TIME, GERTRUDE.
OR HAVE YOU FORGOTTEN WHAT HE DID THE LAST TIME YOU HELPED HIM?
FAWOOSH!

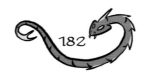

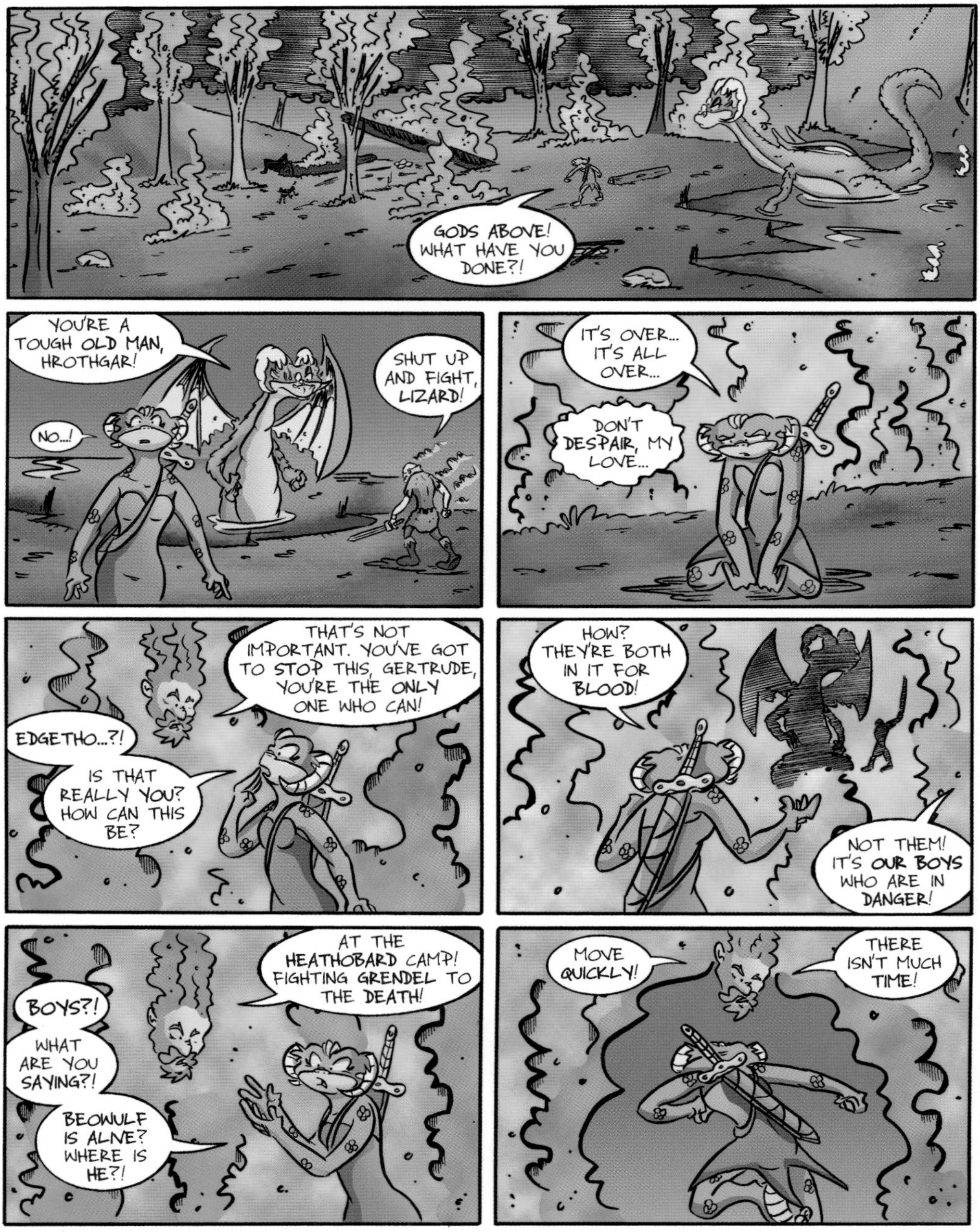
GODS ABOVE! WHAT HAVE YOU DONE?!
YOU'RE A TOUGH OLD MAN, HROTHGAR!
SHUT UP AND FIGHT, LIZARD!
NO...!
IT'S OVER... IT'S ALL OVER...
DON'T DESPAIR, MY LOVE...
THAT'S NOT IMPORTANT. YOU'VE GOT TO STOP THIS, GERTRUDE, YOU'RE THE ONLY ONE WHO CAN!
EDGETHO...?!
IS THAT REALLY YOU? HOW CAN THIS BE?
HOW? THEY'RE BOTH IN IT FOR BLOOD!
NOT THEM! IT'S OUR BOYS WHO ARE IN DANGER!
AT THE HEATHOBARD CAMP! FIGHTING GRENDEL TO THE DEATH!
BOYS?!
WHAT ARE YOU SAYING?!
BEOWULF IS ALIVE? WHERE IS HE?!
MOVE QUICKLY!
THERE ISN'T MUCH TIME!

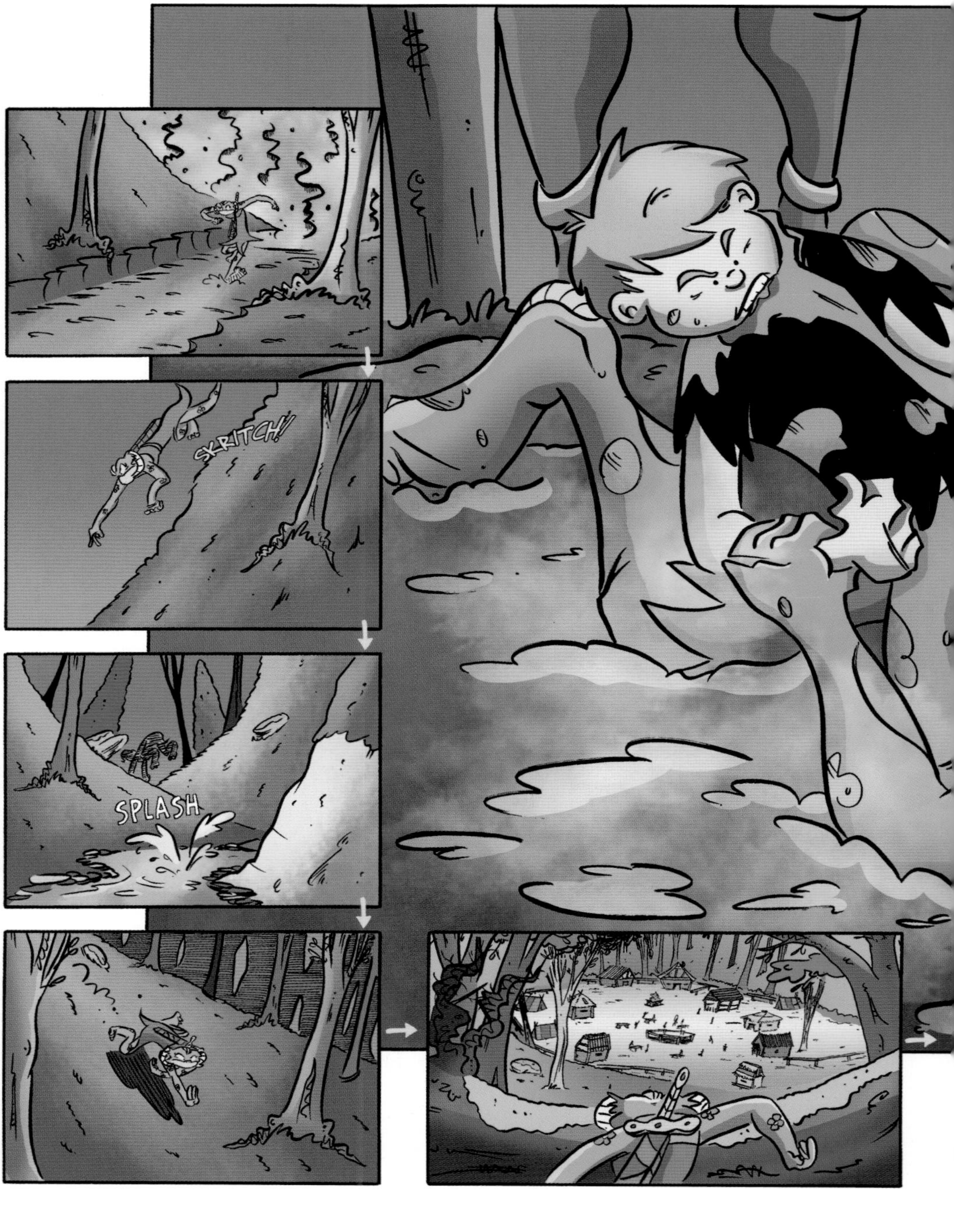
SKRITCH!
SPLASH

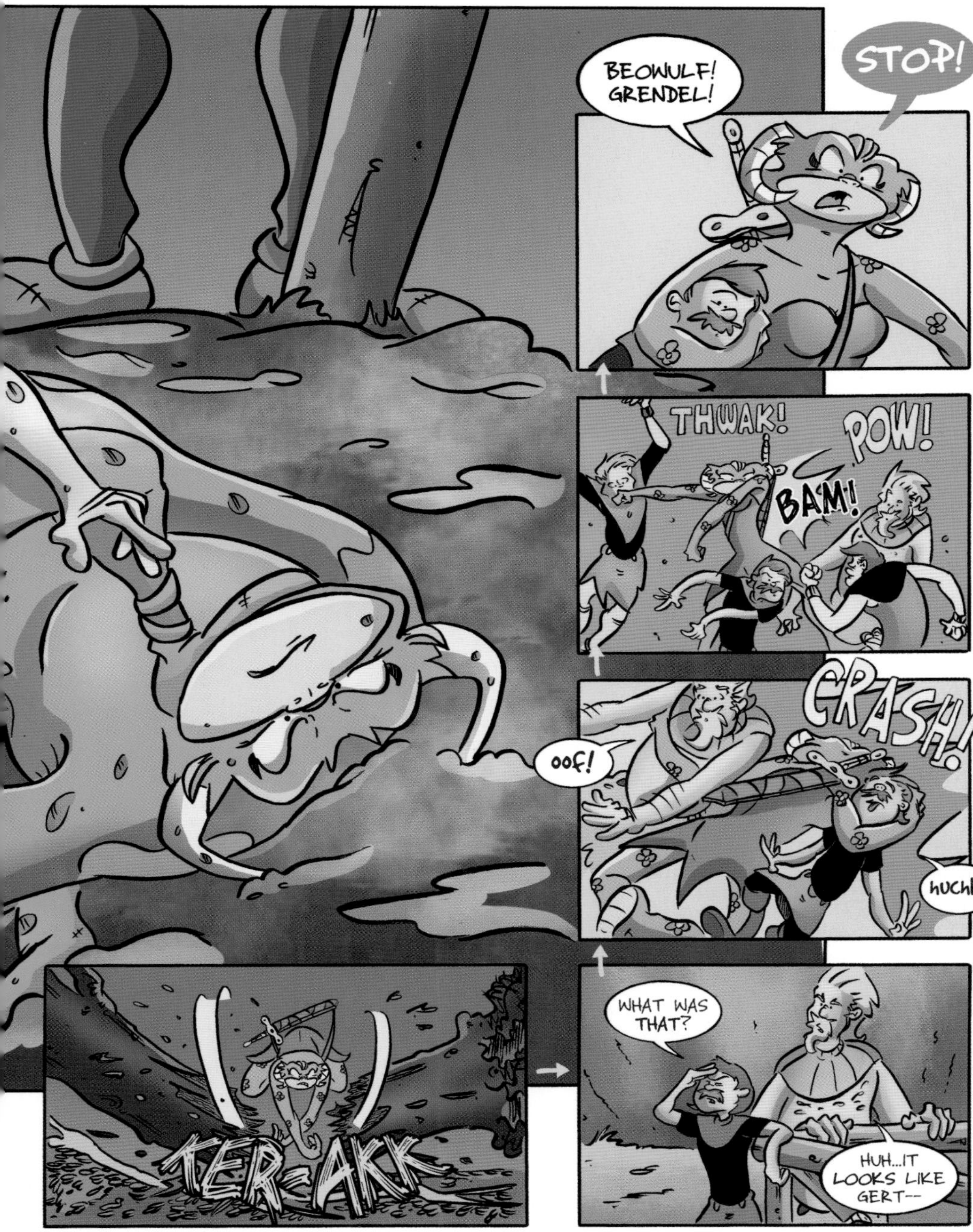
TER-AKK
WHAT WAS THAT?
HUH...IT LOOKS LIKE GERT--
oof!
CRASH!
huchk!
THWAK!
POW!
BAM!
BEOWULF! GRENDEL!
STOP!

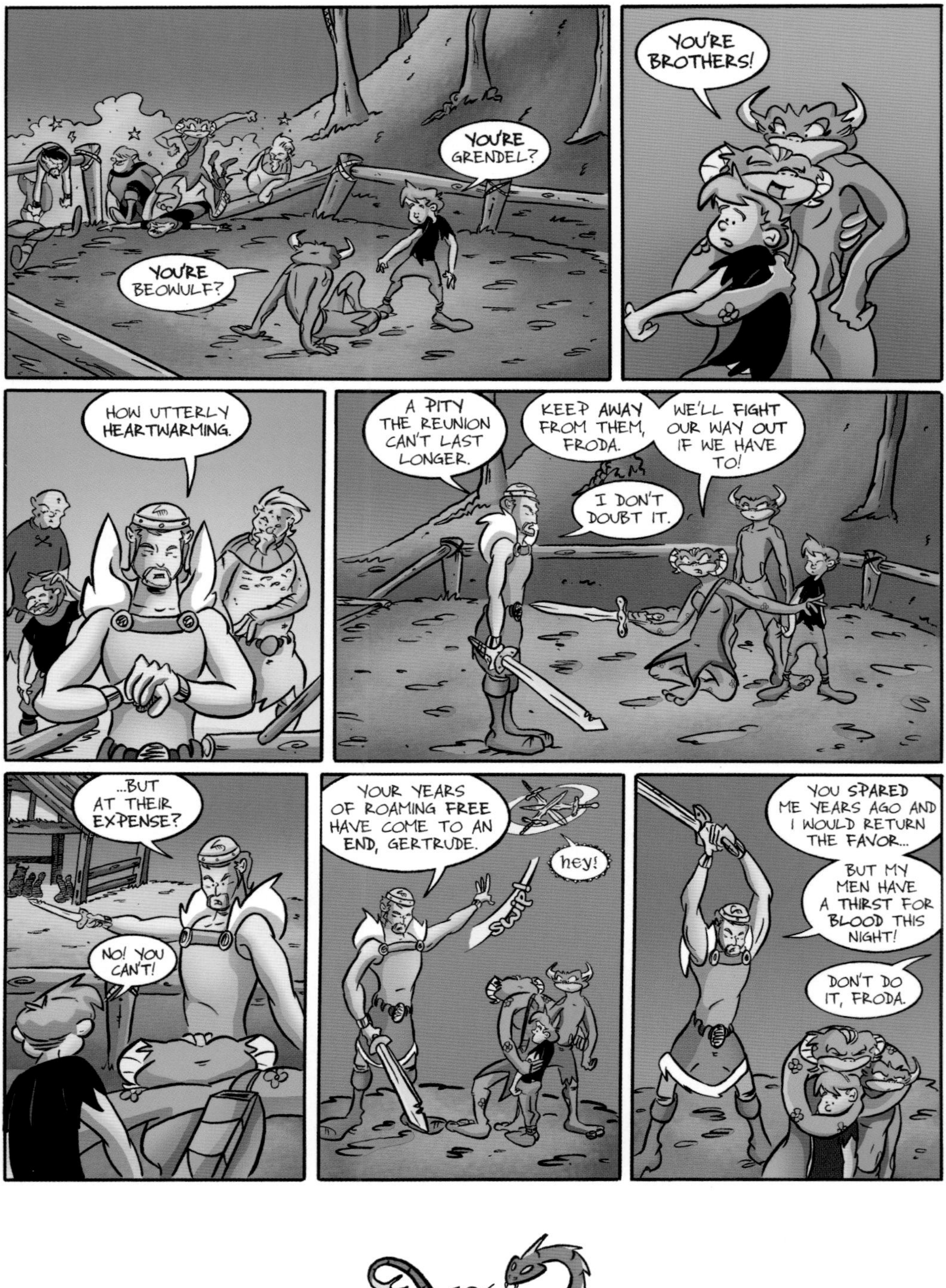
YOU'RE GRENDEL?
YOU'RE BEOWULF?
YOU'RE BROTHERS!
HOW UTTERLY HEARTWARMING.
A PITY THE REUNION CAN'T LAST LONGER.
KEEP AWAY FROM THEM, FRODA.
WE'LL FIGHT OUR WAY OUT IF WE HAVE TO!
I DON'T DOUBT IT.
...BUT AT THEIR EXPENSE?
NO! YOU CAN'T!
YOUR YEARS OF ROAMING FREE HAVE COME TO AN END, GERTRUDE.
hey!
swip
YOU SPARED ME YEARS AGO AND I WOULD RETURN THE FAVOR...
BUT MY MEN HAVE A THIRST FOR BLOOD THIS NIGHT!
DON'T DO IT, FRODA.

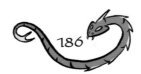

HROTHGAR? FOR SIF'S SAKE-- WHAT HAPPENED TO YOU?

LET HER GO, FRODA.

AND WHY SHOULD I? IF SHE'S WORTH SOMETHING TO YOU, THEN I'LL SLAY HER WHERE SHE STANDS!

YOU CANNOT!

SHE IS YRS'S, DAUGHTER!

WHAT? YRS...? HOW CAN THAT BE...?

IT'S TRUE. GERTRUDE IS HER DAUGHTER...

GERTRUDE IS MY DAUGHTER.

DAUGHTER? HOW...?

AND THESE BOYS THEN...?

ARE MY GRANDSONS.

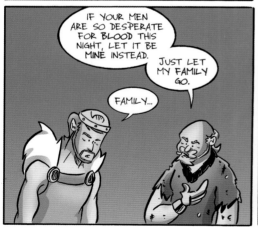

IF YOUR MEN ARE SO DESPERATE FOR BLOOD THIS NIGHT, LET IT BE MINE INSTEAD.

JUST LET MY FAMILY GO.

FAMILY...

AND WHY SHOULD I WHEN ALL YOU DID WAS TEAR MY OWN FAMILY APART?

YOU EXPECT ME TO BELIEVE YOU'D SACRIFICE YOURSELF FOR THEM?

THEY'RE ALL I HAVE LEFT.

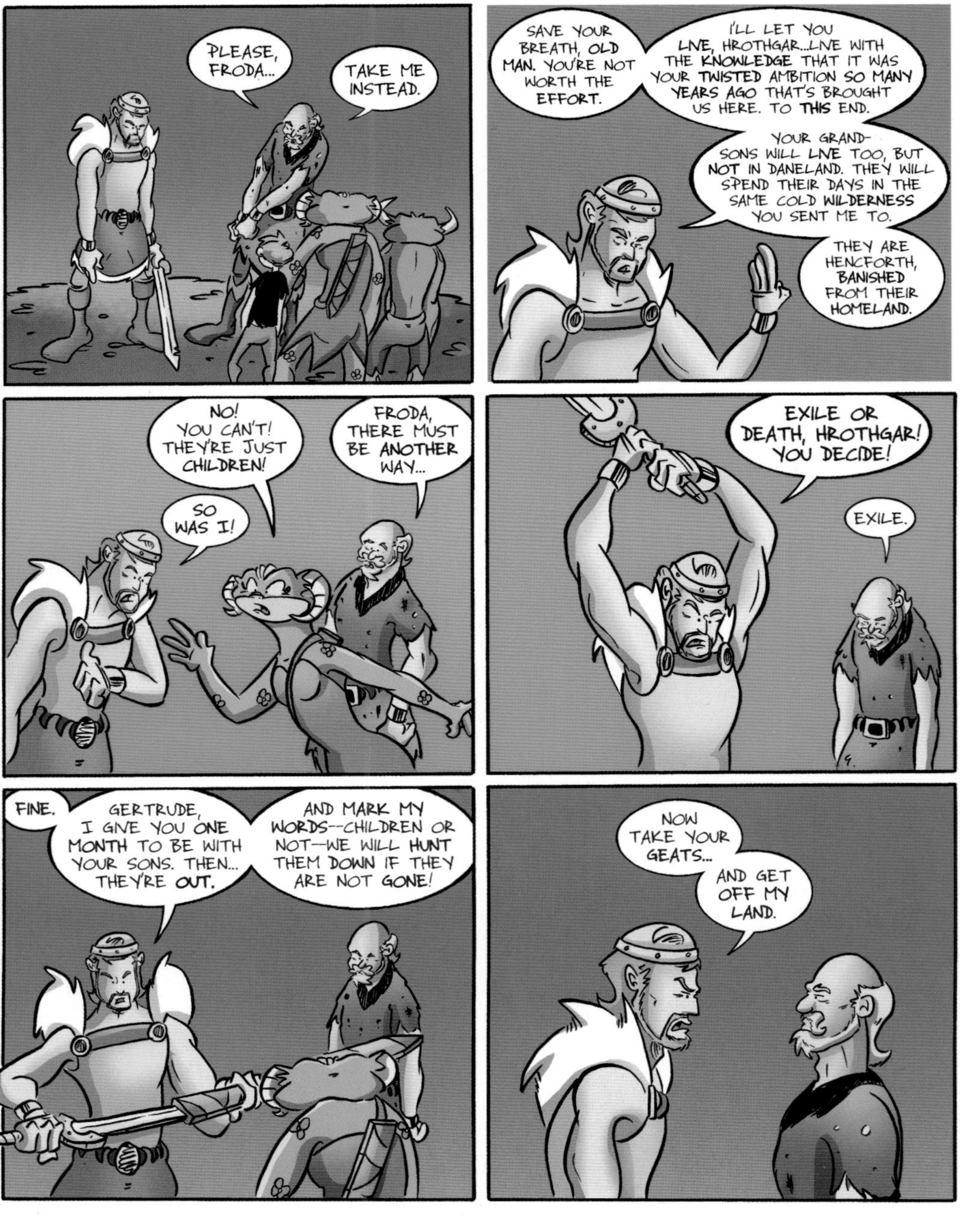
PLEASE, FRODA...
TAKE ME INSTEAD.
SAVE YOUR BREATH, OLD MAN. YOU'RE NOT WORTH THE EFFORT.
I'LL LET YOU LIVE, HROTHGAR...LIVE WITH THE KNOWLEDGE THAT IT WAS YOUR TWISTED AMBITION SO MANY YEARS AGO THAT'S BROUGHT US HERE. TO THIS END.
YOUR GRAND-SONS WILL LIVE TOO, BUT NOT IN DANELAND. THEY WILL SPEND THEIR DAYS IN THE SAME COLD WILDERNESS YOU SENT ME TO.
THEY ARE HENCFORTH, BANISHED FROM THEIR HOMELAND.
NO! YOU CAN'T! THEY'RE JUST CHILDREN!
SO WAS I!
FRODA, THERE MUST BE ANOTHER WAY...
EXILE OR DEATH, HROTHGAR! YOU DECIDE!
EXILE.
FINE.
GERTRUDE, I GIVE YOU ONE MONTH TO BE WITH YOUR SONS. THEN... THEY'RE OUT.
AND MARK MY WORDS--CHILDREN OR NOT--WE WILL HUNT THEM DOWN IF THEY ARE NOT GONE!
NOW TAKE YOUR GEATS...
AND GET OFF MY LAND.

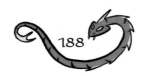

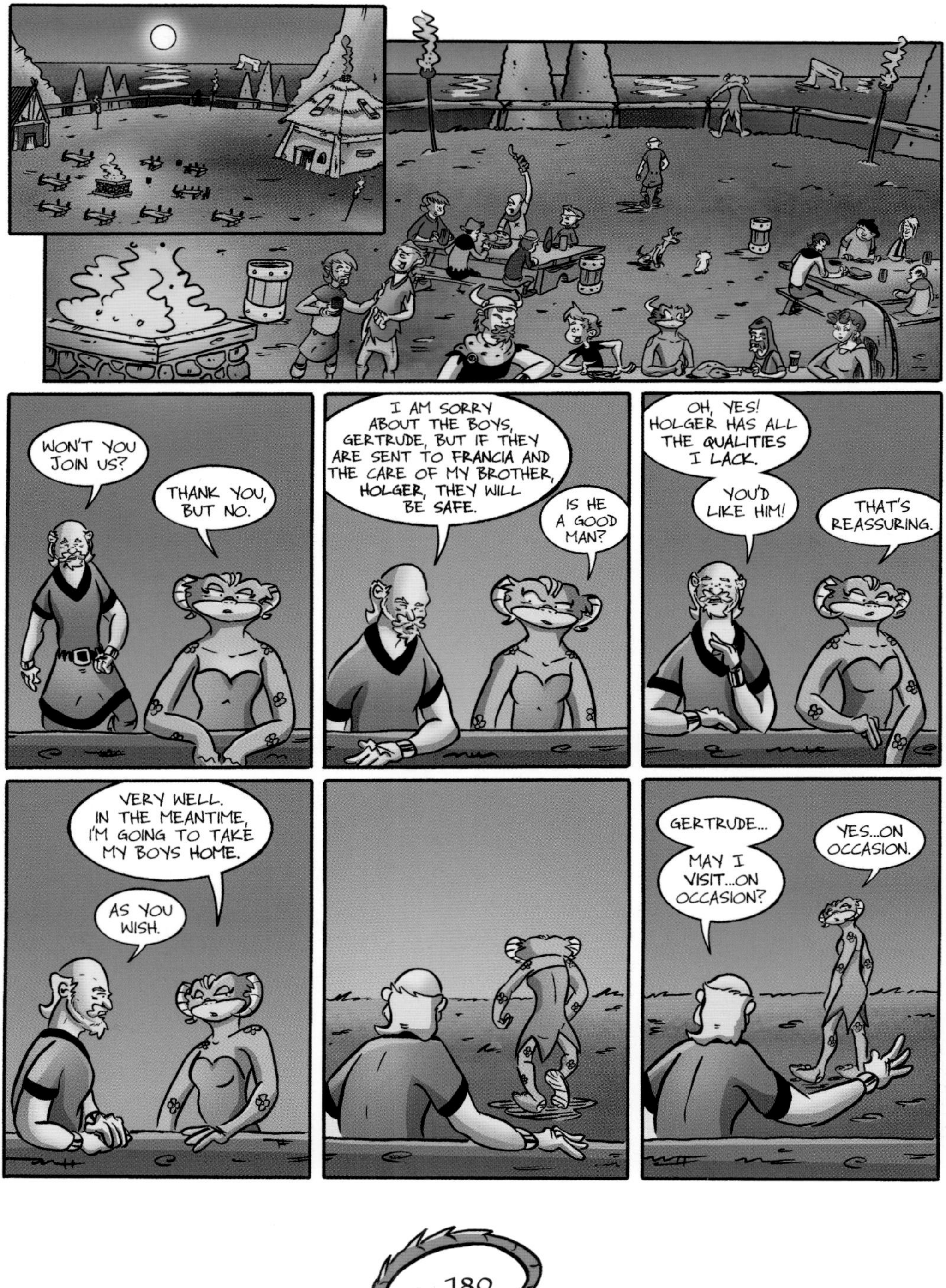
WON'T YOU JOIN US?
THANK YOU, BUT NO.
I AM SORRY ABOUT THE BOYS, GERTRUDE, BUT IF THEY ARE SENT TO FRANCIA AND THE CARE OF MY BROTHER, HOLGER, THEY WILL BE SAFE.
IS HE A GOOD MAN?
OH, YES! HOLGER HAS ALL THE QUALITIES I LACK.
YOU'D LIKE HIM!
THAT'S REASSURING.
VERY WELL. IN THE MEANTIME, I'M GOING TO TAKE MY BOYS HOME.
AS YOU WISH.
GERTRUDE...
MAY I VISIT...ON OCCASION?
YES...ON OCCASION.

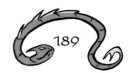

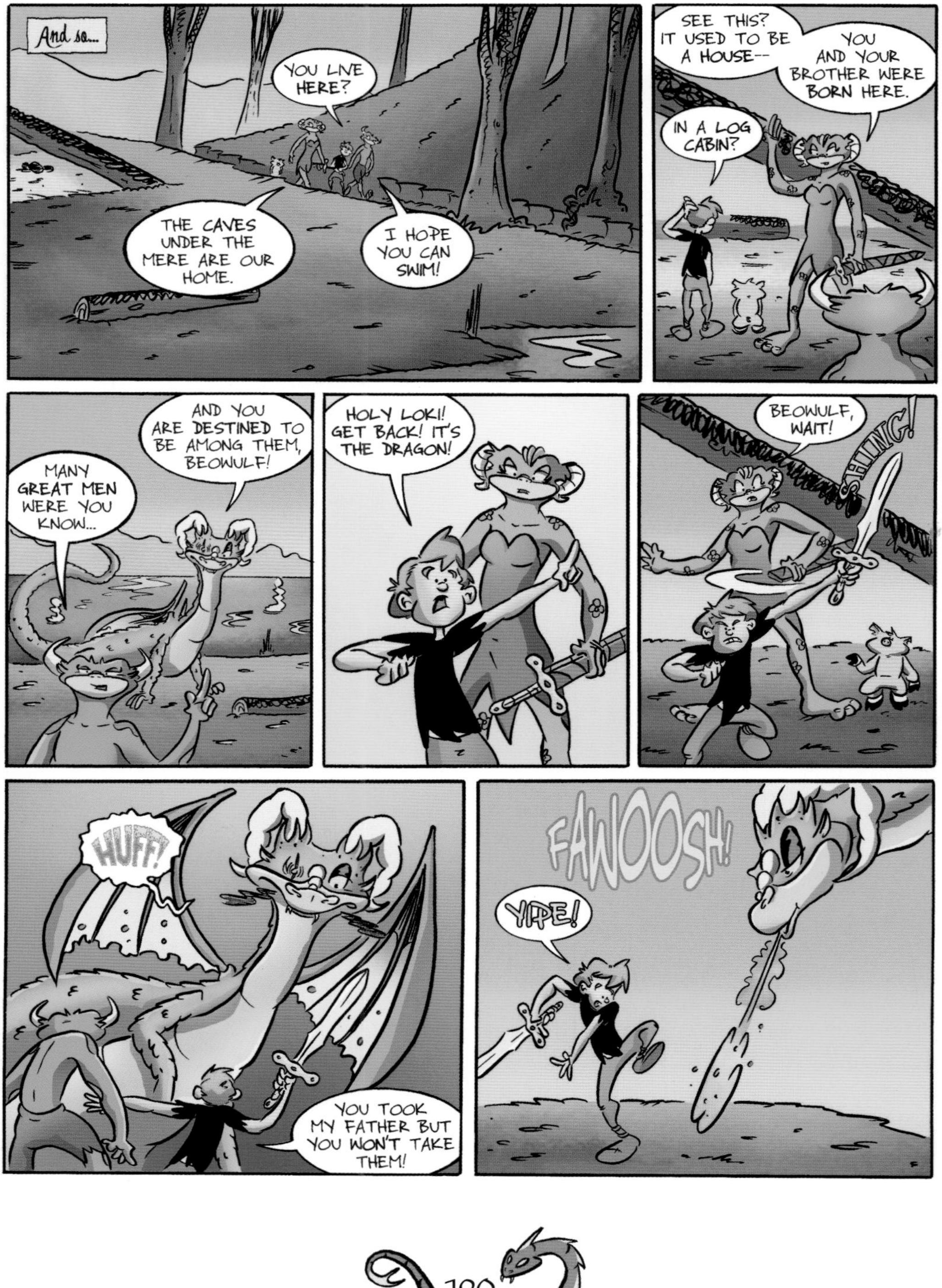
And so...
YOU LIVE HERE?
THE CAVES UNDER THE MERE ARE OUR HOME.
I HOPE YOU CAN SWIM!
SEE THIS? IT USED TO BE A HOUSE--
YOU AND YOUR BROTHER WERE BORN HERE.
IN A LOG CABIN?
MANY GREAT MEN WERE YOU KNOW...
AND YOU ARE DESTINED TO BE AMONG THEM, BEOWULF!
HOLY LOKI! GET BACK! IT'S THE DRAGON!
BEOWULF, WAIT!
SHING!
HUFF!
YOU TOOK MY FATHER BUT YOU WON'T TAKE THEM!
FAWOOSH!
YIPE!

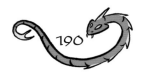

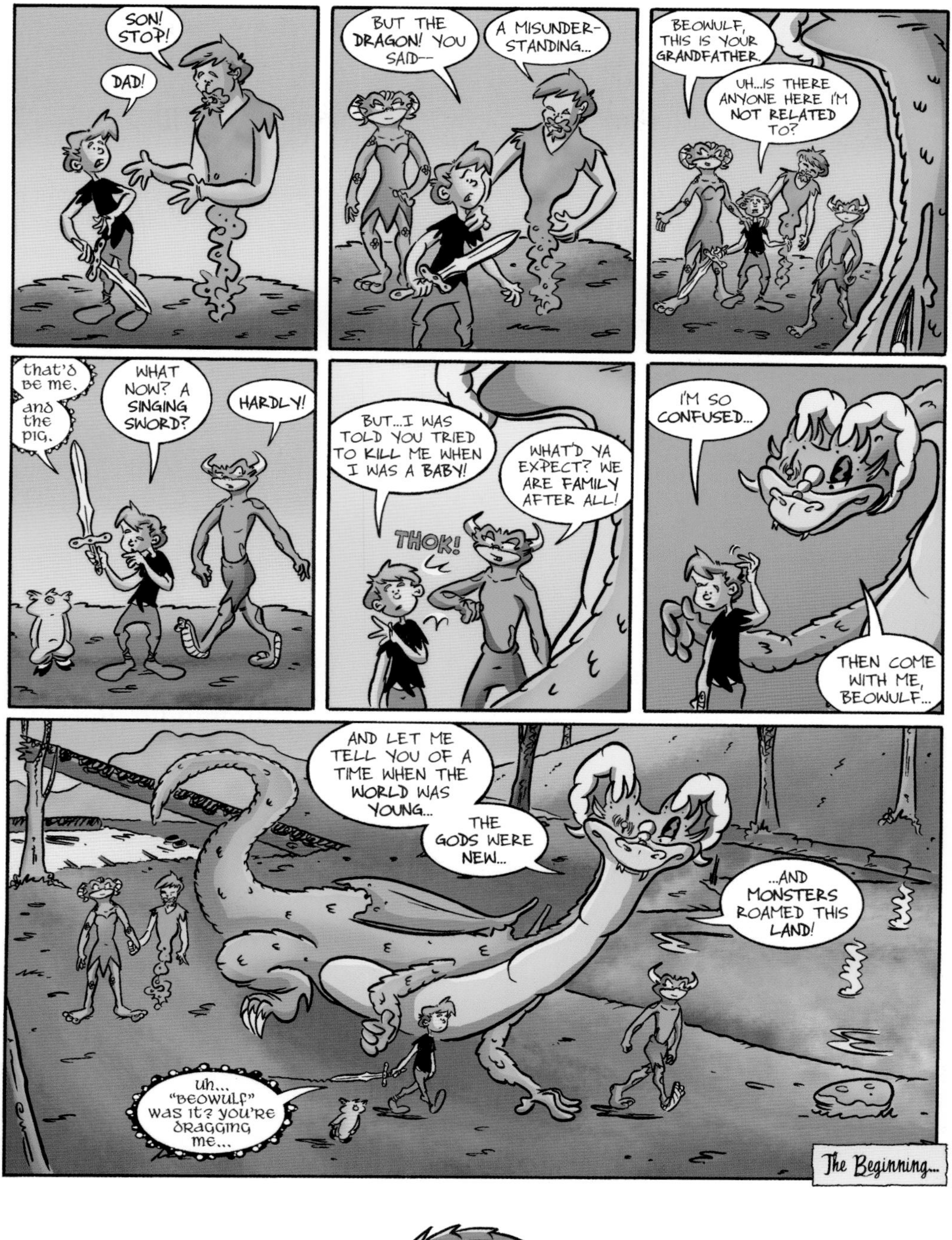
SON! STOP!
DAD!
BUT THE DRAGON! YOU SAID--
A MISUNDER-STANDING...
BEOWULF, THIS IS YOUR GRANDFATHER.
UH...IS THERE ANYONE HERE I'M NOT RELATED TO?
that'd be me,
and the pig.
WHAT NOW? A SINGING SWORD?
HARDLY!
BUT...I WAS TOLD YOU TRIED TO KILL ME WHEN I WAS A BABY!
THOK!
WHAT'D YA EXPECT? WE ARE FAMILY AFTER ALL!
I'M SO CONFUSED...
THEN COME WITH ME, BEOWULF...
AND LET ME TELL YOU OF A TIME WHEN THE WORLD WAS YOUNG...
THE GODS WERE NEW...
...AND MONSTERS ROAMED THIS LAND!
uh... "Beowulf" was it? you're dragging me...
The Beginning...

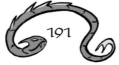

MORE
TO EXPLORE!

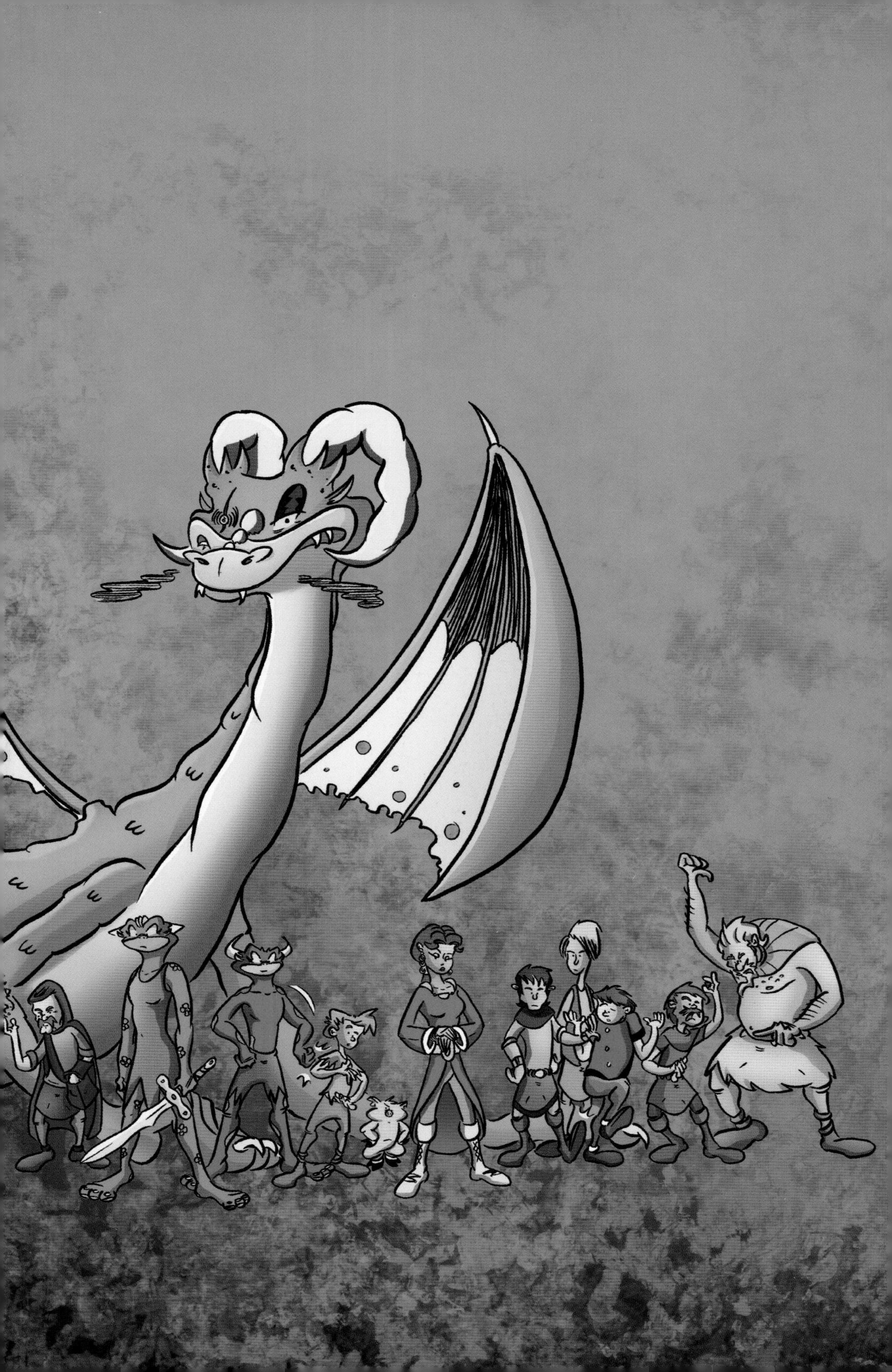

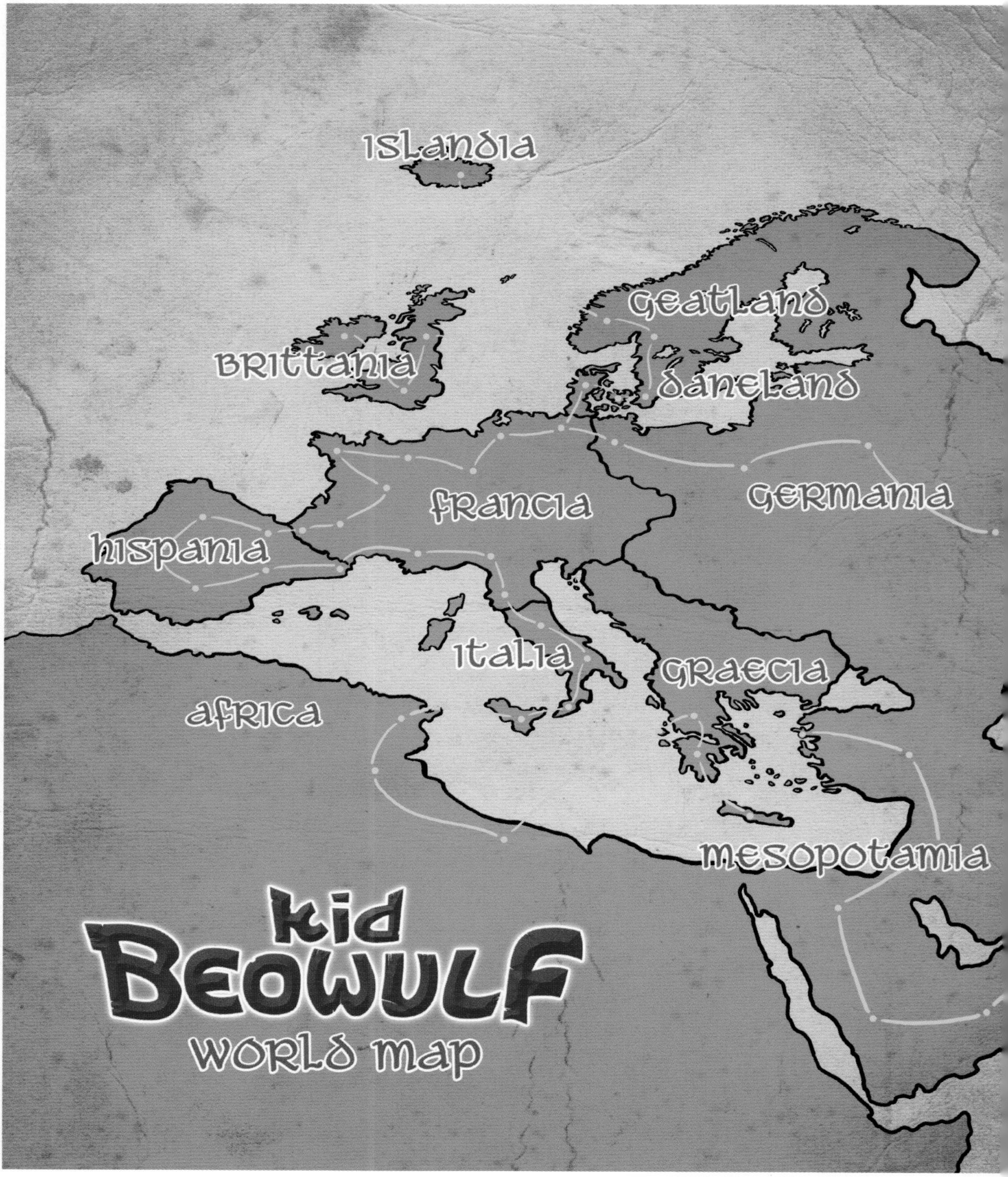
ISLANDIA
GEATLAND
BRITTANIA
DANELAND
FRANCIA
GERMANIA
HISPANIA
ITALIA
GRAECIA
AFRICA
MESOPOTAMIA
KID BEOWULF
WORLD MAP

The world map is on the inside cover of each book, and it is an important piece of the *Kid Beowulf* series; not only does it tell us where Beowulf and Grendel are, but it clues us into where they might go next.

Each country listed is another potential adventure in the series as the brothers make their long road trip through mythology. Can you guess where they will go next and which heroes they will meet there?

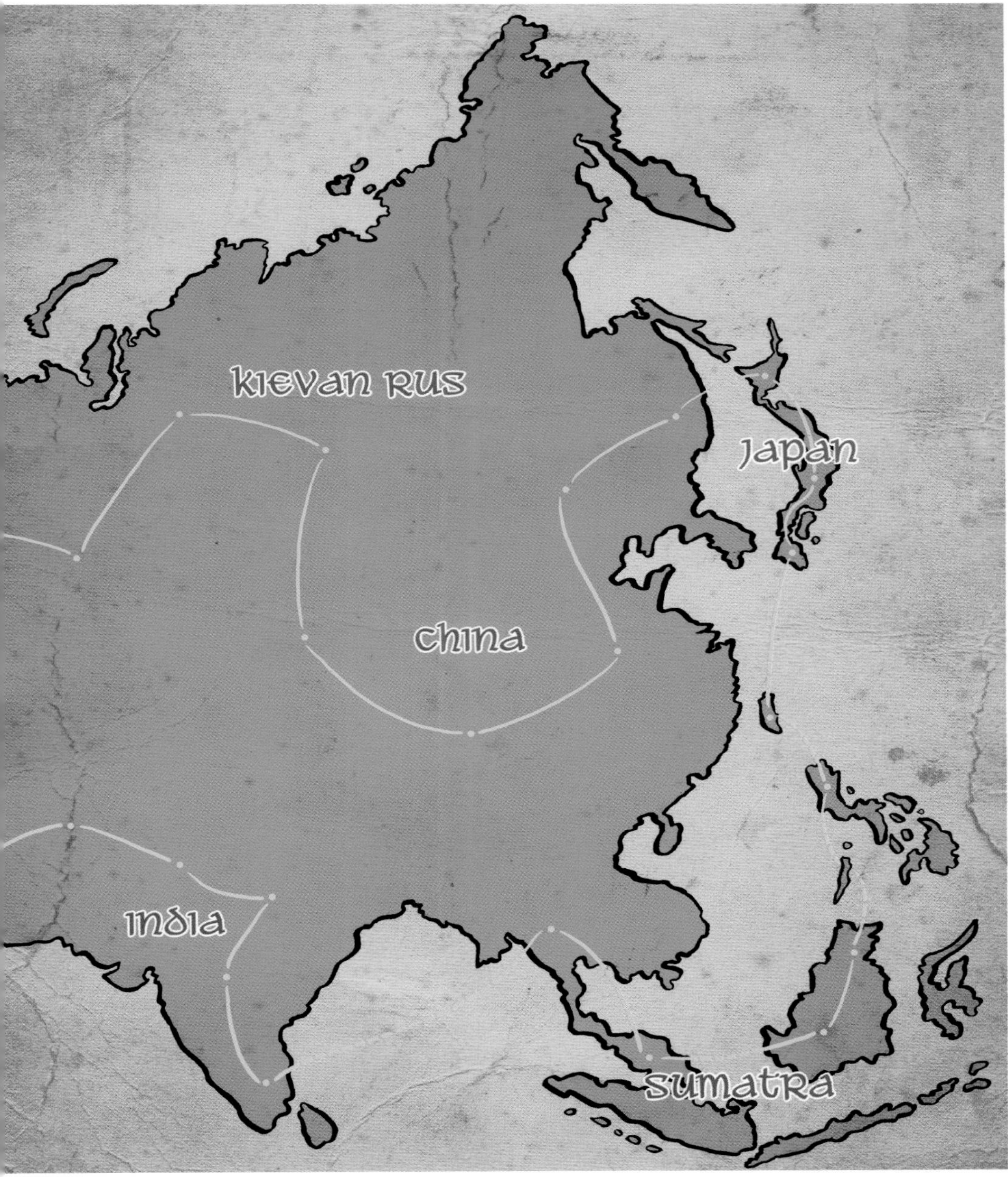
KIEVAN RUS
JAPAN
CHINA
INDIA
SUMATRA

The world is full of countries all with their own stories, legends, and heroes that have influenced their culture. With each new place Beowulf and Grendel vist they will encounter these new lands and heroes. The brothers will grow up along the way and learn from the people they've met and the places they've been. Beowulf and Grendel's long road home will lead to self-discovery and their ultimate destiny!

Daneland Circa 450 A.D.

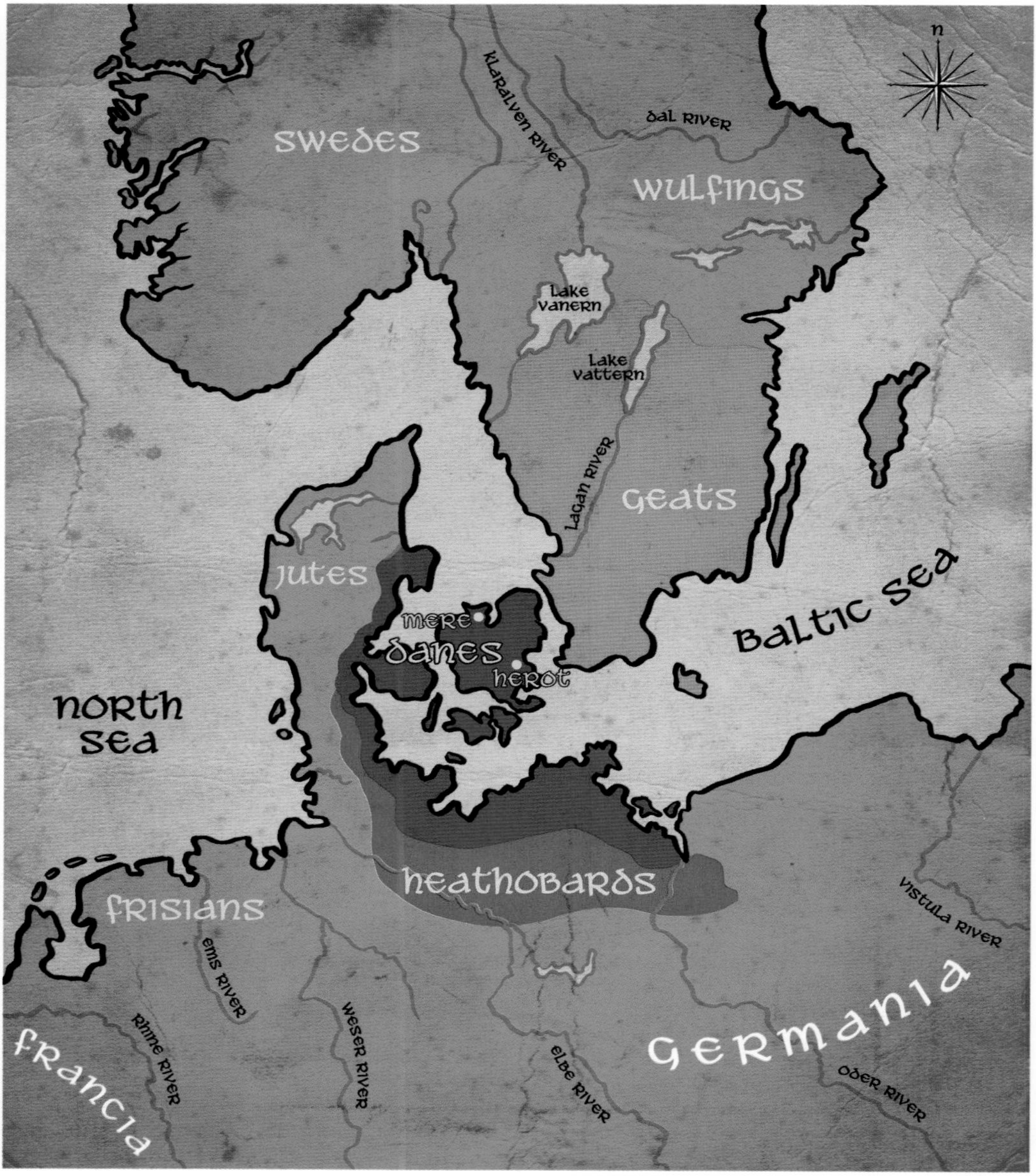
n
Dal River
Klaralven River
Swedes
Wulfings
Lake Vanern
Lake Vattern
Lagan River
Geats
Baltic Sea
Jutes
Mere
Danes
Herot
North Sea
Heathobards
Frisians
Ems River
Rhine River
Weser River
Elbe River
Vistula River
Germania
Oder River
Francia

Book one in the *Kid Beowulf* series takes place around 450 A.D. in Daneland (modern-day Denmark) and Geatland (modern-day Sweden). During this time Daneland was populated by small clans. The most powerful clans during Beowulf's time were the Danes, the Geats, and the Swedes. When clans went to war, blood-feuds would rage for generations. In *The Blood-Bound Oath*, a small clan originating from Germania, called the Heathobards, is encroaching on the Danish land and threatening the Danes' supremacy.

key terms

Blood-feud is a feud with a cycle of retaliatory violence, when the relatives of someone who has been wronged, dishonored, or killed seek vengeance by punishing the culprits or their relatives. Blood-feuds were common in the time of *Beowulf*, and in *The Blood-Bound Oath*, Froda swears vengeance against Hrothgar for attacking his people and abducting Yrs, thus creating a blood-feud that will last for generations.

Danes are the ruling clan of Daneland and are led by King Shild. They are allies with the Geats, a strong clan just across the sea. The Danes are enemies with the Heathobards, a clan moving in from Germania. When King Shild dies, his kingdom goes to his son, Hrothgar.

Geats are a clan across the Baltic Sea and are led by King Hrethel. They are longtime friends of the Danes and often aid them in battle with the Heathobards. When King Hrethel dies, his kingdom goes to his son, Higlac.

Heathobards are a clan led by King Dagref and hail from Germania. They have warred with the Danes for many years. When King Dagref dies, his kingdom goes to his son, Froda.

Herot means "heart" and is the name of a great meadhall built by Hrothgar. Hrothgar decides to build Herot in an attempt to unite all the warring clans and leave something permanent to his kingdom. In an act of revenge, Froda and the Heathobards burn it down. In the original epic poem, *Beowulf*, Herot Hall is terrorized night after night by Grendel.

The **mere** is a mysterious swamp in the highlands of Daneland where it is rumored a dragon and other monstrous creatures live. No one goes near the mere if they can help it.

Ragnarök is a series of cataclysmic events in Norse mythology when gods war with giants, the earth crumbles, and the world is subsumed in water. It is often referred to as "the twilight of the gods" as many of them die in battle (including Odin, Thor, and Loki). Ragnarök is the end of a cycle, after which the earth will resurface anew and fertile, the surviving gods will return, and the world will be repopulated by human survivors. The Dragon refers to Ragnarök when he first meets Hrothgar in his cave.

Valhalla is also from Norse mythology and is a majestic meadhall ruled over by the god Odin, where slain heroes go to live out eternity while they drink mead, eat good food, and relive past glories.

Character Glossary

Beowulf (**bay**-oh-wolf) is Grendel's twin brother and the son of Getrude and Edgetho. As a baby, Beowulf washed upon the shores of Geatland and was raised by his uncle, Higlac. Beowulf never knew his true lineage until he made a trip to Daneland and soon discovered everything.

Dagref (**day**-griff) is king of the Heathobards, a migratory people from Germania. Dagref has fought many battles against the Danes to carve out a home for his Heathobards. His son, Froda, will one day be their chief.

The Dragon is the oldest living creature in Daneland. He adopted Gertrude when Hrothgar abandoned her and is grandfather to Beowulf and Grendel. He resides deep below the mere but knows about everything that happens above ground: past, present, and future!

Edgetho (**edge**-thoe) was adopted by King Hrethel and raised as Higlac's brother. On a trip to Daneland, Edgetho discovered Gertrude and fell in love. He is father to Beowulf and Grendel and died protecting Beowulf during a fight with the Dragon. Years later, Edgetho returns as a fire spirit.

Esher (**esh**-er) is a Frisian and is a longtime friend and adviser to King Shild. For years he has kept an eye on the young princes Hrothgar and Holger. Later, he advises King Higlac and looks over Beowulf. Esher has long known about the Dragon and the world of monsters and their slayers.

Froda (**froh**-duh) is the son of Dagref, the Heathobard chief, and will one day be king. Froda has a contentious relationship with Hrothgar. When the Dane takes Froda's wife, Yrs, away from him and exiles Froda from Daneland, Froda swears retribution on Hrothgar and his family.

Gertrude (**grr**-trood) is the daughter of Hrothgar and Yrs and was adopted by the Dragon when she was a baby. It was the Dragon's blood, mixed with Hrothgar's human blood, that gave Gertrude a half-breed appearance. She fell in love with Edgetho and is the mother to Beowulf and Grendel.

Grendel (**gren**-del) is Beowulf's twin brother and the son of Getrude and Edgetho. Grendel was raised in the highlands of Daneland by his mother and his grandfather, the Dragon. He grew up thinking his brother died as a baby and is totally surprised to discover his twin twelve years later!

Hama (**ha**-ma) the pig is from Geatland and was sent to Daneland as supper. Hama got shipwrecked with Beowulf in Daneland and the two became fast friends. Hama accompanies Beowulf and Grendel on all their adventures. The brothers are lucky to have this smart and stalwart companion.

Higlac (**hig**-lack) is Hrethel's son and heir to Geatland's throne. His best friend, Edgetho, was adopted at an early age by Hrethel, and the boys grew up as brothers. When baby Beowulf washed up on Higlac's shores he raised his nephew like he was his own son.

Holger (**hole**-grr) is Shild's son and Hrothgar's little brother. He was never meant to rule, but when Hrothgar went missing and Shild died, leadership of the Danes fell to Holger. Holger kept peace with the Heathobards until Hrothgar returned and made war. Holger left soon after to seek redemption in a new land.

Hrethel (**reth**-el) is king of Geatland and a longtime friend of the Danes. When Hrothgar became king, Hrethel sent his sons, Higlac and Edgetho, to Daneland to become men. When Hrethel dies, leadership of Geatland will pass to Higlac.

Hrothgar (**roth**-gar) is Holger's older brother and the son of King Shild. He is in line for the Danish throne. Hrothgar hates the Heathobards but falls in love with one of them, Yrs. When Hrothgar meets the Dragon he makes a blood-oath and becomes powerful, but he abuses that power. He abducts Yrs, and their child is Gertrude, a human-dragon hybrid and the embodiment of all that Hrothgar hates.

Ingeld (**ing**-eld) is a Heathobard and an old friend of King Dagref. He is a smith by trade, and comes to Daneland to forge weapons for Dagref. Ingeld brings his daughter, Yrs, with him. When she is taken by Hrothgar, Ingeld vows vengeance and plots with his son-in-law, Froda, for many years to come.

Nagling (**nag**-ling) means "nailer" in Old English and is an ancient sword forged by the great smith Weyland from ages past. It has been wielded by gods and demigods, heroes and heroines. Nagling is imbued with the power of speech and likes to be heard (though no one likes to listen).

Shild (shilled) is the father of Hrothgar and Holger, and is king of the Danes. He built his kingdom out of many battles, the first of which was against the Dragon (who mistook Shild for his slayer); Shild lost his hand that day, but gained the knowledge that one day the Dragon's slayer would come from his own bloodline.

Unferth (**un**-firth) is a Danish boy who has grown up listening to the stories of when the Danes were proud, ruled the land, and built Herot Hall, but those days are long past. Unferth scrounges for food with his friends and has to beat back Grendel, the monster who roams Daneland's forests.

Welthow (**well**-thoe) is Hrothgar's second wife and the queen of Daneland. She is unaware of Hrothgar's checkered past—including his daughter, Getrude, or the blood-feud he started with Froda and the Heathobards. When Hrothgar leaves to confront the Dragon one final time, leadership of the Danes falls to Welthow.

Wulf (woolf) is Hrothgar's faithful dog whom he has raised since he was a pup. Wulf makes no judgments and stands by his owner even during Hrothgar's darkest and loneliest hours. Wulf's favorite food is grilled firesnake.

Yrs (yerz) is Ingeld's daughter, and she is the smartest and prettiest woman in the Heathobard clan. She falls in love with Froda but is abducted by Hrothgar. Through mysterious circumstances she gives birth to Gertrude but dies on the night of the birth.

kid BEOWULF
family tree

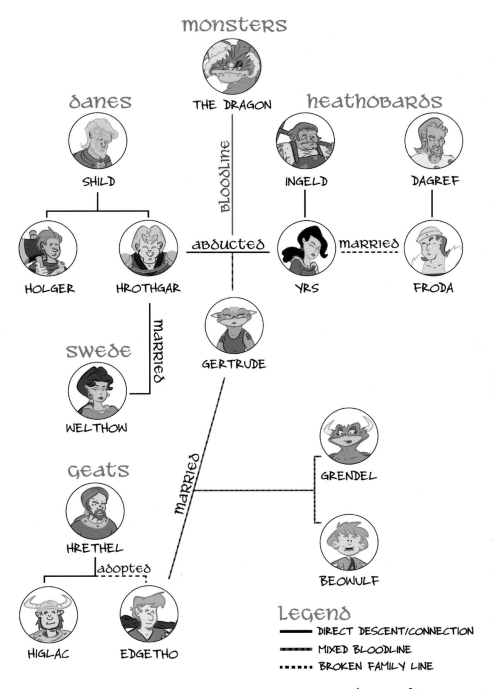

monsters

THE DRAGON

danes

SHILD

heathobards

INGELD

DAGREF

BLOODLINE

HOLGER

HROTHGAR

abducted

YRS

married

FRODA

swede

married

GERTRUDE

WELTHOW

geats

married

GRENDEL

HRETHEL

BEOWULF

adopted

HIGLAC

EDGETHO

LEGEND

— DIRECT DESCENT/CONNECTION

▬▬ MIXED BLOODLINE

····· BROKEN FAMILY LINE

BEOWULF

ORIGINS OF THE EPIC POEM

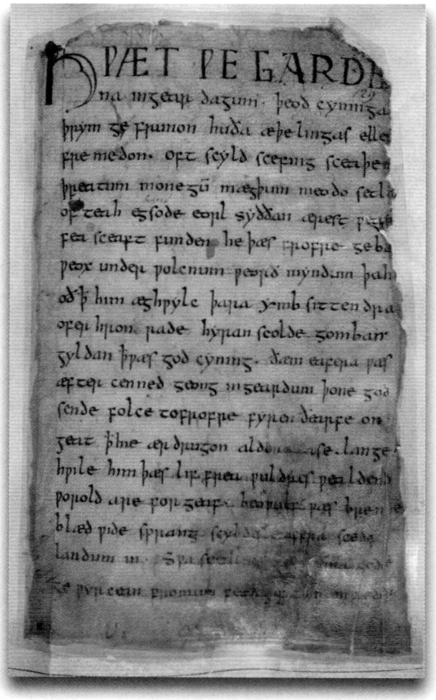

Top: Opening page of the original Old English manuscript, circa 700 A.D. This copy barely survived a library fire in 1731, which is why the right side of the page looks ragged and burned.

Originally sung by bards about events from the early fifth century, the epic poem *Beowulf* takes place in Daneland (modern-day Denmark), in a kingdom plagued by a horrific man-eating beast named Grendel. No one can defeat the mere monster until Beowulf, a hero from the northern neighbor, Geatland (now Sweden), arrives on Daneland's shores and boasts of Grendel's demise.

In perhaps the greatest showdown ever told, Beowulf and Grendel fight in the Great Hall of Herot. The battle culminates in Beowulf ripping Grendel's arm off barehanded!

But Beowulf's fight has just begun, because now he must contend with a monster fiercer than Grendel: Grendel's mother, the Sea-Hag! The hero tracks her down to her fire-swamp, dives down deep into the monster's lair, and attempts to fight her. Grendel's mother does not go easily, however, and, when Beowulf's blade breaks against her thorny hide, he fears the worst . . . until he finds an ancient sword buried amid the monster's gold. With the last of his strength, Beowulf takes a final swipe at the Sea-Hag and kills her.

Below (from the prologue): When Beowulf first encounters the Sea-Hag he is surprised by her strength.

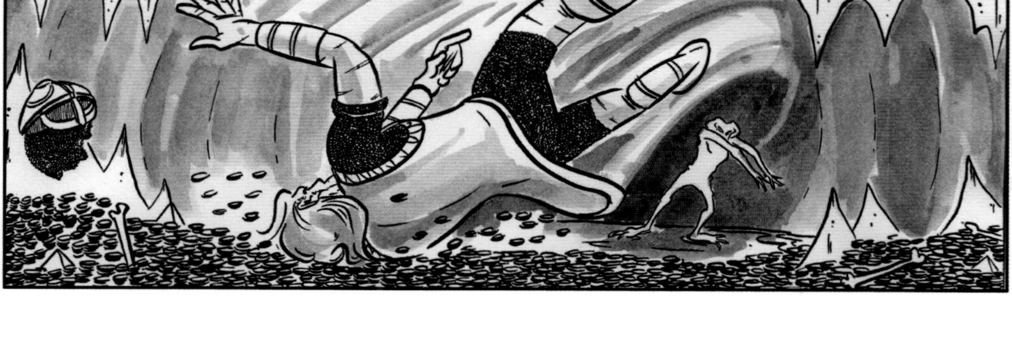

Beowulf leaves Daneland a hero and piles his ship high with gold and tribute. When he returns to his native Geatland, he gives his winnings to his king, Higlac, and becomes his faithful thane. Many years later, Beowulf is awarded kingship of Geatland and he rules for fifty long years, until one day another threat looms on the horizon: a Dragon. Beowulf must go out one last time to defend his people; he takes his ancient sword and faces down the beast, knowing he'll surely die in battle. Beowulf fights valiantly and with the help of his lone kinsman, Wiglaf, he defeats the dragon and dies alongside it.

The dragon's bones are tossed into the sea, and Beowulf's body is cremated in a funeral fit for the hero and king. His name and deeds lived on in song for centuries until they were finally committed to the page by a nameless monk around 700 A.D.

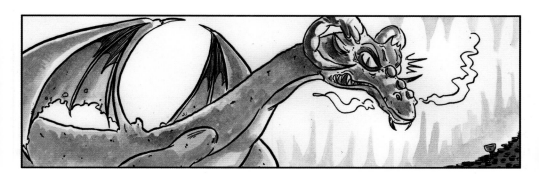

Even though the story is over one thousand years old, its themes and symbols still resonate today. *Beowulf* gives us a glimpse into a world that is very different from our own but whose ideals of wisdom, fortitude, reputation, destiny, and the peril of growing old are not foreign to us. *Beowulf* is the story of harsh landscapes and harsh people, when all that people had to rely on were their words and actions and the renown (or notoriety) that sprung from them.

The poem has been studied, translated, and puzzled over by scholars such as J. R. R. Tolkien and Seamus Heaney, and the poem has inspired countless pop-culture iterations taking form in novels, comic books, games, and movies. Just like the hero it's named for, the epic poem's fame lives on, and *Beowulf* will likely be read, analyzed, interpreted, taught, and enjoyed for another thousand years.

MONSTER SLAYERS

Monster slayer myths are common across many cultures, and are one of the earliest types of stories we have. Heroes like Herakles, Perseus, Theseus, Siegfried, Gilgamesh, and Beowulf are all monster slayers, and I've always liked the straightforward nature of these stories. There is a primal quality to them that's alluring, and it's in the seemingly simple premise of a hero setting out to kill a monster where all sorts of complex ideas can take root: things like fate and faith, destiny and destruction, might and magic.

Above: Other famous monster slayers from left to right: Theseus, Jason, Siegfried, and Oedipus.

In *Beowulf* there are three monsters he must vanquish: Grendel, Grendel's mother, and the Dragon. Inspired in part by John Gardner's depiction of the dragon in *Grendel*, my Dragon has a fatalistic view of the world and of men in particular. He is powerful and has an elemental magic to him, but he knows he's not immortal and is part of some larger cosmic scheme.

As invulnerable as the Dragon may seem, like all monsters before him, he has a counterpart slayer who will one day challenge him.

Right: The original design of the Dragon did not change much in the final book.

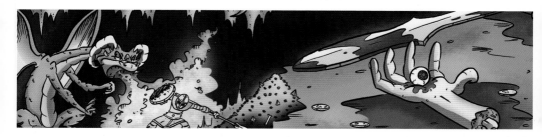

In the *Blood-Bound Oath*, when Hrothgar first meets the Dragon he is told about monsters and monster slayers. I wanted to lay the foundation for Beowulf's bloodline and make the connection back to the Dragon, who, generations before, mistook Beowulf's great-grandfather Shild for his slayer. Shild and the Dragon fought, and that's how Shild lost his hand and the Dragon lost his eye! A generation later Hrothgar comes calling, and the Dragon almost makes the same mistake but soon realizes Hrothgar is not his slayer either.

YOUR BLOODLINE IS STRONG, HROTHGAR AND SOMEWHERE MY SLAYER RESIDES IN IT. BUT HE HAS NOT COME THIS DAY.
BUT HOW DO YOU KNOW FOR SURE?! MAYBE IT IS ME!
I DON'T MAKE THE SAME MISTAKE TWICE...
YOUR DESTINY IS AMONG MEN...
NOTHING MORE.

In order to fulfill his destiny as a monster, the Dragon must confront his slayer and has a deep desire to do so. When he meets Hrothgar, he knows the slayer is somewhere in Hrothgar's bloodline. Perhaps out of boredom or curiosity the Dragon makes a pact with Hrothgar and decides to imbue him with a drop of his dragon's blood . . . maybe Hrothgar's child will become the mighty slayer the Dragon has been waiting for? Instead, Hrothgar abuses his power, and some say his only child—the half human/half monster Gertrude, is the embodiment of that broken oath. It's only a generation later, when Gertrude has twins, that the magic splits: the result is a monster boy and a human boy, and Beowulf is the human slayer that the Dragon has been waiting for all along!

how to draw Beowulf

Our hero Beowulf is a scrappy, scrawny, twelve-year-old orphan boy. One day he'll be a strong and wise warrior, and people will sing of his deeds far and wide. Until that day arrives, he is trying to figure out who he is and where he came from—and get along with his newly discovered twin brother! Now you can learn how to draw him, following the steps below.

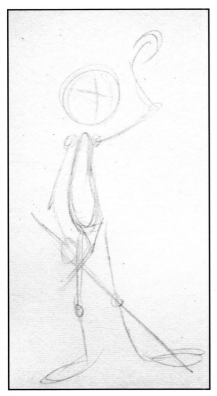

⬅ STEP 1 - ROUGHS

The key to drawing well is to work in layers. Build up your character from a very basic pose (called a rough) and focus on getting the gestures and proportions right before you move onto any details. I always start by drawing the head, and then create the pose from there. The torso is generally a kidney-bean shape, and then I use small circles to place the knees, feet, shoulders and hands. Connect these parts with a loose armature.

STEP 2 - PENCILS ➡

In the pencils stage you start to fill in the details of the character. Some things to keep in mind about Beowulf: He's got big ears, a small button nose, and cowlicks in his hair! He's also scrawny so don't make him muscular. I draw with a blue pencil, which does not smudge like graphite or get picked up by scanners and copiers.

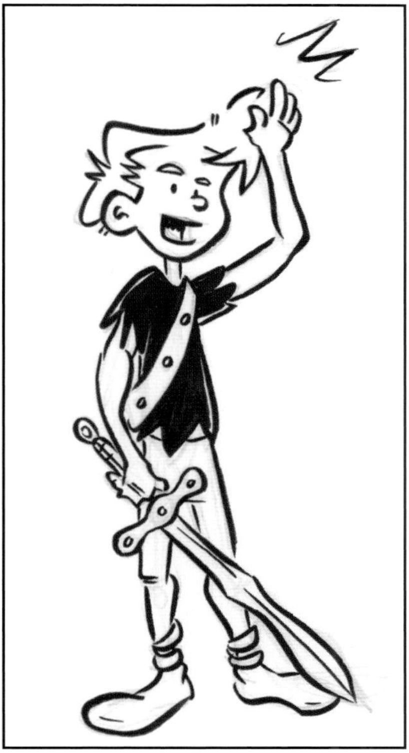

← STEP 3 - INKS

Now on to my favorite part: inking! You can ink with whatever tool you like best, (brushes, markers, sharpies). Experiment with a variety and eventually you'll find what works best for you. I use brush pens which help me get a "thick-to-thin" line. Remember, inking is not "tracing"—this is the stage when the pencil drawing comes to life, so stay loose with the brush and try to bring some bounce to the drawing through the pen strokes.

tools of the trade

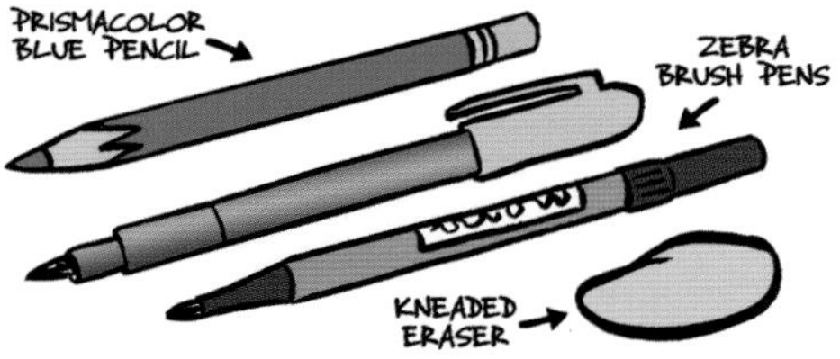
PRISMACOLOR BLUE PENCIL
ZEBRA BRUSH PENS
KNEADED ERASER

STEP 4 - CLEANUP & COLOR →

This step is just what it sounds like—time to erase the under drawing so the inks can shine through. There are all sorts of erasers, but I like to use "kneaded erasers," which are soft and pliable (like Silly Putty) and won't rip your paper! When you color Beowulf, his hair is orange, and he wears blue pants and either a black or gray shirt. He's also got a red sword belt slung over his shoulder. You can use whatever tools to color that you want (crayons, colored pencils, or even a computer).

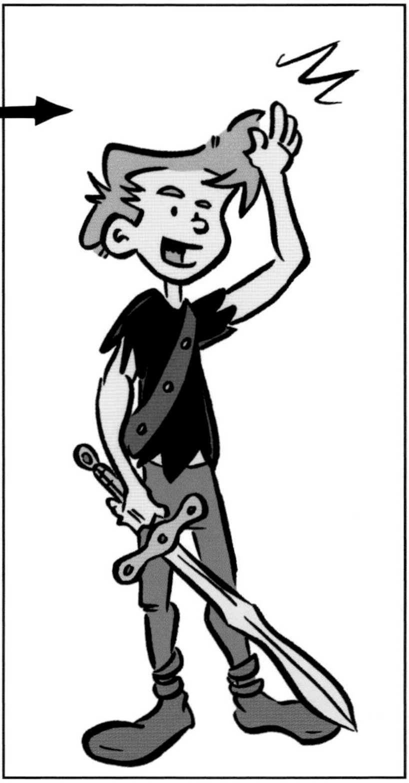

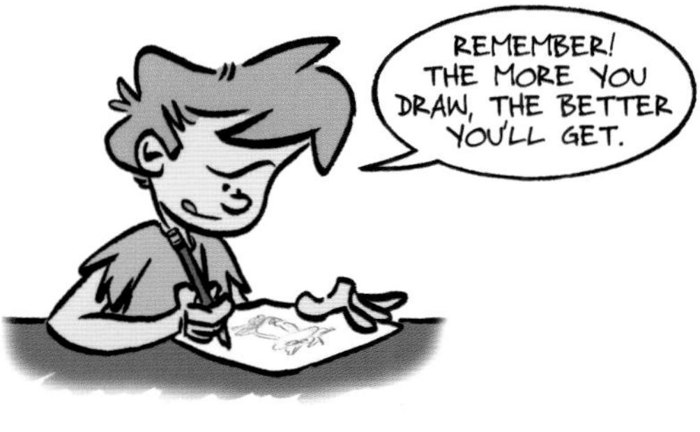
REMEMBER! THE MORE YOU DRAW, THE BETTER YOU'LL GET.

anatomy of a page

There are many stages to creating a comic book. Every artist works differently, and the method I use in crafting a story below is just one variation on the many different ways you can make comics.

STEP 1: SCRIPT & THUMBNAILS

Once I've done all my reading and research and I feel comfortable with the story I want to tell, I start to write the script. My scripts are not too different from a screenplay: I break down the page in terms of panels and then describe the action and setting within each panel. I like to write the script on one half of the page and leave the other page blank for my **thumbnails**. A thumbnail is a small, quick drawing that shows the panel layouts I wrote in the script. A thumbnail is a way to remind yourself what you want your penciled page to look like, or to help work out storytelling from one panel to the next.

Page 2: 4-panel layout

Panel 1: Wide landscape shot of small settlement. This is the Heathobard encampment. It is comprised of a main hut (where their leader Dagref and his son, Froda, live), which is ringed by several other huts and small shacks. It has the makings of a small town. It is afternoon and many of the Heathobards are bustling about, working through their day.

Panel 2: The camera shifts to the wooded hills above the Heathobard village. Rocks and bushes mingle among the trees. Behind one of the larger rocks we can see the tops of two heads spying on the Heathobards below: the young Danish princes Hrothgar and Holger.

Holger (looks a little worried): "I don't like this Hrothgar. We shouldn't be spying..."

Hrothgar: "Sorry, Holger—old habits die hard. Dad wanted us to check in on them, that's all we're doing."

Panel 3: Conversation continues between the brothers. Holger: "But aren't we friendly with the Heathobards now? If they catch us like this, they'll think something's up!"

Hrothgar: "Dad's peace is tenuous at best. You know it and I know it. Everybody down there knows it. If Dagref wants to start another war, I'd welcome it."

Panel 4: Holger (a little wary of his brother's bloodlust): "Is that what we're doing here?"

Hrothgar: "Ha! You worry too much, little brother—we're just the welcoming committee!"

Holger: "For who?"

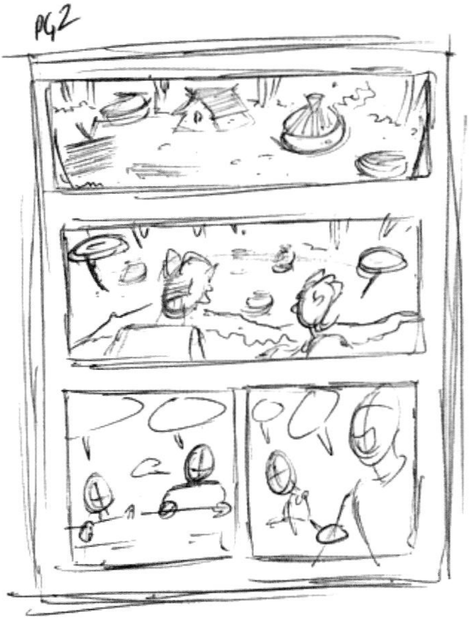
PG2

STEP 2: PENCILS

After the script and the thumbnails are done I'm ready to start penciling the book. I draw my pages on 11x14 Bristol board with a half-inch margin on all sides. From there I divide the page into panels. For this page I tried to make each tier the same height and width, dividing the last tier into two panels, just like my script and thumbnails told me to.

• **Bristol board** is a heavy paper that will not rip or tear when drawing or inking. I like the Strathmore 300 Series Smooth surface/100lb.

• I draw my pages with a **non-photo blue pencil**. This means when I ink the page I won't have to erase the pencils because the scanner will not pick up the blue.

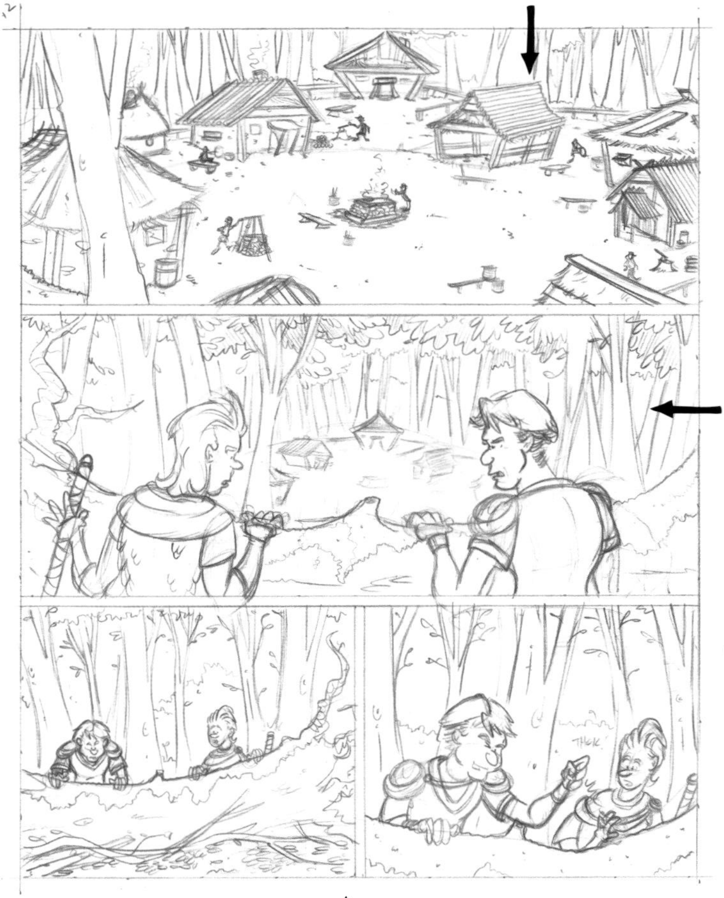

• Hey! Where are the words? I do all my **lettering** in a later stage but I try to leave enough space around the characters for word balloons and sometimes will draw balloons in for placement. It's a good practice to look at your pages without words and see if you can still follow the action and emotions of the characters and get an idea of what's going on in the story. Remember, this is comics, so it's about **visual storytelling!**

Believe it or not, penciling is tough! It takes a lot of concentration, energy, and brain power to pencil a page (at least for me). Depending how complex a page is, it may take me at least two hours to do one page!

• Take a look at the **thumbnail** and the final **penciled page**—you'll see that I switched the positions of Holger and Hrothgar in the final layout for clearer storytelling.

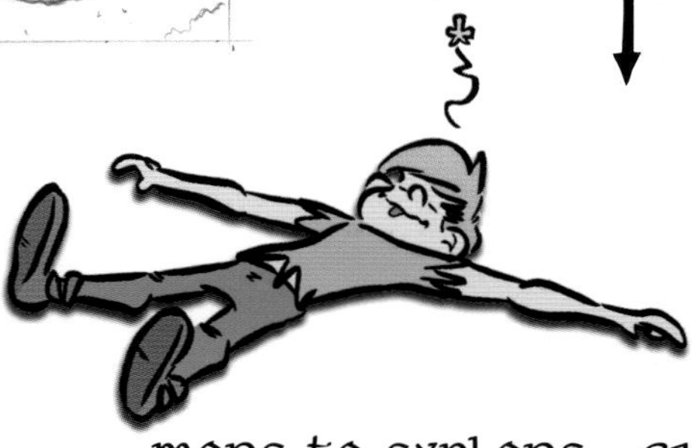

STEP 3: INKS

After I have a batch of penciled pages done, I like to take a break and start my favorite part of making comics, which is inking the pages! Inking is not tracing; it's another layer of drawing but with a pen or brush instead of a pencil. It gives you the opportunity to refine your penciled page, correct mistakes, and add some life to your characters and the page with dynamic linework, shading, and detail. You can use whatever tools you like best when you ink. Some people prefer brushes; others like hard-nib pens. I use a variety of Japanese brush Zebra pens.

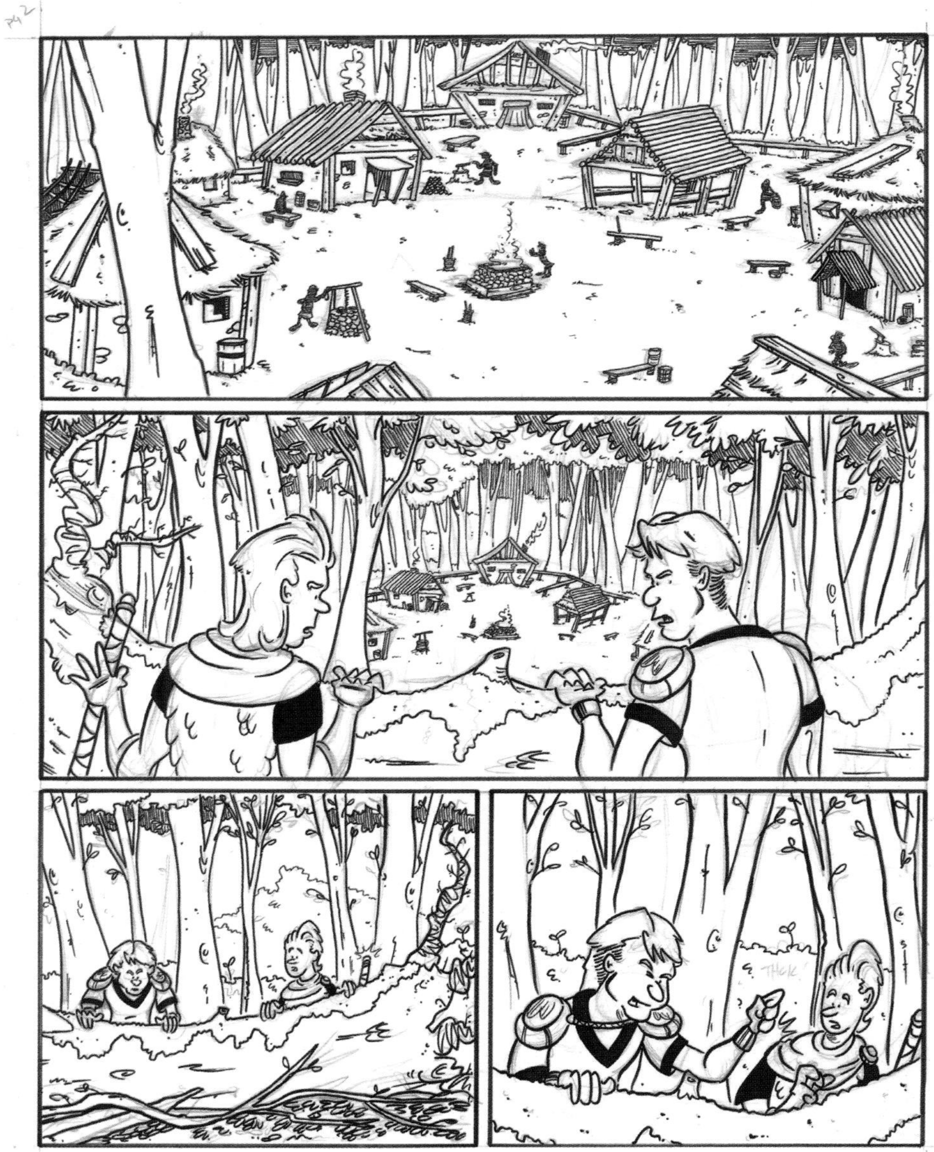

STEP 4: CLEANUP & COLOR & LETTERS

Once my pages are inked I scan them and they become a digital document. The rest of the work will be done on the computer using Photoshop. The first step is **cleanup**, which is basically getting rid of the blue pencil lines and making the black inks look as clean and dark as possible. That's when I send the pages to **color** and my colorist, Jose. While he colors on his computer, I start **lettering** the pages on mine.

• Jose does two stages of coloring. The first is called **flats,** which is basically filling in all the areas of the page with color (right). This will make the second stage of **final color** (below) easier because he can select any area and color it, adding special lighting effects to the the characters and the environment.

I DON'T LIKE THIS, HROTHGAR. WE SHOULDN'T BE SPYING.
SORRY, HOLGER. OLD HABITS DIE HARD...
DAD WANTS US TO CHECK UP ON THEM, SO THAT'S WHAT WE'RE DOING.
BUT AREN'T WE FRIENDS WITH THE HEATHOBARDS NOW...?
OUR PEACE IS TENUOUS AT BEST.
IF DAGREF WANTS ANOTHER WAR, I'D WELCOME IT.
IS THAT WHY WE'RE HERE?
HA! YOU WORRY TOO MUCH, LITTLE BROTHER.
WE'RE JUST THE WELCOMING COMMITTEE!
FOR WHO?
THOK!

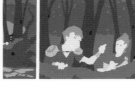

• I have a **font** that is made from my hand lettering so when I type the letters it looks hand written. It makes editing easier. I also draw all my **word balloons** and **sound effects** and place them in the page. This also gives the final comic page a handmade look and feel.

Of course, many cartoonists do their own lettering on the original page they drew, too. The wonderful thing about making comics is that there is no single way to do it. Experiment with the form and start telling your own stories!

fun facts

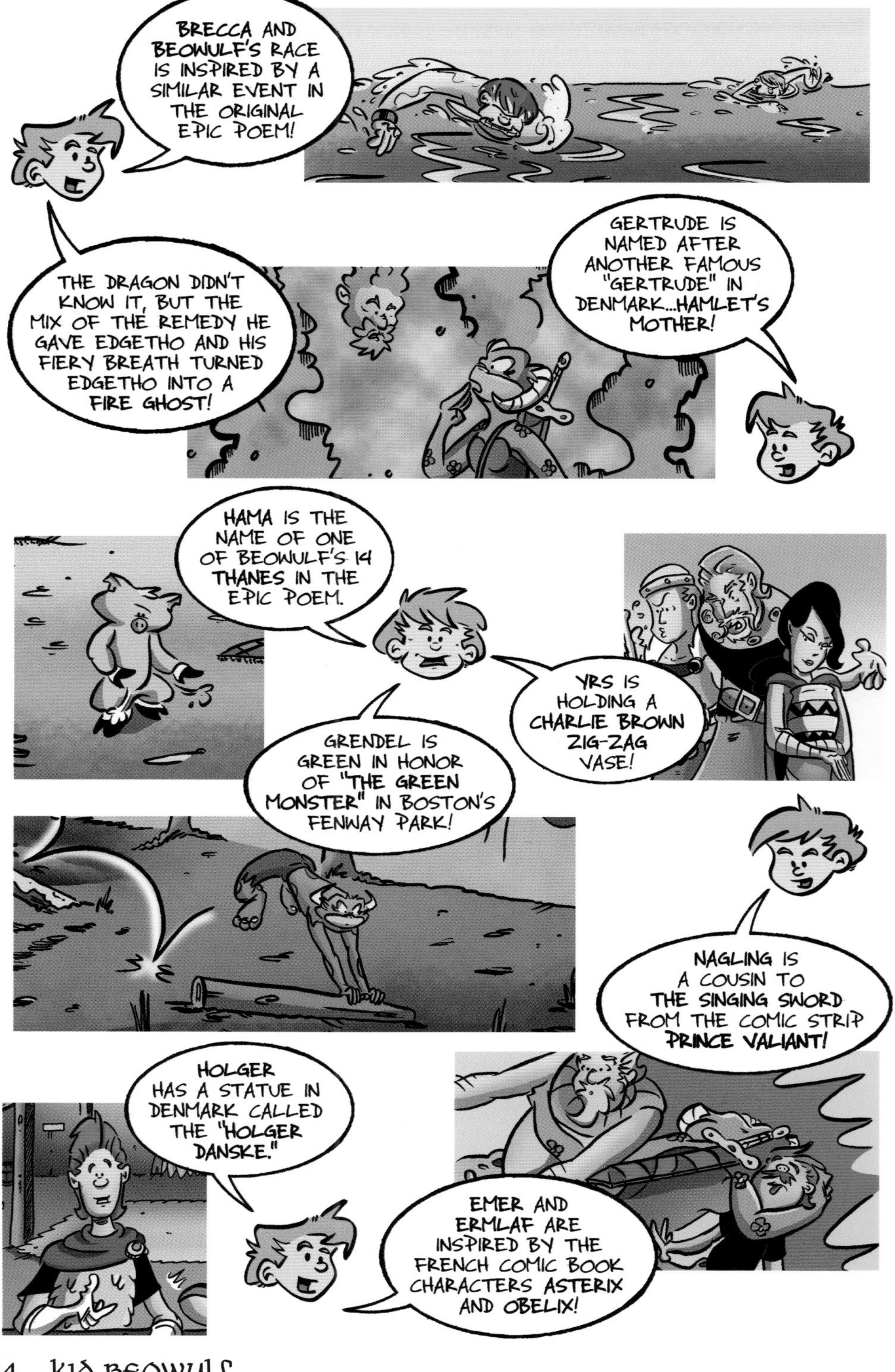
BRECCA AND BEOWULF'S RACE IS INSPIRED BY A SIMILAR EVENT IN THE ORIGINAL EPIC POEM!
THE DRAGON DIDN'T KNOW IT, BUT THE MIX OF THE REMEDY HE GAVE EDGETHO AND HIS FIERY BREATH TURNED EDGETHO INTO A **FIRE GHOST!**
GERTRUDE IS NAMED AFTER ANOTHER FAMOUS "GERTRUDE" IN DENMARK...HAMLET'S MOTHER!
HAMA IS THE NAME OF ONE OF BEOWULF'S 14 **THANES** IN THE EPIC POEM.
YRS IS HOLDING A **CHARLIE BROWN ZIG-ZAG** VASE!
GRENDEL IS GREEN IN HONOR OF **"THE GREEN MONSTER"** IN BOSTON'S FENWAY PARK!
NAGLING IS A COUSIN TO **THE SINGING SWORD** FROM THE COMIC STRIP **PRINCE VALIANT!**
HOLGER HAS A STATUE IN DENMARK CALLED THE **"HOLGER DANSKE."**
EMER AND ERMLAF ARE INSPIRED BY THE FRENCH COMIC BOOK CHARACTERS **ASTERIX** AND **OBELIX!**

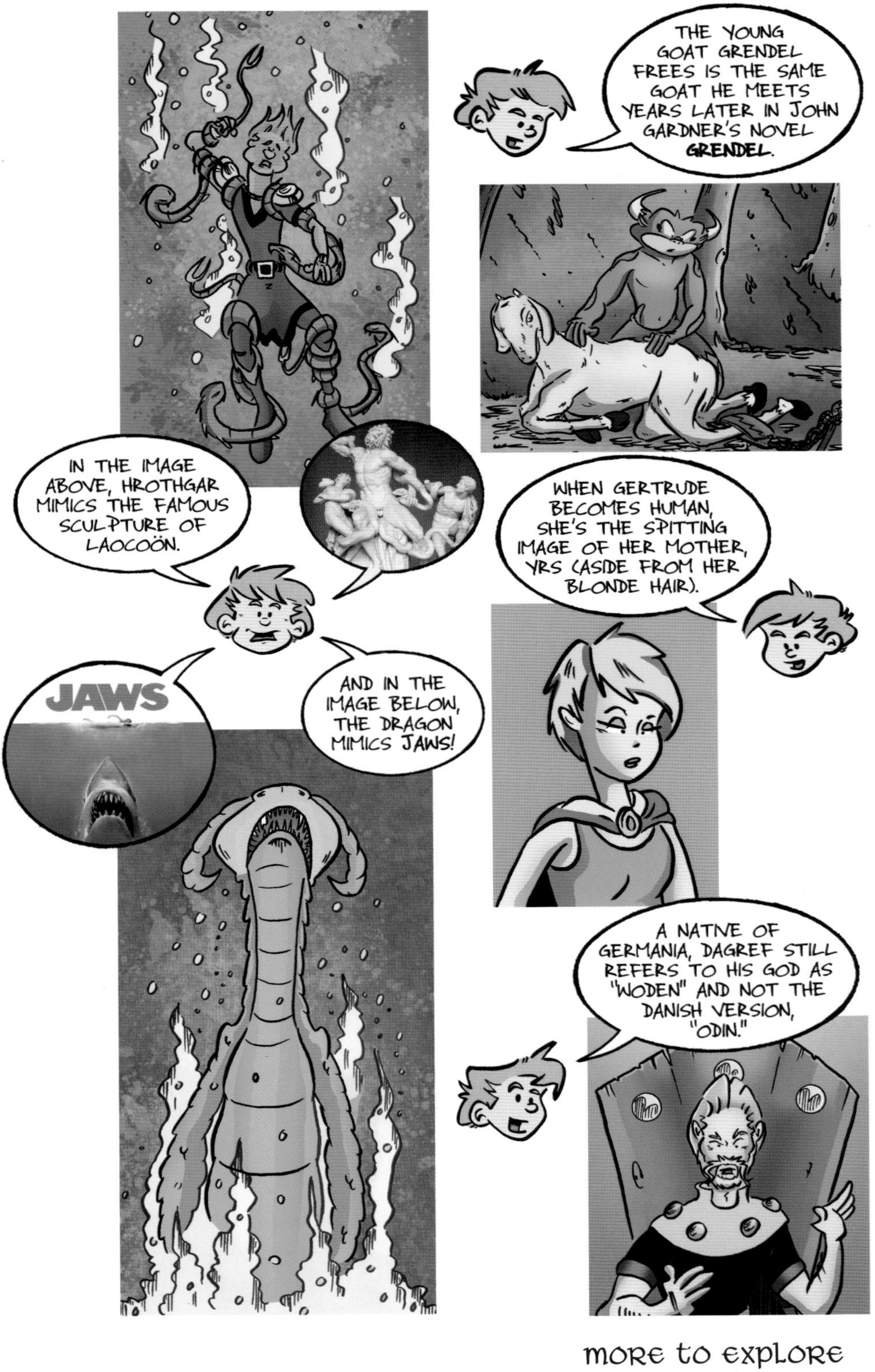
THE YOUNG GOAT GRENDEL FREES IS THE SAME GOAT HE MEETS YEARS LATER IN JOHN GARDNER'S NOVEL **GRENDEL**.
IN THE IMAGE ABOVE, HROTHGAR MIMICS THE FAMOUS SCULPTURE OF LAOCOÖN.
WHEN GERTRUDE BECOMES HUMAN, SHE'S THE SPITTING IMAGE OF HER MOTHER, YRS (ASIDE FROM HER BLONDE HAIR).
JAWS
AND IN THE IMAGE BELOW, THE DRAGON MIMICS JAWS!
A NATIVE OF GERMANIA, DAGREF STILL REFERS TO HIS GOD AS "WODEN" AND NOT THE DANISH VERSION, "ODIN."

Bibliography

These books were used during the research and writing of *Kid Beowulf*.
All come highly recommended!

Beowulf
Translated, and with an Introduction by
BURTON RAFFEL

BEOWULF
SEAMUS HEANEY

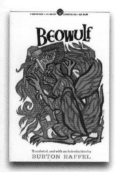

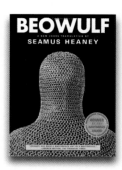

There are multiple translations of *Beowulf*, and each has its strengths. My favorites include Burton Raffel's 1963 version and Seamus Heaney's 2000 edition. Raffel's descriptions are particularly vivid though Heaney is perhaps more accurate and also comes with the original Old English version printed alongside the translation.

J.R.R.
TOLKIEN
BEOWULF
SELLIC SPELL
Edited by CHRISTOPHER TOLKIEN

J.R.R. TOLKIEN
THE MONSTERS AND THE CRITICS

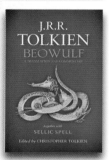

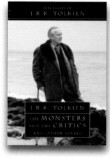

J.R.R. Tolkien did a "working" translation of *Beowulf* (meaning he never finished it). This was published recently along with his well-received collection of essays *The Monsters and the Critics*, which has great insight into the epic poem.

BEOWULF

Gareth Hinds's graphic novel adaptation of *Beowulf* is as grim, gritty, and as beautiful as the original epic.

JOHN
GARDNER
Grendel

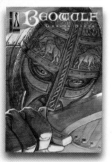

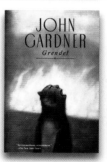

John Gardner's *Grendel* is a terrific novel that retells the epic poem *Beowulf* from the point of view of the tragically misunderstood monster Grendel.

JOSEPH
CAMPBELL
THE HERO
WITH A
THOUSAND
FACES

Joseph Campbell's timeless work *The Hero with a Thousand Faces* chronicles the hero's journey through multiple mythological lenses.

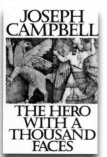

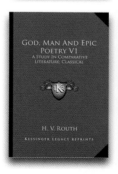

GOD, MAN AND EPIC
POETRY VI
A STUDY IN COMPARATIVE
LITERATURE: CLASSICAL
H. V. ROUTH
KESSINGER LEGACY REPRINTS

God, Man and Epic Poetry by H. V. Routh is a terrific collection of essays on epic literature and the similarities and differences among a variety of classic epic poems.

a special preview of book two

Kid Beowulf

the song of Roland

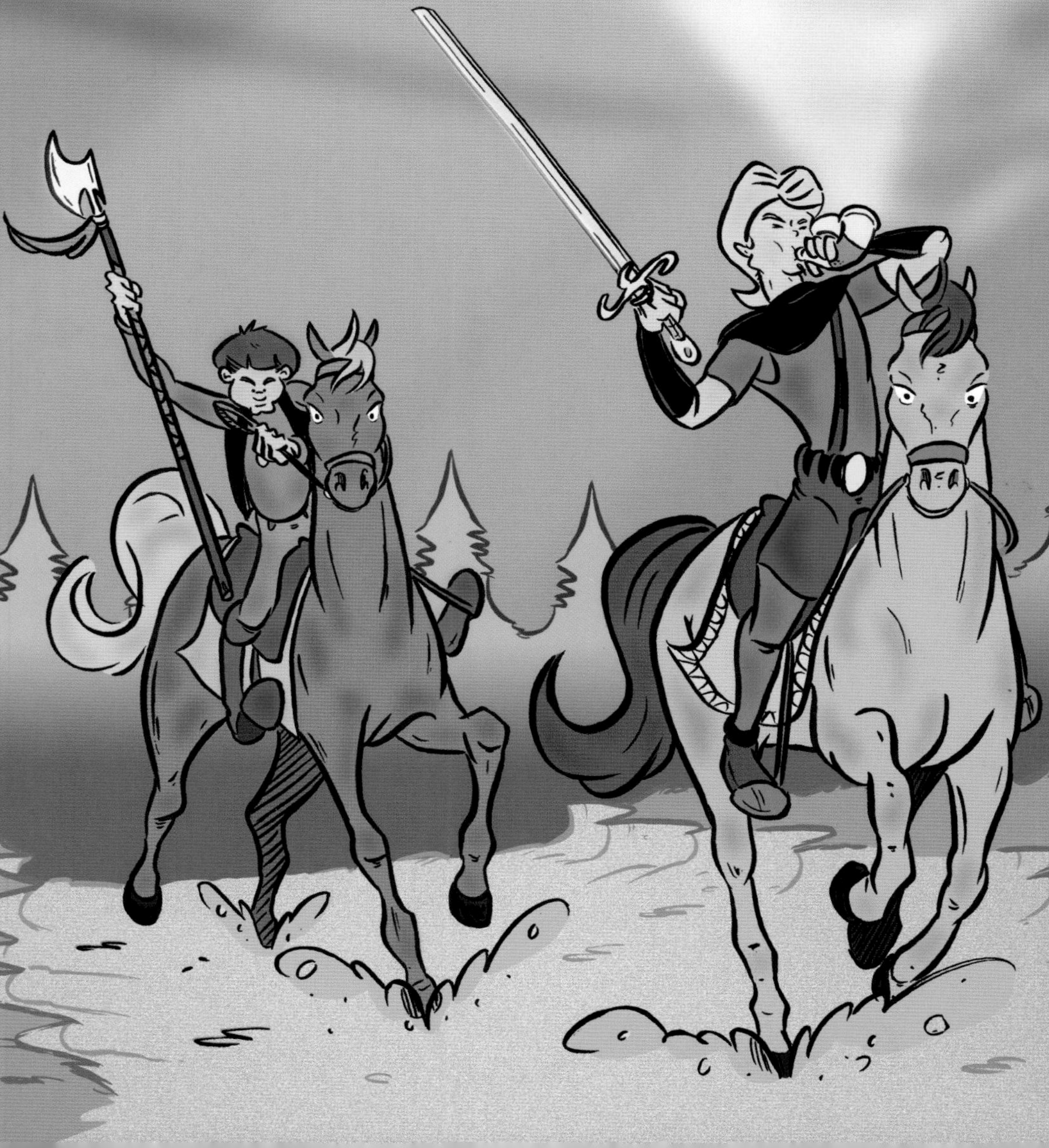

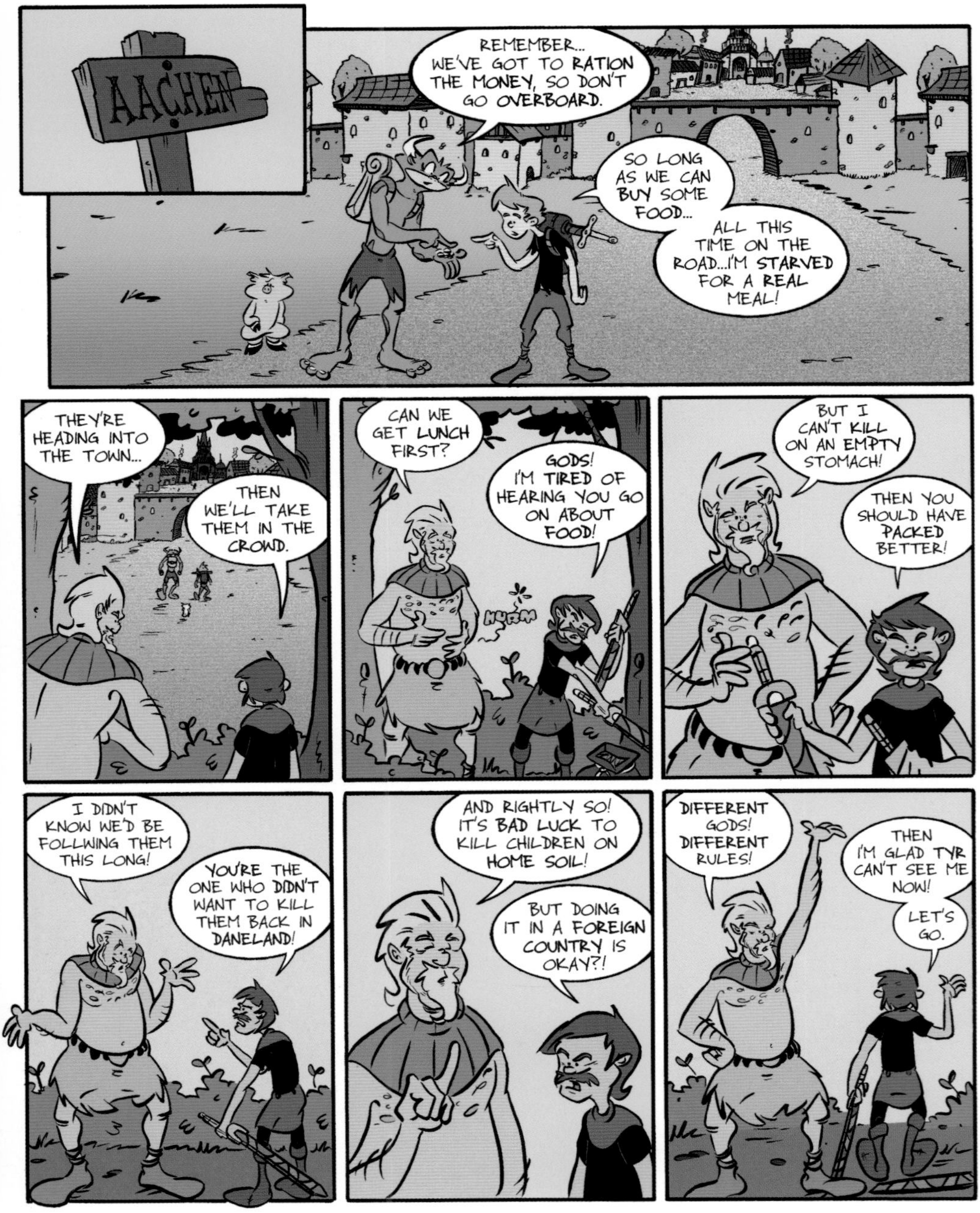
AACHEN
REMEMBER... WE'VE GOT TO RATION THE MONEY, SO DON'T GO OVERBOARD.
SO LONG AS WE CAN BUY SOME FOOD...
ALL THIS TIME ON THE ROAD...I'M STARVED FOR A REAL MEAL!
THEY'RE HEADING INTO THE TOWN...
THEN WE'LL TAKE THEM IN THE CROWD.
CAN WE GET LUNCH FIRST?
GODS! I'M TIRED OF HEARING YOU GO ON ABOUT FOOD!
HURM
BUT I CAN'T KILL ON AN EMPTY STOMACH!
THEN YOU SHOULD HAVE PACKED BETTER!
I DIDN'T KNOW WE'D BE FOLLWING THEM THIS LONG!
YOU'RE THE ONE WHO DIDN'T WANT TO KILL THEM BACK IN DANELAND!
AND RIGHTLY SO! IT'S BAD LUCK TO KILL CHILDREN ON HOME SOIL!
BUT DOING IT IN A FOREIGN COUNTRY IS OKAY?!
DIFFERENT GODS! DIFFERENT RULES!
THEN I'M GLAD TYR CAN'T SEE ME NOW!
LET'S GO.

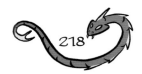

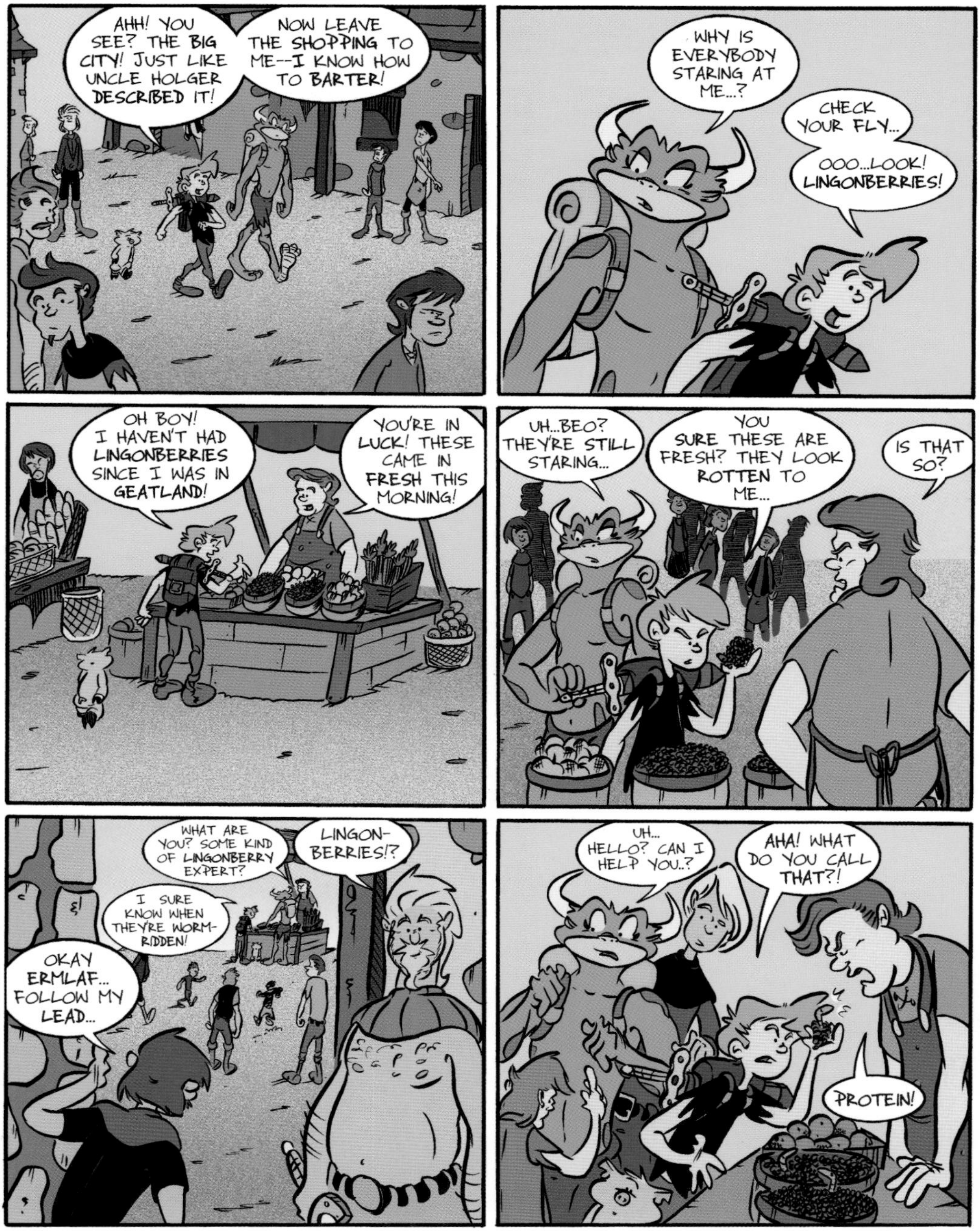
AHH! YOU SEE? THE BIG CITY! JUST LIKE UNCLE HOLGER DESCRIBED IT!
NOW LEAVE THE SHOPPING TO ME--I KNOW HOW TO BARTER!
WHY IS EVERYBODY STARING AT ME...?
CHECK YOUR FLY...
OOO...LOOK! LINGONBERRIES!
OH BOY! I HAVEN'T HAD LINGONBERRIES SINCE I WAS IN GEATLAND!
YOU'RE IN LUCK! THESE CAME IN FRESH THIS MORNING!
UH...BEO? THEY'RE STILL STARING...
YOU SURE THESE ARE FRESH? THEY LOOK ROTTEN TO ME...
IS THAT SO?
WHAT ARE YOU? SOME KIND OF LINGONBERRY EXPERT?
LINGON-BERRIES!?
I SURE KNOW WHEN THEY'RE WORM-RIDDEN!
OKAY ERMLAF... FOLLOW MY LEAD...
UH... HELLO? CAN I HELP YOU..?
AHA! WHAT DO YOU CALL THAT?!
PROTEIN!

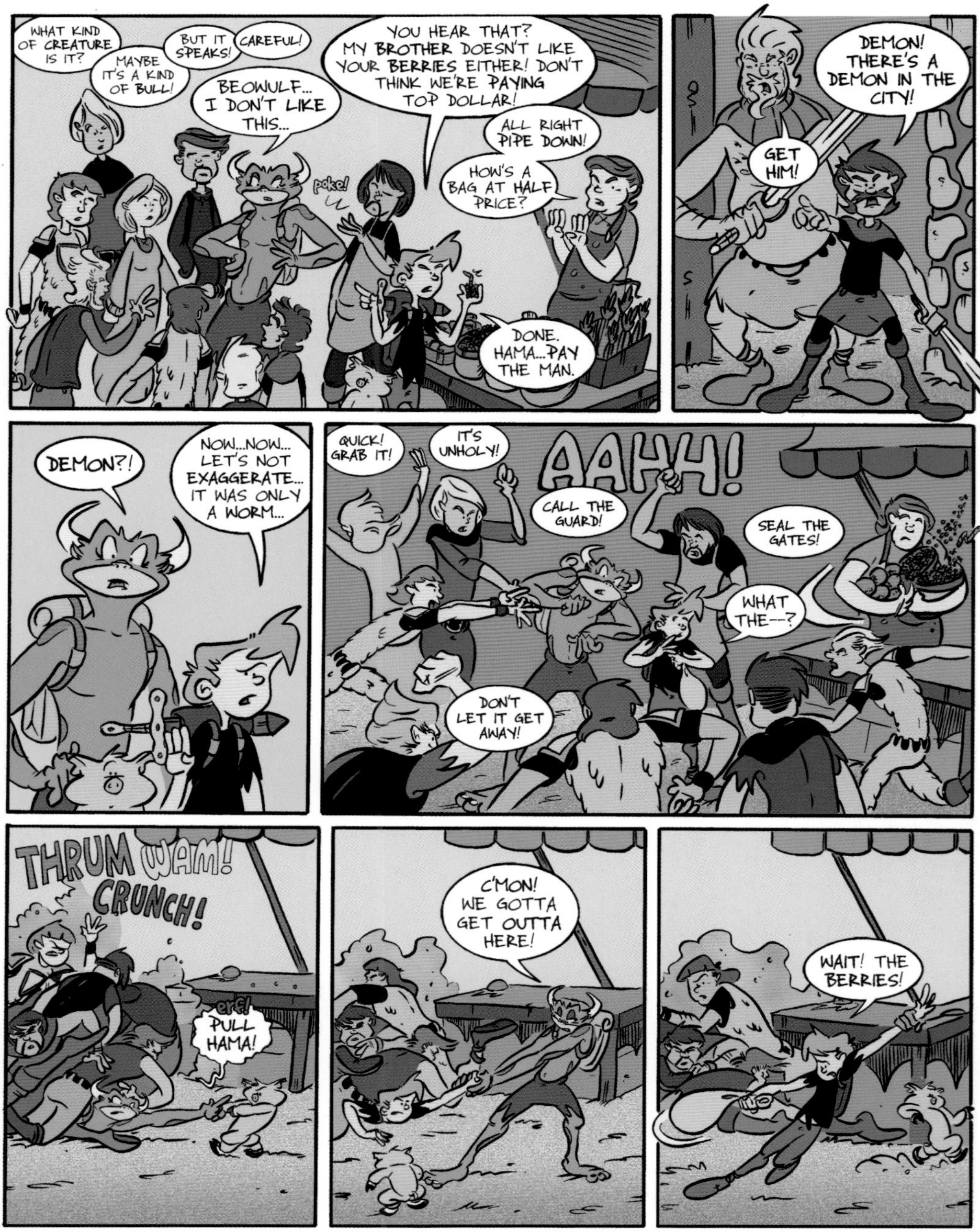
WHAT KIND OF CREATURE IS IT?
MAYBE IT'S A KIND OF BULL!
BUT IT SPEAKS!
CAREFUL!
BEOWULF... I DON'T LIKE THIS...
YOU HEAR THAT? MY BROTHER DOESN'T LIKE YOUR BERRIES EITHER! DON'T THINK WE'RE PAYING TOP DOLLAR!
poke!
ALL RIGHT PIPE DOWN!
HOW'S A BAG AT HALF PRICE?
DONE. HAMA...PAY THE MAN.
DEMON! THERE'S A DEMON IN THE CITY!
GET HIM!
DEMON?!
NOW...NOW... LET'S NOT EXAGGERATE... IT WAS ONLY A WORM...
QUICK! GRAB IT!
IT'S UNHOLY!
AAHH!
CALL THE GUARD!
SEAL THE GATES!
WHAT THE--?
DON'T LET IT GET AWAY!
THRUM
WAM!
CRUNCH!
erf!
PULL HAMA!
C'MON! WE GOTTA GET OUTTA HERE!
WAIT! THE BERRIES!

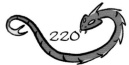

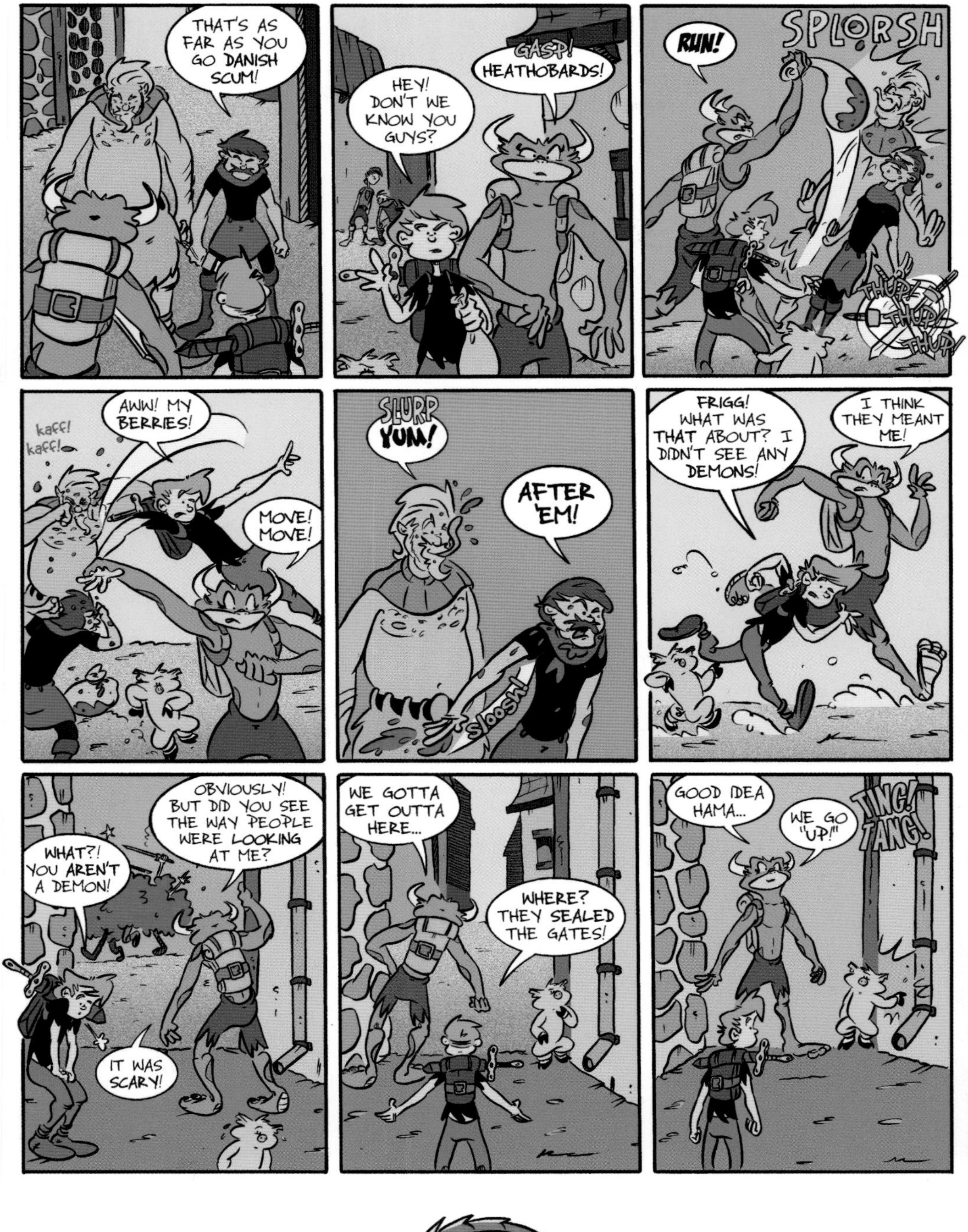
THAT'S AS FAR AS YOU GO DANISH SCUM!
HEY! DON'T WE KNOW YOU GUYS?
GASP! HEATHOBARDS!
RUN!
SPLORSH
THUP! THUP! THUP!
kaff! kaff!
AWW! MY BERRIES!
MOVE! MOVE!
SLURP YUM!
AFTER 'EM!
sloosh!
FRIGG! WHAT WAS THAT ABOUT? I DIDN'T SEE ANY DEMONS!
I THINK THEY MEANT ME!
WHAT?! YOU AREN'T A DEMON!
OBVIOUSLY! BUT DID YOU SEE THE WAY PEOPLE WERE LOOKING AT ME?
IT WAS SCARY!
WE GOTTA GET OUTTA HERE...
WHERE? THEY SEALED THE GATES!
GOOD IDEA HAMA...
WE GO "UP!"
TING! TANG!

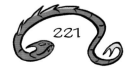

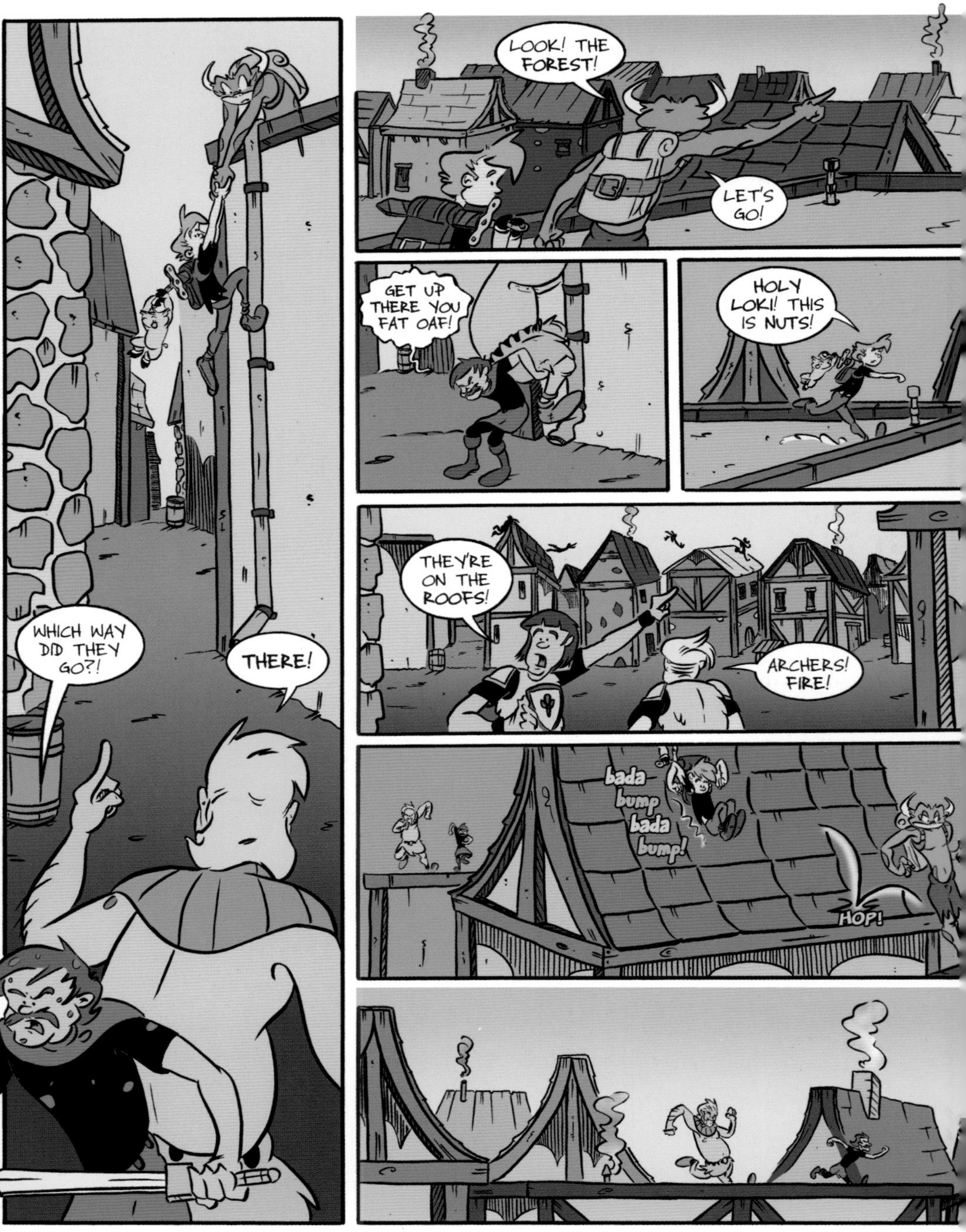
LOOK! THE FOREST!
LET'S GO!
GET UP THERE YOU FAT OAF!
HOLY LOKI! THIS IS NUTS!
WHICH WAY DID THEY GO?!
THERE!
THEY'RE ON THE ROOFS!
ARCHERS! FIRE!
bada bump bada bump!
HOP!

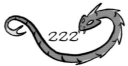

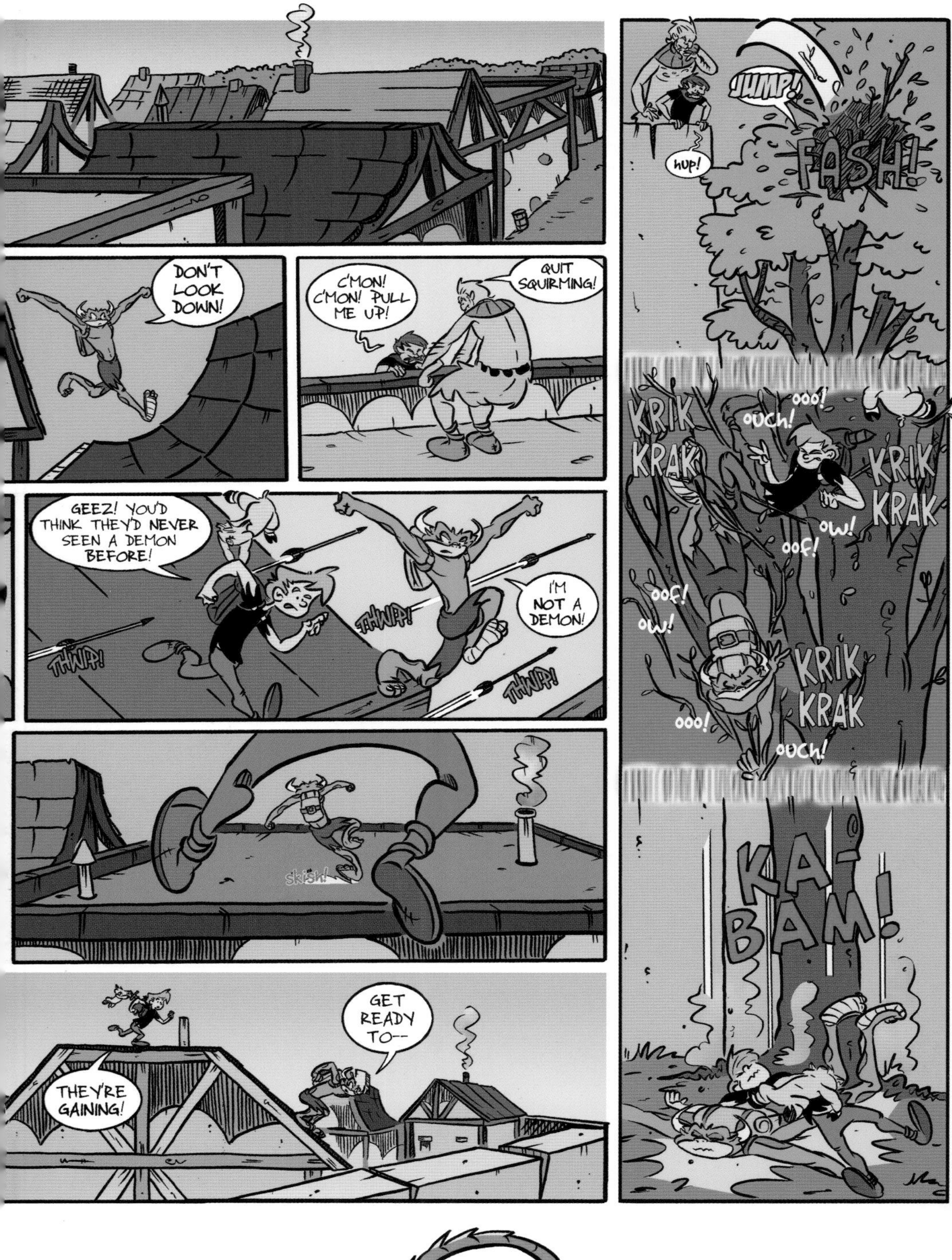
DON'T LOOK DOWN!
C'MON! C'MON! PULL ME UP!
QUIT SQUIRMING!
GEEZ! YOU'D THINK THEY'D NEVER SEEN A DEMON BEFORE!
I'M NOT A DEMON!
THWIP!
THWIP!
THWIP!
SKISH!
THEY'RE GAINING!
GET READY TO--
JUMP!
HUP!
FASH!
KRIK KRAK
OUCH!
OOO!
KRIK KRAK
OW!
OOF!
OOF!
OW!
KRIK KRAK
OOO!
OUCH!
KA-BAM!

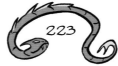

about the author

photo by Cathy Barrett

Alexis E. Fajardo is a student of the classics—whether Daffy Duck or Damocles—and has created a unique blend of the two with *Kid Beowulf*. When he's not drawing comics, he works for them at the Charles M. Schulz Studio in Santa Rosa, California. Lex does not live in a castle but would like to one day with his wife and his dog, Loki.

Follow Lex on twitter *@lex_kidb*
Discover more at *kidbeowulf.com*
Become a fan on *facebook.com/kidbeowulf*

Andrews McMeel Publishing
a division of Andrews McMeel Universal
1130 Walnut Street, Kansas City, Missouri 64106

www.andrewsmcmeel.com

17 18 19 20 21 SDB 10 9 8 7 6 5 4 3 2

ISBN: 978-1-4494-7589-5

Library of Congress Control Number: 2016934687

Creative Director: Tim Lynch
Production Editor: Maureen Sullivan
Production Manager: Chuck Harper
Demand Planner: Sue Eikos

Made by: Shenzhen Donnelley Printing Company Ltd.
Address and location of manufacturer: No. 47, Wuhe Nan Road, Bantian Ind. Zone, Shenzhen China, 518129
2nd Printing - 3/27/17